Ian Irvine was born in Bathurst, Australia, in 1950, and educated at Chevalier College and the University of Sydney, where he took a PhD in marine science.

After working as an environmental project manager, Ian set up his own consulting firm in 1986, carrying out studies for clients in Australia and overseas. He has worked in many countries in the Asia-Pacific region. An expert in marine pollution, Ian has developed some of Australia's national guidelines for the protection of the oceanic environment.

The international success of Ian Irvine's debut fantasy series, *The View from the Mirror*, immediately established him as one of the most popular new authors in the fantasy genre. He is now a full-time writer and lives with his family in northern New South Wales, Australia, where he can be contacted at ianirvine@ozemail.com.au

Find out more about Ian Irvine and other Orbit authors by registering for the free monthly newsletter at www.orbitbooks.co.uk

IAN IRVINE

A TALE OF THE THREE WORLDS

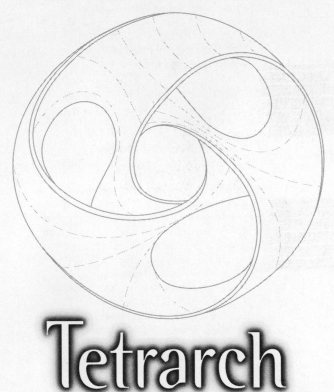

Tetrarch

Volume Two of THE WELL OF ECHOES

orbit

www.orbitbooks.co.uk

An *Orbit* Book

First published by Penguin Books Australia 2002
First published in Great Britain by Orbit 2003

Text copyright © Ian Irvine 2002
Maps copyright © Ian Irvine 2002

The moral right of the author has been asserted.

A CIP catalogue record for this book is
available from the British Library.

ISBN 1 84149 210 8

Printed and bound in Great Britain by
Creative Print and Design Wales, Ebbw Vale

Orbit
An imprint of
Time Warner Books UK
Brettenham House
Lancaster Place
London WC2E 7EN

CONTENTS

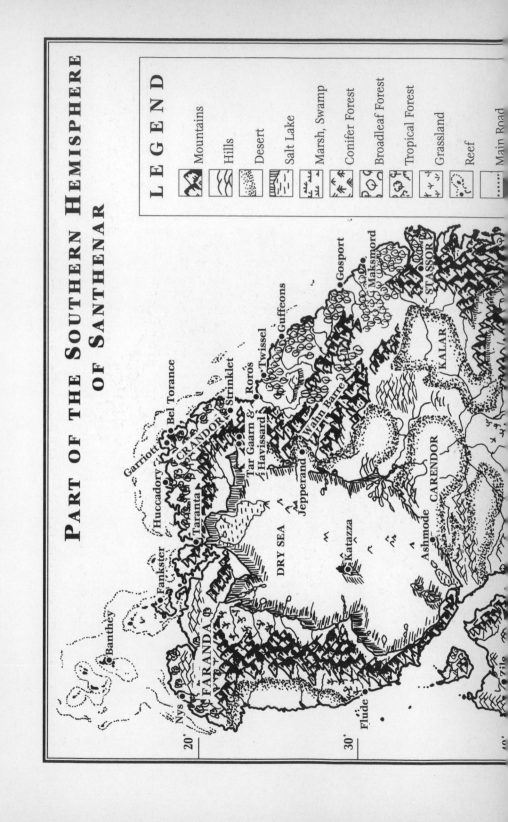

PART OF THE SOUTHERN HEMISPHERE OF SANTHENAR

L E G E N D

- Mountains
- Hills
- Desert
- Salt Lake
- Marsh, Swamp
- Conifer Forest
- Broadleaf Forest
- Tropical Forest
- Grassland
- Reef
- Main Road

Banthey

Fankster

Garriott • Bel Torance

Huccadory

CRANDOR

Taranta • Strinklet

Nys

FARANDA

Flude

Roros

Twissel

Tar Gaarn &
Havissard

Jepperand

Guffeons

Wahn Barre

Ashmode

CARENDOR

Katazza

DRY SEA

Gosport

Maksmord

STASSOR

KALAR

20'

30'

SCALE

KILOMETERS

0   100 200 300 400 500 600 700 800 900 1000

LEAGUES

0   40   80   120   160   200

Maps by the author

Tiksi

Tirthrax

Burning
Mountain

MIRRILLADELL

LAURALINP

Fiz Gorgo

KARAMA MALAMA
(Sea of Mists)

OOLO

SHAZABBA

LUUMA NARTA

Oguir

HA-DROW

Steppe

Noom

KARA AGEL
(Frozen Sea)

Grinding

50˚

60˚

70˚

MIRRILLADELL AND THE GREAT MOUNTAINS

GREAT MOUNTAINS

Tirthrax

Itsipitsi

MIRRILLADELL

L. Faell

TARRALLADELL

Tatusti

MISTY MERES

Flaha

Runcil

MILMILLAMEL

Thryss

DROW

Kaer Slass

HA-DROW

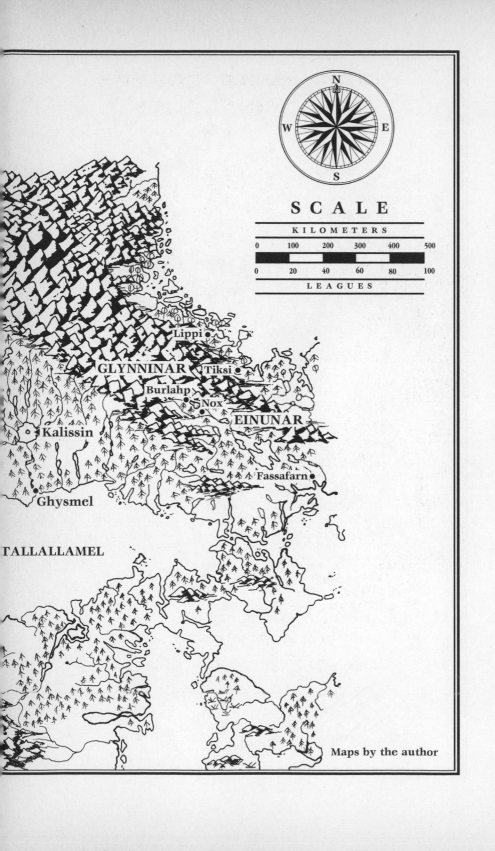

N

W E

S

SCALE

KILOMETERS

0 100 200 300 400 500

0 20 40 60 80 100

LEAGUES

Lippi

GLYNNINAR Tiksi

Burlahp

Nox

EINUNAR

Kalissin

Fassafarn

Ghysmel

TALLALLAMEL

Maps by the author

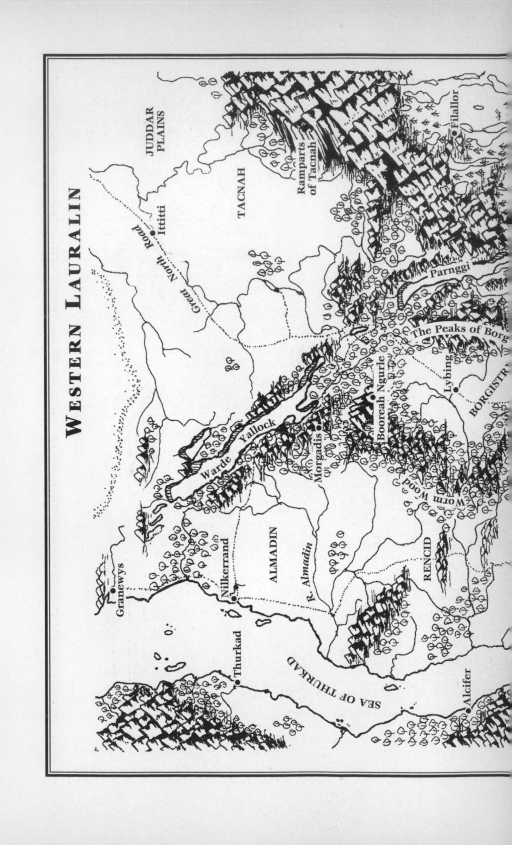

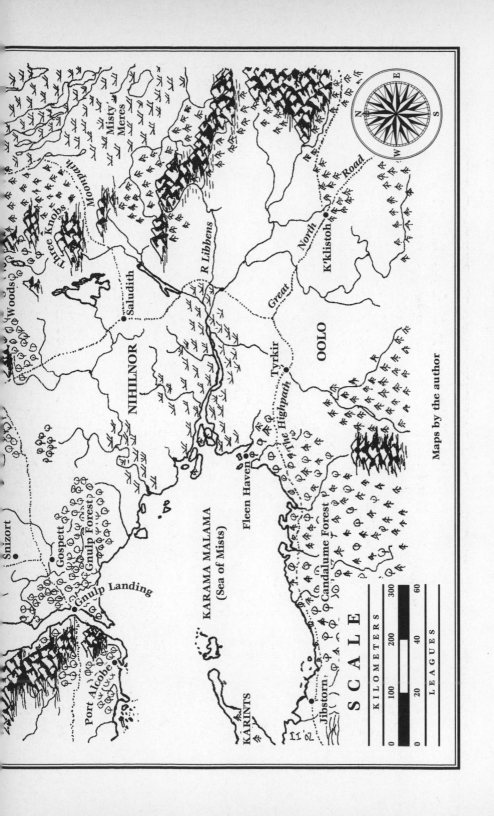

Maps by the author

SCALE

KILOMETERS
0   100   200   300

LEAGUES
0   20   40   60

Three Knobs.

Misty Meres

Woods

Mount Moonath

Saludith

R Libbens

NIHILNOR

North Great Road

K'klistoh

OOLO

Tyrkir

The Highpath

Fleen Haven

KARAMA MALAMA
(Sea of Mists)

Gnulp Forest

Gospett

Gnulp Landing

Snizort

Port Alcobe

Candalume Forest

Jibstorm

KARINTS

PART ONE

MATAH

ONE

Tiaan had been carrying the dead child for the best part of a day before she realised that something was following her. She was being hunted through an abandoned city.

She scanned her surroundings, but nothing moved in that vast chamber. An oval ceiling, carved from the solid heart of Mount Tirthrax, arched high above. Caverns ran off in five directions, though none were lit. She was somewhere inside Tirthrax, the Aachim's most magnificent city, though she had no idea where.

Her life lay in ruins. Tiaan had trekked halfway across Lauralin to save Minis, her lover-to-be, but he had cast her aside. The Aachim people had callously taken advantage of her soft heart, but in saving them she had betrayed her world. And little orphan Haani, her adopted sister, was dead – killed by an Aachim javelard in a terrible, senseless accident.

Laying Haani on the dusty floor, Tiaan sat beside her, but felt so weak she had to lie down. Her whole body was trembling. In the distance, a walkway of wires and crystal spiralled through floor and roof. She had climbed several like it in her dismal trudge through the empty city. Each time she encountered a stair, Tiaan had gone up. There was no reason for it; her feet had just taken her that way.

Haani's cheek was waxy pale; her striking, lime-green hair

had gone limp. The clothes she had dressed in so carefully were filthy. Feeling a tear welling in one eye, Tiaan ground it away with her fist. If she allowed that, she might never stop.

First she would find a suitable place to lay the child to rest. Somewhere pleasant, by a window, if there was one in this accursed city. Then she would lie beside Haani and they would sleep together, forever.

A noise roused Tiaan; a footstep on one of the crystal treads of the stair. Had the invading Aachim come back to finish her and seize the amplimet, the magical crystal that had allowed her to open a gate from here to Aachan? Let them have it. She never wanted to see it again. Though Tiaan had left the amplimet behind, she felt no withdrawal. She had felt nothing since the gate had opened.

Tiptoeing across to the hole through which the stair passed, she peered over the rim. Far below, she saw the top of a man's head. Further down on the looping staircase, no more than crystalline treads strung on taut wires, crouched a woman with a black band over her eyes. She had a small, pale face and hair like colourless silk. Her arms were wrapped around the side wires of the stair.

The man went down to her. It was Nish from the manufactory! Cryl-Nish Hlar, her enemy. Tiaan had once rejected his advances and he had never forgiven her. He must know about the gate and the Aachim. If he caught her, it would mean a death sentence.

Tiaan pulled back from the edge, out of sight. How had he found her here, hundreds of leagues from the manufactory? It did not seem possible, yet here he was. The manufactory must be determined to get her back.

Haani's body lay like a rag on the dusty floor, as cold as the glacier that had broken through the side of the mountain when the gate opened. Her hair was now covered in feathery frost. Tiaan picked the child up and for the first time felt her weight. She was so tired.

She looked around despairingly. Far off to her right Tiaan

spied another stair, this one a ribbon of metal swirling up to what, in the dimness, appeared to be a landing. She slogged across to it, and up a dozen steps before grinding to a stop.

She forced her foot up one step, then another, but halfway to the landing her strength and courage failed. Why *should* she go on? Nothing mattered any more. Why not plunge off the stair, the child in her arms, and put an end to it? Their bones would lie together in the empty city for as long as it endured.

Sagging on the treads, Tiaan stared sightlessly through the supporting meshes. Such a handsome man Minis had seemed when he called her from across the void; and so lost; and in such pain. His world, Aachan, was being torn apart by volcanic eruptions. She had trekked across the continent of Lauralin to save him; risked her life to make the gate. She had done it all for him.

But he had come with a host of Aachim in thousands of constructs, mighty engines of war – the greatest army ever assembled on Santhenar. The rustic battle clankers built by human manufactories could never match such sleek, deadly machines. The Aachim must have been preparing for war long before Minis sent out his call. They had used her, betrayed her, and she had betrayed her world. Now she was paying for it.

'She went that way, Nish!' A high, colourless voice echoed in the great room.

Tiaan scrambled to her feet and the stair rocked as she took up her burden. Every step hurt. Three-quarters of the way to the top she looked down. Nish was running straight for the base of her stair. Letting out an involuntary gasp, Tiaan climbed harder. The triumph in his eyes, his crowing over her downfall, would be unbearable.

Finally, when she could not go another step, Tiaan reached the top. Glowing spheres lit up, pointers that would not allow her to hide. She was in an empty chamber with seven sides of unequal length. Aachim designs were often asymmetric. Small archways led through each side, though all the passages were dark. To one side of the centre was the most extraordinary set of stairs Tiaan had ever laid eyes on.

5

Five separate staircases arose from a slab of polished crystal one step high. Each stair spun out and up in irregular whorls, carving arcs through the air before looping back to the centre, coiling about the others and exploding out again. It was a ludicrous extravaganza, architecture for the sheer delight of it. The stairways were built of shining metal and faceted crystal, each different, and at the top they spiralled up into darkness.

It mattered not where they went; Tiaan could not have climbed them even if a nylatl had been at her heels. She did not think of laying down her burden. 'I will never leave you,' she had promised the dying child.

Below, Tiaan could hear Nish's feet on the treads, his gasping breath. It was inconceivable that anyone could have found her here, but somehow he had. Why? She had been a fine artisan, the best in the manufactory, but not so brilliant that they would chase her halfway across the world. It *had* to be the amplimet: the strange, glowing crystal that had allowed her to reach across the void to Minis in the first place.

She became aware, deep down, of faint stirrings. Not withdrawal, just an indefinable longing for the crystal. She had been parted from it too long. Tiaan put the feelings out of her mind. If Nish wanted the amplimet, let him have it. It had been the cause of all her troubles. Dear Joeyn, the old miner who had been her first and closest friend, had died getting it for her.

The footsteps came closer. Taking up Haani, Tiaan staggered into the archway directly opposite. Spheres lit up, revealing a stone passage that curved away into darkness.

On she trudged, along a passage that seemed to have been curving forever. Tirthrax was unfathomable. It was as if she was inside an exuberant work of art, built solely for the pleasure of mastering its materials.

Her mouth was powder dry. She had not had a drink since opening the gate, a day and a night ago. Another passage slashed across the first and she turned left into it, but some twenty or thirty paces along, the passage ended in native rock. Or did it? As she headed back, from the corner of her eye the rock seemed to shift sideways into a cavity darker than black itself. She moved towards it, thinking it might be a place to hide. The blackness went back to rock.

Tiaan reached out with her free hand. Rock, unquestionably, but again as she moved her head came that flash of blackness, like a tunnel extending into the mountain. The moment she looked directly at it, it changed back into wall.

She turned her head back and forth. Blackness, wall, blackness, wall. Could she get through? There was an enchantment here and since Nish had no talent for the Art he probably could not follow.

Tiaan touched the crystal hanging on a chain around her neck – just an ordinary hedron — thinking it might help her to see more clearly. The rock vanished and a black tunnel opened up before her. She edged inside.

After several minutes, the blackness gave way to a faint glow which had no particular form, but quivered gently. It felt more like a soap bubble, but gave before her, sliding wetly over her fingers.

Any refuge was better than none. Tiaan pushed into the clinging stuff, its resistance broke and she was through. It was even colder here, and so dark that she could see nothing but the shimmering edges of a second bubble, a cube with curved faces that contained within it another, smaller cube, and inside that another, and another, and another. The hair stirred on her head. Infinity blocked her way – infinity and nothingness. This was a forbidden place.

She spun around but behind her now felt like rock, even when she touched her hedron. Tiaan moved toward the cubic bubble. Its walls began to wobble, and so did the inner cubes, vibrating faster and faster until she could no longer see them.

Shifting Haani on her shoulder, Tiaan lowered her head and pushed at the bubble. The wall parted but inside was like the previous one, though smaller. Her head touched the upper face of the cube, which was freezing. The nested cubes extended to an infinity that frightened her.

Since there was no way back, Tiaan pushed through the wall of the next cube. The first breath burned her lungs. With the next, she felt frost forming in her nostrils. She tried to back out but the wall resisted her. Panicking, she kicked the face of the cube in front of her. It was much more solid – more like flexible glass than bubble – and her sandal bounced off.

Steadying Haani, Tiaan lifted the hedron over her head. At once she saw the coloured energy patterns of the field swirling around her like a psychedelic tornado. She drew power into the hedron and reached out. As her fingers touched the wall, it thinned, so she scored the crystal across and back. The bubble vanished with a faint tinkle and a blast of freezing air. One by one, the other cubes popped until the tunnel lay open before her. Unfortunately it was also open behind. The illusory barrier had disappeared.

Some distance along, she emerged in an open cavern of rough-hewn stone shaped like a cone standing on its base. It was strikingly different from the rest of Tirthrax, where the stone had been carefully polished and intricately decorated. The rock here looked deliberately unfinished.

The cavern was dimly lit by something circular, high on one wall. Her eyes adjusted. It was a shaft that ran up through the mountain at a steep angle. Icicles hung from its lower lip and the light was daylight, deep blue as if filtered through ice. It must be morning outside.

Moving on, she passed through a blue corona like illuminated mist, though more solid. She distinctly felt its resistance. It was one of a series of concentric coloured rings lit by the light from the upper shaft. Each ring was a deeper hue than the one sur-rounding it. A circle of indigo, almost black, filled the centre. Tiaan pushed through the rings and almost fell into another shaft, a continuation of the first.

Laying Haani beside it, she peered down. The shaft was a smooth bore through the rock, its sides as polished as glass. She could not tell how far it went, though wisps of dark mist coiled lazily around the walls, and in the depths it had the look of a frozen whirlpool. She wondered what it would look like if it unfroze. Taking up a chip fallen from the ceiling, she dropped it in. It clicked off the sides a couple of times, she heard nothing for thirty or forty heartbeats, and at last a frosty tinkle. The shaft was deep. It would do.

The sounds came echoing back in reverse order: the tinkle, and a long time later the clicks, greatly magnified. The last click thundered out, whirling the coloured rings about, and silence fell once more.

The child looked to be sleeping but her little chest was sunken, the broken ribs driven into her lungs by the blow from the javelard. A smear of blood tinged her lower lip. Tiaan wiped it off, smoothing the pale hair with her fingers.

Taking Haani in her arms, she sat beside the shaft, rocking. A tear trickled down one cheek. Little Haani had been the happiest of children, living a carefree life with her mother and aunts by the lake, until Tiaan came. Until the nylatl – a creature of mad savagery – gorged itself on Haani's mother and aunts. The awful memories went round and round.

'There she is!'

Nish's cry of triumph reverberated from the tunnel. Tiaan was still cradling Haani and, before she could move, he threw himself at her.

Haani fell beside the shaft. Nish forced Tiaan's arm up behind her back so hard that she cried out. She kicked with her heel, striking him on the shin. He yelped but did not let go. As she tried to pull free, one foot went over and a pain sheared through her guts at the thought of falling. No, dying was all she had left. Tiaan threw herself into the bore.

Nish landed hard on his knees and cried out. She made no noise, nor tried to save herself, as she swung on his arm. He was a small man, not much taller than she. He could hardly hold her for long.

Her wrist slipped. 'Let me go, Nish.' Tiaan forced herself to speak calmly. 'I want to die.'

Nish's hard fingers bit into her wrist. 'I'm sure you do!' Perspiration beaded on his eyebrows, freezing even as she watched. 'You've betrayed your friends, your family, your manufactory and your world. I *won't* let you die.'

'Please, no,' she begged.

'I'm taking you back – *for justice*!'

'Revenge,' she gasped. 'That's all you care about.'

'Whatever!' He strained with all his strength.

Terror seized Tiaan. She could imagine the nightmare trip back to the manufactory, Nish tormenting her all the way. She would be paraded before her thousand former workmates, and down in her home town of Tiksi in front of her vindicated mother. After a public trial she would face a drawn-out execution, a gruesome and grisly spectacle by some method officially prescribed for the artisan she had once been. All would be lovingly recorded in the Histories and a hired teller would turn it into a cautionary tale, that the whole world know of her crime and its punishment. The Council of Scrutators required everyone to know their justice, and to fear it.

Thrashing her legs, Tiaan tried to make him drop her. Terror twisted his face as he was dragged closer to the edge. One knee slipped over. She would never have expected such desperate courage from Nish. Why didn't he let her go?

'Ullii,' he gasped. 'Help!'

The tiny woman flitted back and forth like a butterfly, her colourless hair streaming out behind her. She caught at Nish's arm, let out a piercing squeal and disappeared again.

'Ullii!' he bellowed. 'For pity's sake. I'm going to *die*!' He was on the brink now, so precariously balanced that a child could have pushed him over.

Ullii danced back, plucked at his arm then let go. Her mouth was wide open. She still wore the mask over her eyes.

'Help me!' he screamed, his terror echoing off the rough stone walls.

Lightning quick, Ullii darted forward, caught him by the belt and heaved. They swayed on the edge. It was touch and go whether they might all fall; then, with a mighty wrench, Nish had Tiaan up and over to safety. He collapsed beside Ullii.

Tiaan scrambled to her feet. He threw out an arm but she wove to one side and, letting out a cry of anguish at leaving Haani behind, fled into the darkness.

'Stop her, Ullii,' Nish wailed, but Ullii did not move.

Tiaan wept as she ran, for abandoning Haani, but she had to. Nish would never give in. She ran on, to nowhere in particular. All directions led to the same end.

She kept going for as long as she could. Always she took the central way, if there was one. Whenever she came to a stair, and she encountered many, Tiaan climbed it. Finally she could run no further. Her legs felt as if they were cooking in their own juices. She slowed to a walk, to a slack-kneed stumble. Her tongue felt like a leather strap.

She must be high in the city now. Tiaan felt dizzy and her head was throbbing. She could not seem to draw enough breath. After crawling to the top of that stair, she pushed herself onto the next floor and collapsed. Her limbs felt like glue. The outfit she had chosen for Minis was reduced to filthy, bloodstained rags. She laid her head on the floor, looking sideways at the top of the stair, awaiting her fate.

It was not long in coming. Nish walked like a man in the last throes of exhaustion. *Thump-clump*, *thump-clump*, he came. His round head appeared, capped with dark curls that clung to his skull; his spotty, unhandsome face; his strong shoulders. His jaw was set, his mouth compressed into a scar, but when he saw her lying there he gave a wolfish grin.

'Oh, Tiaan, how I'm going to enjoy your trial.

Two

Nish looked like a general who had snatched victory from the abyss of ruin. His triumph turned her stomach. Only her eyes moved as he stalked toward her.

Nish took no chances this time. Rolling her over, he put one foot on her wrist, the other across the back of her neck, and pressed hard. She did not resist. He tied her wrists behind her back and bound her to him with a length of rope.

'You'll pay!' he snarled. 'You evil, vicious traitor. You'll never stop paying until the day you die. Get up.'

Tiaan was incapable of moving. She *was* a traitor. She had betrayed her world.

He nudged her in the ribs with a boot toe. 'Move, artisan.'

She heaved, gasped and fell down. Whatever he had once felt for her, it was long gone. All she could see was contempt.

'I loathe you, artisan,' he said through clenched teeth. 'With every bone of my body I despise you. My father is a mutilated horror because of you.'

She could never forget that terrible battle on the edge of the plateau. Nish's father, Perquisitor Jal-Nish Hlar, had been struck down by a lyrinx, his face, arm and chest torn apart by its claws.

Nish lifted her to her feet by the ropes, then had to hold her up. To Tiaan's shame, her breasts were exposed through the rags of her blouse. When Nish did not even glance down, she truly knew she was finished.

'Don't try to play on my better side.' He thrust his face against hers. 'After seeing the doom you brought upon our world yesterday, I have none. *Move!*' He prodded her toward the stairs.

'I can't go down,' she said, staggering. 'I'll fall.'

He looked around, spying another stair in the dim distance. 'That way then. It'll give you time to recover.'

'Hadn't you better warn your companions?' she croaked, hoping to discover how many there were.

'I have none, only Ullii –' He broke off. '*My* first thought was for my duty. I've already sent a message to the manufactory, by skeet, warning the scrutator of the invasion.' He calculated. 'It's two hundred leagues as the skeet flies. And it flies fast: the message should be there tonight.'

'I'm glad,' she said, not that they could do much about such a mighty force of Aachim. So, she only had these two to deal with. There must come a chance, on the long journey back.

'Bah!' Nish prodded her again.

Tiaan was getting her breath back, though her knees were still wobbly. 'How did you find me?' she said, hoping Nish could not resist displaying his cleverness.

'Ullii can see the Secret Art in all its forms. Irisis and I taught her to hunt you down.'

Beautiful Irisis, Tiaan's rival at the manufactory. She might have known. Tiaan considered what Nish had said. He was clever and liked people to know it. Perhaps she could learn more.

'How did you get here so quickly?'

'We floated all the way on an enormous balloon, and it was I who first thought of it.'

'A balloon?' Even speaking hurt.

He described the device and how it worked. Tiaan listened with one ear only. Having spent her life making controllers for the eight-legged mechanical war carts called clankers, she saw the potential of flight at once. She also saw the danger, in a world where the technology of magic seemed to be escalating out of control.

13

Clankers were powered by the *field*, a nebulous aura of force surrounding naturally occurring *nodes*. That power was drawn through particular crystals called hedrons, which artisans like Tiaan shaped, *woke* and tuned to the field. But clankers required so much power, and there were now so many of them, that they had been known to drain a node of its field. One node, not far from Tiaan's manufactory, had simply failed. Hundreds of soldiers had died.

But that was not the worst. Not long ago, a convoy of racing clankers had drawn so much power that it had turned the field inside out. A thousand soldiers had been struck unconscious and when they revived, a squadron of clankers and all their crew had vanished, never to be seen again. Now the war would take to the air. How much power would that require, and what would the consequences be? Could the field survive? But if it did not, could humanity?

'Get moving, artisan.'

Tiaan took one shuffling step, attempted another, and her knees collapsed.

Ullii, who had been flitting back and forth in the shadows, crept to her side. 'She is ill, Nish,' Ullii said in a strange, empty voice.

'She's pretending. Get up, artisan.'

'You are unkind, Nish. She is very ill.' Taking a flask from her belt, Ullii held it to Tiaan's lips.

A few drops spilled onto her lower lip. Trying to lick them off, Tiaan could hear the dry rasp of her tongue. Ullii sent a small surge of water into Tiaan's mouth. Half went down her windpipe; she coughed the rest out again. Another surge; she held it this time. After running and walking and climbing leagues inside the vastness of Tirthrax, she could have drunk a bucketful.

When she'd had enough, Nish passed a wrapped food packet to his small companion. 'Give her this. I can't bear to touch her, much less waste our precious food on her.'

Ullii broke a kind of sweet, rich bread into pieces, feeding them to Tiaan with her fingers. Tiaan wondered about the small woman. She wore a black silk mask over her eyes, her ears were covered with padded muffs, yet she seemed to hear everything and know where everything was.

All too soon, Nish pulled Tiaan to her feet. She let out a faint cry as the rope tore her wrist. He only jerked it harder. Tears formed on Tiaan's lashes as she stumbled after him. She blinked them away.

'You are *cruel*, Nish,' said the small woman.

'No more than she deserves!' he snapped, and kept going.

Ullii stopped dead, crouched and slowly began to curl up, covering her face with her arms. Nish was slow to realise that she was not following. 'Ullii?' he said, looking around.

There was no reply. Tiaan expected Nish to fly into a rage but he hurried back, dragging her by the rope, and fell to his knees beside Ullii. 'I'm sorry,' he said softly. 'I'm really sorry.'

Ullii remained curled into a tiny ball. Nish took off his pack and Tiaan was amazed at the change in him. She had always thought him a lecher and a layabout, and today, a monster; but he genuinely cared for Ullii.

'It's nine in the morning. We'll camp until four.' He tossed his cloak at Tiaan's feet.

She rested on it. It was cool on this level, though not unpleasantly so. Tiaan was desperately tired but there was too much in her mind for her to sleep. The past day contained a lifetime of trauma and tragedy. Minis's betrayal, and the Aachim's treachery from the very beginning, she could not deal with.

Haani's broken body still lay beside the shaft, abandoned. I promised that I would never leave you, but I was too afraid, Haani. I had the chance to do the honourable thing. If only . . .

The day passed. Tiaan dozed but woke as tired as before and aching in every muscle. Ullii had not forgiven Nish. She did not even look in his direction when he spoke to her.

They ate in silence. Nish tied Tiaan's rope to the stair and disappeared with the water bottles. Ullii squatted, watching with her masked eyes. Tiaan did not think the seeker was doing sentry duty. What would Ullii do if she tried to escape? Tiaan did not attempt it. No doubt Nish was not far away.

After he returned, Ullii gave Tiaan a generous swig from her bottle. They headed off, Nish leading, Tiaan stumbling at the end of the rope, Ullii padding behind her. Tiaan closed her eyes. This was worse than anything she had endured in the breeding factory; worse than being held captive by the lyrinx and forced to aid them in their ghastly flesh-forming.

She sank into a dazed daydream. Tiaan had always been a dreamer, her escape from a miserable childhood in the clanker manufactory. Her daydreams arose from romantic tales her beloved grandmother had told her.

She conjured up the image of her mother's mother. Tiaan thought, and remembered, in pictures, so Grandma Aaloe's face was as clear as if she was walking beside her. A small woman, almost as wide as she was high, Aaloe had a face as round as the moon and an embrace like a warm pillow. Her man had been killed in the war when Aaloe was nineteen and Tiaan's mother, Marnie, had just conceived. Aaloe had not partnered again but her tales were full of handsome young men rescuing beautiful maidens, or as often, maidens going to the aid of lost lovers.

Minis had been Tiaan's personal dream, but within minutes of meeting him that had been destroyed. She hated him for his treachery, but despised him for being so weak. He had said he loved her, but could not stand up to Vithis. Vithis ordered Minis to repudiate Tiaan. And Minis had.

'Get a move on, artisan!'

Nish jerked the rope so hard that she fell to one skinned knee. She gave him a hate-filled glare. His returning smile reminded her of a jackal.

It had been her dreams, and her longings, that had got her into this trouble in the first place. All her life she had been a misfit. Everyone was required to mate but, being so shy, she had found one excuse after another to avoid that duty. Why could she not have settled down at the manufactory like the other artisans, taken the best partner she could find, produced the required number of children, and worked hard at the craft she had come to love?

The evening dragged on. They made slow progress, the thin

air barely enough to sustain them. No one knew where to go. Nish had tried countless ways but all doubled back on themselves as if enchanted.

Long after midnight they stopped for dinner and a nap, after which Tiaan's hands were untied and she was permitted to go into one of the bathing rooms to relieve herself. As he followed, she snapped, 'Still a little pervert, Nish?'

He went scarlet. 'Go with her, Ullii,' Nish said coldly. 'Don't take your eyes off the traitor.'

Obediently, Ullii followed Tiaan into the room but took no further notice of her. Ullii wandered about, touching everything with her fingertips. She pulled down a lever and water gushed from a device like an upside-down funnel. The small woman jumped, began to curl up, then unfolded with all the grace of a ballet dancer. Creeping back to the tap, she wiggled her fingers under the flow, entranced.

Tiaan slipped around the corner to a washing trough, beyond which she spied another door. Could it be this easy? Ullii was paying her no attention. Edging it open, Tiaan found herself in a set of chambers like many she had seen in Tirthrax. She went through the bedchamber, out the far door and tiptoed around a gentle curve. Passages led three ways. Straight ahead lay a stair entirely made of glass. More extravagant than any she had looked at so far, it looped back and forth across the room like the flourishes on the end of a queen's signature. She would be seen on it from top to bottom. But it led up, and that felt right.

As Tiaan reached the first loop of the stair she heard Nish's bellow of rage. She bolted.

'There she is!' He took the glass treads three at a time, shaking the stair with every step.

She fled up and up. Nish gained slowly. At the top she encountered another stair, made of obsidian, then a third, a simple spiral barely wider than her hips. It was so steep that to look down caused sickening lurches in her stomach.

Light appeared above her. Daylight – a way out. She hauled herself up by her arms. A cavern opened out before her, a hemisphere scooped from the native rock of the mountain. The floor, walls and roof were like polished granite, the flat side a single sheet of glass five spans high. Outside lay a platform with a high-backed stone seat, and beyond that a sea of peaks and snow and ice went all the way to infinity. The sun was rising.

Tiaan ran up to the glass and stopped. It was inset into the stone on all sides. She pressed her hands against it but had to snatch them away – the glass was bitterly cold. If there was a door she could see no sign of it, nor any other way out. Putting her back to the glass, she waited. Nish was scarlet in the face, his step as unsteady as hers, but he drove himself on.

'Don't move!' He lashed at her with the rope. One end caught her on the cheek. She cried out, he jerked her to him and swiftly bound her hands.

'Call me what you like,' he gritted, 'I'll not untie you again until we stand inside the gates of the manufactory.'

Ullii came creeping up the steps. After slowly circum-navigating the room, she looked out through the glass with her masked eyes.

When Tiaan was so bound that she could move neither hands nor arms, Nish ran a length of rope from her to him. 'Go down!' he croaked, harsh as a raven.

Dead inside, Tiaan obeyed. Should she take the first opportunity to fall and carry him with her? She had just set her foot on the top step when, with a whirr, the glass wall slid into the stone.

Nish spun around. 'What's that, Ullii?'

'I can see the Art,' Ullii said softly.

Someone rose from the seat. The figure turned, tossing back her hood. As she approached, the sun caught her hair, illuminating a few flame-red strands among the grey. Her hands were bare, the fingers remarkably long, almost twice the length of her palm. *Aachim!* Chills fizzed up and down Tiaan's backbone.

THREE

The woman stopped inside the door. She was taller than Tiaan, about the height of a human man. Her pale face was lined, though that took nothing away from an austere and ageless beauty. Large grey eyes held just a hint of green. The red eyebrows were fluffed with grey. Her small ears were perfectly circular.

'What are you doing here?' she said in the common speech. Her voice was soft, low and without accent.

No one spoke. Tiaan glanced sideways at Nish, who was staring at the woman, brow furrowed.

'Who are you?' he burst out.

The woman turned those ice-grey eyes on him. 'I am Matah. I am Tirthrax.'

'What are you doing in this lyrinx nest?'

The Matah laughed, which made her young again. Tiaan found a smile. Nish was not as clever as he thought.

'Tirthrax,' the Matah said, 'is the greatest city of the Aachim on Santhenar. It is more than three thousand years old. No lyrinx has ever come through its doors. Nor has any human, *uninvited*, until this day. I am Matah of Tirthrax. You will explain your-selves.'

Nish jerked Tiaan's lead rope so hard that she fell. 'What's going on?' Flecks of spittle spattered Tiaan's face. 'Who have you betrayed us to, artisan?'

19

'Release her,' said the Matah, in a tone cold as chips from the glacier.

'Keep out of it, old woman!'

Ullii let out a squawk as the Matah spread her arms then slowly brought her hands together in front of her. A tiny golden bubble drifted from one fingertip. Floating through the air, it struck Nish on the forehead, bursting with a spray of sparkles. He went rigid, arched his back and gasped. His teeth snapped closed on his protruding tongue. With a muffled grunt, he fell to his knees. A scarlet bead formed on his lower lip.

'I asked you to release her,' the Matah said mildly. 'Please do so.'

Ullii hooked her fingers into claws. Her breath simmered in her throat and she looked set to spring on the Matah. Despite her anger with Nish, Ullii would not tolerate any attack on him. How had he come to inspire such loyalty? Tiaan could not fathom it.

The Matah turned to Ullii, reached out with an open hand, and smiled. 'I will not harm him, little seeker.'

Ullii went still, confused. She looked from the Matah to Nish, to the Matah again.

'Ullii, help me,' he gasped.

'Give me your hand,' said the Matah.

Ullii was a mixture of emotions: delight and terror. She slowly extended her tiny hand. The Matah's fingers wrapped all the way around it, holding the grip for a long interval. Ullii let out an extended sigh and bowed her head, smiling enigmatically.

'Ullii!' Nish wailed, but she paid him no heed. He strained against bonds he could neither see nor feel.

The Matah flicked those long fingers and Nish was himself again. She inclined her head towards Tiaan. Moving as if he ached in every bone, he untied Tiaan's ropes. He looked frightened and she took fleeting pleasure from it.

'What is this talk of betrayal?' the Matah asked.

'Ask *her*!' Nish spat. 'She sold our world. Tiaan brought an army of constructs here through a gate.'

For an instant the Matah's self-possession left her. She clutched at the glass to support herself.

'*Constructs*? Through a *gate*? Is that why the mountain shook yesterday? Explain, humans! Who are you and where did you come from?'

Tiaan gave their names, then began on a halting explanation. 'I was an artisan at the manufactory near Tiksi –'

'You're a long way from home, artisan.'

Tiaan acknowledged that. 'I made controllers for battle clankers, which are armoured war carts driven by eight iron legs –'

'I know what clankers are. What about your controllers?'

'Mine were the best.' Tiaan said it without pride. 'I could see the field more clearly than anyone, and I was better at tuning the hedrons. I began to have strange crystal dreams. I dreamed that a young man cried out for help, because his world was exploding with volcanic fire. His name was Minis.'

'Minis!' the Matah said sharply. 'That is an Aachim name. An ancient one.'

'Aachan was dying,' Tiaan said, 'and Minis with it.'

'And so will we because of your folly,' said Nish. 'Why could you not do your duty like everyone else?'

'I *was* doing my duty,' she replied coldly, 'until you and your slut Irisis had me thrown out of the manufactory, and all because I refused to bed you.'

Again the Matah turned those glacier eyes on Nish, who tried to stare her down, flushed and had to look away.

'*It is the duty of every one of us to mate,*' he recited, '*to replace those who give their lives in the war.*'

'Not against her will, surely?' The Matah's voice was frosty.

'The population is falling,' said Nish. 'Will has nothing to do with it.'

'In the breeding factory they kept a bloodline register,' cried Tiaan. 'A stud book!'

'Is this what the world has come to?' said the Matah. 'What happened to the great romance?'

'Romance has nothing to do with mating,' Nish said loftily. 'Mating is duty, love mere unruly passion.'

'And you had a passion for Tiaan, or was your lust *mere* duty? Go on with your tale, Tiaan.'

21

Tiaan explained how Joeyn had found that strangely glowing crystal in the mine, one that had seemed to be drawing power from the field all by itself, without ever needing to be woken. And she told how she had fled with it.

'Minis called to me,' said Tiaan, 'when I was trapped in a blizzard, dying of cold. He taught me about geomancy, the greatest magic of all.'

'A most foolhardy young man,' said the Matah. 'A wonder it did not kill you.'

'He taught me just enough to draw power into the crystal and save my life. The Aachim called it an amplimet and –'

'An *amplimet?*' The Matah gripped the edge of the glass.

Tiaan nodded. 'In return for my own life, I promised to help the Aachim. They asked me to bring the amplimet here to Tirthrax. After many trials, including being captured by the lyrinx and forced to help them with . .' Her voice cracked. She shuddered. 'I suffer dreadfully from withdrawal when the crystal is taken away. At least, I used to before the gate was made. Using that weakness, the enemy forced me to channel power for their *flesh-forming.*' She told that story, including the tale of the nylatl. 'Eventually I managed to escape, using the crystal, and brought it here.'

'Here?' the Matah asked hoarsely.

'Minis told me to give it to your people, but I found Tirthrax abandoned.'

'Not abandoned,' said the Matah. 'My people have gone, en masse, north to our other city, Stassor. The war comes ever closer and they are meeting to see what may be done about it. They won't be back until next year. It is a long and hazardous journey.'

'By the time I arrived,' Tiaan continued, 'the Aachim were too weak to do anything with the crystal.' She glanced at Nish, then away. 'I had to save them. They told me how to assemble a gate-making device, which I called a port-all. I put the amplimet into the core of it, followed their instructions and created a gate.'

'*You* made a gate, from here to Aachan?' cried the old woman. 'Alone?'

'Yes,' Tiaan said faintly.

'Where is the port-all now?'

Tiaan moved close and whispered in the Matah's ear, watching Nish all the while. 'It is in the hall by the great glass gong.'

'Ah!' said the Matah. 'Continue, if you please.'

'I did all the tests and called Minis. The gate opened but the Aachim began to come through, in *constructs*.' She described the sleek metal machines and the way they hovered above the ground.

'I know all about constructs,' the Matah interrupted. 'I saw the first one ever built. How many were there?'

'I don't know,' said Tiaan. 'Thousands, certainly, and each contained ten or fifteen people.'

'There were more than eleven thousand constructs,' said Nish. 'I counted the ranks as they passed. They have gone down to the lowlands to wage war against Santhenar. You have betray-ed your world, Tiaan.'

The Matah looked wan. 'I must sit down.' She slumped on the floor with her head resting on her knees.

'As *I* was betrayed,' said Tiaan bitterly. 'They must have been planning this invasion for a long time, for such a fleet of con-structs would have taken decades to build. They used me and killed little Haani, who never hurt anyone in her life.' Tears ran down her cheeks. 'Vithis offered money in exchange!' She glared at the old woman. 'That was the grossest insult of all.'

'Reparation must be paid,' the Matah replied. 'How did it happen? Did you threaten them?'

'How could I threaten eleven thousand constructs?' Tiaan raged. 'She died because they were afraid. The Aachim are liars and cheats, and as timid as rabbits.'

The Matah tightened her lips. 'You may call them cowards if you dare, though it sounds like an accident to me. But know this, Tiaan: to impugn our honesty is a mortal insult that every Aachim will fight to avenge.'

'They callously and deliberately deceived me about their intentions, and about the gate. They said they were just a few thousand. A lie. They said –'

23

'I will leave it to them,' said the Matah hastily. 'But tell me – have they mastered all the secrets of Rulke's lost construct? Did the machines fly?'

'Not that I saw.' Tiaan dashed her tears away. 'They just hovered above the floor. Vithis called me an incompetent fool, after all I had done for him. Minis turned his cheek to me, and then they went away.'

'We can be arrogant,' said the Matah, 'but Aachim are rarely rude, unless unbearably provoked. Who were the leaders?'

'I met three,' said Tiaan. 'Tirior of Clan Nataz, Luxor of Clan Izmak, and Vithis. Are you related?'

'We Aachim of Santhenar broke the clan allegiances long ago. My house was Elienor, named for our most famous ancestor, though it was always the least of the clans. Many of Clan Elienor have red hair, as I did once.'

'I did see people with red hair,' said Tiaan.

'That is good. I would see my lost house again. What of Vithis? Did he name his clan?' The Matah looked as if she already knew.

'He named it Inthis – First Clan,' said Tiaan.

'Ah, Inthis!'

'But the gate went wrong and his entire clan was lost in the void, save for Minis. Vithis blamed me. He is a hard, cruel man.'

The Matah's eyes sparked. 'Inthis was ever the greatest clan – and in excess, too. We have been led by them more than by any other clan, sometimes to disaster. Tensor was such a man; a great leader driven to folly. Yet he strove for the good of all Aachim, not out of clan rivalry which ever held us back on Aachan. The gate went wrong, you say?'

'Vithis said I had built the port-all the wrong way around, left-handed instead of right, and that made the gate go awry. But I built it exactly as I was instructed. I still have the image in my mind. I will never be rid of it.'

'Left-handed?' said the Matah. 'I recall something about that, from our Histories. Yes, what is left-handed on Aachan is right-handed here, and that includes crystals that bend a beam of light one way or the other. Handedness cannot be discerned from afar, but the matter was known to the ancients. Vithis should have checked before he instructed you in the making of the gate. Even so, that should not have made it go wrong.'

Tiaan searched for a memory of that terrible day. She had a feeling there was something else, but it would not come. Had she blundered, condemning thousands to death in the void?

'I'll take a look at the port-all later,' said the Matah, shaking her head at some thought. 'The loss of First Clan is a cataclysm for Vithis and a blow to every clan, for all their rivalry. I fear what will come from it. Did he take the amplimet?'

'Vithis said it would have been corrupted by the gate, or by me. I think he was afraid of it.'

'He showed sense, in that at least,' said the Matah, her mouth down-curling. 'And then?'

'Vithis said, "We have a world to make our own," and they went out the side of the mountain.'

The Matah sat, thinking. 'Peril hangs over us and only I to stop it. I felt the ripples in the field, even before the mountain shook. I tried to ignore it. Ah, and I was so close. *I was on my way.*'

Eventually it was Nish who asked the question. 'Where were you going?'

'I was on my way to the Well.'

'The Well?' he echoed.

'The Well of life and rebirth. The Well of fate. I was going to The Well of Echoes.'

'You were going to kill yourself?' Nish said sneeringly. 'How pathetic!'

The Matah sprang up, looking, for all her age, rather sprightly. 'How dare you thrust your twisted values on me, old human! You are not even my *species.*'

Nish backed away.

Tiaan shivered, for it was freezing. The Matah placed a hand against the wall and the glass slid closed. 'Alas, I cannot go *now.* Neither can I be in three places at once.' She paced across the hemispherical chamber. 'How came you here?' She addressed the question to Tiaan.

'I walked from Itsipitsi,' Tiaan replied. 'Before that, I sailed by iceboat upriver from the sea.'

'And you, artificer?' said the Matah.

'By *balloon*,' he said proudly. 'All the way from the manufactory near Tiksi. And it was my idea.'

'Balloon?'

'A gasbag ten spans high, filled with hot air from a stove.'

'Do you still have it?'

'It lies on the slope of the mountain, directly below us.'

'Take it back to warn your people.'

'I sent a skeet the day before yesterday.'

'It may not get there. Hurry! This is urgent, artificer.'

'I can't find the way out.'

Taking a piece of paper from her pocket, the Matah sketched swiftly. 'This point, here, is the stair behind you.'

'First I have to gather fuel,' said Nish. 'There are no trees where the balloon is hidden, only bushes. And the winds –'

'I'm sure you'll find a way. After all, *it was your idea*. Go at once!'

He did not move. He was still looking for a way to get Tiaan away. 'But –'

'Begone!' roared the Matah, 'or you shall feel real power.' She swept her hands together and more of those golden bubbles quivered there.

Nish held his ground. He was brave enough, Tiaan thought grudgingly.

'Take food from the lower storerooms, should you require it,' said the Matah.

'I –'

'*Now!*' She hurled the bubbles at him.

One struck his cheek and a yellow blister swelled there. Nish cried out, dashed the bubble away and bolted down the stairs.

'And you?' the Matah said to Ullii. 'What will you do, little seeker?'

Ullii came to her. The Matah put her fingers around the small woman's head. A golden nimbus shimmered like a halo, lifting her colourless hair into drifting tendrils.

'Go, child,' said the Matah. 'Follow your mate, and beware.'

'Nish will never hurt me,' Ullii said serenely.

The Matah searched her face, then touched her on the shoulder. 'I pray that you are right, though I fear otherwise.'

Ullii went after Nish. The Matah turned back to Tiaan. 'What will you do with your life?'

'I ought to end it, to make up for all the evil I have done.'

'You know nothing about evil, Tiaan. I pray you never will.' The Matah held her gaze until Tiaan looked down.

Pressing her palm to the wall, the Matah went outside to stand at the edge of the platform. Tiaan followed, shuddering in the cold. Her bare toes began to ache. The mountain towered above them, for they were barely a third of the way up it. Ahead and to either side stood peaks and glaciers as far as the eye could see, and that was very far in the crystalline air. Below lay a vast ice sheet, breaking away into glaciers all along one side.

'It's lovely,' she sighed.

The Matah glanced at her. 'I never tire of it. I come here every day that the weather permits. But you are cold.' Taking the coat from her shoulders, she wrapped Tiaan in it.

Tiaan took it gratefully and shuffled to the edge, looking down on a sheer drop of at least a thousand spans. The great horn of Tirthrax hung directly above her. She had never been this high before, and her lungs strained at the thin air. 'It would be so easy,' she said aloud.

Tiaan expected the Matah to talk her out of it, but she sat on the stone seat, saying nothing. The eyes were penetrating, though Tiaan could read nothing in them.

'Do you not care if I live or die?' Tiaan asked, trying to provoke a reaction. Why had the Matah saved her from Nish, only to ignore her now?

'I care,' said the Matah, 'for I see you have much to offer. But if you really did plan to take your life, and I convinced you not to, you would do it as soon as my back was turned.' She stared at the ice cap. The wind whistled around the edge of the platform.

Tiaan regarded her blue, throbbing toes. Better get inside before she got frostbite. She was not going to end it after all.

'I have a great deal to put right.' Tiaan turned away from the edge.

'I hoped you would think that way,' said the Matah, 'since I foresee that you have a part to play in the coming war. Come in out of the cold.'

Tiaan made no reply, but as the glass closed and they headed down the stair, she was thinking: I *will* have my revenge on Minis and all his kind. I will bring them down if it takes the rest of my life. Her gaze settled on the grey head below her. The Matah was also Aachim. Must she destroy her as well?

The Matah waited for her at the bottom. 'Anything else you'd like to tell me, Tiaan?'

Tiaan flushed. 'No,' she said softly. 'I don't know what's going on. Why do folk do the things they do?'

'Because they must.'

'I've never been able to understand people. Machines are so much easier, and more reliable.'

'That would appear to be your problem.

FOUR

They went down, then up on the other side, to a small set of chambers simply furnished in metal and fabrics as smooth as silk. They ate together. It was plain fare – black grainy bread, preserved meat so hard that the Matah shaved curls from it with a knife, cheese layered with mustard seeds and something yellow that had the crispness and pungency of onion. The meal was settled with a glass each of a sublime green wine.

The Matah rose. 'You must excuse me. Thanks to you I have urgent business to attend to.'

Tiaan quaffed her wine. The fumes went up her nose, her head spun, she had a vague memory of the Matah laying her on a pallet and drawing a cover over her, and that was all.

When she woke, the sun was streaming in through a glassed porthole high on the western wall. It was mid-afternoon. Tiaan stretched aching limbs and rose. Food had been set out on a stone table and a set of clothes laid over the end of the bed. Nearby was a bathing room. Pressing down the levers for water, she tore off her stained rags – clothes selected so she would look her best for Minis. Tiaan looked back on that morning, only two days ago but a lifetime away, contemptuous of the naïve trembling girl she had been. She *had* been a girl, though it had been her twenty-first birthday. That person, that life was over.

With a shudder of disgust, Tiaan hurled her rags into a refuse basket. Taking off the plaited leather bracelet Haani had made for her birthday, she laid it carefully on the bed. It was her most precious possession now. She stood under the warm water, brooding. She despised Minis for his fickleness, his treachery, but most of all because she had loved him with all her passionate heart and he had been too weak to stand up for her. Love was for fools! She would never love again.

On the way back, she caught sight of herself in a metal mirror mounted on the wall. Tiaan stopped to stare. Mirrors were rare in her part of the world and she had never seen a full-length one.

Neither tall nor short, Tiaan had a slender yet womanly figure which the matron of the breeding factory had rated well enough. Her skin was her best feature – it was silky smooth and the colour of honey dripping from a comb.

Pitch-dark hair, cut straight just below her ears, framed a neat oval face whose most striking feature was a pair of almond eyes, so deep-brown that they were almost purple. In better times they'd had a liquid sparkle; now they were fixed in a hard stare. Her mouth, full enough to be called sensuous, was compressed into a ridge that hid most of her remarkably coloured lips, the reddish-purple of blackberry juice.

Tiaan jerked away from the image. Neither face nor figure had moved Minis in the end. Dressing in the blouse and loose pants the Matah had left, she took enough food and drink to satisfy her. There was a kind of bread, or cake, stuffed to bursting with dried fruits, nuts, seeds and candied peel, then sliced so thin that she could see through it. There were roses and other flowers crystallised with solutions of honey. The flavours were so subtle and the creations so delicate that Tiaan could scarcely bear to touch them. There were exotic vegetables, none of which she recognised, preserved in oil as red as cedarwood.

Having eaten her fill, she was at a loss. Her dreams of revenge were foolish; futile. That armada of constructs must be twenty leagues away by now. Feeling her resolve fading, she went looking for the Matah and eventually found her on the frigid balcony.

'Good afternoon, Tiaan,' she said, without looking around.

Tiaan stood there, uncertainly. The Matah patted the stone seat. Tiaan perched uncomfortably on it, for the cold went right through her trousers.

'What will you do now?' the Matah said softly.

'I must lay Haani to rest.'

'Where is the child?'

'I left her beside a great shaft that plunges down toward the mountain's heart.'

'What?' The Matah sprang to her feet. 'How came you to the Well of Echoes?'

Tiaan scrambled off the seat. 'N-Nish hunted me there. I meant no harm.'

'Be calm, child. You could do no harm there, though it might well have harmed you. How did you get into that place? It should not have been possible.'

Tiaan explained what she had done, and why. Coming up close, the Matah lifted the hedron on its chain but let it fall. She put her palms on Tiaan's cheeks, thumbs resting on either side of her nose, the long, long fingers wrapped around her head. She stared into Tiaan's eyes for a good while, then let go, shaking her head.

'There is something about you, Tiaan . . .'

'What?' Tiaan said uneasily.

'I cannot say, though it rings alarms. You are in peril. Either that, or you *are* peril. Come, I will take you to the Well!'

The Matah dissolved the re-formed cubic barrier with a gesture and they entered the tunnel. Tiaan had forgotten the cold of that place, even worse than outside. The smooth-as-glass walls of the tunnel were networked with feathery patterns of ice crystals. The whole tunnel felt to be breathing cold, for little whooshes of wind would rush past, ruffling her hair, only to turn and blow down the back of her neck.

Even when the breeze blew from behind, Tiaan found it difficult to move forward. Each step proved more difficult than the last. How had she entered so effortlessly the previous time? The Matah, who had been only a few strides ahead, had now disappeared around the corner. Tiaan forced herself on. It felt like the time she had tried to put the crystal into the port-all, before she opened the gate and brought her world to ruin.

She had done too much and could do no more. When the Matah came back, Tiaan was on the floor, hunched up against the cold. The Matah lifted Tiaan to her feet, taking her hand, and at once the opposing force was gone. Tiaan followed her to the room and the Well.

Though the room was a simple cone of rough-cut rock, its magic was manifest. Deep blue light from the shaft cut through the dark space, highlighting mist that drifted in lazy coils centred on the Well. The air was so fresh and crisp it tingled with every breath. Scattered snowflakes floated above the shaft. One landed on Tiaan's sleeve and it was a perfect, six-pointed star, a crystal so lovely that she wished Haani could have seen it.

Haani lay beside the shaft as if sleeping. There was frost in her hair. Tiaan took her icy hand. The Matah went to her knees, probing Haani's chest with her fingertips. 'Poor child. Why is it always the young ones?' She seemed lost in some tragedy of her own.

Tiaan stood with head bowed, waiting silently.

Eventually the Matah turned to her. 'Is there a death ritual you wish to observe?'

'I don't know the customs of her people,' Tiaan said. 'As for my own, we bury our dead, but I can't dig a hole through rock.'

'Nor should she lie in the catacombs filled with our dead. Her spirit could not dwell comfortably in such a culture-haunted place.' The Matah circled the shaft.

Tiaan looked in. Blue tendrils rotated down as far as she could see. The Well seethed with power, like a spring under tension.

The Matah put one knuckle against her lip and gnawed at it, then bent to stroke the hair out of Haani's eyes. As abruptly, she stood up.

'Wait!' She strode off along the further extension of the tunnel.

Tiaan sat beside Haani, holding the frigid wrist, not thinking at all. After a long wait, the Matah reappeared with a basket in one hand and a roll of fabric in the other. Placing it on the floor, she offered the basket to Tiaan. It contained small bunches of cuttings from a black, glossy-leaved plant, at the tips of which were small flowers, purple outside and white within, crimped in the form of five-pointed stars.

'We Aachim cleave more to metal and stone than we do to gardening,' she said, 'but there are one or two among us who care for growing things. These are the best I could find in this part of the city.'

'They're beautiful,' Tiaan said. 'Haani loved trees and flowers.' Folding the child's arms across her broken chest, Tiaan placed a bunch of flowers in her hand.

The Matah unrolled the cloth, woven of a thread like metallic silk in subtle patterns of green and gold. They wrapped the child in it, leaving just her face exposed.

'I would, if you see fit,' said the Matah, 'send Haani to the Well. It is an honour accorded to the greatest of us after death, and occasionally taken before that, if we so choose.' She looked sideways at Tiaan. 'I do not know . . .'

'She is dead!' Tiaan said more harshly than she felt. 'She does not care.'

'The ritual is for the living as well as the dead. But only if you judge it fitting.'

'I would honour her to the limit of my ability.'

'Just so.' Again the Matah went up the passage, returning with a metal object like a sled with three runners. Of blue-black metal, it was chased all over with intricate, interwoven patterns.

They lifted Haani onto the sled, binding her there with silken cords. She looked tiny. 'Make your farewell,' said the Matah, 'then push her to the centre. The Well will take her in its own time.' She walked away.

Tiaan stood over the child, thinking of all that might have been. Tears spotted Haani's face, forming frost marks there. Tiaan murmured a prayer, remembered from her childhood, and then could stand it no longer.

She thrust the sled into the shaft. It sat in mid-air as if resting on a sheet of glass. Scooping a handful of flowers from the basket,

Tiaan sprinkled them over the body. Errant petals moved about as though on a current of air. Some drifted around the shaft.

The sled moved down, almost imperceptibly at first. Staring at the little pinched face, Tiaan felt such a pang in her heart that she thought it was going to tear apart. Letting out a great cry of anguish, she leapt into the Well.

She landed on an invisible barrier that would not let her through, no matter how she screamed and clawed at it. The Matah had anticipated her. Tiaan went still, watching the sled drift down. The Matah, hands out, drew her back. They looked at one another.

'The Well is only for those at peace with the world.'

'And if you are not?' said Tiaan.

'I made sure it would not take you.'

'*You* were going to the Well.'

'I felt my time had come. Did you not say that you have much to put right?'

'I'm sorry. I don't know what came over me.'

The hand released her. 'Don't stand too close,' the Matah said.

Haani's body drifted down and out of sight. A long time later there was a bright flash in the depths. A shiny bubble came rolling up the shaft. Tiaan ducked out of the way as it burst with a set of silver rays and a faint scent of flowers.

'The Well has taken her,' said the Matah. 'Come.'

Rubbing her eyes, Tiaan followed the Matah back to her chambers, where she unsealed a flask of turquoise liquor, so thick that it oozed. Pouring a hefty slug into two goblets, she passed one to Tiaan.

'Thank you, Matah.' Tiaan picked up her goblet but did not taste it.

The Matah smiled. 'Matah is a title, not my name.'

'What does it mean?'

'It's hard to say in your language. "Flawed" or "ambiguous" hero, perhaps.'

Tiaan's curiosity was aroused. 'Why flawed?'

'My people are in two minds about my role in the Histories.'

'What is your role?'

'*Was*,' she corrected. 'It was a long time ago. I have outlived my own expectations. My people felt that I worked too hard for humanity, in all its forms, and not hard enough for my own Aachim kind. I am venerated, yet an outcast. That is why I remained in Tirthrax when everyone else went to Stassor last year. I was not welcome at their meet.'

Tiaan took a sip of her liquor and immediately regretted it. Its thickness clung to her tongue, trickling pulses of a burning floral pungency up her nose and down her throat. She would not have been surprised if steam had burst from her nostrils. It cleared her head though, blasting the last hours clear away.

'Who are you?' she said raspily, feeling the hot passage of the liquor all the way to the pit of her stomach. She put the goblet aside, searching through her memories of the Great Tales, and the lesser, for clues to the Matah's identity. Many were the brave, and noble, and ultimately futile deeds done in the struggle with the lyrinx. Four Great Tales had been made in the last hundred years alone, though the Matah must predate them.

'I played a part in what was once known as the greatest of all the Great Tales,' the Matah said. 'The *Tale of the Mirror*. Sadly, that tale has fallen out of favour with your scrutators.'

That reminded Tiaan of something old Joeyn the miner had once said to her. He'd said that the Histories had been rewritten. A question for another time.

'I've heard that tale,' said Tiaan. 'Who are you?'

'My name is Malien.'

Malien! A famous name from the Histories. The Aachim could be long-lived, Tiaan knew, but she could hardly take it in. She was in the presence of a legend. 'You always seemed to be strong, yet kindly.'

Malien met her eyes. 'I can be hard as stone if I must.'

In the early hours of the morning, growing feelings of longing for the amplimet, and growing unease, drew Tiaan down to the chamber with the glass gong. It was not exactly withdrawal, for she had not felt that since putting the amplimet inside the port-all and opening the gate.

35

She had often thought that the amplimet had some purpose of its own, developed over the thousands, if not millions of years it had lain in that cavity in the mine, after it had *woken*. Had she freed it to work on some purpose as aged as the very bones of the mountains? And what care would such a mineral *awareness* have for petty humans and their transient lives and deaths? Maybe it had been using her. How could she hope to understand the purpose of something that could, with perfect patience, wait out a million years? Tiaan was afraid of the amplimet now, yet she could not give it up.

She approached the hall tentatively, for it reeked with bitter memories. It was as cold as outside. An icy wind, whistling down the glacier from the ice cap, whirled in through the side of the mountain, frosting everything in its path.

Tiaan had entered from a stair that ended near the outer wall. As she paced toward the port-all, every step was a nagging reminder. Over to her right was the pile of rubble and ice Haani had sheltered behind. Before her lay one of the bags of platinum Vithis had thrown to her, wealth enough to buy the manufactory and everything in it. The bag had burst open, scattering slugs of precious metal across the floor.

Her boot struck something that tinkled. She bent down, then drew back. It was the ring, woven of precious metals, she had made so lovingly for Minis. Every strand held a wish or a dream. Impossible to identify with those girlish longings now.

Picking it up, Tiaan drew back her arm to hurl it out onto the glacier, but stopped in mid-throw. 'I will use it against him,' she said aloud. 'I will see him beg for it, then spurn him the way he did me.'

Putting the ring on the chain about her neck, she gathered up the platinum. It might also be useful in her quest to bring the Aachim down. After some minutes she reached the place where the gate had opened. The stone floor was scorched and the three constructs that had locked together in the gate were nearby. One lay on its side, its skin of shining blue-black metal crushed. The second was upside down. The third sat on its base but the front was smashed in.

A little thread of curiosity tugged at her. How did the constructs work? Were they like clankers, or completely different? Tiaan wondered if they might be repaired. She walked around the machines but kept going. The call of the amplimet was stronger.

She continued to the room where she had assembled the port-all. Scattered mounds of rubble had been blasted out of the wall as the gate formed. Tiaan expected to find the port-all a slaggy heap of metal and glass but it looked exactly as she had built it.

Memories of using the port-all, and opening the gate, stirred her hackles. Why, when she had built it exactly as shown, had it gone so wrong? She ran through the memories. Could it have been the wrong-handedness of it? She tried to reconstruct her recollections but again something eluded her.

As she hurried forward, longing for the amplimet etched molten tracks across her heart. She ran around the side of the machine, trying to see through the network of glass, metal, wire, ceramic and shaped stone. She was looking for the soapstone basket that held the amplimet. There it was, inside that de-formed doughnut of glass that Haani had called the twisticon.

With trembling fingers Tiaan reached out to open the basket, already seeing the amplimet in her mind's eye. It was a bipyra-mid of quartz, inside either end of which were radiating balls of needle crystals. Single, extended needles ran down the long axis of the crystal, separated by a little central bubble half-filled with liquid. Most unusual of all, the crystal had glowed, faintly when it was a long way from a node, strongly when close. Here in Tirthrax, radiance had positively flooded out of it.

There was no resistance this time. Her fingers went straight to the catch. She flicked it and the soapstone basket sprang open.

Tiaan let out a cry of anguish.

The amplimet was gone.

Malien! Earlier, the Matah had not been able to control her desire for it. She must have come for it in the night. A pang of rage twisted Tiaan's insides. Despite her vow, she could not bear anyone else to have it. Joeyn had died getting it for her.

Malien was not in her chamber. Tiaan searched her rooms but

the amplimet was not there. Sinking on the bed, she put her throbbing head in her hands. Malien might have hidden it anywhere.

She became aware that Malien was standing in the doorway, staring at the mess. Tiaan felt an irrational surge of rage. Keep calm; don't give yourself away. All in vain. She threw herself at the older woman, beating at her with her fists. 'What have you done with it?'

Malien held her easily. Aachim were strong, even old ones. 'What is the matter, Tiaan?'

'The amplimet is gone!'

Malien turned and ran.

'Where are you going?' Tiaan ran after her. The old woman was moving faster than Tiaan's weary legs could run. 'Wait.'

Malien allowed her to catch up. '*I* haven't taken it, which can only mean one thing.'

Nish, of course. Tiaan felt such a fool.

'I should never have left it there,' said Malien. 'What if it falls into the wrong hands?'

'What do you mean by the *wrong hands*?' Tiaan panted.

'Any hands but yours.'

'Or *yours*?'

'Even when I was young, I never wanted power. Besides . . .'

'What?'

'You had the crystal for months, and used it to do mighty works. By now it will be so imprinted with you that others may only use it at their peril.'

That was not as convincing as it sounded. Tiaan had seen the look in Malien's eyes when first the amplimet had been mentioned.

At the door to the port-all chamber, Malien checked, as if afraid to go in. 'If only this were a dream and I could wake from it.' She passed a hand over her eyes and pushed through the door. 'After the Forbidding was broken, we thought we were free of gates and what they brought. Only one man knew how to make them – old Shand – and he swore he would take the secret to his grave. I'm sure he did. We never thought *that* knowledge

38

would return from across the void. Who would have thought it could?

'Ingenious,' Malien continued, walking around the port-all, giving Tiaan curious looks as she did. 'You are quite a mechanician, Tiaan.'

'I just put it together from a pattern Minis sent to me. I don't claim to understand it.'

'Few Aachim could have built this from a mental image.' Malien sat on a piece of fallen stone, deep in thought.

Tiaan fretted. 'He's getting away, Malien.'

'Let me think this through. It has to be your friend, Nish. Take this.' She handed Tiaan a rod, about the length of a sword, made of black metal, though it was comparatively light.

Tiaan handled it as if it was about to explode. 'What is it for?'

Malien chuckled. 'To whack him over the head, if necessary. Have you clothes for outside?'

Tiaan ran to the room where she had left her pack, days ago, and dressed in her old down-filled pants, coat and boots. When she returned, Malien was standing by the crashed constructs. She wove her long fingers into a knot, tore it apart, then began to make another, which she also wrenched undone.

'These things are just like Rulke's machine. I'm afraid, Tiaan, as I have never been before. Afraid of my own kind.'

'Were you not afraid of Rulke?'

'Very. But he was only one man with one construct, and we knew his character, for we had the Histories to guide us. Rulke, within his own strange code, was an honourable man. This is different. Vithis, embittered by the loss of his clan, now leads a mighty force. It will tip the balance.'

'What are you going to do?' Tiaan said anxiously, yet glad Malien was taking charge.

'I don't know.' Malien stepped back, eyeing the constructs. 'I wonder if these might be repaired . . .'

'Are you a mechanician too?' Tiaan cast anxious glances at the entrance.

Malien smiled thinly. 'The least among my people, though I

am not entirely without talent.' She cocked an eye at the construct which was smashed at the front. 'This one does not seem to be badly damaged.' She gave Tiaan a long, assessing glance. 'Maybe later.' Malien headed for the entrance.

Among the tumbled columns and heaps of rubble and ice, they looked down. Just below, the glacier had gouged out the side of the mountain in a curving scar, forming a surface like a road, though the broken, up-jutting slate would be difficult to walk on. Beyond ran a river of blue ice a good league across, scarred with crevasses large enough to swallow whole villages. The glacier, the fastest in the world, could be heard plucking and grinding at its bed. Every so often a crevasse would crack open, the sound echoing across the valley. How would they ever find Nish in this wilderness of rock and ice?

Malien began to climb down. 'Are you coming, Tiaan?'

'He's probably floated away in his balloon already,' she said miserably.

'He'd have to gather fuel first and that could take days.' Malien picked her way down the side of the mountain as if she knew exactly where she was going.

'Can you sense the amplimet?'

'I wish I could.' Malien looked more at ease now. 'He said the balloon was directly below us and the only fuel was bushes, so it must lie above the tree line. It can't be more than a few hours down the slope, and a gasbag ten spans high will be visible from a long way. We'll find him.'

They rested every half-hour. The downhill walking was unexpectedly tiring. On their second stop, as Tiaan was sipping from her flask, there came a monumental crash that shook the rock beneath her. She dropped the flask and scrambled for it as the water gurgled out.

'What was that?' The start of an avalanche, she imagined.

'Icefall,' said Malien. 'The glacier runs over a precipice. See, just there. Every so often, the overhanging ice breaks off and falls a thousand spans to the plain.'

They continued, more warily now, though the jumbled rocks here provided plenty of cover. Shortly Malien stopped. 'Ah, this is hard on my old knees. Creep up onto that rock, Tiaan, and see if you can see anything.'

As Tiaan put her head over the top she saw a black, swelling mushroom, not a third of a league below. 'It's just down there,' she hissed.

Malien climbed up beside her. 'Ingenious design.' She shaded her eyes as she stared at the balloon. 'It looks nearly inflated. We'd better hurry.'

They had not gone far when Tiaan felt a pang in her right temple, a stabbing pain that disappeared as quickly as it had come. She let out a gasp.

Malien stopped at once. 'What's the matter?'

'Just a headache. It's gone now.'

'Take some more water,' Malien advised.

Tiaan took another few sips, though she knew dehydration was not the problem. The pang reminded her of something she had put out of mind a long time ago and did not want to think of now.

A little further on, Malien crouched down between the boulders. 'I don't like this,' she muttered.

'What is it?'

'We're being watched.'

Tiaan scanned the sky. 'I can't see a thing.'

'I can. Come, quickly! There are three of them, and since they're flying . . .' Malien pointed high in the western sky, where Tiaan now discerned a speck, and then two more.

'Lyrinx!'

FIVE

Nish slammed his way down the stairs, so angry that he dared not speak, lest he take out his frustrations on Ullii. One minute he had succeeded against all the odds and made up for his previous follies. The next he had lost and was good for nothing but to be sent to the front-lines in the hopeless war against the lyrinx. Nish was a proud and ambitious young man who took failure hard.

At the bottom he waited for Ullii. The little seeker moved confidently, despite the mask. Nish never ceased to marvel at her agility. It would be easy to fall off, which would be fatal, but she made not a single misstep.

'You are sad, Nish,' she said as she reached the floor, not even out of breath.

Another wonder: how someone who took no exercise could be fitter than he. Nish's heart was still pounding. 'What am I going to say to the scrutator, Ullii? He'll have my head for this.'

'No one could fight the Matah, Nish.'

Ullii could see the Secret Art in all its forms, as knots in a lattice she created in her mind. It was her special talent, one that made her worth a thousand of him. 'You were very friendly to her,' he said harshly, and immediately regretted it. He moderated his tone. 'What did you see, Ullii?'

'Matah is old. She is wise and kind, but sad too. She has lost a whole world.'

That was food for thought, though not what he was looking for. 'What kind of knot does she have, Ullii? Is she a powerful mancer?'

'Matah is very strong, but she did not use her strength against you. Be careful, Nish.'

'Ha!' He headed down the next set of stairs, which were made of alabaster. Nish was no coward, but he knew which battles to fight and which to keep away from.

At the bottom of the next set of stairs, as Nish was consulting his map, Ullii said, 'I can see Tiaan's crystal.'

He dropped the map, just managing to catch it before it fluttered through the hole to the next level. He'd assumed that the Aachim would have taken the amplimet. 'You mean it's still here?'

'I can *see* it.'

She meant in her lattice. Of course she could; she had tracked it all this way from the manufactory. And Tiaan too – Ullii had found her after Tiaan had been missing for months. 'Where is it? Quick, before they think of it.'

Using the map, it took less than an hour to regain the level where the gate had been made. Nish looked around him. They were in an oval chamber, so large that a good-sized town could have been built inside it, with doors and subsidiary chambers everywhere.

'Over there.' Ullii pointed.

Nish ran, looking over his shoulder all the way. There had been too many failures; too many disappointments. Inside the room he was confronted by a strange-looking machine, all glass and crystal, ceramic and wires, ghostly in the dim light. He roved around, trying to make sense of it. Nish did not know what the amplimet looked like. He had never seen it, and the port-all contained dozens of crystals.

'Ullii?' he shouted. The sound echoed back and forth for ages. That made him afraid, too.

She came creeping through the door as though trying not to attract attention. Her life was avoiding people. Ullii looked troubled, as if expecting him to yell at her again.

'I can't find the amplimet,' he said softly.

She walked up to the port-all, reached out and took the crystal from a soapstone basket. Nish was amazed that it could be so easy.

She held it in her hand, gazing curiously at it. The amplimet resembled other hedrons Nish had seen in the manufactory, except for one small detail: it glowed.

'It's different now.' Ullii turned it over in her hand.

Alarm choked him up. 'What do you mean? Is it damaged? Ruined?'

'No,' she said softly. 'It's just as strong, but it has a different knot.'

'What can you tell about it?'

She put her hand over the mask as if to block out the least glimmer of light. 'It is as old as time. It is dreaming at the core of the world.'

Ullii's pronouncements sometimes bordered on the mystical and he could make no sense of this one. Further questioning proved useless. She could not put what she sensed into words. It did not matter. He had the amplimet, more important than Tiaan now. If he got it back to the manufactory, that would make up for everything.

He reached for it. *Snap!* It was as if a spiky ball had embedded itself in his palm and was gouging its way through. He wrenched his hand away and the amplimet went flying through the air. 'No!' he cried as it fell toward the stone floor.

Unerringly, Ullii snatched it out of the air.

'I think you'd better carry it,' Nish said. It felt as if the amplimet had rejected him.

She packed it in her little chest pack and fastened up the straps.

Casting a last look behind him, Nish said, 'Come on.' They hurried out of Tirthrax.

After some hours of scrambling down the mountain, Nish realised that Ullii was no longer behind him. He called her name but she did not answer.

He set down his pack, rubbing the palm of his hand. The pain still lingered and the centre of his palm had gone white in the shape of a spiky star. 'Ullii!' he roared, and knew that could only make things worse. If she was close by, the racket would make her retreat into herself and he might get nothing out of her for hours. Retracing his path, he found her fifty paces up the slope, huddled under a rock. She did not look up as he approached.

'What's the matter?' He squatted beside her. She did not answer and he had to give her his hand to sniff before she would rouse. Whenever she was distressed, the smell of him seemed to comfort her. He did not understand that either.

'Tired,' she whispered. 'Feet hurt.'

She had thrown off her boots and socks, and her feet were resting on a patch of snow. The little toes, as small as a child's, were red and one heel had a large blister. He clicked his tongue in vexation.

'I'm sorry, Nish,' she wailed. 'I tried really hard.'

Ullii never lied or exaggerated, and was so sensitive that walking in those boots must have been agony. There was no possibility of her wearing them again. Nor could she go any distance in bare feet. It was too cold.

'Climb onto my shoulders, Ullii. I'll carry you.' She probably would not like that either but there was no choice.

She did so willingly enough, and once up there she smiled. 'I can smell you, Nish.' Lifting the blindfold, she peered down the front of his shirt.

'Whatever makes you happy,' he muttered. She was no heavier than a ten-year-old but even that was a hefty burden to carry down the mountain.

By the time they reached the balloon, whose basket was wedged between two boulders, he was drenched in sweat and Ullii's smile was broader than ever. Setting her down in the weak sun, he lay beside her.

'I love you, Nish,' she said.

Had Nish been standing up, he would have fallen over. All he could do was gape. Ullii never made remarks like that. What did she expect of him? He could hardly reciprocate. He liked Ullii, cared for her, and many a night had lain awake burning with desire for her sweet little body, but he could never, except perhaps to get that desire fulfilled, have said that he loved her.

Taking her hand, he drew it to his lips. She shivered and her eyelashes fluttered. He could have screamed with frustration. Why now, when he could do nothing about it? To hide his confusion, he climbed up to look at the balloon, ignoring her little whimper. Tonight, he thought. When everything is prepared.

The gasbag was flaccid, though being formed around a series of struts and stretched wires, it maintained its shape. The air inside had gone cold and he would have to burn the brazier for at least half a day to lift off. First he must gather fuel, for all he had was a large flask of distilled tar spirits. It was useful for burning wet wood but could not be used by itself in the brazier, or the explosion would have blown balloon and boulders back up to Tirthrax.

There was little fuel here, just scrubby heath and a few patches of grass. If he filled the basket with the stuff, it would barely lift the balloon. No time to waste. He headed for the nearest patch of vegetation.

By the middle of the afternoon, Nish had gathered a great mound of shrubbery. As he'd expected, it burned quickly, generating plenty of ash but little heat. After an hour the balloon was almost as flaccid as when he had started. Already he had exhausted the closest supplies of fuel. What if the witch-woman (as he thought of the Matah) was already on her way?

Forcing down panic, he considered other options. The rocks were hung with feathery strands of lichen. Perhaps if he tied that into bales and soaked it in tar spirits? Nish began collecting the material but soon gave the idea away. It took an hour to gather a small bag of lichen and it weighed nothing. There could be no heat in it either.

By then the sun was going down. The sky was clear; the night would be cold and they would need a fire; more precious fuel wasted. He trudged off for another armload of scrub.

On his return Nish could not find Ullii anywhere. He felt like screaming, but did the sensible thing and lit the fire before he went looking for her. She was not far away, just down the slope at their original campsite. Ullii had discarded her mask in the evening and was drawing on a slab of sand-coloured rock with a black lump of pencil-stone.

'I wish you'd told me where you were going,' he said irritably.

For once she did not cringe. 'I knew where *you* were.' She gave him such a sweet smile that it was impossible to be angry with her.

'Come up. It's time for dinner.'

He followed, admiring her figure. Nish prepared dinner, a gruel made of mashed and boiled grains for her, since she could not bear any kind of strong flavour, and much the same for him but with hot spices and smoked meat added.

Nish ate his dinner moodily. If he began the instant it was light, he might just manage to collect enough fuel by darkness, and that was not good enough. The witch-woman might have discovered that the crystal was gone. She could stop him with a single flaming arrow, for the tar-sealed silk would burn like a torch.

By the time he had cleaned up, Ullii was asleep and Nish knew better than to disturb her. He spent a frustrated, agonising night, punctuated by trips to replenish the brazier, and before dawn gave up hope of sleep.

The day crawled by. Nish set Ullii to keep lookout for Tiaan and the Matah. Each time he returned with his burden of fuel, the brazier was out. By lunchtime the balloon had begun to fill but it was a long way from lifting off. Ullii sat beneath the boulder, still scribbling with her pencil-stone. The patterns made no sense at all. He was gnawing on a lump of smoked meat when the seeker gave a whimper and curled up.

'Ullii?' he whispered. 'What's the matter? Is it the witch-woman?'

She did not answer, which meant it was a major distress. He felt for his knife, though it was useless against the likes of the Matah. Climbing the rope ladder to the brazier, Nish scanned the surroundings. He saw nothing in any direction. Nothing

47

moved but a white eagle soaring on the updraught above the ice-fall. Its beak was bright yellow.

When he reached the ground, Ullii had partly unfolded. He tried to discover what had scared her but she was unable to articulate it. 'Hooks and claws,' she said over and over again, referring to something seen in her lattice. He tried to put it out of mind.

Nish was about to go for another load when he noticed the lump of pencil-stone in her hand. The manufactory sometimes burned it in the furnaces. 'Where did you get that, Ullii?'

'Up mountain,' she said in a barely audible voice, still suffering.

He took her hand. 'Is it far? Can you show me?'

'Not far.'

After a short climb they reached a steep face where the dark and light rock stood on end, dipping back into the mountain like layers in a cake. At head height the soft rock had weathered away, leaving an elongated cavity the width of Nish's hips. Several lumps of black, shiny pencil-stone were stuck to the overlying slate. Inside, the cavity was half full of chunks the size of his fist.

Nish climbed in and began to scoop them into his bag. To his amazement, Ullii joined in with the work, and soon the bag was bulging. 'Beautiful fuel,' he said, laughing for joy.

Back at the balloon, he stuffed the brazier, packed lichen all around and carefully poured in half a cup of tar spirits. The pencil-stone would need a hot fire to burn. He flew down the ladder, afraid he had used too much spirits. Nothing happened for a couple of minutes, then with a whoomph the fuel went up and flames roared out the top of the flue.

'More!' They raced up the slope, filling another bag each. The balloon was starting to swell visibly as they returned, though they would need more fuel to take them any distance.

He had come back with a third load and was topping up the brazier when Ullii choked and dropped her bag, spilling pencil-stone across the ground. 'What is it?' he called.

The little seeker looked as if she was having a fit. Her teeth were bared, her eyes staring. She tried to tell him something but managed only incoherent squeaks.

The hairs stood up on the back of his neck. He scanned the mountain and immediately saw two figures, only minutes away. One was the Aachim witch-woman, the other Tiaan. As he ran down the ladder, something broke the air in the west. Three winged shapes, too big and bulky to be eagles or even skeets. They were lyrinx, and heading directly for the balloon.

He fled down the ladder, frantically undoing the ropes, though the balloon was not quite full enough to rise. Moreover, the basket had jammed between the rocks in its fall and would have to be worked free.

Nish hurled in his bag of pencil-stone, the packs and what remained of Ullii's load. 'Ullii!' he yelled. 'There's no time. We've got to go.'

She made not a sound. He lugged her up, thrust his knife in his belt, decanted half a mug of tar spirits and scampered up the ladder. Lifting the lid off the brazier, he tossed the liquid in. It exploded in his face; Nish felt his hair frizzing. Slamming the lid, he leapt onto the nearest boulder and gave the basket a heave. It did not budge. It was jammed tight. Despair coiled around his heart. Not only was he going to lose the crystal but probably his life as well.

Jumping down between the boulders, he put his shoulder under the basket and heaved. It moved a fraction but jammed again. He tried the other side. The edge of the basket dug painfully into his shoulder. The basket scraped along the rock, then stopped.

The balloon was now as round as a globe and the ropes that held it to the basket were taut. It was ready to lift. Scrambling up the side, he shook the basket. It moved but did not free.

The lyrinx were descending rapidly now. The witch-woman was just fifty paces away. She threw out her arm, pointing at him.

Nish ducked. Golden sparkles burst in his eyes but he was otherwise unharmed. The witch-woman clutched at her chest as if in pain, then tottered forward. Nish shook the basket and felt something give. It lifted a handspan before jamming again.

If only he had a branch; anything to use as a lever. 'Come on,' he screamed, shaking it. 'Just move!'

It did not. The witch-woman plodded around the boulders to come at him from the other side. She looked distressed. Nish wished a heart attack on the old fool.

'Give up the crystal, artificer,' she called.

'Be damned!' he snarled, ducking behind the basket for a rock.

She put out her hand, fingers hooked as if she were holding an egg, and slowly closed them. It was as though they had closed about his throat. Nish could not breathe. His face began to swell; his tongue was forced out through his lips. He gave a grunting squeal, which was answered by a moan from inside the basket.

Tiaan began to climb the rock. She had a length of metal in one hand. With a tremendous effort of will, he tore away from the Matah's illusion and gasped a breath of air.

'Ullii,' he choked. 'Save me.'

Ullii's head appeared over the side of the basket, bobbing up and down. 'Don't know what to do,' she quavered.

'Throw something at the witch-woman. Try to knock her out.' He groped for his knife.

Ullii hurled out her half-filled bag of pencil-stone, which flew wide, scattering black lumps everywhere.

'Not the fuel!' he screamed. 'Haven't you got a brain in your head?'

The seeker moaned. Then, to Nish's horror, her chest pack, with its infinitely precious amplimet, soared out of the basket and struck the witch-woman in the face, knocking her down.

The pressure on his throat eased but before he could move Tiaan threw herself at him. He swiped at her but his knife was in the wrong hand and the blow missed. Tiaan thrust out the metal rod. He yelped, thinking she was going for his groin, but the rod went between his knees. She wrenched it sideways, his left knee collapsed and he toppled off the rock.

The fall seemed to take a long time. Nish thought he was going to land on his head, then his back. As he tumbled over, he realised that the knife was pointing up and he was likely to impale himself on it. He twisted in mid-air, slammed into the ground and felt a burning pain in his side.

He rolled over, groaning. Wetness flooded his shirt. A few steps away, the witch-woman was on her knees. Tiaan hurled herself on the pack. With a cry of triumph, she held up the amplimet.

Ullii wept. Nish groaned. His eyes met Tiaan's, then slid sideways to where the wings of the descending lyrinx darkened the sky.

'Enjoy your triumph!' he gritted. 'It won't last long.'

'Nor your tragedy,' said Tiaan. 'Goodbye, Nish. I hope we never meet again.'

'We will,' he said. 'Oh yes, we will, artisan. *Traitor!*'

He hauled himself onto the rock. Tiaan was helping the witch-woman up the hill. Near the point where he had first seen them, they stopped, their backs to a jagged outcrop, and prepared to defend themselves.

Two lyrinx came gliding down in spirals. Was it better to flee, or hang around in case the battle gave him a chance to recover the crystal?

The first seconds dashed that hope. The witch-woman held out her arms and another of those shining bubbles, a huge one this time, burst forth to explode against the chest of the leading lyrinx. The creature seemed to freeze in mid-air, rolled and landed on its back. The second flapped away. He could not see the third.

Nish had seen enough. The witch-woman was too strong. The crystal was lost. He shook the basket and it moved up. Climbing in, he took hold of the balloon ropes and pulled down hard. It came a little way and rebounded. The ropes snapped taut and with a tearing of cane the basket slid out. They were away.

At last they were free of the heavy earth, where every step was a labour and the smallest river an impassable barrier. Up here, Nish felt in control of his life again. He did not have Tiaan, nor the crystal, but he had done the best he could. Most important of all, he had warned the scrutator about the invasion. Nish settled back. Just for a few minutes he was going to enjoy the ride.

The balloon shot up. Well above the level of the glacier, a strong wind pushed it away from the mountain, to the west. Nish frowned. He wanted to go east. Perhaps he should go down again, in some isolated place, and wait for a wind that would carry them the right way. That could be a long wait at this time of year. He reached for the release rope.

'No!' cried Ullii, holding her hands over her ears. 'No, no!'

She was turning round and round, facing up at the sky. Her hands batted at the air; then, to his utter astonishment, she tore off the mask, exposing her naked eyes to the daylight. They were watering so much that pink tears ran down her cheeks.

'*Noooo!*' she screamed.

The third lyrinx had remained high up, on watch. Now it soared effortlessly after them. It was smaller than the others, no larger than a big man. Its outer, armoured skin was so transparent that he could see the more human inner skin beneath. It looked delicate, almost fragile, until Nish caught sight of the finger-long, extended claws.

Blood trickled down his side and Nish felt a momentary dizziness. Clutching one of the ropes, he stared at the approaching lyrinx. How would it attack? The basket was difficult to get at from the air; the creature would not want to risk tangling itself in the ropes.

Perhaps it would swoop down and come at them from below, or even try to knock him out with the Secret Art. All flying lyrinx were mancers – that was how they kept their massive bodies aloft. *More lyrinx have died trying to fly on our heavy world than have been killed in the war*, he recalled Scrutator Flydd saying. If he could distract it in some way he might have a chance.

Nish held out his sword, which made him feel better. He weighed the rope in his hand, balancing on the balls of his feet. The creature would have a harder job than it thought.

He was wrong. The lyrinx had no intention of attacking him. It altered course, darted for the side of the balloon and, with a single swipe of its claws, tore through the fabric.

Air hissed out. The balloon plunged toward the rocks, far below.

Ullii stopped screaming.

SIX

'Are you all right?' Tiaan yelled as the second lyrinx lunged towards them. Backing under the overhanging rock, she whacked at it with her rod. The lyrinx retreated a step. She held no threat but it was wary of Malien.

Malien was breathing hard. 'I've not used the Art to defend myself in two hundred years. Just give me a minute.'

Lowering her head, she took several deep breaths. 'After the last time, I swore I would devote myself to peace. You have undone all that in a day.'

'I'm sorry –' Tiaan began.

'Hush! I'm not blaming you.'

Malien peered out from under the rock. The first lyrinx still lay on its back, one leg moving feebly. The other was three or four paces away, standing with wings spread, watching them. It was a massive creature, many times Tiaan's weight, and all of it bone and muscle. The armoured skin plates made it difficult to attack, even with sword or spear. The large mouth was agape, revealing hundreds of grey teeth. Its eyes, under prominent brow ridges, shone with intelligence. Beautiful colours shimmered across its chameleon skin, iridescent blues, greens and reds. Skin-speech: used for communication, to frighten enemies, and sometimes just for the joy of it.

'Even three would not have troubled me when I was in my

prime,' Malien muttered. 'Of course, that was a long time ago and this is a poor place to defend. If there are more of them around, we can't hold out. We've got to get back inside.'

'They'll just come after us,' said Tiaan.

'Tirthrax has defences. Keep an eye out for the third lyrinx.'

Edging out from under the shelf, Tiaan scanned the sky. She saw the creature at once, swooping toward the balloon, which was now just a small black teardrop in the western sky.

'What's it doing?' she said as lyrinx and balloon merged. The balloon fell out of the sky and disappeared. The lyrinx turned back towards them.

Tiaan felt sick. For all her hatred of Nish, she did not want him to die that way. Nor Ullii, who seemed harmless and had been kind to her. 'It's torn open the balloon. Now it's on its way back.'

'Flying drains them. We'd better move before they recover. Give me the rod.'

Tiaan passed it to her. Malien slid her hands back and forth along it, and Tiaan felt the hairs on her arms rise up. Malien pressed forward, holding the rod out toward the standing lyrinx. A silver bead formed at the end, swelling and glowing like molten glass on the end of a glassblower's tube. When the bead was about the size of a melon, she thrust it at the lyrinx.

The creature clapped its hands together. The globe broke out in bright speckles, like metal filings sprinkled into a fire. Malien's neck sinews stood up. The lyrinx went rigid, straining to overcome an invisible force. Malien muttered under her breath. The globe burst and the lyrinx went tumbling backwards down the slope.

She fell to her knees, dropping the rod. 'That hurt,' she gasped. 'How are we doing?'

Tiaan picked the rod up. 'The lyrinx isn't moving but I don't think it's dead. The flying one will be here in a minute or two.'

'No, it's not dead. I'm not a killer, Tiaan. Give me a hand.'

They made their way up the slope, Malien's weight heavy on Tiaan's shoulder. The flying lyrinx began to circle around them. Tiaan stopped abruptly.

'What is it?' Malien asked.

'I know her.' Tiaan was staring at the transparent-skinned creature. 'Her name is Liett. She was one of the lyrinx at Kalissin; a flesh-former.' That roused unpleasant memories.

'What will she do?'

'I have no idea,' Tiaan said. 'I spent three months as their prisoner, but I knew little more about them at the end. Though . . .'

'Yes?'

'They are deadly in battle, but when you get to know them . . . I found them to be honourable creatures.'

'That's encouraging,' said Malien, 'yet I can't say I want to get to know them.'

They watched the circling lyrinx, which now turned and flapped towards the two fallen ones. 'She's given up.'

'They know where we are. They can come back at any time, with an army.'

The lyrinx did not attack again, though as Tiaan and Malien made the weary climb up the mountain, Tiaan twice saw Liett circling high above. After they passed into Tirthrax, Liett flew east.

'What do we do now?' Tiaan asked as they rested in the entrance.

Malien unwrapped a food packet. 'Have some filuvior.'

Tiaan took a chunk of something that looked like green, crumbly cheese but dissolved smoothly in the mouth. It had a taste she could not put words to, a combination of aromatic, creamy and acrid. Her mouth tingled afterwards but she did feel better.

'What is this stuff, Malien?'

'A tonic for exhaustion, body or mind.'

She took another piece. Tiaan did too.

'This level of the city is undefendable,' Malien went on. 'And that's a pity, because there are things here I would sooner the enemy never saw, not least of them the wrecked constructs. Fortunately I can seal off the upper and lower entrances. We have greater treasures there. I wonder what brought the lyrinx here?' She looked questioningly at Tiaan.

'The amplimet, I expect. They can track such things.'

'How do you know that?' Malien said sharply.

'At the manufactory, when I was an artisan . . .' Memories of her lost life came rushing back and for a moment Tiaan could not speak. 'The enemy were locating our clankers from afar, and we could not tell how. I discovered that they could sense the aura given off by a working crystal.'

'How? I've never heard of such a thing.'

'I was never sure. They used something that resembled a large, leathery mushroom. I don't know whether they made it, grew it or –'

'Flesh-formed it,' Malien said, with an uncharacteristic shiver. 'Go on.'

'I developed a way of shielding crystals from them.'

'What did you do?'

'I wrapped the crystals in gold foil, sealed them tight and covered everything with pitch. That cut off the aura and prevented the crystals being sabotaged by heat, too.' She looked away. 'I miss my work.'

'What a remarkable young woman you are,' said Malien. 'I wish –'

'What?'

'No matter.'

Malien activated sentinels – squat black cones – at the entrances to the lower and upper levels. Tiaan's eyes lingered on the broken constructs as they went by. The design, and the workmanship, was magnificent. Were they powered by the field, as clankers were, or did they draw on an entirely different source? She wanted to get inside one and find out. Tiaan really missed her craft.

They went up. It was not far, now that Tiaan knew the way, but they had to climb eight long swirling flights of stairs, one after another. By the last, the old woman was shaking.

'This day has been rather too much for me. I'll see you in the morning.' Malien went into her room and closed the door.

Tiaan had a drink of water and sat down until her heart stopped hammering. She was overcome by a deep melancholy.

Such a small decision to care about Minis, such mighty consequences. Was the world already at war with the Aachim? Were innocent people being slaughtered while she sat here in luxury?

Tiaan sprang out of the chair. She felt a mad urge to hurt herself, to make herself suffer as a way of connecting with Haani. Flinging the door open, she hurtled up the stairs to Malien's lookout, rejoicing in the ache in her side. She slapped the opener with her palm. The glass wall slid back and Tiaan pushed out into the gale.

The balcony was icy. Tiaan slipped, cracking her shin against the stone seat. Limping to the edge, she looked over. The air was perfectly clear, the distant peaks like etchings on glass. A low sun glinted bronze off the ice sheet.

The view was magical but Tiaan could not see it, any more than Malien did in the hours she spent here every day. Malien looked across the void to Aachan, the ancestral world her people had been cut off from thousands of years ago. Now they would never return. The small, cold globe that was Aachan was no longer habitable. They were forever exiles.

As was she. By the time the red sun plunged into a lake of mist, Tiaan was practically frozen to the seat.

'What the blazes do you think you're doing?'

Malien was shaking her. Tiaan could see nothing, and for an instant of horror thought her eyes must have frozen solid. The Aachim picked crusted snow off her eyelids, rubbed them with a warm palm and Tiaan's eyes cracked open.

Back down below, her fingers wrapped around a mug of a custardy-thick, sweet red drink, Tiaan began to feel rather foolish. The emotions that had taken her outside felt alien now.

'I suppose . . .' she said haltingly, 'I was punishing myself.'

'What a *stupid* thing to do! If you have done harm, do something to make up for it.'

Tiaan sipped her drink. Malien was right. She must do something, but what? Maybe she should try to get back to the manufactory and resume her artisan's work.

Malien was turning the pages of a small book bound in yellow calf, though not reading it.

'Is something the matter?' said Tiaan.

Malien laid the book to one side. 'I cannot tell you what a shock it was to hear of the gate, and see those constructs. Arrogance was ever an Aachim failing, and so many constructs, and such power, would breed hubris in the meekest of breasts. Vithis is a type I know well – a brilliant, blind fool. After the loss of world and clan, he will not compromise. He has suffered – why should others not suffer equally? We have had many such leaders in our Histories, but all looked backwards to a time when we were great, while knowing that such times were past.

'Vithis is different. Having lost everything that mattered, nothing can moderate him, and now he has the opportunity of a lifetime. With his mighty force, the most powerful ever assembled, he comes to a world ruined by war. What will he do?'

'Take it,' Tiaan said softly. 'But . . . we are all humankind. Maybe he will ally with us to defeat the lyrinx.'

'*I* would,' said Malien, 'but why would Vithis? Many Aachim think of you old humans as primitive, even sub-human, and from what you say of him Vithis holds to that view. He may prefer to let the lyrinx win, or even side with them to destroy humanity.'

Tiaan's blood congealed. 'He would not,' she whispered. 'He could not.'

'Look at your own Histories, Tiaan. The more advanced races, or the more powerful nations, have wiped out hundreds of the lesser.'

'But humanity has a great and ancient civilisation. How could anyone think . . .?'

'Look to your Histories, I say.'

Tiaan could not countenance it. That Vithis might destroy humanity, and all its culture and Histories, as carelessly as one might kill a cockroach, was incomprehensible.

'And nothing can be done about it?' she said in a daze.

'I wouldn't say *nothing*,' said Malien. 'Vithis must have weaknesses as well as strengths.'

'I saw none, apart from clan rivalry.'

'Which would disappear the instant the Aachim were threatened.'

'And perhaps your own people would join with them to make an even stronger force.'

'If pushed hard enough, *they* probably would.'

'But not *you*, Malien?'

'I will never betray my own kind, Tiaan. But I will do what I can for all humanity.'

'And I!' Tiaan swore. 'Since I brought the Aachim here, I must make up for it.' How, though? She was trapped by geography, hundreds of leagues from anywhere.

Malien sat forward on her chair, looking down at her boots. Her veined hands shook. She rested them on her knees. 'I –' She broke off.

Tiaan said nothing. What could Malien offer her but words? Words could change nothing.

'You can never know what I felt when I heard about the amplimet,' said Malien.

Not expecting that, Tiaan felt a surge of jealous anger. 'Why?' she said coolly. 'What is it to you?'

'The chance to look back to lost Aachan.'

'You can't have been born there.' The Histories were clear on that.

'I was not. We came to Santhenar thousands of years ago, mostly as slaves of the Charon. For that reason, few of us feel perfectly at home on Santhenar. Nor do I, despite that my children and my partners lie in their graves here. We forever look back to Aachan, mourning the world that we lost. We always hoped and planned to return. Now we never shall. But still I would use the amplimet, if I may, to take a last look at our lost world.'

'But Aachan was destroyed,' said Tiaan. The anger had gone but she still felt reluctant to let Malien have it, however briefly.

'With the amplimet, and a strong enough will, I might look back into the depths of time. I might even see beloved Aachan as a paradise, before the Charon took it from us. Ah, Tiaan, you cannot know how I yearn for that.' Malien shook her head and tears fell from her ageless eyes.

Tiaan found herself moved by the old woman's anguish. 'Take it,' she said, unfastening the little pouch hanging between her breasts. 'Look back to Aachan and be at peace.'

'I'm afraid,' Malien said softly, and the power and the confidence were gone. She was no more than an ageing woman whose life had seen more of tragedy than triumph.

'That the amplimet has been corrupted by the gate?'

'I fear that, but not as much as I fear what I will see on Aachan.'

Malien did not elaborate and Tiaan asked no more questions. She did not have the right. The crystal lay on her hand, glowing in a way that seemed vaguely menacing. They both stared at it.

Malien shuddered, then reached out to lift it away between fingers and thumb. It dragged as if anchored to Tiaan's palm with sticky threads. Something went snap and suddenly the crystal was tumbling through the air, exploding with light. She cried out but Malien's long fingers closed around it and the light was cut off.

Malien rose. 'Come with me.'

Tiaan followed her to the stone bench on her lonely eyrie. 'What do you want me to do?'

'Nothing, apart from being here.' Malien sat on the bench.

Tiaan stood by the glass door, where it was a little warmer. There was still a core of cold in her from before, and Malien having the amplimet only added to that.

'Isn't it dangerous using it so close to the node?'

'It is.'

Malien held the amplimet between her fingers, which were pressed together as though in prayer. The end of the crystal extended past the tips. She rested her elbows on her knees. Her posture was so rigid that Tiaan moved toward the edge of the precipice, the better to see.

Malien's head turned sharply and Tiaan was shocked at her expression. She looked afraid. The amplimet, normally a luminous white or blue-white, had gone a baleful red. The glow

60

rose and fell, and with each flare Tiaan felt a wrenching in her middle.

The crystal pulsed faster, more erratically. Some kind of struggle seemed to be going on between it and Malien, and Tiaan recalled Vithis's fear – that it had been corrupted. Would it be a danger to her too, when she got it back? *If* Malien gave it back.

Abruptly the glow was gone. The illuminated globe inside the door also went out. The sun had set long ago and the night was black, apart from a shimmer of starlight on the distant ice sheet. That seemed ominous. Malien shuddered from head to foot, then rose from the bench until she was standing on tiptoe. She held the crystal above her head and let out a great cry that could have been ecstasy or anguish.

The crystal shone so brightly that Tiaan saw the blood running in Malien's veins. It slowed, slowed, slowed. What was she doing? Tiaan tried to move but the world vanished and the next she knew, she was picking herself up from the frigid stone.

Some time had passed, for moonlight now glistened on the peaks and the icefield. Malien still held the crystal above her head, pastel rays streaming out between her fingers. It looked as though she had frozen in place. Gelid tears hung on her cheeks but beneath her eyelids her eyes were moving.

Tiaan crouched near the edge of the precipice, afraid to disturb her. The rays slowly thinned and dulled until they could barely be seen, until the light illuminated only Malien's fingertips and her face, and finally even that went out.

Reaching up, Tiaan touched Malien's hand. To her surprise it was warm. A great weight left her and Tiaan took the crystal from Malien's fingers.

Malien turned stiffly, like a statue coming to life. Her eyes opened, shedding crescents of ice. 'Tiaan,' she said haltingly, as if so long had passed that she barely recalled how to speak.

'Come inside.'

'Go to the warm. I will follow directly. I have a deal to think about.'

Tiaan was reluctant to go, so concerned did she feel for the old woman, but she was freezing. She went creakily down the stairs to Malien's chambers but could not get warm until she drew a bath of steaming water and slid in to it.

There Malien found her, hours later, fast asleep in the tub. She touched Tiaan on the shoulder. 'Dinner is ready.'

'What did you see?' Tiaan asked after they had finished another magnificent repast, every item of which was strange to her. She was sitting in a comfortable chair, clad in a silky dressing-gown with a glass of something that vaguely resembled coffee, though richer and more aromatic, at her elbow. 'I'm sorry. That was rude of me.'

'I did not see what I expected,' said Malien, 'and I will not speak of that save to my own kind.' She took a sip from her glass, made to say something, then went silent.

Tiaan did not prompt her. Aachan meant nothing more to her than visions, through Minis, of volcanoes and ruins. She finished her glass, went to bed and did not dream.

It was not until the following afternoon that Malien came to her. 'You deserve an explanation, Tiaan. I must –'

'Aachan is your affair. I don't want to pry.'

'Hear me. Aachan involved itself in your affairs and you must know what is going on. I believe Vithis did deal dishonestly with you, or if he did not, other Aachim used or manipulated him. You were right to impugn the honour of the Aachim of Aachan; I was wrong to rebuke you. Someone is playing a deadly game and the consequences could be more dire than anyone imagines.'

Tiaan opened her mouth but Malien held up a hand. 'There is more, and this concerns you personally. The amplimet *has* been corrupted by the gate, or by what Vithis did to change the gate. That appears to have roused something in the amplimet that was formerly dormant.'

'What?' Tiaan whispered.

'I don't know. Perhaps a kind of mineral instinct.'

That was too close to what Tiaan had been thinking. From the very first, there had been something different about it. She had not needed to wake it to draw power, as with a hedron.

The amplimet had already been drawing power, *by itself*. 'What is it up to?'

'I can't say. Its purpose may be benign, malignant or indifferent, but it will try to follow it no matter what.'

'Should we destroy it?' Her voice broke. It was perilous for an artisan to destroy any hedron she was intimately linked to. But to destroy an amplimet . . . She dared not think what that would do to her.

'No!' Malien cried. 'It may be perilous but it is still a treasure. Guard it, protect it, and above all, beware of it, for make no mistake, it is deadly.'

'To use, or just to have by me?'

'I don't know. You must leave as soon as you are able. The amplimet is . . . incompatible with the node here, and the Well. You're lucky something drastic hasn't already happened.'

'What do you mean?'

'I'll be looking into that tonight.'

'Maybe *it* made the gate go wrong,' Tiaan said hopefully.

'No. The gate corrupted the amplimet.'

More to think about. 'Where am I to go?'

'Where best your knowledge, and your skills, might be employed to bring good out of ill.'

'If I went back to the manufactory it would take a year to get there,' Tiaan mused, 'if I got there at all. *And* if I dared risk their punishment. Going west would take months of equally dangerous travel. By then it would be too late, even if I knew what to do.'

'You must work out your own path. I can't advise you. But before you go, there is one thing you can do for me.'

'Yes?' said Tiaan, sure she was not going to like it.

'You're a skilled artisan,' said Malien. 'Perhaps you could pull the crashed constructs apart and make a working one from them.'

SEVEN

It shivered Tiaan from the roots of her hair to her toenails. From the moment she had set eyes on the constructs, she had longed to see how they were powered, controlled and built. It was fate.

'I'll begin right away.' She leapt up. 'This minute!'

'I was about to prepare dinner.'

'What if the lyrinx come back? I don't dare miss the chance.' In truth, she longed to feel metal in her hands again. Devices were logical, predictable, reliable. They did not lie or cheat or betray.

Malien smiled, though it had a faraway edge. 'Dinner will be ready shortly.'

Tiaan hurried down the stairs, her heart pounding. As an artisan, new ways of seeing and doing had always fascinated her. Everything about these constructs must be new, since they had come from another world.

Down on the gate level, she walked around the three machines, frowning. Without understanding how they worked, it was difficult to know where to start. The one that lay on its top looked the worst damaged, and no doubt righting it would cause more. The second had its front smashed in; the third, one side crumpled, and its upper part warped. Tiaan tried to pull the metal back into place but could not budge it. Though just a thin, curved sheet, it had the strength of the plate armour on the side of a clanker.

Climbing the construct with the crushed front, she looked in through the hatch. It was more spacious than it had appeared, though it must have been dreadfully crowded with a dozen passengers inside. Above and behind the hatch, a cramped turret was fitted with a javelard-like weapon, similar to the one that had killed Haani. She turned her back to it.

Inside the hatch was a small ovoid compartment with space for half a dozen people to stand close together. Seats pulled out from the rear wall. At the front was a curved binnacle of coloured glass, the pale green of young lemon leaves. Below that was a bank of finger-shaped levers, several coin-sized wheels and many coloured knobs or buttons. Between the binnacle and the seat, a hexagonal rod came up from the floor, sprouting into a six-sided trumpet with a studded knob on top. The trumpet could be moved back and forth as well as from side to side and up and down. Nothing happened when she tried it. On the floor beside it were five crescent-shaped pedals.

She wiggled the levers and pressed the buttons and pedals, to no effect. Perhaps the mechanism was damaged, or there was a secret way of operating it.

To the left of the trumpet an oval hole gave access to the lower level. Stepping onto the top rung of a metal ladder, Tiaan went down tentatively. A lightglass began to glow. The egg-shaped interior was decorated with inlaid silver and other precious metals in the intricate Aachim way. Handles ran down the wall in front of her. She pulled one and an ingenious bunk unfolded. Another revealed a small cupboard containing mugs, plates and cutlery. A third seemed to be a weapons cabinet, though all it contained was a sword shaped like a cutlass and quarrels for a crossbow. A fourth held tools of unfathomable purpose.

Lifting a recessed hatch in the floor, she found what she assumed to be the driving mechanism. Some of its components resembled those she had used to build the port-all: crystals of various kinds, thick and robust glass tubes in the form of doughnuts and twisticons (as little Haani had called them), and other structures of ceramic and metal. The familiar shapes and components were comforting. The port-all had worked, therefore she might be able to make this construct operate.

Going back to the operator's compartment, she checked it more thoroughly. Everything was as dead as before. Climbing out, she walked around the machine. It did not *seem* badly damaged, though a vital part might have been broken in the collision or the subsequent fall from the gate. But surely the Aachim would not build a war machine that could be disabled so easily?

She checked the one on its roof. The top of the machine was crushed; she could not get in. It was hard to imagine its vital parts surviving such an impact. The third construct, lying on its side, proved similar to the first but was badly damaged inside.

Returning to the first construct, she began to remove the damaged front section. The work required the utmost concentration, for she had to deduce how every part worked, and the right tool to use with it. Tiaan became so engrossed that she lost all track of time. She had part of the damaged section in pieces when she realised, with a start, that Malien was standing right behind her.

'Where did you spring from?' Tiaan exclaimed.

'Whistling while you work,' said Malien. 'This *is* a change from yesterday.'

'I've missed my craft. Is it dinnertime already?'

'It went cold ten hours ago. I came to call you to breakfast.'

Tiaan was astounded. Yes, dawn was outlining the hole in the wall of the mountain. 'I had no idea. I'm sorry.'

'It doesn't matter. Why are you taking the whole front to pieces?'

'I was planning to replace it with parts from one of the others.'

Malien squatted beside her, reached underneath and did something with her long fingers. There was a soft click. She did the same at the top and on the other side. 'Pull this.' She indicated a strut.

Tiaan did so, Malien tugged on the other, and the front section slid onto the floor.

'How did you do that?' Tiaan cried.

'I understand Aachim design,' Malien said.

Half an hour later, the undamaged front section of the other construct had been installed. Tiaan wiped her hands and stood back. The repaired construct, apart from the dust, looked as if it had just been built.

'There's still the bigger problem to solve,' said Tiaan. 'How to make it go.'

'Best leave that for later. Aachim machines can be booby-trapped and even an expert would not work on one after a sleepless night. I'll come down later and teach you a few words of our tongue. To understand what you're doing, you'll need to know the names of things.'

While Tiaan was sleeping, Malien returned to the Well. Even before she entered the conical chamber, she noticed that things were different. The entry passage was less frigid, the barrier cubes more brittle. The blue-illuminated mist around the Well was as thick as cream and now extended higher than her head. Malien felt resistance as she pushed though it to the Well.

She peered down anxiously. What if it had begun to unfreeze? She listened for the telltale tinkle of cracking ice – the first sign. Nothing. The tendrils still coiled lazily inside. The Well was silent, the depths still. She relaxed. Not yet. Malien was not sure she could restrain it by herself. Not sure that any one person could.

On the way back, she debated whether to tell Tiaan about her worries. Malien decided to keep them to herself for as long as possible. It would not benefit Tiaan to know.

That afternoon, Malien began to teach Tiaan the rudiments of the Aachim tongue, focussing on the words needed for this kind of work. Though Tiaan spoke three languages – the common tongues of the south-east, the west and the north – as most people did, Aachim speech proved difficult. It was always a relief to get back to the real world of her work.

She spent days studying the construct but could understand neither how it was powered nor what mechanism it used to hover and move. Maybe it was beyond her understanding. Vithis, and the other Aachim, had emphasised their mastery of geomancy and the limited scope of her own abilities. Eventually, more exhausted by this failure than by all her previous labours, she went to sleep inside the construct.

Malien woke her, bearing a mug in each hand. While they sipped their zhur, as the thick red spicy beverage was called, Tiaan explained why she was so downcast.

'With your clankers,' said Malien, 'can anyone operate them?'

'Of course not! The operator has to be tuned to its controller, and when he leaves he always takes it with him. Without it, nothing can make a clanker go.'

'Except another operator with his own controller, presumably?'

'Well, yes, but not always. Do constructs operate the same way?'

'I don't know,' said Malien.

'That isn't much help,' Tiaan snapped.

'After Rulke built the very first construct,' Malien said carefully, 'at the time of the *Tale of the Mirror*, our finest thinkers devoted much time and thought to such devices. How they could be built, powered and controlled. They failed. The problem was too difficult.'

'But later, humanity discovered how to use the field,' said Tiaan. 'Nunar's Theory showed us how, and then we learned to build clankers.'

'A primitive machine,' said Malien. 'I mean no insult,' she added when Tiaan bridled, 'but the one can hardly be compared to the other.'

You just can't help yourself, Tiaan thought. Your Aachim superiority is bred into you. She spoke aloud, 'Your people in Aachan succeeded.'

'They were *more* desperate. And they had Rulke's original to use as a model, wrecked though it was.' She regarded Tiaan expectantly. 'So there must be a key for the machine.'

'I imagine they took it with them to prevent anyone else using it.'

'There may be a way around that. Leave it to me.'

Tiaan climbed inside, took off the lower hatch to reveal its workings, and sat with her legs dangling into the cavity. She created a mental image of the mechanism and turned it this way and that, trying to *know* it. Not just the way an operator knew his clanker, but the way a master controller-maker knew the vagaries of the ever-fluctuating field that was the source of all power. Her talent for thinking in pictures allowed her to do that, and it had often helped her to solve problems.

How *could* a construct float above the ground? What held it up? She could not work it out. The controller mechanisms seemed wrong for the field as she knew it. But of course constructs did not use the weak field, so presumably they must employ one of the strong nodal forces Nunar had speculated about. Deadly forces, even to experienced mancers.

A thought occurred to her. One problem an artisan had to solve, each time she made a controller, was how to tune it so that it did not react against the field but drew power smoothly from it. But what if a controller was tuned to *resist* the field? It, and whatever it was in, might be *repelled* by the field. Could that be done?

In her mental image she worked the mechanism trying to see what made it go, and noticed something curious. Behind the glass binnacle a small, cup-shaped receptacle rotated on a shaft, and as it reached the vertical its cap flipped open. It was about the right shape and size to take a small hedron. Looking beneath the binnacle, Tiaan found the receptacle. It was empty but she picked up faint traces of a crystal's aura. What if she put the amplimet in it?

She unfastened the drawstring, feeling that oneness she always felt when her fingers touched the glowing amplimet. She was about to slide it into the cup when Malien spoke from above.

'I wouldn't, if I were you.'

'Why not?' she asked testily.

'I told you – the amplimet is deadly. And the people who built this construct had not seen one in four thousand years. Whatever crystal they used, it was nowhere near as powerful. The mechanism might burn out, or blow apart. Or melt the construct, and you and me, into puddles. If you must try such a dangerous experiment, do it with a lesser crystal.'

Tiaan could see the sense in that. 'I've got an ordinary hedron. Should I try that?'

'If you must; only know that anything you do here is a risk.'

'Why?'

'The Tirthrax node is one of the greatest in the world, and working so close to it may have unexpected effects. And then there is the Well . . .'

'What about it?'

Malien hesitated, as if reluctant to speak of it at all. 'It has a somewhat . . . uneasy balance with the node. I would not want to upset that.'

'I don't understand.'

'These are Aachim secrets, not for outsiders' ears.'

'How do you expect me to fix the construct if I don't know what's going on?'

'Very well! There are some things I can tell you, but you must promise to keep them secret.'

'Of course,' said Tiaan.

'The Well of Echoes has been captured but not tamed. Improper use of power might change it in an unpredictable way, or even allow it to *break free*! We are always careful with the Art here, and so must you be.' She turned away abruptly, ending the conversation.

That raised a dozen questions but Tiaan knew better than to ask them. She took her hand off the amplimet. The more Malien told her, the less she understood.

Putting it away, she weighed her hedron in her hand. Her jaw was clenched tight. Tiaan tried to relax. Reaching down, ever so carefully, she lowered the crystal into the cup, then whipped her hand out of the way.

Nothing happened. She looked up at Malien questioningly. 'What should I have expected?'

'I don't know.'

Tiaan was about to take it out when Malien said, 'No, leave it there. Something else may be required.'

'What?' Tiaan cried in frustration.

'Leave it until tomorrow. Things always seem better after a good night's sleep.'

'I like to keep going until I can't do any more.'

Malien's gaze was penetrating. 'I wonder about you, Tiaan.'

'What do you mean?' said Tiaan uncomfortably.

'What do you enjoy, apart from work?'

Tiaan did not understand the question. 'I love my work.'

'And I mine, but it is not *all* of me. What are you hiding from?'

'I'm not hiding from anything,' she yelled, turning away. 'It's why I'm such a good artisan; because I work harder than everyone.'

'How old are you? No, you've already told me. You were twenty-one the day the gate opened.'

Tiaan hurled her wrench onto the floor. 'So?'

'Do you know my age?'

'You look about sixty, but Aachim age slowly. And I know you were alive at the time of the Mirror. So I would guess, 250?'

'I'm 385, a hundred years more than I ever expected to live, and I've a good few years in me yet, if I don't take the Well. I've lived eighteen of your lives, Tiaan, and learned a thing or two. You can't work all the hours of the day, and you can't cover up other failings by staying at your bench day and night. You have to live!'

'My *mother* used to say that.'

'If you won't listen to me, take her advice. Go to bed early and get up in the morning, refreshed. What is hard now will seem easy then. It may come to you in your dreams.'

Tiaan dreaded her dreams these days, though as she headed up the stairs she muttered, 'I'm glad you're not my mother.'

She had not thought of Marnie in ages. What would she be doing now? Tiaan could almost see her on the great bed, gorging

71

herself and pulling her latest lover down on her enormous, fleshy expanses. Her mother did nothing *but* live.

'I'm worried the lyrinx will come,' she said as they reached the top. 'This is the greatest opportunity of my life and I don't want to miss out on it.'

'I'm worried too,' said Malien. 'I think I'll go to my eyrie for a while. I need to think.'

'What is it? There's something else on your mind, isn't there?'

After a long hesitation, Malien said, 'I've been keeping a close eye on the Well. It seems to be unfreezing.'

'What do you mean?'

'The Well is a dynamic object, like an energy whirlwind. It wants to run free, but that freedom would come at the expense of everything in the natural world that is fixed – rocks, forests, life of any kind! Tamed as it is, it's a treasure. Set free within the plane of the world, it spells ruin for every solid thing it touches. It has been frozen in place ever since we came to Tirthrax, but now it appears to be thawing. Should it thaw completely, I would be hard pressed to hold it.'

'Why is it thawing?'

'I don't know. Have you noticed anything different about the amplimet lately?'

'No. You warned me against using it.' She passed it over.

Malien studied it. 'I don't see anything, but keep an eye on it, and tell me if anything unusual happens.'

'Do you expect it to?'

'I don't know. The thawing may have nothing to do with the amplimet. It might be due to the gate opening, or all the power the fleet of constructs took from the node.'

'But you're worried?'

'I'm very worried.'

EIGHT

The tear was two-thirds of the way down the balloon but the air still gushed out. The balloon fell, not quite like a stone, but fast enough to be frightening. The lyrinx did not wait to make sure of them, but turned back toward Tiaan and the witch-woman.

Nish wondered what it would feel like to be splattered across the rocks. He hoped the pain would not last long. Ullii whimpered and tried to climb into her basket.

'That won't do any good. Come here.' Nish took her in his arms.

Ullii pressed herself against him as if she was trying to get inside his skin. He hugged her tightly. The tearing wind had carried them a few leagues west of Tirthrax and down over the precipice. They were now dropping towards one of the spreading mounds below an icefall. The ice would be as hard as stone.

A sudden whirling updraught caught the balloon, driving them past the ice mound in the direction of a moraine of boulders, then beyond it toward an island in a frozen outwash river. Nish was sure they were going to smash right through the ice. However, the wind pushed them towards the forest covering the centre of the island.

The trees loomed up, tall conifers rather like fir trees, though the needles were blue. The balloon was not completely deflated but as soon as they hit the trees, a branch would tear the side right out.

Nish felt quite calm about dying. He had done his best; however, as with so many other people in this war, circumstances had been against him. His only regret was that his family would never know what had happened. Their Histories would just say 'disappeared in Mirrilladell'.

The balloon was falling directly towards one of the larger trees of the forest. They were going to hit the top, full on. 'Hang on!' he said uselessly to Ullii.

She clung to him. Nish gripped the sides of the basket. The base struck the top of the tree, snapping it off, and the broken trunk thrust up through the bottom of the basket like a magic beanstalk. Blue needles and pieces of shredded bark and cane whirled like snowflakes. The basket kept going down, stripping off the small upper limbs until it slammed into a pair of solid branches. The tree swayed across the sky, went *creak-crack* and Nish thought it was going to snap again. It moved back and forth a few times then stopped. They had, somehow, survived.

The stripped trunk had thrust up beside the brazier and gone some distance into the open neck of the balloon. The tree now appeared to have a black mushroom sprouting from its top. The last of the air rushed out and the balloon went flaccid, bent in the middle where its supporting wires had warped out of shape.

Nish looked at Ullii. 'Well, at least we're alive.'

'I knew we'd be all right,' she said.

The climb down was unpleasant. Though Nish was not afraid of heights, the knife wound troubled him and Ullii did not seem to understand how high they were, or how to get down. The branches were spaced uncomfortably far apart and she had no idea which ones would support her weight and which would not. He had to check her every step, as if she were a two-year-old.

Eventually they did reach the ground, where he was at a loss what to do. The black balloon could be seen for leagues and he was tempted to burn it to make it harder for the enemy to find them. Of course, he could only do that from underneath the tar-soaked fabric. Besides, a fire in the treetops would be even more visible.

Nish did not think there was any possibility of repairing the balloon, which was a pity. He could see no other way out of here. There had been no sign of habitation from above and they would soon starve to death in this wilderness.

His side began to ache. Taking off his jacket, jerkin and bloody shirt, he inspected the self-inflicted injury. A long shallow cut ran up his ribs almost to his armpit. The wound had closed over but was rather painful. It was getting late. Having no idea what to do, he put the decision off until the morning.

'We'll have to camp here.' He unpacked the tent. 'Could you find some firewood please, Ullii?'

She stared blankly at him.

Nish suppressed the urge to slap her. Ullii had never learned to do the least thing for herself and had no concept of cooperative labour. That was just the way she was. She was not going to change.

'We must have a fire, Ullii,' he said patiently, 'and I've got to put the tent up. Could you collect some wood, please?'

He pointed to a branch on the ground. She tried to pick it up, found it was too heavy and just stood there looking at it. Sighing heavily, Nish showed her two others that she would be able to carry. By the time he had erected the tent, she had brought back the two pieces of wood and was squatting by them, shivering.

'That's not enough, Ullii. We'll need ten times that much to get us through the night.'

He had to show her, piece by piece, and then help her to bring them back, so he might as well have done the work himself. Finally, when the fire was blazing, Nish looked around for the dinner bag. It was still in the basket at the top of the tree, with their packs.

It was getting dark but they had to have food. The climb, a good thirty spans up, then down again in the gloom, was not one he cared to think about afterwards. But he made it with no more damage than a lot of skin off his hands and the departure of what remained of his temper.

'I'll make the dinner, Ullii . . . ' He was speaking to empty air.

Nish swore. Where had the wretched woman gotten to? About to roar out her name, he heard a gentle snore coming from the tent. Ullii was inside, curled up in his sleeping pouch, fast asleep.

'All the more dinner for me,' he said selfishly, and set to with the frying-pan.

On the morning after the crash, Nish discovered that the minor injury, which he had been too weary to tend the previous night, had become infected. It was now an angry red from one end to the other.

'This is all I need,' he muttered, peeling off his shirt.

'Don't die, Nish,' Ullii wailed, thrusting her head hard against the wound.

It was agony. Nish cried out and shoved her away, biting back tears. Ullii put her hands over her ears and ran into the forest.

'Come back,' he yelled once the shooting spasms had eased. She did not answer. Well, let her go; she would not run far.

He boiled water, cleaned the wound, then put on salve from the medicine kit and bound it up in the cleanest cloth he had. With the rest of the water, Nish made a brew of liquorice tea, sweetened with great quantities of honey from a comb. The tea was too hot to drink, so he leaned back against the tree and closed his eyes, the better to think.

The balloon carried a small repair kit: needles, thread, a length of silk cloth and a pot of tar to seal it with, though Nish doubted if there was enough fabric for this job. The tear was long, with subsidiary rips radiating out as far as the seams in the material. Without them the top of the balloon would have torn off.

Still, he had to try: the idea of walking out of here was laughable. He had already consulted the map which, even if it was accurate, showed no town within ten leagues. Ten leagues of frozen waste that was rapidly unfreezing, turning even small streams into impassable barriers.

He could, he supposed, attempt to build a raft of logs tied together with the ropes from the balloon. That would be easy enough for someone with his artificer's skills, and he had an axe. As long as the green wood floated. But rafts were difficult to steer and at the first set of rapids it would be torn to pieces, dumping him, Ullii and everything they owned into the icy water where, if they survived the rocks, they would quickly drown or freeze to death on the shore.

Repairing the balloon was the better gamble, and he'd better get started. Leaving Ullii to return in her own time, Nish shinned up the tree next to the one they had landed in, so as to gauge the repair job. He was inured to the climb now, though his wound hurt more than before. At the top he took a firm grip on the trunk and leaned out. He was level with the top of the balloon, which was sheltered from the wind by the surrounding treetops. The damage was worse than he had expected, the main tear a good three spans long. How could he possibly repair that?

On the ground again, he found Ullii in the tent, curled up into a ball, but he was sure she was awake. He did not go in, just made sure she knew he was there, and in sound health.

He spent the rest of the day by the fire, considering possibilities for repairing the balloon, and rejecting them all. The infection grew more painful and, by the afternoon, climbing the tree was impossible. He went to his sleeping pouch as soon as the short day ended.

For the next three days, snow fell lightly all day and wind whistled through the branches. It was too cold to risk exposure up in the trees, for he could not work bundled up in his cold-weather gear. He spent the time carving and shaping pieces of wood with the blade of his axe and the tip of his sword. It was awkward work. The time dragged, the only comfort being that the lyrinx did not come back. Nish saw them wheeling in the air on occasion, in the direction of the mountains, and wondered what they were up to.

One day, trudging down to the river for water, he saw a white shadow thumping the water with a flat paddle, making a booming sound that could have been heard half a league away. Nish slipped behind a tree. It was a great Hürn bear, scarcely visible in its shaggy winter coat. It was in the water now, scooping stunned fish out onto the bank. A magnificent animal, this one was bigger than a lyrinx.

As he watched, its head turned in his direction. Nish went still. Hürn bears were not vicious but they were territorial, and even a backhanded blow from those paws would be the end of him. As soon as it went back to its fishing, he slipped away to the camp. He and Ullii spent a cold and uncomfortable night halfway up the tree. Nish did not sleep. A Hürn bear could climb better than he could.

On the following morning he woke to feel no pain in his side, just the tightness of healing flesh. The sun was out, already melting the snow on the branches. He went up at once. Though they had plenty of food, the supply was not inexhaustible and every day they stayed here increased the risk of lyrinx coming to investigate. Or Hürn bears.

He assembled the shaped pieces of wood into a small block and tackle. Passing the rope through it, he tied one end to the tree and tossed the other across to the neighbouring trunk. Climbing down, then up, he passed the rope around the trunk and threw it back to the first.

By the time Nish had gone down, then up the first tree again, he was practically treating it like a footpath. He used the block and tackle to pull the two trees closer, then lashed them together. He constructed a platform by cutting one of the sides out of the basket and tying it to the branches. Now the real job would begin.

It went painfully slowly, for the upper part of the tear curved away from the trunk and he had to lean out just to the point of toppling. At the end of the day he had done less than a third of the sewing.

The job took another two days, at which time the cloth ran out when he still had half a span to go. Nish sewed one of his shirts over the remaining slit. The cloth was heavier than silk, but the balloon had less to lift than before, so he hoped it would suffice.

When all was finished, and sealed with tar, he stood back. The repair did not look strong enough. What if they got up into the air and it tore out? Their escape had been miraculous. It would not happen a second time. Unravelling a length of rope, he reinforced the repair with a network of strands and tarred them down. It would have to do. He had no tar left.

It took another day to cut up enough dry fuel, and then he had to carry every stick up on his back. Nish tied the section back into the basket, roped everything down and wove green twigs together to repair the hole in the floor, should he ever succeed in raising the balloon.

'Amplimet is gone,' Ullii said suddenly.

'What?'

She pointed to the west. 'It went that way.'

'Do the lyrinx have it?'

'I don't know.'

'What about Tiaan?'

'Tiaan too.'

He mulled over that while he worked, but there were too many possibilities and he had no way of distinguishing between them. Finally all was ready. Firing up the brazier, he cut away any branch stubs that would impede their upward progress and helped Ullii into her basket. He was stirring the fire with a stick when three things happened at once.

To the east, in the direction of the great mountain, a yellow cigar-shaped object passed across the sky. It looked like a gourd or squash, though tapered at either end. Underneath hung a smaller, elongated container. Nish squinted at the object, wishing for a spyglass. Was it a lyrinx machine of war, brought here to attack Tirthrax?

Ullii let out a screech that made his hair stand on end. Nish spun around, wondering what had so terrified her. She was not looking that way at all. The seeker was staring towards the base of the tree.

'Hooks and claws,' she moaned. 'Hooks and claws.' Ullii threw herself into her basket and wrenched the lid closed.

Nish caught an unpleasant reek, like hot rotting meat. What was it? Ullii had said something similar before they'd gone up in the balloon. Was it a predator nearby, or just something she had seen in her mental lattice? Better find out. The brazier would not fill the balloon for hours. Thrusting his battered sword through his belt, Nish began to climb down.

Near the bottom, the decaying reek became stronger, until he began to gag. It did not have the smell of a dead animal; more like a live one that had burrowed through decaying flesh.

Nish went still. The noise sounded like a low, purring growl. The purring bothered him more than the growl. Something began scratching at the bark at the back of the trunk.

Drawing his sword, Nish peered down. He could not see anything. Edging around the tree, he looked again. Still nothing. He lowered himself onto the next branch and ducked his head through the twigs. The beast slid around the tree and stood up on all fours, staring straight at him.

NINE

Tiaan lay on her bed, puzzling about the construct until she drifted to sleep. Perhaps that was why she dreamed of the forbidden book, Nunar's *The Mancer's Art,* which she had found hidden in the manufactory. At the very least, discovery would have meant the end of her career, if not her life, so why had she kept it? Partly for the thrill of the forbidden, though she had never been a rebel. But mostly because the night she had read the thoughts of the great Nunar on the nature of power Tiaan had been touched by something.

The basis of mancery, the Secret Art, was the field. Though artisans were mere craft workers, whenever she plied her trade Tiaan felt kinship with the greatest mancers of the age. But until she'd read Runcible Nunar's book she had not understood what she was doing. The field was just one of several forces that mancers speculated about, and the weakest of all. No one knew how to use the strong forces, or even if they existed. At least, if anyone had, they had not survived to record it.

Minis had taught her the rudiments of geomancy, the greatest of all the Secret Arts, which drew on the forces that shaped and moved the earth. Tiaan had not understood that either, though the Aachim had implied that their geomancy employed one of the strong forces.

Jerking awake, she dug *The Mancer's Art* out of her pack

where it had lain, carefully wrapped, for months. It was a small, slim volume written in a fine hand on silky rice paper. Tiaan turned the pages, searching for anything to do with geomancy. She did not find that Art mentioned by name, though late that night when she could barely keep her eyes open, she did discover something else.

The Strong Forces and the *General Theory of Power*

It is my contention that a node may generate as few as four strong forces, or as many as ten. These forces must be mutually orthogonal, and therefore only three can ever manifest themselves in our familiar world. The remainder must lie in other dimensions and can neither influence our physical environment nor be drawn upon by any refinement of the mancer's Art about which I am competent to speculate.

There followed a theoretical discussion of the strong forces, written in such abstruse language that Tiaan could make no sense of it. And then she found this:

Though I cannot prove it, I believe that the peril of the strong forces lies in their sheer intensity. The weak field is diffuse, so mancers were able to draw upon it without necessarily hazarding their lives, though those who were unlucky, or greedy, frequently made that sacrifice. Cautious mancers could master their Art from nebulous areas of the field, before drawing upon more concentrated parts.

The strong forces offer no such comfort. Essentially planar rather than three-dimensional, they would contain prodigious amounts of power within the plane but virtually none immediately adjacent. They would also be difficult to sense. Thus, any attempt to draw power from a strong force would almost certainly result in annihilation. No mancer could react quickly enough to control it.

Others have argued that a controller device could be fashioned to overcome this limitation. Not in my understanding of the Art. I believe that such forces are forever beyond the tampering fingers of humanity, and rightly so.

Had the Aachim discovered the answer after all? Tiaan recalled her image of the construct mechanism. Surely its controlling parts were in the wrong arrangement to be sensitive to the strong forces, much less to control them – unless the great Nunar was completely wrong? That was possible. *The Mancer's Art* had been written a hundred years ago, before the first controller had been invented.

That night, Tiaan had crystal dreams for the first time since opening the gate. They vanished on waking, as usual. She did not leap out of bed, as she was accustomed to do, but lay with the covers pulled well up, thinking about the problem. The Aachim must have a special way of controlling the construct. Could she read that from the aura?

She dozed, woke, dozed and woke again with a rudimentary design in her mind. After another hour she had worked out the details of her sensor, but only when she heard Malien moving about in the kitchen did Tiaan get up.

'Good morning,' she said, springing out of bed.

'You're cheerful today. The sleep must have done you good.'

'It has. I know what to do.'

Tiaan spent all afternoon building an array of interlinked hexagons of wire and crystal that mimicked the amplimet's form and structure. It was set around a little glass doughnut she had taken from one of the many storerooms in Tirthrax. The amplimet lay at its heart, in the soapstone basket from the centre of the port-all. She now felt anxious about that. Every time she touched the amplimet, she mentally flinched. Using it was no longer a comfort but a threat.

Sitting on the operator's seat, she slipped her fingers in through the wires of the hexagons and touched the amplimet. It was warm. Stroking along its length, she closed her eyes.

The amplimet began to pulse; she could feel the light beating against her eyelids. Tiaan did not try to control the crystal – this close to the great node of Tirthrax she was afraid to. She merely allowed the pulsation to wash over and through her, drifting with it until, finally, the field sprang into view. It was the greatest she had ever felt.

Tiaan traced the construct's aura into a black metal box whose contents she could not visualise. The aura came out the other end, twisted through the bowels of the machine and went up behind the green glass binnacle in front of her. There she lost it in murky tangles which she could not penetrate. It was like trying to make out a blueprint written in mist. Her eyes ached. The workings must be *protected*.

But a lock protects nothing if you have the key. She just had to decipher it. Feeling unusually tired, Tiaan rested her head on the glass. Was her obsession with her craft just a way to avoid other responsibilities, as Malien had implied? She did not want to think about that. Better keep going. She was terrified that the lyrinx would come back, and take the construct before she could understand it.

That black container in the bowels of the machine was another mystery. Putting her head through the lower hatch, she peered around, holding out one of Malien's glowing spheres. The box was up in the darkness at the front.

She was trying to sense its purpose when she felt an odd prickle and the image of wires and crystals froze in her mind. It was so quiet that Tiaan could hear her heart thumping. Going up, she traced the aura on the green glass, but the glass lit up and a spiralling red line began to rotate.

Tiaan jumped. Other markings appeared on the surface: blue circles that shrank and expanded again, yellow lines arcing from one side of a rectangle to another, rows of characters that were undoubtedly some kind of writing.

The shapes and colours changed, the writing flowed endlessly, but nothing else happened. As she crouched beneath the binnacle, probing with her inner sight, an alarm shrieked in her ear; then something clamped around her forehead and began to squeeze.

It was a trap and she had fallen into it. Metal fingers gripped her skull. Tiaan tried to tear them off but received a shock that singed her fingers. Her arms flopped uselessly by her sides. She began to shake uncontrollably as echoes of the shock raced up and down her limbs.

Tiaan felt disconnected from her body. Her tongue expanded

to fill her mouth, her eyes rolled down as far as they would go, and stuck. She could see her hands hanging like floppy spiders, but she could not move.

It was hours before a grinning Malien appeared and freed her – hours of helpless terror that she would never move again. And hours of crystal dreams that she remembered all too clearly, for she was dreaming awake. She dreamed that she was trapped inside the amplimet, paralysed or frozen, and it was feeding upon her essence as a wasp feeds on a spider. And the whole time, she could see the amplimet in her mind's eye, the central light flashing on and off like a signal lamp.

Her head felt fuzzy; it hurt to think. 'What's so funny?' she said curtly.

'The look on your face,' Malien chuckled. 'Next time, have the good sense to ask me for help. Did I not tell you that there could be traps?'

'I was worried that the enemy would get here first.'

'Better *they* kill you than you do it yourself. How are you feeling?'

Tiaan sat up. 'A bit shaky.'

Malien gave her a hand. 'We'd better get to work.'

'Yesterday you were lecturing me about working too hard.'

'The lyrinx weren't out there yesterday.'

'*What?*'

'I saw one this morning, circling high in the eastern sky. I wouldn't want them to get hold of a construct.'

By the evening, Tiaan felt that she understood most of the controls, though she had not discovered how to make the construct operate. 'There's still something missing,' she said.

'Like a key for a lock? I wonder . . .'

'What?'

Malien touched an isolated button at the base of the binnacle. A curved tube with hexagonal sides slid out from beneath. 'This leads to a cavity above that black box, low down. Can you sense what used to be in there?'

'I was trying to when it trapped me.'

'I think it's safe now.'

Tiaan sensed out the lingering aura. 'It held some kind of woken crystal.'

'What kind?'

'I can't tell. Do Aachim use crystals the way we do?'

'Not exactly, but I expect I can find a hedron or two, if that's what you're getting at.'

They spent half the night searching the storerooms, and found a number of woken crystals that would fit, though none had any effect on the construct.

'I can't do any more,' Tiaan said, when it was well after midnight.

'Wait a minute,' said Malien. 'Have you got the amplimet here?'

Tiaan took it from its pouch. Light streamed forth; steady light. 'What do you have in mind?'

'Putting it into that cavity.'

'But yesterday you said it would be too powerful to use.'

'I'll try to moderate it.'

Tiaan moved the amplimet from hand to hand, wondering if they might not be doing *its* will.

'Put it into the tube, Tiaan. No, the other way round.'

Tiaan did so.

'Now, push the tube down, very carefully. I'll stand ready, just in case.'

When it had gone all the way, she heard a gentle click as the crystal settled into the cavity. They waited, holding their breath. The colours on the glass plate brightened.

'Close the cap,' said Malien.

Tiaan pushed it down. There came a metallic screech from below and the whole construct shuddered. Orange rays streamed from the open hatch. Something began to thump against the floor. Malien hit the button; the amplimet shot out of the tube. Tiaan caught it and stuffed it into its pouch. The racket stopped. They looked at one another.

'It's too powerful.' Malien looked drawn. 'Let's go. I can't do any more tonight.'

'I'll stay for a while. I need to think.'

'Don't do anything foolish.'

'I won't,' Tiaan said absently, her mind on the problem.

With a hedron, power did not flow at all without the artisan drawing it from the field. In the hands of an experienced artisan, power could be controlled delicately. However, the amplimet drew power all the time and, here, even a little was too much.

It seemed to be drawing more than ever now – a flashing glow was visible through the leather pouch. A worm inched down Tiaan's backbone. She opened the flap but the crystal just shone steadily. She closed it. The flashing resumed. She lifted the flap, fractionally. The amplimet was flashing at a furious rate, just as in her dream.

Closing her fist around it, she ran up to Malien's chambers. 'It's blinking!' she cried, bursting through the door.

Malien rolled over, touching a globe to the faintest light. 'What on earth is the matter?'

Tiaan thrust the pouch at her. 'The amplimet was blinking furiously but as soon as I opened the pouch it stopped. Now it's doing it again.'

Malien shot up in bed and touched out the light. The flickering glow could be seen through the pouch, and when she lifted the flap, again it stopped.

She slid her legs out of bed, pulled on her boots and shrugged a cloak around her. 'Come with me. Leave it here.'

Tiaan sat the pouch on the table beside the bed. 'What is it, Malien?'

'I don't know. I've never seen anything like it before. I think –'

'What?' Tiaan had to trot to keep up.

'Let's just see, without prejudice. How does the field look to you?'

'I can't see it. I left my hedron down in the construct.'

Malien shook her head and walked faster. Tiaan ran after her. The tunnel to the Well was now distinctly warm. At a sweep of Malien's fist, the cubic barrier smashed into shards that vaporised in the air. The mist in the conical chamber whirled higher and faster, and the light from the shaft now had an oily green tinge. Moonlight, or an exhalation from the Well?

Malien was standing at the brink, her toes over the edge. She was breathing hard.

'It looks the same to me,' Tiaan panted.

'It's not!'

'Is it –?' Tiaan peered down fearfully.

Malien laid a hand on her shoulder. 'It's not as bad as I thought. It's still bound – just! And . . .'

'What, Malien?'

'I think the amplimet is communicating with it.'

'What's it saying?'

Malien looked her up and down, wordlessly.

Stupid question. Communication between a woken crystal and a frozen whirlpool of force might take any form. And might have any purpose.

'You'd better get back to work,' Malien said abruptly. *'And hurry.'*

Tiaan turned away. Malien did not move. 'Are you coming?'

'I hardly dare,' said Malien. 'I'll have to keep watch. Run, this is an emergency!'

Tiaan thought through her problem on the way back. She needed to choke down the flow, yet allow more power through when the construct was further from the node. What if she set the amplimet in a golden box, to contain the aura, but with a rotor at the open end, powered by the flow from the field? The blades, also made of gold, would lie flat. If there was not enough power to spin the rotor, the power would come though. Once the rotor began to turn, the golden blades would rise into position, choking down the flow. Tiaan was sure it would work. It had to – she desperately wanted to make this construct go.

The fabrication was painfully slow but she dared not rush it – the box must seal perfectly and the rotor work every time.

In the afternoon she was so tired that she had to take a nap. She dozed for an hour and roused to find her cheeks damp with tears of longing. She had dreamed that the construct was hers.

By that evening she had built a golden box and assembled her rotor. Tiaan put the boxed amplimet into the tube and closed the cap. Now she saw a field, though it was not the one she normally used. This was different, flatter, weaker; and probably just as well.

The hum resumed. It was lower now, more like the sound the constructs had made when she first encountered them. There was no thumping. Tiaan experimented with the buttons, which did no more than change the images on the green glass. She played with the finger-shaped levers. One lit up the area all around the construct, another changed the sound of the mechanism below from a hum to a whine, a third opened the turret behind her with a *whirr-click*.

A fourth shook the machine, which slowly rose in the air until it stood hip height above the floor. At last! Tiaan's heart crashed painfully about her ribcage. Now, if she could just get it to move.

She wiggled the studded knob on the trumpet-shaped lever and was hurled sideways as the machine spun like a top. Her arm grew so heavy that she could barely hold it up. Forcing with all her strength, she managed to push the knob the other way but as the rotation slowed she went off-balance, forcing the trumpet further over.

The construct spiralled sideways across the floor, directly towards one of the main roof pillars. She jerked the knob. The machine spun the other way. Tiaan let out a screech. Her brain seemed to be spinning inside her skull. Each new movement sent the machine a different way. As it whirled toward another pillar, Tiaan saw Malien with her hands cupped around her mouth. What was she trying to say?

Tiaan could not hear a thing. The machine was out of control, spinning so fast that everything became a blur. She felt herself losing consciousness.

Golden sparkles burst in her eyes and the whine stopped. Malien must have cut off her view of the field. The machine came to rest just a handspan from the pillar. Tiaan climbed out, reeled about drunkenly and collapsed on the floor.

'That was the funniest thing I've seen in a long time,' Malien chuckled.

'I'm glad you think so,' Tiaan choked. 'I could have wrecked it in the first minute.' As she sat up, the world tilted, so Tiaan lay down again. 'I don't feel very well.'

'It'll pass. Tiaan, a construct is not a clanker. Strength with delicacy is the hallmark of our work, whether it be a bridge spanning the mightiest of abysses, or a dressmaker's needle. The gentlest movements are all it takes to control a construct.'

'I'm not sure I want to control one,' said Tiaan, feeling as though she was being lectured.

'I know you do,' said Malien. She placed one hand on the flank of the machine. 'There's something strange about it.'

'What's that?'

'Except for the fitting out and the turret at the back, it's just like the one Rulke made two hundred years ago.'

'I suppose the Aachim copied his design.'

'We are artists first, engineers or craft workers second. We never make the same object in the same way twice, yet these three constructs are almost identical. From what you say, the others were too.'

Tiaan recalled the images to mind. 'They were all sizes, but the shape was always the same. So what?'

'It suggests that they didn't dare make changes, because they had copied what they did not understand. Not the way Rulke did.'

'What are you trying to say?'

'Rulke's construct didn't just hover, it flew through the air. I saw it with my own eyes.'

The freedom of the skies! How she wanted it. Tiaan bit down on those feelings. 'Maybe so, but all the cleverness of the Aachim has failed to uncover that secret.'

'Perhaps they were looking in the wrong place.'

'What are you up to, Malien? Do you hope I will solve it for you?'

Malien laughed, though it had an odd ring to it. 'My adventuring days are well behind me.'

They returned to the machine. 'What I don't understand,' Malien continued, 'is *how* they could have rebuilt it. I saw Yggur's blast pass across the void and turn Rulke's construct into a glowing cinder. We all did, who were there that fateful day. How could they recover its design after such ruin?'

She answered her own question. 'Metalmancy. They used mancery to recover the form and purpose of every part of it. That must have been a labour indeed, though they had two hundred years to do it, and the resources of a world. But even metalmancy could not have recovered the most fragile parts.'

'They never saw it used,' Malien mused. 'Not the way I did. Rulke's machine was as hot as a furnace beneath, after it had flown.'

'The Aachim constructs weren't hot,' said Tiaan. 'They passed over snow and ice without melting it.'

'*Did they now!* Vithis can't have discovered the secret of flight at all.' Malien turned away. 'I'm going back to check on the Well.'

Tiaan, consumed by the thought of flight, the ultimate secret, hardly noticed her going.

She spent all the following morning practising with the construct, bringing hand and eye into coordination. It was more difficult than it seemed, especially under the pressure of time, though after a couple of hours she could manoeuvre it without too much risk.

She went back over everything the Aachim had taught her of geomancy. The more she compared that to what Nunar's book had taught her, the clearer it was that someone was wrong. The construct did not seem designed to detect, much less draw upon, the strong forces. It used a weak field she had never bothered with.

A few hours later, Malien came down the stairs, exhausted. Tiaan told her what she had learned. 'Maybe Nunar was wrong, and the strong forces do not exist.'

Malien sat on a carved bench and closed her eyes.

After several minutes, Tiaan said, 'Malien?'

'What? Oh, give me a look at the book.'

Tiaan showed her the passages in *The Mancer's Art*.

Malien looked thoughtful. 'I think I know how to test your theory. Wait here.'

She returned with two sheets of a glassy mineral somewhat like mica, though brittle. Laying one sheet over the other, she held them up to the light and rotated the top sheet. At one point it went black. 'Make yourself a set of goggles from these. Put the goggles on, then use the amplimet to envision the field.'

Tiaan did so, and as soon as she put them on, the field streamed all around her.

'Rotate the upper lenses until they go black,' said Malien. 'Now what do you see?'

'Nothing. The field has completely disappeared.'

'Nothing at all?'

'No.'

'Concentrate, as though you're searching for a distant field.'

'Still nothing.'

'You're too tense. Relax. Just let it flow.' Malien's hands went around her head, over the goggles.

Tiaan tried to relax. One of the lenses moved, allowing in a multi-coloured loop of the field. She moved it back to the dark position and saw a white-hot cross made of three planes intersecting at right angles. She cried out, the lenses slipped and the cross vanished. And then the truth came to her.

'I saw it!' she cried. 'The strong forces do exist.' Tiaan began to laugh.

'What is it?' Malien said, anxiously.

Tiaan took particular pleasure in telling her. 'Vithis *can't* be using the strong forces. The Aachim don't know how.'

'I don't understand. Come, sit down. Tell me what the matter is.'

'The Aachim always act so superior. To their mind they *are* superior, and make sure everyone knows it. Yes, you too, Malien. But they're not even using the node field, just little local fields.'

'Stress-fields,' Malien said crossly. 'They're strong on Aachan but weak here.'

'They don't know as much as we do,' Tiaan chortled.

'Beware pride!' snapped Malien, nettled.

'Or *false* pride,' Tiaan retorted. 'The Aachim could never have made the construct fly. Flight requires power that only the strong forces can provide, as well as the ability to see them.'

'Once the secret is out, they will soon learn. So, are you saying you can make the construct fly?'

'I'm prepared to try.'

'Try very hard.'

'Is something the matter?'

'The amplimet is still communicating with the Well, in spite of all my efforts. The Well is drawing power from somewhere and rapidly unfreezing. I can't allow that to happen.'

'What are you saying?'

'Either the amplimet leaves here, or I'll have to destroy it, whatever the consequences.'

TEN

'No!' cried Tiaan. 'You can't.'

'Do you think I want to?' said Malien. 'No one knows better than I do, how precious it is. I know what destroying it would do to you, too. But should the Well unfreeze and break the bonds that hold it here, the consequences would be catastrophic.'

'How do you mean?'

'Possibly, no more Tirthrax – city *or* mountain.'

'How long do I have?'

Malien hesitated. 'I've sent a skeet to Stassor, but no Aachim could get back here in less than two months. The construct would be no quicker – the country is too rugged for a hovering craft. But with flight, it could be there in a week. I sense that we're close to uncovering the last secret of the construct. Dare I risk it? Come upstairs. I'm going to my eyrie. I need to think.'

Tiaan followed. Malien walked out the opening and stood staring down at the glacier. Tiaan watched, hoping and praying she would come up with something. Destroying the amplimet would surely drive her insane. To miss the chance of flight would be almost as bad.

Malien came running back, her cloak flapping behind her. Tiaan held her breath.

'You have until tomorrow,' said Malien. 'I believe I can hold the Well that long. If you haven't found the answer by then, we must come to a decision: to take the amplimet away, or destroy it. And I dread what will happen if it leaves here – whose hands it will fall into. The choice almost makes itself.'

'Please,' said Tiaan. 'I'll take it. To destroy it would be to destroy myself. Though I don't know where to go.'

'In that case, I may have to come with you. Get to work and I'll do the same, and tomorrow I'll decide what is for the best.'

Tiaan studied the strong forces through her goggles. She had to know them perfectly before she could tailor the controller to them, and even then they would be deadly.

The hours raced by. She felt that she was making no progress at all. Malien came and went a number of times during the day, looking ever more careworn. Time was running out.

'No luck?' she asked that night.

'No.' Tiaan was exhausted too, but that was due to her own failure. 'How about you?'

'It's holding, for the moment. Let me have a look down below.' Malien went down into the construct. A good while later she came up with the black box in her hand. 'This surely has to be the key.'

'It isn't connected to anything.'

'The original must have been.'

'Then why didn't the Aachim's mancery reconstruct it?'

'Perhaps the vital parts were no longer there.' Malien seemed to be looking right through Tiaan to the far wall. She often appeared lost in another world, or a distant time. Or perhaps she was *holding* the Well from afar.

'I have no idea what you're talking about,' said Tiaan.

'I hardly know myself. I'm thinking as I go. The original construct was destroyed by Yggur's blast –'

'Completely?'

'There's little in a construct to burn, but its parts would have fused. The crystals commonly used in the Art would not melt, though they may have shattered. Traces would remain, enough for Aachim metalmancers to reconstruct what was there. And yet . . .'

'What?' said Tiaan.

Malien looked frustrated. '*I don't know*. Rulke's construct flew. These are as exact copies as could be made, but they cannot fly. What did Vithis miss? What have I?'

Tiaan prised the top off the black box, which contained metal coils and shaped pieces of magnetic iron, as well as a number of evenly spaced ceramic plates on which were mounted rows of metal sockets. She held the box up to her eye. 'There are dozens of tiny little holes in the back.'

Malien raised the box to the light. 'Fifty-four of them. I wonder what they're for?'

'Perhaps it gets hot inside and they let the hot air out.'

'They're too small.' Malien counted the metal sockets. 'Also fifty-four pairs. That can't be an accident.'

'They're meant to hold something.'

'Whatever it was, all were the same size and shape.'

'Small crystals?' Tiaan said doubtfully.

'How could small crystals draw such power that the construct would grow red-hot beneath? And why was no trace found of them?'

'There are crystals that, when heated, simply evaporate, though none are any use in mancing . . .'

'That's it! Tiaan, name those crystals.'

'Ice, sulphur, iodine . . . There must be others, but none are good for making hedrons –'

'Some mancers use brimstone crystals.'

'Not for drawing power. It would shatter them.'

'Agreed. What else?' Malien leaned forward eagerly. 'What is the most powerful crystal?'

'Diamond, of course, but diamonds are generally too small to use in controllers. And large ones are too precious.'

'Not if they're the only thing that will do,' said Malien. 'And Rulke had the best of everything.'

'But diamond is the hardest of all. Why didn't they find it?'

'Because, unlike other crystals, diamond burns. That must be the answer: these pairs of sockets once held small hedrons made of diamond.'

'How were they connected to the amplimet binnacle?'

'Perhaps through these tiny holes in the back, no bigger than a cat's whisker? And look, there are also fifty-four holes in the back of the amplimet cavity.'

'If they were connected to the crystal there, why did metalmancers not recover the wires?'

'Because they were not metal, and also vanished without trace.'

'How can that be?'

'What wires would disappear when heated, Tiaan?'

'Ones made of thread, or spider-silk, or hair, though none are useful in the Art as I know it.'

'Nor I. Wait here.'

Again Malien disappeared in the direction of the storeroom. She was gone for ages. It was after midnight. Tiaan lay on the warm floor of the construct. Only hours left . . .

Malien thumped into the operator's compartment, waking Tiaan from a deep sleep.

'Any luck?' Tiaan called. She went up the ladder.

'Possibly.' Malien opened a small case that contained dozens of pink diamonds, all the same, and a leather sheet wrapped around a black cord made of braided threads. She drew out a single thread. 'These are hollow whiskers made from soot, as is diamond itself. The whiskers are stronger than steel, yet they too would have burned leaving no more than a trace of smut. And the crystal calls to the whiskers, for elementally they are the same. It's a perfect geomantic design, just right for controlling the strong forces. Feed them through.'

Tiaan fed fifty-four whiskers through the holes in the black box and up to the cavity while Malien inserted fifty-four woken diamonds in place. They made a three-dimensional pattern that seemed peculiarly appropriate to the strong forces. Once the whiskers were connected, everything looked so right that Tiaan knew this was the way it was meant to be. It was so beautifully simple.

They looked at one another.

'Go on,' said Malien.

'I hardly dare,' Tiaan said. 'It was dangerous enough just scooting above the ground. I wouldn't know how to control it, using the strong forces.'

Malien edged her out of the way without repeating her offer. 'Then let me try.'

Tiaan was uncomfortable with that idea, and more so as Malien took the goggles and put the amplimet in. She hoped, selfishly, that the older woman would fail. If Malien could operate it, what chance was there for Tiaan ever to do so?

Tiaan pressed the amplimet down and closed the cap. The construct shook, rumbled and rose smoothly from the floor. Malien flicked down one of the finger levers and a blast of heat coiled up the sides. She pulled on the knobbed trumpet and the machine kept rising. She directed it around the ceiling, then took it down to the floor again.

'You knew what to do all the time,' Tiaan accused.

Malien had drops of sweat on her brow. It must have been harder than it looked. 'I did not even suspect it until you discovered those little holes.'

'Well, you've done it!' It was a momentous discovery, an awesome moment. The world would never be the same again. What was Malien going to do now?

'My people have sought this secret for two hundred years, here and on Aachan.'

'But they didn't find it. Is an amplimet necessary for flight?' said Tiaan.

'Probably not, if the hedron is strong enough, and the operator skilled.'

'Did Rulke have one?'

'I don't know. Your turn, Tiaan.'

'You're going to let *me* fly it?' It did not seem possible.

'Why not?'

'I just thought . . .'

'The trumpet-shaped controller works the same way, but you pull up on it to climb and push down to descend.'

Tiaan took hold of the knob. Her heart was pounding.

'Remember, do everything gently,' said Malien beside her.

Tiaan swallowed, then pulled up the knob the way Malien had done. The construct jerked into the air.

'Put it down, quick!'

'What's the matter?' Tiaan cried. 'What have I done wrong?'

Malien pointed in the direction of the opening.

Tiaan set the construct down.

A lyrinx was descending onto the rubble in the entrance. Another settled beside it, a third, and then many more, too quickly to count.

ELEVEN

The beast was the size of a large dog, though lower to the ground, and all tooth, claw and spiky armour. Its head was massive, the maw surrounded with teeth and the crested head coated in rings of spines. The body was protected by segmented armour plates, spiny above and underneath. The tail was a knotted and spiked club. That was not the most frightening thing about it. Nor was the truly repulsive smell.

What scared Nish most was the lurking cunning, and the madness, in its eyes. It looked like a beast that lived to torment; to rend and devour. It could only be the nylatl Tiaan had mentioned. It must have tracked her down and he was to be a snack as it went by.

With those claws it could run up the tree as quickly as he could walk down a path. If he leapt to the ground, he would have a better chance with the sword, but that would leave Ullii defenceless. The creature would follow her scent upwards and devour her at its leisure. Nish imagined her terror, confronted by the beast. He could not give it the chance.

Here, on the lower branches, was a poor place to defend. The trunk was too big and the creature could come at him from behind, or even climb past him in a rush. He screwed a heavy green cone until it broke off. Thrusting the sword into his belt, Nish shifted the cone into his right hand and threw hard at the unblinking eyes. It went true, striking the nylatl on the ridges above and below its left eye. The creature yelped and scurried into the bushes.

The injury was minor, at best. The nylatl would be back in a minute. Nish scrambled up, hand over foot, faster than he had ever gone before. Five or six branches higher he missed a foothold, almost plunging all the way down again. After that he was more careful, but before he had climbed much further Nish knew that the monster was after him.

At a point where the trunk was no wider than his chest, and there was no way for the nylatl to get past, he prepared to defend. Here the branches stuck straight out from the trunk, as good a footing as he would find anywhere. The sword was not a long one, though its reach extended below his feet. Far enough to get in a good hack if the creature attacked that way, as it must.

It did not. Nish was searching the underlying branches, cursing himself for not having spent more time practising his swordsmanship when he had the chance, trying to stop his heart from bursting out through the wall of his chest – when he felt eyes on the back of his neck. The nylatl was staring at him from the branches of the neighbouring tree. It had crept up the far side of the trunk without making a sound.

The creature was about three spans away. It was a heavy beast. Could it leap that distance? It certainly seemed to think so. The muscles tensed in its back legs. Bracing himself against the trunk, Nish thrust out the sword, making a hissing whistle that came out ear-piercingly shrill.

The nylatl squealed and reared up on its hind legs, as if the sound had hurt it. Nish did it again. The creature's mouth gaped and a rolled blue tongue extended, but it was not, as he thought, another distress signal. The tongue squirted something at his eyes.

Nish went backwards but not quickly enough; the spittle struck him on mouth and chin. The putrefying smell went up his nose and he threw up so violently that vomit projected out of his mouth and nostrils.

'Aaargh!' he gasped as the venom began to burn and blister. As he scrubbed at the venom with a sleeve, the skin peeled off. Nish could feel his lips swelling, bleeding.

The pain was excruciating. It felt as if his lips were splitting apart. He steadied himself, held out the sword and eyed the nylatl. It crouched, its back legs tensing and relaxing.

'Haaahh!' he screamed, waving his weapon.

The nylatl swayed backwards. It was just a slight movement but it gave Nish hope. The creature was uncertain how dangerous he was. Once it launched itself at him, it could do little to evade the point of his sword. It scrabbled up the trunk, watching him over its shoulder.

Sheathing the weapon, Nish climbed too. He could not allow the nylatl the advantage of height.

Once or twice it stopped, crouching and staring at him with those cunning eyes, but Nish waved his weapon, whistled or shrieked and did his best to look intimidating, and the nylatl kept on. In this way Nish reached the bottom of the balloon basket, where he realised his vulnerability. He would have to move out on the branch toward the creature, then climb the rope ladder with his back to it.

The nylatl went up another branch and stood watching him. Nish prayed that it would stay where it was. If it leapt into the basket, it could dine on Ullii at its leisure and attack him as he tried to climb over the rim.

Nish tapped on the bottom of the basket with his sword. 'Ullii,' he hissed.

She did not answer. He hoped she just had her earmuffs on, for if she had gone into one of her states he would never get her out of it.

'Ullii!'

Still no answer. The nylatl raked its claws along the branch, tearing the hard bark into curling shreds. Its back legs tensed.

'Ullii!' he screamed, loud and shrill. He wasn't pretending. 'Help. It's going to eat me.'

Again the nylatl reared back as if in pain. Above him, the lid of the basket creaked open. He could hear the seeker's teeth chattering. Poor Ullii.

'Nish?' she whispered. 'Where are you?'

'Under the basket.'

'I'm very frightened, Nish.'

'I'm frightened too.' Somehow he had to force her to act. A threat to her might not be enough, since her normal defence was to retreat into herself. Then he had it.

'Ullii, look over the side.' No answer. 'It's hurt me, Ullii, and now it's going to *eat* me.'

She peered over, caught sight of his bloody, grotesquely swollen lips and let out a wail. 'Nish, poor Nish!'

'Ullii, can you see S'lound's sword?' S'lound, their guard from the balloon trip, had died in the landing at Tirthrax.

'Yes,' she whispered. 'It's under his pack.'

'Hold it out in front of you.'

He heard a rasp as the sword came from its scabbard.

'That's good. Now watch the beast while I climb up to you. Can you do that?'

'I'm scared, Nish.'

'It's going to eat me, Ullii.'

Nish went out on the branch towards the dangling rope ladder. The nylatl rolled its tongue. He whistled and lunged forward, slashing with his sword. The creature went backwards, but not very far. Something flickered in its eyes. It wasn't fear. It had worked him out.

Not daring to put the sword through his belt, Nish caught the ladder with one hand and tried to pull himself up. He slipped but managed to hook his arm through the rung. His back was to the nylatl now. Nish could feel the eyes on him. He was so terrified, he could almost see into the mind of the creature, feel its bliss as the talons raked down his back and the jaws went for his throat.

Heaving himself onto the next rung, he felt the sweat dripping from his armpits. Another rung. Only three to go. Two.

'No!' Ullii screamed. 'Nish. Nish!'

The nylatl sprang. He saw it out of the corner of his eye. As Nish tried to swing around, one sweaty hand slipped on the rope. He snatched at the rung with his other hand and, horror of horrors, the sword slipped from his grasp. He tried to catch it with the toe of his boot but missed.

As he swung off the rope, the nylatl thumped into the side of the basket above his head. Its backside was right above him. Had he not lost his sword, he could have skewered it in one of the few places where it was vulnerable. He could not go up and dared not go down. Nish did the only thing left. He caught hold of one back paw, below the spines, and tried to tear the nylatl off the basket.

Futile hope. Nothing could relax those mighty claws. It kicked backwards, luckily at an awkward angle, or the claws would have torn his arm off at the elbow. As it was, they opened him up from wrist to the inside of his upper arm. Nish cried out; he could not help himself.

'Nish!' Ullii wailed. 'Are you all right?'

'No,' he groaned, grasping the paw again. A spine pricked into his wrist but he dared not let go. All the nylatl had to do was spin around on the basket, lunge and bite his face off. There was nowhere for him to go.

Then, a sight that brought tears to his eyes, little Ullii was up on the edge of the basket in her bare feet, balancing like a tightrope walker. She had the long sword in both hands. She looked down, saw the gore all over him and let out a bloodthirsty cry of rage.

The nylatl lunged but Nish was holding it back and Ullii was lightning quick. The sword flashed and danced. One blow opened up a cut across a crusted nostril, a second below the eye. The nylatl retreated and its backside struck Nish's head. A spine slanted into his scalp; the poison burned. Thinking that the creature was going to come down on top of him, he let out a shriek.

Ullii wailed and hacked at the beast with all her strength. The sword clove three of its toes off and went a handspan through the wall of the basket. Blood poured from the damaged limb, all over Nish's face.

Wrenching out the sword, Ullii thrust the tip at the creature's eye, but it had had enough. It sprang off the side of the basket and landed on a lower branch, scrabbling at it with its injured limb. Jumping for the trunk, it went head-first down the tree.

Nish lost sight of it as the beast's blood trickled into his eyes. He hung dazedly on the ladder until Ullii took his hands and dragged him into the basket.

She said nothing until she had wiped the blood away and discovered that he was not badly injured, whereupon she lay on him and wept until her tears washed his face clean. 'I was so afraid,' she sniffled, putting her soft mouth on his lower lip, which was swollen like a sausage.

He kissed her. 'You are the bravest woman in the world, Ullii.' Nish meant every word.

The tree creaked in the wind and he jerked upright, terrified. She pushed him down. 'I will know, Nish,' she whispered. 'If it ever comes back, I will know.'

She poured water onto a rag and began to clean him, as gently as if he had been her baby. Afterwards they lay quietly on the floor of the basket, holding each other, until Nish realised, from the rising warmth, that his clothes stank of the nylatl's blood. Pulling off his shirt, he tossed it away and felt in his pack for a clean one.

'My clothes smell too,' Ullii said, staring at his chest.

Nish was reaching for her pack when he realised what she was saying. She lifted her arms while he peeled the bloodstained coat off, and her trousers, which were not stained at all, followed by the neck-to-ankle underwear of woven spider-silk that protected her overly sensitive skin. Ullii, standing naked above him, was sweet and lovely and so very desirable.

They slept afterwards, until the cold woke them. A breeze moved the treetops as they dressed, giving each other sideways glances, still wondering about what had happened. Every so often Ullii would look up at him from beneath her colourless lashes, smile to herself, then glance away. Her eyes were watering but she did not put on her mask, and that was odd.

Nish was gnawing at a stale slab of flatbread, baked in the ashes days ago, when he remembered that strange vessel drifting across the sky. Standing up on the side of the basket, he peered through the treetops but of course could see nothing. Nish climbed to the level of the brazier, staring into the east. The sun reflected off the side of the mountain. There was no sign of the air-floater.

He yawned, stretched, and looked the other way, across the flatlands of Mirrilladell, dotted with a hundred thousand lakes now thawing in the spring. As he did, he caught a movement from the corner of his eye. The air-floater was coming directly for them and its intentions did not look peaceful.

TWELVE

'What are we going to do?' Tiaan yelled as more lyrinx flapped down into the entrance. She could see at least thirty already.

'I'll seal this level off,' said Malien. 'Run up and hide.'

'They'll slaughter you.'

'This isn't your battle. Anyway, Tirthrax has defences and so do I.'

'I'm not going to leave you to fight alone.'

'All right. Stay in the construct. I'll set the sentinels.' Malien hurried away.

Tiaan took hold of the controller knob but had to let it go for her arm was shaking. The construct was too precious to risk. She had no idea how to defend herself anyway, apart from driving straight at them, which could do no more than knock one or two down. She could not rely on its strangeness. The enemy were used to clankers. And to destroying them.

Two big females were flying towards her, accompanied by a smaller but more heavily muscled male. Above them soared a slight, unpigmented lyrinx – Liett again. The other lyrinx fanned out across the floor. There were too many of them. She couldn't do it. But you fought the nylatl, Tiaan told herself. You're not completely helpless. It was not convincing.

She concentrated on her breathing – deep, slow breaths. Her

heart stopped thumping; her arm steadied. She hovered the construct. Tiaan dared not try to fly it. She moved the controller, ever so gently, and the construct went around a quarter-turn. She did it again, until she was facing the enemy. She felt a mad urge to race straight at them, out through the entrance and away.

Where *was* Malien? Tiaan felt desperately alone. She directed the construct toward the stairway with many a lurch and hop, for yesterday's control had deserted her. The opening to the higher levels was closed. Malien appeared, wrestling with a black sentinel.

Tiaan drifted the construct that way. Malien looked up, flashed Tiaan a tight smile and said, 'It wasn't working properly. I had to *renew* it.'

'Is it all right now?'

'I believe it will do.' She climbed in.

'What are they doing?' said Tiaan. The fliers were circling halfway down the hall, directly above a wedge of lyrinx on the floor. 'Do you think they're afraid of us?'

'No, but they *are* wary. There's a great civilisation here that they knew nothing about. For all they know, Tirthrax might have another thousand constructs ready for battle.'

'And we could be luring them into a trap.'

Malien laughed. 'If only. And of course, they must know of the great construct fleet by now. They may even have encountered it.'

'How long can your sentinels keep them out of the upper levels?'

'Days, at best. They're watchers, not weapons, and not designed to defend an empty city.'

'Then if Tirthrax is not to fall –'

'Why would they want it?' said Malien.

'Because you have it. And because a mighty node lies here, which might be of benefit to them in their flesh-forming.'

Malien pursed her lips. 'There are nodes aplenty in Santhenar, but if they want this one I will give them a show they will long remember. Though I fear . . .'

'What?'

'They'll most remember that we are alone.' She climbed up over the back.

'What are you doing?'

Malien lifted the rear hatch and settled herself into the turret. One just like it had fired Haani's fatal missile. Whirring gently, a spear-throwing device resembling a large crossbow rose from a concealed cavity. Malien swivelled the weapon back and forth, slid in a rod with a stone fist on the end, and wound the crank until the wires creaked.

'I imagine I can do some damage with this. Go towards them, slowly. Try not to show any fear.'

One or two javelard missiles would make no difference. Tiaan prayed Malien had a stronger defence. With much concentration, she managed to keep the machine straight and steady, though it must have been clear that it was driven by an amateur. Did it have any other weapons? She should have explored that question long ago.

Tiaan moved to within fifty paces of the point of the wedge, then stopped. The fliers were all down now, except Liett. It required a considerable exertion of the Secret Art to stay in the air and they would not want to waste their strength. Liett, one of the best fliers of all, was just for show.

'Why do you trespass in the city of the Aachim?' came a cold voice from behind Tiaan. 'I am Malien, Matah of Tirthrax. State your business, lyrinx!'

The largest female stepped forward. 'I am Wise Mother Cordione,' she boomed. 'Until now, we have had no quarrel with the Aachim. You have kept to your cities and taken no part in the war.'

'That is so,' said Malien, 'but you have not answered my question.'

'Our business is eleven thousand machines of war like this one! Built in secret and now pushing across the world on half a dozen fronts. To what purpose, Matah?'

Malien did not answer straight away. 'You know them better than I do, Tiaan,' she whispered. 'Is it better to say we built the machines here, or that we brought them from another world?'

109

'I don't know,' Tiaan whispered back. 'Either way confirms the value of this place.'

'They know that already.' Malien raised her voice. 'These constructs were not built here, Wise Mother, though they could have been. They came across the void from Aachan, through a gate. Their passengers are refugees from a dying world.'

'Then they do their own business and you cannot negotiate for them.'

'They are still my people,' said Malien. 'My own Clan Elienor is numbered among them.'

'Come they in war or in peace?'

'They came, like your own kind, for survival. Should they be accommodated by Santhenar, they will have no need to fight.'

'War, then,' said the Wise Mother. 'I thought as much.'

Tiaan held her breath. The lyrinx now showed violent red and black skin colours. Were they going to attack?

'We are an honourable species,' said Malien. 'There will be no war without a declaration.'

The skin colours flashed brighter than before. Even Malien seemed alarmed. The moment stretched out, then the colours faded.

'It best not be long in coming, for the march of your constructs is an act of aggression. Be sure we are ready to match it.'

The Wise Mother, yellow waves shimmering over her green crest, bowed low. Malien did the same. Cordione spread her glorious wings and climbed into the air. The others followed.

Malien's javelard followed them to the entrance. Only then did she release the tension.

'That was close. They're not fooled, Tiaan. Nothing has changed here in weeks. If Tirthrax had any strength at all, we would have cleared away the rubble and sealed off the opening.'

'What will they do?' What am *I* to do, Tiaan thought desperately. I can't destroy the amplimet, and I can't leave with hungry lyrinx outside.

'They will watch and wait. Once a declaration comes, they will return in force.'

'And you?'

'Tirthrax has stores enough to feed an army, and hiding places they will never find. You need not fret for me.' She got down.

Tiaan followed her. 'Malien, I –'

'You'd better go.'

'But they'll eat me.'

'If you're flying the construct they'll never catch you.'

Her heart lurched. 'Where are we going?'

'I'm not going anywhere. I don't dare, with the Well in this state.'

Tiaan did not know what to say. 'But the construct isn't mine.' How she wanted it!

'It was abandoned in my city. I give it to you, freely and unencumbered.'

It was the greatest gift in the world. Too great a gift, undeserved. Why did Malien offer it? 'Thank you,' said Tiaan uneasily, 'but . . . why not keep it for yourself?'

Malien walked across the great hall, head down, hands tucked in her loose sleeves. Tiaan watched her go, and return.

'You've got to take the amplimet away, far and quickly. How else can you do that? The construct won't fly without the amplimet, so it's no use to me here.'

'You could hide the amplimet outside until the Well has stabilised.'

'It would still be too close. The amplimet must be taken a hundred leagues, at least. Since I cannot take it, you must. And also, Tiaan, in my heart I know that old humans and Aachim are both forms of humanity. Perhaps Minis was drawn to you for a reason. Maybe he *can* see the future and you are vital to it. There *is* something about you.'

Something small, frightened and helpless, but Tiaan did not argue. She had coveted the construct for too long.

'The machine is well provisioned,' Malien continued, 'but take what you want from my storerooms. Anything at all.'

'Thank you.' What conditions would she put on the gift? Nothing came without an obligation.

Tiaan was exhausted but there was no time for sleep. She

spent the rest of the day checking everything and practising. The strong force took a deal of getting used to, for it either flowed like a torrent or not at all. It required much more control, and affected both her mind and her sight. Once, her vision went blue for a minute before flashing back to normal. Another time she thought she was seeing double, a strange hallucination where what she saw through her left eye was a few seconds later than her right. She shook her head and the effect vanished, but another problem remained. Her view of the strong force tended to slip 'off plane', which would be disastrous if she was flying. If not for her visual memory, she could not have done it at all.

She would never master the machine in time. Tiaan was terrified of the strong forces; she knew so little about them and Malien could not help. She had to understand them on her own.

'The design of the flying controller seems a little primitive for Rulke,' said Malien that evening. 'Perhaps that's the problem. There may be something about the original design we haven't discovered. You'd better get some sleep.'

'But the Well . . .'

'I can hold it a little longer. The morning will be fine, but don't sleep in.'

That was not comforting. Tiaan kept practising and, by late that night, felt she could operate the machine in relative safety, in its hovering state. Flying was a different matter. When high up, she could not tell how fast she was moving and, if the visibility was poor, it was hard to know whether she was going down or up. But it would have to do.

Rising at first light, she returned to the machine, disabled the sentinels the way Malien had taught her, filled containers with water and did her last checks.

As she climbed out, Malien appeared with a basket and steaming mugs, and a rolled map. 'This may be of use to you in your travels.'

The map was entitled *Part of the Southern Hemisphere of Santhenar,* and depicted all the lands between the tropical Isle of Banthey in the north and the frozen Kara Agel in the south.

'Thank you,' said Tiaan. 'It's beautifully drawn. It must be very old.'

'Very,' Malien said dryly. 'I drew it last night.'

They sat beside the machine for a last meal together.

'I wish you luck with your construct,' Malien said.

Tiaan frowned. 'I don't like that name. It's cold, like Vithis.' She thought for a moment. 'I shall call it *thapter*.'

'Good choice,' Malien laughed. 'Where will you go? Back to your own people?'

Tiaan had spent half the night thinking about that, but had not come to a decision. 'I don't know. The manufactory is a long way from here. I may go west.'

'You'll see plenty of the enemy. The war is at its worst over there.'

'Then the thapter will be needed.' Tiaan stood up. Malien was more a mystery than ever. 'I'd better go.'

'I hate long farewells.' Malien embraced her and stood back.

Tiaan climbed in and reached for the controller.

'Wait!' called Malien. 'I have a gift for you.' She tossed something in the air.

Tiaan caught it. It was a small piece of worked metal in a swirling pattern that was hard to look at, for it seemed to double back on itself, inside, then outside, then inside again. She had seen it somewhere else in Tirthrax. Markings had been inlaid into it, silver on black. Just to look at it was calming.

'Thank you,' she said. 'What is it?'

'A symbol of the Well of Echoes,' Malien replied casually. 'It signifies infinity, the universe and nothingness. Or to put it another way, the importance, as well as the insignificance, of humanity in the great cosmos. It's just a token but I've laid a virtue on it that may help you find what you are looking for.'

Tiaan put it on the chain around her neck. She knew what she was looking for: revenge! Though even that had lost its force lately. 'I'll cherish it always. It will remind me of you.'

Malien smiled and raised her arm.

'You've not said what you require of me,' Tiaan said after a long interval.

'I don't know that I'm wise enough to require anything.'

'You've given me the greatest gift I could hope for. You must want something in return.'

'The thapter may turn out to be a poisoned fruit, Tiaan. It may ruin your life, or destroy it. I also give it to you because, through accident or design, the amplimet has been imprinted by you. If you cannot use it to the betterment of humanity, who can?'

'I might be taken by the enemy straight away.'

'All might be lost in a dozen ways. Even the greatest seer sees only fragments of the future and can never know if what they predict is for good or ill. That's why I place no condition on you, save to do what you think is right, calmly and clear-headedly, and never out of calamitous passions.'

Was that a warning? Surely it was. 'I'm afraid.'

'To live is to be afraid. You'd better go, Tiaan. It's getting harder to hold the Well.'

Tiaan clung to the controller knob. Already the gift had become a burden. It was not hers at all, but then, how could it be?

'I feel so alone, and I've not a friend in the world.'

'Apart from me,' said Malien, with the most fleeting of smiles. 'And if you should ever need me, come back. Or send word.'

'I will,' said Tiaan.

She drew power and the mechanism whined into life, lifting the thapter above the floor. She turned it to face the opening.

'One last thing,' Malien called.

'Yes?'

'Take care. Whatever you do to Vithis, or Minis, will come back on you tenfold.'

Tiaan went rigid. Malien had known her purpose all along, and still had given her this marvellous thapter. Almost afraid to look, Tiaan sketched her a stiff salute and pushed the knob. The thapter shot forward, much faster than she had expected, and she was hard put to control it as she careered toward the ragged opening in the side of the mountain. She lifted the machine over the piles of rubble, down again to avoid pendant slabs of roof rock, and out into the sunshine. A soaring eagle had to brake in mid-air and was sent tumbling by the shockwave of her passing. Above the glacier, the thapter turned east and disappeared into the mist.

Malien stood watching until the mist concealed it. Already the pain of holding the Well had begun to ease, thankfully. She was near the end of her strength. She would just sit down for a while, then go up and renew the great spell that kept the Well shackled inside Tirthrax. In a way, it *was* Tirthrax.

Malien sat on the bench behind the remaining two constructs, following Tiaan in her mind's eye, and fretting about her. She was flying into a maelstrom and Malien could do nothing about it. If only she could have gone with her. Perhaps she should have sent Tiaan to Stassor. No, better to avoid that dangerous complication.

'I could not even protect my own children,' she said aloud. 'I could not save either of them.' That was the worst part, and it made her unexpectedly long life all the more bitter. A mother should not outlive her children.

Not wanting to start all that again – the useless self-reproach, the futile dwelling on what might have been – she forced against the exhaustion of body and mind and got up. Hard work would keep those thoughts at bay, for the moment.

Passing by the port-all chamber, Malien recalled that she'd previously planned to check it. She spent an hour there and all the while her disquiet grew. Tiaan had assembled the port-all perfectly, so why had it gone so wrong? It took a potent, subtle spell to find out.

As Tiaan opened the gate to Aachan, the Aachim had stampeded up that spiralling ramp. All that was very clear. Vithis, realising that the port-all was left-handed, not right, and fearing it, had ordered his clan to stay back. They had ignored him and were first into the gate. In desperation he had snatched control from Tiaan, but the gate had gone wrong, hurling all those inside it across the unknown void. The failure had nothing to do with Tiaan.

But the more Malien studied the port-all, and divined what

had happened, the more she felt that she had missed something. Or that something had been carefully covered up.

It took hours of the most exhausting toil to uncover it, hours she could not spare. Malien was uncomfortably aware of the unstable Well, and the risk she was taking by not attending to it. But this might be even more important, and once started she could not stop her divination, else those hidden vestiges would vanish like smoke.

And at last she had it. As Vithis took control of the gate, someone had twisted the wormhole, linking it to Tirthrax, inside out. Just for a fraction of a second, but everyone inside had been lost: the entirety of Clan Inthis and some hundreds of other Aachim.

Who could have committed such a monstrous, genocidal deed? Could it have been another Aachim clan? She prayed that it was not. If it had been, Tiaan was flying right toward them. And if not, who on Santhenar had the power, and the malice, to do such a thing?

With a heavy sigh, Malien headed up the stairs to set the Well to rights.

THIRTEEN

The thapter turned over the icefall and headed west, which was where Tiaan's troubles began. The controller jammed and the thapter kept turning until it was facing Tirthrax again.

She hovered above the blue, deeply crevassed ice not far from the icefall, and disconnected the flight controls. As the thapter settled, clouds of steam hissed up all around. She worked the trumpet but could find nothing wrong with it. She hovered again; the controller was fine now. Tiaan checked the linkages from one end to the other. Everything worked perfectly.

Setting off, she turned and headed west, and again the machine kept turning. It was as if it did not want to leave, though that was absurd. As she drew more power from the field, for a fleeting instant Tiaan saw coloured streaks streaming toward the mountain, and swirling into it. The amplimet must be trying to keep her here.

She set down hard in a vast billow of steam, trying to work out how to overcome the crystal. It was not alive. It could not move or speak. Tiaan could not understand how to deal with it. What could an inert piece of mineral want?

The crystal had already been awake when Joeyn had found it in the mine. It might have been in that state for a million years, and who knew what slow intelligence might have developed in it over that time? Why would it want to free the Well? And what next? She did not dare imagine. Tiaan wished Malien were here to advise her. She thought about going back, but that might be disastrous if the Well had unfrozen further. And whatever the amplimet wanted, she should try to do the opposite.

This time she took off and drew all the power she could handle before flinging the controller over hard. The thapter spun so sharply that her vision went black, but still it turned the other way. She took it down to the base of the cliff and again hovered. Removing the amplimet, she put it in her pouch. Tiaan disconnected the carbon whiskers as well, just in case. Drawing power through just the hedron in its cup, the thapter would no longer fly, only hover like any ordinary construct. Turning west, she thrust on the controller.

The thapter moved forward, away from Tirthrax, without resistance. She kept going all day. It was slow travelling in the broken country at the base of the Great Mountains and she had to constantly detour south around boulder fields, mounds of broken ice at the bottom of icefalls, gorges and other obstacles. The hovering thapter could not rise high enough to cross them.

By the end of the day Tiaan was less than a dozen leagues from Tirthrax. She ate her dinner on top of the thapter, watching the setting sun, then locked the hatch and slept inside. Next day she continued, making better time across untracked snow and through spindly forest, and by the morning after, felt that she might risk flying again.

This time she felt no resistance when using the amplimet – they were beyond the influence of the Well. Tiaan flew on. She was bound to the amplimet now, reliant on it, yet it could not be trusted. Would it do the same thing when next she approached a powerful node? Or would it betray her at the most inopportune time?

Tiaan knew what she had to do – fly straight to the nearest large city, find its scrutator or army commander and turn the thapter over to him. Humanity must be in despair at the Aachim threat. The thapter would give them hope, as well as a weapon better than anything the enemy could field against them.

But every scrutator would know her name by now, and what she had done, for Nish's skeet would have reached Flydd many days ago. While a far-sighted scrutator might recognise her value, a vindictive one would see only a traitor who must be made example of. From what Tiaan knew of them, the vindictive scrutators outnumbered the other kind, so she would be gambling with her life. First she must do something to prove her loyalty and her worth.

She decided to shadow the fleet of constructs, find out where they were going and, if she could, what their plans were. That would be valuable intelligence and the best she could hope for. Revenge was out of the question.

It did not take her long to pick up the trail, even after all this time. So many machines travelling close to the ground had left an unmistakable path of beaten-down bushes and broken branches. Where they had passed over snow, the crystals had clumped together like grains of sand.

Tiaan followed every winding league of their path. She did not have to, for she could have tracked them from a thousand spans up. But she needed time to master flying the thapter and time to think, though that only emphasised her inadequacies. She had no place dealing with the mighty – she was quite out of her depth.

At night she slept inside, in the most secluded place she could find. Tiaan was not afraid, thinking that most folk would avoid the alien machine on sight, but she did not want anyone to know she was there. She saw few people – the north-west quarter of Mirrilladell was an empty land.

The fleet had headed west from Tirthrax, following the rind of the Great Mountains. Some hundred leagues to the west, the mountain chain turned south, and here the Aachim had spent days searching for a way across. Tiaan followed their trails up one path and another, but all ended in country that not even constructs could cross. They could not negotiate steep banks or cliffs, rugged or very rocky land, nor climb slopes greater than one-in-one.

Finally they had turned south and, near a vast landscape of

swamps and mires called the Misty Meres, the dwindling range broke into strings of windswept hills that allowed them through into the west. Ruined guard towers crowned the hills like grey teeth in brown gums, last remnants of the Mirrillim, an insecure people long gone.

Winter had not completely relaxed its grip in Mirrilladell but the lands beyond the mountains now rioted in the luxuriance of spring. A narrow road, the Moonpath, ran west between two large lakes before meeting a broader north–south highway, the Great North Road. It ran north across Lauralin for hundreds of leagues, and south nearly as far. Here the force of constructs had separated. Near Saludith she counted five trails splitting off the main one.

On her tenth day of travel she saw the fleet in the distance, running north toward a rich land ringed by forest and mountain. The map named it as Borgistry, and just south of Borgistry she found their camp. The deciduous trees of the Borgis Woods were already springing into leaf.

It was night when she drew near, keeping low to the ground to avoid being seen, though that was unlikely. The passage of the fleet had raised a dust cloud five spans high. On the other hand, they might have sensing devices that she knew nothing about.

Tiaan flew east then north along the Great Chain of Lakes, to the point where a scattered line of volcanoes thrust up through the skirts of the forest. Judging by the luxuriance of the vegetation, it was a long time since any of them had erupted, though several were smoking. Setting down her craft halfway up the slope of the nearest peak, Tiaan checked her surroundings, made a campfire and prepared dinner. From here she could soon tell if the fleet moved.

She did not sleep that night. The promise, or threat, of tomorrow kept her awake. And also, though she suppressed the thought each instant she had it, of Minis. He was a lying, treacherous man whose word meant nothing to him. He had betrayed her. And still the memory sent her heart pounding.

Before dawn broke she was in the air, meaning to conduct a reconnaissance over the fleet. Tiaan hoped that, at this time of the day, and high enough up, she could do that undetected. If she did nothing else, she could learn valuable information about the disposition of their forces.

Her hand shook on the controller trumpet. She wanted to render the constructs useless. Wanted to see the Aachim left helpless, abandoned, bereft. And she wanted Minis to suffer. Or was she following Minis because, despite what he had done to her, she could not keep away from him? Was she truly that weak, that pathetic?

Yes, she was. She was bound to him by hatred now, because breaking free would be even more painful. And she would never be free until she felt neither love nor hate, only indifference.

That realisation was a release of sorts, though she was not strong enough to put Minis behind her. With her emotions fluttering like a butterfly in a cage, she cruised across the camp, high in the dark sky.

The machines were drawn up in a seven-sided array around an open space, in the middle of which several large tents, and dozens of smaller ones, had been erected. The larger tents touched each other, leaving a shadowed space in the middle. The area was lit by globes on poles and she saw vast selections of weapons, piles of supplies, and ranks of soldiers practising battle manoeuvres or firing at targets. They were preparing for war.

As she passed across the centre, Tiaan sensed a great distortion in the field, as if it was being warped by something centred on the array of constructs. Some device there was drawing mighty amounts of power, even more than the gate had taken. They must be testing some new kind of weapon. She had to get a better look.

Five larger constructs were near the main tents but the warping was not coming from them. Perhaps from one of the tents? The field distortion was spiralling in like a whirlpool. Was it some terrible weapon they had developed on their own world?

The whirlpool pulled her in one direction as she passed over the large tents, then pushed her hard the other way. Incredibly, it seemed to be interfering with the controller. She looked down into the space walled around by the tents. *What was that?*

Spinning the thapter around, she headed back, aiming to go right over the walled space. Again the warp wrenched her off course, though this time she managed to correct enough to see down. Peering through her fingers, she looked into a whirling red hell, like a captured tornado, that distorted everything around it. As she went over it, a rod of blue light burst forth from the centre of the red hell, like a searchlight.

For an instant she thought she was being attacked, but the light angled away into the heavens as if searching the very void. It blinked on and off many times, then vanished. Were they signalling the other fleets to war? She had to go to the scrutators now.

Tiaan turned the thapter away from the camp, climbing toward the safety of a ridge of cloud. As she did, the sun rose and its first bright ray highlighted the thapter, a spark curving across the pale sky. She prayed that no one would notice, but a crowd of Aachim ran into the open, pointing to the sky, and a series of streaks rose up. Before they even knew who she was, they were shooting at her.

Since she'd been discovered, she might as well learn as much as she could about that strange device. Such intelligence could be vital. Flinging the front of the thapter down, she headed towards the largest tent, which was rapidly emptying. More glowing spheres came on, lighting up the clear area as bright as day.

A group of Aachim converged on a tall lean man, the last to exit the tent. Tiaan recognised Vithis instantly. He had a spyglass trained on her. Vithis reeled backwards, gesturing furiously to the guards behind him. He must have recognised her. Two soldiers raised a kind of heavy crossbow to their shoulders and fired. Tiaan hurled the controller sideways, skidding across the sky.

A bolt slammed into the machine just behind her head. Others struck the outside with a clatter like hail on metal. She had done nothing to them, yet they were trying to kill her, just as they had killed Haani. Bloody rage exploded and all her resolutions, her promises to Malien, went over the side. Vithis or her, it was time to end it. Flinging the thapter about, she went low to the ground and hurtled up between the rows of constructs. Aachim, running everywhere, threw themselves out of the way.

She roared through the open centre, coming at Vithis's command tent from the rear. Guards were shouting and loading weapons. More bolts struck the thapter. Tiaan went left, right, left, then saw Vithis straight ahead. She slammed the trumpet lever forward as far as it would go. Acceleration thrust her backwards and the thapter hurtled straight toward the leader of Clan Inthis.

Just before she hit, Tiaan realised that Minis was behind him. Vithis hurled Minis to his left and tried to go the other way, but the slick metal skin of the thapter caught the clan leader on the hip, sending him tumbling across the ground. She tried to turn but the tent came up too quickly. The thapter crashed through it, fabric wrapping itself around the machine. All she could do was pull up on the knob and pray.

The thapter soared, fabric flapping, ropes lashing the sides, then the wind tore it away. She looked back but could not tell whether Vithis was dead or alive. Alive, she felt sure. Directly below, she caught a last glimpse of that hellish tornado, and the searchlight spinning like a top. Its blinking blue light struck the machine, a blast of heat and dazzle. Her mental control failed, the controller slipped off-plane and suddenly she was falling in silence.

Tiaan waggled the lever but nothing happened. The machine arced down toward a patch of trees on the far side of the camp. The impact would turn her to jelly. She could not see the strong force at all. Tiaan reached under the binnacle and popped the cap, thrusting her hand in until her index finger touched the amplimet. The field flashed before her eyes and the thapter whined into life. She climbed away from the camp while she tried to work out what had happened. The blue ray fingered the sky as if they were trying to cook her alive. She hurled the thapter around to avoid it.

The mechanism stuttered but came to life again. Was that ray interfering with the machine, or the field? She couldn't think straight. Why, why hadn't she slipped quietly away as soon as she was seen? Her attack had been an insult to the pride and might of the Aachim, and to Vithis personally. She had brought disaster upon herself, risked everything for a moment of self-indulgence.

This thapter, and the secret of how it worked, was worth a nation. Flight could win the war; the world. What warlord, general, scrutator or Aachim would not kill to get it? She was friendless in a desperate world, and every time she set down to sleep or buy supplies, she would be in peril.

The first priority was to get well away and pray she did not lose the field again. Then, find a general or scrutator, and give him the thapter as well as her intelligence about what the Aachim were up to. That was her duty and she must do it. And then plead for her life. What she knew might be enough to save her.

She headed north along the Great Chain of Lakes, which ran up through the Borgis Woods before curving north-west to the Sea of Thurkad, a couple of hundred leagues away. To her right loomed the southern arm of the Great Mountains. To her left, up ahead, stood the jagged white pinnacles of the Peaks of Borg. Between them she made out the vast elongation of Parnggi, second-greatest of the lakes. Cloud covered this area and she passed into it grate-fully, guided only by the thin disc of the sun above.

Tiaan felt numb. They had tried to kill her. Now that Vithis knew about the thapter, he would hunt her to the four corners of the globe. Everyone else would do the same. She was doomed. Why, why had she been so foolish as to let him see her? Why hadn't she heeded Malien's warnings? Every time she allowed her emotions to govern her, it made things worse.

The Aachim had shown that Haani's death was not accident, but policy. She wanted to hurt Vithis and Minis, to humiliate them and, beyond all else, to thwart them in their plans for Santhenar. Most of all, she wanted to repay Malien's confidence in her.

But first she had to find a scrutator and work out what to say. Tiaan flew on, making plans and rejecting each. All foundered on the same reef – how to find the right person, and tell her story, without being attacked or seized as a renegade.

She finally passed beyond Parnggi around the middle of the night. Moonlight showed her the way. Forest still clothed the hills in all directions, though through a gap in the clouds she saw clear land well ahead and, some way to her left, a cluster of volcanoes dominated by one much larger and taller than the rest. Its flanks were covered in dense forest, part of the endless Worm Wood. She checked the map. It was Booreah Ngurle, the Burning Mountain. It seemed to call to her, but she would not find a scrutator there.

Further back and to her left she made out a road – the Great North Road again – cutting through a rich and fertile land that must be Borgistry. Its principal city was Lybing. Surely it would have a scrutator.

There was no way out of it. Time to give up the thapter, and herself. She moved the controller to turn left. It moved back to centre. She tried again but the thapter was set on its course and would not turn the way she wanted.

It was flying north-west, quite slowly, for as the day passed it had grown ever more sluggish. Dense forest passed beneath. The thapter seemed to be heading for the cluster of volcanoes; for Booreah Ngurle. What was the amplimet up to now? Whatever it *was* doing, she could not prevent it, for there was no place to land. Nothing but forest in every direction.

The moon was hidden now. At least no one could see her. Unfortunately she could not see either. She dropped low over the shadowy trees, still flying toward the distant mountain.

Twice more she tried to turn away, and twice the controls refused to answer her. Just after dawn, the thapter approached the peak of Booreah Ngurle. She saw a great building off to her left, on the inner rim of the crater, and tried to turn towards it. The controls jammed. Why had it brought her all this way only to thwart her again? The node, of course – an unusual one here, a double with one centre larger than the other.

Her fury flared again. She was not going to allow it to master her this time, or ever again. Tiaan looked for a place to set down, planning to take out the treacherous amplimet and smash it against a rock, and curse the consequences!

The ground was steep here, extremely rugged and clothed in

dense forest – the worst possible place to land. Spotting a tiny clearing, Tiaan hovered above the trees, planning her route down. As she nudged the lever forward, the field vanished. The thapter fell like a rock and crashed through the treetops in a cloud of leaves and shattered branches. It bounced off a leaning tree and hit a fallen trunk with an almighty thump. Tiaan was hurled against the binnacle and after that felt nothing, not the fall down the ladder, nor the impact with the floor below.

A long while later she came to. Something was running into her eye. She wiped blood off her forehead. It did not feel like a major injury, though her head had begun to throb and her ears were ringing. She could not work out what had happened, but she had an alarming suspicion that the amplimet had cut off the field. She prayed that the construct could still be made to hover.

Tiaan tried to get up, and that was when she realised that things were badly wrong. She could not move her legs. Tiaan lifted her head. Her pants were torn from hip to ankle and there was a long gash on her thigh, but she could not feel a thing. Again she tried to move her leg. She could not even wiggle her toes.

Her back was broken.

PART TWO
REFUGEE

FOURTEEN

Nish checked the balloon, which was nearly inflated. He crammed in as much fuel as would fit and opened the damper all the way. Flames roared up the flue. Racing down the ladder he began hacking at the cane floor where it encircled the trunk.

'What is the matter, Nish?'

'Someone's coming!' He pointed in the direction of the yellow floater. 'Can you sense anything about it?'

'No, Nish,' she said, giving him sweet and loving looks.

He was too panicky to reciprocate. 'It can't be lyrinx, or you would see them in your lattice.'

'I can't see anything in my lattice.'

'What!' he roared.

Ullii slapped her hands over her ears, her face screwed up in pain.

He lowered his voice. 'What do you mean? Is it gone?' Had their lovemaking destroyed her talent? There were folktales about that kind of thing but he had always sneered at them.

'My lattice isn't gone.' She smiled a secret smile. 'I just can't see it. I'll have to make a new lattice.'

Nish cursed, but under his breath. What a time to lose the only talent that could help them. He looked up. The balloon was taut. The danger would come when it lifted, for the stripped trunk went up through the neck. If anything caught, it would tear the flimsy fabric apart.

The air-floater was getting closer every minute. Nish leapt out and gave the basket a heave. It lifted but stuck. He climbed in and rocked the basket from side to side. It freed itself from a snag and shot up; he had to brake it with S'lound's sword against the trunk.

The balloon rose steadily, the trunk slid from the neck and they were free, rising above the treetops. Nish could have wept. Their survival was truly a miracle; a series of miracles. He held his breath, staring at the patch. Let the wind not be too strong. Let the patch hold.

The patch held and there was no wind at this level. They simply drifted above the forest, slowly rising. The air-floater altered course, heading directly for them. How could it do that?

The minutes went by with agonising slowness. The balloon caught the gentlest of breezes and sailed beyond the forest. The air-floater approached. Nish could make out people standing in the smaller compartment underneath. Human, or Aachim? If human, were they friend or foe?

Nish picked up S'lound's sword, not that it would be any good against archers. He rubbed his chin, which hurt. It was blistered from the nylatl venom. The air-floater closed the gap, swung side-on, and at least a dozen soldiers, armed with spears and crossbows, stood along the side. Nish swallowed.

'What the blazes are you doing?' bellowed a familiar voice across the gap.

Nish searched the faces. A lean, gaunt-looking man forced his way between the ranks. 'Don't hang there like a bloody fool. Go down.' It was Xervish Flydd, the scrutator.

Nish yanked the release rope and the balloon drifted down. What was the scrutator doing here? Nish had no idea what he was going to say to him.

He rehearsed his lines all the way to the ground. The scrutator was the most powerful man in the land, and the most feared. A combination of secret policeman, spy and inquisitor, he could do just about anything he wanted. He had sent Nish out on this suicide mission, to bring back Tiaan, and the crystal. Nish had recovered neither.

The balloon slowly reached to the ground. Nish jumped out, closed the valve and tied the tethers to a log. He stood waiting as the air-floater slid to earth not a hundred paces away. Soldiers sprang over the rails, hammered stakes into the ground and roped the vessel down fore and aft.

The craft held sixteen soldiers. He counted them off, as well as the scrutator and Mechanician M'lainte, who looked like a squat scrubwoman and did not appear to have changed her clothes since he'd last seen her. The mechanician was a genius and it did not matter how she looked, but Nish was conscious of his own shabbiness. Appearances had always been important to him, as if to make up for his short stature and indifferent looks.

The whirring, that had been in the background ever since the craft approached, slowed to a gentle tick. Some kind of mechanical contraption at the rear was attached to a twelve-bladed rotor similar to those he had seen on windmills, though this one was driven by the field. It enabled the air-floater to go where it pleased, even against the wind as long as it was not too strong. The cabin of the craft was built of canvas reinforced with light timbers, to weigh as little as possible. Sandbags hung on the sides, for ballast.

'Well, artificer?' The scrutator, a small man who looked as though every scrap of flesh had been pared from his bones, clambered over the side. He walked awkwardly, as if those bones had been broken in a torture chamber and put back together wrongly, and they had. Taking Nish's arm, Flydd led him back toward the balloon. 'What have you got for me?'

'Er . . .' said Nish.

'Did you recover the precious crystal?'

'No – I mean, I did recover it, surr, back there at Tirthrax, but a witch-woman took it from me and gave it back to Tiaan.'

'A witch-woman? What bloody nonsense is this? Explain yourself, artificer.'

Nish felt his life hanging by a thread. 'A noble Aachim, surr.

A woman of advanced years. She called herself Matah of Tirthrax.'

'Matah? What did she look like, boy?'

'She was this tall,' Nish held his hand a little above his head, 'with grey hair that once must have been as red as the setting sun. A very handsome woman, for all that she was old . . .' He selected his words more carefully, not wanting to insult the scrutator. 'She looked the age of a human of sixty, but she talked about the time of the Forbidding as though she had been there. I −'

'Malien!' said Flydd between his yellow teeth. He turned away in some agitation, muttering to himself, as he often did. 'Well, well. The Council of Scrutators will want to hear of this.'

'You mean *the* Malien, from the *Tale of the Mirror*?' Nish said, awed. 'How can she still be alive?'

Flydd did not bother to answer. 'She is no witch-woman, artificer, but a mancer of considerable subtlety. I will not hold it against you that she took the crystal away. You are not made for that kind of foe. You did not manage to take Tiaan either?' he barked.

'I had her, twice, and twice she got away from me.'

'Twice?' The scrutator wrinkled the single brow that ran across both eyes. '*Twice*, boy? To lose her once is bad enough. Twice looks distinctly like −'

'She was . . . clever,' Nish said lamely. 'I caught her a third time, tied her up, and was determined that nothing could free her.'

'Where is she? I don't see her?' The scrutator pretended to look around.

Nish went along with the game, knowing how deadly it could become. 'The witch − Malien, surr. She freed Tiaan and befriended her. I tried,' he pleaded, 'but Malien used her magic against me.'

'Enough!' snapped the scrutator. 'I have no doubt that you tried, but you failed.'

'And Tiaan is gone, with her crystal.'

'What?'

'This morning, surr. Ullii said that they had gone west.'

'The lyrinx, or the Aachim, must have taken her.' Flydd growled. 'She's out of the game! You've let me down.'

Unable to think of any defence, Nish stood, head hung, awaiting his fate.

'So!' Flydd measured him up and down. 'You seem to have grown up since I saw you last.'

'There have been a number of trials, surr,' Nish said softly.

'I'm sure there have. You shall tell me the entire story, later, and my chronicler will write it down. At least you have not lost the seeker, eh?'

'No,' said Nish inaudibly.

Flydd ratcheted his way across to the basket, spoke to Ullii and gave her his hand. For some reason Nish would never comprehend, she got on well with him. She stood up on the side, wearing mask and earmuffs now, protection as much against people as against the elements. Ullii stepped lightly down. Flydd threw her pack over his shoulder.

They ate lunch inside the lower section of the air-floater, since the ground was a snowy slush. Nish was seated next to M'lainte, and Ullii beside the scrutator. Nish told his tale, which earned the undivided attention of the group, and even several grunts from Flydd that might have constituted approval. At the end, when he described the repair of the balloon in the treetops and the subsequent beating off of the nylatl, both he and Ullii were given a cheer by the soldiers.

Even Flydd, a man who rarely praised anybody, reached across to grip him by the shoulder. 'You might be a second-rate artificer, lad, but I can't fault your initiative.'

'Thank you, surr,' Nish said without a trace of irony.

Flydd showed no such restraint with Ullii. 'If courage is measured not by the deed but by the terror overcome, surely you are the bravest of us all.' Shaking her little hand, he said, 'You are one of my finest, seeker.'

Ullii pulled off her mask. Her eyes were huge, luminous and moist. She kissed his withered hand and swiftly pulled the mask up again, though she could not conceal the colour that crept up her cheeks.

'Is something the matter?' said Flydd.

'Ullii has lost her lattice,' Nish interjected.

'I was not speaking to you! Ullii, what happened?'

Ullii blushed, her colourless skin going the colour of blood.

'Is there something the matter? Something I should know about?' Flydd continued.

'No, Xervish,' she said faintly. 'I will make a new lattice.'

'My skeet arrived safely?' Nish asked, for that had not been mentioned. 'That is what brought you here so swiftly?'

'It arrived only two days after you sent it. That was a good bit of work, lad. Fortunately I had other skeets at the manufactory and could send out the warnings right away. Within three days every city in Lauralin had been alerted to the invasion, though I don't know what good it may have done us.'

'How did you build this air-floater so quickly?' It was much bigger than the balloon, which had exhausted all the silk cloth in the city of Tiksi and taken more than a month to construct.

'We didn't,' said M'lainte. 'I had the idea not long after our first balloon flight, but we were not sure that it would work, so it was built in secret at another manufactory. It was already being tested when you left.'

Nish looked up at the great airbag and for the first time noticed something missing. 'Where is the furnace, and the fuel?'

'Not needed,' said M'lainte complacently. 'A mine in the mountains produces floater-gas. We simply filled the air-floater with it.'

Nish had heard something about floater-gas. 'Isn't it . . . explosive?'

'Horribly. And it leaks through the tarred seams, so we must return soon or there will not be enough to lift us. Going back will be slower than coming.'

'Why did you come?' Nish asked.

'To see what we could see,' said the scrutator. 'To test this new air-floater. And to bring back whatever you had found. The wind seldom blows east at this time of year so, even if you had recovered Tiaan or her crystal, you would have had to walk home. That would have been too late.'

'And to bring back Ullii, of course,' Nish said quietly.

'You are expendable, alas, but we can't do without her.'

'How is my friend Irisis?'

Ullii jumped, then clenched her little fists.

The scrutator gave Nish a hard stare. 'I'm pleased to say, since you've been gone, she has settled down to her work. There'll be no more of that nonsense.'

'No, surr,' Nish said faintly.

The mechanician was concerned about the leaking floater-gas, so as soon as lunch was finished they prepared to leave. Nish was heading to the balloon for his gear when one of the guards shouted, 'Lyrinx, surr, in the north-west!'

'Are they heading this way?'

The guard put a spyglass to his eye. 'Not at the moment, surr. They're watching the hole in the great mountain.'

Flydd paced back and forth. 'Is it better to be in the air or on the ground? In the air, I think. At least we can move, and defend ourselves. But on the ground, should they drop something on the envelope, we're done.'

'And we can soar up high,' said the mechanician, 'where the air is too thin for their wings.'

'We won't be able to breathe,' said Flydd.

'There'll be enough. *We're* not doing the hard work of flying.'

'True. Gather your gear, everyone. We're going now.'

Nish ran. 'Make it snappy, artificer,' roared Flydd. 'I won't wait on anyone.'

Nish was climbing the rope when Ullii cried out, something that in all the shouting he did not catch. Then she screamed.

'Get moving!' yelled Flydd.

Nish went over the side into the basket, and froze. On the other side, just across the hole in the floor, crouched the nylatl. And he was defenceless. S'lound's sword was over by the air-floater.

He tried to throw himself out but the nylatl sprang and caught him by the calf muscle. Nish kicked, the teeth tore through his flesh and the nylatl fell through the hole in the floor. He hobbled to the side but, before he could leap over, the horned snout came at him again.

There was a knife in S'lound's pack. Nish wrenched out the long blade, then hurled the pack at the creature, hoping to create enough of a diversion to get over the side. He caught a fleeting glimpse of Ullii, screaming and struggling in the arms of one of the guards. The scrutator was shouting. 'We can't wait, even for you, Nish. Come now or *stay behind*!'

Nish heaved himself onto the rim. The nylatl's teeth went through his boot, just missing his toes. It tossed its head and the force went close to breaking his ankle. Nish was dragged into the basket, slashing wildly at the beast. One blow carved the top off the main spine on its snout. The nylatl squealed, drew back and sprang again. This time the vicious teeth closed around his leg.

Nish hardly felt it, the way the adrenalin was surging through his veins, the blood lust singing in his ears. He stabbed down with the knife, whose blade was long enough to pass between the poisoned spines. It skated off an armoured plate, found the crack between it and the next, and went in deep.

The nylatl reared up, its eyes wide, and let go. Nish knocked it down with one boot and kicked it in the head with the other. It fled through the hole.

He clambered over the side but was too late: the air-floater was taking off without him. Nish slashed the tethers and the balloon shot up. His leg began to throb. Sagging against the basketwork, he took toll of his injuries. The muscle of his calf was torn in three places and there were tooth punctures on both sides of his leg, almost to the bone. It could have been worse. Much worse.

The balloon had gone up faster but the air-floater was swiftly overtaking him. There was still a chance. He waved and some-one waved back. The air-floater altered course, though Nish could not see how they could take him off in mid-air.

He was wondering how to manage it when the nylatl, which must have been clinging to the underside of the basket, came over the side right behind him. Its smell alerted him as it was about to sink its teeth into his neck. He dived across the basket. This had to end, *now*.

The nylatl limped around the rim, its back legs dragging. He must have done it some damage. How to kill it? The flask of tar spirits, carried all the way from the manufactory, gave him an idea.

Hefting the flask, he backed away from the creeping beast and jerked out the bung. The creature eyed him. He feinted with the knife, and as the nylatl went the other way, heaved a great spurt at its face. It squealed as the stinging liquid went into eyes, nostrils and gaping mouth. Nish gave it another whoosh, then dropped the flask and attempted to attack while the nylatl was blinded.

It did not work; the creature seemed to sense his position and slashed with its right paw. The sole remaining claw raked down Nish's wrist, sending the knife flying across the floor and out through the hole. He was defenceless.

From the corner of his eye he saw an archer standing at the rail of the air-floater, but the man could not get a clear shot. The nylatl sprang down. Nish threw himself onto the rim, crawled around and his head bumped the hanging rope ladder up to the brazier.

Without thinking he went up hand over hand, all the way to the top. The nylatl came to its hind legs to follow. The air-floater, which had been standing by, suddenly veered away as fast as its rotor could go.

Must have read my mind, Nish thought. Nothing mattered but to rid himself of this ravener. Flipping open the lid of the stove, he reached in with his bare hand, pulled out a handful of red-hot coals and hurled them into the basket. Then he pushed head and shoulders through the rope ladder and hung on for dear life.

The coals scattered. One landed on the creature's snout. Flame burst out in all directions. The nylatl let out the most hideous scream and raced around the basket, flame following it to every drop of spilled spirit. Nish's hand began to burn and there was worse to come. He closed his eyes, gritted his teeth and waited.

The blazing nylatl ran full tilt into the half-empty flask of tar spirit. Flame licked it, then bottle, basket and nylatl were blown apart in an explosion that sent flames bursting out in all directions.

The ladder burned away from below Nish's feet. His trousers caught fire. He beat them out. Nish opened his eyes to see the remains of his nemesis falling in a sheet of flame. It surely had to be the end of it.

The balloon, freed of most of its load, shot upwards, higher than it had been before. There it caught a gale blowing west.

Nish climbed up next to the warmth of the brazier. Tying himself to the ladder, he thrust his hands into his sleeves. The air was numbingly cold, but it eased the pain. It was thin, too. So thin that he could hardly breathe. He closed his eyes.

FIFTEEN

Ullii screamed herself into a fit and had to be sedated, for she kept trying to jump out of the air-floater in mid-air, as if she could fly to Nish. When the drug had taken effect, the guards bound her hands and took her inside the cabin, a flimsy structure of canvas attached to stretched rope and a few bracing timbers.

The scrutator stood with the mechanician, arms folded, watching Nish's desperate struggle with the nylatl. 'Dare we go closer, M'lainte?' he asked at one point.

She took a long time to answer. 'We dare not. We can't get near enough to take him out of the basket, and if we tried, chances are the brazier would set off our floater-gas. I don't want to end our lives as a firework.'

'He might kill the beast,' said Flydd. 'If he does, can we risk landing to pick him up?'

M'lainte eyed the three lyrinx, which were circling some distance away. 'They don't look as though they're going to attack.'

'I was referring to our shortage of floater-gas.'

'We're already taking a risk,' said the mechanician. 'Ask me if it happens.'

They watched in silence until Nish began to hurl liquid about the basket. 'What's in that flask?' the scrutator asked sharply.

'Tar spirits.' M'lainte swung around but the scrutator was quicker.

'Away!' roared Flydd. 'Away and all speed!'

The air-floater veered off. The complement of the vessel was leaning over the rail now, willing Nish to succeed.

'Faster!' yelled the mechanician. 'Get over the other side, you lot. You're ruining our trim.'

'What's he doing?' cried Flydd, for they were now a long way off.

'He's up at the brazier,' said the watchman with a spyglass. 'He's reaching into the brazier with his bare hands. He's . . .'

They watched, holding their breath as flames appeared in the basket. Suddenly it was blown apart and dark objects fell, trailing flame. The balloon shot upwards, was caught by high-level winds and disappeared towards the west.

'Well?' Flydd said to M'lainte.

'Not a chance. Nothing could catch it now.'

The scrutator turned away, shoulders slumped. 'A pity! He had a great future, that lad.'

'We can't be certain he's dead,' said M'lainte.

'If not now, then soon enough, when the balloon comes to ground in the wilderness. Let's go home.'

Despite the danger, Flydd changed his mind as they whirred past the great mountain. Tapping Pilot Hila on her slender shoulder, he pointed to the ragged entrance. The air-floater landed just inside and the guards formed a ring around it, aiming their weapons at the circling lyrinx, while scrutator and mechanician walked into Tirthrax.

'I hope . . .' began the scrutator.

M'lainte raised an eyebrow.

'I must speak with Malien.'

'To make alliance with her?'

'Just to talk, first. I . . .' Flydd smiled self-consciously. 'My childhood was spent elbow-deep in the books of the Histories.'

'You *had* a childhood?' M'lainte was making one of her rare jokes. 'I thought you were born scrutator.'

'I loved the Great Tales as much as any child alive. It's ironic, now that I look back . . .'

'What?' she said.

'No matter. Malien is a legend, one of the few surviving from ancient times. Just to talk about the past –'

'I understand, Xervish. This place is a marvel,' M'lainte went on as they passed yet another staircase made of little more than a ribbon of metal. 'The Aachim know so much. It's tragic that we've not been able to make an alliance with them.'

'Aye,' said Flydd, 'but they are a people much governed by history, tradition and a powerful sense of their own worth. The affairs of other humans are of importance only when they touch theirs, and in their increasing isolation, that is seldom.'

'Until now!'

The scrutator looked morose. 'What has this fleet of constructs come for? Is Aachan really dying, or is it the first wave of an invasion?'

'The Aachim of Santhenar will take their side, whatever their purpose.'

'And we're in the middle. But can we persuade them to take *our* side against the lyrinx?'

'We are both human species.'

'The lyrinx are not as alien as they might appear,' the scrutator said enigmatically.

They stopped beside the two wrecked constructs. 'Nish's message said there were three,' Flydd went on. 'Where is the other?'

'And Tiaan gone too,' said M'lainte shrewdly.

'Well, better her than the enemy.'

'I dare say. Beautiful metalwork,' the mechanician observed.

'Aye.'

She walked around and around, making notes on a scrap of paper. 'They float above the ground, Nish said.'

'Yes, and we must try to get Tiaan's back.'

'She could be hard to find.'

'There's not much the scrutators can't find if they want it enough. I'll send a skeet at once, in case we don't get back.' Flydd cast an anxious glance at the entrance. 'We'd better go, M'lainte. Those lyrinx may have called their mates. We're vulnerable here.'

'To say nothing of our leaking floater-gas. Write your message, surr. I'll just have a peep inside.'

The scrutator flexed his twisted fingers. 'Make it a quick one, old friend. I'd hate to lose you.'

'I'd hate to lose myself!' M'lainte looked down at her thick body and grinned. 'Not much danger of that.'

The scrutator wrote a note and took it to the skeet handler, who was standing mournfully outside the cage. The skeet lay on the floor, quite dead.

'What the bloody hell's happened?' Flydd began.

'Jellybeak,' said the handler. 'There was an outbreak in Tiksi but I thought our birds were clean.'

Cursing, Flydd returned to the constructs. 'Come on, M'lainte!' He was not worrying about her being killed, and least of all himself, but if they did not get back to tell all they knew, the war effort would suffer.

'I'm coming,' she said from inside. She did not appear.

He went across to a broad set of steps guarded by a black conical object like a witch's hat. Flydd knew it to be a sentinel. He looked up. The stair passed through a hole in the stone ceiling, as did all the others. He edged closer. Closer. *Crack!* The shock curled his toes and it was just a warning. If he tried to go up it would be far worse.

He considered using his Art on it. Scrutator magic was designed for sneaking, spying, interrogating and manipulating, and the breaking of locks and protections. Only rarely did it involve outright power, but he had that too, in words of power, charged crystals and other artefacts. Flydd thought better of it. The Aachim had used sentinels for ages and had defences for most of the Arts.

He walked up the other end of the vast chamber, looking all around. The sentinel would have sounded an alarm in the floors above but Malien did not come to check on it. Finally, when the mechanician had been inside for a good hour, Flydd rapped on the hatch with a knuckle.

Her head popped out. M'lainte's eyes were gleaming. 'Marvellous!' she said. 'Just marvellous.'

'Remember our leaky floater-gas.'

'I've finished.' She hauled herself out. 'Well, of course I'm *not* finished. I could spend a year here.'

'Can you make one like it?'

'Probably not. Some of the innards are sealed and I have no idea what's inside, and we'd not master such fine metal-working as this –' she slapped the smoothly curving side, 'in a hundred years. Still, I've learned a thing or two.'

The scrutator left it at that. M'lainte was the best mechanician in the south-east, and did not make promises she could not keep. It was better than nothing.

'Malien's not coming,' Flydd said dispiritedly. 'Come on.'

The air-floater took off as soon as they climbed in, heading east. There were no enemy in sight. It was something over two hundred leagues back to the manufactory and they would probably have to rotor all the way.

They had taken on rock ballast at Tirthrax so as to fly extra low, for at high altitudes, strong winds blew directly against them. They floated along the line of the mountains, enjoying the magnificent vista of peaks and glaciers. Below and south as far as they could see lay a flat landscape, a monotonous vista of snow-clad plains, swamps and ragged lakes, many still frozen. The forests were straggles of spindly, impoverished pines.

The trip was slow but uneventful. Night fell. They continued, and late in the morning, at a place where the Great Mountains were less high and they could see across the range to another in the distance, the air-floater dropped its ballast and turned north-east to make the crossing.

'We should reach the manufactory within the hour,' said M'lainte in the mid-afternoon, trying to consult her map as the air-floater lurched and bounced.

'I'll be glad to see it,' the scrutator replied curtly. He had paced all night and was not in the best of humours, and the rough flight made his head spin.

'At least the air-floater has worked well,' she said cheerfully.

'Don't jinx it!' he snapped.

M'lainte went up the other end, to stare over the rope rail. Flydd inspected his scarred and gnarled hands, trying not to think of the events that had made them that way. The knot in his stomach was painful.

'How is the seeker?' he called to the soldier on duty inside.

'Still sleeping, last I checked.'

'Check again.'

The man ducked away, then came back. 'She's stirring. Should I give her another dose of poppy?'

'Of course not! Keep an eye on her. Bloody idiot,' the scrutator said, more out of habit than annoyance. His mind was on other matters.

They floated over the last range and saw smoke everywhere. 'What's going on?' cried Flydd. 'We've only been gone four days.'

'It's early in the season for a forest fire.' M'lainte had come up to the rail beside him.

'Far too early. That's Tiksi; the city is burning. Circle round,' he roared to the man at the helm. 'See what's going on. Hurry!'

They veered left, sliding through smoke clouds all the way. The air-floater bucked and rolled in the updraughts. Flydd choked back on nausea uncomfortably similar to seasickness.

The air-floater broke out of the smoke. Tiksi lay dead ahead. The city wall was broken in three places, the eastern quarter ablaze. On the plain outside the main gates a battle raged, four clankers against dozens of lyrinx. Dead lay everywhere, and Flydd counted fifteen broken clankers. Behind the clankers a small force of troops stood together, shields up, spears out.

They circled, weighing the damage. Flydd's escort stood by with their heavy crossbows, in case of an attack, though there were no lyrinx in the air. Flydd allowed half the soldiers to fire on the enemy. Several lyrinx fell. The others retreated, but not far.

'It's not as bad as I first thought,' said the scrutator. 'They would have beaten the enemy off without us. There's no fighting inside the walls.'

'But bad enough!' It was his sergeant, Ruvix, a short, broad man who was a solid slab of muscle. 'Those are storehouses burning.'

144

'Still, the damage can be repaired.'

'As long as they don't come back in force. It'll take a week to fix the wall breaches, and with only four clankers left . . .' Ruvix muttered oaths.

'Do you want to go lower?' called the woman at the helm.

'I've seen enough. Wait.' The scrutator pulled out a piece of paper and began scribbling. 'Take us over the master's palace.'

They hovered over the magnificent building, which was unscathed apart from minor damage from catapult balls. Flydd finished writing, stamped his seal at the bottom of the paper and snapped his fingers. A soldier came running with a leather envelope.

Another shouted to the crowd gathered below. The soldier dropped the envelope, someone caught it and ran inside.

'To the manufactory,' said the scrutator. 'And don't muck about.'

The manufactory had also been attacked though it was not badly damaged. The air-floater landed on the gravelled area outside the front gates, disgorged its passengers and took off to replenish the floater-gas. Scrutator and mechanician watched it away, then went inside, where Flydd called Overseer Tuniz, all eleven foremen, Captain Gir-Dan and Crafter Irisis to a meeting.

'Your reports, if you please,' said the scrutator. 'Captain?'

Captain Gir-Dan had recently arrived from one of the coast garrisons. A handsome man, dark-haired and broad-shouldered, he had set many hearts aflutter since his arrival. Scurrilous rumour, however, put a question mark over his behaviour on the battle lines, and said that he had been sent here 'for evaluation', as the quisitors put it.

'One attack, surr.' Gir-Dan was not a loquacious man. 'Two days back, it were. Five of the beasts, with a single 'pult. We did three of them with the javelards mounted on the wall. The others fled.'

'Very good.' The scrutator swung around to face Tuniz, a tall, dark-skinned woman with wiry brown hair and filed teeth. A native of Crandor, a steamy land in the subtropical north, she stood out among the smaller, honey-skinned and black-haired natives of this region. 'Overseer, what news from below?'

The captain scowled, for military matters were his province and to be passed over in this way was a deliberate slap in the face. Knowing better than to show it, Gir-Dan composed his features. The scrutator was not a forgiving man.

Tuniz smiled. Her filed teeth made the gesture threatening though she was, by nature, cheerful and friendly.

'The enemy have come out of the ranges all along the coast, surr. As you may have seen, Tiksi has been attacked and badly damaged.'

'We've been down there,' Flydd said flatly. 'It's bad, but they're holding out.'

'Then your news is more recent than mine, surr. There have been attacks on most cities between here and Gosport. Maksmord is likely to fall; Guffeons is sorely pressed. We don't know as much as I'd like; the enemy are targeting skeets now and some messages have not come through. I have the despatches here.' She held out a leather wallet. 'Some are for your eyes only.'

The scrutator took out the papers, riffled through them and sorted them into two piles. He began to read the pile at his right hand. No one spoke for the ten minutes it took him to finish.

Flydd cleared his throat. 'It is worse than I thought. The enemy now hold most of the lands about the Dry Sea, save for Crandor. The mountains of Faranda are theirs, though not the lowlands, and some of the arid lands north of the Great Mountains. And of course Meldorin fell last year, save for the southern peninsula. Thurkad was a crippling loss. We still hold the east coast, the fount of our wealth, central Lauralin and everything south of the Great Mountains. But the east coast is in peril now, and with the Aachim flooding across Lauralin . . . Well, we shall see about them in due course.'

He set his jaw and eyed them one by one. All broke under his glare, save Irisis. 'We will never give up, not even if all we have left is desolate Luuma Narta. Anything else, overseer?'

'We will meet our target again this month, surr, or better. Three clankers, I'm pleased to say.'

'Very good. Crafter Irisis?'

Irisis also stood out in the manufactory. She was tall, though not as tall as Tuniz, but with pale skin, bright blue eyes and hair as yellow as butter, a sight few people here had seen before her arrival. She had a breathtaking figure, which meant that, despite the shortage of males, she could take her pick. Irisis had been Nish's lover at one stage, though by the time of his departure that had changed to an abiding friendship.

As crafter, she was in charge of the artisans who made controllers for the clankers built here. Twenty artisans now worked to her direction, and fifty prentices. Because their work was so fine, completed controllers were being shipped to other manufactories.

'We have also exceeded our target,' she said. 'We've built eleven controllers this month . . .'

'But?' snapped Flydd. 'What is the problem, crafter? Remember you are on probation.'

'I could hardly forget it, surr!' Irisis stood up to everyone, and sometimes it got her into trouble. 'The problem is crystal. We've used up almost all we have and the miners can't find more. And since Ullii went away . . . We need the seeker to sense it out. I'm told you brought her back, surr?'

'I did, but I'm not sure what use she will be. She has suffered a considerable trauma and lost her talent.'

'*Lost it?*'

'It may come back. The healers are looking at her now.'

'This is bad, surr. How can I find the crystal I need?'

'I've no bloody idea. Discover a way.' He turned to the first of his foremen.

'One more thing, surr, if I may.' Irisis was unaccountably tentative.

'What is it?' the scrutator snapped. 'I've got a war to win, crafter.'

'What . . . happened to Nish, surr?'

'We lost the damn fool!'

147

'Is he dead?' she whispered, rod-straight and hands clenched by her sides.

'Almost certainly. Maybe Ullii can tell us, if she gets her lattice back.'

'She can't.'

'What?'

'Ullii can only see the Secret Art, and Nish has no talent.'

'Useless fellow. He'll be no bloody loss. M'lainte can tell you the tale, when our important business is done.'

Irisis joined the mechanician in the refectory afterwards, and over bowls of cabbage soup M'lainte told her what had happened.

'Scrutator was practically in tears,' said the mechanician, slurping from her bowl, 'and that's a sight I've not seen in the thirty years I've known him. Nish did well, notwithstanding that he did not recover the crystal nor get Tiaan back. A boy left us a month ago. At Tirthrax I saw a man, transformed.'

'And now he's dead!' Irisis said bitterly. Despite their many fights, little Nish had been good to her and he was the only man she really cared about.

'You never know. I've got work to do.' M'lainte stood up abruptly.

Irisis remained where she was. She had work to do as well, but her workshop was running smoothly and she needed to think. The loss of Nish changed everything.

Many people had died in the war. Very many men. The population was falling and it was the duty of everyone to mate and produce more children. Irisis had done that duty eagerly, with a number of partners, but so far without result. She had considered bonding permanently with Nish, but that would never happen now. There would be pressure on her to take another partner. For the first time, Irisis found the idea unappealing.

'Done all your work, crafter?'

She jumped, for the scrutator had come up behind her without a sound. 'Sometimes I just need a quiet place to think.'

'I have to talk to you.'

'I'm listening.' She reached for her bowl of ginger and lime tea.

'Not *here*. Come outside.'

They went through the front gate and Flydd turned right. Irisis had expected him to go left, down in the direction of the crystal mine. She walked beside him up the path, under the aqueduct and towards the tar mines, where fuel was obtained for the furnaces. They lay four hours up a steep path. Irisis hoped he was not planning to go all the way.

After labouring up a steep incline, the scrutator turned left and settled onto an upthrust boss of pale rock, a dyke that ran across the slope like a series of knobs on a backbone. 'Sit down, crafter.'

She perched beside him. 'If this is about my work, surr . . .' Had he learned the terrible truth about her, that she had lost the most crucial talent an artisan could have – the ability to draw power from the field? That to cover it up she'd become a liar and a fraud, despite her undoubted ability to manage her team of artisans.

'I'm happy with your work, Irisis.'

She relaxed, just a little. Some day she would be exposed, but not today. 'What is it, surr? Something to do with the war?'

'Everything is to do with the war, crafter!' Flydd snapped. 'There's a problem that I didn't wish to bring up, in there. People talk, despite themselves.'

'*I* don't!'

'You already know something about it. Do you recall a time, some months back, when a vital node went dead, stranding fifty clankers on the plain of Minnien?'

'It was before Tiaan's fit of crystal fever. Just before she was sent to the breeding factory . . .'

His dark eyes probed her. 'About which the least said the better. The lyrinx destroyed every one of those clankers and we have been trying to find out what happened to the node, or at least to its *field*, ever since.'

'What have you discovered, surr?'

'Very little, and now it has happened again.'

'Where?'

'A number of places. Two are Maksmord and Guffeons, way up the coast, where the enemy have had their greatest successes.

It's a great blow to us, Irisis. A terrible blow. Without clankers, we have no hope.'

'Why are you telling me this, surr?'

'No one else has been able to solve the problem. I'm going to give you a try.'

'*Me?*'

'I have confidence in you, crafter, but you won't be going alone. You've worked well with the seeker in the past. I'll send her with you, once she regains her talent.'

'What do you want me to do?'

'Find out why the nodes are failing. Are we draining them dry, or has the enemy found a way to block or destroy them?'

'Not much is known about nodes, surr.'

'Then you will have the thrill of discovery,' he said dryly. 'Get your work done and organise the best artisan here to take your place. You have a week to be ready.'

'What if Ullii has not recovered by then?'

'She'd better have. Choose two artisans, best suited to the task. You'll go in the air-floater, with guards.'

'Go where?'

'To Minnien, then to the next node, if necessary. And the one after that. Be prepared for anything.'

He got up, then sat down again. 'Another matter. A minor one but I thought you'd be pleased to hear about it, since you're under suspended sentence of the place.'

'I've no idea what you're talking about.'

'In the attack on Tiksi, the breeding factory was burned to the ground.'

She smiled. 'I'm delighted to hear it.'

'I dare say it will be rebuilt soon enough.'

She tapped her fingernails on the stone. 'Tiaan's mother was there. What will she do, I wonder?'

'She's a wealthy woman. She'll survive better than most.'

'I dare say.'

Marnie was not surviving well at all. Only weeks before, as the war approached, she had sold everything and converted it to gold, which she kept in a chest in her room. She had been downstairs when blazing balls crashed though the roof, and the fire had burned so fiercely that there was no chance to recover anything.

She went back in the morning, before the ashes cooled, tramping through the rubble in a pair of workman's boots found in the gardener's shed. She tracked back and forth for three days, until there was not a handful of ash she had not sifted. Marnie found the half-burned leg of her chair and the brass bands of a chest with her name engraved on it, but that was all. The scavengers had already been. The gold was gone.

All she could do was join the thronging destitute who had lost everything but the clothes they were wearing, and hope someone would take pity on them and give them a few scraps to exist on. Marnie knew her life was over. The breeding factory would be rebuilt but they would never take her back. She was past it.

SIXTEEN

Irisis sat with Ullii in her darkened room every day, making
time where there was none to be had. The seeker spoke not a
word. She had taken to throwing her clothes away again and
most times squatted naked in a corner, rocking on her bare feet,
staring at the wall but seeing nothing. Then, on the third day, she
uttered a single word, 'Nish!'

'What is it, Ullii? Can you see him in your lattice?'

'Nish!' she screamed. 'It's got Nish! It's eating his leg! Claws,
claws.' She began to sob. 'Myllii, Myllii, Myllii.'

'Who is Myllii?'

Ullii did not reply and Irisis could get no more out of her, for
the seeker went back into that silent state.

Returning to the workshop, Irisis sat at her stool and considered her artisans. Of the twenty, there were only three that she
would consider taking with her: Goys, a woman of sixty, brilliant
but erratic and past her best; young Zoyl Aarp, equally clever but
inexperienced and naïve, his head turned by every woman who
paid him the least attention; and Oon-Mie, no genius but level-
headed and a master of every aspect of her craft. Fistila Tyr, now
back at her bench after the birth of her third daughter, was also
steady but she must stay here. No one else could be relied upon
to get the work done and manage the prickly personalities that
most artisans were.

So Oon-Mie had to come; Irisis also needed someone she could rely on. Should the other be Zoyl or Goys? Experience or youth? Several teams of artisans and mancers had already worked on the problem and failed. In this hierarchical world those teams would have been packed with experience. A brilliant insight was required here, and that was the province of the young. Zoyl then, and Oon-Mie would balance him.

Everything was ready, and Irisis was awaiting the arrival of the air-floater, when a lightning raid on a shipment heading down to Tiksi resulted in the loss of six newly built controllers.

The scrutator was beside himself. 'Those controllers were needed desperately. The node mission will have to wait. How quickly can you make a new lot, crafter?'

'We have the mechanisms already, surr,' said Irisis. 'But without crystal we can't make them work, and we have no suitable crystal left.'

'What the hell are the miners doing?'

'The mine is practically worked out. The last vein Ullii found, before she went away, contained only three suitable crystals. We've used them all.'

'There must be more somewhere.'

'No doubt, but our miners can't sense it through solid rock.'

'And Ullii is no better?'

'No.'

'This is bad, crafter. I don't know what we're going to do.'

'There is one possibility, surr.'

'Oh?'

'If we could discover where Tiaan came by her special crystal there might be others there like it.'

'I doubt that.'

'Or at least another vein we can use.'

'Does anyone know where she found it?'

'Only she, and old Joeyn, but he died in a roof fall before she fled.'

'So presumably he had only just discovered the crystal.'

'Possibly.'

'Where was his body found?'

153

'On the sixth level.' Irisis gripped the sides of her stool.

'What's the matter?' said Flydd.

'I was thinking about being trapped down there.'

'You're not afraid of the underground, surely?'

'No,' she said softly.

'Well, get miners in and find the place.'

'The roof collapsed. Joeyn's body is still there. Two miners died trying to bring it out.'

'Did anyone survive the collapse?'

'I believe so.'

'Find them; locate the spot as precisely as you can and drive another tunnel into it.'

'That level is forbidden, surr,' said Irisis.

'Do you think I don't know that? I take full responsibility. Get it done!'

Mining was slow work and all the pep talks and offers of double pay could not measurably speed it up, especially on the unstable sixth level. Moreover, skilled miners were in short supply and even in this desperate situation the scrutator did not want to risk them in unnecessary haste. He had set two teams of miners to the problem, tunnelling in from either side, offering a quile of silver to the team that got there first, but nearly a fortnight had gone by before the slow creep of the tunnel face brought the first team around the collapsed area towards the vein of crystal on the other side.

'We've just about done it, surr,' said Peate, the senior miner on the team. 'Next shift, according to my survey, we should break though. And win the prize.'

'Glad I am to hear it,' said the scrutator. 'The Council has not been pleased so far. I hope this will restore their faith in me. *And in this manufactory . . .*'

Irisis shivered, as did everyone. Bad enough that they had a scrutator breathing down their necks every day. Far worse to know that, even if he was happy with their efforts, his superiors were not.

She went back with Peate, for it had been a week since Irisis had had the time to go down the mine. She had no fear of confined spaces. It was the thought of being trapped down there and slowly starving to death that terrified her.

'Here we are,' said Peate, squeezing under a hard layer glistening with golden mica. Two miners, naked to the waist, were using hammer and chisel to break the rock while another shovelled it into a hand cart.

'The rock's different here, is it not?' Higher up in the mine it was pink granite, all sheared and vein-impregnated, but here the granite was blue-grey and the veins were the width of tree trunks.

'It's different *everywhere*.' Peate levered a shattered piece of rock out of the face with his pick. Seeping water had stained the granite in brain patterns.

'How far, do you think?'

'Two spans; at most, three.'

'And you can dig that far in a day?'

'We can do two spans in this kind of rock, since we're digging on such a narrow face. Probably not three. Definitely not if we have to prop up the roof, though I don't think we will.' He turned away.

Irisis watched them for some time; but as she was about to leave, a muffled crack sounded off to the side, where no one was working. 'What was that?' she yelled. 'Is it the roof?'

'It's the team working on the other side,' said Peate. 'Won't do 'em any good, poor sods.' He laughed, a strangled gasp. 'They'll never catch us. The silver is as good as ours.'

'Would we hear them through all this rock?'

'Sound travels strangely through stone. Sometimes miners can be working five spans away and you won't know they're there, while in another place you'll hear them from half a league. Who can fathom it? I'm going home. Come back tomorrow afternoon if you want to see the breakthrough.'

Irisis returned at midday to find the team hammering and shovelling like fury, stripped down to loincloths and covered in sweat. 'I've never seen anyone work so hard,' she marvelled.

The scrutator, perched on a rock like an emaciated vulture, snorted. 'The other team kept going all night. When Peate's mob got in this morning, their opposition had only a span and a half to go. Peate hasn't taken a break in five hours.'

'He'll kill himself,' said Irisis. The miners were staggering about like zombies.

'No one ever worked themselves to death!' Flydd said carelessly.

'Won't be long now,' she said a while later, then realised that she was talking to herself. The scrutator had gone to check on the progress of the second team. She followed the tunnel around the other side. Here the roof rock, which was greatly sheared, was held up with a forest of props and beams. She edged between them, afraid that if she bumped one the whole roof would come down. Four miners crouched, their faces yellow in the lamplight.

'We're through,' grinned Dandri, the leader of the team. She poked her stubby finger into a cup-sized hole. 'Careful now. And remember, no yelling and cheering when we're in the cavity. We'll just sit there, drinking our tea and waiting for them to break through. That'll teach the buggers to gloat.'

'I would give you the same advice,' said the scrutator.

'But *we've* done it.'

Flydd and Irisis stood back while they dug out a hole large enough to step through. Frantic hammering echoed from the other side. Someone laughed.

'Going to tear down the old hut and build a new one with my share,' said a panting miner.

'This way, if you please, surr,' said Dandri.

Flydd took the offered lantern and eased sideways into the cavity, which ran vertically here and was as wide as his shoulders. Holding the lantern out, he turned around, then his lipless mouth curved down at the corners.

'What's the matter, surr?' cried Irisis.

'No crystal,' he said in a dead voice.

'This is the place, surr,' Dandri pleaded. 'I checked the survey twice.'

Irisis put her head in. 'Are you playing a joke, surr? There's crystal everywhere.'

'Indeed, but it isn't any good. I can sense proper crystal, the stuff that can be woken into a hedron, and there's none of it here. This is just ordinary quartz, as dead as we'll soon be.'

'But how can that be?' cried Irisis. 'This has to be the place where Joeyn found the wonder crystal.'

'It's the place, all right. The aura makes my skin prickle. Good crystal *was* here, buckets full of it. But it isn't here now.' He indicated an oval shaft that slanted down towards the seventh level. 'Someone has tunnelled up and taken the lot!'

Xervish Flydd said not a word for the rest of the day, which was far more frightening than the half-joking threats he was wont to issue in normal conversation. A brief, grim meeting was held, where he put the disaster to overseer, foremen and captain, and dismissed them.

A volunteer soldier followed the shaft, which zigzagged back and forth through weaknesses in the stone, down to the disused seventh level.

'It had better be lyrinx!' said Overseer Tuniz, for once without the least trace of good humour, as the soldier scrambled from the hole.

The crisis had a personal dimension for her. The scrutator had promised that she could go home after a year, if the manufactory met all its targets. Home was Crandor, four hundred leagues north. Tuniz had left her work there without leave, to search for her shipwrecked partner, only to discover that he had been captured and eaten by the enemy. She had not seen her little children for a year and without the scrutator's leave might never see them again.

'It *was* lyrinx, overseer,' said the soldier. 'I found their dung all around the exit. Trod in it, in truth, and right horrible, stinking stuff it was.'

Irisis could smell it on his boots. She moved backwards out of the way.

157

'How did they know the crystals were there?' said Tuniz, rubbing her eyes.

'I imagine they tortured it out of Tiaan,' Irisis surmised. 'They know how desperately we need crystal.'

'What are we going to do about it?' demanded the overseer. 'We'd better have an answer by the time the scrutator gets up tomorrow, or . . .'

'What?' said the soldier, snappy because his bravery had not been recognised.

'Or our lives may well be forfeit, and Flydd's as well. The Council does not like failure and these past six months we have had nothing else.'

'Time the seeker got over her self-indulgence,' said Irisis. 'I'll see if I can shake her out of it.'

'What good will that do?' asked the overseer.

'She saw crystal in several places in the mountain, before she went away with Nish. I'll have her search out the best of them, and then we must dig for our very lives.'

Irisis was unable to rouse the seeker from her self-absorbed state. Something drastic had to be done. When it was nearly midnight, she went to see the scrutator. His door was closed. She knocked. There was no answer. Irisis knocked again.

'Go to bloody hell!' he roared, so loudly that she jumped.

Taking her courage in both hands, Irisis lifted the latch and pushed the door open. Xervish Flydd was sprawled in a wooden chair, a flask of pungent parsnip whisky dangling from one gnarled hand. An empty flask lay on the floor. He was naked but for a loin rag and his skeletal body was as scarred and twisted as his face and hands. Whatever had happened to him, whoever had tortured him and broken his bones, they had spared no part of him.

'What the blazes do you want?' he snarled. Flydd's voice was clear despite the quantity of liquor he had consumed. 'Go away! I'm sick of the lot of you.'

A half-written letter, presumably confessing the manufactory's difficulties to the Council of Scrutators, rested on the table.

'I have an idea!' she said.

'I don't want to hear it.' Tilting the flask up, he drained the contents in one swallow, then reached for another.

The death wish was rising up in her again. Snatching the flask from his hand, she hurled it out the door, where it smashed satisfyingly.

The scrutator rose to his battered feet, swayed and steadied himself on the table. 'You could die for that, artisan.'

'Crafter!' she snapped. She wanted to run away screaming, but Irisis forced herself to meet his eyes, to hold his gaze. She had never met anyone as tough as Xervish Flydd, and she had to be just as strong. 'If you don't pull yourself together we could all die, scrutator. How is that going to help the war?'

'You lecture *me*?' he said incredulously. 'The penalty for insubordination is death, crafter.'

'If I'm going to die, it might as well be of my own choosing!' Irisis gave him the kind of glare she used to quell importunate lovers and idle prentices.

He glared back, quite as fiercely. They held their positions, each waiting for the other to break, then finally the scrutator barked with laughter and pointed to the other chair.

'Spill your idea, Irisis.'

'Come with me, and together we will cajole the seeker, or force her if we must, out of that state. Then we get her to find the biggest cluster of crystals the mountain has to offer and we dig for them, night and day. I'll take my turn with pick and shovel, if there's a shortage.'

'Not much of a plan, crafter, but it's better than anything I can come up with. Shall we go?'

With her hand on the knob, Irisis looked back. 'It might be an idea to dress first, surr. Wouldn't want to alarm her unnecessarily.'

The scrutator looked down at his grizzled nakedness, grinned, and said, 'Quite!'

Ullii squatted in the corner, exactly as she had for the past couple of weeks. Though it was cold today, she wore only her spider-silk undergarments.

'Seeker?' the scrutator called from the door.

The rhythm of her rocking did not alter.

He came up close. 'Seeker?'

Nothing at all.

'What are you thinking about, seeker? Are you remembering your friend, Nish?'

She might have rocked a little faster, though more along that line of questioning yielded nothing.

'Here is your other friend, Irisis. Do you remember her?' He beckoned Irisis in.

Not by so much as a blink did Ullii react, nor could he gain one from any other approach, though he spent half an hour trying.

'I don't know what else to do,' he whispered to Irisis, over by the door.

'Since being kind has not worked, maybe you should try being nasty.'

'Better that *you* be the nasty one,' he snapped. 'You've had more practice.'

She ignored that. 'Come outside.'

She led him out and around the corner, so that Ullii, even with her hypersensitive hearing, could not overhear.

'I can't force her,' she said, 'else I will lose her trust. I'll need it when we go to examine the failed nodes.'

'True enough. What is she afraid of most in all the world?'

Irisis considered. 'Apart from Nish's father, Perquisitor Hlar?'

'Precisely! Go away. Best that you're nowhere near.'

The scrutator went inside, this time taking a bright lantern and leaving the door wide open. Ullii groped around for her goggles and mask but he got there first and held them out of reach. She began to moan and flail her arms in the air.

'Well, at least that's a reaction,' he said aloud. 'Ullii?'

She dropped back into her slack-jawed rocking. Was it an act? Perhaps she was sulking, or punishing him for losing Nish.

He slammed the door a couple of times, opened it again and turned the lantern up to maximum brightness. Ullii put her arms over her face and began to make a keening sound in her throat.

'Stand up, Ullii,' he roared, knowing it would hurt her.

She did not move.

'What are you afraid of, seeker? Are you frightened of me?'

No reply, though for an instant one eye peeped out through her fingers.

'Do you remember Perquisitor Jal-Nish Hlar, Ullii? Nish's father?'

She wailed and covered her ears.

He dropped his voice. 'If you don't wake up and help us, seeker, do you know what will happen? The Council will cut off my head.'

Ullii went still and her fingers slipped away from her ears, so he knew she was listening.

'What will happen then, Ullii? You don't know, do you? Well, listen good. The perquisitor will come!'

Ullii let out a little gasp, 'No!'

'Yes, Jal-Nish Hlar will come, *for you*! Right here, to this room.'

'No!' she wailed.

'*Yes*, he will smash your goggles and rip your earmuffs apart. He will tear off your spider-silk underwear and cast it into the furnace.'

She screamed and threw her head from side to side but the scrutator did not relent. Squatting in front of her, he took her by the shoulders. Her wide eyes stared into his.

'And then, little seeker, he will beat you and scream at you. He will torment you in ways so horrible that I cannot bear to say them. He will stake you out in the sun and leave you there *to die*! That's what kind of a man the perquisitor is, seeker!'

'No, no, no!' she screamed, leapt up and raced around the room, so distressed that she cannoned off the walls.

The scrutator allowed her that freedom for a minute or two, then turned down the lantern, closed the door and, as she fled past, handed her the mask and earmuffs.

Ullii snatched them and put them on. Fleeing to her corner, she crouched down, rocking furiously.

'On the other hand,' said Flydd gently, 'you could agree to help us. We know your talent has come back, Ullii.' He was guessing about that, but Flydd felt sure that her loss of talent was due to a temporary trauma, long over, and she was pretending otherwise for her own perverse reasons.

'Only sometimes,' she muttered. 'I don't have it all the time.'

'Better than nothing, seeker. So you will help us?'

'Yes!' she mumbled.

'That is very good. Thank you, Ullii. We will start down the mine after lunch.' He tiptoed to the door.

'I hate you,' hissed Ullii. 'You are a nasty, cruel man!'

'I am,' he replied. 'But not as nasty nor as cruel as the perquisitor.'

SEVENTEEN

'Master, the pipes are calling!'

Gilhaelith, known locally as the tetrarch on account of his obsession with numbers to the power of four, threw himself out of bed, eyes firmly closed. 'Where is my gown?'

The servant wrapped it around Gilhaelith's gangling frame. Gilhaelith tied the sash with awkward jerks, sat on the bed and raised a pair of large and profoundly ugly feet. Leather slippers were pulled on. He put out a hand, blindly, for he still had not opened his eyes. The servant pressed a two-handled cup the size of a serving bowl into Gilhaelith's fingers. The yellow liquid was too thick to ripple. Even the steam rose sluggishly.

Gilhaelith put the cup to his nose, inhaling pungent fumes of mustard-water that was more mustard than water. His head jerked back; his eyes sprang open.

'Aah!' he gasped, draining half the cup in a long series of swallows that bobbed his larynx up and down like a cork in a pail. 'Aaaah!'

The servant, ever ready, wiped Gilhaelith's streaming nose with a kerchief the size of a tablecloth. Gilhaelith gulped the rest of the mustard-water and sprang to life. 'Aaaaaaaah! Very good, Mihail; a fine brew this morning. Take me down the outside walkway, if you please.'

'I . . . dare not, master.'

Gilhaelith smiled. The ritual was an old one. It pleased him to ask, and to have the servant refuse. He would have been irked had Mihail answered differently.

'Meet me in the pipe chamber then.'

'At once, Gilhaelith.'

Gilhaelith frowned at the familiarity. But after all, Mihail had served him nearly fifty years, and Mihail's father for thirty years before that. 'Be ready,' he said. 'I am hungry this morning.' He said that every morning. Gilhaelith strode out, the mustard-coloured, mustard-stained robes flapping about his bristly shanks.

It was still dark outside as he walked across the terrace. A thumbnail paring of moon, low in the sky, gave barely enough light to see. That did not matter – Gilhaelith had trodden this path most days in the hundred years since Nyriandiol, the ultimate creation of his life and work so far, had finally been completed.

The night was a little too cool for what he was wearing but his belly radiated a satisfying warmth. Gilhaelith paused under a vine-covered pergola while a mustard-flavoured belch made its wobbly way up. His slippers rasped on the paving stones as he turned down the walkway.

A swooping suspended path of stone, the walkway curved along the outside wall of Nyriandiol, which itself swept in and out. At the far end, the path took a zigzag down and ran back the other way, and so on right down the eight levels of the monstrous building. The path had no steps and no rail. Its surface undulated like waves in the ocean. It was a colossal conceit and a dare, for there was nothing beneath it but the dull gleam of water hundreds of spans below, and to fall meant death. Many workers had died building the path; only one man dared to walk it.

Gilhaelith knew it like the most familiar parts of his body but every day it was a challenge that left his heart racing. Presently it was damp with condensed moisture from the lake, slippery in unexpected places, and if he relaxed it would claim him with profound indifference. Walking this path was a good way to start the day, or the night for that matter.

Safely at the lowest level, he grasped the handle of a door carved from solid red jasper and jerked it open. No need for locks here. The corridor was unlit. He made his way through the blackness to a small chamber, out through whose door yellow light streamed.

Mihail waited inside with breakfast – a platter of freshly salted slugs covered in foaming yellow slime. Gilhaelith downed the delicacies whole, two at a time, smacking his lips and licking the foam off his fingers. On each corner of the tray was a quartered, pickled red onion the size of a grapefruit, with which to cleanse his palate. Gilhaelith selected a quarter, inspected it, found a minute blemish and put it back. The others also failed his scrutiny; the whole sixteen quarters were blemished. Fortunately Mihail knew what to do. He deftly peeled the outer layer off the first quarter, presenting Gilhaelith with a perfect inner segment.

'It's too small,' Gilhaelith said for the sake of form, but took the onion and crunched it noisily.

The servant presented a finger bowl half full of sulphur-water. Gilhaelith waggled his fingers in it, dried them on the proffered napkin and was ready for work.

'You may go, Mihail.'

The servant withdrew. Gilhaelith took up the lantern and went through into the adjoining room, a chamber so vast that neither its ceiling nor far wall could be seen. He set the lantern on the floor, shuttered it completely and stood in the dark, listening.

The pipes *were* calling. He made out a low note, a fluttery tremble that he could feel through his slippers, and then a higher, eerie keening. Gilhaelith cocked his head. He had not heard either sound before and could not work out what their ultimate source might be.

Unshuttering the lantern, he made his way up the room. The light picked structures out of the gloom – pipes of wood and metal, most in clusters of four by four, rarely nine by nine. The values were important. He would have used larger numbers but Nyriandiol was not big enough to accommodate them. Some clusters were horizontal, though most stood upright. The end of the room was taken up by countless arrays of organ pipes, the tallest stretching up to the ceiling, which here stood the full eight storeys of Nyriandiol above them. Gilhaelith sat in a chair around which were clustered, in symmetrical arrays, more pipes of all sizes, down to ones smaller than a pencil.

The organ was a geomantic device designed to listen in to, and give sound to, the harmony of the spheres. So far, though he had spent a century refining it, Gilhaelith had been frustrated in that endeavour. The subtle vibrations of the planets in their orbits could not be detected by his geomancy, even funnelled through the largest pipes he could create. However, the organ did pick up other vibrations, other tones, and for more than fifty years he had been noting these and trying to discern the underlying patterns and the numbers behind them. Many vibrations seemed related to nodes or to their fields. Fields that in some cases were being drained dry by the power drawn by humanity's squadrons of clankers, and other machines powered by the Secret Art. Another puzzle he was keen to solve.

Gilhaelith had constructed a model of the main nodes he knew about, trying but failing to understand them. His organ was powerful, for he drew upon the great Booreah Ngurle double node to drive it. But it, or perhaps he, lacked sensitivity. He could not tell how to overcome that.

There was something strange about the tones he was now hearing, and he needed to pinpoint them. On a bench across the room, on a pedestal of ebony wood, sat a perfect sphere some half a span across, surfaced with glass. The sphere contained a model of Santhenar, or at least the parts of it for which there were reliable maps. It showed Lauralin and the surrounding islands in detail, including the mountains in relief, though all of that lay beneath the smooth surface of glass.

Drawing on a pair of silken gloves, Gilhaelith passed his fingers over the surface of the geomantic globe, close but not touching. Wisps of cold vapour followed his movements: for sensitivity, the sphere had to be bitterly cold. It was kept that way by what lay at its core.

Beneath his hands, tiny pinpoints of light sparkled. He put on a pair of spectacles, each side of which contained a trio of lenses set within wire coils, like springs. Pulling down on the coils to separate the lenses, he squinted at the markings. With a grimace he lifted his hands and repeated the operation, no more successfully than the first time.

Gilhaelith returned to his chair, which stood in front of a curving console carved from a single block of cedar wood two spans across. It contained a number of organ keyboards whose yellow triangular keys alternately pointed toward him and away, as well as a variety of stops, buttons and pedals. Drawing out some stops and pushing in others, he set his big fingers to the keys and began to play, attempting to duplicate the low, fluttering tremble. He could not, which vexed him. Nor could he work out where the note came from, which bothered him even more. To unmask the source, he must first record the location on his scrying globe.

Gilhaelith was a geomancer of great power, though power itself held no interest for him. He cared about nothing except knowledge. He was wealthy, but likewise wealth had only one value – it allowed him to pursue his drive to understand geomancy in all its subtlety. Geomancy was the Art that underpinned the heavenly bodies and the forces that controlled them, and he sought to master it to the limit of his ability, though in truth he rarely used that power. When he did need to use the Art he relied on mathemancy, which he had developed and of which he was, as far as he was aware, the only practitioner in the world. Wielding an unknown Art had its advantages.

Neither could he precisely reproduce the higher sound that came from the pipes, though Gilhaelith had perfect pitch and knew which pipes made it. That irritated him even more. However, he was able to identify one remarkable feature of the call. *It was moving.*

That was strange. His organ could pick up the sounds associated with the great forces that shaped and moved the world, but they were always in the same place. It could not detect the harmonies associated with the planets, the moon, wandering comets or other celestial bodies. Occasionally a meteor might be large enough, and come close enough, for him to detect its song – a high squeal rising in pitch before abruptly being cut off – but neither of these sounds was remotely like that.

They were moving slowly. Definitely not a celestial body. A delicious puzzle. He enjoyed puzzles – Gilhaelith had been playing the world game for most of his adult life and was a long way from solving it. What could this object be? The organ was not sensitive to the tones from minor forces such as hedrons, clankers and other devices that employed the Art. He had no interest in the works of vulgar humanity. But this was different, and something in the notes was slightly, hauntingly familiar.

Shuttering the lantern, he sat in the dark, listening and remembering. His stomach crawled as though his breakfast was still alive. Some weeks ago, a strange disruption had frosted his globe and wrung a sobbing note out of the worldwide ethyr itself. That had not happened before in all his years of listening. The ethyr was only a carrier, normally intangible, and for it to sing meant that a monumental disruption had taken place.

Gilhaelith had not yet discovered what, or where. If some natural force, it must have been a cataclysmic one, though a huge earthquake, eruption or landfall would have reverberated for ages. It had been nothing like that. Nor had it to do with the war. Neither humanity nor the lyrinx had that kind of power.

The sounds were still moving. He put his hands on the keys, again struggling and failing to duplicate them. His curiosity would not let go, but though he played for hours with such intensity that his mustard-stained gown became drenched in sweat, Gilhaelith could not get close. He wanted to draw the source to him but did not know how. For all his geomantic power, he was helpless. Should he go to the bells? He glanced over his shoulder at the cloth-shrouded carillon and shuddered. No, he was not in the right frame of mind for that particular kind of struggle.

When Gilhaelith finally left the organ, the pipes no longer sang. In disgust, he closed the door and climbed the obsidian stairs to the top of his observatory tower, to draw solace from the ever predictable motions of the celestial bodies.

Gilhaelith's house stood at the top of the volcano whose name was Booreah Ngurle, the famous Burning Mountain, and it was the strangest house in the world. He called it a house, though really it was a great rambling workshop, laboratory and library. Gilhaelith was a polymath, a man interested in everything and master of many disciplines. He was more than one hundred and fifty years old, but in society might have passed for forty, not that he was ever in society. He lived alone apart from a flock of servants whose families had served him for generations.

Gilhaelith spent the rest of the night in his observatory, at the top of the tower near a vine-covered terrace. He was searching for comets, which were more frequent at this time of year, but as the dawn brightened he fell asleep at his 'scope. A servant woke him an hour later with a mug of stout, heated to boiling by plunging a red-hot poker into it. Black liquid foamed over the sides, flecked with shreds of mace.

As Gilhaelith reached for the mug, the greatest pipes of his organ, which had not sounded by themselves in all his years of watching, groaned. The sound was so low that it shook the whole of Nyriandiol. The drink quivered in his servant's hand. A few seconds later something flashed past the rim of the crater. It could not have been a comet, for it was black and the rising sun glinted off it. Swinging the spyglass around, Gilhaelith caught another flash of black, now dropping sharply to disappear below the rim.

He leaned back in his chair and, putting his lanky legs up on the rail, grated a good third of a nutmeg onto his stout. Stirring it in with a pair of brass dividers, he took a cautious sip. Spice-crusted foam caught on his upper lip. 'What can it be?' he said to himself.

He puzzled about the incident until mid-morning, working through all the possibilities he could think of. It did not occur to him to go down into the forest and take a look. Gilhaelith was not a man of action. However, he did check the organ and look into his globe again. Neither told him anything. Frustrated, he occupied himself with other activities, to cleanse his mind of the puzzle.

Late in the morning Gilhaelith was composing a poem in his library – an ode on the power four – when his eye caught an engraving of a scene from the famous but debased *Tale of the Mirror*. It portrayed the tragic funeral ride of Rulke across the Way between the Worlds to Aachan, his body bound to the side of the construct. The engraving had been on his library wall for ninety-seven years, so long that Gilhaelith had ceased to notice it.

Laying down his quill, he peered at the engraving. The fleeting black image seen earlier resonated with this image of the construct, a congruence so remarkable that he began to contemplate a radical action – actually going down to the forest to investigate. 'Curious,' he said. 'Will I or won't I?'

He tested the omens by raising a selection of random numbers to the fourth power, then reading the pattern. It was mostly harmonious. 'Yes, I'll go down and take a look.'

Being a methodical man, he returned to the tower, took a sighting on the spot where the falling object had disappeared, and marked it on his map. Taking off his robes he donned a dark green shirt, red walking boots and baggy pants which revealed hairy, skinny legs knobbed in the middle by kneecaps as square as pieces of toast.

Gilhaelith tossed a shapeless pack over his shoulder. It contained a length of rope, a hatchet and a large bottle of stout so black that it could have been used to dye soot. Fully equipped, he told the servants where he was going and strode off along the rim of the volcano as though there were springs in his knees.

Booreah Ngurle was dormant at the moment, emitting only wisps of steam and an occasional puff of ash. One day, however, it would come to life and erupt violently, blasting cubic leagues of rock into the air and destroying everything for five or ten leagues around, including Nyriandiol and, if he was in residence at the time, himself.

Gilhaelith enjoyed that uncertainty almost as much as his

morning walk on the suspended path. Life on Santhenar was fragile, death often brutal and sudden, and living here reminded him every day. He knew the science of the earth better than anyone, and monitored the tremblers and the gaseous emissions of the volcano as methodically as he did everything in his life. Gilhaelith hoped to predict the eruption and make his way to a safe vantage point, the better to observe it. But if he failed, that would also be interesting, albeit briefly.

Crunching along the ashy ground, which was sparsely covered in silky lamb's ears and other hardy plants, he looked over the outer side. Further down, weeds gave way to grey shrubs, beyond which the vegetation became increasingly luxuriant. From the halfway point, the slopes were clothed in tall forest that extended into the vastness of Worm Wood in all directions, concealing what lay below. He felt sure the falling object had gone down there, somewhere.

Though Gilhaelith was familiar with this part of the forest, it took him what remained of the day to find the machine. A lesser man might have given up but, once set upon a course, Gilhaelith never did.

It *was* a construct. He marvelled at that. Gilhaelith knew the Histories well and understood the significance of this machine. It, or the events that had brought it here, would change the world. Just what was the connection with that disturbance of the ethyr weeks ago?

The construct lay on its side, partly embedded in the mouldering remnants of a pair of rotting logs, forest giants that had fallen many years ago. The metal skin was crumpled, the front and side stoved in. He walked around it twice, noting everything for future consideration and making sketches. He might do a painting one day and hang it in his library.

The hatch was closed. 'Hello?' he called. 'Is anyone here?'

There was no answer, so he heaved it open. Constructs had always fascinated him, because no one knew how they worked. In his boyhood, before reality crushed such ambitions, he had dreamed of flying one.

It was growing dark. Gilhaelith slid in through the hatch.

It was completely dark inside but his exploring hand struck a glass sphere, which began to glow. Everything about the machine was strange and, to a geomancer, fascinating. He discovered that it bore similarities to clankers, but also had many differences. The most notable: its flight had been powered by one of the strong forces. To the best of his knowledge, no one had ever mastered such forces. Did he have a rival more advanced than himself?

Then he discovered the amplimet. In all his life he had seen nothing like it. He spent ages there, oblivious to everything else, studying the amplimet without ever touching it. He was wary, for the danger was obvious. Yet he coveted it, and the construct too. Within them lay the answers to questions he had puzzled over for a very long time. How he would enjoy that journey of discovery.

A faint scraping sound from below reminded him that the construct must have had an operator. 'Hello?' he called.

A groan answered him. He climbed down into the darkness. The globe on the wall was broken so he conjured a glimmer with his fingers – the simplest magic of all. A young woman lay on the tilted floor. Gilhaelith had little use for people but she was different from the women of these parts, and quite lovely. He gazed at her.

The woman was small compared to his female servants, and slender, with hair so black and glossy that even in this dim light it shone. Her colouring, and her eyes, suggested that she was from the south-east of Lauralin.

Gilhaelith had no currency with women, apart from the elderly matrons who worked in his villa. He had not spent time with a young woman in a hundred years. From his early life, Gilhaelith knew that human relationships caused only misery. Nonetheless, he did not like to see any creature in pain.

Squatting beside her, knees popping, he called to mind the common speech of the south-east, which he had learned in his youth but seldom had cause to speak. 'My name is Gilhaelith. Who are you?'

'I am Tiaan Liise-Mar.' Her voice was the barest exhalation.

He inspected her from head to foot, probing her skull with

bony fingers. 'You've taken a nasty knock, but I think no harm is done. Take my hand; I'll help you up.'

'I can't feel my legs. My back is broken.'

Gilhaelith rocked back on his heels. Broken backs could not be repaired by any healer's skill, nor any form of the Secret Art he was aware of. What was he to do with her?

'Have you friends or family?'

'Not within two hundred leagues,' she whispered.

Beautiful and doomed. What to do? He would take the glowing crystal. He could have his servants bring the construct to Nyriandiol. It would not be easy but it could be done. And Tiaan Liise-Mar?

It would be a kindness to put her out of her misery, as he would do for any animal with the same affliction. He considered it dispassionately, but the practicality of suffocating her, or breaking her neck, under the gaze of those dark eyes, was beyond him. Better to expose her on the floor of the forest. A predator would take her within a day and it would be a quick death, though not a pleasant one. He would not want it for himself, and the waiting would be worse. Gilhaelith lidded his eyes, the better to take the omens. The numbers all fell badly, so he could not expose her either. There was only one thing to do, though he felt sure he would regret it.

'I will have you brought to my house, Nyriandiol,' he said heavily. 'It is not far.'

She closed her eyes. Gilhaelith stood by her for a minute. He could carry her that distance, had there been no option, but was reluctant to. Her back *might* not be irretrievably damaged, but if he picked her up it would be, and then he would never be rid of her. He would bring down his most reliable servants, a healer and a stretcher.

'I will be gone a few hours,' he said. 'Will you be all right for that time?'

'I'm not going anywhere,' Tiaan said, with an empty laugh that chilled him.

He gave her the last of the stout from his bottle. It went down the wrong way, causing her to cough. Black stout dribbled down her chin. He wiped it off, and with a last backward glance went up the ladder. Outside he closed the hatch and climbed the mountain as fast as he could in the dark. Red-faced and dripping sweat, he crashed into the hall not long before midnight.

'Mihail, Fley,' he roared. 'Get up! An accident down the mountain. Have we a stretcher?'

Mihail, a portly man with a pink, shiny complexion like fresh scar tissue, put his head around the door. 'Healer Gurteys has one, I believe, Master Gilhaelith.'

'Rouse Gurteys and Seneschal Nixx out of bed. A young woman lies injured in the forest. Her back is broken.'

Fley came trotting out of the infirmary with the stretcher under one arm. He was a big man, as muscular as a butcher, but completely silent, for Fley was a mute. Gurteys, his wife, was lean and wiry, with webbed fingers, a perpetual scowl and a voice as raucous as a cockerel.

'As if I haven't enough to do in the daytime,' she said in a whine that caused Fley to clench his fists. Staring at the back of his wife's neck, he opened his fingers into claws, then crushed them closed. That appeared to satisfy him for he followed in silence.

Nixx met them at the front door. An ill-shaped man, the seneschal had a nose so hooked, and a chin so pointed, that he could have held a walnut between them. His eyes were black buttons, his ears pendulous and his egg-shaped skull completely bald. Nixx was polite, efficient and completely loyal. And he had one feature that to Gilhaelith was worth more than all the others – he was the fourth son of a fourth son, and the fourth of his line to have been seneschal to Gilhaelith.

It was around three in the morning by the time the procession of lanterns reached the construct. Gurteys the healer, well back from Gilhaelith's hearing, complained all the way. The servants stared at the fallen machine but did not ask questions. Inside, Gilhaelith and the healer held Tiaan's head while Mihail and Fley rolled her just enough to slide the stretcher underneath. They bound her to it and Gurteys gave her a dose of green syrup that closed her eyes within a minute. The bearers carefully manoeuvred the stretcher up and out of the hatch. Gilhaelith gave orders for them to return with a canvas, to conceal the machine while he worked out what to do with it.

It was a slow trip back. Gilhaelith paced ahead of the stretcher, worn out after his second night without sleep. His belly throbbed, high up. What was he to do with Tiaan? Near the summit he looked back and saw that her eyes were open. She quickly closed them.

Dawn had broken by the time they reached Nyriandiol. Gilhaelith saw Tiaan settled in the room beside his, next to the front door, and left her to the healer. He spent hours pacing the suspended walkway, oblivious to the danger. Usually he found the scenery exhilarating. Now he did not notice it.

When the healer had finished, Gilhaelith met her at the door. Taking Gurteys by the sleeve, for he did not like to touch, he led her out to the main terrace. They stood by the stone wall, looking down into the crater. Below, a man clad only in a loincloth toiled up a winding path, carrying a laden basket on his head. It was piled high with chunks of native sulphur, which condensed around vents inside the crater. Sulphur had always been valuable. The war had made it priceless and Gilhaelith's supply was the purest in the world.

That was another worry. For the past century the war had been so far away that it did not matter, but it was coming closer all the time. The lands immediately east of the Sea of Thurkad looked set to fall before next winter. The scrutators might be thinking it was time they secured their supplies directly rather than paying his outrageous prices. The lyrinx, who had never bothered him, could equally be planning to seize the source to deny it to humanity. Though he loved Nyriandiol more than anything, Gilhaelith saw a time coming when he would have to abandon it, if he was to continue his work.

'What have you found?' he asked the healer.

'Her back *is* broken,' said Gurteys. 'It's not a bad break, as such things go. It will heal. Unfortunately the spinal cord has been severed. There's nothing I can do about that. She will be paralysed from the waist down until the day she dies.'

Gilhaelith treated his people well, though he had never concerned himself with their lives or problems. Now, as he stared down into the crater, all he could see was Tiaan's face, bleached under the amber skin, and the eyes staring up at the ceiling.

It made him uncomfortable. Gilhaelith had no friends, nor wanted any. People were unreliable. People rejected, spurned and betrayed. His only desire was to play the great game to the limit of his ability, but if Tiaan remained here that would be disrupted. Yet how could he rid himself of her without compromising the crystal and the construct?

The amplimet, carefully wrapped, hung like a lead weight in his pocket. The construct oppressed him too. He wanted to master them, whatever it cost. If the scrutators knew the construct was here they would march on Nyriandiol with an army. To say nothing of the construct's true owner, and he knew that was not Tiaan. The machine was of Aachim make and they must be hunting it even now. Why had she stolen it?

By keeping it secret he risked everything, but he was going to try. He had to. The construct offered knowledge that could give him the advantage in the game.

That reminded him of something. Hastening to the library, he took up a secret book of geomancy his agents had only just uncovered. After ten minutes he had not taken in a single word. Tossing it on the table, Gilhaelith looked for his poem, but did not bother to pick it up. He could see nothing but Tiaan's tormented features.

One remedy had never failed him. In the cool of the cellar at the back of the seventh level, Gilhaelith tapped a foaming mug of his favourite stout. The black brew went down untasted, and another two after it. They proved no use at all.

Since Tiaan had stolen the amplimet and used the construct, she must have some minor talent. Perhaps he could use her. Gilhaelith was a fair man and would pay her for that service. Was there anything he could do to get her legs back?

His library was one of the best in the world, for books were the first treasures to be sold when war swept across a city and drove its citizens onto the road. The world was awash with rare

176

manuscripts; treasures could be had for a few gold coins and his agents were constantly sending him more.

Calling his librarian, Gilhaelith instructed her to find every document that bore on the subject of broken backs, necks, and recovery therefrom. There was plenty; he read all day and half the night before collapsing on his bed for a few hours of sleep. Late that evening he visited the patient, who lay as still and silent as before, then went on with his work.

Gilhaelith ploughed through the rest of the tomes, scrolls and parchments. Though they contained a good lading of miraculous cures, most he was able to dismiss as quackery. He found no reputable healer's opinion that disagreed with his own.

EIGHTEEN

Tiaan roused from the potion while they were still in the forest. She remembered everything except the fall that had broken her back. The bearers were carrying her up a steep slope through forest that had a rich decaying smell. The lanterns were golden orbs swaying across her vision. The night was silent, apart from the tramp of footsteps and an occasional mutter of 'No, this way,' or 'Give us a hand up here.' The man who had discovered her was just a shadow, well ahead.

Was Gilhaelith friend or enemy? Most likely the latter. In her travels across Tirthrax, Tiaan had often considered how she might defend herself against attackers. She had not imagined being helpless to do so. This man could use her, or abuse her, in any way he wanted. He could give the thapter to the enemy, or sell her to the most evil man in the world. There was nothing she could do. She wished she had died.

Hours later, as dawn broke, they carried her out of the forest up through a patch of thorny bushes, over a barrens of black rock and scree that slipped underfoot, and onto the rim of the crater.

The summit of Booreah Ngurle was elongated like a bean seed and consisted of a large crater at the western end overlapping a smaller one at the east. Ahead, Nyriandiol hung inside the northern lip of the larger crater. Long and low, it extended for several hundred paces around the rim. Apart from a slender tower, from the approach road it appeared to consist of only a single storey.

The road, a rutted and gullied track deliberately maintained in poor repair, curved around onto the stony rim, here no more than fifty paces wide. The area outside the front of Nyriandiol was paved with roughly worked stone, forming a terrace that had been partly roofed and provided with stools and tables. Other parts were covered in climbing vines. A series of benches had been cut into the welded rock of the mountaintop, forming lower terraces that looked down into the crater.

From here, as they carried her across, Nyriandiol appeared to grow out of the mountain's rim, which had been cut away on the inside to accommodate it. Subsequently the rubble had been put back so that, from the outside, only the upper storey and roof could be seen. From the lowest terrace, however, the full magnificence of the place was visible.

Sinusoidal walls of dark stone curved down for another seven levels. Enormous windows of coloured glass set in small panes made up parts of a giant mosaic which could only properly be viewed from the other side of the crater, with a spyglass. The panes, in groups of nine by nine, were linked by patterns of stone inlaid in the walls in geomantic themes: swirls, bridges and arcs of stone each laid according to secret numbers. The steep roof was covered in shingles of red jasper and even these were set down in numerical mosaics. Nyriandiol was a geomantic masterpiece, designed to safeguard its owner and enhance all his efforts in the great room on the lowest floor.

The front door, made of a single slab of chalcedony swinging on massive brass hinges, was an oval two spans high and two wide. The door surroundings had been cut from yellow jasper.

They lugged her inside. The villa was built entirely of stone, the lower floors being vaulted to bear the weight of those above. She was brought into a large room and placed on a bed. Someone saw that her eyes were open and gave her another dose of syrup. Tiaan surrendered to it gratefully.

179

She woke in the most mortifying position of her life. A metal dish had been jammed under her and someone was pressing hard on her bladder, forcing her to urinate. She prayed that it was a woman and not the odd-looking scarecrow, Gilhaelith. Whoever it was, they let out a muffled grunt with each thrust. Tiaan kept her eyes firmly closed. Was this a prescription for the rest of her life, having to be helped with every bodily function? If so, she prayed she would not live long.

Life conspired to devalue her in her own eyes. Each time she gained something it was snatched away. Minis's rejection had been the ultimate demonstration of her worthlessness.

Tiaan had always known that she would mate and have children. It was every person's duty, after all. She often dreamed about it, in an overly romantic way, but now it would never happen. She might still do her artisan's work sitting down, but the few men available could take their pick, and who would want a mate such as she?

There had been so many visitors in the day that Tiaan began to feel like a circus exhibit. Several people spoke to her, but she did not answer. The drug had left her listless. Overwhelmed by the disaster, and unused to being waited on, she could not think of anything to say to them.

The nurse gave an especially loud grunt and Tiaan heard footsteps cross the room, away from her. She opened her eyes. Gilhaelith stood by the head of the bed, staring at her. What a strange, ill-put-together fellow he was. His nose was a triangular chunk sawn off the corner of a plank, his mouth seemed to take up half his face, while his chin was so big and square it would not have been out of place in a carpenter's toolbox.

Gilhaelith had hair the colour of beach sand, the individual hairs crinkled and lying apart from their fellows in a frizzled mass like the unbraided strands of a rope. It looked as if he had mopped the floor with his head. His eyes were smoky grey, though not hard, as pale eyes could often be – he looked contemplative, even philosophical. They were his only appealing feature.

Who was Gilhaelith, and what did he want? He was taller than Minis, which made him *too* tall, and big-framed but skinny. His bones looked too large for his muscles; he had the oddity of broad shoulders but a narrow chest, and his legs made her want to laugh.

She studied him from half-closed eyes as he went back and forth in the room, walking with a springy, bent-kneed step. He kept staring at her then looking away. Now he was coming toward her. He could walk; she never would. Tiaan did not know how to deal with him either. She closed her eyes and pretended to be asleep. After standing beside her for a few minutes, he went away.

The room was empty at last. Tiaan looked around. Soft cords ran across her chest, waist and hips, binding her tightly to lengths of timber. She could move only her arms and her head.

The roof beams seemed to be massive trunks of petrified wood. The room was large and kidney-shaped, the walls built of chunks of dark volcanic rock cemented together with pale mortar. The floor was cleaved stone, slabs of irregular shape also set in mortar then varnished to the colour of beer. The walls were bare apart from three large watercolours depicting scenes from the Histories, all by the same artist.

In the far corner, a curved bookcase had been fashioned to fit the shape of the wall. It was hand-carved from thick pieces of a dark, highly figured timber, but was the work of an enthusiastic amateur, an artist rather than a master craftsman. The maker had used the natural curves of the timber, shaping them only when necessary. To Tiaan, used to furniture that was simple, geometric and functional, it was a shocking piece, self-indulgent and wasteful.

The books might as well have been on the far side of the world. She turned the other way. Her bed was enormous, also hand-carved, though from a darker, straight-grained timber. The sheets were fine linen. There was one blanket of blue lamb's wool, quite unlike the scratchy material in the manufactory, and a quilt filled with down so light she could barely feel it.

The luxury felt sinful; even the space did. In the manufactory, twenty people would have been crammed into this room. The floor was scattered with brightly patterned rugs in earthy reds, oranges, yellows and browns. A pot beside her bed contained a succulent plant covered in large white flowers. She could smell

181

the nectar. No one in the manufactory had a plant in their room; nothing would grow in such cold and gloom.

This room had three huge windows, each of plain glass in many small panes grouped in threes, flooding the chamber with light and colour. In Tiaan's experience only rich people had a window to themselves. Gilhaelith must be as wealthy as the legendary Magister of Thurkad.

She looked through the nearest window. All she could see was blue sky with wisps of high cloud. To someone who'd spent her life in the manufactory, that was a welcome novelty. The sun had not been much in evidence in her long winter's trek across Mirrilladell either. She longed to feel it on her face.

A shadow passed by the end window – Gilhaelith again. She hoped he would not come in. He knocked at the door. She did not answer but after an interval he entered. He was now dressed in long yellow robes which concealed his ungainly figure. She imagined he had come to interrogate her.

'You are better, I hope?' he said in her tongue, which he spoke with a rather flat accent, as if he had learned the language from a book.

'Yes, thank you. Apart from my broken back!'

'I'm sorry,' he said formally. He looked down the line of her body under the covers.

'It's done.' She wished he would go away. The conversation was pointless.

'Is there anything you would like?'

'I'd like to go out in the sun.' It came out without her thinking about it.

'I will arrange it at once.'

He went to the door. Shortly two servants wheeled in a small bed and slid her onto it. Gilhaelith pushed her out of the door, around the corner and along a suspended, undulating stone walkway.

Tiaan caught her breath at the view, not to mention the drop into the lake. 'How can you live at the top of a volcano?'

'Booreah Ngurle, the Burning Mountain,' said Gilhaelith, misinterpreting the question. 'Welcome to Nyriandiol. My house.'

She counted the windows as they went by. Eighty-one. And there were another seven levels below this one. 'House' was not the word for it. It was almost the size of the manufactory.

Gilhaelith parked the bed on a small paved area at the rear of the building. Some distance away was a stone skeet house. She could hear their harsh cries. To her right the arid inner slope of the crater swept down, not quite barren of life, but nearly. Steam wisped up from vents, discoloured yellow or brown. Workers, the size of ants, could be seen toiling at them. Below, occupying perhaps a third of the floor of the larger crater, the lake was as brilliantly blue as lapis lazuli. Nearby a large fat-tailed lizard scratched among the rubble. The crater aroused a deep-seated fascination; she had never seen anything like it.

'What's that lizard doing?' she wondered.

'Looking for a suitable place to lay its eggs.'

'Isn't this a dangerous location to do that?'

'Indeed, and for us too, though I have dwelt here more than a century.'

She opened her mouth and closed it again. In her part of the world the normal lifespan (for those not sent to the war) was less than sixty years, though a few people lived longer. Gilhaelith clearly was not a normal old human like her. And yet he did not appear to be Aachim, as Malien was.

The sun slanted in on her face. It felt wonderful to be warm. 'Could I look over the other side?'

He wheeled her across so she could see down the outer slope to the forest. It was luxuriantly different from the impoverished forests around her manufactory.

'That's where I . . . crashed?' she asked.

'Back the other way.' He pointed. 'The construct is damaged, but I think it can be repaired.'

She did not have the strength for question and answer, nor for thinking about what had caused the crash. For some reason she couldn't explain, she did not want him to know about the capricious amplimet. 'It doesn't matter. Nothing matters now . . .'

The sun was beating down on her head. She felt ill and Gilhaelith's looming presence discomforted her.

'I'd like to go back to my room, please.'

The servants wheeled her away, but an hour later she was still sweating. Gilhaelith had not questioned her. He must want something from her, otherwise he would not have treated her so well. What was it? Her helplessness was terrifying.

Tiaan's second day began the same way as the first, with embarrassing toilet operations by Alie, a pale fleshy woman with a figure like a bale of wool and a square face utterly devoid of expression. Breakfast was spooned into her as if she was a baby. Alie talked the entire time she was in the room, but her words were empty. It was so tiresome that Tiaan closed her eyes and turned away.

'Bitch thinks she's better than us,' Alie said to the healer on the way out.

'And she can't even wipe her arse,' Gurteys agreed. 'What is the master thinking?'

Tiaan bit her lip. Why did they resent her so? She hadn't said a thing to them.

Gurteys plied her healer's art with all the indifference of the true professional, and so roughly that it hurt. In the afternoon she reappeared with a contraption made of wood and leather. Rolling Tiaan onto her side, she propped her in place with cushions and pulled her gown down to the waist.

'What are you doing?' Tiaan asked.

Gurteys fitted the rows of straps around Tiaan's chest, belly and hips and pulled them tight until they pinched the skin. She adjusted the position of the wooden spars. 'The brace will ensure the bones set in place.'

The brace was uncomfortable lying down. Tiaan could not imagine what it would be like sitting up. 'How long will I have to wear it?'

'How would I know?'

'Well, you're *supposed* to be the healer.'

'A month. Two? Until your back is healed.' A bell rang and Gurteys hurried out, leaving Tiaan's garments around her waist.

Gilhaelith thrust the door open. He had been in several times today, but this time, realising that she was half-undressed, he spun on one foot and dashed from the room, shouting orders. Gurteys reappeared, roughly jerking Tiaan's gown over her shoulders. 'You're more trouble than you're worth!' she said between clenched teeth.

'I didn't say a thing,' cried Tiaan, but the healer had gone. Why had Gilhaelith reacted that way?

NINETEEN

The balloon, carrying no more weight than Nish and the brazier, drifted high and fast. The streaming winds carried it across the Filallor Range, which ran south from the western end of the Great Mountains, separating frigid Mirrilladell from the more equable western lands. The forests of central Lauralin passed beneath unseen. Still out of it, Nish drifted north of Booreah Ngurle in the dark, slowly descending. The brazier had gone out hours ago and the air in the balloon was cooling rapidly. The craft skimmed the top of a solitary tree, floating over scrub towards a broad, sluggish river.

As the sun rose, the balloon just cleared a palisade around a vast encampment crowded with the meanest of dwellings, a refugee camp for some of the millions who had fled the fall of the great and wealthy island of Meldorin. From the top of the hill the Sea of Thurkad could barely be seen. It had rained in the night and the bare earth was an ocean of mud. Nish drifted between two decrepit dwellings before his dangling boots struck the earth and the balloon lay on its side, the last air sighing out of it. Its long voyage had ended.

Nish, roused by his impact with the mud, groaned. Though he was half-frozen, his injuries throbbed. Within a minute he was surrounded by people, all dirty, hungry and staring. Paying him no heed, they took the balloon and brazier apart with ruthless efficiency. In ten minutes every scrap had disappeared, even the scorched rope ladder he had tied himself to. They went through his pockets, removing everything but the lint. The coat vanished from his back but they left him the rest of his clothes. Then the crowd evaporated.

He sat up, still dazed. He had no idea where he was, though it was not cold enough to be Mirrilladell. The place stank of sour water and human waste.

Someone shouted. Drums rattled. He was about to call for help when a small figure came flying out from behind the nearest hut.

'Quick!' hissed a young voice. It was a boy of eleven or twelve, a skinny lad. He used the common tongue of the west, in which Nish had become fluent during his days as a merchant's scribe. 'Guards coming.'

'That's just as well,' said Nish. 'I've been robbed and I –'

'Come on!' The boy hauled him by the hand. 'If they find you, they'll beat you senseless.'

'But I don't come from here,' Nish began. Prudence overcame outrage. He staggered after the boy, around the corner, down between the rows and into a sodden space underneath one of the huts. It was barely high enough to crawl through. When he was well inside, the boy shoved a rotting piece of timber against the entry.

'Shh!' he said.

'But –' Nish began.

'Wait!'

Nish peered through the crack. The rattle of drums came closer and shortly a squad of guards passed by. Two of them kicked open the door of a hut and stormed inside. Dragging an elderly man from the hovel, they began beating him about the back and body with their sticks. 'Get to work, you lazy swine! No work, no eat!'

The other soldier made a mark on his slate. They proceeded to the next hut, and the one after, all the way down the line. The old man reeled off in the other direction.

'What is this place?' Nish asked. It was all too much to take in.

'It's supposed to be a refugee camp,' said the boy. 'It's really a

187

slave city. We work fourteen hours a day, every day of the week, and all we get for it is pig swill.' The boy seemed older than his years. No doubt kids grew up quickly here, those that survived.

A hundred questions swirled in his head but Nish was too dazed to ask them. 'My name is Cryl-Nish Hlar, son of Jal-Nish Hlar. He is the perquisitor for Einunar.' It could not hurt to establish that at the beginning.

'A perquisitor!' whispered the boy.

'I'm just an artificer. I fix weapons, and clankers.'

The boy seemed, if anything, even more impressed. 'Back home, I used to watch the clankers go by. I always wanted to ride up on top with the shooter. Can you get me a ride?'

'I will, when I get out of here. You can call me Nish, if you like.' He held out his hand, forgetting the burn.

'I'm Colm,' said the boy, squeezing hard. A blister popped and Nish winced. 'My home was in Bannador, but I have no home any more.'

'Where's Bannador?' Nish asked.

'Across the sea; in the mountains.'

'What sea?' Nish had no idea where he was.

'The Sea of Thurkad, of course,' the boy said scornfully. 'Don't you know anything?'

'I come from a long way away.'

'Where are you from?'

'Einunar.'

'Never heard of it.'

'It's on the other side of the world. So this camp is near the sea?'

Colm pointed. 'It's only half a league, that way.'

'Are we near a city?' The Sea of Thurkad was long and Nish was desperately trying to find some geographical point to hang on to.

'Nilkerrand is up the coast. Not far.'

'I don't know that place,' he said. 'Can you give me any other names?'

'Nilkerrand is directly across the sea from Thurkad. Surely even *you* have heard of it?'

'Of course I've heard of Thurkad,' said Nish. For millennia it had been the most famous city in the world, the richest, and certainly, to the prudish minds of distant Einunar, the wickedest. 'It fell to the enemy a while back, didn't it?'

'Last autumn. Why were you hanging onto that . . . bladder thing?'

'I floated across the Great Mountains on it.'

'Just like that?' Colm asked, incredulously.

'There used to be a basket but I was attacked by a savage beast called a nylatl, the most horrible creature you have ever seen. It's got claws as long as my fingers, and teeth nearly as big. Its spines are poisoned and it squirts venom out through a blue tongue. I set fire to the basket and exploded the beast to bits. It was the only way to survive.'

'Really?' said the boy, in a tone that suggested he did not believe a word of it.

'Yes, *really*!' Nish pulled up his trouser leg, showing the savage lacerations to his calf and the teeth marks on either side, which were red, swollen and hot to the touch. 'And see this,' he probed his still-swollen lips with a fingertip, 'that's where it got me with its poison. It was aiming for my eyes.'

Colm was impressed. 'I've never met a real hero. I bet you could fight a lyrinx and win.'

'I bet I couldn't,' said Nish. 'A real hero knows when to fight and when to run.'

'Like everyone here,' sneered Colm. 'The camp is full of cowards. Even my father ran when the lyrinx came.'

'My father didn't,' said Nish, 'but I wish he had. A lyrinx ripped his face open and tore his arm so badly that we had to cut it off.' He clenched his fist, grimaced and examined it in the dim light. There was a blister the width of his palm, and smaller ones along his fingers.

Now Colm was positively awe-stricken. 'Was that where you wiped the venom off?'

'No, that's where I pulled red-hot coals out of the brazier to set fire to the beast.'

Colm went quiet. Nish looked out through the crack but the yard was empty. All he saw was beaten earth and mud. There was not even a weed to be seen. Everything burnable had been burnt, and everything edible, eaten.

'I've been praying for a real hero,' the boy said softly. 'We really need help, Nish. Our home is gone, where we lived for more than a thousand years. We've even lost our Histories, all but what mother and father remember, and they won't talk about it any more. They've given up! I hate them sometimes. Why won't they fight? Will you help us, Nish?'

'I'm on a secret mission,' Nish replied, thinking fast. He needed aid and only this lad, and his parents, could give it. However, the island of Meldorin was swarming with lyrinx, and anyone who went there would be eaten. 'For the scrutator! I'm sorry, Colm. It's the war.'

'Of course,' Colm said dully. 'I understand. Where were you going?'

'I can't tell you that. But there is something you can do for me.'

The boy's eyes were shining. 'But you're a hero.'

'I've lost my balloon, and those thieves stole everything I own. I've got to get out of here and . . . do my job.'

'Of course I'll help you. I'll do anything. And in return . . .' He caught Nish's eye, a desperately young lad. 'In return, when all this is over, will you help me get back my heritage?'

What could Nish say? 'I give you my word, Colm. When the war is over, I will help you.' He held out his hand. The lad took it and there were tears of gratitude in his eyes. 'But first, I have to get out of this place.'

'The guards won't let anyone go.'

'I'll tell them who I am. That will make them sit up.'

'Do you have papers or a special pass?'

Nish had nothing. Most of his gear had been lost when the basket burned; the rest stolen the instant he arrived. 'No, but I represent the scrutator.'

'Not ours! They don't like foreigners in this country and the guards have heard every story in the world. They won't listen. They'll just beat you senseless and throw you in the mud. They say we should have been left to the lyrinx.'

'People must come in and out, in a camp this big.'

'Only soldiers. Sometimes they take the young women out, but they don't bring them back. My big sister is hiding.'

Nish could imagine why, all too well. The war was tearing society apart and in places like this the only thing that mattered was power. Getting it and keeping it.

'Perhaps I could dress up as a woman,' Nish said, half-joking.

Colm inspected Nish's swollen face and sturdy body. 'They wouldn't take *you*, Nish.'

I deserved that, Nish thought. 'Could I dig my way out?'

'The soil is only this deep.' Colm spread his fingers. 'And under it, there's rock.'

'What about over the fence?'

'The guards hang the bodies on the spikes. *After* they've finished with them.'

Nish shivered. His options were rapidly running out. 'Do your mother and father know anyone important?'

'I don't think so,' said the boy. 'I'll take you to meet them when it's dark. It's not safe in daytime. You haven't got a sign.'

'A sign?'

Colm held out his hand. On the back was a red, raised scar of jagged lines, like a jumble of triangles.

'Did the guards do that to you?'

Colm nodded. 'They did it to everyone, even the babies. With quicklime!'

'It must have hurt.'

'It still does, sometimes, and that was six months ago.'

'You've been here *six months*?'

'Yes, but we lost our home a long time before that. On my ninth birthday.'

'How old are you now, Colm?'

'Twelve and a half. I can join the army when I'm fourteen, if I'm big enough.'

'Don't be in too much of a hurry,' said Nish.

'I'll be signing up on my birthday,' said the boy proudly. 'We have to fight for what is ours, else we may as well lie down and die.'

Nish felt a thousand years old, though he was only twenty. Colm would be sent to the front with minimal training and would probably be dead in a month. The tragedy had been played out a million times and was not going to end until humanity was no more. Well, perhaps what he, Nish, knew might make the difference, if only he could get out of here and find someone in authority.

From not far away came the barking of hounds. Someone screamed. 'Come on!' said Colm. 'They've brought the dogs in. If they catch us, they'll beat us half to death.'

Nish wormed his way out, the boy beside him. 'Where are we going?'

Colm had his head around the corner. 'It's clear. Follow me.'

They ran a zigzag path between the hovels, Nish doing exactly as the boy told him to. Everything stank here. They dropped into a gully running with human waste, leapt the brown stream and continued along the other side. The ground was bare apart from bright-green, slimy strands of algae growing in the flow. Further down, Colm ducked into an embayment where a flood had undercut the bank, leaving a hollow the size of a small barrel.

'This isn't much of a hiding place,' Nish said doubtfully.

Colm dug a chip of stone out of the wall with one finger, tossed it aside and excavated another. 'We'll only be here a minute. Give me your hand.'

Nish held it out. Colm turned the chip of stone around until he had a sharp edge and scored it across the back of Nish's hand.

Nish yelped and tore his hand away. 'What are you doing?'

'You've got to have a mark,' said the boy. 'Without it, you're *nothing*!'

Nish gave him his hand. The boy pressed harder, making a series of bloody cuts. Nish flinched.

'It's only a scratch,' Colm said scornfully.

'Heroes still feel pain, Colm.'

When it was done, Colm dabbed the surplus blood away, comparing the marks with the raised red welts on the back of his own hand. 'It's not very good, but it will probably look like the real thing, from a distance.'

'What if they check it and discover it's not?'

'You could run for your life, but it'll be worse when they catch you. Best thing is to just take the beating.'

'Why do the guards hate us so much?' Already Nish felt it was 'us' and 'them'.

'It's not the guards who will beat you in the workhouse. It's the boss refugees. They don't want any attention, in case their own schemes are found out.'

They were off again, up the stinking gully, then towards a large ramshackle building made of reused timber. It looked as if a dozen houses, all different, had been pulled down to make it. A sentry, dressed in clothes as ragged and filthy as the boy's, stood outside.

'How do we get in?' Nish hissed.

Colm did not answer but, after checking that the sentry was not looking, darted across the space between the gully and the side of the building, lifted a couple of loose boards and wriggled inside.

Nish only just managed it, his shoulders being as wide as the opening. He emerged in a gloomy space with timbers running along above his head, and more in front of him. Beyond were dozens of pairs of dirty feet. He was under a wide workbench that ran along the side of the building.

Colm turned right, crawling down next to the wall. Before long he stopped by a pair of grubby feet. Next was a smaller pair, clad in sadly stained and tattered slippers.

'Stay down until I say so,' he whispered in Nish's ear, and with a twisting movement like an eel on a hook, Colm was out, up and standing between the two pairs of feet.

'Where have you been, Colm?' came a weary, worn-out female voice. 'I've been worried sick about you.'

'Just around,' said Colm. 'I –'

'Get to work, son.' The man's voice was equally lifeless. 'We're behind in our quota and your slackness –'

'I've found him!' Colm hissed.

'Can you fix this one?' said his mother as if he had not spoken. 'It doesn't want to go together again.'

193

Silence, in which there was an occasional click or rattle, a muffled curse.

'I've found the man who floated in on the balloon.'

'Lose him! They're looking for him and we don't want to attract attention to ourselves, boy. I've told you that a hundred times.'

'But –'

'It's dangerous, Colm,' said the dead voice. 'Keep your head down. Do your work. Say nothing. Never catch anyone's eye.'

'I might as well be *dead*!'

'He's a spy! Or in the pay of the enemy. We could all die if he's linked to us. And there's your sisters to think of, Colm. It'll be worse for them. I didn't think I'd have to remind *you* of that.'

'He's a hero!' Colm said stubbornly. 'He's going to help us get Gothryme back.'

'It's gone forever,' snapped the man. 'We're refugees and we will never get anything back. We're lucky to be alive.'

'We're *unlucky* to be alive,' said Colm. 'What's the point to life when we've lost everything, even our Histories?'

'We can't eat our Histories.'

'I'm going to go back if it takes me all my life. Gothryme is my due and I won't give it up.'

'Anything you can't carry on your back is worthless; it's like chaining yourself to a rock.'

'You don't even tell us our family Histories any more.'

'If you cling to the past, you'll never make a new future.'

'This man can help us. You should hear what he's done, father. He's a hero.'

Smack. Colm fell to his knees. For a second his eyes met Nish's, then he climbed to his feet again.

'I *won't* hear another word, son,' said the father. 'The man is a liar and you're a little fool for being taken in by him.

TWENTY

Nish pulled himself against the wall, where it was darkest. His pockets were empty. He had not a copper nyd to his name, nor anything else he could use to buy or bribe his way out. He had no weapons, no means of defending himself. All he had were his wits. He might have given way to despair, but lately Nish had thought his way out of a number of difficult situations. Leaning back, he closed his eyes and went through his options. He could only see three.

Declare himself to the guards at the gate, tell them who he was and where he had come from. Likely result: a merciless beating and being thrown back into the camp, where the powers that ran it could well give him another beating. It didn't seem worth the risk.

Try to get over the palisade in the night and escape. Colm's little remark made that into an unpalatable option, though Nish knew that guards were seldom as vigilant as rumour had it. On a dark night, or a rainy one, there must be a chance.

Failing that, let's see what he could do with the boy. Colm had proven trustworthy but Nish was wary of pressing him too hard. Family always came first.

He spent the whole day under the table. It grew increasingly hot and humid until Nish could think of nothing but cool water. His last drink had been with the scrutator the previous day. Had he really come all this way in only a day? He had no idea how long he'd been unconscious. It felt like another year; another life. The scrutator would not be back to the manufactory yet, and Ullii . . . Poor Ullii. How was she coping? He could still hear her screams.

The hours dragged by. The building stank of unwashed bodies. There was not a breath of fresh air to be had and he felt as if he were suffocating. Nish looked up at the underside of the bench, where the grain of the timber made sawtooth patterns reminiscent of the crest of a lyrinx. He swallowed.

Considering so many people worked here, the workhouse was uncannily quiet. All he heard was the shuffle of feet, an occasional clearing of the throat and the muted tap and click of mechanical parts being put together. Nish manoeuvred an eye to a gap between the boards, looking up along the bench. The workers were putting together small clockwork mechanisms, possibly for something like a clanker.

Thwack. Someone let out a reedy scream, quickly cut off.

'Half-rations for three days. Work harder!' The voice was close by.

Nish made himself as small as possible but felt sure he would be discovered. A thick pair of hairy calves went by, attached to the filthiest feet he had ever seen. They smelled like ordure.

The feet stopped. Something struck the bench above Nish's head so hard that small objects jumped. He did not dare to breathe. He could hear the heavy breath of the supervisor. The room was completely silent. Everyone else was as afraid as he was. Nish's nose began to itch but he resisted the urge to scratch it.

'Get on with your work!' the man roared and the dirty feet moved away. The clicking and tapping resumed.

Nish endured the day. Should he declare himself, or leave it to the boy? He waited. In the early afternoon the work stopped briefly while lunch was taken at the benches. Nish could smell the water by then and had begun to shake with hunger. He was practically fainting when a thin hand reached below the bench, holding a battered wooden mug.

Nish drained it in a single swallow and immediately regretted that he had not made it last. He put the mug into the waiting hand. Shortly it reappeared with a generous chunk of black bread.

Nish eked that out, taking the tiniest of nibbles, which was just as well since it was full of hard, burnt grain and grit he might have broken a tooth on. After that he pillowed his head on his arms and slept.

When he jolted awake it was dark outside but the work was still going on. What had disturbed him?

'Don't start that again,' Colm's father hissed. 'You're not too old for a beating, boy!'

'He's *here*,' Colm whispered.

'What are you talking about?'

'The man is right here, under the bench. His name is Cryl-Nish Hlar and his father is a *perquisitor*.'

The silence stretched out, then the man dropped a wooden spanner, bent down to pick it up and stared at Nish.

Nish held his gaze. 'It's true,' he said softly. 'He is Jal-Nish Hlar, Perquisitor for Einunar, and I have come all this way on scrutator's business. I beg your help in his name.'

The man ducked away again, forgetting his spanner. Reaching forward, Nish handed it up to him.

'Which scrutator?' Colm's father said out of the corner of his mouth.

'Xervish Flydd!'

The work resumed on the bench, and only some minutes later did Nish hear any more.

'You have ruined us, Colm,' his mother muttered. 'This will be the end of your family.'

'Why couldn't you mind your own business?' his father said. There was no anger in him now; just despair. 'Why, Colm?'

'You taught me to do what I thought was right, no matter how painful.'

'Those rules don't apply any more,' his father said in a low voice.

'Just look at the poor man! He's got wounds everywhere but it hasn't stopped *him*.'

Both mother and father bent down, inspected Nish, then stood up again.

'Of course you can't denounce him,' said Colm's mother. 'That would also attract attention.'

'We have to,' said the father.

'He's not much more than a boy,' muttered the mother. 'He doesn't even have a proper beard.'

'Tell him to go, boy,' said Colm's father.

'I won't betray him. *You* tell him.'

Again Nish heard a slap, but thankfully Colm remained defiant.

'If he is a perquisitor's son,' the mother quavered, 'and on scrutator's work, to refuse him will mean our deaths.'

A metal cover-plate was knocked off the bench. The father's face appeared in front of Nish. The mother and son closed up on either side. 'What business?'

'I can't tell you, but I carry information vital to the war. I must find a way to escape and meet a querist or perquisitor. Or failing that, an officer in the army.'

'Very well,' said the father. 'I know my duty. We will be leaving shortly to go back to our quarters for the night. When I give the signal, come out between me and Colm. Walk carefully, looking down. Show me your hand.'

Nish held it out and the man examined the bloody scratches. 'It *may* do, if they don't look too closely. We have no friends here, but people know us, and in this camp anyone will betray their neighbour for an extra bowl of fishhead soup.'

The call came. Nish ducked out from under the bench and stood up between Colm and his father, who was a big man, nearly a head taller than Nish. He took a sideways glance. The building had three aisles and a line of people was forming along each of them. There would have been hundreds. Most were as haggard, thin and dirty as the boy. Few looked anywhere but at the earth floor.

The line crept forward. Nish felt a fluttering in his stomach. He had saved himself several times, by his own initiative, assisted by a generous helping of good fortune. Fortune could turn against him just as swiftly, and then he would die.

They approached the door, where each of the workers was delivered a dollop of gruel into their mug, and a slab of black bread. Nish had no mug. He was going to fall at the first hurdle. Panic told him to run but he fought it. He looked back. The father had realised the problem but did not know what to do about it. Nish was going to be discovered with the family and they would all be punished.

It was too late to get out of the way; they were only half a dozen places from the end of the line. Nish leaned forward. 'I've no mug,' he whispered in Colm's ear.

Colm passed his own back, picked up a fragment of metal lying on the bench and, with an unobtrusive flick, sent it flying down the row. It struck a hairy man on his protruding ear. He whirled and swung a blow at the man behind him, who struck back.

The fellow serving the slops came out from behind his bench, flailing at the struggling men with his wooden ladle. Colm snatched a mug from the back of the bench and held it out.

The fight was over quickly. No one wanted to attract the attention of the guards outside. The line paced by, Nish received his ration of slops and his lump of bread, the serving man taking no notice of him, and then they were through the door.

He passed the guards and was halfway across the yard when one yelled, 'Hey you!'

Nish froze, whereupon a hard hand went down on his shoulder and squeezed. 'Keep going. Don't look around.'

Nish did as he was told, expecting the soldiers to come running after him, but no one did. As he rounded the corner he saw, out of the corner of his eye, an unfortunate fellow being beaten between three laughing guards.

'It's their game,' said the father. 'Some poor wretch always turns around, and then they beat him for it.'

It took an anxious ten minutes to cross through the labyrinth of huts, shacks and hovels to the dismal space Colm and his family called home. Built from scraps of timber and canvas, chinked in with grass and mud, it was meaner than the hut of any primitive tribesman.

Inside it was barely long enough for the father to lie down. The earth floor was covered in bracken and reeds. The walls were hand-smeared mud, the roof a piece of rotting canvas smaller than a single bedsheet. They had nothing else in the world.

Two girls crouched within. The older, who might have been fifteen, was a small, unattractive creature, her hair positively dripping grease, her face full of spots and scars, and her teeth horrible black stumps. The younger, no more than five, was pretty, with wavy chestnut hair and green eyes.

'This is Cryl-Nish Hlar,' said the father, whose name was given as Oinan. 'He is an important man. He will stay with us for a little while and we are going to look after him. No one will ever mention his name. Cryl-Nish, this is my wife Tinketil, my older daughter, Ketila, and my other daughter, Fransi.'

Ketila hid her face, and a flush crept up her throat. Poor girl, Nish thought, to suffer such a handicap, especially when her sister is such a beauty. He shook hands with Oinan, with Tinketil and with a solemn, staring Fransi. Ketila would not look at him. Her hands fluttered over her mouth.

'Ketila,' said Oinan sternly.

Putting one hand behind her back, she held out the other. Nish took it and she gave him a little shy smile that went all the way up to her eyes. It revealed perfect white teeth, and it quite transformed her. She must have been wearing something in her mouth to make them look so horrible. Perhaps the spots and the scars were fake too.

'Teeth, Kettie!' snapped Oinan.

'They hurt, father,' Ketila said, soft and pleading.

'Oh, let her be,' said the mother. 'Have you no brains at all, husband? She can put them back if anyone comes.'

Tinketil boiled a tin mug of water over a handful of roots, cleaned Nish's wounds and covered them with precious lard.

The parents said no more about Nish, nor spoke to him either. After a while Ketila and Fransi settled on the bracken against the far wall. Nish lay on his side facing the entrance. Oinan and Tinketil whispered to each other for a long while, a furious argument for all that they spoke so softly. Nish did not catch a word of it and finally he slept.

He was woken before dawn by a flickering light at the back of the hut. Tinketil was kneeling in front of Ketila, applying the spots to her face with a clump of hair glued into the split end of a twig. The smaller girl was still asleep. Oinan was not there.

Shortly he reappeared, carrying his dinner mug. 'Hold out your hand, Cryl-Nish.'

Nish did as he was told and Oinan applied white powder to the back with a spoon, tracing out the pattern Colm had scratched the previous day. The mixture immediately began to burn and Nish had to grit his teeth.

'It only takes a few minutes,' the man said.

They were all staring at him. He wanted to weep with the pain, but they had gone through it and so could he. He counted down the seconds, then Oinan washed the quicklime off. It had taken most of the skin with it, leaving raw, weeping flesh.

'You're one of us now,' said Oinan.

A gong sounded and everyone hurried to their workhouses. So the day passed, much as the previous one had, except that Nish now had to work. Like everyone else, he was required to assemble the clockwork mechanisms, and for all his years of artificing Nish proved the slowest of all.

Back in the hut that night, as Tinketil mended a shirt by the light of a pithy reed smeared with rancid fat, Nish became aware that Ketila was watching him, though every time he looked in her direction she glanced away. She had washed her face and tied back her hair. She was not as beautiful as Fransi, but she was charmingly fresh and lovely, and Nish liked her.

Six months ago he might have taken advantage of her, had the opportunity come, but he was a wiser and a less selfish man now. Nish was no saint, but he could see her yearning. Not for him, particularly, and certainly not for the kinds of fleshy grapplings he dreamed about. Ketila was becoming a woman and wanted to be seen as one, and to be taken seriously.

'This land is so different from where I come from,' he said.

'Where do you come from, Cryl-Nish?' Her back was pressed against the wall but Ketila inclined her head towards him. Her mother noted it and smiled.

Nish looked different from the other people in the camp; there was a mystery about him. He had flown into the camp hanging from a huge balloon, and he came from the other side of the world. He had an important father and a powerful master and Ketila knew, because Colm had told them, about his great deeds and heroic struggle with the nylatl. She had seen the tooth and claw marks in his leg, when Tinketil dressed the wounds. To her, he was not short, plain and lacking in a beard. He was fascinating, exotic, bold and brave. And he spoke to her as if she was important.

'I was born in Fassafarn,' said Nish, 'which is almost as far as you can go east from here. It is the chief city of the province of Einunar, at the furthest end of the Great Mountains.'

'What is it like there?' she asked softly.

'There are enormous mountains covered in snow all year round, and valleys so deep you can hardly see the bottom . . .'

'I was born in Bannador,' she said. 'We also have big mountains.'

'These ones are so big that when the wind blows they write their names in the sky, and the glaciers . . .'

'What are glaciers, Cryl-Nish?'

'Rivers of ice that flow down from ice caps half a thousand spans thick, grinding out the bottoms of mighty valleys and not stopping until they reach the sea. Sometimes they break into chunks of ice as big as islands and float across the ocean. Many a sailor has seen an iceberg loom up out of the foggy night and knows that his little ship was going straight to the bottom and he with it, never to see his wife and his darling daughters again.'

Nish was enjoying his rhetoric, though at the last the girl bit her lip and he turned to safer waters. 'We have great snow bears in the mountains, white beasts so big that they could not get through the door of a house. I saw one once and it was almost two spans high. It could have eaten a lyrinx for breakfast.'

Ketila brightened at that. 'Are they not dangerous?'

'Very dangerous, though they seldom attack people unless they get between a mother and her cubs.' Nish's eye met Tinketil's for a second.

'Have you ever killed a snow bear?' asked Ketila.

Nish felt the urge to make up a heroic story, but suppressed it. He was not sure why. 'No, Ketila, I haven't. To tell you the truth, I don't like killing things much, and snow bears are magnificent creatures.'

'You killed the nylatl.' They had all heard that tale.

'I had to, or it would never have stopped trying to kill me. It was mad, the poor creature. The lyrinx flesh-formed it out of nothing. Did I tell you that?'

'No,' she breathed.

The whole family was listening as he told the tale of the lyrinx attack, the flesh-formed little monstrosities he had found in the ice houses on the plateau, and all that he had learned about the depraved Art since. It was a long tale, and both girls' eyelids were drooping by the time he finished it.

'Thank you,' said Ketila. 'That was a wonderful tale. You are so brave. Good night, Nish.'

'Good night.'

When they were asleep he said quietly to Oinan, who had been out earlier in the evening, 'Have you had any luck so far?'

'No. It's a delicate matter, Cryl-Nish. I have to be sure we won't be informed on before I ask my favour.'

Since there was no more he could do, Nish settled down to sleep. It was not a good start.

The weary days went by. One night, something roused Nish in the early hours of the morning. It had been a noise, far off. He looked out through the opening of the hovel. It was still pitch dark. Crawling outside, he stood up and stretched. The night was mild compared to what he was used to. The stars glittered in a clear sky. He wandered around the huts, relieved himself, yawned and headed back. Again came that noise, a faint, distant roar like an angry mob.

Fleeting across to the palisade he peered through a knothole.

It was dark outside, which was strange. Normally the guards patrolled with blazing torches, calling to one another. He went further along, to a gap between two poles, and heard that faint roar again.

Nish pulled himself up the palisade. There was not a guard in sight. He slipped his leg over and sat atop the fence as if it was a saddle. The roar was louder from here and he made out a glow in the north, from the direction of Nilkerrand.

A not-so-faint glow when he stood up, one foot on the outside rail, the other in the valley he had been sitting on. It looked like a fire. He knew there was no forest up that way, and it was too early in the season for the fields to be burning. It must be in the city.

The sound came on the wind, louder now, a terrified mob. Flames shot up. Nilkerrand was burning, its hundred thousand inhabitants running for their lives, and the guards of the refugee camp had fled. The battlefront must have moved faster than anyone expected. It was almost on them.

Racing back to the hovel, Nish shook Oinan and Tinketil awake. 'Get up!' he hissed. 'Nilkerrand is burning and the guards have run away. The enemy is upon us.'

They must have been used to fleeing in the night for they woke instantly and pulled their boots on. Nish felt for his own. Tinketil woke the children, who were just as silent and grimly efficient. In a reed-light Nish saw Ketila's eyes on him again.

'I'll wake the camp,' Nish said, crawling out.

Oinan caught his leg. 'There'll be a stampede. We'll never get out.'

'I can't let everyone be slaughtered in their beds. How will I find you?'

'Which way, Colm?' cried Oinan.

'Down the gully where the waste runs,' said the boy without hesitation. 'We can get through the fence at the far end, if there are no guards at all.'

'I'll meet you there,' said Nish, 'but if I don't come, go without me.'

204

He ran down the row to where the great gong hung by the workhouse. Snatching up the mallet, he thumped the gong, one, two, three.

There were cries all over the camp. 'Wake!' he roared. 'Nilkerrand is burning and the enemy is upon us. Wake!' Giving it one last thump, he dropped the mallet. Then, thinking that it was a better weapon than his bare hands, Nish tucked it under his arm.

People were running everywhere, shouting, screaming and crashing into each other. Down the row, one of the hovels was ablaze. As he turned the corner, Nish was swept off his feet by a stampede. Holding his arms over his head, he scrunched up and waited for them to go by.

Once they passed, he crept along the walls of the buildings. A flame leapt up to his left: someone had set fire to a shanty and in its light a mob was attacking the gate. A dark figure went over the top and hurled the bar off. The gate burst open.

Nish kept going. Most of the camp was behind him now. Stumbling along in the dark, he fell off the edge of an embankment, skidded in greasy clay and slid all the way to the bottom. Judging by the putrid smell, he was in the gully. The drain must be just to his right. Well, that saved him looking for it.

He picked his way down. Several others must have had the same idea, for he could see figures further along. Perhaps it was the family. Nish did not call out in case it was not. A vibrating shriek of terror came from behind, then screams from hundreds of massed throats. Was it the enemy? He had to know. Scrambling up the side of the gully, Nish climbed a mound, stood on tiptoes and stared towards the gate, clearly visible in the flames.

People were streaming back, screaming and trampling each other in their desperation to get away. He knew what was behind them but had to see it with his own eyes.

A great shape came over the palisade, landing in front of the flames. The silhouette was unmistakable – a massive body, crested head and leathery wings. A lyrinx. Others stormed through the gate.

Nish could not bear to watch. He hurtled down the gully, splashed through the stinking muck in the bottom and along the other side, running and running despite the agony in his injured leg. He could not ignore it, but it was a reminder of what it would be like to be eaten alive. Nish rounded the corner and the fence stood in front of him. Several of its poles had been torn away. Someone was just going through the gap. He squeezed after them, tearing his shirt.

On the other side he looked around for Colm's family, but they were nowhere to be seen.

TWENTY-ONE

Ullii was down the mine with Irisis, her only friend now that the scrutator had betrayed her and Nish abandoned her, and even Irisis was suspect. True, she had defended Ullii previously, but she had also been Nish's lover. Ullii resented that with all her jealous little heart, and took pleasure in defying Irisis whenever she could get away with it.

Dandri and Peate, the leaders of the two mining teams, were there as well, to make sure artisan or seeker did not wander into unsafe ground, and also because it was their mine and they did not like outsiders poking around in it. They were accompanied by a pair of soldiers armed with heavy crossbows. The loss of the crystals, and the discovery of that secret tunnel, had been a shocking blow. The mine was no longer their haven from the world, but an unknown and threatening place where at any moment they might find a lyrinx behind them.

They were now completing a survey of the seventh level, working in the section below Joeyn's vein. It was a dangerous area, with many sections out of bounds because the roof was too unstable. It had been a frustrating week and Ullii had found no crystal at all.

Please find something, Ullii, Irisis prayed. *Anything!* I can't bear to tell the scrutator no again. He's afraid. I saw it in his eyes last night.

'I can't see *anything*.' Ullii was standing against the wall, her arms and hands pressed to the stone. She had been saying that all day.

'All right,' said Irisis tiredly. When had she last had a decent night's sleep? 'Where to now, Dandri?'

The miner held out her map, on which she had marked in red ink all the places Ullii had been. 'We've finished this level. There's nowhere to go but down to the eighth, if the scrutator permits it.'

'I already have his authorisation,' said Irisis.

'We must have it in writing,' Peate interjected, 'since that level was expressly forbidden by the previous overseer.'

He referred to Overseer Gi-Had, her second cousin, who had been slain in that terrible battle up at the ice houses. Irisis could never forget that. Gi-Had had been a decent man, despite the fact that he'd had her flogged. Her back would bear those scars until she died.

Irisis handed Peate his copy of the letter. The miner placed his mark on it and put it in his pocket. 'Then let's make a start.'

'Tired,' said Ullii, whose sentences grew more abbreviated the more weary she became. 'Can't do any more.'

'Please, Ullii,' said Irisis. 'Just for an hour. The scrutator –' She broke off, realising her mistake.

'Lost the lattice,' Ullii said, pleased to refuse her. 'Going home.'

It was not long after dark when Irisis returned to the manufactory, but Xervish Flydd had already retired to his room. She could hardly deny him his report on the grounds of lateness, so she went there directly. The door was ajar, as if she was expected. She knocked once and pushed it open.

The room was warm, for a charcoal fire burned in a corner grate. The scrutator was at his table, clothed this time, surrounded by maps and papers. Flydd had a ruler in his hand and was measuring the distance between a series of red marks on the map, then entering figures into a column on a sheet of paper.

Unusually, he laid down his pen as she entered. 'You don't need to tell me,' he said. 'You found nothing.'

'I'm afraid not, surr.'

He leaned back in his chair and put his battered feet on the table. 'Shut the door. Sit down. Would you like a drink?'

'I can't say I'm that fond of parsnip whisky.'

'That's not what I'm offering.' He selected a green glass bottle, carefully wrapped, from one corner of his chest, levered out the bung with a little silver tool and poured a healthy slug into two glasses. 'This is *real* brandy; one hundred years old.'

They were proper glasses, made of crystal. Irisis's parents had some at home, but she had never seen any in the manufactory. She warmed the glass in her hands and took a careful sniff. It went up her nose and made her gasp.

'What are you celebrating, surr?' she asked after her eyes had stopped watering. Irisis touched her glass to his and took the gentlest of sips. It was splendid stuff, the best she'd ever tasted.

'I drink this at wakes, not weddings.' He tossed half the glass down his throat. 'You think I'm all-powerful, don't you, Irisis?'

'Er, well, I once did, surr.'

'I too have my masters, crafter, and they are less forgiving than I am. And there is another consideration. The higher you climb, the further there is to fall. I can climb no higher, for which I'm glad, though don't tell anyone I said so.'

'You have had a reprimand from the scrutators?'

'You might say that, though the Council won't couch it so bluntly. The letter begins, *Be assured, Xervish, that we are not saying we are displeased with you.* Of course, that means they are *highly* displeased. Furious!' He chuckled, which she found odd.

'What's going to happen to you? And to us?'

'You're worried that when the tower falls, it will smash all the little ants to bits. I suppose it will, *if* it falls. But I'm a fighter, Irisis, and I'm a way from beaten yet. I have friends on the Council, as well as enemies.'

She relaxed, leaned back and took another sip of the glorious brandy. Irisis seldom drank and the fumes seemed to be floating around her head, inducing a delicious haziness.

'Don't feel too reassured,' he went on. 'Another failure and I may well be done. The war is going worse than ever.'

'You can't be blamed for that!'

'I would be quick enough to take the credit, were it going well. And I *can* be blamed for the Aachim invasion, as we are calling it. Without Tiaan, it would never have occurred.'

'But you weren't anywhere near here. If anyone should be blamed, it's me!'

'Don't remind me!' he growled, draining his glass and filling it again, along with hers. 'Einunar is my province. I'm supposed to know everything that's going on, and be in control of it.'

'How badly *is* the war going?'

'Very badly!'

'People have been saying that for a long time.'

'It's been going badly for a long time, but it's going worse now. We've been losing territory for years, but not gaining any. It could be all over in twelve months, and then we'll be in pens, waiting to be eaten.'

'Is it really that hopeless?' She took a sturdy pull at her glass.

'No. We're working on a lot of . . . secret weapons. If one or two of them come off, it could make all the difference.'

'What sort of secret weapons?'

'If I told you, they would not be secret, would they? Think of the ways clankers have changed warfare compared to foot soldiers and cavalry, and apply that Art to everything we do. We could use controllers to power dozens of different kinds of devices – night lights, weapons, pumps, boats. And indeed we must, for we no longer have the labour to do otherwise.'

The thought was less comforting than it seemed. 'We're already overusing the Secret Art,' she said, 'and seeing nodes drained of their fields. I would be worried about the consequences, were I on the Council.'

'Thankfully you will never be,' he said smoothly, 'so you can leave that worry to us.'

'The enemy also have secret projects, like their flesh-forming. What if that succeeds?'

'We'll need our own devices to combat it.' He looked away. He did not want to talk about that.

Irisis had a sudden thought. 'Wasn't the querist studying their flesh-forming? I haven't seen Fyn-Mah for months.' Fyn-Mah, the querist or spymaster for the city of Tiksi, answered to the perquisitor and therefore, indirectly, to Flydd.

'She was and still is.'

'Where is she?'

'Away on Council business. Don't ask that kind of question.'

'What about the Aachim and their eleven thousand constructs? Are they with us or against us?'

'We don't know. There has been contact with them, though it wasn't fruitful.'

'What do you think?' She held out her glass for more brandy.

'I'd say they are too bitter to negotiate. Bitter that the Charon kept them as slaves on their own world. Doubly bitter that since the Forbidding was broken their world has become uninhabitable. I hear they blame us, which is a worry. We have no answer to their constructs, and maybe the lyrinx don't either. We're both weak after so much war. The Aachim are strong. What they choose to do will decide the fate of the world.'

'So how important is our work? *Really*?'

'Finding out what happened to the node is vital.'

'Then why don't we do that first?'

'Because without crystal this entire manufactory, and the others we supply with controllers, are useless. If we can't produce them, my head will soon be hanging over the gate and a new scrutator will take over. You would be out within a week. You're tainted, Irisis.'

'Who would the new scrutator be?'

'I can't talk about things like that. However, I can tell you one thing – I was premature to write off Nish's father. Perquisitor Jal-Nish Hlar has fought back from his injuries. He will always be a horror to look at, he will always be in pain, but that has only hardened his ambition. He still wants to be scrutator and there's only one way he can get there. Over my maimed and mutilated body.'

She wrapped her arms around herself. It felt as if something had just scuttled over her coffin and was clawing at the lid, trying to get in. 'Were you ever friends?'

'No. I was his mentor for a time, but that was terminated by mutual agreement. Jal-Nish is too ambitious, and ambitious people can't be trusted. They're always looking out for themselves.'

'Coming from someone who has been scrutator for thirty years, that's a bit rich!'

'I was made scrutator because I was better at what I did than anyone else. I never wanted to be on the Council, though having got there, I cling to it because I know what happens once you let go. I still think I can do the job better than anyone else, in spite of the last few months. Ah, it's hot in here. You don't mind if I take off my shirt, do you?'

'I've seen your chest before,' she said with a chuckle. 'I don't expect to lose control.'

He pulled it over his head, revealing a scarred and sinewy torso that looked as though all the flesh had been gouged out from under the skin.

'I wonder about you,' she said, fascinated. He was ugly but not grotesque. The scrutator was such a likeable man, once you got to know him, that his appearance became irrelevant.

'People do.'

'Who did such terrible things to you?'

He emptied his glass but did not answer.

She held out the bottle. 'More?'

'No, thank you. I've a job to do later on and I'll need my wits for it. The Council of Scrutators did this to me. At least, it was done at their command.'

'Why would they torture their own?' she said, appalled.

'I was not scrutator then. I was a perquisitor; a young and handsome one, rising fast. I became too full of myself, and too curious. As you know, the scrutators have the best spy network in the land. We pride ourselves on knowing everything, though of course there's no such thing as perfect knowledge. I was too clever. I pored over what everyone else had looked at, and saw something no one else had seen. I saw a pattern. People had been a little careless.'

'What are you talking about?'

He rubbed his chest, pointedly. 'Do you really want to know?'

She did not. She sipped. He reached for the bottle, drew back, then filled his glass after all. They sat in a companionable silence, listening to the crackling of the fire.

'It was about our master,' he said, now slurring just a little.

'The Council of Scrutators?'

'No, our real master. The Numinator.'

'I've never heard of him.'

'No one knows who the Numinator is, but be assured, there is a power behind the Council, working to its own purpose. It may not care who wins the war. It may have manipulated everything that's happened since the Council was formed.'

'The Numinator?' she said thoughtfully.

'Don't mention that name again! It's a death certificate. I must have had more brandy than I thought.' Suddenly he looked frail and rather vulnerable, which she found strangely endearing.

'I've also had more than is good for me,' she said, moving close. She traced the scars on his chest with a fingertip. 'You must have suffered so.'

'I did,' he said, 'and would rather not be reminded of it. Besides, you have also felt the lash.'

'And I have the scars to prove it, though they are nothing like yours.'

'I'm sure they are.'

'Would you like to see them?'

'As a matter of fact, I would.'

She unbuttoned her shirt, pulled it off and draped it over the back of the chair. Irisis had a magnificent bosom, though the rest of her did not put it to shame.

His eyes passed over her, and again. Finally he said in a hoarse voice, 'I see no scars.'

She turned her back. The creamy skin was marked across with welts that, even after half a year, had a purple tinge. He laid a hard hand on her back, quite gently. A shiver went up her neck.

'I've seen enough,' he said.

'Really?'

'Of your back, I meant.'

She turned around.

213

'Would you like to see the rest of my scars?' he said.

'That depends.'

He raised his forehead-wide eyebrow. 'On what?'

'On whether every part of you is as emaciated as your chest.'

He took off his trousers.

Irisis considered him thoughtfully. 'Am *I* the job for which you needed your wits about you?'

'You are.'

'You're not the handsomest of men, scrutator, nor the youngest. What gave you the idea that I would be interested?'

'I told you. We scrutators pride ourselves on knowing everything.'

Twenty-two

Well, thought Irisis, smiling to herself after Flydd had gone to sleep. The things they teach you in scrutator school! Easing out of bed, she looked down at him. They must have appeared quite the oddest couple, when they were at it, for he was her opposite in every physical respect. Tucking the blankets around him, she dressed, went to the bathing room and after that to her own room, but not to sleep.

Her room was small, dark and airless, like every chamber in the manufactory, and even after all this time she found it confining. As a child of the wealthy House of Stirm she'd had a room bigger than some people's homes, with views of meadow, lake and forest. Having been surrounded with beautiful things, the profound ugliness of this place was a drain upon her soul. Her work was, too. Irisis had always wanted to be a jeweller but her family would not hear of it. For four generations they had been crafters or better, and it was her duty to raise them back to the pedestal they had slipped from.

Irisis hated them for it, but with the world at war she had no choice. Family and Histories were everything to her and she could not go against them. She had become an artisan, and was now crafter, but her mother demanded more. She must rise to chanic, the pinnacle of the artisan's profession. Irisis was going

215

to, though not for herself. She still planned to be a jeweller once the war was over.

Her gaze wandered the walls, which were decorated with things she had made in her spare time, mostly miniatures created of silver, plentiful here, and semi-precious gems. They gave her more pleasure than anything she had done as an artisan. It was a canker in her soul. Many women in the manu-factory wore jewellery she had made, which was remarkably fine. But making jewellery did not aid the war, and the war had to come first. She understood that, and accepted it, but it was not enough.

Irisis sighed and turned her mind to duty. The mountain might be full of crystal but not even Ullii could sense it through a league of rock. However, if the miners could get her close enough, Ullii would see the crystals like plums in a pudding, and then it would just be a matter of mining them out.

The failing nodes were another matter. Finding out what had gone wrong with them was vital to the war, and for the scrutator to have given her the job meant that he was unhappy with the work of the other teams.

But I don't know enough, Irisis thought. I don't know any-thing about nodes, except that's where the field comes from. This is a job for a mancer, not an artisan, and I'm neither. I can't do it.

It became clear, as the night wore on, that she really only had one option. She must go to the scrutator and confess.

She knocked on his door at six in the morning, carrying a loaded tray.

'Yes?'

She put the tray on the bed, since his table was littered with work. Flydd laid the pen aside, rubbed his temples and sniffed appreciatively.

'That smells nice. I'll bet a bottle of last night's brandy you didn't get it from the refectory.'

'I made it,' she said. 'Specially.'

He gave her a keen stare, picked up the tray and placed it on his maps and papers. He took the cloth off to reveal freshly baked buns, a piece of grilled fish, still hot, and a bowl of ginger tea.

'Will you join me?' He indicated the other chair.

'No, thank you. I've already eaten.' That was a lie, but she did not want to share food with him. It would make it even harder.

'All the more for me.' He broke a piece of pink flesh from the fish with his eating sticks and ate it with relish. 'Very good!' He tore a bun in half. 'Is there nothing you *can't* do well, Irisis?'

She did not answer, just sat watching, enjoying his pleasure in the meal. He sipped his tea, stirred honey into it with a crooked finger and looked up at her.

'Of course I know you want something, crafter. What is it?'

The lump in her stomach felt like a pumpkin. She caught his eye and for once had to look away. She liked the man; they had been lovers. How could she let him down like this? But then, how could she not tell him? He had to know.

'I want to confess. No, that's not true. I *have* to confess. I cannot bear it any longer.'

He considered his plate, selecting a choice morsel of fish, and licked his lips. How could he be so casual?

'Confess, Irisis? You surprise me. What can you possibly have to confess to *me*?'

It burst out of her. 'I'm a fraud, scrutator. I can't draw power from the field. I lost the talent when I was a child of four and I've never been able to get it back. I've been lying and cheating ever since. I can't do the job and I can't possibly help you see into the node and find out what's gone wrong with it.'

'But you *do* do the job, Irisis. This manufactory produces the best controllers in the east, and more quickly than most. The Council is rather pleased with *your* work.'

'But . . .'

'Besides, we *know* you have drawn power. You did it up on the high plateau when the clanker controllers had to be re-tuned to that strange double node. Fyn-Mah told me so.'

'That was . . . Ullii showed me the way, surr.'

'I don't answer to "surr" from my lover, Irisis.'

'Xervish –' The name felt wrong; she could hardly bring

217

herself to use it. 'It was Ullii's doing, Xervish. She showed me the path and power just flooded from the field. I could not have done it on my own.'

'But I'm sending Ullii with you to the node. Where is the problem?'

'I'm not what I'm supposed to be.'

'None of us are what we're supposed to be. I'm a pragmatic man. It's the result that counts. You worked well with the seeker so I trust you will again, artisan.'

'I don't answer to artisan from my lover, Xervish.'

'I'm sorry. The scrutator in me.'

'I prefer the other meaning,' she said wickedly.

He smiled. 'Ah, yes. Very good. Might . . !' He hesitated, unsure of himself for once. 'Might there be further opportunities in that regard, do you think?'

She pretended to consider it, blank-faced. Her eyes met his. 'I'm mindful that we each have a duty to perform, Xervish.'

'I prefer the other meaning,' he grinned.

'Er, I'm not sure I take your point, Xervish.'

'You will, later! A duty, to *perform*!'

She lay back on the bed and closed her eyes, listening to the clacking of his eating sticks. The scrutator was a noisy eater and drank his tea with loud, appreciative slurps. It did not bother her; that was good manners in the country he came from.

She felt very tired. Irisis had not slept all night, and sparring with Flydd was emotionally exhausting. What was more, it still had not solved the problem.

'Another thing, Xervish.'

He gulped the last of the bowl, wiped his mouth on the cloth and swung around. 'You're thinking that you don't know enough about nodes. That this is really mancer's work and you can't do it.'

'Precisely.'

'You won't be going alone,' said Flydd.

'Who will be going with me?'

'I'll let you know when the time comes.'

Irisis was not at her best that day. They were now surveying on the eighth level. She was desperately tired and not up to dealing with a fractious, childlike Ullii who suffered constant headaches and would curl up in the dark at the least provocation. The miners, a rough lot at the best of times, were having trouble restraining their tempers. They were bitter about the loss of the reward, more so that the enemy had infiltrated their mine, not to mention anxious at the danger of working beneath such unstable rock. Dandri had already shouted at Ullii twice. If it happened again, it would put paid to any useful seeking for the rest of the day.

'This is hopeless,' Irisis said to Peate as they trudged down another tunnel so narrow that the sides scraped against her shoulders. 'Isn't there any way to tell where to look for crystal?'

'The veins wander where they want to. And often, in this mine, the best veins are in the most dangerous areas. Like –' He looked away down the tunnel.

Irisis sensed that there was something she was not being told, or shown. They seemed to have been going around in a circle.

'Could I see the map of this level, please?'

'That's miner's business,' he muttered, rolling it up.

She put out her hand.

He held the map behind his back. 'You have no right? Anyway, you'd never understand it.'

'Would you like me to get an order from the scrutator?' she said coldly.

'Just give her the blasted map, Peate!' shouted Dandri, and marched off into the darkness.

Peate's arm dropped to his side. He did not offer her the map, nor resist when she took it. His face had assumed that mulish expression she had seen so often on miners over the years.

The map was, of course, perfectly comprehensible. The tunnels were marked with double lines whose width varied according to the size of the tunnel. Shafts were shown with circles; arrows indicated whether they went up or down. Markings along the sides of the tunnel were in symbols she did not understand, though she presumed they described the character of the rock and the sources of ore or crystal. The places Ullii had surveyed, fruit-lessly, were marked in red. The red marks formed an irregular 'U' shape around a central core of tunnels.

'We've not been in this area at all,' she said to the miner.

'Too dangerous,' said Peate.

'Is that what these black jags show? Bad rock?'

'Yes!'

'I'd still like to go in there.'

He threw down his pick. 'Then you can go alone!'

'I will. Give me your lantern.'

He passed it to her, Irisis called Ullii and led her away. Around the corner, she said to the seeker, 'We must go down here. Is that all right?'

'Yes,' said Ullii. 'We can go anywhere you want.'

'You're not afraid to go without the miners?'

'Don't like Peate. He is an angry man.'

'The rock is bad down here,' said Irisis. 'It might fall and kill us.'

'I know you'll look after me.'

Irisis sighed. 'Let's get to work.'

'Nothing *here* either?' said Irisis about six hours later. The silent darkness of the mine was getting to her. She had been edgy from the moment she'd entered.

Ullii shook her head. 'Head hurts. Want to go home.'

'Let's just look around the corner first.'

Irisis trudged off. Ullii plodded after her. It was no wonder the seeker's head was aching; the air was really bad down here. It had a faintly sulphurous smell, overlain by the odour of stagnant water, though the map showed no water on the eighth level. Where could it be coming from?

Around the corner the tunnel narrowed between two bosses of massive white quartz, free of any kind of crystal. Irisis held her lantern out. Ahead she could see only sheared pink granite in walls and roof. Wet mounds of crumbled rock, nearly waist high, partly blocked the tunnel. The roof must be really unstable. Water dripped all the way along.

'Well, that's one place we're definitely *not* going.' Turning away, Irisis rotated the half-shuttered lantern so it would not dazzle Ullii.

The seeker slipped by her and went up to the obstruction, staring into the dark and sniffing. Irisis kept going. Ullii needed no light; in fact, she could employ her seeker's talent better without it.

Irisis had been walking for some five minutes before realising that Ullii was not behind her. She held the lantern up. There was no sign of the seeker. No point yelling or cursing her, that would only make things worse. Irisis returned to the roof fall. Ullii was not there, though there was a small print in the clayey muck.

'Ullii,' she called, not too loudly.

Grit sifted down from a crack in the roof. Irisis felt afraid. Rotten wet rock was far more perilous than dry stuff. She squeezed through the gap, scraping breasts that were still tender from the previous night, and edged forward. A flat piece of granite detached itself from the roof, landing with a plop in front of her. Irisis shuddered and kept going.

The rotten rock continued as far as she could see, which was not far here. At a shallow bend, she peered around. Something crouched down the other end of the tunnel, but Irisis could not make out what it was. It might even have been a lyrinx.

At the thought, terror rose up within her and she almost screamed. Get a grip on yourself! A lyrinx would not even fit in this tunnel. She held up the lantern, the shapes shifted and became the seeker, crouching with her arms against the wall.

'What are you doing?' Irisis said crossly. 'This place is too dangerous. We've got to go back.'

'I can *see* something,' said Ullii.

Irisis resisted the urge to run. 'What?' she whispered when she got there.

'Crystal. Good crystal. *Big* crystal!'

'Really? Are you sure?'

'*Biiiig* crystal!' Ullii turned around and around, as if searching for something she could not quite locate.

'Where, Ullii? Which way?'

Her outstretched arm revolved, slanting down towards the floor. 'There.'

'Is it close?' Ullii could never be precise about distances, although directions were usually accurate. To be so fuzzy was unusual.

'Not . . . so close,' said Ullii.

That meant down a fair way. The ninth level was also unsafe and partly flooded, the level rising and falling with the seasons. It had not been too bad last autumn: Tiaan had been able to escape that way. That could be different after a winter of heavy snowfalls that were rapidly melting. If the crystal was below the ninth level they might as well forget it, for the water would come into the excavation faster than their primitive pumps could extract it.

'Let's go, Ullii. We'll come back in the morning.'

For once, Ullii seemed reluctant. She lingered by the wall, feeling it with her fingers. Her face was animated.

Irisis felt the sleepless night catching up with her. She caught Ullii by the arm. 'Come on. It's late.'

The seeker resisted. 'Leave me alone!'

Irisis was so astounded that she took a step backwards. 'What's the matter?'

'It's talking to me!'

'What is it saying?'

Ullii gave her a strange look, somewhere between pity and contempt. 'You can't understand.'

Irisis did not have the strength. She squatted against the wall and closed her eyes, but sprang up as the rock shook and a crash thundered along the tunnel. Air rushed past, carrying a wet, clayey smell. More of the roof had fallen.

Irisis looked back the way they had come but could see no further than the bend. She inspected the roof with her lantern. It was fractured all the way along.

'Ullii?'

The seeker had not moved, nor did she answer. There was nothing to do but wait. Irisis settled down again. Her eyes drifted closed.

I'm ready now.' Ullii was shaking her shoulder.

'What?' Irisis said thickly, roused from deep slumber. She opened her eyes to utter darkness. 'Where –' She remembered. 'What's happened to the lantern?'

'It went out ages ago.'

Irisis felt for it and gave it a shake – it was empty and cold. It had burned all its oil. How were they going to find the way back to the lift shaft? The eighth level was a maze of intersecting tunnels.

'Ullii,' she whispered. 'I'm afraid. I don't know the way back. What are we going to do?'

The seeker made a muffled sound in her throat, which Irisis took for a sob. Panic began to close her throat over.

A warm little hand found her cold fingers. 'It's all right,' Ullii said soothingly, the way Irisis had often spoken to her. 'I know the way.'

Being treated like a child was irritating, but Irisis tried not to show it. Maybe the seeker did know the way out. Perhaps she could see it in that lattice in her head.

Ullii pulled her gently along. 'This is the wrong way,' Irisis hissed, sure that she had gone to sleep against the right-hand wall, which meant that the way back was on her left side. They were going the other direction.

'No, it's not,' Ullii said calmly.

Irisis did not argue. The seeker was at home in this environment and she was not. Maybe she had turned around in her sleep, or after she stood up. It was so easy to become disoriented down here.

The tunnel turned sharply, then back the other way, like the bends of an 'S'. Irisis shivered.

'It *is* the wrong way, Ullii. We *definitely* did not come around those bends.'

'Shh.' Ullii patted her hand. 'I know where I'm going.'

Perhaps the fall had blocked the way they had come. After that, and turning into a different tunnel, and then another, Irisis kept her mouth shut. Hopelessly lost, she had no choice but to rely on the little seeker.

They had been walking for a long time when Ullii stopped

suddenly. Irisis, so tired that she could not think straight, kept going. Ullii jerked hard on her hand.

'What's the matter?' Irisis asked dazedly.

'Hole in the floor. *Shouldn't be there.*'

How could she possibly know that? 'Does that mean we have to go back?'

'Stay here.' Ullii let go of her hand.

'Ullii?'

'Shhh!'

Irisis sat on the damp floor. This puts a whole new shade on being kept in the dark, she thought wryly. The silence settled around her. Absolute silence. It was broken by a faint echoing click.

What was the seeker doing? Was she trying to climb down the hole and up the other side? Irisis did not fancy that in the dark. She wanted to cry out, to hear the reassurance of the seeker's voice. Now *that* was ironic.

What was taking her so long? Had she gone down and could not get up again? Irisis felt very alone. To pass the time she began counting, but after reaching a thousand gave up because she could no longer concentrate. Suddenly, out of nowhere, Ullii was beside her.

'I smell clawers.'

It was her word for lyrinx. 'Where?' Irisis whispered.

'Down. Ninth level.'

'Did they make this hole?'

'Think so.'

'Does it go all the way down?'

'Yes,' said Ullii.

'What do they want?' Irisis said to herself, then answered it. 'They want crystal and they're also after the big one. Can we get past the hole?'

'Think so.'

Getting information out of the seeker was like pulling teeth. 'Come on!' said Irisis. 'We can't let them trap us here. I don't want to end up in the belly of a lyrinx.'

It was the wrong thing to say. Irisis heard the seeker's muted squeal of panic, then nothing.

'Ullii,' she whispered.

There was no reply. Feeling around, she came upon the seeker, curled up like the armadillo that was her favourite animal. Irisis felt just as panicky. Now what was she supposed to do?

Leaving her there, she crawled to the hole. It was absolutely dark. Feeling around the ragged edge, Irisis smelt a familiar musty, meaty odour. The lyrinx were not far away.

It was unpleasant work in pitch blackness, knowing that if she overbalanced she would fall head-first and dash her brains out on the floor of the ninth level. Her hands met the wall, but leaning out as far as she dared Irisis did not find the other side. As she hesitated there, her heart clattering in her chest, something else struck her. If she could smell the lyrinx, they could probably smell her.

Her probing fingers found the narrowest of shelves on the left side, too narrow to walk across. She had to know how wide the hole was. Her pockets were empty but for fluff. No, there was something caught in the seam.

It was a holey nyd, a copper coin with the centre punched out. She weighed it in her hand. The small sound it would make had to be weighed against the risk of not knowing how far across the hole was.

Standing at the edge of the hole, she tossed the coin. It fell short, bounced off one wall of the hole, then the other, and landed with a distinct *ching* at the bottom.

'Slazzhik?' a lyrinx called, the sound echoing along the tunnel.

'Glunnra!' another replied. 'Tynchurr.'

Running back on tiptoes, she shook Ullii. 'Wake, seeker! The enemy knows we're here. We must run.'

Ullii moaned and curled up even tighter. Irisis felt like kicking her. She grabbed the seeker, who lashed out, catching Irisis in the left eye. 'Stop that!' she hissed, and when Ullii continued to struggle, Irisis slapped her.

Ullii went rigid, then curled up again. Holding her in her arms, Irisis felt her way up the tunnel. As she neared the hole, or shaft, it was outlined by a glow from beneath. They were coming.

Irisis peered down. The light was still moving; she smelt something like incense. They were burning sticks dipped in tree gum. The hole looked a couple of good steps wide. She would have to jump it, for the rim of stone along the left side was definitely not wide enough to walk on. Irisis checked the roof. No point leaping high and knocking herself out.

Ullii was like a hard little ball, which was not going to make it any easier. Irisis took three long steps backward, ran up to the hole, knew she was not going to make it and baulked at the last instant. She bent over, gasping for breath.

Something appeared at the bottom, the shadow of a beast with wings, and roared. She had to do it this time. Irisis ran, one, two, three. The load in her arms kept shifting and her mind could not calculate how much further, how much higher she had to jump. She stopped, overbalanced and almost fell down the shaft.

She managed to recover, spinning on one foot as she did so, but lost her footing and was forced to drop the seeker. Ullii landed on her bottom, let out an aggrieved howl and fleeted across the tiny ledge of floor. Without looking back, she hared off up the tunnel.

You little cow! Irisis thought as the seeker disappeared. After all I've done for you. A dark silhouette was moving up the shaft. No choice now. Jump or die.

She ran backwards, took two deep breaths and ran. As she came near, the creature's head emerged. The torchlight lit up its face from below: eyes and teeth. Jump high and fast, or you're dead. She took off, leaping as high as she possibly could. The lyrinx threw up its arm, its claws scraped her ankle, caught on her boot seam and it tried to pull her out of the air. Irisis kicked, connected with its forehead; and then she was over, landing on hands and knees.

The lyrinx roared and threw itself out of the shaft, holding up the torch. The tunnel ran straight for about thirty spans. Irisis fled. When she was nearly to the bend, the light disappeared. All she could see was the silhouette again. The creature had put the torch behind it, so as to hide the way ahead of her.

Slowing to a trot, she put her arms out. Even so, it came as a shock when she ran into the bend. She felt around it and moved forward at a shuffling walk. That would not save her if she encountered another shaft.

Irisis prayed for a narrow pinch that her pursuer could not get through; there had been several like it over on the other side. Here, the tunnel was almost as wide as a road. It took many a turning, and each time she had to go blindly into the dark. Each time the silhouette appeared behind her, it was closer.

She went harder, but it sped up too. There was a stitch in her side. She felt as if she had been running all her life. Suddenly the lyrinx let out an almighty roar that seemed to shake the tunnel. It had a note of triumph. Gravel and grit fell on her head. Something thumped behind her; a lump of roof.

The roar echoed back the other way. Or was another lyrinx ahead? She saw a flickering light, panicked, and when a smaller tunnel loomed up on her left, Irisis turned into it. Unfortunately it was not a tunnel, just a dead end, but in the darkness she could not see that. Irisis ran into the wall.

TWENTY-THREE

Gilhaelith had gone to see Tiaan several times but she always pretended to be asleep. She was hiding something. He had left off questioning her for the moment, for he had much to think about. War now raged in northern Almadin, and that was not far away. The lyrinx had defeated an army and razed a city. Neither the vastness of Worm Wood nor the slopes of the mountain could deter a determined attack. And the amplimet was preying on his mind. He had spent hours each day, watching it and wondering how it had formed. He had not touched it yet – each time he read the numbers they told him to wait.

On the fourth day after the crash, there came a tap on the door and Nyrd the messenger hurried in, his satchel bulging and a leather envelope in one hand. With his pointed nose and chin, elongated ears and skin so thick and wrinkled it could have been a leather suit, Nyrd looked like an oversized gnome.

'What is it?' asked Gilhaelith.

'The war!' said Nyrd with a quizzical glance. His eyes were as small and black as cherries. 'Better take a look at this one first.' He passed over the leather envelope. 'It just came in by skeet.'

Gilhaelith untied the red cords, withdrawing the wax-sealed packet inside. Noting the origin of the seal, he stiffened. 'Thank you, Nyrd. I won't need you until after lunch.'

After Nyrd closed the door on the way out, Gilhaelith broke

the seal. The letter was from his factor in Saludith and contained no identifying marks, though it bore the previous day's date.

Surr,

I have the most alarming news. A horde of battle constructs, modelled on Rulke's that was destroyed in Aachan two centuries ago, have come over the mountains from Mirrilladell. Their number is 6118, and presently they are camped beyond the southern boundary of Borgistry, near Clew's Top. They are said to have come from Aachan. Though I do not see how that could be true, they speak in

a most barbarous accent and are armed as for war. Other fleets are believed to have gone south to Oolo, Candalume and K'Klistoh, as well as west toward the Karama Malama.

I am awaiting reports on those movements.

The main force is led by Vithis, an arrogant and unlikeable man, very bitter and uncompromising, according to those who have had dealings with him. Vithis has made no declaration though surely his plans are predatory. The enclosed papers contain more detailed information, maps and sketches of these constructs.

Finally, and most urgent of all, I have heard reports of another construct, *a flying one*. It flew over the main force three days ago, attacked the camp recklessly and knocked down Vithis, injuring his leg. It then disappeared in the direction of Parnggi and the Peaks of Borg. Vithis is said to be out of his mind with rage. He has, for the present time, turned aside from his military objectives and is exerting all his strength to finding this renegade machine and its operator.

I will send more the instant I have it.

Chiarri

Chiarri, not her real name, was one of his most reliable factors. Crushing the letter in his fist, Gilhaelith called for a jug of stout and went to sit on the terrace, a favourite thinking place. He stared down into the crater.

Aachan! That meant a gate, and its opening had something

to do with that reverberation of the ethyr he had felt weeks ago. Was this the first strike of a war of the worlds? Why, why had Tiaan brought the flying construct here? But of course, when the pipes had sounded days ago, he'd done his best to draw her here. Whether her coming was due to his efforts, or to sheer chance, here she was and he must deal with her and all her baggage.

How had she stolen the flying construct, and why had she attacked the Aachim so recklessly? The situation was out of control and for the first time in a century Gilhaelith felt afraid. The prize might not be worth the risk. He ran the numbers but this time the pattern was ambiguous, the worst result of all.

The best option would be to take Tiaan back to the site of the crash, put her next to the construct and leave her to die. She was so intimately mixed up with the gate, amplimet and construct that whoever found the construct must come looking for her.

He resolved, reluctantly, to do just that. Gilhaelith was not going to risk his life's work for a thief and cripple, no matter how haunting the look in her eyes. He'd seen that look before; nothing good ever came out of it.

The amplimet was another matter. The Art and Science of the earth were his life's work and this crystal could take him to the core that had always eluded him. He would not give it up unless he stood to lose everything. And so he might, if he did not quickly discover why Tiaan had stolen the flying construct. And there lay the problem. Any competent mancer could read the aura given off by the amplimet, inside and outside the construct. If he left the construct where it was but kept the crystal, the first place they would look was here.

It was all or nothing, and whatever his decision, he had better make it quickly. Was the amplimet worth it? If not, the choice was made for him. He went down to the organ to see what he could make of the crystal.

Gilhaelith worked the lever that uncovered the skylight far above, allowing the thin rays of the crescent moon to shine vertically on the bench, the frosty globe of the world and the amplimet which lay on a piece of crumpled black velvet. The crystal glowed strongly but the central spark sometimes fluctuated in intensity. Strange and intriguing.

He reached out with gloved hand, then drew back as one of the larger organ pipes soughed, just on the lower edge of hearing. It was like the murmuring of bees in the far distance – a warning. He'd had that whenever he tried to investigate the amplimet.

It was frustrating. The crystal was powerful *and* sensitive. What wonders might he uncover if he could learn how to use it properly? The little thief could not have employed a fraction of its potential.

Making a sudden decision, he wrapped the amplimet in its velvet and carried it beyond the keyboard to a spot where arrays of organ pipes – some vertical, some slanted and the remainder horizontal – formed a series of fans converging on a single point. At that spot stood a hollow star with eighty-one points, each a matched crystal. Gilhaelith eased the amplimet into the hollow, settled it in place and removed the velvet.

Reaching for a stop on his organ console, he carefully, carefully pulled it out, withdrawing a golden mask from the centre of the star. He held his breath. A nerve throbbed painfully in his stomach. Anything might happen. Or worse, nothing.

The glow from the crystal died down. The spark vanished. At the same time a cloud must have passed in front of the moon, for the silvery beams coming through the skylight disappeared. Frost seemed to settle on everything. When he moved his foot, the floor crackled.

As he eased the lever the last fraction, the frost deepened. Then, with a shrieking, roaring rumble, every pipe of the organ sounded at once, a noise so violent that it tore at his skull. He clapped his hands over his ears but that made no difference. The sounds were inside too. A wooden pipe burst, embedding a dark splinter fingernail-deep in the back of his hand.

Gilhaelith kicked the stop in and the cacophony cut off, though not before more pipes exploded and a metal array sagged as if made of putty. Wrapping his hand in the piece of black velvet, he reached into the star. Gilhaelith would not have been surprised had smoke risen from his fingertips. The crystal was unchanged except, perhaps, a little colder than before. Its glow was subdued.

He did not know what had happened and shuddered to think what other mancers would make of that disturbance to the ethyr. He prayed that no one could tell its origin. The crystal was more potent than he had thought, and more dangerous. Something had transformed it but he could not tell what. He had to have it, though Gilhaelith did not plan to risk his life testing it. That seemed to leave him with only one alternative.

Let's see what the little thief knew about it. But first, one thing must be done urgently. He called his foreman.

'Guss, put together a detail, only your most reliable people. Go down to the forest and bring the machine back. Leave no trace of it and keep it covered as it is brought up. Can that be done today?'

The foreman considered, rubbing his shiny forehead. 'I'll take twenty men. That should be ample. Not far from the site there's an ancient lava tube, if you recall, which we've previously used as a covered road. We'll bring it up that way, and the last distance under cover of night. It'll be in your deepest cellar by midnight.'

'Swear the men to secrecy, even from their partners.'

'It's a little late for that, master. No one has spoken about anything else for days.'

Gilhaelith frowned. People were so ill-disciplined. 'I'll speak to them myself. No more talking. The others need not know it's here. Better still, I'll send them around the rim. The glanberries are starting to fruit already, are they not?'

'The winter flowering ones are, on the warmer northern slopes.'

'Good. I have a fancy for glanberry pie tonight. Oh, and one other thing.'

'Yes, Gilhaelith?'

'It might be an idea if you and your men were not around to be questioned for a while.'

'There's plenty to do below,' said the foreman. 'We'll work there until you give the word.'

'Very good. Tell the men to stay clear of my best stout.'

The foreman laughed. 'Every man has his weakness, and I imagine you're referring to me rather than them. I'll keep it in mind, though it'll be a thirsty duty, master.'

His loyalty deserved a reward, though Gilhaelith offered it with a tinge of regret. 'When you come up, you shall have a barrel of the stuff.'

Gilhaelith spring-stepped to Tiaan's room. Hitherto she had dodged all his questions. Now he had to know.

Her head rotated as he entered. Her eyes were dull; she did not seem to be interested in anything. Pulling up a chair, he sat down. She resumed staring at the ceiling.

He leaned forward, unfolded the letter from his factor and began to read it. She ignored him until he mentioned Vithis, whereupon her hands fluttered under the covers. She bit down on a gasp. He kept reading. At the end, her eyes turned to him and he saw naked terror there. Just as quickly she hid it.

'You must tell me everything,' he said sternly.

'There's no point. Just take me down the mountain and leave me by my thapter.'

'Thapter?'

'The flying construct.'

'I am thinking of doing just that.' He inspected her as dispassionately as he would have done the least of his servants. There was no room for sentiment, not for a thief. 'Why did you steal the thapter?'

'I didn't. It's mine.'

The claim was nonsensical. 'Tiaan, Vithis is searching for the thapter, and you, and won't rest until he has interrogated every witness in the land. I cannot resist him, even if I wanted to. You are a thief who wantonly attacked his camp and tried to kill him. I must give you up.'

'Please, no!'

'Then talk to me.'

'He is a liar who callously betrayed me, and attacked me first. I am not a thief.'

He did not believe her. 'Go on.'

'I did not steal the thapter,' she blurted. 'It's mine.'

'Come, Tiaan, patently it was made by the Aachim.'

'Malien gave it to me in Tirthrax.'

He drew in a breath. 'Malien is still alive?'

'She is old, but in health.'

'How very interesting. Were the other constructs made at Tirthrax?'

'They were built on Aachan. I created the gate that brought them to our world, for their own is dying in volcanic fire.'

He got a tale out of her, with much probing, and many pauses on her part that made him sure there was little truth in it. It was well into the evening by then. A shiver went up his spine as he understood, at last, the source of that ethyric convulsion weeks ago. *Someone* had made a gate but it could not have been Tiaan. She was not old enough to have mastered the basics of geomancy, far less the greatest of all magic. Gilhaelith was so unsettled that he shouted for a cup of mustard-water.

'But, master,' said Mihail, 'you never drink mustard-water in the evening. Shall I fetch you –'

'At once, dammit. And tea for Tiaan.'

Gilhaelith sat back in his chair. She could not have made a gate, so who had? Malien, most likely. The situation was more dire than he had thought: for the world, for himself, and of course for Tiaan. Her attack, even if it had been self-defence, would have been the ultimate humiliation for the proud Aachim. And the thapter was worth a continent. Who had made it fly, as Rulke's original had, two centuries ago? Tiaan had not revealed that. Vithis would do everything possible to recover it. With mastery of the air his forces would be unstoppable; humanity's clankers would be no more useful than hay wagons.

And then there was the amplimet. Even if Vithis dared not use it himself, it was required for the thapter to fly. Vithis might be capable of scrying out the path flown by the thapter, given time. It would be a difficult task, but not impossible for someone with unlimited resources. Sooner or later he would end up here. *I haven't thought things through,* Gilhaelith thought. *Should I*

234

call Guss back? Perhaps I should tell Vithis where the construct is, and earn the reward.

'Tell me about the amplimet, Tiaan.'

'I've already talked about it.'

'There's much you haven't told me. It's a deadly crystal and I can't see how you survived using it, even briefly.'

Tiaan flushed and looked down at the bed. Mistaking her reaction for guilt, he reared up over her and said sternly, 'I have been testing the amplimet and I know you're keeping much from me. My patience has run out. Tell me, or it will go badly for you.'

'The c-crystal is alive,' she stammered.

She was less intelligent than he'd thought, but he'd humoured her. 'How can you tell?'

'It was drawing power from the field all by itself, without ever being woken.' She told him about finding it. 'And in Tirthrax, since the gate opened, it was talking to the node.'

'Talking to the node? Preposterous!'

She explained about that, and how it had taken over the thapter's controls. He did not speak after she had finished, but paced the bedchamber, analysing what she had said and calculating probabilities. He *could* not believe her.

'What are you going to do?' she said. She seemed to be going through some kind of internal struggle.

'I don't know.'

'Vithis must not get the thapter. You've got to give it to the scrutators. It will make all the difference to the war.'

'You're a fine one to talk about duty, after running away from your manufactory.'

'I was on my way to Lybing to give the thapter to the scrutator, but the amplimet brought me here instead. It cut off the field to make sure I couldn't fight it.'

One absurd lie after another. Did she take him for a fool? But still, there *was* something about her, and her story, that made him pause.

'Please,' she said in tones that would have wrenched at the heart of any normal man. 'Vithis is a monster. He plans to take our world.'

Gilhaelith was not a normal man, but he could not think with her tragic eyes on him. He rose abruptly, sending the chair skidding back. Her head whipped around and he saw terror in her eyes.

He stalked around the rim of the crater, stumbling over the rubble in his agitation. He was not defenceless. Gilhaelith had been born with a talent for the Secret Art, one he had worked hard to master. Nonetheless, the Aachim force must contain many adepts greater than he, and if they discovered what he had done they would destroy him. He could not play that kind of game. Better be seen to be helpful, while hiding his true design.

Or should he give the thapter to the scrutators? A good decision if it helped them to win the war, but a foolish one if, as he suspected, they were going to lose. Gilhaelith took the omens but the numbers were ambiguous. He took them again – different numbers, yet the uncertainty was the same. The choice went three ways and his decision could alter the future of the world. One option was right, the others likely to be disastrously wrong, but for all his auguries and all his logic he could not separate them. The future was scrambled. Randomness, the greatest curse of all, looked like being crucial.

In the early hours of the following morning, Gilhaelith sat in his chair in the basement, a jug of stout at his elbow, staring moodily at the thapter. He could not bring himself to believe Tiaan's outlandish story about making the gate. A student of geomancy for a century and a half, he knew just how long it took to master the Art. The notion that the amplimet had some will of its own was even more absurd. And yet . . . there had been that strange reaction when he had tested it with his organ.

Gilhaelith had not got to where he was by having a closed mind. If it did have some kind of mineral awareness, he would discover it. But what *could* a piece of crystal want?

He spent a day and a half cunningly investigating it with the subtlest of his instruments. It shone steadily all the while – unusual, but not unprecedented. It did not blink once. It was not communicating at all – that was just another of Tiaan's fantasies.

Once he had gone, the amplimet's glow faded to the dullest of glimmers, but the central spark began to blink rapidly and, after some hours, the field of the Booreah Ngurle double node started to pulse in unison. Several minutes passed. The spark died and the field went back to normal.

TWENTY-FOUR

The thapter was another puzzle, though one more amenable to logic. Gilhaelith's smiths had removed its crumpled metal skin and were now beating it back to shape. He had studied every part of the machine's workings but had not discovered how it hovered, much less flew. It vexed him that a little liar and thief had been able to do what he could not.

Two days later, Mihail came running to Gilhaelith, who had just gone in to check on Tiaan.

'Master, master!' he cried, bursting through the door.

'What is it?' Gilhaelith snapped. He hated chaos and emotion.

'Klarm, surr. The dwarf scrutator.'

'What? On his way up the mountain?'

'He's turning onto the terrace right now.'

Gilhaelith jumped. How had Klarm climbed the hill without anyone seeing him? Scrutator magic! 'Keep this door shut!' he snapped and ran out, ignoring Tiaan.

Klarm was scrutator for Borgistry, the land south of Booreah Ngurle. Strictly speaking he did not have any authority here, for Gilhaelith held an ancient charter that declared his little kingdom independent. It suited the leaders of the surrounding nations, and more importantly the Council of Scrutators, otherwise they would have repudiated it long ago. But the war had changed the world and Gilhaelith was uncomfortably aware of his vulnerability. He had to please everyone, offend no one, and maintain his usefulness to the scrutators. And still he could not make his choice. Should he give the thapter to Klarm, or lie and pray he got away with it? Even if he did, he would soon have to abandon Nyriandiol and all he had done here. But if Klarm suspected the thapter was being kept from him . . .

'Scrutator Klarm!' Gilhaelith said as he went out the circular front door. 'It's very good to see you. Come down.'

Klarm's groom trotted across with a footstool and stood it beside the stirrup, for Klarm had not grown properly and, standing on tiptoes, his large round head reached no higher than Gilhaelith's waist. Despite his dwarfism he was a cheerful fellow, though as ruthless as anyone ever to take the robes of scrutator.

Klarm clambered down, nodding to the groom. He walked with a rolling gait, like a man who had spent too long on the deck of a ship. With a dazzling smile, the scrutator threw out his hand. He was a handsome man with a noble mane of brown wavy hair that enclosed his neck like a collar. His eyes were the brilliant blue of the crater lake below. 'It's a pleasure to be back, Gilhaelith.'

Gilhaelith bowed low and took the outstretched hand. He had always liked Klarm, though he did not trust him. Scrutator first, friend a distant second. 'And to you, my friend. How long has it been? Too long, certainly.'

'Eleven months to the day.' Klarm always knew such details.

'Come into the shade. Shall I bring up a jug of my finest stout?'

'Porter, I think, but don't be mean. Bring the whole damned barrel.'

A servant was despatched and Gilhaelith led Klarm under the vines. They talked about the splendid weather and the beauty of the blue lake, as custom dictated, until the drink arrived. The first servant bore a jug the size of a large bucket. Another carried a tray of delicacies – the pickled intestinal organs of lake fish, arranged in squares four to a side, for Gilhaelith, and more traditional tidbits for Klarm.

The scrutator wrinkled his nose. 'Nothing changes with you.'

He chose a cube of blue cheese, which he roofed with slices of gherkin before swallowing it whole.

'And why should it?' Gilhaelith selected a pair of small, liver-pink organs between finger and thumb, admiring the colouring. Red-brown material oozed out. He slurped them down.

He poured the scrutator a large tankard of the boot-polish-brown brew. They touched porcelain to porcelain and Klarm drained his in a single swallow. It was his habit to begin a session that way, though he seldom lost his wits no matter how much ale he had taken. He poured another, sinking it as quickly, and a third, which he merely sipped.

Gilhaelith, knowing his limitations, took a sturdy pull at his own drink, sat it on the table and looked the scrutator in the eye.

'I know you'd come a tidy distance to drink a porter as fine as mine,' he said. 'Are you passing by, or have you come about this other matter that everyone is talking of ?' No one passed by Booreah Ngurle, for it was a winding twenty leagues through Worm Wood from the Great North Road, and not on the way to anywhere.

'I figured your spies would have told you of it,' Klarm said. 'Whatever happened to this flying construct, it's checked the progress of the Aachim, and that's a blessing. They raced halfway across the continent in a couple of weeks, but since the machine disappeared they've not moved their main camp. I need not tell you what a shock their appearance was. They came from Aachan, Gilhaelith. *Through a gate!* What do they want? Are they really refugees, or an advance guard come to bring the rest of their people across? Will they ally with us against the lyrinx, or take their side, or fight us both? On the answers to these questions our very future depends.'

'And the Aachim's too. I'm glad you came, Klarm, for I've been mulling over the business ever since I first heard of it. And one thing puzzles me more than anything else.'

Scrutator Klarm raised an eyebrow.

'The earliest rumours were that they were imminently preparing for war. Since then, all reports show them to have lost their purpose.'

'Reports they could have tainted,' Klarm retorted.

'I doubt that even these Aachim are as calculating as the scrutators,' Gilhaelith said with a cheerfulness he did not feel. 'They mill all over the place, and every day their advantage is diminished. This is no way to win a war. If they planned to attack us, *or* the lyrinx, why not do so at once?'

'A question the Council also asks, you may be sure. The Aachim have had a number of shocks since they arrived. Recall.' Klarm dipped a stubby finger in the head of his porter then held it up, licking at the tip with a neat pink tongue. 'The last they knew of Santhenar, we were just a collection of primitive and warring nations, easy prey. Now they find a world united, organised for war, well-armed and hardened after generations of conflict. We have vast fleets of clankers, as well as other weapons powered by the Secret Art. What else do we have that they know nothing about, nor how to deal with?'

Another finger. 'The lyrinx are an equally formidable enemy and they too are legion. They also have developed the Art in directions the Aachim do not understand, such as flesh-forming.'

Finger number three. 'The Aachim would have expected their own kind, who have dwelt here for thousands of years, to support them, for they see themselves as the original and unsullied people of Aachan. But I know our Aachim and I see it differently. They will regard these interlopers as primitives who place clan above kind, who over four millennia never united to throw off the yoke of the Charon.'

A fourth foam-covered digit. 'The flying construct is a secret they do not have, despite the fact that they built all the others: more than ten thousand, I am told. Who is this genius who transformed their work so quickly, and so radically? The Council of Scrutators will pay one million gold tells for the secret of flight. For the flying construct, or the person who stole it, ten thousand apiece.'

Gilhaelith was staggered. A soldier's pay for a year was a single gold tell and the scrutators were notoriously miserly.

'And there is friction among the invaders,' Klarm went on. 'The clans resent Vithis for his arrogance and his inflexible command. And he, it is said, condemns those who cannot focus on the prize.' He drained his porter and poured another. 'Whatever his plans are, losing this construct has stalled them. In order to get it back, he has given away the element of surprise.'

'You're saying they can't agree what to do?' said Gilhaelith.

'They're disunited. It gives us an opportunity, though one that will vanish the instant war is declared. But first we need answers. What have you heard about the woman who stole it?' Klarm's eyes were unnaturally bright.

Last chance. If he gave up the thapter, and Tiaan, would Klarm let him keep the amplimet? Of course not. Without it the thapter could not be made to fly. No doubt that problem could be solved in time, but humanity did not have time. *I can't give up the amplimet*, Gilhaelith thought. I've worked a hundred and fifty years for this. Humanity must fend for itself.

He met Klarm's eyes. 'Nothing, save that she attacked their camp,' he lied. 'And you?' There was no going back now.

'She is old human, an artisan from Tiksi who used to make clanker controllers. Very good ones. Her name is Tiaan.' Klarm licked foam from the rim of the tankard. 'It took me a while to work out who she was. So many despatches to remember. She fled the manufactory last year after a . . . distasteful incident. The last I heard, she had been taken by the lyrinx. My colleague Xervish Flydd was trying to get her back. And here is the most important question of all: did she discover how to make the construct fly? Or if she did not, *who did*?'

'How could she? That would require mastery of the Secret Art, surely? You imply that she has a history of crime. She is just a clever thief. I would look to the Aachim of Santhenar.'

'Why?'

'Rumour says the gate was made at Tirthrax. The Aachim have the resources and the Art. Who else does? I don't, and I doubt if even the Council –'

'I wouldn't take that line of reasoning any further, if I were you.'

'*Meddle in the scrutators' business at your peril*,' Gilhaelith quoted.

Klarm waddled to the wall, which was the height of his head, and hopped up on it facing the crater. Gilhaelith perched beside him.

'I'm terrified,' said Klarm, and he did look distressed, a rare expression for a scrutator. 'Though I say it to no one but you. If the Aachim do unite, and I'm sure they will when it comes to it, their constructs will destroy us. Flight is the only answer, *if we get it first*. I hear what you say but we've got to find Tiaan before Vithis does. Our future depends on this machine. I must send messages right away.'

Any other man might have felt guilty. Gilhaelith felt not a twinge. Klarm began scribbling notes, after which they walked around the back of Nyriandiol to the skeet house. Gilhaelith gave Klarm three message wallets and the scrutator placed one letter in each.

'Where are they going?' Gilhaelith asked.

Klarm told him. 'How long will it take to school your skeets to the destinations?'

A sharp pain struck Gilhaelith in the stomach, high up, and he bent over, clutching at the spot.

'Are you all right, my friend?'

'A touch of colic.'

'No wonder, the gruesome stuff you feed on.'

'It's made me what I am today.'

'I've no doubt of that,' Klarm said dryly. 'Can I do –?'

'It's just gallstones. The pain will pass.'

'Not too quickly, I'll warrant. My apothek has a sovereign remedy for stones.'

'If it persists I may well call on his services.' Gilhaelith forced himself to straighten up. 'How much time, you asked? None at all.' He took seed crystals from labelled jars on a shelf and popped one into each wallet. 'The bird homes by following lines of force. I've already set these crystals to the correct destinations.'

'A clever innovation.' Klarm passed the wallets to the handler. 'We must do business. Lost messages are one of our greatest problems.'

'You may have as many crystals as you want,' said Gilhaelith. 'With my compliments.'

Klarm bowed. They watched the skeets released, with an interval between each so they would not attack one another, then returned to the front terrace, Gilhaelith walking bent over.

'It will not be easy to find her,' said Klarm, 'nor to carry her and the construct away if we do. Vithis's spies and informers are everywhere.'

'I shouldn't wonder. Whoever finds this flying machine, and can crack its secrets, will win the war.'

'Whoever finds it and tells me,' said the scrutator, 'will bathe in a solid-gold tub for the rest of his life.'

'I wish I had it!' Gilhaelith forced a smile. 'Mine is of humble rhyolite.'

'You haven't done so badly.' Klarm ran his eye along the length of the villa.

'It's taken me a long time.'

'And all could be lost so quickly,' said Klarm.

'Indeed,' Gilhaelith sighed, ignoring the ever-so-subtle threat. 'In the twinkling of an eye.'

'On a different matter entirely, isn't your brimstone contract up for renewal soon?'

'It is, but if you don't want to renew it . . .'

'Of course we do,' said Klarm, 'though many considerations have to be weighed up. The war, other suppliers . . .'

'I'm sure we can satisfy each other, Klarm. As you know, I am the most flexible of men. And if there's any other way I can help the scrutators –'

'Do you have anything specific in mind?' Klarm feigned disinterest, not entirely successfully. Gilhaelith had developed a rare ability to read people, even the trained impassivity of the scrutators.

'One rumour has it that the construct disappeared in the northern part of Worm Wood. I am doing everything I can to find it, and if I do . . . well, I have no need of such a device.'

'Any merchant who had it would make a fortune,' said Klarm.

'But he wouldn't keep fortune or construct for too long,' said

Gilhaelith. 'Nor his head! I prefer to stay attached to mine. If I hear anything, I will send word at once, by skeet.'

'Thank you,' said the dwarf, draining his tankard. 'As always, it's a pleasure doing business with you.'

'Another porter, my friend?'

'Not this time. The Council runs us harder than ever. I must go.'

Tiaan lay in her room, trying to hear, though she caught only a sentence or two. The air of controlled power the little man gave off frightened her, but better him than Vithis.

The door opened. Gilhaelith came in. 'Scrutator Klarm is a dangerous man. A good friend, as long as you don't cross him, which I have just done, but a deadly enemy.'

Tiaan closed her eyes. Two deadly enemies, and both were hunting her. 'You're going to give the thapter to him, of course?' She held her breath for the answer.

'No.'

'Why not?'

Gilhaelith scowled. Clearly he was not used to being questioned by inferiors. 'I need the amplimet, so I cannot give up the thapter either.'

'But it's vital to the war!'

'There's always a war somewhere. The amplimet may hold the key to the great game.'

She could not believe anyone could be so greedy or stupid. 'You fool!' she cried. 'What use will your precious secrets be if there is no one alive to see them?'

TWENTY-FIVE

Nish scanned the flame-shot darkness. A solitary figure ran along the wall but nowhere did he see a family group. He risked a shout. 'Colm! Oinan, Tinketil! Ketila! Fransi!'

No reply. Perhaps a lyrinx had circled around the palisade and got them. More likely they had dared wait no longer. He could not blame them. In this race, the stragglers would be eaten. He was sorry, though. They had risked their lives for him and he would have liked to thank them.

Taking up his mallet, Nish slid like a spectre into the darkness. Which way? In the field of war you could never tell. Even if you guessed right, an hour later it might become the wrong way.

He was skidding down the gully when something crashed through a thicket to his left. It was probably another refugee as miserable as himself, but Nish was taking no risks. He crouched down so that he would not show against the glowing skyline. Someone hurtled out of the bushes, straight for him. Nish tried to get out of the way and the man – it *was* a man, by the size – swung something at him. Nish thought it was a sword, and that he was going to lose his head.

Foolishly, he threw up his arm. A piece of wood snapped against it, just a brittle stick, luckily. Nish swung the mallet hard and low, into the fellow's midriff. He went down without a sound. Nish fled along the reedy gully until he smelt salt water. The Sea of Thurkad lay ahead.

To go right would take him in the direction of Nilkerrand, which was still burning, and the enemy. He turned left. The coastline curved west here and, as he reached the shore, Nish saw flames reflecting on the water. Such a pretty sight, from this distance.

As he continued on sand that squeaked underfoot, it began to grow light. Making out a low promontory, Nish broke into a trot. A flying lyrinx would easily spot him on the beach or in the dunes behind it.

He reached the promontory as the sun rose. The headland was layered sandstone, as grey as the water. A rock platform, weathered into rectangular blocks, surrounded it. Sullen waves crashed over the edge. Picking his way across, he came upon a band of oyster shells. His mouth watered. Nish pounded an oyster with the mallet and shell fragments flew everywhere, one catching him in the corner of the eye.

The oyster was just a smear on the rock. Nish found a pebble in one of the tidal gutters and attacked another shell, more carefully. He managed to crack it in half and picked out the oyster. It was not very big, nor did it look appetising, but he was too hungry to care.

He ate about thirty of the little creatures, only stopping because they were salty and he had nothing to drink. Nish climbed the sandstone stack at the back of the promontory to look for a stream.

From the top he could see the towers of Nilkerrand, still burning. The westerly wind drifted a greasy brown plume across the landscape. Smoke trailed upwards from several parts of the refugee camp and lyrinx circled in the air over it.

To the south a long curving beach extended as far as he could see. Behind the beach were dunefields and salt marsh, country difficult to cross, easy to get lost in. There were hundreds of boats on the water, from majestic barges to little dinghies with scraps of sail. All were heading away from Nilkerrand, well out to sea where the lyrinx would not dare attack. He waved in the faint hope that one might come to his aid. None did.

To the east Nish saw a road crowded with refugees. It offered the safety of numbers and the possibility of begging for food. Further on, a meandering line of trees appeared to mark a creek. Nish set off in that direction.

Two hours later he was sitting in the shrubbery next to the road, thirstier than ever, watching the refugees go by. He had not reached the creek. His leg throbbed after the long walk through the dunes and he did not think he could go much further.

The refugees comprised every kind of humanity imaginable. Passing him now was a fat merchant or lawyer, staggering under bags of silver plate and precious metal chains. His fine clothes were tattered and soot-stained; he was drenched in sweat and scarlet of face. He would not last long, nor his equally plump and beringed wife.

Behind them trudged a mother and four young children, the youngest a babe-in-arms. They were dressed in peasant's drab, coarse brown cloth that hung in baggy folds. They would not last long either. Then Nish saw the knife in the woman's belt, the fixed look in her eye, and was not so sure. He would not want to get between her and her cubs.

A farmer's cart followed, a rickety affair with a wheel that squealed at the top of every rotation. The mournful nag looked as if it wanted to lie down and never get up again. An aged woman and her equally weathered man sat on top.

The dismal procession continued. Nish was looking for someone who had been in authority and was still strong and capable. He planned to ingratiate himself, which was not going to be easy – people would be more suspicious than ever. Failing that, after his accidental success with Colm he would try to find a child to befriend, in order to get into the good graces of the parents.

Hours went by. He kept watch for Colm and his family but did not see them. Nish saw few people who looked more competent than himself. However, around midday his eye was caught by two girls, about twelve years old, coming up the road arm-in-arm. They looked to be identical twins. Both had the same coppery-brown wavy hair, the same dark eyes and sturdy figure. Each was dressed in plain green blouse and pants, their faces shielded by broad-brimmed hats. Their little packs were identical. Superficially they could have been any children on the road, but their clothing was of fine weave and well cut. But they were alone, and that was no good to him. No point, if they had already lost their parents.

One of the girls was limping. She sat down on a stone at the edge of the road, not far away. Taking off her boot and sock, she inspected a blistered heel.

'I don't think I can go much further, Meriwen,' she said. 'My foot *really* hurts.'

'Remember what father said. If we were separated we must keep going, and *never* stop, until we get to Kundizand. He will find us there.'

'My foot is *killing* me.'

'It's not far, Liliwen.'

'It *is*! It'll take us all day and half the night.'

'The sooner we start the quicker we'll get there.'

'You sound just like Mother,' said Liliwen crossly.

Another group of refugees, wearing straw hats and labourer's drab, passed by. No one gave the twins a passing glance. The world was full of lost children.

'They'll be *really* angry if they can't find us. You know Father has to go back to the army tomorrow.'

'If there *is* an army,' Liliwen muttered.

'Of course there's an army! There will always be one.'

'The beasts might have eaten Mother *and* Father,' said Lili-wen, clearly the pessimist of the pair.

'Stop it!' shouted Meriwen. 'Don't talk like that!'

Nish, desperately thirsty and in considerable pain, could see no better prospect. Cutting through the scrub, he came out behind the girls, who were still arguing as he limped by. The wound in his leg was agonising. He walked on a dozen steps, then perched on a boulder. Pulling his trouser leg up, he began unwrapping the bandages.

The rents in his calf muscle had been healing, but one had torn open with the night's exertions and was trickling blood. The tooth marks were red, swollen and filled with pus.

The twins were walking towards him. As they came by, Nish probed the wound, groaned and looked up. 'I don't suppose you've got any ointment, have you?'

The first girl stopped. They weren't absolutely identical. Liliwen had thicker eyebrows than Meriwen, a rounder face, and the beginnings of a bosom. 'I'm sorry,' said Liliwen. 'Mother has some but she's . . . not here.'

'Is she coming?' said Nish, looking down the road. 'My leg is killing me.'

'Liliwen!' hissed Meriwen, standing some distance away. 'We're not allowed to talk to strangers.'

'That's very wise,' said Nish, knowing that he must look a fright. 'There are all sorts of wicked people on the road. My name is Cryl-Nish Hlar, but everyone calls me Nish. Actually, I hate that name,' he said confidentially, 'but it doesn't seem to make any difference.' He held out his hand.

Liliwen took it in a way that suggested she had never shaken hands before. 'I'm Liliwen. This is my sister, Meriwen.'

'Hello, Meriwen,' said Nish.

'Hello,' she said grudgingly, keeping well away. 'You sound strange.'

'I come from the other side of the world. I'm not very good at your language.'

'Come *on*, Liliwen.'

Nish rose and limped beside Liliwen. Meriwen kept to the other side of the road.

'Do you live in Nilkerrand?' Nish asked.

'Yes.' Liliwen looked up at him. 'At least –' She suppressed a sob.

'What happened?'

'The enemy came, those horrible flying beasts. Everything was on fire. Our lovely house was burnt, and all my toys, and . . .' she began to sob, 'poor Mixy.'

'Who was Mixy?' he asked gently.

'Her old tomcat,' said Meriwen, still uncomfortable with him.

'I'm very sorry. I lost my cat too, when I was a kid, about as old as you.'

Liliwen wiped her eyes. 'What happened to him?'

'Her,' said Nish. 'Finn was her name. A cart ran her over in the street. I cried for days.'

'*Did* you?' Meriwen thawed a little.

'I loved my old Finn,' said Nish. 'She used to sleep on the end of my bed at night. She kept my feet warm in winter. I can still hear her purring sometimes, when it's dark.'

They continued along the road. 'What's the matter with your leg?' asked Meriwen.

'I was attacked by a nylatl,' said Nish. He showed them the wounds. 'It nearly killed me.'

'What's a nylatl?'

He explained, and though it was a bright day, both cast a glance at the undergrowth and moved closer to him.

'Have you lost your parents?' Nish asked a while later.

'They're going to meet us down the road,' Meriwen said quickly.

'They're not!' Liliwen wailed. 'We've lost them and we'll never see them again.'

'How did you become separated?'

'We were waiting outside the front gate,' said Liliwen. 'Mother and Father were trying to get something from the house. All these people came running down the road, screaming. Millions!' she said hyperbolically. 'We got carried along with them and when we went back, our house was on fire. Mother and Father were gone.'

'It burned to the ground,' said Meriwen. 'We waited for ages but they didn't come back. Then people started screaming and running away, so we ran too.'

'Your parents are probably up ahead,' said Nish. 'Waiting for you.'

'I hope so,' Liliwen said doubtfully.

This was developing the wrong way. He could not afford to take on someone else's problems. Two girls, alone on the road with no one to look after them, did not bear thinking about. He told himself that this situation must have been repeated countless times in the war, but it made no difference. He knew the girls now and could not abandon them.

The day grew hot, and Nish's leg more painful with every step. Liliwen was struggling too. They came to a rivulet trickling across the road, its reeds trampled into mud. Nish eyed the brown water, swallowing raspily. If he drank here it would probably make him sick.

The girls stood by. 'I can't go any further.' Liliwen wiped away tears of pain.

Her sister pointed upstream to where a pair of umbrella-shaped trees leaned towards each other. 'It'll be cool in the shade.'

'I don't think it's a good idea to stop yet,' said Nish. 'The enemy –'

'We don't need *your* help,' said Meriwen, eyes flashing.

'Yes, we do. Don't be silly, sis.'

The shade looked beautifully cool, and Nish's throat was as dry as the soles of his boots, so he accompanied them up the wooded stream, gripping his mallet. It was a good place for an ambush. There were all kinds of vermin on the road, desperate for whatever they could get.

His stomach began to bubble and churn. The stream was about a long leap across, and here flowing clear and clean. The girls cooled their feet in the running water. Nish drank until he was bursting, then looked for fruit, nuts or anything else edible. He found nothing; it was too early in the season. Judging by the trails twisting through the scrub, plenty of game came to drink, though he doubted if anything would be slow enough for him to thump with the mallet.

'I don't suppose you've got flint and tinder in your pack?' he said to Meriwen.

'Of course! Do you want to make a fire?'

'I need to boil water and bathe my wounds.'

She handed him a flintstone, a small packet of tinder and a little cooking pot with a wire handle. Nish gathered dry wood and soon had a fire going. It gave off just the faintest trail of blue smoke. He heated water, cleaned his wounds, then poked the dirty bandages under the boiling water. After a few minutes he fished them out with a stick and, when they were cool enough, wrapped the wounds again.

His stomach was now churning like a milk separator. Those wretched oysters! Nish hobbled into the scrub to relieve himself. It took a long while, and he had just turned back when he heard a muffled cry.

The girls! Why had he gone so far from the fire? He ran a few steps before realising that he was heading in the wrong direction. Everything looked the same in this scrub. Walking in a circle until he found his footmarks, he followed them back. When he finally burst into the clearing by the rivulet, the girls were gone.

If he lost them, Meriwen and Liliwen were as good as dead. Their abductors would take them away from the crowded road. Which way? They might have gone up the stream, or off into the scrub. He hunted for tracks.

There were tracks everywhere. Hundreds of refugees had filled their water bottles here. Nish hobbled back and forth, feeling panicky. Why hadn't he been more careful? He'd had a bad feeling about this place from the beginning.

Tracks ran into the scrub here and there, though none were the right size. Wading the stream, he searched the other side and came upon several sets of marks leading upstream. Among them he saw a small bootprint. Nish limped that way.

There could have been two abductors, or even three. Bad odds, especially if they were armed. One man with a sword would make short work of his mallet. Hopefully they would not take the children too far, or Nish's injured leg would beat him. He followed the tracks for a few hundred paces by the water, came into a clearing and lost them on hard ground.

Now what? Nish stopped, cupping his ear. Was that a groan? No, just the wind rubbing two tree trunks together. Had they gone back across the stream? He could see no tracks there. He took the risk and kept going. Despair crept over him. If he lost them he would never be able to forgive himself.

There – a footprint in the soft mud of a dried-up pool. It

belonged to one of the girls, and the dry grass was crushed beside it. He followed stealthily and, anxious minutes later, caught a flash up ahead, perhaps the sun reflecting off a pack buckle. Creeping forward, he peered between the trees.

There were two of them: big, unshaven ruffians in filthy clothes. Each had hold of a struggling girl but, as Nish watched, the taller of the men struck Meriwen across the face and threw her down on the grass. Nish had a moment of panic, a failure of nerve. There was no way he could attack them both. He closed his eyes, feeling sick. Then Meriwen screamed.

He hurled himself through the trees, ignoring the agony in his leg, and swung wildly at the man who held Liliwen. His leg folded up and the blow missed. Thrusting Liliwen to one side, the man lashed out.

The blow caught Nish on the side of the head, making his skull ring. He staggered backwards. The man came after him, arms flailing. Nish did not have the strength to lift the mallet above his head. All he could do, as the bearish man lunged, was to swing it up, underarm.

The amateurish attack took the man by surprise and the heavy, iron-bound mallet caught him fair under the chin. His head snapped back so hard that his feet lifted off the ground. He fell, legs thrashing.

The other fellow flailed at Nish with a cudgel, which caught him on the elbow. The mallet went flying and Nish's whole arm began to go numb. The backswing crashed against his ribs. The third blow was aimed at his head.

Nish ducked but the cudgel clipped the top of his skull, knocking him to his knees. His vision blurred; he could hardly see. His hand, scratching on the ground, found a pebble. Nish hurled it at the ruffian's face. It missed.

The man kicked Nish's legs from under him. Nish went sprawling. The man lunged. Hands big enough to throttle a steer went around his throat. The fellow gave out a horrible, black-toothed grin and squeezed.

TWENTY-SIX

Nish tried to push him off but the man pinned his shoulders with his knees. Then he tried to knee the ruffian in the groin but was in the wrong position. He kicked and squirmed. It was no good. The huge thumbs dug into his windpipe.

Tossing his head from side to side, he managed to gasp, 'Please, don't!'

The man spat in his face. As Nish began to black out, he gave one last, despairing heave. It failed.

There came a nauseating pulpy thud and the man collapsed on top of him, his eyes wide open. Nish choked; the fingers had locked around his neck. He tried to push the fellow off but he was far too heavy. Nish managed to get his fingers under the man's thumbs and prise them away. Liliwen was on her knees, heaving on one arm. Together they rolled him to one side.

Nish could not stand up. He wiped his face and gasped, 'Thank you. Are you all right?'

She nodded stiffly, avoiding his eyes.

'What happened?'

'I whacked him in the back of the head with your mallet,' whispered Liliwen. 'I'm sorry. I didn't know what else to do.'

'You did well,' said Nish, clasping her hands in his. 'You saved my life. No one could have done better, Liliwen.'

Meriwen was sitting up, looking at the other man, who had

stopped kicking. Judging by the angle of his head, his neck was broken.

'They did not harm you?' Nish asked Meriwen.

'No,' she said in the faintest whisper. 'We're both all right.'

'We'd better go,' said Nish, 'before they recover.'

'Yes.' Liliwen was still staring at her victim.

He was not going to recover either. Liliwen's blow had crushed his skull and killed him instantly. Nish suspected she knew that. A difficult thing for a twelve-year-old to cope with. Difficult enough for him, for that matter. Nish checked the other ruffian. His neck *was* broken. He, Nish, had killed a man.

'Come on!' he said. 'There may be more of them.'

Nish wiped the bloodstained mallet on the ground when he thought Liliwen was not looking, and led the way back to the road. The girls collected their packs and they kept going all day without stopping. Liliwen did not complain about her blisters. The girls said virtually nothing. As did Nish, though his leg was in agony, his throat was so swollen that every breath hurt, and he was seeing double. He was too caught up with what had happened. He had killed. The fellow had been a villain, certainly, but hadn't desperation driven him to it? Could he, Nish, end up like that one day?

'Is it far to Kundizand?' Nish asked when the day was near its end. He did not want to spend the night out here.

'Not far,' said Meriwen.

They turned a corner at dusk and the lights of the town were twinkling ahead of them. They had not seen a lyrinx all day but he could not allow himself to relax until, finally, they reached the gates.

They were passed through without question. The normal checks had been suspended; just to be human was a passport. The town was bursting with people. As well as its normal population of eight thousand, there were at least thirty thousand worn out, desperate refugees. Every bed had been taken long ago. Every street was jammed; people were bedding down in the alleys and everywhere else that was out of the way of direct traffic.

They fought their way through the throngs, Nish keeping close by the twins. It would be easy to lose them and impossible to find them if he did.

'Where were you to meet your parents?' he asked.

'In the town square, by the wind clock.'

The square was an explosion of people – it took a good fifteen minutes to struggle from one side to the other. Eventually they reached the clock, which was striking the hour of seven. Its screw-shaped scarlet sails twirled merrily in the breeze, though down in the square the air was still and stifling. Nish and the girls worked back and forth for an hour without finding anyone the twins recognised.

Liliwen burst into tears. 'They're dead, I know it.'

'Father said he'd be here,' Meriwen said soothingly. 'He never breaks his promises, Liliwen. We have to keep looking.'

Nish thought he saw Colm's sisters, Ketila and Fransi, across the square. He shouted their names but the sound was swallowed up in the din, the crowd closed again and he could not find them.

By the time the clock struck nine, Nish could barely move. 'We'd better find a place to sleep –' he began, when a tall woman screamed, pushed through the crowd and threw herself at the girls.

'Meriwen, Liliwen! Where have you been? We thought we'd lost you.'

Meriwen burst into tears. 'We went home, Mummy, but you were gone. We were so afraid –'

'But you did as you were told. Good girls!' The woman embraced Meriwen, and then Liliwen.

'Where's Father?' Liliwen asked anxiously. 'Is –'

'He's just over there,' said the woman. 'Troist!' she yelled. 'They're here!' Shortly a stocky, handsome man in a lieutenant's uniform shouldered through the crowd, beaming from ear to ear.

He embraced his daughters, gathered the family up and was shepherding them away when Meriwen said, 'Wait, Father. I must thank this man –'

Troist spun on his heel, inspecting Nish and evidently not

much liking what he saw. 'Who the blazes are you, fellow?' he demanded, his lip curling.

'My name is Cryl-Nish Hlar, surr, and I –'

'If you have rendered my daughters a service, I thank you for it.' He reached into his coin pocket.

'Father,' said Liliwen, 'he saved our lives! Two horrible men grabbed us and took us into the forest –'

'What?' cried Troist. He spun around to his daughters. 'Are you all right, girls? They did not harm you? By heavens –'

'We are untouched,' said Meriwen calmly. 'But only because Nish attacked them with his mallet.'

'Give me their descriptions, man,' cried Troist. 'I'll see they hang for this.'

'They're dead,' Nish said softly. 'I broke the neck of one of them, and the other your daughter struck down with this mallet when he had his hands around my throat.' Nish pulled down his collar, revealing the bruised and blackened flesh.

'The devil!' cried Troist. 'I owe you an eternal debt, man. Name it and you shall have it.'

'I want no payment,' said Nish, 'but . . . I see you are an officer in the army. You may be able to advise me.'

'Oh?' Troist said warily.

Nish lowered his voice. 'It is a matter of the utmost secrecy. I must speak to a senior officer, the master of the city, or a representative of the Council of Scrutators.'

Troist took another look at him. 'You are not from these parts.'

'I have come all the way from Einunar.' Nish said no more. He did not know whom he could trust and the news he carried was a great burden to him.

'The master of Kundizand is not here,' said Troist. 'Neither is any representative of the Council. Perquisitor Unibas was in Nilkerrand when it was attacked and has not been heard of since. We are quite as lost as you are, I'm afraid.' He shook his head wearily.

'And the army?' said Nish.

'Slain, or scattered to the four posts of the compass. The enemy's favourite trick is to attack the command tents first with

258

flying lyrinx. I fear that all my senior officers were killed, else there would not be this chaos now. Had I not been on leave I would be dead too.'

Nish turned away in despair. He had no money, no papers, no friends. If he did not get treatment for his leg, he was likely to lose it. He had to trust someone and this fellow had an honest look about him. And you could tell a lot about people from their children. Meriwen and Liliwen were bright, resourceful and well brought up. He turned back to Troist.

'Then I must trust you, surr. I am in the service of Scrutator Xervish Flydd and carry vital intelligence about the war.'

'I wondered about your accent. You'd better come with us, Cryl-Nish. We cannot talk of such matters here.'

He introduced Nish to his wife, Yara, who was an advocate. She was a half-head taller than Troist, with a lean, horsy face, big teeth and flared nostrils, though she had an elegant manner. Her dark hair hung in a single plait all the way down her back.

Troist was short and muscular, with a small head capped in sandy curls, a blunt nose and a square jaw. His eyes were blue, his shoulders broad, his fingers thick and blunt. He exuded capability.

It took an hour to force their way through the crowds to their inn, though it was only a few blocks away. Cramped and musty, their room was considerably better than the hovel Nish had last slept in. He lay on the floor with his head in his hands and could scarcely believe that he had survived.

There was no possibility of a bath, for the overcrowding had exacerbated a water shortage, but Yara announced that dinner was on its way. Shortly a skinny lad staggered in under a laden tray. The smell made Nish drool. He had not had a proper meal since leaving the manufactory a month ago, and this smelt better than anything he had eaten there.

The girls told their story over dinner, then Nish his, leaving out only such details about the amplimet and the Aachim invasion as might be considered strategic information. These he would reveal after the children were asleep.

'So, your father is Perquisitor Jal-Nish Hlar?' said Troist.

259

'Yes. Do you know him?'

'No, but I've heard much about him. Hmn.'

What did that mean? Nish's father had a lot of enemies.

Troist questioned Nish in detail about his father. No one could be too careful, for the enemy had been surprisingly successful at recruiting spies and impostors. Finally he seemed satisfied, whereupon Yara began, for she had travelled to Tiksi a good few years ago. Nish must have answered to her satisfaction, for she made a sign to her husband, to which Troist nodded. He glanced across to where the twins were curled up together on the small bed asleep.

'Well, Cryl-Nish,' said Troist, 'your tale astounds me, and that doesn't happen often. It was a happy day when you ran into our daughters on the road, and I will never forget your service.'

'Thank you, surr. If I may, I will tell you the rest of it, for I'm deathly tired and my head still throbs from the blows I took.'

'Does it?' said Yara, coming up close with her candle. She checked his skull with long cool fingers, turned his head from side to side and looked into his eyes. 'I don't think there's any damage, apart from a minor concussion. I'll mix a potion for you.'

While she was busy, Nish told Troist about the amplimet, what he knew of Tiaan's geomantic abilities, and all she had done at Tirthrax.

'There has been rumour of an enormous fleet of craft, that resemble clankers, coming over the mountains from the west,' said Troist. 'No doubt our leaders have the scrutator's despatches, though no news has come down to me. But of course I am only a junior officer.'

'Though a brilliant one,' said Yara, handing Nish a mug. 'Drink this.'

Troist bowed in her direction. 'Yara is the genius of the family,' he said. 'She will be Advocate-General one day. I am merely diligent and hard-working.'

'Pfft!' said Yara, attending Nish's leg. 'You will be commander of all our forces before the children are grown.'

'I would like to be,' said Troist. 'I make no secret of that. But neither hard work nor good connections are enough. One must

260

also have the good fortune to be where it matters, and the ability to seize the opportunity when it comes.'

'And win it!' said Yara.

'Perhaps we can help each other,' said Nish.

'Perhaps,' Troist said in a non-committal way. 'What is it you want, Cryl-Nish?'

'Since I lack the means to go home, I must do my best for the war, and for myself, here. As you know, I am an artificer by trade and have seen combat with the enemy. And with my knowledge of the Aachim constructs, I may be able to help plan to defeat them, should it come to war.' That was a faint hope, since he had seen them only at a distance, but it was the one advantage he had.

'Indeed,' said Troist, who seemed to be thinking fast. 'And what can I do for you?'

'Take me on as your adjutant.'

'Only the commander has an adjutant,' said Troist, looking to Yara as if seeking her advice. She was a cool, reserved woman except with her family. It would be hard to fool her. But Yara nodded, almost imperceptibly.

'Tactical assistant, then. Call it what you will. I would like to make my career in the army, by your side. Can this be done?'

'I don't see why not,' said Troist. 'You are well spoken, well connected, and you have valuable experience. I will see about it as soon as we rejoin my unit. That, unfortunately, could be more difficult than you might think.'

'Why is that, surr?' asked Nish.

'The defeated army has been scattered. I hope enough have survived to make a small fighting force, but first I must find them. I am leaving in the morning. You may come with me.'

They slipped out of town the following morning, heading east. Nish had expected it would just be himself and Troist, but the family accompanied him, along with five soldiers discovered among the refugees. They were all mounted. Nish had no idea where the horses came from but it spoke considerably of Troist that he had been able to obtain them in such chaos.

261

Troist was busy all day, despatching his troops one way or another, conferring with new soldiers who appeared out of the dust, some mounted, armed and ready for war, others footsore, worn out and weaponless. Nish tried to keep up but it was a long time since he had sat on a horse and his head still throbbed. Finally, catching him deathly pale and swaying in the saddle, Troist said curtly, 'Your place is back at the camp. I'll see you tonight.'

It was not a reprimand, though it felt like one. Nonetheless, Nish was glad to return. The camp was hidden in a scrubby gully scarcely visible from a distance. Three soldiers stood guard. Yara was working in an infirmary tent which already had half a dozen casualties in it, and more coming in all the time. Meriwen and Liliwen cleaned wounds and applied bandages. Clearly it was not the first time they had done it. Everything looked efficient and well-organised, though there was much worried talk about their lack of supplies and weapons. Nish lay in a corner, closed his eyes and fell asleep.

He was woken by someone roaring out orders like a drill sergeant. A soldier was directing the laying out of the camp, which now comprised almost a hundred troops.

As it grew dark a squad of a hundred and fifty marched in, followed by smaller groups and a mounted troop. There was no sign of Troist but as the mess tent began serving dinner Nish heard an unmistakable squeak and rattle.

His professional interest aroused, he limped to the edge of the firelight. Four clankers appeared, one after another, their eight mechanical legs moving in rhythmic pairs. They were a different design from the ones he was familiar with, lower and broader, with the overlapping armour plates shaped like leaves rather than oval shields. The shooter's platform on top contained seats for two shooters: one to load and fire the catapult, the other for the javelard that could fire its heavy spears right through the armoured body of a lyrinx.

Troist came galloping in, close to midnight. Sliding off his horse he gave it an affectionate pat, greeted his wife and daughters and immediately went to the command area, a patch of stony ground covered by a canvas slung on long ropes from tree branches. Nish was called in as well.

The tent was crowded. A small map was spread out on a folding table. 'We are here,' Troist said, indicating a spot on the map about six leagues south-east of Nilkerrand. 'We'll break camp at dawn and head south-east, across the plains of Almadin in the direction of the Worm Wood. That's an enormous forest,' he said to Nish, circling it on the map. 'Quite the largest in eastern Lauralin. Our next camp will be here,' he stabbed at a location with his forefinger, 'or failing that, here. I hope we can find more soldiers on the way. If General Boryl escaped –'

'He did not, surr,' said a bald man with a bandage around his bare chest. 'I'm his adjutant. I saw him fall.'

'Slain?' asked Troist.

'The blood would have filled a bucket. His head was practically severed –'

'Later!' Troist glanced at his wide-eyed children. 'What of the other officers?'

'Most are dead, surr. The enemy broke into the command tent and slew them in a minute. Had not I been outside they would have killed me too. You are the most senior officer alive, surr. If you can't rally the troops, I fear all Almadin will be lost.'

'I thought as much,' Troist said heavily. 'Well, there's not much I can do with a few hundred troops and a handful of clankers, but whatever can be done, I'll do it.'

He turned away, and Nish, standing at his elbow, caught a strange gleam in the man's eyes. Troist's chance had come. Should he be able to seize it, it would be the making of him. If he failed, none of them would survive.

Almadin was a largely treeless land, flat apart from residual mounds topped in black rock, the tells of towns abandoned in ages past. The soil was barren, salt-crusted, and supported only yellow grass. Here and there were round saltpans, quite bare of life. Carrion birds circled in the distance.

They wound back and forth across the arid land for days. Troist spent all the daylight hours in the saddle, combing the countryside for survivors of the battle and sending them back to the camp. All the troops he could spare were doing the same. The trickle of battered, dispirited soldiers became a flood.

More clankers began to come in. Many had been lost in the battle, for as soon as the officers had been slain the enemy turned the attack to the clankers' shooters, exposed on their platforms atop the machines. Once the shooter was dead a clanker operator could do nothing but flee. Some machines had only an operator, others as many soldiers as could fit inside and cling to the sides and top.

Troist greeted each one, no matter what time they arrived, and ensured they were fed, given a place to sleep and had their wounds attended. Nothing was too much trouble. He scarcely seemed to sleep at all.

On the fifth night he took a detachment out on a raid, on horseback and in half a dozen clankers fitted with the new sound-cloaker that reduced their rattling squeal to a whisper. Nish was not invited to go with them and knew nothing of their objective. Yara, who did but would not say, paced the whole night. Her worry infected Nish. If Troist and his bold team did not return the little army would fall apart.

Dawn came and there was no sign of them. Noon went by. Yara was still pacing, rigidly now. The sun went down, and finally a dust cloud appeared on the horizon.

'It's Troist!' cried Yara, her reserve failing for an instant. Tears glistened on her eyelids.

In they came, weary and brown with dust but grinning broadly. The clankers were packed with swords, crossbows, camp implements, tents, provisions and other gear abandoned by the defeated army. Hastily constructed wooden sleds, piled high, were towed behind.

'This should solve the supply problem for a while,' said Troist. 'You could not call it a victory, since we were unopposed. We're still running from the enemy but not as fast as before.'

'Where are the enemy?' Nish asked.

'We saw them in the air above Nilkerrand, and doubtless

264

some still occupy what remains of the city, but most, I am told, went back across the sea to Meldorin.'

'So the attack on Nilkerrand was a raid, not an invasion?'

'A raid and forerunner to the invasion.'

'When will that occur?'

'If I knew that, Cryl-Nish, I wouldn't be wasting time listening to your inane questions.' He turned to his wife. 'Now that things are more secure, I'd like you and the children to go back to Kundizand.'

'No, Daddy!' cried Liliwen. 'Don't send us away again, please.'

Meriwen, normally conservative and responsible, supported her. 'We wouldn't feel safe without you, Daddy. And if you get hurt, you'll need us to look after you.'

'I'm not going to argue –' he began, but Yara laid a hand on his.

'Just a few more days,' she said. 'The enemy can fly across the sea to Kundizand in hours. We're safer here.'

'Oh, all right, but as soon as the chance comes . . .'

'Of course,' she said.

The army slowly swelled as they travelled. Troist had begun to form it into fighting units, and as the news got around, soldiers appeared from everywhere. After ten days they had a force numbering three thousand, several hundred of them mounted, as well as a fleet of seventy-one clankers. Five more machines needed repairs before they could go into battle, and Nish worked long days helping the other artificers get them ready. He learned more about his trade in that short period than he had in his years at the manufactory. Many more clankers lay abandoned at the battlefield east of Nilkerrand, or in flight, but until operators could be found or trained, they were useless. Troist had done a wonderful job so far, though he was worried that the scrutators would not let him keep his command.

In the evenings Nish sat with Troist and another tactician, telling them all he knew, or had deduced, about constructs. Together they began to formulate tactics to attack the machines, tactics for defence, and plans for all kinds of contingencies. They worked until after midnight every night, each taking one side or the other and fighting imaginary battles in a variety of terrain.

This night, the twelfth since leaving the inn, Troist tossed his lead pieces aside before the midnight bell had struck. He rubbed red eyes, yawning.

'Games are all very well but they count for naught when the battle starts. Out there, we can't see what's going on after the first few minutes. Our messengers are slain, or the field simply changes so quickly that our orders are useless.'

'They don't make the kinds of mistakes we do in battle,' said the other officer, Lunny. 'It's as if the enemy can communicate with each other.'

'What if we were to send up an observer in a balloon?' said Nish. 'He could see the whole battle and signal us what was really going on.'

'Until the wind blew it away,' said Troist, 'or a flying lyrinx tore it open, which they would do at once.'

A messenger ran in, saluted and handed Troist a folded piece of paper. Troist read it, frowned and stood up.

'We will find out soon enough, gentlemen. A sizeable force of lyrinx are moving in our direction; many hundreds. We must prepare to do battle in the morning.'

He looked every inch a commander, though as his eyes rested on Yara, who sat up the back winding bandages, Troist stiffened. Tomorrow could see the brutal end of his family, but it was too late to send them to safety. Why hadn't he taken the chance while he had it?

PART THREE

DIPLOMAT

TWENTY-SEVEN

Irisis woke with terrible roars and cries ringing in her ears. She felt her throbbing forehead, which sported a lump the size of a small potato. Lights, surrounded by haloes, danced along the corridor. They seemed to be moving closer. She rubbed her eyes, trying to see what they were, but they only separated into paired images.

She supported herself on the rock wall, struggling to recall what had happened. She had been on the eighth level of the mine. A lyrinx had come after her and Ullii had fled.

'Who . . . are you?' Irisis said to the first pair of lights.

The scrutator chuckled. 'How quickly they forget.' Bending down, he whispered, 'It's your lover, Xervish Flydd, come to rescue you.'

'How did you know –?'

'Peate turned up with a story about you going off with Ullii into the forbidden section, so I came to find out why. We had just about given you up when Ullii hurtled out from a tunnel that isn't even on the map, crying for us to save you from the clawers. So here we are.'

'How did you manage it?'

'Mancer's secrets, crafter. Mancer's secrets.'

Taking her arm, he helped her to the lift, which was not far at all. Within the hour, Irisis was tucked up in bed with a cool compress across her forehead and a steaming bowl of willow-bark tea on the bedside table.

The scrutator took the map, which was still crumpled in her hand, and unfolded it. 'The seeker said something about good crystal. A *big* crystal.'

'I've marked it on the map, with a red circle.'

'Here?' He held the map out.

'That's where Ullii sensed it, but down at an angle. Like this!' She mimicked the gesture. 'The ninth or tenth level.'

He frowned. 'It had better not be lower than the ninth. We'll get started in the morning.'

That being miner's work, Irisis went back to her own, directing the twenty artisans and fifty prentices in the making of clanker controllers. Once a day Ullii was taken down to check that the miners were driving in the right direction. Irisis sometimes accompanied her. Working on the eighth level was perilous and slow. The miners were guarded by squads of soldiers with heavy crossbows, but they saw no further sign of the lyrinx.

They reached the ninth level, which was dry here, but found no crystal. Ullii still pointed in the same direction so they continued sinking the shaft towards the tenth. Water began to trickle into the workings and they had to bring in a pump, powered by two workers on a treadmill, to keep them dry. Below the tenth, the trickle would become an unstoppable flood.

A couple of weeks after Ullii's discovery of the crystal, Irisis woke to the familiar crash of a catapult ball against the wall of the manufactory. She was running to her station, up on the wall near the front gate, when the scrutator caught her by the arm.

'What is it?' she yelled, for already the racket was deafening.

'Take no risks!'

'I have to get to my post!' She tried to pull away but he did not let go.

'I mean it, Irisis. I can't replace you.'

'Plenty of women are prepared to warm the scrutator's bed!' she snapped, deliberately mistaking his meaning.

'Don't be a fool, crafter. I need you: to make controllers, to support Ullii and, most of all, to work with me on the node problem.' Nodding curtly, he let her go.

Irisis ran up the stairs, feeling guilty that she had not done better, but she could not make controllers without crystal. On the wall, crossbow in her hands, she soon forgot the scrutator's warning. In the light of the watch flares Irisis could see eight lyrinx, and from the clamour on the far walls, there must be just as many on that side.

A catapult ball sang overhead, smashing into one of the furnace chimneys, which collapsed in a shower of bricks. The masons and bricklayers would slave for a fortnight to repair it.

Crouching between the battlements, Irisis sighted on a large, green-crested lyrinx that seemed to be directing the attack from the eaves of the forest. Stay where you are, just another second. She fired. The lyrinx jerked, then slapped a hand to its breast. The bolt had gone low, embedding itself in the breast plate. The creature would be sorely bruised but no real damage had been done. It raised its fists to the sky in a voiceless cry.

Irisis was reloading the clumsy weapon when someone cried, 'Look out!' and she was struck hard between the shoulders. The crossbow skidded down the paving, struck the wall and went off, firing its bolt into the stone.

Irisis was on her knees, trying to work out what had hit her, when she was lifted in the air. A hovering lyrinx had her in its claws, flapping desperately. She must have weighed more than it had anticipated.

She thrashed her arms and legs. Her coat tore and she fell free but the creature slashed out and its claws went through her collar. The beast wobbled in the air as it tried for a better grip. She kicked, caught it in the groin and it went close to dropping her. Its eyes were staring, its breath coming in tortured gasps.

Irisis tried to pull out of her coat but could not get her arms free. She smacked at the face of the lyrinx, which snapped back, almost taking her hand off. Its wings beat irregularly as it struggled to gain height. She attacked again and managed to poke it in the eye with a finger. It canted sideways, its eye closed and she thought it was going to fall over the edge.

271

Its head lunged, the great teeth snapping so close that she smelt its hot breath. The abduction had failed; now it was trying to kill her. Irisis drew her legs up and kicked it in the jaw. The lyrinx howled and almost fell out of the air. She was a heavy burden for a creature that required the Secret Art to keep its own weight aloft. Irisis touched the artisan's pliance hanging around her neck and could sense the distortion the lyrinx was making in the field.

She kicked again but it held its head well back now. Its free hand went for her throat, but so slowly she had time to get her arm across. The claws tore harmlessly through the heavy fabric of her coat. The lyrinx gained control, the great wings beat and it lifted. Irisis could see the guards, their weapons tracking the creature, but no one dared shoot for fear of hitting her.

The scrutator came running up the steps, only to stop at the top as if he had run into a wall. The beast was gaining height now, drifting out toward the edge, its wings thumping the air. Just a couple of spans and it could let her go. She heard its rumbling purr. Irisis struggled but its grip was too tight. She had no knife or any other kind of weapon. She kicked and missed. Kicked again.

The creature rotated in the air. Time seemed to be going so slowly. Flydd was up on the edge of the wall, then he whirled, racing for the steps that led to the lookout above the gate. What was he doing?

Appearing at the top of the watch-tower, he took a flying leap out across the angle of the wall. She felt sure he was going to fall to his death, but the lyrinx drifted underneath and he landed with a thump that drove it out of the air. Irisis crashed into the battlement, the creature landing on top of her with stunning impact. It slid down onto the walkway, its skin flaring bright orange, claws scraping the stone beside her face. Lowering its head, it thrust forward. Her arms were trapped. All she could do was draw her knees up before her face. The lyrinx wrenched them apart and kept coming.

The scrutator's knife dug in between the neck plates and dragged across. Hot blood exploded from its throat, spraying the stone, her face and her hair. The lyrinx stopped struggling. Two soldiers dragged her out from underneath and she watched the great beast die, its eyes slowly closing, the head drooping. The death colours – mottled yellows, greens and scarlets – kept on flickering long after life was extinguished.

Irisis could not stand up. Flydd wiped the blood off her face, sat her with her back to a battlement and put her crossbow in her hands.

'I told you to be careful. Get your breath. We've a long way to go.' He ran down the wall.

A ball smashed stone into stinging gravel. Another crashed through the light-tower, scattering blazing tar-soaked straw everywhere. Little fires began on the roofs. Attendants scrambled to put them out.

A boulder struck the massive iron gates below their section of the wall, tearing one off its hinges. Another ball hurtled through the gap, followed by a third, equally large. A splintering crash was confirmed by the doorman's shout.

'To the gate! The inner gate is broken.'

Levering herself to her feet, Irisis peered over. The lyrinx charged in a group. In the gloom she could not count their numbers. One fell outside the iron gates, another on the step, struck down by a lump of rock dropped from the wall, but it got up again. She fired her crossbow as fast as she could load it, though soon there were no targets left. The survivors were inside the manufactory.

The attacks on the wall continued, the catapults firing from the edge of the forest. In the dark it was almost impossible to hit them, while the soldiers on the wall were easy targets. A splatting thud signalled the end of another guard.

Not long before dawn she saw Flydd hauling himself up the stair by the railing. He looked as if all the blood had been sucked out of him.

'What's happening?' Irisis yelled.

'They drove us right through the manufactory, but we ambushed them near the furnaces, firing red-hot bolts. They didn't like that at all. We killed five and injured the others, and they fled out the back door.'

'Red-hot bolts,' said Irisis. 'Whose idea was that?'

'One of the artificers. He's dead, now. It turned the battle though; changed minor wounds into disabling ones.'

Irisis, imagining the agony of such a wound, felt ill.

'We've suffered terrible casualties,' he went on. 'At least sixty dead and as many wounded. We can't take much more, Irisis.'

'They're only firing intermittently now. I'd say they've had enough.'

'There were sixteen and we've killed eleven, at least, but don't think this is the end of it. They'll be back.'

'They're deadly accurate with those catapults,' said Irisis. 'Do you think the attack on me was deliberate?'

The scrutator was aiming through an arrow slit with a borrowed crossbow. He fired. 'I do. They've kidnapped artisans before. It went straight for you and would not let go even when that risked its own life. They don't usually go for suicide missions so they must have wanted you badly.'

'Or wanted me dead. Thank you, Xervish.'

'We also want you badly,' he said dismissively.

Shortly afterwards the attack ended, the surviving lyrinx fading into the forest. By daybreak there was no sign of them. Flydd called a meeting in the refectory to review the damage.

'The gates and front doors will have to be completely rebuilt,' said the chief mason. 'We'll make a temporary wall out front, not that it'll do much good. If they attack tonight with as much force, I don't see how we can survive.'

'I'm sure they will attack tonight,' said Flydd. 'They'd be fools not to.'

There was worse news and it was not long in coming. Chief Miner Cloor, a little nuggetty fellow whose pores were so impregnated by mine dust that it looked as if he was covered in blackheads, stumped in.

'The lyrinx have taken the mine, surr.'

'How many?' asked Flydd. He did not look surprised, though his scrawny shoulders drooped even further.

Irisis felt for him. Since he'd arrived there had been one disaster after another. He would be blamed for them all.

274

'Can't tell, surr. We saw five or six behind the grid. That could be all . . .'

'Or there could be another hundred down there,' said the scrutator bleakly. 'Evacuate the miners' village, chief miner. We can't defend it as well.'

Cloor nodded and stumped out again.

After the night's exertions, few people were able to work. In the case of Irisis's artisans, it hardly mattered, since they already had a large store of controllers assembled, awaiting hedrons to complete them. That was looking increasingly unlikely now.

Irisis snatched a few hours sleep then returned to the refectory, where she found the scrutator sitting at a table in the far corner with the chief miner, Overseer Tuniz and Captain Gir-Dan. Maps of the various levels of the mine were spread out in front of them.

'They must have come in through the lower tunnels,' said the captain. 'The enemy had captured the mine before the outside guards knew a thing.'

'Unless they had skived off from their duty,' the scrutator said darkly.

'Let's have no talk of neglect of duty, if you please, *surr*,' said Cloor. He was as irascible as Flydd, with little respect for any authority save his own.

Flydd gave him a black stare. The chief miner glared back. Neither broke. 'Enough,' Flydd said finally. 'The fault does not matter. What can we do about it?'

'I've talked with my surveyors. We're sure they're getting in this way.' Cloor's battered fingernail indicated a long tunnel down on the ninth level. 'If we could drop the roof here, we'd have them trapped and it would just be a matter of winkling them out.'

'Deadly winkling,' said the captain. 'A dozen lyrinx would be a match for fifty of my men, down there in the dark.'

'I'd starve them out,' snapped Cloor. 'Not even lyrinx can go a month without food.'

'I can't wait a month for crystal. How long would it take to bring down the roof?' asked the scrutator.

'We could do it in a few hours in this section.' Cloor's finger marked an 'X' on the map. 'And it's relatively close to the workings. Of course, we'd need a strong guard.'

'At least forty men,' said the captain.

'If I send that many down,' the scrutator mused, 'and they attack here, as they are bound to do . . . We might well lose the manufactory.'

'Without the mine there's not much point to the manufactory,' said Irisis.

The scrutator dismissed that with an irritable sweep of the hand. 'The mine is just a hole in the ground, but to replace this manufactory would take five thousand people working for four years.'

'What do you want us to do?'

'Get some rest. We'll be on the wall again tonight, I'll be bound.' Flydd rose. 'What do they want?' he muttered on the way out. 'Do they aim to deny us the crystal, or is there something more sinister at work?'

That night, on the gong of midnight, the lyrinx attacked again. Irisis had just dozed off when a catapult ball, fired up at a steep angle, came smashing through the roof a few doors away, demolishing the room of one of the recently arrived artisans. The silence was followed by her screams, then shouts as the manufactory scrambled out of bed.

Irisis was the first to get there. The artisan lay in the splinters of her bed, unharmed but screaming her lungs out. More balls began to fall, so swiftly that the catapults must have been firing many at a time. Though only the size of melons, they wrought terrible damage. Not all the sleepers were as lucky as the first.

Irisis dressed and put on the metal hat she wore down the mine. It would not save her from these missiles, but might protect her from the slates that were falling all around.

There was a lull of a minute or so. She ran into the scrutator in the corridor. 'What are we to do?' she shouted.

'It's not this I'm so worried about,' he said, 'though it's doing damage enough.'

She looked up through one of the holes in the roof. 'What *are* you worried about?'

'Fire –' As he spoke, a flaming ball descended from the sky, hit the roof and slid in through a hole to land in one of the ruined rooms. Flames leapt up. Irisis grabbed a fire bucket and emptied the sand on it.

'What is it?' the scrutator yelled.

'Rock dipped in tar.'

Soon blazing missiles were falling all around. Irisis and fifty other people were kept busy putting out the fires. They still had many to go, and the fire team were attaching their canvas hoses to the hand pumps when the barrage stopped. At once the attack on the walls and front gate resumed.

'I don't think we're going to survive this time,' said the scrutator as their paths crossed again. 'Better pack up your gear.'

She stopped, staring at him. 'What do you mean?'

'We're *leaving*.'

'How?'

'I try to plan for all contingencies. The air-floater is standing by, up in the mountains. I've signalled it to come.'

'It'll be a sitting target, floating over the manufactory.'

'It will drop down behind the ridge. We'll sneak up inside the aqueduct where the enemy can't see us.'

'The air-floater won't carry a thousand people.'

'Not even twenty. The rest must stay behind.'

'To die!'

'More likely they'll be left alone once we're gone.'

'I've worked with these people for most of my life,' she said. 'I'm not leaving them.'

'I'm ordering you to. Anyway, we'll be in more danger than they are.'

Alhough Irisis was quite selfish, she could not bear the thought of running away. 'I've got work to do!' she snapped and went back up. The fires were under control now and Irisis preferred the danger of the wall; at least she could see what was coming.

They were losing. The lyrinx had an uncanny sense of where

to aim and their catapults picked off the guards one by one. Half were dead now, and most of the survivors carried injuries. Their replacements were just ordinary workers who did little damage to the enemy and were slain in droves. The dead still lay where they had fallen hours ago, for no one could be spared to carry them away. Irisis had known them all for years.

She checked the sky. Dawn was not far away but there was no sign of the air-floater and the scrutator had sent no message. Finally she dragged her exhausted body down for a drink and a bite to eat, a few minutes' relief from the hell that was the wall.

The scrutator was in his room, writing furiously. 'What's happened to your air-floater?' she said sarcastically. 'Another failure?'

Irisis regretted this the moment the words left her lips, but Flydd did not react. He looked numb.

'There's been nothing since I signalled. The lyrinx must have caught them.'

'Then we're finished,' she said.

'It seems so. I'm sorry.'

'Oh, well. I've been here before. And survived too.'

'I doubt you will this time,' he muttered.

'It was borrowed time anyway.'

There was a great roar outside. 'See what that is, will you?' he said, without looking up.

Irisis ran to the front gate, where she encountered Tuniz. The overseer had blood all down her front, though it was not her own. 'How are we doing?' Irisis gasped.

'We beat them back but I don't think we can do it again.'

Irisis peered through the broken gate. 'It's not long until dawn.'

'That won't stop them this time. They're too close to victory.'

Irisis ran back to report. 'The gate still holds,' she said to the scrutator, 'though it can't last long.'

'We'll be overrun by sunrise.' He carried a stack of papers to the furnace and heaved them in. They burst into flame and were sucked up the chimney.

Light began to spread through the manufactory. Irisis was on her way to the wall to make a last stand when a massed cheer sounded. She ran up the steps three at a time. A panting scrutator appeared beside her.

Over the ridge to the west, between the mountains, appeared a flotilla of clankers. These were bigger than the ones the manufactory made. The great, ten-legged monstrosities had a pair of javelards at the front as well as the catapult at the rear.

'Twenty-seven clankers,' said Irisis. 'That's the most beautiful sight I've ever seen.'

All along the wall the soldiers were laughing, cheering and embracing one another. The workers of the manufactory began streaming up the steps to rejoice in the sight. Already the lyrinx were pulling back, melting into the forest and disappearing. It was over.

She looked across at the scrutator. His face was twisted into the most bitter anguish Irisis had ever seen on a man.

'What's the matter?' she asked, laying her hand on his arm. He did not respond. 'Xervish?'

He turned that gaunt face, pared of all superfluous flesh, to her. 'Do you see the ensign on the leading clanker?'

'Yes, of course. What of it?'

'That is the flag of my most bitter enemy; and yours, Irisis. It belongs to the man who will not rest until he destroys us both. Perquisitor Jal-Nish Hlar!'

TWENTY-EIGHT

Irisis tried to breathe and found that she could not. The air felt as thick as the gruel they served in the refectory. She could not get it down. 'What will he do to us?' she gasped.

'He'll watch, and wait, and bide his time. He likes to drag these things out, the better to torment his enemies. We should go down. At least, I must. Stay back – better that he does not see you straight away.'

Flydd trudged down the steps, back bowed, and her heart went out to him. The scrutator was as tough as boiled leather. A hard man but, underneath, a decent and honourable one. He had done his best. It had not been enough.

Gathering her crossbow and a pocketful of quarrels, Irisis headed for the rear of the manufactory. Most of the workers remained atop, to cheer the clankers in. She went out of the rear door and down to the ravine over which the wastes were dumped into the river. It was a horrible, reeking place suited for nothing except despair. She wandered along the cliff. Irisis had not been this way since her failed suicide attempt, when all that had saved her had been Nish going over the edge and ending up in Eiryn Muss's air-moss farm.

She could hardly remember that self now, so long ago did it seem. What had happened to Muss? He had not been a halfwit at all, but the scrutator's prober, or spy. Muss had disappeared just as his secret was revealed.

Irisis missed Nish. Could he still be alive? It seemed unlikely, but Nish was resourceful. If anyone *could* survive it would be him. She paced along the escarpment. The smooth rocks were coated in brilliantly green spring moss, so soft she felt like taking off her boots and walking barefoot across it. Why not? Enjoy life's small pleasures while you may.

It was peaceful here. The damage to the manufactory could scarcely be seen. It looked an architectural abomination, but not the scene of a bloody and murderous battle.

Irisis sat by the drop-off. The lichens made a patchwork of colours – green and grey, brown and yellow, and even red. They gave her an idea for a brooch. She began to plan it in her head, knowing she would never make it now.

It was funny the way life could turn out. Who could have imagined this just a few short months ago? She tossed a pebble in her hand, reached out to throw it over the edge, but drew back. Nish had done that, and look at the consequences. She saw them cascading on into the future for as long as time existed. The thought paralysed her, for a few seconds, then Irisis smiled, and shrugged, and dropped her pebble on the ground. She could not live her life that way. Dusting her hands, she headed back.

She reached the gravelled expanse out the front at the same time as the leading clanker. It clattered to a halt. The shooter leapt down and stood by the rear hatch with his hand gripping the lever, but did not open it. The rest of the clankers rattled in, almost filling the yard. All but the first disgorged armed, hard-bitten veterans, ten from each. They stood by their machines, at attention.

Xervish Flydd emerged from the shattered front gate, a small, withered man, standing alone. The rising sun caught the angles and planes of his face. He looked almost as ruined as the front of the manufactory.

The shooter of the leading clanker flung the hatch upwards. A figure emerged, straining to make it look easy, but unable to conceal the pain. His feet crunched on the gravel, he swayed, then snapped upright.

The perquisitor had once been a roly-poly little fellow but the plumpness had been etched away, revealing a stocky frame hard with muscle. His right arm had been cut off at the shoulder, which made him look lopsided. Irisis, who had done it to save his life, would remember his screams for all her remaining hours.

Jal-Nish's face had been torn apart in the attack and he had lost an eye. Irisis could not forget the torn ball of jelly dangling from its empty socket. The wounds had not healed in the weeks-long journey back to the manufactory.

The damaged parts of his face were now covered by a burnished platinum mask that hid the lost eye, the hideous red crater that had once been his nose and the warped and twisted mouth and cheek. It curved across below the other ear, where a thin band of the same silvery metal swept around the back of his round head to join up on the other side. Another band ran across his forehead and around, making an open helmet. A mouth opening, like a downwards-curving crescent moon, revealed nothing. He might have drunk through it using a straw, Irisis thought, though surely he would have to take off the mask to eat.

Irisis moved closer, walking on the paved path that ran along the side of the manufactory. She had to see the confrontation between the two, which would reveal her own fate. She was only a dozen steps away when the perquisitor's head whipped around. The single eye fixed on her. Irisis froze. The face showed no expression at all, but she sensed such feelings of rage and loathing that she could scarcely breathe.

He did not move for a handful of heartbeats, then turned away in a manner that dismissed her as worthless, and crunched across the gravel to the scrutator. She held her breath.

'Perquisitor Hlar!' The scrutator inclined his head. 'Never have we seen a more welcome sight.' He held out his hand.

Jal-Nish hesitated for a second, then took it. 'Scrutator!' His voice had once been rich and warm; now it was slurred as if he had been drinking. His ruined mouth could barely shape the words. He bowed and Irisis held her breath in case the mask came off. It did not. 'We would appear to be just in time.'

'The enemy have been unrelenting, Jal-Nish. They know the worth of this place, and its people.'

'Things have not gone well since you moved your station here,' said the perquisitor.

The words held a threat and Irisis was not the only one to notice it.

'I inherited a difficult situation.'

'That was some time back. I'd have expected that you would have sorted it out long ago.'

That was no way for a perquisitor to speak to his superior. Jal-Nish was hiding something.

'How goes the war, down on the coast?' the scrutator enquired.

If he was hoping to discomfort his enemy, it misfired.

'Badly, though we would do better if we had the clankers that sit here, rusting and controllerless.'

'Aren't you in charge of the node failures?' asked Flydd. 'What progress has been made there?'

'None so far,' Jal-Nish said grudgingly. 'I have put a new team on it, though, and I expect results very soon.'

'What team?'

'It is led by Mancer Flammas.'

The scrutator raised part of his eyebrow. 'A courageous choice, perquisitor. No doubt you have your reasons.'

'*He* won't let me down.'

'I'm sure. But you've travelled a long way, and in haste. You must be as tired as we are. Come inside; breakfast is ready.'

'I'll inspect the damage, if you don't mind, then go down to the mine.'

'The mine has fallen into enemy hands.'

'What?' bellowed Jal-Nish. The soldiers swung around, their boots grating on the gravel. He lowered his voice. 'This is bad, scrutator. The Council, I need not remind you, is unhappy. When they hear this news . . . I can't say how they will react, *surr*.'

'I am also unhappy, *perquisitor*, but I cannot do the impossible.

It would take an army to defend this place against the forces gathered nearby and the Council has not seen fit to give me one. However, I do have a plan. I'll tell you about it while we do our inspection.' He drew the perquisitor toward the shattered gates.

Irisis relaxed. The confrontation was not going to be as violent as she had expected, though it had been bad enough. For Jal-Nish to speak to his superior that way showed considerable support on the Council, and little for Flydd.

She went back to her work, checking on the progress of each of the artisans and prentices, and inspecting every completed controller for flaws of any kind. There were none; her team was working well, though several of the prentices had to be reprimanded for not keeping up with their lessons.

Irisis could not blame them; neither could she concentrate. The perquisitor had disliked her from the moment they had met, but on the hunt for Tiaan, across the snowy plateau, that had turned to contempt. She felt the same way about him. After his callous attack on little Ullii, Irisis had struck Jal-Nish down, smashing his noble nose. Jal-Nish had ordered her death but the sergeant had refused to carry it out. The perquisitor had hated her ever since.

But that was nothing compared to her next crime. Horribly mutilated by Ryll the lyrinx, Jal-Nish had begged that they let him die but Nish had pleaded for his father to be saved. Irisis had done the ghastly operation out in the open, while a blizzard roared across that desolate plateau. Jal-Nish had survived, deformed and in constant torment. Now he lived for the opportunity to take an equally horrible revenge on Irisis. What's more, he had the perfect hold over her. He was convinced she had lost her artisan's talent and had been lying for years to cover it up.

It was not Jal-Nish's way to strike at once. He would draw it out, the longer the better. She went to bed early that night, falling into an exhausted sleep in which she was tormented by a vengeful perquisitor. Jal-Nish loomed over her, pulling away the mask to reveal torn, festering flesh. Yellow liquid oozed onto her forehead . . .

She jerked awake and struck her flint striker at the lantern, needing light and lots of it. The room was empty, of course, and the door locked. She failed to go back to sleep.

Ullii had spent the past two days under her bed. She often slept there, curled up in the darkest corner. The noise was the worst. The screams, the impact of stone against walls, the crumbling of masonry, the clashing of weapons, the constant screaming, could not be blocked out even with earplugs and muffs. There was too much sound. The impacts shook the whole building.

Worse, she had lost the ability to sink into the catatonic state that had saved her so many times. In it she felt nothing and not even a beating could rouse her. She had been sliding into that state when the lyrinx came after them in the mine, but had not been able to find it since. That frightened her, as did the sudden unreliability of her seeker's talent. Her life was changing and she did not know why. Ullii was losing the control she had worked so hard for.

Finally the battle noises stopped. She heard cheering and the rattle and squeak of clankers. Ullii already knew they were coming. She could have told the scrutator hours before, had he thought to ask her. The clankers' controllers had appeared in her mental map the previous day.

She knew it was the perquisitor. Having some talent for the Secret Art, as all perquisitors must, Jal-Nish made a recognisable knot in her matrix. He had struck her, that terrible day beside the frozen river. Ullii would never forgive him for it and would always fear him. In her experience, the strong preyed on the weak.

If only Nish were here. But Nish was lost with the balloon and she could not tell if he was dead or alive, for he left no trace in her lattice at all. Nish, Nish, Nish. She could not stop thinking about him. That day in the balloon basket, for the first time in her life, she had truly known love. Skin on skin. Flesh in flesh. Ecstasy. She had replayed it every day since, and every night, sometimes many times.

But the brilliance was fading like a message repeated too often. The memory was losing its power to move her. She wanted more of it, but Nish was gone. He had abandoned her, just as Myllii had. Her beloved twin brother was the only other person she had cared about. Love led only to abandonment. Her longings turned to despair.

Her nose picked up a faint, putrid odour. 'Come out, seeker! You are required down the mine.'

It was that hated voice, the perquisitor himself. Ullii dared not disobey him. His knot in her mental lattice was different, now. It was much larger than before, a swollen clot of jagged tangles. That alone would have told her to avoid him.

'Seeker! *At once.*'

She crept out from under the bed. The perquisitor stood at the door, with the scrutator behind him, and a dozen soldiers. The putrid odour was strong now, and it came from behind the mask. Ullii stood up, caught a stronger whiff and vomited on the floor.

A single speck landed on the perquisitor's shiny boot. He quivered and Ullii quaked, expecting him to smash her down. He tore the cover off her bed, wiped his boot with it and tossed it aside.

'Clean her up and bring her!' he said coldly.

Less than an hour later they were gathered at the entrance to the mine, along with four clankers and forty heavily armed soldiers. These were led by the perquisitor's captain, a completely bald man, even lacking eyebrows, but with a dense black beard clipped to the length of a week's growth. Four of his front teeth had been knocked out. His compact frame was densely muscled.

The grid was up and the entrance appeared empty. 'How many lyrinx can you sense in the tunnel, seeker?' rasped Jal-Nish. Lantern light danced on the cheek of his mask.

The mask terrified her, for what was behind it, and what it allowed. Hidden behind it, no horror would be beyond him. 'There are two,' she said, and felt a deep foreboding. 'And another one down near the lift.'

The captain relaxed visibly.

'Do your business, captain,' said the perquisitor.

The captain signalled. Soldiers moved forward in pairs, labouring under the weight of crossbows so large and heavy they had to be carried on a body frame. The clankers moved into position, well back from the entrance, two out on either side. Their javelards were trained on the tunnel portal.

The soldiers went in. The pair behind the first held up bright lanterns on poles. The lead soldiers readied their weapons.

'Come with me, seeker.' Jal-Nish reached for her hand.

She shuddered, but allowed him to take it. Ullii knew the penalty for disobedience.

'There's one!' a lantern-carrier roared. The leading pair of soldiers fired their curiously shaped crossbows.

The lyrinx screamed, the sound echoing and re-echoing through Ullii's head. The soldiers fell back to reload their weapons. Another pair took their places.

'It's clear down to the lifts,' someone called.

They pushed forward to the fallen enemy. The lyrinx was dead, its chest a horrible mess. Ullii could smell the blood. She wanted to run away but the perquisitor would not allow her.

'This weapon was my idea,' Jal-Nish said conversationally to Ullii. She tried to get away from the body but he held her easily. 'I thought of it after the disaster at the lyrinx ice-houses. Do you remember that, Ullii?'

She did not want to, but she did. All too well.

'The enemy are too fast, agile and tough. They are hard to kill, yet one lyrinx can destroy half a troop of soldiers. How can we even the odds, I kept asking myself? And I came up with this answer – a crossbow that shoots not one bolt, but six. The centre one goes where it is aimed and the other five fan out around it. Six chances to kill the beast. If you're close, they all hit the target. No need to worry about an injured lyrinx getting up again. Clever, eh?'

Ullii could feel a scream building up. She hated violence of any kind.

'I'm speaking to you, seeker. Answer, or by the powers –'

'Yes,' she whispered. 'Very clever.'

'I had my artificers make one up and it worked so well they're building five hundred more. A weapon like this could turn the war, seeker.'

'Yes,' she said faintly.

They found and killed another two enemy in the tunnels. The new crossbows were deadly here, for once spotted the lyrinx could go only forward or back, and either way they were vulnerable. Their chameleon ability did not help them, since Ullii always knew where they were. Before the end of the day the soldiers had secured the mine down to the seventh level, posting pairs of guards at the entrance to each, and half a dozen on the long tunnel where the creatures had gained entry. They kept going through the night. At sunrise the perquisitor returned to the manufactory. Standing in Flydd's doorway, he reported with some smugness that the long tunnel had been collapsed, eight lyrinx were dead and the mine was secure.

'What you failed to do in all your time here, I have done in a day,' said Jal-Nish from behind his shining platinum mask. He nodded formally to the scrutator, who was sitting at his table. 'I'm writing my daily despatches to the Council, if you have *anything* to report . . .'

Flydd did not reply.

'I will also be reporting on your crafter's incompetence.'

'What are you talking about?' snapped Flydd. 'Her controllers are the best we've ever had.'

'If you don't know, it is another black mark against you. Irisis gets her artisans to do the work she cannot do herself. She is a liar and a charlatan, hardly fit to be called artisan, much less crafter.'

'Nonsense,' snapped Flydd.

'Where are her controllers? We have not seen any in a month.'

'They only await suitable hedrons.'

'Tell me,' Jal-Nish said, 'who is in charge of ensuring that suitable crystal is always available?'

The trap was sprung. Flydd did not bother to answer.

'Crafter Irisis has failed and must pay the price.' The perquisitor went out, then returned. 'You can come out now.' He was gone.

The cupboard door swung open and Irisis stepped forth. She looked haunted. 'I could *smell* him, Xervish. It got into the cupboard and stayed there. Blood and dead flesh.'

'And cloves and garlic,' said the scrutator. 'He's addicted to nigah. That's something I wasn't aware of.'

'After he was savaged by the lyrinx, we must have fed him a bucket of the stuff. He was so violent that we had to keep him sedated the whole time.'

'He's still in pain and has to take nigah constantly. The addiction is not going to help.'

'What does it do, apart from taking the edge off pain and cold?'

'And fatigue. He hasn't slept for days. I made a study of nigah, once, to see if it was worth the risk.'

'Was it?'

'It was, if used carefully. Some mancers take it for the brilliant insights it offers, but addicts eventually lose track of reality and it exaggerates whatever failings they have. In Jal-Nish's case, I'd expect him to become more paranoid, more angry and more unstable.'

'That gives us something to look forward to,' she said.

TWENTY-NINE

Ullii spent all her waking hours underground. The perquisitor had taken charge of the project to find the crystals and since he had little need of sleep, everyone else had to work until they were ready to drop.

Today she was riding down to the mine with Jal-Nish in his clanker. 'What's the matter?' he snapped at the operator, a beard-less boy with startlingly blue eyes. 'Why are we going so slowly? I can walk faster than this.'

The operator was so terrified that he could not look at the perquisitor. The clanker lurched, stopped, lurched again then continued more smoothly. 'It's the field, surr,' he squeaked.

'What about it?'

'It . . . it's weak today. Much weaker than before.'

'Go and talk to one of the manufactory operators. Find out how much it changes.'

The clanker kept going.

'Now!' roared Jal-Nish. 'We'll walk the rest of the way.'

Ullii had traced the source of crystals to a point below the partly flooded ninth level. The miners walled off the place, pumped it dry and began excavating a shaft in the floor. Before they had gone down the height of a man, water began to pour in. The miners scrambled from the hole.

'It's beyond us,' said Cloor, chief miner. 'The water –'

'Damn the water, man!' snarled Jal-Nish. 'Keep working.'

'It's coming in faster than we can pump it out.'

'Bring in more pumps.'

Soon the area around the shaft was thronged with screw pumps and the many people needed to work them, all gasping and grunting as they pounded their treadmills. They forced most of the water out and the shaft-sinking resumed. A day later it happened again, the water coming in so quickly that it went over the heads of the two miners. One caught the rope that Cloor threw to him and was pulled to safety, but the other miner did not come up.

Cloor was over the side in an instant, to disappear under the roiling water. Ullii held her breath, then his head broke the surface and he waved. The miners pulled and the other man's head appeared. Someone went down on another rope and between them got the miner over the edge.

He had swallowed dirty water and was taken to the infirmary. Another pump and treadmill was called for. While it was being brought down, Jal-Nish called Overseer Tuniz across and spoke urgently to her. She sketched something on the floor. Perquisitor, overseer and chief miner spoke among themselves.

'Get to it,' said Jal-Nish. 'No – wait. With fifty people on the treadmills there'll be no room to move. Do something about that too.'

'What did you have in mind, surr?'

'Find a way of powering those pumps with the field, *and get it made.*'

'I'll speak to Irisis. She –'

'Irisis isn't going to be here,' he grated. 'Put a competent artisan onto it, overseer, *if you have one.* I want it done by the morning.'

'Impossible, surr.'

'If it's not done, you'll be cleaning out the drains for the rest of your life.'

'We don't have the crystal. That's why –'

'They're *pumps*, not clankers. Surely the scrap crystals will do?'

'I'll speak to the artisans.' Tuniz ran.

The perquisitor's clanker operator appeared, looking around uneasily.

'Well?' barked Jal-Nish. 'Don't stand over there, boy.'

The lad crept forward, staring at the floor. 'The field is unusually weak at the moment, surr. They haven't seen it this way in the past ten years, which is how long the artisans have been mapping it.'

'Incompetent fools. They'll learn to do better when I'm in charge.'

That afternoon, as the shaft was finally pumped dry, one of the clankers hauled down two great curved sheets of iron. They were lowered to the ninth level and manoeuvred into the shaft, where they were fitted together to form a cylinder about two spans across and the same deep. The joins were liberally coated with tar and the two halves tightened with bolts to form a watertight lining. Pumps drew water from the outside. The miners kept sinking the shaft, cutting away the rock beneath the cylinder, while those on top hammered it down and added another section.

The following morning, just before noon, Tuniz and Artisan Oon-Mie brought down a mechanism to drive one of the pumps. It was a strange device of iron pipework topped with a bare controller, no more than a jumble of wires and crystal.

'What the hell is that?' snapped Jal-Nish.

Tuniz and the artisan had been up all night and the overseer had had enough. Tuniz stood up to her full height, a head taller than the perquisitor, and bared her filed teeth. 'Are you questioning my competence, surr?' she said in a silky-soft voice. 'You asked for a pump controller and we have given you one.'

For a moment it looked as though Jal-Nish would explode, but he thought better of it. 'If it works, I'm happy. If it does not . . .'

They set it up and attached it to one of the pumps. Oon-Mie drew power into the controller and water ebbed from the outlet of the pump.

'Good,' said the perquisitor. 'Take its treadmill away and attend to all the others. By tomorrow.'

The miners worked at an equally furious pace. 'I don't like it,' said Cloor the following day, as a third section was bolted on. The shaft was now five spans deep. 'The water pressure is too great. If we hit a big fracture, water will burst in underneath and flood the shaft in seconds.'

'Then put ropes around your miners so you can pull them out,' said Jal-Nish, who seemed to have a solution for every problem. 'How the hell did you ever come to be chief miner? Seeker, are you ready?'

Ullii nodded stiffly. They had rigged up a rope chair for her. She climbed into it and two miners lowered her into the pit. She liked the moist, quiet darkness and normally felt at home in the mine, but the further into the pit she went, the more uncomfortable she became. She could sense the water swirling on the other side of the iron. It felt like a malevolent creature waiting to burst in and drown her. Ullii was inclined to personify the forces of the world, and think that they were directed against her.

Then she felt it. There was crystal everywhere, a whole pod or vein not far below her. Good crystals. And among or beneath them was a huge one that felt to be beating like a heart. It was different – a master crystal, the source of the field, perhaps the node itself.

But it was not beating regularly. In her lattice she could see it, fluxing strong to weak, fast to slow to fluttery. It was as if the huge crystal, or the node, was sick. When she'd first sensed it, up on the seventh level, it had filled her with ecstasy. She had spent hours listening to it and feeling it. Now she felt a twisting, aching sorrow and could not tell why. Tears streamed down her face.

'Take me away!' she choked.

They pulled her up.

'What is it, seeker?' cried Jal-Nish. 'What's the matter?'

'Crystal!'

'What about it? It's not there? The lyrinx have taken these crystals too?'

'Crystal is there. Good crystal. Node is sick; dying.'

Jal-Nish spun around so quickly that the mask slipped on his face, though not enough to reveal what lay beneath. 'The enemy has got to it! That's why the field is so weak. The worthless scrutator –'

Breaking off, he ran toward the lift, his one arm scything. 'Keep working,' he shouted over his shoulder. 'Don't stop until you find the first crystal; then call me.'

A pretty young aide burst in through the door of Flydd's room. 'Perquisitor's coming, surr, and he looks mighty angry.'

'Thank you, Pirse.' She ducked away. 'Get out of sight, Irisis.'

Irisis disappeared into the manufactory. The scrutator kept on with his work. Within a minute, Jal-Nish burst into the room. 'Your incompetence has gone too far this time, scrutator.'

Flydd looked up from over his papers. 'I would remind you, Perquisitor Hlar, that I am your superior. I'm doing a report on you now.'

'I've already done one on you, *surr*, and I'm expecting despatches from the Council at any time. You won't be so smug then.'

'You realise the penalty for appealing over my head, should your judgment prove to be faulty?'

'It won't!'

'What is the problem?'

'The problem,' gritted the perquisitor, 'is that the node is failing. The field has lost near half its power already.'

'The field fluctuates,' replied the scrutator. 'There's no evidence –'

'The seeker thinks differently,' Jal-Nish said. 'She says that the node is dying. You allowed the enemy into the mine and they've attacked the node. You've failed to protect what was most vital of all, scrutator. This will be the end of you and your lying, cheating lover.'

'We can't protect what we don't understand,' said Flydd. 'We don't even know how nodes, and their fields, come about.'

A different aide rapped at the door, an equally pretty young man. 'Yes?' said Jal-Nish.

'A skeet is coming in, surr. From the Council of Scrutators. Shall I bring the message down?'

'At last!' crowed the perquisitor. 'No, I'll come to the skeet house. We'll speak again, scrutator!' There was a savage glint in his bloodshot eye.

When he had gone, the scrutator recalled Pirse. 'Would you tell Crafter Irisis that I will meet her in the refectory? Be quick.' Pirse ran off.

Flydd took several articles from the desk and put them in the leather satchel that he carried with him. He went to his trunk, extracting a small book. Finally he opened his door, looked out and went by a roundabout way to the refectory.

Irisis was already waiting, head down, writing on a tablet. He admired her from across the room. She really was a magnificent creature, and a fine artisan too; one of the best. If only she had not lost her talent. Selecting a bowl of tea and some sugared plums – he must look casual – he hobbled across. His bones were troubling him more than usual today. He reflected on the torment that had made them that way.

She smiled as he sat down. It warmed him. If only . . . Don't be an old fool! Flydd told himself.

'Good news or bad?' said Irisis.

'The worst. The field is weakening daily and Ullii says the node is sick. Jal-Nish thinks the enemy has got to it, and blames me.'

'The field has been fluctuating strangely of late.'

'I didn't know that.'

'Just since the lyrinx captured the mine. We didn't realise at once, what with the attacks and everything. Do you think the lyrinx could have done something to the node?'

'That's possible, though it lies below level ten, which is completely flooded. How could they have got down there? They're afraid of water and we've found no diggings. Anyway, there's no time for that now. The perquisitor is about to move on me. Despatches are coming in and Jal-Nish seems very pleased with himself.'

'What are you going to do?'

'I don't know, but when I fall, he'll have you in the cells within minutes. He wants you in his power, Irisis, even more than he wants to crush me.'

She twisted her elegant fingers together. 'I can't do anything about that.'

'How quickly can you be ready to flee?'

She touched the crystal in the artisan's pliance that hung about her neck. 'This is the only thing I cannot do without. In an emergency I could leave right away. I would like to have my artisan's toolkit, though.'

'Get it, anything else you require, and a weapon you can conceal. Wait for my word.'

'In the artisans' workshop?'

'It's too easy to seal that area off.' Flydd rotated his chair so he could see the door.

'There's a stair up onto the wall between the cistern and the privies.'

'But you'll be just as trapped on the wall. We can't risk it.'

'I'm not afraid to die, surr, if it's come to that.'

'I don't want you to die, crafter. I've that node job for you, and with the news we've just heard it's more urgent than ever. When I fall, Jal-Nish will abandon my work. He believes in military solutions, but that'll do us no good against the lyrinx.'

'He's done pretty well with those new crossbows.'

'In the mine! They're too heavy and unreliable to be used in battle, as he'll soon learn.'

'How would you get me away?' said Irisis.

'You can climb into the aqueduct from the top of the outer-most cistern. Follow it up over the hill and across the valley. Stand up on the side and wave. If everything goes well, the air-floater will pick you up.'

'And if it doesn't?'

'I suggest you jump.'

Irisis swallowed. 'I'll wait in the clanker sheds. I can be checking the strength of the field there, and if necessary, get out the side gate.'

'It's a long run from there to the cisterns.'

'I'll manage it. Do you mean me to do this job on my own?'

'I've others already spirited away.'

'Is there a mancer among them?'

'Yes.'

'What about Ullii? She was going to help me read the node.'

'That's impossible now. I'd never get her away from the perquisitor. Get going. Jal-Nish will be here any minute.'

'But . . . you can't leave Ullii to the mercy of Jal-Nish.'

'She'll be safe enough. He needs her.'

'She'll be terrified out of her wits. She'll think we've abandoned her.'

'Do you think I don't know that?' he snarled. 'If I could do anything, I would. But I can't. Now clear out.'

She went. Flydd took another bowl of tea, called Pirse and gave her final instructions. She waited by the door. He was halfway through his ginger and rose-hip tea when the perquisitor appeared.

Flydd tried to still his racing heart. There were procedures for the demotion, and even the dismissal, of a scrutator, and Jal-Nish must follow them. He was not in mortal danger *yet*, though he would soon be.

The perquisitor's face, behind his mask, showed nothing; however, the eagerness of his stride suggested that he carried bad news for his enemy. He marched to the table and his single eye was ablaze.

'You're finished, scrutator!' Jal-Nish tossed a document on the table.

Flydd steeled himself to show no reaction at all. Reaching for the parchment, he unrolled it and checked the seals and signatures. There were six of each. Six of the eleven on the Council had signed it. Enough to doom him.

He read the document. He was suspended, pending a scrutator's quisitory, or inquisition. Jal-Nish had been appointed acting scrutator in his place. Having once in his life been before a quisitory, Flydd had no wish to repeat it. He still bore the scars, inside and out.

On the other hand, suspension was preferable to dismissal.

He still had his rights as a scrutator, which were considerable. Had he been dismissed he would have become an outlaw, a non-citizen, and Jal-Nish could have done whatever he wanted to him.

Acting scrutator was a temporary position and conferred few of the rights of scrutator. Jal-Nish would have to justify his every action. Even so, the tables had been decisively turned. And, of course, if Jal-Nish got him alone he could have him slain and deny everything afterwards. No doubt that was his plan. Scrutators were as adept at covering up evidence as they were at ferreting out the truth.

Flydd tossed the parchment aside and his arm knocked the tea bowl off the table. It smashed with a loud crash. Pirse touched her cap and slipped out.

His eyes met Jal-Nish's. 'I don't think you've quite beaten me yet, *surr*.'

'An acting scrutator outranks a suspended one.'

'In certain circumstances.'

'These, to be precise.'

'What are you planning to do? Have me quietly killed when there are no witnesses around?'

Something showed in Jal-Nish's eye, though he tried to prevent it. 'I don't want you to die, Xervish. I want you to live and be ruined. That would only be just, considering the damage you've done us by your incompetence.'

A soldier came up, saluted and whispered something in Jal-Nish's ear.

'Where is the crafter?' said Jal-Nish.

'How would I know? Try her workshop.'

'We already have.'

'Irisis has many responsibilities,' said Flydd. 'She could be anywhere. Now, if you'll excuse me, I have the right to prepare my defence.'

Irisis was in the vast clanker sheds, standing at the back hatch of one of the clankers, when the little aide appeared at the door. Irisis waved and Pirse ran across.

'Scrutator Flydd bids you run, at once.'

'Thank you. Get out of sight.'

Pirse ducked in between the row of machines. Irisis fleeted toward the side gate. She was just going through when the inside door was thrust open. A brace of soldiers stormed in, closely followed by the perquisitor.

'Crafter!' roared Jal-Nish. 'Stay where you are.'

She bolted through the gate. Which way? Left was closer to the cisterns but if the soldiers took a shortcut through the manu-factory they would be outside the front gate before she reached it. She turned right, pounding for the corner. If she could get out of sight, they would have to search both ways.

Irisis just made it. On her left was the parade ground, at present empty. To her right was the long stretch of wall enclos-ing the barracks and winter training yard. Ahead were the gardens and orchards. They would be busy with workers at this time of year but no one there would move against her.

'There she is! Stop or we'll shoot, crafter.'

Stop *and* we'll shoot. Irisis kept going, weaving from side to side. She was a couple of hundred paces ahead, outside the accurate range of a crossbow, though that did not make her feel secure. A lucky shot could kill her at twice that distance.

Ahead, a rounded buttress curved around the corner of the training yard. The pack was thumping against her chest, her breasts were bouncing painfully and it was a long way to go.

A cluster of crossbow bolts screeched off the stone, carving grey streaks in the moss-covered wall. They had not been far away. She sidestepped, skidded and went down, sliding on her palms across the mossy paving. Gravel tore a gouge in the heel of one hand. Irisis scrambled to her feet, looked back and saw the other crossbowman aiming at her.

She scratched across the ground on hands and knees, trying to get around the corner. Bolts smashed into the buttress just in front of her, stinging her face with stone chips and grit. A piece stung her in the eye.

Rolling around the corner, she came to her feet and kept going. It was only a short distance to the next corner. On her right were the pitch, ore and firewood bins, to her left the slag heaps, the half-filled ancient holy well and, beyond, the ravine into which the wastes were dumped.

Let there be no guards at the back gate, she prayed, and there were not. She kept going, more slowly now, for she was tiring rapidly. She prayed that the soldiers, lugging those heavy crossbows, were more tired. Irisis could not see out of the injured eye and had no time to pick the bit of grit from it, so she kept it closed.

She scrambled over the pottery pipes and drains, around the corner and across another set of drains coming from the metal-pickling troughs. The acid fumes made her choke. Up between the manufactory wall and the weavers' building, which lay outside. Not far to go, but she had a horrible feeling Jal-Nish would be waiting at the other end.

On she panted, past the stinking slaughterers and butchery, and the barns and stockyards which were nearly as offensive. The stitch grew worse: it felt as though a screw was being twisted in between her ribs. Ahead were the three cisterns and the mouth of the aqueduct, which discharged into the outer cistern. The cisterns were massive, each more than ten spans across. Irisis ran for the outer one and the ladder that led up to safety.

Jal-Nish stood in the way, two soldiers flanking him. They were armed with crossbows, aimed right at her.

'Hold your hands high!' he yelled. 'Move suddenly and they'll fire.'

She should have kept running. A quick death by sword or bolt was preferable to the agony Jal-Nish had in store for her. But having stopped, her legs no longer wanted to move. She waited for the soldiers to take her.

'This is a happy day, crafter.' Jal-Nish was grinning under his mask; she could tell from his voice. 'I've thought about it every minute since you hacked my arm off.'

'I did it to save your life,' she said.

'I wanted to die. You should have let me.'

'Give me your sword. I'll be happy to remedy my error.'

He struck her in the face, intending to break her nose as she had broken his. She took the blow on her cheek and it knocked her sideways.

Irisis forced herself to remain calm. 'Your son, Cryl-Nish, begged me to save your life.'

'I have no son by the name of Cryl-Nish. He's dead, and so will you be, eventually. But first I'm going to take your arm, and then your face, so you can understand what you did to me. Soldiers, hold out her arm.'

The soldiers showed no reluctance. No doubt they were inured to his brutal whims. One held her while the other extended her arm.

Irisis was filled with a bowel-crawling horror. He was going to do what the lyrinx had done to him. Mutilation was the one thing she could not face. She had always been vain about her appearance.

'No,' she pleaded. 'Please don't. I'll do anything you want.'

'I'm sure you would, because that's the kind of person you are. But it's too late, Irisis. The day you struck me down it became too late. Nothing on earth could make me save you.'

THIRTY

Gilhaelith's smiths proceeded with the repair of the thapter, working methodically, leaving untouched every part that he did not understand. He questioned Tiaan about it every day but since his betrayal of Klarm she had refused to answer him. Why had the little thief stolen it, and why attack the Aachim camp? It made no sense, unless she was just a lovelorn fool.

One day, Gilhaelith's cook was on the outer slope, picking mountain parsley that grew around a seep, when she saw the triplet of constructs gliding up the track. They were taking it slowly, the road being narrow and the hairpin bends exceedingly tight. Cook was too plump to run, and the day was hot and the hill steep. But she did hurry, so they had the best part of an hour to prepare.

Gilhaelith ran, which made him look even more ridiculous, for he lifted his knees above his waist and bounced as if springs were attached to his boots. Bursting into Tiaan's room, where she lay on the bed clad only in a sleeping gown, he cried, 'The Aachim are coming.'

'No!' she gasped. For an instant her striking eyes pleaded with him. She put one arm out but let it fall. Tiaan regained control and her face went blank.

'I've prepared you a hiding place. It's so bound about with

spells of concealment that they could tear Nyriandiol down and not find it.'

'Is Vithis among them?'

'The lead construct flies what I understand to be his flag.'

She seemed torn by a terrible dilemma. 'I must see them!' she burst out. Tiaan had tried to eliminate all feelings for Minis, but had not succeeded.

'Why?'

'To see the man who betrayed me!' she choked.

'You would risk everything just for that?'

'Yes,' she whispered.

She *was* a lovelorn fool, and he could use that weakness against her. Dare he take the risk? If he failed, or she gave him away, all would be lost. But the game was everything and this might give him an advantage.

'And will you cooperate afterwards?'

'Yes,' she said quietly.

'And help me repair the chapter?'

'I will.'

A proven thief and liar, her word meant little. But should she break this promise, he had ways of forcing truth and would use them ruthlessly.

'If you do not, you will rue the day you were born.' Gilhaelith's eyes met hers and she shrank before the fury in them. He intended that. He was not a brutal man but he required obedience.

Gilhaelith slid one arm beneath her knees, the other under the back brace, and lifted her easily. 'Put your arm around my neck.'

Carrying her to the door, he looked out, saw no one and scooted down the hall. He slid into a storeroom, used a rod to pull down a concealed trapdoor, climbed the unfolding ladder and laid Tiaan down on a platform in the ceiling.

'Where am I?' she said.

'Nyriandiol has many hiding places. No one knows this one except me, and it is heavily bespelled. You can see out.'

He crawled to the far side, half-carrying, half-dragging her.

There he placed her on her side by a tiny gap in the jasper shingles covering the gable end.

'Don't make a sound.' He crawled backwards to the trapdoor.

Within a minute, the storeroom had been returned to its previous state. The trapdoor was not visible. He checked everything with an egg-shaped scanningstone, then wiped his dusty hands and went to dress for his visitors.

Gilhaelith put on the most extravagant mancer's robes he could find, scarlet and black with diagonal threads of gold. He selected a wide-brimmed hat of the same material, with a crown of crumpled scarlet fabric. With his lanky frame it gave him an air of lofty dignity, but also of harmless eccentricity, the image he hoped to cultivate.

Before he was buttoned up, Gilhaelith had a thought that led him to run all the way to the lowest level, where the thapter lay hidden. It had taken most of one night to lower it down on a pair of winches, ease it in through the window hole and put the window back. He had since paced out the entire path from the forest, checking with his scanningstone and using his Art to erase all trace of the thapter's aura. Now Gilhaelith withdrew the amplimet and the other crystals, slipped them into a lead box and sealed the lid. You never knew what emanations, or auras, the Aachim might be able to detect.

They might also scry for wisps of aura that could indicate the amplimet's present location. He scuttled across to the organ chamber and, selecting a crystal that bore a close physical resemblance to the amplimet, passed it back and forth across the frosty glass sphere, scrying for traces. He found none, nor did the organ sound when he put the crystal into the eighty-one-point star. That did not mean all traces of the amplimet were hidden, but it would take more than casual scrying to find it. At the least, a room-by-room search of Nyriandiol. He had a plan for that contingency too, but hoped he would not have to use it. It involved dead Aachim, the destruction of Nyriandiol and flight through secret forest paths to a distant refuge.

'They're coming,' Nixx shouted.

Gilhaelith followed him to the front terrace. He waited there, restraining the urge to glance up at the gable behind which Tiaan lay hidden.

The three machines came whining and puffing dust around the corner, onto the gravelled expanse outside the front door of Nyriandiol. Swinging into an arrowhead formation, they stopped as one. At the back of each machine a soldier sat behind a kind of javelard in a turret. The weapons were armed – most discourteous. Nothing happened for what Gilhaelith recognised as a carefully calculated minute. Good. It was a warm day and his robes kept him cool, but it must have been sweltering inside the black machines. Had they considered the much hotter climate of Santhenar when they built them?

The top of the first machine cracked open, followed by the others. A lean, hatchet-faced man appeared. There were black circles around his eyes and deep creases etched into the sallow skin of his face. He leaned on a platinum-topped cane.

'Are you the master here?' he said. He employed a deceptively slow manner of speaking. Arrogance showed in every word, every gesture, in the tilt of his head, the way he thrust himself forward, and the down-curving of his upper lip as he glanced around him.

'I am,' Gilhaelith said, putting on a merry smile. 'Gilhaelith is my name. And who may you be, master, with your gleaming new clankers?' He used the word deliberately.

'Don't confuse *our* constructs with your primitive war carts,' the man snapped. 'Surely even in this backwoods place you've heard of us by now?'

'No, master,' said Gilhaelith. 'I can't say that I have.'

'I am Vithis, of Clan Inthis, First Clan of Aachan.'

Gilhaelith took a calculated step backwards and threw up his hands. 'Aachan, master? Surely you are having a joke at my expense. Even I know that the Way between the Worlds has been closed these two hundred years and more, and cannot be reopened.'

Two more people appeared on the platform, holding what seemed to be a wire and glass dish about the size of a large plate. They moved it slowly, scrying for traces of the thapter, or perhaps the amplimet. It was a dangerous moment. Gilhaelith tried to remain calm.

Vithis turned to them, his words carrying, as no doubt he intended. 'The man's a damn fool.' He spun on one heel, military fashion. 'Aachan is dying,' he said to Gilhaelith. 'I command a mighty force of constructs and there is nothing on your world that can resist them. You would be well advised to cooperate.'

'I am happy to cooperate,' said Gilhaelith, spreading his empty hands, 'should you state what you want of me. It's not necessary to use threats. And if you say you are from Aachan, *of course* I believe you.' He put all the doubt he could muster into those words. 'How may I help you, master? Please, come down. You must be sweltering, cooped up in those little rattle boxes in the blazing sun. This is the hottest spring I can ever remember. Take a chair on my terrace, and a cool drink.'

He clapped his hands. An attendant came running. 'Ale, man, from the deepest, coolest cellar! And if there is any ice in the chest, crush a few buckets. Bring platters of my *favourite* tidbits. Hurry!'

'I am perfectly comfortable,' said Vithis, though sweat was running down his face.

The scriers were still scanning the building. If their device was unusually sensitive it might pick up traces of aura he had missed. Gilhaelith grinned like a yokel, but his liver was crusted with ice. 'What can I do for you, master? I am at your complete disposal.'

'I seek news of a construct like this one,' said Vithis, indicating the smaller machine to the left of his own. 'It resembles it in every respect, save one. *It flies!*'

'It flies!' Gilhaelith echoed, his mouth hanging open. 'A marvel! How on earth did you make such a machine?'

'That is not your business,' Vithis said with a grimace. 'The construct was stolen from us by a young woman. Tiaan, her name is, a skinny, sneaking creature with black hair. The wretch tried to kill me and must be punished. I will pay well for information about the construct, *or about her.*'

So she *was* a thief. The twinge of disappointment surprised Gilhaelith.

'A young woman!' he exclaimed. 'She must be a resourceful lass indeed, to have stolen your most prized machine.'

'How do you know it is prized?' snapped Vithis.

'*Your* constructs did not fly here. You came creeping up the road, eating the dust and sweltering in the heat. Ah, it is truly terrible today.' Gilhaelith went backwards under the shade of the terrace roof. The scriers had put away their dish. Was that good or bad? He could not tell.

'But since you ask, I did hear rumour of a flying machine, some days back.' Gilhaelith was on dangerous ground here, especially after pretending to know nothing of the Aachim. Better to tell them straight out than deny everything and have them suspect him. 'Being well read in the Histories, I recognised its value. I asked my factors for news of this extraordinary machine.' This was true; he had sent people out to ask for news and to spread disinformation, but only after the thapter was safe in his cellar.

'Really?' said the Aachim. 'And what did you learn? Quick, man, out with it!'

'I will tell you,' Gilhaelith said slowly, 'if you allow me the chance. You are an impatient young fellow, surr!'

Vithis's face darkened, but someone put a hand on his shoulder and he restrained himself. 'Go on.'

'There was no news from nearby, though that isn't surprising. The forest surrounding us is dense. Only hunters and sap collectors dwell there, and they are a taciturn lot.' Gilhaelith held his breath. What he had said was mostly true, though if the Aachim already had reports to the contrary it would undermine what he said next. 'But north and east the forests thin, especially close to the great lakes of Parnggi and Warde Yallock. There are many small settlements near the lakes. At one of them, people saw the flying machine sweeping north.'

Vithis pounced. 'At its nearest point, either lake is a good thirty leagues from here. Considerably more, the way the forest paths run. You could not have walked there and back in time. *So how do you know?*'

'My information came by skeet, of course,' said Gilhaelith. 'I have factors in the larger towns on the lakes. I trade in a number of commodities.'

'What is a skeet?' asked Vithis.

'A large, vicious carrier bird, widely used on Santhenar for carrying messages. Would you care to see my skeet house?'

'I would,' said Vithis, climbing down from the platform, probably as a face-saving way of getting out of the heat. He winced as he reached the ground, stabbing at it with his cane.

Gilhaelith led them along the paved pathway. The twenty Aachim were discreetly armed, a breach of courtesy which Gilhaelith ignored. His sentries were concealed in all manner of unlikely places. Their heavy crossbows could have sent a bolt right through the metal sides of the constructs, though to do so would have meant the end of Nyriandiol, Gilhaelith and themselves.

The path paralleled the outer rim before curving back to the rear of the villa. Gilhaelith talked all the way, pointing out the sights within the crater and without.

Vithis was sizing the place up. Nyriandiol was easily defended from a minor onslaught, the upper sides of the crater being too steep and rugged to be traversable by clankers or, Gilhaelith suspected, by these marvellous constructs. The road could be blocked if need be. The arrangement of terraces and walls that surrounded Nyriandiol on three sides was designed for defence and he could stop a sizeable force, though not an army.

The skeet house was a small stone building with metal lattice across the front and back. Leaning against one side, Gilhaelith noted that only sixteen Aachim had followed Vithis. The others would be scrying, and spying. He pretended not to notice, but inwardly Gilhaelith was smiling. Sixteen was the fourth power of two, a potent number in his mathemancy. The number of spies, four, also worked to his advantage. They would find nothing.

'We keep the birds in separate pens,' said Gilhaelith, 'else they would tear each other to pieces. This one still has the message pouch on its left leg.'

Inside the first pen was a dark-plumed, hook-beaked raptor, as big as a good-sized eagle. Its yellow eye was flecked with red and when Gilhaelith poked a stick in through the bars the skeet shredded the bark with a single swipe of its talons.

'Many a keeper has lost an eye or a nose to a skeet,' he went on. 'Or a throat! Unpleasant animals, but we could hardly conduct our lives without them.'

'Or the war,' said Vithis.

'I dare say. The war is not my business.'

'Ah yes, business,' Vithis said. 'You trade in certain commodities that could affect the course of the war.'

'If they were available to you and not to humankind?'

'Precisely.'

'My given word is an unbreakable contract,' said Gilhaelith. 'I'm sure you, as the leader of a noble species, appreciate that?'

'Of course,' said Vithis, a little too quickly. 'But I doubt that everything you deal in is spoken for.'

'It is not. Am I to take it that you wish to trade?'

'In due course,' said Vithis, 'I will send a representative.'

'Your representative will be made most welcome.'

Back at the terrace, Vithis accepted the offer of drinks, and the troop of Aachim sat in the shade of the vines, which were just coming into full leaf. 'This is my foster-son, Minis,' he said, waving a young man across. 'He and I are all that remain of Clan Inthis, First Clan.'

'I am sorry to hear that.'

'The world will be sorry one day.'

THIRTY-ONE

Tiaan felt her throat close over when the Aachim appeared. The sight of Vithis, standing so arrogantly on the platform of his construct, had set her heart racing. How she hated the man. Had she a crossbow, it would have taken all her self-control to hold back from shooting him.

Snatches of his conversation with Gilhaelith drifted up, and when Vithis offered a reward for news of Tiaan, terror gripped her. This talk of using the amplimet was a fantasy. Gilhaelith must realise the peril he was in. If he gave her up, he could have all the wealth he ever wanted. He must betray her. He would.

She could see Vithis's face clearly. What would he do when she was in his clutches? Pain spread outwards from her stomach. Gilhaelith seemed to be playing some kind of game with the Aachim. What a fool! Vithis was the leader of a world in exile, Gilhaelith just a rustic eccentric who lived on a mountaintop because he was too strange to survive in the real world. Once they discovered what he had done, he would die, and so would she.

Tiaan did not like Gilhaelith. She could not work him out at all, and he disturbed her. Though he was always perfectly mannered, the way he stared at her reminded her of Nish. Perhaps, living out of society, he did not know any better. And yet . . . When he had carried her in his arms, for an instant she had felt safe.

They disappeared from view and she lay waiting for the sound of their big feet on the ladder. It did not come. Perhaps Gilhaelith had taken them to see the thapter first. Despite the secrecy about the recovery operation, she knew it was here. A noise had woken her one night and, looking out her window in the moonlight, she had seen them carrying a long, canvas-covered shape. Fourteen strong men had it up on their shoulders, tied to poles, while others held it steady with ropes to left and right.

She imagined them downstairs now, Gilhaelith drawing back the canvas to reveal the beautiful machine. His wealth came from trade, after all. Perhaps they were counting out the first allotment, and he was gloating and rubbing his skinny hands together. How many pieces of platinum did it take to buy you, Gilhaelith? And what does Vithis *most* want, the thapter, or the person who learned how to make it fly?

Her miserable thoughts were interrupted by Gilhaelith's hearty laugh. The Aachim were now gathering on the terrace. Servants hurried back and forth with foaming jugs and trays of delicacies. They must be sealing the deal with a drink. Everyone was smiling; they were shaking hands.

It was hot in this airless space, directly under the roof. She was desperately thirsty. She waved her free hand in front of her face but the breeze was not enough to cool her.

Who was Gilhaelith talking to now? He looked so very familiar. Her skin prickled. It was Minis! Gilhaelith led him out to the edge of the terrace and they leaned on the rail together, chatting like friends. Tiaan felt sick. Her heart hammered; her eyes watered. Minis looked magnificent but he was jelly inside. She despised him for it.

Gilhaelith shook hands with Minis, a handsome, dark-haired young man. He could see why the fellow had appealed to Tiaan. Minis had a pleasant, open face with a hint of vulnerability, and not a trace of the arrogance of his foster-father.

'I'm pleased to meet you, Minis,' he said, offering the jug of ale. 'Come this way. Let me show you the view.' He drew the young man over to the stone wall at the inner edge of the crater.

311

The lake was particularly blue today. 'This lake goes up and down with the seasons, and is warm enough to swim in, even in the winter. I often do so.'

'On Aachan, our winters are bitter,' said Minis, 'though they don't last long. Our year is little more than half of yours, I believe, yet our day is longer. But Aachan is a cold world compared to Santhenar.'

'Winter here is cold enough, and lasts for a good hundred days,' said Gilhaelith. 'Don't be fooled by today's weather. It's unseasonably hot for this time of year but, should it turn southerly, we could have snow next week. The weather is changeable here, and we are high up. Tell me, what is your profession?'

'I . . . am in flux.' The young man looked self-conscious. 'My foster-father would mould me into a force commander.'

'And that is not entirely to your liking?' Gilhaelith enquired.

'I will do whatever he requires of me,' Minis said formally.

Gilhaelith changed to the subject he was really interested in. 'The tale of this flying construct must be a fascinating one, though perhaps I should not ask questions of matters that may be . . . strategic.'

'I would prefer that you did not,' said Minis.

'This woman who stole it – Tiaan, I think your foster-father named her – is not Aachim, surely?'

Minis started, and a tic developed at the corner of his mouth. 'Tiaan is old human; from the province of Einunar.'

'Einunar! That's a long way from here. I would like to hear the tale of how she came to steal your *flying* construct. She must be a most talented woman.'

Minis began to sweat. 'Most talented,' he choked, and his admiration for her could not be disguised.

Well, well, thought Gilhaelith.

Minis looked over his shoulder at Vithis, who was in a huddle with the scriers, and went on. 'Tiaan did not steal the flying construct, for we have not learned how to make them fly. She must have made it herself.'

'Made it!' Gilhaelith exclaimed.

'We abandoned three damaged machines in Tirthrax.'

Gilhaelith had difficulty concealing his astonishment. Could Tian's preposterous statements about the gate and the amplimet also be true?

'How could she make it fly?' He did not expect an answer to such a strategic question, but Minis, with another glance in the direction of his foster-father, continued.

'I don't know. We have sought Rulke's secret for two hundred years, without success. But Tiaan is –'

'How did she come to be in Tirthrax?'

'I told her how to get inside the city, so she could make the gate.'

'Are you saying Tiaan *made* the gate that brought you to our world?' Oh, to have an hour alone with this indiscreet and desperate young man.

'Yes, she did. Without her the Aachim of Aachan would be extinct. And in return we betrayed her. I can never forgive –'

Gilhaelith, seeing Vithis heading in their direction, cursed inwardly and interrupted him. 'Perhaps, should we meet again, you could tell me the rest of the tale? I must rejoin your father. I have forgotten my manners.'

'I would be happy to tell you now,' Minis said. 'She is –'

'Ah, Vithis,' Gilhaelith said breezily, quaffing his mug of ale, 'would you care for a snack?'

He snapped his fingers and a servant presented a tray on which was arranged a series of shrivelled, oily, yellow-green objects. They made a square, seven to each side.

'What are they?' said Vithis, wrinkling his nose at the smell, which was nauseating.

'The preserved gonads of the Parnggi walking fish,' said Gilhaelith, picking up seven with his free hand and flicking them into his mouth with his thumb. The numbers, as well as Vithis's reaction, gave him a little more control.

Vithis looked disgusted. 'They smell rotten.'

'An ancient method of preservation that greatly enhances –'

'We must go,' Vithis said tersely. 'A large area to search and much else to do. I thank you for your hospitality.'

He limped back to the machines. The others followed and the constructs headed down the mountain road.

Gilhaelith watched them out of sight. He *thought* he had fooled Vithis, but if the man found a single witness to say otherwise, the Aachim would be back to take the place apart stone by stone.

So Tiaan *had* been telling the truth. When he'd believed her a thief and a liar, it had coloured his view of her talents. Now he veered to the opposite extreme. She must be a masterly natural geomancer, the rarest of geniuses. What might she be capable of if that talent was properly schooled? She could greatly help him with his own quest. He must find a way to gain her cooperation.

Tiaan was still tormenting herself when she heard the creak of the trapdoor and Gilhaelith crawled across. Though she hated and despised Minis, the sight of him had been unbearable.

Gilhaelith carried her to her room and sat in the chair beside her bed, offering her a piece of cream linen the size of a small tablecloth. She wiped her dusty face and hands.

'You thought I was going to betray you?' he said, regarding her fixedly.

He had strange eyes, she noticed. The pupils were slightly oval and of the most unusual colour, a streaky though warm blue-grey. 'Yes,' she whispered, and the admission broke something in her that had been holding her back all this time. 'Why didn't you? They must have offered you a great amount of platinum.'

Most men would have been offended by the implication, even if they *had* been tempted. He showed no sign that he was offended. He just kept staring at her.

'Don't you know that it's rude to stare?' she snapped.

He looked away, turned back, caught himself doing it again and angled his face to the window. A touch of colour appeared on his cheeks. 'Is it? I did not know that.'

Something was different about him. He seemed less cold and machine-like. It was almost as if he cared about her. 'It makes me uncomfortable,' she said softly. 'I feel as if . . . as if you're feeding on me.'

'I'm sorry. I would not have you think me ill-mannered.

I have lived alone, with only my servants for company, for so long that perhaps I have not learned what I should. Or forgotten it a century ago.'

'A century –?'

He smiled, which almost cracked his ugly face in half, but lit up his eyes. He no longer seemed so strange. 'I am not offended. As it happens, I am 180 years old – a number with several unusual properties. The sum of consecutive cubes –'.

'I'm sorry,' she said, flushing.

'What for?'

'For so insulting you a moment ago.'

'What about?'

'Accusing you of being bought by Vithis.'

'I might have turned you in, at one stage, but never for money. Anyway, you have a precious talent and I would prefer to foster that.'

Something *had* changed and, for whatever the reason, she had to use it. 'Why would you jeopardise what you have here, for me?'

Gurteys put her head around the door, scowling at the pair, but at Tiaan's words a convulsion of rage transformed her unattractive features. Tiaan shuddered. Gilhaelith turned toward the door but the healer had gone. More trouble.

'The volcano could destroy it all tomorrow,' said Gilhaelith. 'That uncertainty keeps me vigilant.'

'Vithis might also destroy you.'

'In that case, I would be dead and it would not matter. All that matters, Tiaan, is my work. You are safe with me.' He was staring at her bosom, oblivious.

She put her arms across her chest. 'But what do you *want* of me, Gilhaelith?'

'Not what you might be thinking,' he said, belatedly realising what was bothering her. 'I am a celibate. I have been so all my life.'

'*All your life?*' Tiaan's own urges were strong, though she had not yet mated. For a man to live to his age and remain celibate seemed impossible, not to mention *wrong*. In her country, not

315

mating at all was a crime. 'Is there . . . something *wrong* with you?' She blushed scarlet. 'I'm sorry. *Again*.'

His face set hard. 'I never liked any woman enough to consider it. I never knew *how* to like a woman – I'm not good with people.'

'Did you have a strange childhood, like me?'

'I suppose so. Certainly no one liked me. I was too different, and I refused to conform. I always felt that it was me against the world, a game I couldn't win. Instead of fighting, I rejected everyone and played the game *I* was best at – numbers.'

'I was different, too,' said Tiaan, 'though I didn't want to be. I just wanted a proper family, like other kids had. I only have half my family Histories.'

'I have none of mine,' he said bitterly.

'Who were your parents?' she said softly.

'I don't want to talk about it.' He hurled himself from his chair so violently that she cried out and covered her face with her hands.

He stood over her, breathing hard, then rushed out of the room. Before she could work out what had happened he was back. Tiaan shrank into the pillow.

'Forgive me.' He went down on his knees beside the bed. 'I didn't mean to frighten you. I would not deliberately hurt any living thing. I . . . my past causes me pain and I find it hard to control.'

He was trying hard to be what he was not – a man who could relate to a woman. 'Tell me about it,' she said.

'I was born of a dead woman, dragged screaming from a bloody corpse. I must have been the unwanted child of an important man, for I was carried away in the night by my loyal nurse. Far, far away we went, but she died of the plague when I was five, and then I had no one. I was brought up in an orphans' home.'

'I have a mother,' she said, 'but no father. He was killed in the war soon after my birth.'

'A common thing in these times, to lose a father. I wonder about my own. It was hard, having no heritage at all, and being so different.'

Her eyes were on his but she said nothing, so he continued. 'I spoke with my nurse's accent, and I looked strange. The other children found me awkward and ugly. It hurt, but I learned not to care, for I knew I was cleverer than they. I could not play at ball-and-stick but I was better than my teachers at mind games. I pursued that world to the exclusion of everything else, until I became arrogant in my superiority. The other children were afraid of me – my first taste of power.

'When I grew up, I wanted to play in the real world, so I took on the local merchants and traders. Before they knew what was happening, I had become immensely wealthy at their expense. Business was just a game to me, one I easily mastered. I knew everyone's strengths and weaknesses, but I also knew the perfect time to buy and sell.

'Within a few years, a whole city hated me, so, tiring of the game, I converted my wealth to gems, found a place where no one dared to live, changed my name and began to build Nyrian-diol. That took forty years and I did not show my face in the world all that time. By then, my enemies were dead. No one knew who I was, not even the recently formed Council of Scrutators. I watched and played against them for years, and began to recognise a pattern behind what they did and said. But I abandoned that game as well – I was bored with the petty intrigues of humanity, ever the same, and always destructive.

'By then I had no interest in rejoining the world, though I still traded, a good cover for my real work. I had become interested in the greatest game of all – the Art and Science of the earth and the heavens. The forces of geomancy: the natural processes that move and shape the sun, the earth, the planets and their moons.

'Geomancy was the deadliest of all the Arts, but that gave it all the more appeal. The greater the risk, the greater the reward if I succeeded. I sought to understand, and then to master such forces. I knew that was an impossible dream for any mancer, though I had devised an entirely new Art – mathemancy – in order to do so.

'I built greater and greater geomantic devices – my organ, my carillon of bells, my scrying globe – but mastery has always

317

eluded me. The earth and planets are ever changing, and my knowledge of the forces that drive them must always be imperfect and behind the times. I could never learn enough.'

'Is that why the amplimet so fascinates you?' she asked shrewdly.

He hesitated long before answering. 'It could help me to scry into secrets that no one has been able to uncover . . .' He trailed off, deep in thought.

'But if it *is* talking to the node –'

'That would be something entirely new. Incomprehensible.'

'What if nodes are the key? If a crystal can talk to a node, what would happen if a node talked to another node?'

Gilhaelith leapt up. 'Do you realise what you're saying?'

'I just thought of the question. I don't know the answer.'

'Nor do I, but maybe I've been looking at the problem the wrong way round, all along.' He sat, thinking, and did not move for ages.

Tiaan was still wondering about him. 'You chose to be a celibate?'

Gilhaelith nodded. 'I did.'

'We have something in common. I am also a virgin.'

He rolled the word around in his mouth. 'Virgin seems wrong applied to myself, but that is what I am. I do not regret it. It made an impossible life possible. I've lived a rich life of the mind. I wonder . . .' He stared at her.

The admission built him in a new light, not so threatening. 'What are you going to do now?'

'I was wrong about you, and I apologise. Minis told me all you have done.'

So that's why he had changed – he wanted to make use of her talents. Tiaan was not upset. Everyone had their place in this world and she needed to be a useful part of it.

'I cannot make you walk again,' he said, 'but if there is anything I can do for you, I will.'

'And, in return, what do you require of me?'

'The amplimet has been overprinted with a new pattern, I think due to you. It's too dangerous for me to use. Or anyone else.'

'Or anyone else,' she repeated. So whoever wanted the amplimet must have her too. A lifetime of being used. Still, it was better than the alternative. Why not cooperate, though she could not see Gilhaelith lasting long. All the more reason to get what *she* wanted – a working thapter she could take to the scrutators, and finally know that she had done her duty.

Could he be trusted? Tiaan thought so, but she had trusted Minis and would never be so gullible again. 'Can the thapter be repaired?'

He considered the question as he paced. 'My smiths have beaten the metal skin to shape. It's not as fine as before, but it'll fit. I've had them do some repairs to the mechanisms and left others I did not understand. Unless something vital has been broken, I expect it can be put right. I've a good workshop.'

'I'll help you,' she said, 'but I want the thapter.'

He took a long time to answer. 'You may have it, but not the amplimet.'

His eyes met hers but she could not tell what he was thinking. Could the thapter be made to fly without the amplimet? Malien had thought so, though it would not be easy. Still, that was as good as she was going to get.

'Agreed.' She held out her hand.

He took it. 'You shall direct the repairs. I'll have a wheeled chair built for you, which you can move with your arms. Not as good as walking, but better than lying on your back.'

'When can we start?' she asked eagerly. Too eagerly. Control yourself, Tiaan. Don't appear too enthusiastic. *Don't trust!*

'The sooner the better, if you are strong enough. I'm afraid –' He broke off and went to the window, looking down into the crater.

'Of what?'

'There is no power on Santhenar who will *not* want the thapter, once they hear of it, and I am not fool enough to think that it can be kept secret. Even *my* servants can be made to talk, if the reward is great enough. Or the torment!

'And then,' he went on, 'there is *you*.'

'What are you talking about?'

'You are a great prize, Tiaan.'

'A cripple who can do nothing for herself?' she said scornfully.

'An artisan with a brilliant mind; one who can solve a problem that has eluded the genius of the Aachim for two hundred years – the secret of flight.'

Tiaan did not doubt that she was clever, but she could not consider herself brilliant. Her mother, and her superiors at the manufactory, had always talked her abilities down. Besides, Malien had made the key discovery, not she.

'It was mere luck; I just happened to have an amplimet.'

Having changed his mind about her, Gilhaelith would not be dissuaded. 'And the ability to use it. Tiaan, you made a gate between the worlds. You are a master geomancer.'

'The slightest prentice! I understood nothing.'

'Ah, but when you are trained –'

This conversation made no sense. 'I have no one to teach me, even should I want to study the Secret Art.'

'Why do you think I built my home on the edge of this mighty and perilous volcano?'

'I have no idea.' Now she was staring at him.

'I have studied the Geomantic Art all my adult life. I am its greatest master, and it's time I took a prentice.'

This was moving too fast. But suddenly, though Tiaan had never thought about it before, she did want what he was offering. She had felt such fulfilment, using her tiny geomantic skills to save the lives of the Aachim. Using power to do good. Artisans were just craft workers and had to do what they were told, but mancers were a law unto themselves. Geomancy meant freedom and she would seize the offer with both hands.

Out the window, wisps of steam trailed up from a sulphur-crusted fissure. On the terrace, Gurteys was talking to a group of servants. They all turned and stared at her window. Tiaan looked away from their hostile eyes.

'I've always been interested in such things,' she said. 'Since I was little I wondered what forces could be so strong as to cause the earth to tremble, and volcanoes to burst forth flame and liquid rock. Why *do* the tides rise and fall? I wonder about that, too.'

320

'Then will you become my prentice?' His voice was a trifle unsteady.

Gilhaelith was an enigma, one she was not sure she was capable of dealing with. She had seen him lie to Klarm and Vithis. Why would he not do the same to her? 'I'll think about it tonight. I . . . my life is changing so constantly that I can't keep up.'

'Make your decision in your own time. I have been waiting for decades.' He turned his head. 'What is it, Nixx?'

His seneschal was standing in the doorway. 'I felt you should know at once, master.'

'Know what?' Gilhaelith sounded as if he resented the inter-ruption.

'We watched the constructs, Gilhaelith, from the entrance of a lava tunnel halfway down the mountain. They could not have seen us.'

'Get to the point, seneschal.'

'Near the bottom they stopped. Six Aachim got out, carrying large packs, and went into the forest. To spy on us.'

Tiaan shivered. Sooner or later she must be discovered. So little time; so much to learn. Seize the opportunity while you have it. She looked up at Gilhaelith.

'I will be your prentice.'

THIRTY-TWO

Nish spent the night before the battle lying awake, as no doubt Troist was too, and Yara. His vivid imagination told him exactly what would happen in the morning – bloody ruin! The lyrinx force was at least eight hundred, more than a match for their own force, even counting the clankers.

The troops were roused well before dawn, knowing the lyrinx liked to attack at that hour. They did not attack. The sun came out, swiftly burning off the mist that had formed in hollows and along the line of the creek behind them. There was not a cloud in the sky and the wind blew warm from the north. It was going to be a bright, hot day.

'Why don't they attack?' muttered Troist after an hour had gone by. The tension was telling on everyone. 'Go and speak to the watch, Nish.'

Nish ran across to a tall tree with its roots in the sandy creek. A soldier sat in the crook of a branch, two-thirds of the way up, a spyglass to his eye. It was a dangerous job, for scouts and watchers were among the first targets of the enemy.

'What's going on, Kahva?' Nish called up.

'They're moving!' said the soldier.

'Which way? Quick, man?'

'They're moving slowly south-west, away from us.'

'It must be a trick.' Nish raced back to the officers' tent. 'They're moving, surr, away from us.'

Troist ordered a runner to the tree. Shortly the man came pounding back. 'There's dust in the north, a big, broad cloud. Must be hundreds of the buggers.'

'That's why the main force is going around,' said Troist. 'They plan to pinch us between the two. What should I do – retreat or fight here? Orbes, what do you think?'

Orbes, the strategist, was inept at everything, even walking in a straight line, but had one vital ability. He never forgot any detail of his work, and kept in his head a description of every battle fought between humans and lyrinx in the past hundred and fifty years. At least, every battle where a human had survived to report it.

The strategist scratched his head, dislodging a clump of wispy hair which drifted away in the breeze. His hair was falling out, exposing a pink skull crusted in ragged blisters. The skin of his arms and legs was flaking off. The man looked as if he was falling apart.

'Could do either,' he said unhelpfully, 'depending on what they're up to. The country is flat as a table round here so you'll find no better place to defend. Nor a worse one!'

'Then we'll stay.' Troist gave his orders. Runners went back and forth to the scouts, who reported that the enemy were still circling and were now south of them.

The day grew hotter, the tension thicker. Nish had sweated enough to fill a bucket. He moistened his mouth with muddy water which tasted like something small had died in it – it was the only kind they had. The dust cloud grew. Yara went back and forth, as cool as ice, though her knuckles were white. Liliwen was crying, while Meriwen remained desperately stoic. Nish wished he could look as calm. It felt as though terror was carved into his brow for all the world to see.

'It's Romits, surr!' cried a runner.

The entire force turned as though they were iron particles lined up by a piece of lodestone. 'What?' Troist whispered.

'It's Captain Romits in the north. He's come out of the dust. The scout recognised his flag, flying from a clanker.'

Troist ran to the tree and scrambled up. 'It *is* Romits!' he roared, dancing up and down on the branch, to the peril of his scout and himself. 'He's got nine, no ten, no twelve clankers, and troops hanging all over them. There must be a couple of hundred, at least.'

It was not long before everyone could see them through the billowing dust. 'Not enough.' Troist was on the ground again. 'But welcome nonetheless.'

Soon after Romits's force joined them, the scouts reported that the enemy had turned south and were moving rapidly away.

'That's strange,' said Troist. 'Orbes?'

'I'd say our reinforcements just made the difference. Lyrinx don't like to fight in broad daylight unless they have a clear advantage.'

'I'd have said they did.'

'They would have, if they'd been able to fight at dawn. But their eyesight is poor in bright sunshine and they don't like the heat either. After all, they came from the void, which is a cold, dark place. Or so the Tales tell.'

'Maybe they get confused in such conditions,' Nish speculated.

'They're clever and cunning fighters, in small groups, but they aren't great tacticians.' Orbes examined a wisp of hair pinched between fingers and thumb. 'When we *have* beaten them unexpectedly, it's been in large, complicated battles where our forces have been all over the place but held to the battle plan.'

'They rely on darkness, and superior strength and speed. I'm starting to think of a plan,' said Troist. 'I've been making for the Worm Wood, as you know, but that place would advantage them more than us. Perhaps we're better off remaining on the plains where they can't come on us unexpectedly, and the conditions are more to our liking than theirs. Let's go through our tactics again, for when they do attack.'

They remained on alert until midday when the scouts reported that the enemy had retreated over the horizon. Nish walked down the lines with Troist as he explained what had happened. The soldiers muttered among themselves.

'Why won't they stand and fight?' said a weedy-looking fellow who would not have lasted five minutes once the battle started.

'You'll get your chance, Mamberlin,' said Troist, clapping the soldier on the shoulder.

Nish lingered after Troist had moved on. 'Surely you aren't in a hurry to fight?' said Nish. 'A lyrinx would kill you in ten seconds.'

'Or I might kill it,' said the soldier. 'Fighting is what we're here for, and it'd be a lot better than waiting.'

Nish did not think so but, not wanting to give the man the wrong impression about himself, said, 'Good luck, Mamberlin,' and kept going.

The army continued south-east across Almadin, still gathering men and clankers. The lyrinx continued to shadow them, which kept everyone on edge, though Troist now led a formidable force. On a hot spring day, around noon, they came to a broad, meandering river and had to track upstream for an hour to a point where the clankers could get across. There were tall trees here, and vast head-high reed beds.

'A perfect place for an ambush,' said Troist, riding round in circles.

They crossed in safety, disturbed by no more than a herd of angry buffalo. The following morning the scouts brought word that a large force of constructs had massed to their south, on the border of Almadin and Rencid.

'Are they friend or foe?' Troist said to Nish.

'More likely the latter.'

'The Aachim are an honourable species. I will send out an embassy.' Troist riffled through his papers, eyed Nish speculatively, and bent his head.

Something was up. 'Sounds . . . dangerous,' said Nish.

'It could be, so I'd need the right person to lead it.'

Nish felt an urge to slip out of the tent and disappear.

'I had you in mind, Cryl-Nish.'

'Me!' cried Nish.

'I can't leave the army leaderless with lyrinx massing so near.'

'But surely one of your officers . . .?' Nish began.

'They're good soldiers but I need Romits. Lieutenant Floid never speaks without an obscenity, Prandie stammers so badly that he can hardly get a sentence out, and as for Buffon –'

'He's a dirty slob. Even so . . .'

'The Aachim would be mortally insulted. Vithis is the leader of his people and the representative of another world. My officers have neither nobility nor high rank.'

'Neither have I.'

'But you have been a scribe and translator to great merchants. You know the protocols and courtesies.'

'Not for the Aachim.'

'I have someone who can instruct you. Moreover, you are of good family and your father is a scrutator.'

'Perquisitor only,' said Nish.

'According to the latest despatches, which came by skeet last night, he has been appointed acting scrutator in place of your patron Kser . . .' he stumbled over the name, 'Kservish Flydd, who has been suspended.'

'Xervish suspended!' cried Nish. 'What for?'

'It does not say.'

What was going on back at the manufactory? If his father was in charge, how were Irisis and Ullii faring? Nish had not had time to think about them in the past weeks. 'I'm sorry to hear that. Flydd is a decent and honourable man.'

'Can't think why he became scrutator then!' Troist looked over his shoulder in case anyone had heard the uncharacteristic and heretical utterance. 'Nonetheless, your father is now among the mighty. The Aachim will respect you the more for it, despite your youth and . . . well, stature. They are great believers in nobility, or at least breeding, and the hierarchy of power.'

'What will I say to them?'

'I'm sure you'll work it out. Be polite but firm. Observe all the protocols.'

'I don't know what they are,' Nish cried.

'Then invent some and then follow them rigidly afterwards!' snapped Vithis. 'Make no concessions, for you have no power to do so. Keep our interests in mind at all times.'

'How do I know what they are?'

'Imagine you are at the bottom of a deep pit, with hungry beasts on the one side and brutal slave-owners on the other. You want to get out of there alive, but you don't want to be eaten, or become a slave. Those are our interests.'

'And we could do a hundred things that might advance ourselves, or ruin us.'

'Indeed. You must use your own judgment about that. But when in doubt, say you must consult your masters. I'll have the tailors make an appropriate uniform for you. You'll leave in the morning.'

'Not alone, I hope.'

'You'll have a small guard and such assistants as protocol requires.'

There was no way to get out of it, though the fear of failure had never been stronger. This mission was bound to be a disaster.

He left at the instant of dawn, dressed in a smart blue and maroon uniform that two tailors had spent the whole night on. A spare was carefully folded in his pack. His guard consisted of just two soldiers, and one was a raw youth considerably younger than Nish's meagre twenty years.

'Your escort awaits you,' said Troist. 'Though I cannot spare the horses, you must be mounted. No embassy could go forth on such a vital mission on foot. Here is your charter. My scribe worked most of the night on it.' He handed Nish a rolled piece of parchment tied with a scarlet ribbon.

The document, written in the most florid hand, full of whorls, loops and curlicues, declared Marshal Cryl-Nish Hlar, son of Scrutator Jal-Nish Hlar, to be the officially appointed legate to General Troist, Commander-in-Chief of the armies of Almadin and presently Military Governor of the Central Almadin Region.

'Marshal?' said Nish.

'It would be the grossest of insults to send anyone more junior,' said Troist.

'But . . .'

'As commander I am entitled to confer such a rank,' said Troist, 'if that's what's worrying you.'

'I . . . I don't know what to say.'

'This may be the biggest gamble of my life. If you fail me, you'll be broken to a common soldier as quickly as you have risen, Marshal Cryl-Nish.'

'And if I succeed?'

'You may very well keep the rank. Look sharp now, it's coming dawn.'

His head whirling, Nish shook hands with Troist and hurried outside. His escort stood waiting by their horses, as well as a woman of middle age with coarse skin and silver hair turning to white. She presented him with another parchment, unsmiling.

'I am Envoy Ranii Shyrr,' she said. 'Here is my commission. I will advise you on Aachim protocol.'

'My mother's name is Ranii,' he said, scanning the parchment. 'I'm glad to have you. Where have you come from, Ranii? Are you a kind of charlatan, like me, thrown into the water without knowing how to swim?' He realised his mistake immediately. 'I mean no insult. It's just –'

'That you don't know how to put it?' she said stiffly. 'A considerable failing in an ambassador, to my mind. Fortunately I have spent my adult life in one embassy or another, and the last five years as legate at the city of Stassor, which is –'

'The principal city of the Aachim of Santhenar,' Nish said, wondering if Ranii felt herself hard done by. She had been passed over for the position he held and doubtless resented it. 'I know of Stassor, though I've never been there.'

'Well, that's a start,' she said. 'Though I can't believe –'

'I have, however, ventured into the great Aachim city of Tirthrax, inside the mountain of the same name, and spoken with none other than Malien, Matah of the city, who is men-

328

tioned in the *Tale of the Mirror!* And twice she humiliated me, Nish thought.

Ranii took a step backwards. 'We must speak more of this on the way.'

Nish mounted his horse, trying to look expert, though he'd not much experience with riding.

'I am Marshal Cryl-Nish Hlar,' said Nish to the soldiers, more self-importantly than was wise. 'I go by the name of Nish, except when doing my official duties.'

The soldiers touched their caps, rather more casually than Nish would have liked.

'Sergeant Mounce,' said the one on the left, a short, stout man with arms like knotted tree roots and leathery skin much the same colour.

Nish glared at him and after some time Mounce grudgingly added, 'Surr.'

'Tchlrrr, surr,' said the youth, a handsome fellow with skin as black as the pitch they burned in the manufactory furnaces. Frizzy hair stood out around his head like a halo. His nose was a long beak, hooked at the tip, yet it only added to his striking good looks.

'You know where we are going, Mounce?'

'Yeah,' said the sergeant.

'Then ride! Time is precious.'

Taking him at his word, Mounce and Tchlrrr set off at a gallop that soon had Nish grimly hanging on, terrified he was going to fall and forever lose face in their eyes. He managed to stay on until they splashed through the creek, where the soldiers slowed to a more appropriate pace. Nish caught up to Ranii, who sat her horse as if she had been born to it.

'How is your seat?' She smiled behind her hand, enjoying his discomfort.

'A little battered. How long will it take to reach the Aachim camp?'

'We should be there by tomorrow afternoon, unless they've moved since our scouts last reported.'

They rode hard all day, by which time Nish's backside was so sore, and his thighs so chafed, that he could scarcely stop from crying out as he rode. In other respects it was a monotonous day. The dry plains of Almadin, and then Rencid, looked the same in every direction. The long grass was brown from the winter, though the first green shoots were now sprouting. The land was treeless except where watercourses, mostly dry, wound their way across the landscape. These were marked by ribbons of tall, white-trunked trees with grey or blue-grey leaves. Where there were no pools, water could be found by digging through the sand.

They were approaching one such watercourse at sunset. 'Are we camping here?' Nish asked hopefully.

'We will do as you order, Marshal Cryl-Nish Hlar,' Mounce replied.

'Please call me Nish,' said Nish. 'What do you think?'

'I am a soldier, Marshal Cryl-Nish Hlar. I don't think.'

Nish's heart sank. No doubt they knew that his dizzying promotion was just a confidence trick.

'If we stop here, will we reach the Aachim camp by mid-afternoon tomorrow?'

'Unlikely, surr.'

'Then we'll press on!'

They raced off. At once the ground seemed rougher, his mount's gait more jouncing, and Nish felt every jolt. Riding even harder, they reached another watercourse just as the light was fading. The sergeant continued through the water and kept going.

'A leader must lead,' said Ranii, at his elbow.

'We camp here!' Nish roared. Attempting to dismount, he fell off his horse as the soldiers wheeled around and came cantering back.

Nish picked himself up, rubbed his throbbing backside and began to unsaddle the horse.

'I'll do that, surr,' said Tchlrrr.

'Help Mounce with the camp,' said Nish. 'I'll take care of my own horse. It's the least I can do since I've been sitting on the poor creature all day.'

'He's a warhorse,' said Mounce. 'He's used to carrying a proper soldier and all his gear. A pipsqueak like you won't trouble him.'

The insult was deliberate and Nish could not pretend he had not heard it. What was he to do?

THIRTY-THREE

Nish stopped dead and slowly turned around. It had to be done right away. 'Sergeant Mounce, you are broken to the ranks for insolence. Hand me your badge and baton, if you please.'

Mounce looked as if he had run into a tree. His leathery skin went red, then purple. His mouth opened and closed like a fish trying to breathe out of water.

'You – you can't do that, surr,' he choked.

'As marshal, I believe I can.' Nish held out his hand. It took an effort to stop it from shaking, for he was taking a monumental risk. If the soldier refused, Nish might as well go home, for he would never recover.

It was a contest of wills, one Nish had often fought with his father, who invariably won it. On the other hand, the trials of the past months had grown a few fibres in Nish's soul. He had faced opponents more formidable than this one. The man was just a soldier, used to obeying orders no matter how stupid they might seem. The advantage was on Nish's side.

Taking a step forward, Nish looked the man in the eye. This was a game he had learned from the scrutator, and one of the easiest paths to dominance, if you had the will for it. Nish screwed his down hard. Nothing is going to beat me. *Nothing!* As Troist has seized his chance, I will take mine. I've waited long enough for it.

He put that fire and fury into his eyes. The soldier held him for a minute, then his eyes slid away and Nish knew he had won. The man put out his hand. Nish took the badge and baton.

The former sergeant bowed his head. 'You have broken me, surr. When I go back I will be finished. No soldier will ever respect me again.'

Nish was about to point out that it was on Mounce's own head, until a sudden, rare feeling of empathy came over him. He had been just as low, more than once, and but for the generosity of the overseer one time, and Scrutator Flydd another, might now be a soldier in the front-lines. Or in the belly of a lyrinx.

'You will have the chance to earn back your baton on this journey. Whether you do so is, of course, up to you.'

The soldier did not grovel, for which Nish was grateful, but he did bow. 'Thank you, Marshal Cryl – Thank you, Nish.'

Nish bowed, the man turned away and they all went about their business.

After dinner Nish sat up talking to Ranii, who now tried to conceal her hostility. She briefed him on the character, the manners, the protocols and the Histories of the Aachim.

'You must appreciate,' she concluded, 'that everything I have told you relates to the Aachim of Santhenar, who have dwelt here for four thousand years. A culture and a people can change immeasurably in that time, even one so self-contained as theirs. The Aachim of this world are, no doubt, more like us than these newcomers. You must be cautious; who knows *what* proprieties an innocent remark or gesture might infringe. And yet you must be bold, for they do not respect timidity. Above all else we must avoid the impression of weakness.'

'Which is the true impression.'

'Yes, and no. Militarily, we are weaker than we have been. The war has taken a toll. But we have endured it, and are tougher and more resilient because we have. And even if we *are* weak, we can act strong. We must, just as you faced down Mounce earlier. There are all kinds of strength, Marshal Hlar.'

'I'm just beginning to realise it.'

'The Aachim can be bluffed. The Histories tell us that. And they are at a disadvantage. Their constructs are more than the equal of our own machines, but they have no home base, no friendly lands to provide them with supplies, no safe place to send their wounded. They must carry everything with them and there are but one hundred and fifty thousand of them.'

'Rulke took Aachan from them with a hundred Charon, so the Great Tales say.'

'That was the boldest stroke of all time! But Santhenar is not Aachan and we old humans are not Aachim. We are lesser, yet greater, and we would never give up our world so easily. Besides, these Aachim do not know Santhenar, and that is the greatest disadvantage of all.'

'Though one readily remedied with advisers and scouts from their own kind in Stassor.'

'Stassor is a long way from here and accessible only on foot. Help could be months in coming. We must capitalise on their disadvantage so as to bring them to negotiate.'

'What is our objective?'

'To have them as allies against the lyrinx! Surely you realise that?' She stared at him as if he was an idiot.

Nish flushed. 'I asked Troist but he did not say.'

'It's so obvious I'm astounded you needed to ask.'

'Well, I did.'

'Whatever we do, we must avoid offending them, and from what I hear of Vithis, that will be difficult.'

Nish considered his approach as he bounced on his black and blue backside across the hard soil of Rencid. It would be his greatest test. He was not sure he was up to it..

As they drew near the Aachim camp, a triplet of constructs whined out to meet them. Nish drew level with Mounce and passed him the baton and badge. 'I must have a sergeant while we are here; the toughest and most unflinching in the east. Are you up to pretending?'

'Surr!' Mounce touched his cap, spurred ahead and put up his pole. The blue truce flag cracked in the breeze of his passage. He pounded up to the clankers, wheeled around them in a circle, ignoring the spear-throwers trained on him, skidded to a stop and jammed the pole into the ground. Pulling back on the reins, he brought his horse up on its hind legs, danced all the way round the flag, then turned his back and trotted back to Nish.

Ranii was smiling. 'I think that sets the right tone. The Aachim are not put off by arrogance, since it is one of their defining characteristics.'

'What do we do now?' whispered Nish. 'Should I present my credentials?'

'To a group of soldiers? Of course not!'

'We must state our business, surely?'

'Let's see what they do first. Since they have not come down from their machines they may be an escort. We'll go forward, mounted, and see if they challenge us.'

Nish gestured to Mounce, who fell in beside Tchlrrr. The pair rode forward in perfect formation. Nish followed several lengths back, Ranii at his side. When Mounce's horse was a bare length from the leading construct, its hatch cracked open.

A tall dark woman cried, 'Who are you who ride so recklessly into the Aachim camp? Name yourselves!'

As Nish opened his mouth, Ranii hissed, 'Leave it to the sergeant, Marshal Hlar. Do not assume lackey's duties or they will think you are one.'

Mounce called out their names and business, whereupon the tall woman said, 'You are expected, Marshal Cryl-Nish Hlar. Go ahead. Keep your hands away from your weapons.'

They rode down the rank upon rank of constructs, and even Nish was hard put not to gape like a village yokel. In Tirthrax he had seen the machines only from a distance. Up close, they outclassed the clankers he had worked on as a prince's yacht surpasses a toy floating in the bathtub.

He forced himself to look impassive. Their marvels were no secret: the Aachim were the greatest engineers and designers in the Three Worlds. His horse was the best Troist had to offer, but it was not a construct.

They entered a heptagon of bare ground with the rows of constructs radiating away from it. At its centre was, clearly, the command tent. Mounce and the soldier moved to either side to allow Nish to pass through.

'Ride to within ten lengths of the tent, then dismount,' said Ranii in a low voice. 'This time try not to fall off. Bow and introduce yourself. I will come behind with your credentials.'

She fell back and Nish walked the horse forward. He felt incredibly conspicuous. A wall of Aachim surrounded the open space. He rode the distance, stopped and swung down. His knee wobbled as he struck the ground and for a horrified instant Nish thought that he was going to fall on his face. He steadied himself and waited.

The wait was a long one. As he was wondering why they did not come, the horse defecated noisily, splattering his left boot and lower leg. Nish tried to wipe it off with his other foot.

Three people emerged from the tent. The first was a very tall, haggard-looking fellow dressed in blue-black robes, his cheeks etched with creases and his mouth cast down in bitterness. He was followed by two others, a dark-skinned woman with black curling hair, handsome rather than beautiful, and another man whose close-cropped hair was iron-grey.

Nish bowed. 'I am Marshal Cryl-Nish Hlar; son of Scrutator Jal-Nish Hlar of Einunar Province; Envoy to General Troist.'

'You are not the first, Marshal Hlar,' said the haggard fellow, 'though you are certainly the littlest. What do you want?'

Nish was taken aback by the affront. Having been told that the Aachim were a formal species, much taken up with ritual and protocol, he had expected the formalities to take hours. Moreover, he was paralysed by the thought that he was about to make a major blunder. He could not think of the right words to say, or how to say them.

He opened his mouth and closed it again, but before he could make a complete fool of himself the woman with the curly black hair moved out from behind Vithis. She wore a scarlet blouse, black pantaloons and long black boots.

'Good day to you, Marshal Hlar,' she said. 'I am Tirior of Clan Nataz. Beside me stands Luxor of Clan Izmak. We are both of the Eleven Clans. Our leader, *for the moment*, is Vithis of Clan Inthis. We bid you welcome.'

'Clan Inthis, First Clan!' Vithis snapped.

There came a rebellious mutter from behind him. Others introduced themselves by their clan and given names, all being members of the Eleven Clans. At the end, a red-haired couple came forward. They were smaller of stature and paler of skin.

'I am Zea,' said the woman. 'My partner is Yrael. We represent Clan Elienor and seek news of our Aachim brethren on Santhenar.'

'Clan Elienor!' sneered Vithis. 'Least Clan, Last Clan. Not of the Eleven Clans nor ever will be.' He stepped in front of them, dismissively.

Zea moved to one side. 'We are one with the Aachim kind,' she said gently. 'All Aachim, not just the Eleven Clans, whose rivalry has ever held us back.'

Nish could see that rivalry in the body language of the leaders. Was that an advantage or a disadvantage? 'Thank you, Tirior of Clan Nataz,' he said faintly, perspiring in his uniform. 'Good day to you, Vithis of Clan Inthis and Luxor of Clan Izmak.' He bowed again. 'Thank –'

'Don't overdo it,' Ranii said out of the corner of her mouth.

'Come into the shade,' said Luxor. 'Will you take a glass of wine with us?'

Nish was prepared for this. Aachim wine was notoriously strong and he'd not had a drink in months. He might have begged for water on the grounds of a religious prohibition, which they must respect, but he'd made such a shaky start that Nish did not dare.

'I would be glad to,' he said.

Vithis grimaced, but stood back so that Nish and Ranii could follow Luxor and Tirior into the annexe of the tent. It was an enormous affair with five apexes held up by engraved poles and taut wires.

Tirior showed Nish to a chair and drew others up opposite. He tried to hide his stained boot and trousers, but was uncomfortably aware of the smell of manure. Refreshments were brought. Nish held his glass up to the light, as he knew the custom to be, and praised the colour for being as green as seawater. Vithis sneered. Evidently the comparison was infelicitous. They waited for him to take the first sip.

He did so. The wine was superb. Nish said so. Vithis smiled thinly.

Tirior chuckled. 'It is from my own estate, held by many to be the finest on all Aachan.'

'It may have been once,' grated Vithis, 'though Inthis would dispute that. But the vineyards of Izmak lie under a span and a half of ash and will never sprout again.'

'Alas, true. And so we have come to Santhenar,' said Tirior, 'to make a new life, we few to have survived the calamity. I brought cuttings of the best vines and will plant them with my own hands.'

'Where do you propose to do that?' Nish asked.

'Ah,' said Luxor. 'Wherever we are made welcome. Have you come to talk about that, Marshal Hlar.'

'I have,' said Nish, 'or at least to open a dialogue. Those with the power to negotiate concessions will follow.'

'Bah!' said Vithis. 'This *little* fellow isn't even the watchdog, much less the master. He's just a puppy and all he can do is piss on First Clan boots, as his horse craps on his. Go home, Marshal Hlar. If you *are* a marshal.'

'I am duly appointed to negotiate with you,' said Nish, signing for Ranii to pass forward his credentials. 'These are my papers.'

Vithis gave them a perfunctory glance, then tossed them on the floor. 'Any forger could have done better in a night and a day.'

Nish reached for them but Ranii shook her head. What was he supposed to do now? Pretend it had been an accident? 'My papers,' he said with an apologetic glance at Tirior. 'Would you –'

Picking them up, she handed them to Ranii, inclining her head minutely. Vithis turned his back, which Nish knew to be an even greater insult. He struggled to maintain his temper, though he must at all costs. Surely even Vithis would not attack them under the blue truce flag. Maybe this was a test. Vithis must be baiting him, to test his mettle.

'Let me be honest with you,' he said, looking to each of the three in turn.

'Meaning you weren't honest before?' said Vithis.

Nish took a deep breath. The man was impossible to deal with. 'I will put our situation plainly. We have been at war with the lyrinx for seven generations. They have hurt us badly. We have lost Meldorin and some strategic cities on the east coast.' Better not make themselves appear too weak. 'Nonetheless, we are hardened by war and will *never* give up. We have made many breakthroughs lately: new weapons, and means of delivering them, that will win us the war.'

'I see no sign of it,' said Vithis, facing him again.

'We will reveal our weapons in our own time,' said Nish.

'Time is what you do not have.'

'We have enough. Even so, we would be glad of your aid. With Aachim help the war could be over within a year, and then . . .'

'You ask for everything, yet offer nothing.'

'You invaded our world, *surr*!' Nish snapped. Realising that was undiplomatic, he added quickly, 'I meant that you ask for the greatest prize of all, part of our world. We are listening. Be sure that we will be generous, once –'

'In my experience, true generosity is unconditional.'

'We are honourable people, surr,' cried Nish, knowing that he was losing the struggle but not how he might recover. 'I have come in good faith.'

'That proves what a puppy you are,' growled Vithis. 'I have been reading your Histories since we came here. A more treacherous, lying and deceitful species than old humans has never existed in all the Three Worlds.'

'Surr,' said Nish, reining his temper in with the most tremendous effort, 'I beg you, consider what I have come to say.'

'I can read you like a book, Little Marshal. Old humans are weak. You are losing the war; I'd say you have already lost it. There's no benefit for First Clan – you can never deliver on your promises. You would say anything to get the aid you need so desperately. And if we did win your war for you, you would betray us. There is no gratitude in humanity, only treachery.'

'Clan Nataz have a different view,' declared Tirior, pushing forward.

Vithis held out his arm, barring her way. 'Clan Nataz do not lead. First Clan has that honour.'

'I hardly think that the lyrinx –' Nish began. His blood was boiling. He wanted to smash the fellow in the face, though it would mean his doom, blue flag or not.

'The lyrinx are beasts, but honourable ones for all that. They do not smile and make lying promises, like creeping, crawling, treacherous humanity. Go away, Little Marshal. You have nothing to offer us. Begone!'

Control yourself. Don't react to the provocation. Nish did his almighty best but suddenly his rage exploded. 'I am young, as you point out. Inexperienced too. But if I wanted lessons in treachery,' he said savagely, 'I could have come to no better place and no more experienced tutor!' Behind him Ranii sucked in her breath. His career as a diplomat was finished, but in the glorious madness of the moment, that counted for naught.

Vithis raised a clenched fist. 'How dare you come into my camp with such insults. I'll –'

Nish stepped right up to the tall man. 'I speak nothing but the truth and you know it, *noble* Vithis of Inthis First Clan. The evidence of your deceit and treachery lies all around you.' Nish pointed to the constructs extending in every direction. 'You lied to Tiaan. You used her innocence and her naïve love.'

A handsome young man ran forward, then stopped.

'You must have been building constructs for twenty years before you contacted her,' Nish went on. 'How dare you accuse humanity of treachery when your own soul is as black as your machines? You are a stinking liar, surr.'

Vithis's face went the colour of a leech's intestines. The young man threw himself between them. His strong hands kept clenching and unclenching. 'Foster-father . . .'

Vithis swung him out of the way. 'No, Minis, and a thousand times no!' He seized Nish by the front of the shirt, lifting him off the ground. 'What do you know of Tiaan and the flying construct?'

Nish's legs swung in the air. He restrained the urge to kick Vithis.

'To lay hands on an envoy under the blue flag is an act of aggression, surr,' said Ranii.

Vithis tossed Nish to the ground. 'Well, worm?'

'She met the Matah in Tirthrax,' said Nish. 'I don't know anything about a flying construct.'

'How do you know she met the Matah?'

'I was there when the gate opened. I saw you all pass by. I pursued Tiaan and caught her but the Matah intervened. That is all I know.'

'It's all you will ever know,' cried Vithis, pulling out a black dagger.

Tirior sprang forward, seizing his wrist. Vithis strained but could not break her hold. Luxor stepped to Vithis's other side.

'And under a blue flag!' Nish sneered. 'Once more you prove your character, Vithis of Clan Inthis.'

Vithis shook the pair off, sheathing the blade with an angry thrust. 'Never will we ally with you, Little Marshal. The war will soon be over and you will lose it.'

As Nish turned away, he could not resist one parting sally. 'At least we will be able to say we fought to the bitter end, and that is more than the Aachim ever did. A hundred Charon took your world from you.'

'Get out!' raged Vithis. 'Get out or not even the blue flag will save you.'

Nish was drawing breath for a final insult when Ranii gripped his collar so hard that it hurt. 'I am not going to give away my life so you can score debating points,' she hissed. 'Walk to your horse, get on it and ride away. If you say another word, I will plunge my sword right through the back of your neck.'

THIRTY-FOUR

By the time they slunk past the last line of constructs onto the plain, Nish's madness had worn off. Ranii said not a word. When he looked around she was back with the soldiers. He kicked the horse into a canter, then a gallop, despite the agony it caused his bruised backside and chafed inner thighs. What a fool he had been. Seize the opportunity with both hands. Ha! Vithis had set the trap and he had fallen right into it.

It was growing dark. The horse began to labour. The poor beast had been going hard all day and did not need a madman on its back at the end of it. A line of trees wavered across the plain in front of him. He slowed to a walk, heading toward the largest, and by the time the others caught up to him Nish had the fire going.

Ranii did not speak to him on the return trip but he knew what she was going to say to Troist. He should never have been entrusted with the job; he had taken what should have been hers, against her advice, and stuffed it up disastrously.

The soldiers were silently efficient. Not once did they meet Nish's eye. He *was* a puppy. A failure at everything.

Mounce sought him out as they approached Troist's camp. 'Surr?' he said anxiously.

Nish had no heart to continue the farce. He was no marshal;

343

no command of his could have any force. 'Yes, *Sergeant Mounce?*'

'I – Nothing, surr!'

Nish did not hurry to his meeting with Troist. By the time he dragged himself through the flaps of the tent, Ranii was halfway through her report. He listened to the rest in silence. Yara sat on the far side of the room but did not interfere.

Troist turned a haggard face to him. 'Have you anything to add, Marshal Hlar?'

Nish was in no mood to make excuses. 'No, surr. It is as Ranii says.'

'Come on, man, this does not sound like the son of a scrutator! You must have something to say in your defence.'

'The son is not the father,' said Nish. 'I was unbearably provoked, and finally I broke. I will say only this. Vithis is a man entirely without honour, and was so *before* his clan was wiped out in the passage through the gate. But . . .'

'Yes?'

'The loss of his clan has driven him over the edge.'

'What do you say to that, Ranii?'

'I hate to say it –'

Troist turned on her and his voice was very cold. 'Why would you *hate to say it*? Have you something against Marshal Hlar?'

'I –' she began. 'No, surr, nothing at all.'

'I'm glad to hear it. I'd *hate* to think that you were being obstructive, envoy.'

'No, surr.'

'Go on.'

'Marshal Hlar may be right. I've never met an Aachim who behaved the way Vithis does. Grief must have turned his mind.'

'He was entirely unreasonable,' said Nish, 'and quite without honour. It is impossible to deal with him.'

Troist sighed. 'What does he want, apart from the conquest of this world?'

Ranii began to answer but Nish interrupted. 'Surely to build his clan anew. To make up for four thousand years of slavery on

344

Aachan. Vithis, I feel sure, is driven to make up for the entire Histories of the Aachim. He will never negotiate.'

'How do you know, Cryl-Nish?'

'He said as much to Tiaan in Tirthrax, after the Aachim came through the gate. The Histories tell me the rest.' Poor Tiaan, Nish thought. I was wrong about her at Tirthrax. It raised the uncomfortable thought that he may have been wrong about her other actions as well.

'Is that all?' said Troist.

'Tirior and Luxor seem reasonable people, surr. If something were to happen to Vithis I believe they would be prepared to bargain with us, as would some of the other clans. It seems that they suffer Vithis for the moment, but clan rivalries run deep. He was openly hostile to Clan Elienor, who are not of the Eleven Clans.'

'Do you disagree with any of this, Ranii?'

'No, surr,' after a long hesitation.

Troist looked across at Yara, who made a gesture with one hand. Nish could not interpret it, but the look on her face suggested that she was as disgusted as Ranii.

'Do you have your commission, Cryl-Nish?' said Troist.

'My commission, surr?'

'As marshal! Surely you did not expect to keep it, after this fiasco?'

'Er, no,' said Nish. 'Vithis cast it on the floor at the beginning of our meeting.'

'Vithis threw your papers on the floor!' Troist exclaimed. 'You did not mention this, Ranii.'

'It . . . slipped my mind, surr,' she said hastily. 'I have the documents here.'

Troist took the papers and tore them in half. 'It is clear the embassy was doomed before it began and Vithis had no intention of negotiating.' Troist paced back and forth, as he was wont to do when thinking. 'You may go about your business, Ranii. I'll speak to you in the morning.'

When she was gone he said to Nish, 'I won't pretend I'm happy, Cryl-Nish. Though it seems the mission had little chance, a skilled diplomat *might* just have extracted an offer we could have lived with. I am mindful that you are not a diplomat. Even so, you should have put up with his taunts. You have made things worse and I see no hope of an agreement now.'

'The man is a tyrant, surr. Not striking back would be seen as a sign of weakness.'

'I didn't ask for a lesson in politics, Cryl-Nish. Our situation is more desperate than you know. With the aid of the Aachim we would probably have won the war. If they stay neutral we will probably lose. But if they ally with the lyrinx . . .'

'Yes?' said Nish, when Troist had been pacing for some time.

'It will all be over in a fortnight! Leave us.'

The army continued to grow over the next few days as stragglers, and sometimes large bands, came in from all directions. They now numbered more than four and a half thousand, and their fleet of clankers, ninety-six. A powerful force, though matched by the lyrinx shadowing them in the west. Tension hung in the air, thick as glue. Troist paced more than ever. Fights broke out among the soldiers: brutal, ugly affairs that only ended when one was battered into unconsciousness. The other was whipped bloody, but it made no difference. Within hours, there would be another affray.

The whole camp knew of Nish's fall from grace, and that any chance of an alliance with the Aachim had vanished. He ate alone. Nish had begun to have stomach cramps, so knotted was he inside. He had let Troist down, and everyone else. Why hadn't he kept his mouth shut?

He went back to his old work, assisting with the development of tactics to use against the Aachim constructs, but Nish was conscious how little he knew of them. He did not even know what weapons they carried inside. But at least he had seen constructs in operation, and that was more than the other officers could say.

He realised that someone was talking to him. 'I beg your pardon?' he said.

'If they attack, h-how can we c-c-combat them?' The speaker

was Lieutenant Prandie, one of the most junior officers, even younger than Nish.

'Pits!' said Nish. The idea had just popped into his head. 'Constructs float hip-high above the ground and I don't think they can go any higher. If we were fighting a pitched battle we could dig a series of pits across their path, cover them, and when the constructs fell in, they would not be able to get out.'

'Neither would our clankers, should the battle move that way.'

'But we would know they were there.'

'A useful idea,' said Troist, who had been standing up the back unnoticed, 'but it's not going to win the battle.'

The weather continued unrelentingly hot and dry. The green shoots soon withered and they had to move camp constantly, but still the horses lost condition. Troist was forever worrying about their supplies. The flour was full of red weevils, the casks of salt meat had a putrid tang, and they had not had fresh vegetables in a fortnight. Troist had recovered the fallen army's war chest but money could not buy what was not available.

A bout of dysentery passed through the camp, leaving half the soldiers groaning in their hammocks with vomiting and bloody diarrhoea. Troist, a man who seemed to have constant trouble with his bowels, was among them. Nish was unaffected, perhaps because he had been ostracised by the rest of the camp. Everyone lived in fear of an attack that they would not be able to defend against.

It did not come, and as the days passed, he began to understand how the soldiers felt. Maybe battle, bloody though it would be, *would* be better than this waiting day after day, never knowing what the enemy was doing or even where they were.

In the second week after the failed embassy, clouds began to build up in the afternoon. Instead of being hot and dry it was hot and sticky. Storms threatened but never came. There were more fights than ever, but Troist now turned a blind eye to them. Nish understood that too – it was the only way they could let off steam. Sometimes he felt like punching his fellow

347

officers for no other reason than the way they spoke, or walked, or ate.

This day it looked as if the storm was finally coming. At sunset, towering clouds hung in the south-west, and they were an ominous purply-green. Lightning flashed. Nish was bent over the chart table when he heard pounding hooves and one of the scouts skidded to a stop outside the command tent next door. He ran inside, then came out again. 'Where's General Troist?'

Nish hurried across. 'What is it? Is there news?'

The scout made a rude gesture. 'Not for your ears!'

Troist appeared from the direction of the latrines, hastily fastening his trousers. They went into the command tent. Nish tried to follow but the guards barred his way. Frustrated, he returned to his work, but shortly afterwards was called to the command tent, now empty apart from Troist. The flaps were closed and it was sweltering inside.

'It's war!' said Troist. 'The lyrinx are moving. They must have been waiting for the weather to change.'

Lightning flickered in the west. This was it.

'I have another job for you,' the general continued.

'I'm surprised you still trust me, surr.'

'It's not a diplomatic mission,' Troist said coolly.

'What is it?'

'My wife and daughters are still here. I should have sent them away long ago but . . . I could not bear to be parted from them. You are to take them east to safety.'

'Won't that be rather dangerous?' Lest Troist think he was a coward, Nish added hastily, 'For them, I meant.'

'Not as dangerous as staying here. Will you do it?'

'Of course, surr. I would be honoured. Where are we going?'

'Yara will tell you, once you are gone. I'm not taking any risks.'

'Risks, surr?'

'Spies, traitors,' Troist said impatiently. 'The families of high officers are always targets in times like this.'

'When do we go, surr?'

'You've got fifteen minutes, or until the storm hits. Easier to keep it quiet that way.'

'Am I going alone, surr?'

'Mounce will accompany you. He won't like it, but that's the lot of a soldier. I can't spare anyone else, nor even him. Get ready!'

It was the work of a few minutes to pack, toss his oilskin cloak over his arm and report back to Troist. 'I'll walk with you,' the general said. 'They're waiting over by the horse yards.'

The camp had been darkened for the night, though they could see clearly enough, for lightning flashed continually. Nish's skin prickled in the heat.

Troist embraced Yara, Meriwen and Liliwen. They all looked stoic now. Mounce loomed out of the darkness like a squat bear. 'Storm's almost on us, surr.'

'Mount up!' Troist said harshly. Yara clung to her man as he lifted her into the saddle. The girls went up onto the next horse, one from either side. In the gloom Nish could not tell which twin was which.

He climbed onto his own horse, the one he'd had on the previous mission, and checked his saddlebags, which Mounce had already packed. His sword was at his hip, a crossbow tied down behind him.

Troist passed him up a small packet. 'Your papers, Cryl-Nish.' Nish put them safely in an inside pocket and buttoned the flap. Another packet followed, rather heavier. 'Coin for the journey.'

'Thank you, surr. And afterwards, what would you have me do?'

'If we survive, we'll be long gone from here, I know not where. You'll have to look out for yourself. Use what remains of the coin if you need to.'

Nish nodded. Lightning struck a tree on the creek, not a hundred paces away. The thunder was shattering. Horses whinnied.

Troist reached up his hand. Nish took it. 'Don't let me down, Cryl-Nish.'

'I won't, surr,' he said hoarsely.

Mounce led the way. Yara followed, the twins after her, and Nish last. He looked back as they rounded the corner of the yards. A flash illuminated Troist, a forlorn figure standing with his hand still upraised. His family would probably never see him again.

The storm struck before they had crossed the creek. It was a kind of rain Nish had never felt before, fat stinging drops that were not cold at all. He was used to freezing rain that seeped through everything and made his bones ache. This was so deliciously mild that he caught the drops in his hands and rubbed them all over his face.

He was not so pleased when, a few minutes later, the downpour turned to pellets of hail, large enough to strike him painfully on the head and shoulders. The horses ahead were black silhouettes when the lightning flashed, completely invisible when it did not. Nish prayed that Mounce knew which way to go; he had not the faintest idea.

Lightning struck the trees behind him. Nish's horse reared, screaming in terror. He clung desperately to the mane, expecting to be thrown, but its front legs struck the ground with a jarring thud and it bolted.

He pulled the reins with all his might but it made no difference. The terrified horse galloped into the darkness. The next time there was lightning he could not see anyone. Once again his life was running out of control.

Not this time. Nish hauled the reins back savagely and to the right. The horse reared up, propped and tried to throw him. Letting go of the reins, Nish caught the saddle straps with both hands and hung on. The next heave lifted him in the air. He pulled himself down. 'Stop it, you stupid nag!' he roared. 'There's a bloody war on!'

He went one way, and then the other, but Nish did not fall. The horse was tiring rapidly. It stood still, and the next flash of lightning, closer than the other, only made it rear its head.

Taking up the reins, he gave the horse a pat on the flank, took his bearings and began to ride around in circles that extended away from the creek, each one larger than the previous. On the fifth of these he saw the three shadows, standing quietly, and rode up to them.

'Perhaps we should rope together until the storm is over,' he said to Mounce.

The storm went east; they headed north-east. Within half an hour it was just a mutter on the horizon. They did not hurry, since the ground was too stony for rapid riding in darkness. As dawn streaked the sky ahead, they approached another ribbon of trees. The plain looked exactly as it had for the past month: grey grass, brown stones, and as flat as a table.

'Where are we heading?' he said to Yara.

She sat her saddle upright as a post, though she must have been as weary as he was. She studied him for some time before answering. After his failure as an envoy Yara had barely spoken to Nish, and clearly she had misgivings about him now. With reason, if he was honest with himself.

'A place in the Worm Wood,' she said coldly.

How far is that?' Geography was not one of Nish's strengths.

'The forest is a few days away, if we can ride uninterrupted.' She glanced up at the sky, then back at him as if weighing him up. If a lyrinx spotted them and decided to attack, Nish could not save them.

'I won't fail you,' Nish said, trying to reassure himself as much as her.

'I believe you made that promise to Troist a while back.'

Yara held his gaze until he was forced to look away. She was terrified for her children and counted him as near useless. It was not a good moment.

They camped by a river, the most substantial one Nish had encountered in many days. It actually had banks, a higher set and a lower. They built a fire next to the higher bank, which was a head-high wall of yellow, pebbly earth. There was plenty of dry wood here, and ribbons of twisted bark that burned as bright as a candle, giving off little smoke.

The girls curled up on a blanket and slept. Nish could not – he had to prove himself to Yara and was determined to do so.

'If you're not going to sleep, surr, I'll take a few hours,' said Mounce.

'Do that,' said Nish. 'I'll keep watch.'

Yara rested against a tree, eyes going everywhere, a short sword at her left hand. Nish climbed the bank and looked around. Nothing moved on the flat plain. The other side of the river looked just the same. He walked back and forth, discovering a pair of ancient trees with patterns carved into their trunks. Growth swelled around the markings, partly obscuring them and obliterating any meaning, at least to Nish's eyes.

Mounce relieved the interminable watch at midday and Nish took his turn on the blanket. They set off as the sun was going down, wading the river, which hardly came up to the horses' bellies.

Twice, from his lookout high in a tree, Nish saw riders in the distance. He made sure that Mounce and the others stayed well hidden until the riders moved away. He expected thanks from Yara but got none.

In this way they travelled for three more days, toward a growing smudge on the eastern horizon. Yara barely spoke to Nish and double-checked everything he did. She did not trust him at all. Even the children were quiet.

Hilly country now lay ahead. On the fourth morning they were close enough to see that it was clad in forest.

'Why is it forest there,' Nish wondered, 'and not in Almadin?'

'Good, deep soil,' said Mounce. 'Not this stony muck.' He kicked a pebble.

They rested for the morning and continued after lunch. There was an hour of daylight left by the time Nish, who was scouting ahead, reached the first of the trees. He rode back to confer with Yara about their route.

'I wouldn't call this forest,' said Nish, eyeing the scattered copses.

'There's woodcutting here on the edge,' said Yara. 'You'll see trees enough before we get to where we're going. Shouldn't you be up ahead, scouting out our path?'

That was unfair. 'Which way?' he snapped.

'Don't speak to me like that, *soldier*.'

A bitter retort was on Nish's lips when he heard a familiar, disturbing whine.

'What's that?' cried Yara, jerking her sword from its scabbard.

A construct emerged from the trees to the front of them. Another appeared behind.

'If you've betrayed us, Nish, you're dead!'

THIRTY-FIVE

The soldiers held her arms. Irisis looked around frantically but the blank walls of manufactory and cistern offered no escape. Jal-Nish was going to mutilate her.

He slashed down. Irisis flinched; she could not help herself. The sword stopped, resting on her outstretched arm.

'It's not that easy, Irisis.' Jal-Nish uttered a liquid chuckle, like vomit splashing in a bucket. 'You haven't suffered enough.'

'If you're going to do it, then do it!' she screamed.

'Oh, I'll do it, but not on your timetable.'

He raised the sword. Would he cut this time? Irisis did not think so, but neither was he predictable. He might just take a finger, or her nose. What if he did that, then let her live? She was too vain to endure such an existence. She tried to pull away but the soldiers held her firmly.

'Please,' she said in a throaty whisper. 'I'll do anything you want.' She would have. Dignity meant nothing before the threat of mutilation. She heaved her bosom toward the nearest soldier.

Jal-Nish snorted. 'You'll make no ground there, crafter. They have eyes only for each other.'

Irisis stared at the pair, horrified. 'But . . . that's a capital crime! How can – ?' She recalled that Jal-Nish had a taste for his own sex.

'They've done their duty and fathered soldiers. What they do in their own time is none of my affair.' Jal-Nish pressed the sword point against her shoulder. It went through her coat and shirt, to break the skin. 'Just there, I think.'

He whipped the sword up, but as he was about to bring it down someone bellowed from the top of the manufactory wall.

'Lower your sword, Jal-Nish, or I'll put a bolt right through your good eye.' It was the scrutator's voice.

'Shoot and be damned!' Jal-Nish brought down the sword.

As Flydd spoke, the soldiers had spun around. Irisis jerked free and dived at Jal-Nish's legs. The sword came down so hard that it struck the ground behind her.

Jal-Nish raised the weapon to plunge it through her back, but with a tinny clang his head was jerked sideways. He clawed at the mask. The crossbow bolt, fired with only half-power, had slammed into the platinum cheekpiece, gone two-thirds of the way through, then stuck. Bilious yellow foam oozed from beneath the mask. A clot quivered on his collar, speckled with bright blood.

'Kill her!' he gasped. 'Kill the scrutator too.'

Irisis had her knife out, not that it would be any use against swordsmen. Ducking behind Jal-Nish, she whipped his single arm up behind his back as hard as she could. Putting the blade to his throat she yelled, 'Tell them to stand back or I'll take your head right off.'

'Think you that I care?' he raged. 'Kill her, even if you have to kill me first.'

The soldiers came at her from either side. Jal-Nish was a hindrance now so she put her foot in the middle of his back and sent him flying. Going into a crouch, she swayed from side to side, trying to keep both swordsmen in view at once.

They laughed. She had no chance. The first lunged. She backpedalled but the lunge kept going until the soldier ploughed face-first into the ground. A small bright spot marked the middle of his back. The second sword hacked at her but missed – the soldier's head snapped back as a bolt took him in the temple. She scanned the wall. The scrutator had three others with him. Two were soldiers, armed with crossbows.

They hurled a rope over the side and climbed down, hand over hand. The third man followed, his mancer's robes billowing. Flydd came last, sliding the lower section and hitting the ground hard. She ran to help him up.

The scrutator examined his blistered hands, then gasped, 'Quick, onto the cistern, then up inside the aqueduct.'

The soldiers were near the top of the outside ladder when Jal-Nish sat up, took a small golden horn from his pocket, fitted the mouthpiece through the hole in his mask and blew hard. It gave forth a low, sobbing moan. The adjacent cistern boomed like an enormous drum and a series of misty concentric hoops formed around it, like rings around a planet.

The scrutator, who was lowest, clutched at his heart and fell. The soldiers clapped their hands over their ears. The mancer went rigid, blood burst from mouth and nose and he slid corpse-like off the ladder. Irisis felt a scream building up in her throat but could not let it out. The air seemed to have thickened in her lungs.

She thumped her breastbone against the side of the ladder. The choking sensation eased enough for her to take a breath. 'Go up!' she shouted at the soldiers. 'Get your weapons out and cover me. Take my pack!'

The lower soldier handed it up. Scrambling down, she ran to the scrutator. He was still breathing. The mancer was dead.

The soldier, who had come down after her, took the scrutator's leather satchel. Jal-Nish was staggering towards her, swinging a sword. The blast, or spell, whatever it was, must have affected him too.

'You can't get away!' he slurred. 'I'll have a hundred soldiers here in a minute.'

Irisis heaved the scrutator onto her shoulder. He weighed no more than a bag of bones. She clutched the ladder and began to go up, but knew she was too slow. Jal-Nish would have a free blow at her back and legs.

She dropped to the ground, pulled the knife from her belt and feinted at Jal-Nish. He hacked back, the sword going so close to her arm that it shaved hairs. He was grunting and hawking as if there was something caught in his throat. Come closer, Jal-Nish, and it'll be my boot. Irisis backpedalled, the scrutator's arms and legs swinging wildly. Her knees felt like rubber. Should she drop Flydd? In his state it might kill him, but so might Jal-Nish's sword.

'Shoot!' she screeched at the soldiers, who had reached the top of the cistern. They did not shoot; she must be in the way.

A wild swing took Jal-Nish's sword past her. The knife was around the wrong way so, holding the hilt, she crashed her fist into his temple. Jal-Nish went down, the mask slipped and she caught sight of the horror beneath. She wanted to be sick.

Staggering to the ladder, she stepped over the body of the scrutator's unknown mancer and began to climb. Irisis felt drunk; she could not think straight. Halfway up she stopped and was clinging desperately to the rungs, wondering what to do, when one of the soldiers plucked Flydd from her grasp.

'They're coming,' he said.

Irisis could see only Jal-Nish, who was beginning to stir. The soldier helped her up the ladder.

'What's the matter?' She supported herself on the stone edge that curved around the top of the cistern.

The soldier pointed. More troops were boiling out the front gate of the manufactory.

'Where to?' gasped Irisis.

'This way. I'm Jym. Other bloke's Yorme.' Carrying the scrutator, Jym trotted around the top of the cistern, which was not much wider than the length of his two feet, towards the end of the aqueduct.

Irisis followed. It was a long reach to a ladder which ran up the discharge flume. Yorme had already disappeared. Jym was struggling to heave himself and his pack up, as well as Flydd's inert body. Irisis gave him a push and he caught the bottom rung of the ladder.

'Pass down your bow,' she said.

After a silence, it appeared. The soldier grunted his way up.

Irisis fitted the bolt, wound back the crank and took aim where the lower ladder came up onto the cistern.

Nothing happened for such a long time that she regretted waiting. She could have been halfway up the flume by now. Then, from the corner of her eye, a head appeared over the edge of the cistern. Someone had climbed the side. Irisis was about to shoot when another head topped the ladder. She had just one bolt.

The man on the ladder appeared first. She pointed the weapon at him and fired. He was moving fast and the bolt caught him high in the chest, just below the collarbone. Arms flailing, he went sideways into the water with an enormous splash.

The other man kept coming. Irisis climbed the ladder, awkwardly holding the crossbow. The soldier, moving like lightning, reached the bottom of the ladder before she was at the top. Springing high, he caught the third rung and raced up as if trained as an acrobat. She kicked at his face but he swayed out of the way, grabbed her boot and heaved. Irisis nearly fell. She kicked again, catching him in the mouth. He went down four rungs before he managed to stop.

At the top, rough stone bordered the water channel. It sloped up steeply here. The man was after her again. She was too exhausted to get away. All she had was a knife and a crossbow without any bolts. The man had a sword, against which a knife was useless. The crossbow was no help without bolts but she did not want to abandon it.

Irisis backed up, keeping him in sight, and slipped the knife into the bolt slot of the crossbow, just to see if it would fit. It did, more or less. The soldier was watching her, coming warily now. He laughed aloud at the makeshift weapon, which was as likely to jam and hurl shards of metal back in her face.

Irisis fitted the wire over the hilt. It would probably slip off as she fired. She sighted on the centre of the soldier's body.

'Go back or I'll fire,' she said, and to Irisis's disgust there was a quaver in her voice.

'Go on!' he smirked.

She did. The knife shot out, too fast to see, to embed itself to the hilt in the man's chest. He lost his footing, fell into the flume and slid down, thump-thumping all the way.

Irisis fled, up and up. Before she reached the top the first soldiers appeared below. One went to his knees, aimed at her and fired. It was a steep uphill shot, difficult to calculate, and Irisis was not surprised that it fell short, ricocheting into the channel. The next was closer but by then Irisis had gained the top. Another soldier moved into firing position as she ducked out of sight.

Jym was waiting with the other crossbow and a bag of bolts. She fitted one into her weapon, cranked it and they set off, running together up the now gentle slope. 'Go ahead,' he said. 'You need a break.'

Some break! She pounded up the rough path. Yorme was a long way ahead, lumping the scrutator and his own pack. Irisis was still far from catching him when a shout echoed behind her.

Jym had gone down on one knee, aiming at the throng which had burst up over the rise. They were a couple of hundred paces behind him. He fired at the group and was lucky enough to see one fall.

Irisis now saw the weak point of the plan. If he waited to reload, they would have crossed half the distance and he would still have only one shot, while there were at least a dozen of them. The range was long but with so many firing, one would get them. A lucky shot could even bring *her* down.

She jumped into the dry channel, scrambled up the other side where she had a clear view, took aim and fired. So many soldiers were clustered together that she was bound to strike one. Irisis was dismayed to discover that she had not. They did check, however, enough for Jym to run for his life.

Several bolts came screaming after him, striking sparks out of the sides of the aqueduct, but none hit and she had time to get off another shot before he reached her. This one was better aimed. The man in the lead went down as if he had been struck with a boulder.

That stopped them. Irisis and Jym ran on, on opposite sides of the channel. They were out of range of all but an accidental hit.

'How far is it?' she shouted.

'Best part of a league.'

Irisis forced herself to keep moving, though she could not keep up. By the time she reached the top of the slope, the enemy were back in range. She stopped to catch her breath and a bolt passed between her knees. That gave her just enough impetus to claw her way onto a gentler slope.

Not far on, she encountered the others. Flydd was on his feet now, a trickle of red running from his left nostril. He managed a smile, a horrible, death's-head affair.

Hers was no better. 'How are you, Xervish?' she gasped.

'I can walk,' he said wanly.

'Walking is no bloody good at all! Can you run as though all the hounds of hell were after you? They're gaining fast.'

'I can't,' he said, 'but I may be able to do something better.'

'I look forward to seeing it.'

'You won't. Go on and don't look back.'

'I — But, surr!'

'Do it!' His voice was harsh with strain. '*Now!*'

She stumbled after the others, but after a few minutes Irisis stopped. The soldiers must be coming up the rise. What could the silly old fool do in his condition?

Flydd was standing like a spread-legged skeleton, holding his arms out and up so he had the form of an 'X'. He looked as if he was trying to summon a bolt from the heavens.

The soldiers topped the rise. Two went to their knees, pointing weapons at him. The bolts would tear him apart. Why didn't he do something? Or was he sacrificing himself so that they could get away?

A ball of mist emerged between him and the soldiers. If he was attempting some kind of illusion, it was too late. They would just fire straight through it. She took a couple of steps toward him. The mist grew. The soldiers fired.

Two red streaks appeared inside the mist, swelled, coalesced, and white fire burst out in all directions, so bright that it burned her eyes. She blinked and rubbed her eyes but could see nothing at all. Reeling backwards, she fell into the channel, which fortunately held only a trickle of water.

Irisis came to her knees. I can't see, she thought, panicking. *I'm blind!* She blundered into one side of the channel, then the other. It was as if she had lost all her other faculties as well.

'You bloody fool!' panted the scrutator, pulling her to her feet. 'As if I don't have enough to do. Stand up!'

'I can't,' she sobbed. 'I can't see.'

He struck her across the face. 'You imbecile, Irisis. I told you not to look back. Take my hand.'

She clutched it as if she was never going to let go.

'Take it, I said, don't crush it.'

He dragged her along the aqueduct. It was surprising how hard it was to walk when she could not see. Irisis kept stumbling, and once her balance went she did not know how to right herself.

'What did you do, Xervish?'

'Scrutator magic,' he said with a hoarse chuckle. 'I'm forbidden to speak of it. Keep moving.'

'I don't see what there's to laugh about. I've lost my sight.'

'Serves you right for being such a stickybeak!'

'You might be a little bit sympathetic,' she said forlornly.

'I've got troubles of my own and your stupidity has just doubled them.'

She closed up. This was the old, hard side of the scrutator. She'd forgotten that as their relationship developed.

They caught up to the others. 'Are you all right, surr?' asked Yorme.

'I've been better. And then again I've been worse, though not by much.'

'What's happened to the crafter, surr?' asked Jym.

'Don't stop!' the scrutator snapped. 'Silly cow looked back when I told her not to and has lost her sight.'

Irisis had not expected much sympathy, but a little more than that. 'I was trying to help you,' she sniffed.

'Next time, don't bother. Just do as you are told.'

'There isn't going to be a next time!' she cried, tripping on a broken edge. He pulled her to her feet and they hurried on, faster than before.

'True enough. They're coming again.'

'How did they survive?'

'There must have been fifty or sixty out of sight down the slope. None of them would have been hurt, though it may take them a little time to get . . . past.'

'How do you mean?'

'Is there no end to your infernal questions? My working of the Art has left the place a little *strange*.'

No one spoke. Irisis kept going; she had no idea how. She just concentrated on putting one foot ahead of the other, then moving the first up to it and past, and then the other again. She could only think of one thing and it was far more important than the soldiers hunting them, or wondering what was going to happen at the other end – *I want to see!*

'I've spotted them, surr.' Yorme's voice was deeper than Jym's, a slow, rolling rumble.

'How many and how far back?' asked the scrutator.

'It's hard to count . . . At least forty. They'd be three hundred paces away.'

'They can still do us harm from there,' said Flydd, 'if they realise it.'

'I think they have, surr. A couple are firing but they're shooting over our heads.'

'Keep going.'

Something smashed into the stone not far away. 'Was that a bolt?' Irisis cried wildly. It would not have bothered her had she been able to see, but unsighted it was terrifying.

'They're shooting up into the air, hoping to drop one or two among us.'

They had been climbing gently for some time. Now they topped a rise and began to move along the easiest of slopes.

'There's the air-floater!' Yorme exclaimed. 'Just across the ravine, among the trees. We'll get there yet.'

'Don't be so sure,' the scrutator muttered.

'How far to go?' Irisis yelled. 'And how far back are the soldiers?'

'The same distance as before. It's not them we've got to worry about.'

A deadly chill settled over her. 'What *do* we have to worry about?'

'Can't you hear?'

Irisis could hear nothing but their feet upon the stone and the hammering of her heart. No, there *was* something else – a rhythmic thud-*thud*, thud-*thud*, and groaning rattles. A whole symphony of them.

'Jal-Nish's fleet of clankers is coming over the hill. They're heading straight for the air-floater and they're going to shoot it out of the sky.'

THIRTY-SIX

Fear of Jal-Nish drove Irisis on. She could almost see under the mask; the scarred, unhealing flesh, the foaming yellow muck oozing out and down his chin. Whatever horrors he had endured, she felt no pity for him. Jal-Nish had always been a selfish, unpleasant man, though good looks and an engaging manner had once veneered over his innate viciousness. He was now a monster, inside and out.

'What's happening?' she yelled.

'Don't scream in my ear! I'm right beside you. The soldiers are gaining on us, though slowly. They're wary of me now.'

'What about the clankers?'

'They're closing the gap. The ridge drops away into a little rocky valley with a stream at the bottom. It's stony there, but shallow; they'll have no trouble getting through. Up the other side is a short steep pinch, but not too steep for skilled operators. Beyond that it flattens out and they can get into good firing position.'

'How far is it to where the air-floater is going to pick us up?'

'About a thousand paces.'

'Signal it to come.'

'There's a heck of a breeze out here in the middle of the valley. It'll be difficult for it to put down on the aqueduct.'

'It would be worth it, if it cuts down the time the clankers have to get into position.'

'You're right! I'll call it over.'

He began to wave. Irisis could feel it through his hand. He shook her hand free.

'What are you doing?' she cried, feeling abandoned. They could all run away and she would never know.

'I may have to work my magic again. The soldiers are coming on.'

'*Can* you do it again so soon?'

'Probably not, though they don't know that. At least, I hope they don't.' He did not sound at all certain.

'Where are the clankers now?' Her panic was rising again. Irisis felt utterly helpless, not a feeling she was accustomed to.

Flydd did not respond, though after an interval Jym said, 'Almost down to the stream, marm. It runs directly below us but they're further downstream.'

'Call me Irisis,' she said. 'Has the air-floater lifted off yet?'

'No, mar – Irisis. They're just unfastening the tethers.'

'They're slow,' she muttered.

No one answered. The seconds ticked by with awful slowness.

'Aaah!' Flydd cried.

'What's the matter?' said Irisis.

'Jal-Nish has sent up some kind of mancer.'

'With the clankers?'

'No, she's on the aqueduct. She's strong. I'm not sure I can best her in my condition.'

'What's she doing?'

Now she could hear his teeth chattering. 'A-A-A! Mfgg! Gahh!'

'Are you all right, scrutator?' she cried. Using his name did not seem to be right, in front of the others.

'I don't think he can speak, Irisis,' said Jym. 'He's being pushed backwards, ell by ell.'

'Maybe we should try and hold him,' said Yorme.

'No!' she snapped. 'Don't touch him. You'll just make things worse.'

Irisis began to see images in her inner eye, like parts of the field. Someone was drawing on it and it wasn't Flydd. It didn't look like the clankers, either. It had to be the mancer and she must be a mighty opponent to disable a scrutator so quickly. Jal-Nish must have brought her specially for the purpose.

Irisis fingered her pliance and the field appeared, swirling like a rotor spinning through brown sugar-streaked porridge.

'The soldiers are coming,' muttered Jym.

The field was clearer than she had ever seen it. Was that because she had lost her sight, or was it something to do with the scrutator's magic? She concentrated. Though Irisis could not draw power from the field, she had always been able to change it in subtle ways, nudging its billows and eddies into more suitable shapes. She did that now, folding one loop over on itself, again and again, until the resulting packet contained countless layers of its strange material, or rather, *immaterial*.

Flydd made no more sound, apart from the breath hissing through his clenched teeth, and that became ever softer. She felt like a mouse in a shoebox, unable to get out and knowing that the cat was coming closer. If Flydd was disabled, it was up to her to save them. The soldiers were useless against a mancer.

'What are the clankers doing now?' she said softly.

'They've stopped in the centre of the valley. The nearest are trying to aim their javelards at the air-floater.' It was Jym speaking.

'Has it lifted?'

'Yes. It's coming towards us.'

'Do you think they'll hit it?'

'Could do, though they're at extreme range.'

'And the soldiers in the aqueduct?' asked Irisis.

'Still creeping forward.'

'I suppose they'll be within range soon.'

'A couple of minutes. At the most.'

'Send a few bolts at them, not that it'll make any difference.'

She heard the twang of the crossbows, followed by the sound of the cranks as they were wound back. 'And the scrutator?'

Yorme answered this time. 'He's still on his feet but he seems to be having some kind of a fit. His eyes are bulging out of his head.'

With a fluttering sound, something passed in front of the sun. 'Is that the air-floater?'

'It's above us, high up.'

'Are the clankers firing?' Her greatest fear was of the air-floater being hit and exploding directly above them.

'No.'

'Why not?'

Jym laughed. 'Because the javelards aren't designed to shoot up at such an angle.'

Relief washed over her. 'Then they can't do anything?'

After a pause, he said, 'The shooters are pulling the pins out of the mechanisms. Looks like they're going to point them by hand.'

'That can't be very accurate,' said Irisis.

'It's a big target,' said Jym.

'See if you can shoot them.'

The weapon twanged. 'Not even close. It's too far for a crossbow.'

'So they can't shoot the balloon with their bows?'

'Not unless they come closer.'

'Soldiers are nearly within range,' Yorme called.

'Have another shot at them.'

The weapons fired and Irisis made out a scream. 'That wasn't the mancer, I suppose?'

'She's well back.'

'I've got to help the scrutator, any way I can,' Irisis said.

'What are you going to do?' asked Jym.

'I have no idea.'

She sensed out the field again and, searching through it, picked out two distortions, one so close that it had to be Flydd, the other a little further away.

She pushed that folded-over package of the field in Flydd's direction but he did not seem to be able to use it. Perhaps he hadn't noticed. 'Xervish?'

'I don't think he can hear anything, Irisis.'

The enemy mancer was using another part of the field. Irisis searched frantically for a way to attack her, but it had to be a hidden way. She could not withstand a mancer's attack for a single minute. What if she changed the field so as to starve the mancer of the power she needed? The woman was drawing fiendish quantities as she hurled everything into her attack on Flydd.

Irisis created a map of the local field in her mind, coloured in the shades of the spectrum, the higher energies being associated with indigo and violet. Now to identify exactly where the other mancer was drawing power from. Ah, there: a little hidden sump that glowed deep violet, tending towards black.

Another mancer, or even an artisan, might have drawn on that source so as to deprive her enemy of power. Irisis lacked that ability but she had become skilled at shaping the field in order that others could better use it.

She subtly thinned the field around the sump, but the mancer simply changed the way she was drawing from it and took more power, endeavouring to immobilise the scrutator. Hopeless to think that Irisis, a mere crafter, could outwit a mancer whose whole life had been spent in mastering the Secret Art.

What if she were to nudge that folded package of energy towards the sump? From outside it just appeared as a dark blob. Inside, the lines of force were so concentrated that a normal mind might not be able to withstand it. Of course, mancers did not have ordinary minds. And that could do the scrutator more harm than it did the mancer, Flydd being so weak.

'What's happening now?' she cried.

'The soldiers have stopped,' came Jym's steady voice. 'The airfloater is trying to settle down but the wind keeps pushing it up the valley. Two clankers are getting ready to fire. Yorme, I can see the perquisitor! Jal-Nish is standing up on the shooter's platform.'

'He wants to see us taken. Or dead.' She had to act now. If it killed the scrutator that would be a merciful release, compared to what Jal-Nish had waiting.

Irisis found her little folded packet, disguised it in a billow of the field and nudged that toward the violet sump, which was now pulsing black and white as the mancer sucked more and more power from it.

Irisis was nearly there when the sump glowed a violent purple. Had she been discovered? No, there it went again, *black*, *white*, *black*. She gave her packet one last nudge. It drifted over the edge, hung on the lip and then slid into the sump. Irisis wrenched herself out of the field, just in case.

Nothing happened, though Irisis could feel the tension. The scrutator began to moan in his throat, a hideous shrill wailing that was like barbs being thrust through her tongue. Irisis moaned too – her trick must have backfired on Flydd. His sounds rose in pitch until they were like spines through her eardrums. Something awful was going to happen. She reached out for him.

Thud-*splat*! Flydd screamed and fell on his back, thrashing. She could hear his boots scraping against the stone. Then there was silence but for the whistling of the wind and the whirr of the air-floater's rotor.

'What's happened?' she shouted. 'Jym?'

'Something seems to have burst down among the soldiers. They're all running around. It's all red, and red stuff is flying all through the air. It's . . . Oh, that's –' Irisis could hear him retching.

'A horrible way to die,' groaned the scrutator. 'But better her than me.' He took Irisis's hand. 'I'll thank you properly one day.'

'One night would be better,' she said automatically, not understanding what she'd done.

'Floater's down!' shouted Yorme. 'Jym, grab the tethers. Get up the ladder, surr, quick as you can.'

'You first, Irisis,' said the scrutator. 'We're safe for a minute. They can only see the top of the floater here, in the viaduct.'

'But when we take off –'

'Yes, that's the dangerous bit. Come on.'

She went up, hand over hand, which in her blindness Irisis found decidedly unpleasant. The rope ladder swayed alarmingly and her weight pushed the section she was standing on under the keel of the air-floater, so she felt she was trying to climb around a corner. Irisis had no idea where she was in relation to anything. What if she was hanging over the ravine? Her sweaty hands slipped on the ropes. She gasped.

'Get a move on!' shouted the scrutator. 'It's not a party.'

Strong hands caught her under the arms and lifted her over the side. 'Over there,' said a deep male voice.

'I can't see!'

Someone took her hand and led her out of the way, sitting her on a canvas seat. Someone else thumped beside her. 'That's the lot,' the deep voice shouted. 'Take it up.'

'No!' yelled the scrutator. 'Get it moving inside the aqueduct, then up as fast as you can possibly go. That'll give them less time to aim.'

'The soldiers are still alive,' said the deep voice. 'They're almost within range.'

'All right! Just go!'

'All hands to the ballast, then hang on. Bowmen, ready your crossbows. Pilot Hila, don't let them get a second shot at us.'

The air-floater lurched. 'Ready? Ballast overboard.'

It lurched again, then shot up. Irisis clutched onto the arm next to her in naked terror. The scrutator's hand held hers until the sensation died away. The crossbows twanged. The rotor spun up to a whine.

'Firing, surr. They're going to go close. *Turn it!*'

The machine turned, too slowly for her liking.

'Look out!' the deep voice cried.

Wood smashed and splinters went everywhere; some landed in her hair. 'What's happened?' she screamed. 'We're crashing, aren't we?'

'That was close,' said the scrutator calmly. 'Fortunately the javelard hit one of the timbers of the cabin, not the balloon. It went in one side and out the other. No harm done. No one hurt.'

'Firing again,' said the deep voice. 'Too low. We've done, it, surr. They'll not touch us now.'

'Very good,' said Flydd. 'Steer a course north, if you please, but take it slowly. I don't dare arrive in daylight.'

THIRTY-SEVEN

Irisis could smell herself, and the scrutator. They both reeked of blood, sweat and fear. 'I wouldn't mind a drink,' she said hoarsely, and discovered that she was trembling.

'I'll get us one.' The chair creaked. Presently he returned, pressing a mug into her hands.

She sniffed. It was ale, of a sort, but all that mattered was that it be wet. Irisis downed it at a single swallow. 'My eyes hurt.' She saw not a glimmer.

The scrutator inspected them closely, his fingers holding her eyelids open, put pads over each and bound them on with a thick strip of cloth.

'I'm so tired,' she said. 'I could sleep standing up.'

'Let's talk first,' said Flydd.

'Are we heading for Minnien, Xervish?'

'Yes. To do the job I've been talking about for a month. To find out what's happened to the node.'

'I'll need help.'

'You'll have the guards, another two artisans and a mancer.'

That reminded her of the mancer who had died on the ladder after Jal-Nish's mysterious horn blast. 'Who was the fellow Jal-Nish killed?'

'Mancer Thards. Poor old Thards,' said the scrutator. 'He was always an unlucky man.'

'So now I need another mancer,' she said thoughtfully.

'I've already organised a replacement.'

'When do I get to meet him, or her?'

'You already have.'

'You!' She stared sightlessly in his direction.

'Is that so bad?'

'No, of course not. It's just, well, you're the scrutator!'

'Not for much longer. Jal-Nish will be writing his report right now and there's no one to contradict him. In a few days it will be in the hands of the Council. They'll convene an emergency meeting where my supporters will have no choice but to vote against me. I'll be struck off the list, broken to a non-citizen, and there will be a reward for my head, whether or not it's attached to my body. You'd be well advised to stay clear of me, lest you be tainted the same way.'

'I imagine I already am. It's too late to do anything about that.'

'I suggest you think again.'

'The advice of a non-citizen is as worthless as he is,' she said loftily. 'In any case, that is not the way I do things.'

'So I'm beginning to discover. Just what *did* you do back there.'

'What makes you think I did anything?'

'I may have fallen low but I'm still a mancer, and one of rare subtlety, if I do say so myself.'

'Not one of rare modesty at any rate.' She laid her head on his knobby shoulder.

'Well?'

She told him. Flydd whistled. 'Now there's something I don't think has ever been done before; probably never thought of. The Council may even readmit me, just for telling them how you did it.'

'Really?'

'Probably not, but they'll certainly be interested to find out.'

'Where are my artisans?'

'Up the other end, somewhere. There's Zoyl Aarp and Oon-Mie.'

Zoyl Aarp was a lad of sixteen, big and muscular, but with the face of a ten-year-old, for which he had been ragged unmercifully in the manufactory. He behaved like a ten-year-old most of the time, being prone to temper tantrums and fits of 'poor me'. He was a brilliant, intuitive artisan, though his craftsmanship was rudimentary. He had no patience for fine work and Irisis usually finished his controllers off, but he was right for this job.

Oon-Mie was the opposite, small with a sturdy frame, a broad face marred by a flat nose, and eyebrows plucked to pencil marks. No one would have called her pretty but she had an impish grin that curled up the left corner of her mouth. Oon-Mie had three children in the creche, each by a different father. She had a one-track mind, chiefly concerning intimate relations between men and women, but it was always good-humoured. Everyone liked her and Irisis felt better just knowing she was here.

She could relax at last. She rested her head on her arm and fell asleep.

The air-floater drifted serenely across the skies, heading north-east toward the coast. Nothing disturbed its stately progress. Once, a lyrinx wheeling in the air above a burning town noted it pass by, but before the creature could react, the air-floater vanished into thick cloud. As the sun set, it emerged long enough for Navigator Nivulee to study the land below through her spyglass, and compare it with her map. Like all air-floater crew, Nivulee was small – a bony girl with waves of dark hair cascading down her back. Her uniform was too big for her and her nails bitten to the quick.

'That way.' She pointed a little more east, with a bleeding finger.

Twice in the night the navigator checked their bearings, using the lights of coastal cities, and a little after midnight told the pilot to go down. They went back and forth for an hour while the pilot muttered and an increasingly worried Nivulee checked her charts over and again; then finally she looked out the port side, nodded and indicated a massif that reared up to a double horn.

The pilot went around it three times in the light of a sliver of moon before the scrutator said, 'Over there. Can't you go any faster?'

'We're running on the Gornies field and it's a long way away.'

'Of course,' said Flydd. 'The Minnien field has failed. That's why we're here.'

The air-floater set down as lightly as thistledown. The passengers descended the rope ladder. The scrutator gave instructions to the pilot, who nodded and raised her hand in salute. The air-floater lifted off and soon was just a shadow whirring into the night sky.

'This way,' said the scrutator. 'Let's get under cover before it's light. Then we'll go over the plan again.'

Irisis had slept the whole trip and woke to find herself in darkness. Then she remembered. She was blind.

Someone, not Flydd, helped her down the ladder. Her feet landed on uneven ground that slipped underfoot. It felt and sounded like shale. The air smelt different: a faint salty tang mixed with the sharp odour of a crushed herb whose name she did not know. It was considerably warmer than the manufactory.

So, she was on the coast somewhere, or near it. Minnien was just a name to her and she could not have traced it on a map. There was not even a village here, only a place name so old that people had forgotten where it came from.

But there was a node at Minnien, and it had failed, causing the loss of fifty clankers and hundreds of lives. She closed her eyes and saw the bloody plain, the wrecked machines that had taken years to build, the broken bodies and the red-mouthed, feeding lyrinx. If the enemy had made this node fail, they could do it anywhere. Everywhere – in which case clankers would become useless and the war must be lost. It was up to her to find out why. The job had been daunting when she'd been sighted. Now it felt impossible.

They walked around the side of a steep slope, one foot higher than the other, for a long time. Irisis plodded along, putting her feet where she was told, holding onto someone's hand. No one

374

spoke. She heard nothing but slate sliding underfoot, smelt only crushed herbs and the sea breeze.

Eventually they stopped and her guide sat her down on a sloping slab of rock. Her fingers traced its smooth surface and sharp edges. Food and drink was handed around. Irisis took what she was given, listening to the talk but alienated from the faces behind it.

'Hush!' said the scrutator. 'Irisis?'

'Yes?'

'What have you got to say?'

'Come here.'

He moved to her side, the slab settling under his weight. 'What's the matter?'

She clutched his arm, felt for his ear and whispered, 'I can't do it. I don't know where the node is. I don't even know *what* it is. What are we supposed to do first?'

'You could start by trying to visualise the field.'

'There *is* no field.'

He sighed. 'The node may not be completely dead. Take hold of your pliance and do what you would do if you *were* trying to see the field.'

She did so.

'Tell me what you see,' said the scrutator.

'I don't see anything at all.'

'Are you sure? Other artisans have been brought here since the field failed.'

'Then why don't you ask them?' she said.

'I have. That's part of the reason I brought you here.'

'Oh?'

'You are better at visualising the field than most artisans.'

'Except Tiaan!' she snapped.

'Oh, stop feeling sorry for yourself,' he snapped back. 'Yes, except Tiaan, if you must. Tiaan is quite exceptional. But then, her heritage . . .'

She wondered about that as she tried again. There had always been something strange about Tiaan. Putting the distraction out of mind, she focussed on where the field should be. This time she did pick something up, the very faintest wisp rising from not far away.

Emptying her mind, Irisis allowed the wisp to flow by. Another followed it, as tenuous as mist, though with the slightest blue tinge. She traced it down. It seemed to be coming from somewhere deep underground, though it was impossible to determine where – fields were difficult to associate precisely with the structures that generated them, and anyway, she could not see the peaks.

Giving up on that path, Irisis withdrew, visualising the wisps from further away. That was better; they now made a drifting, smeared-out trail and as she shifted viewpoint again she saw another trail of wisps a long way to the left, and a third to the right.

Pulling back as far as she could go, Irisis realised that they were rising in a kind of squashed figure-eight formation, apparently offset from the twin-peaked hill they were sitting on, as if mimicking not the hill itself but some subterranean structure.

'I think the node is regenerating the field!' she exclaimed.

'What?' said Flydd.

She explained exactly what she had seen.

'An interesting idea. Nunar herself speculated about such a possibility. Maybe that's why you can see it now, when previously a hundred mancers and artisans could not. It may have started to regenerate recently.'

'Or maybe I'm cleverer than they are,' she said, nettled.

He snorted.

'So what do we do now?'

'Investigate the bigger problem. Find out why it failed in the first place.'

'How do we do that?'

'Well, you're the artisan.'

'And you're the mancer!' she said irritably 'Nodes are the home of *forces*, and forces are mancers' work, aren't they? Artisans aren't clever enough to work with forces. Only the weak field for us.'

'There's no need to be sarcastic. We've all got to work together. You're pulling in the other direction, Irisis.'

'I'm sorry,' she said, and was. 'I'm a moody sod. I've had rather a difficult few days.'

'This *is* mancers' work for the most part, but I still value your thoughts. How would you approach the problem?'

'I've no idea . . . Tiaan once made an aura reader, to find out what had happened to failed hedrons. I might be able to make something to do that, though . . .'

'A node is a far more difficult proposition than a hedron.'

'And more dangerous. Oon-Mie, Zoyl, listen carefully.' Collecting her thoughts, Irisis began to describe what they had to make.

'Hist!' said the man on watch. 'Something's coming!'

'What is it?' Flydd said in a low voice.

'I think . . . I think it's a lyrinx.'

'What's it doing?'

'It's well down and across, walking along a ledge.'

'What would a lyrinx be doing here?' Irisis asked.

'Who knows what they do?' said the scrutator. 'Maybe it's a lookout.'

'It's not a good place for a lookout. Over on the next hill would be better.'

'Maybe it has a nest here?' came Oon-Mie's voice. 'Or it sneaks across to mate . . .'

'The lyrinx are not animals,' Flydd said coldly. 'They're as intelligent as we are. Now be quiet. Keep your weapons ready.'

'It's disappeared,' said the sentry.

'Keep still,' Flydd advised. 'We'll wait and see.'

No one said anything for a long while; then Irisis heard whispering. 'Will someone tell me what's going on?' she said waspishly.

'Nothing's happened,' said Flydd. 'Be patient.'

Finally the lookout spoke. 'I can see it again. It's heading back the way it came.'

They watched it move down the long slope, to Irisis's frustration, before the scrutator took her hand, saying, 'I think we can take a look now.'

A difficult climb for a blind woman, on a steep path littered with slipping plates of slate. 'It was just around here,' said the lookout.

They cast about for ages. 'Tracks!' said one of the soldiers.

'The footmarks seem to have been made by someone stepping in the same places all the time,' said Flydd. 'Someone with a lyrinx stride. It's not the first time it's been here.'

After hours of searching they located a ledge under which the lyrinx had crouched when it had disappeared from their sight; but apart from a few curled-up scraps that looked like leathery mushroom, they found nothing.

'Maybe it just wanted a place in the shade to eat its lunch,' said the sentry.

'I thought they et people,' the soldier muttered.

'They eat anything they can find, just like us,' said the scrutator. 'I don't believe in coincidences. It was here for a reason, and it's connected with the node failing.'

'It's here for the same reason as we are,' said Irisis. 'It wants to find out why the node failed, and if it's remained that way, and how it can use this information to defeat us in the war.'

'We'd better scout the peaks.'

Flydd divided the group into pairs and sent them out. 'What about me?' said Irisis as he prepared to go with them.

'Stay here. Take another look at that pattern you saw before.'

'What if the lyrinx comes back?'

'I imagine it'll eat you.'

Alone, blind and afraid to move, Irisis spent the day imagining that the beast was silently hunting her. She could smell her fear. Her armpits were drenched with it.

Nothing happened, however, and she could not remain at the highest pitch of terror all day. She would hear the lyrinx coming, anyway, for nothing could move silently on the shale-littered slopes.

Having decided on a course of action, Irisis felt able to go on with her search. She was surprised to find that the field sprang out at once. It had strengthened further. No longer wispy, it was now a chain of misty tongues like a continuous flame, though still in the shape of a figure-eight. It was a long way from being back to normal, and definitely not strong enough to drive something as massive as a clanker, but it *was* there.

By the time the scouts began to straggle back she knew as much as she was capable of learning. The field was coming back. The question was: why? And how? And did it have anything to do with that lyrinx?

PART FOUR

SCRUTATOR

THIRTY-EIGHT

The construct had its weapon, a kind of spear-thrower, aimed at them. 'Put up your hands,' yelled Nish. 'Nobody move. Mounce?'

'I'm like a post, surr,' said the sergeant.

Yara edged her mount closer to Meriwen and Liliwen.

'Don't run,' Nish hissed. 'You'll never get away.'

'I'll do what I think best for my children,' she snapped, as if he were to blame.

Nish felt that he was. He should have kept a better lookout – should have been further ahead so the others would have had a chance to escape.

The construct whined forward. The one behind them remained where it was. Its weapon was also ready. The top of the first construct snapped open. An altercation ensued; they could not make out the words, but a young man came down the side, sprang lightly to the ground, moved away from the construct and held out his hands to show that he carried no weapon.

'Don't trust him, surr,' said Mounce. 'They're treacherous devils, these Aachim.'

'I don't see that we have any choice.'

Nish rode forward, holding out his hands, wondering what they could want. Not until he was close did he recognise the young man as the fellow who had looked so distressed at the meeting.

Nish put out his hand. 'I am Cryl-Nish Hlar.'

The Aachim put up his own. 'I know you. Greetings, Marshal Hlar! I am Minis Una Inthis. My friends call me Minis.'

'Since our meeting I've been demoted and am no longer marshal. Mine call me Nish. A dubious contraction, in some parts, but I have become inured to it.'

They gripped hands. The Aachim's long fingers slipped right around Nish's hand.

'I wish to talk to you,' said Minis, 'if you will permit it?'

'In ordinary circumstances I would be happy to,' said Nish carefully. At any other time he would have seized the opportunity to learn more about the invaders. He was curious about Minis too, and his relationship with Tiaan that appeared to have precipitated their coming to Santhenar. Such a small affair; such vast consequences. But the safety of Yara and the children was paramount. 'Unfortunately we are hurrying east and cannot –'

'Just a few minutes,' said Minis. 'Please.'

Please? Minis was a profoundly different man from his offensive foster-father. Nish glanced at Yara, who had put herself between Minis and the children. She gave the faintest inclination of the head.

'It's hot here,' said Nish, 'and two of my companions are children. Shall we take tea in the shade?'

'With pleasure,' said Minis. 'Though I can offer a cooling draught, if you prefer.'

'I will speak to my companions.' He went back to Yara. 'Minis is the foster-son and heir of Vithis, the Aachim leader. He is also the man whom Tiaan . . . well, you know the story. I don't believe he means us harm. He's very polite and seems anxious to talk to me. We may do some good by speaking with him.'

Yara was watching the Aachim warily. 'Or it might just be a game before they move against us,' she hissed. 'If they try anything, he dies!' The look in her eye made his blood congeal.

'Let's see what he has to say,' Nish said hastily. 'Don't do anything that will make things worse.'

'How dare you! You led us into this trap.'

'Then allow me to get us out of it.' He whirled and rode back.

'Girls!' Yara snapped, 'you will not stray from my side while the strangers are here.'

'We don't need to be told, Mother,' said Liliwen, trying to look as grown up as possible.

Minis waited among the trees with a young man rather shorter and younger than himself, and a woman who might have been Nish's age, insofar as it was possible to tell with the long-lived Aachim. She was pale of skin but with long straight black hair, and as slender as a reed.

'My friends, Vunio and Tyara,' said Minis, introducing the man and the woman in turn. They both looked troubled, like children out without permission.

Nish shook hands uneasily. If this went wrong, Yara would kill him too. He had no doubt that she could.

Minis said, 'And your own friends . . .? Or perhaps they are your wife and children?'

'Neither.' Nish managed a smile at the thought. 'I am merely escorting them home. These are troubled times in Santhenar. It is not as safe on the roads as it once was.'

'Troubled indeed,' said Minis, 'and our coming has made it worse.'

'This war has changed the world forever. Though . . . it's all I've ever known.'

Vunio opened the basket, which contained a variety of delicacies as well as a box that turned out to be layered with ice. Flasks were set in it. Nish relaxed a little. How could they mean any harm? He had to remind himself that he knew little about them.

'It is sweltering in our constructs,' said Minis, 'so we took a trip up to the mountains and hacked blocks from the snow. Santhenar is a hotter world than our own. The mountains were more to our liking.'

'And it is yet mid-spring,' said Nish. 'These plains are torrid in the summer, I'm told.'

'You are not from these parts?' Minis enquired.

'My home is almost as far west as it is possible to go from here. I also come from a cool place.'

Tyara levered the stopper from the flask and her eyes met Nish's. They were large, oval and brown as chocolate. Beautiful eyes. 'Will you take a glass with us?' she said. 'It is not strong, but you will find it refreshing.'

Nish tore his gaze away, mindful how easy it could be to give offence. 'Thank you.'

She poured the wine into a glass. It was a glorious golden colour. He held it up to the evening light, admiring the luminosity. Taking an appreciative sniff, he waited until the other glasses were poured.

'May I make a toast?' he said.

'*Tost?*' Minis looked puzzled.

Nish explained the word and they all smiled. 'We would be pleased,' said Tyara, giving him a dazzling smile.

'To good food, fine wine, and friendship between all the human kinds,' said Nish. He raised his glass, watching them carefully.

'To friendship between worlds,' said Minis, and the others echoed him.

They seemed genuine. Nish drained his glass; Tyara refilled it, and the others.

'What happened to Aachan is a tragedy,' said Nish. 'The death of a world.'

Minis frowned. 'We hope . . . it will not come to *that*. Already we dream of going home, though it is not something I can foresee.'

They spoke of various matters, after which Minis set down his glass. 'Would you care to take a walk in the forest, my friend?'

Was this a way to separate him from Yara? Well, whatever their intention, there was nothing he could do to change it. His heart beating rapidly, Nish said, 'I'd be happy to join you. And then we really must be on our way.'

They rose and Minis linked his arm through Nish's. Nish felt uncomfortable, for men did not do that where he came from; but after all, different worlds, different customs.

'Our meeting was not an accident,' Minis said as they strolled among the trees.

'I did not think so,' Nish said stiffly.

'As soon as our scouts reported that you had left the army camp I decided to find you.'

'Your scouts' eyes must be keen,' said Nish. 'We saw no sign of you.'

'They *are* keen. I imagine you know what I have come about.'

'I do not assume,' said Nish, 'and would prefer not to guess.'

'Tiaan Liise-Mar,' Minis said, and sighed. 'I treated her monstrously and can never forgive myself.'

Nish made no reply and shortly Minis said, 'Shall we sit by this tree?' It was a giant with a massive trunk of smooth white bark. They rested their backs against it. 'You saw her at Tirthrax, I believe?'

'Yes,' said Nish. 'I had followed her a long way.'

'Do you know her then?'

'Of course.' Nish was surprised that the Aachim did not know that, but then why should he? 'I worked at the same manufactory as her, for three years.'

'What a fortunate man you are,' cried Minis, taking Nish's hands in his and shaking them vigorously. 'She is the most beautiful woman in the world.'

The breath rushed out of Nish as he finally understood. Minis was no danger at all – he seemed to be rather a prat, or perhaps he was just very young, and obviously in love. 'She has a certain charm.'

'Were you friends?' Minis squeezed his hands.

Nish detached them with the minimum of offence. 'We were not, though there was a time when I was fond of her. We are too different, Minis.'

'Tell me about her. Tell the whole story. I must know everything.'

Nish gave him the tale from the beginning, in brief, though glossing over the more shabby aspects of it. Fortunately Minis had ears for nothing but the beauty and the cleverness of his beloved. He seemed not to appreciate Nish's bad behaviour, which was just as well.

'I would give anything just to see her again,' he said when Nish had finished.

'She feels terribly wronged,' said Nish bluntly. 'She feels that you betrayed her and that your people used her, coldly and calculatingly.'

'Tiaan *has* been wronged and I am to blame. I will never forgive myself for not standing up to my foster-father. But we had just lost our world, and all our people who could not get to the gate. Can you imagine that, Nish? Imagine knowing that, even if you escaped, nine-tenths of humanity were doomed.' He broke off.

I cannot, Nish thought, and that should be a lesson to me, not to judge. Yet he did judge Minis and Vithis. It was impossible not to. *He* would not be so weak. And then, because, for all his faults, Nish knew his own character rather well, he added: at least not weak in *that* way.

Minis went on. 'Foster-father had seen (as I did) his clan wiped out in the void – every child lost, every woman, every man, to the most horrible of deaths. That was a terrible time for me. How much worse must it have been for him, who had devoted all his life to our clan! How could I turn against foster-father at such a time? I am his heir and the sole hope of his clan. I just could not do it. But even so, poor Tiaan was treated poorly, and in the hour of her own tragedy.'

'It is understandable,' said Nish, but he thought the less of Minis for it.

'I should have found a way.' Minis put an arm across his shoulders as if they were old friends. Perhaps, in some strange reality, the link between Nish and Tiaan made him a friend. 'I think about her every hour. Every minute! My life is nothing without her. What am I going to do, Nish?'

'I don't know,' said Nish, moving uncomfortably. 'I have little experience in matters of the heart.'

'Can you think where she might have gone with the flying construct?'

Was this what he had been leading up to all along? Had the father sent Minis to do what he was unable to do himself? Nish felt that Minis *was* genuine, and might have been used, as Tiaan had been. Fortunately he could answer the question honestly.

'I have no idea. I have not seen her since Tirthrax, months ago.'

He told that tale too, and at the end Minis sighed. 'Ah, what a life you have lived, Nish.'

'It's better in the telling than the living,' said Nish. 'I've nearly died a dozen times. And despaired a thousand!'

'I've not lived at all,' said Minis. 'Foster-father has wrapped my life in cotton silk. It was bad before, when First Clan was the greatest. Now all his hopes rest on me and he will not let me do *anything,* for fear I will injure myself. When he discovers me gone, he will come after me with a hundred constructs. I'm suffocating, Nish! The only happy times in my life have been those few hours when I spoke to Tiaan through the crystal, mind to mind. I am lost without her.'

What was there to say to this stranger from another world? In the background Nish could see Yara pacing. She probably thought he was doing some deal with the Aachim to betray them. He should make his excuses and go, but . . . Minis was the heir and the key to Vithis. He would make a powerful friend. 'What will you do now?'

'What foster-father requires of me,' said Minis. 'Of course.'

'Must you obey him? Can you not make your own life?'

'I wish I could, but I know he is right – he always is. I cannot stand up to him.'

'He is an angry, bitter man.'

'And was, even before the gate went wrong. He cannot bear to think that we were held in thrall by the Charon for so long.'

'Ah, yes,' said Nish. 'The Hundred.'

'And though they were but a hundred, we *never* rebelled against them. Some say that we wanted to submit to a stronger race. I do believe Vithis would rewrite our Histories to erase that shame.'

Suddenly Minis did not seem such a prat at all, for all that he was in thrall to Vithis. 'Surely false Histories must be a greater shame?'

'*I* think so, but foster-father . . .'

Nish changed the subject. 'Does he mean war against us?' He broke off. 'I'm sorry, Minis. I should not have asked you that, but you *are* a seer.'

'Why not? You want to do the best for your own kind. I'm not the most reliable of foretellers, and the near future is particularly cloudy. However, I will answer your question, not as a seer but as a man and, I hope, some day a friend.

'Foster-father feels himself to be the greatest failure of all his line, and that line stretches back ten thousand years. He must make up for it – you cannot even imagine how desperately he is driven. There is only one way he can do that. To give the Aachim a new home in replacement of beloved Aachan.'

'Our world,' said Nish. 'He means to take it.'

'If you resist him. Though I am sure, in his heart, he would prefer to negotiate for a part of it.'

'I saw no willingness to negotiate. Only arrogance, and an ultimatum.'

'He is . . . not the most flexible of men, I'm sorry to say. I *am* sorry, for he has been a father to me, and a mother.'

'Will he ally with the lyrinx against us, do you think?'

'That would be against his inclination, but Vithis was ever a creature of strange passions.'

'I wonder that he has not attacked humanity already.'

'Ah,' began Minis, but did not go on.

'What is it?'

'The clans are jealous of each other, as you saw the other day. They strive constantly for the advantage. That makes it difficult for us to achieve a common goal, unless a mighty leader can command all the clans by sheer force of will.'

'And Vithis is not such a leader.'

'He could be, should our situation become desperate.'

'What can we do to ensure that he does not ally with the lyrinx?'

'I don't know. There is only one thing . . .'

'Yes?' cried Nish.

'He wants Tiaan and the flying construct.'

'What is this flying construct I keep hearing about?'

Minis told how Tiaan had appeared out of nowhere, in a construct that did not simply float but *flew*. 'She must have made it in Tirthrax from three that were wrecked there. She solved in a few weeks the puzzle that has eluded our finest thinkers for two hundred years – the secret of flight. She flew it right at us, Nish, in the middle of six thousand constructs. A hundred thousand armed Aachim opposed her but she did not care. I could see her staring eyes. She burned for revenge. There is no woman like her in all the Three Worlds.'

No, there is not, Nish realised. Tiaan was unique; a genius. 'That does not seem like the Tiaan I knew. She was never foolhardy.'

Minis looked mortified. 'Once again I am shamed. My people attacked her first, without warning or provocation.'

'Are the Aachim so afraid that a hundred thousand fear one?'

'Perhaps we are. We have everything to lose now.'

The scrutators would want to know this news, Nish thought. If only there were a way of getting to them. 'Does Vithis want Tiaan, or just the flier?'

'He wants it so desperately that all our plans have been put on hold until it is found. Flight would give us the world. Ah, if I could just offer that to foster-father . . .'

'And you want something in return?'

'His respect. He demands that I obey him in all things, but when I do he curses me for being a spineless creature who lacks the courage to make my own life. Nothing I do is good enough. It's eating me alive.'

'My father can be like that too. The war has made people hard.'

'But you are so strong.'

'I'm free of him now.'

'How did you break free, Nish?' Minis asked eagerly. 'What should I do?'

That's what your problem is, thought Nish. 'You have to do it yourself, Minis. No one can tell you how.'

'Vithis is sure that Tiaan's construct was damaged in the

attack,' Minis mused, 'and could not have gone very far. He would give anything to find it.'

'What do you mean *anything*?'

'Whoever were to find it, and deliver it to him, could name their price.'

Nish sat up. 'What if *I* found it? What if I demanded an alliance against the lyrinx?'

'He would agree,' Minis said without hesitation.

'That would win the war,' Nish ruminated. 'What would I not give for that.'

'Then find the construct!'

'And Tiaan, for you,' said Nish.

'Aye. Foster-father would surely agree to Tiaan then.'

Nish did not reply. He felt sorry for Minis. How could he so delude himself? From what he'd heard, Vithis would never allow him to pair with an old human.

Minis continued, 'Though I am not fool enough to believe that *my* problems can be solved so easily. My betrayal was too great to ever expect her forgiveness.' His dark eyes met Nish's. 'Yet I still hope for it.'

'I hope you get your heart's desire.' Nish rose, casting anxious glances back at the camp. 'Shall we go? My people must be wondering what has become of me.'

Once again he was being offered the chance of a lifetime, for after Yara and the children were delivered safely he had no given duties. Could he find Tiaan and her construct, where the Aachim had failed? And if he could, should he give it to Vithis? Would it be worth it to win the war? Or would it be better to deliver the construct to his own people?

The risk was that humanity might not be able to duplicate it, whereas the Aachim surely could. And if humanity had it, the Aachim might go to war just to get it, which would make matters far worse.

But if he gave it to Vithis, and he was able to make fliers of all his constructs, the Aachim would be all-powerful. Once the war against the lyrinx was won, he could turn on humanity and take Santhenar for his own. How to decide what to do? The wrong decision might lose the war, and Nish his head. He wished the flier had never been discovered. His mind was whirling, calculating possibilities, scarcely hearing what the Aachim was talking about. Minis shook him by the arm.

'I beg your pardon?' Nish said.

'You have done so much, Nish. If anyone can find Tiaan it is you. Will you take it on?'

'I have had my share of disasters. And of course,' Nish gave a short laugh, 'you must make allowances. I may have exaggerated my tale.'

Minis shrugged. 'Our spies have been busy. I know more about you than you imagine. I also share my father's talent – my late father. He was an excellent judge of a man and, so I believe, am I. I will pin my faith in you.' His eyes showed that faith; a new experience for Nish.

Nish was touched. He liked Minis. For all his awkwardness and his silly ways, there was no artifice about him.

'I'll try,' said Nish, 'once I've delivered Yara and the children safely. That duty –'

'I understand duty. You do not need to explain.' Minis held out his hand and Nish took it. The wrap-around handshake felt strange, but it also felt right.

'How will I find you again?'

'I will find you, my friend.'

Back at the camp, Nish joined Yara, who sat warily with Tyara and Vunio. She held herself erect and her hand was never far from the knife on her belt. Nish sat down. Minis shook Yara's hand, and the hands of the twins, to their giggly amusement.

'I must go,' Minis said. 'I too have my duties and they are pressing.'

He bowed, the other Aachim did too, and they went back to the construct. It whined away. The second machine, which had remained in the trees all this time, followed some distance behind.

'What was that about?' Yara demanded. 'Why did you sneak off with him so I couldn't hear what was going on?'

'I didn't *sneak* off. He asked to speak to me privately.'

'Why?' she said imperiously. 'What did he have to say that could not be said out in the open?'

'The poor fellow is quite besotted with Tiaan,' said Nish, meeting her eye. 'He hoped I might be able to tell him where she was hiding.'

'And could you?' Yara demanded.

'I did not know her that well,' said Nish. 'She loathes me, as it happens.'

'Why is that?' Yara said sharply.

'I did her a bad turn, I'm ashamed to say. The Nish of those times was a callow, selfish youth. I've grown up since then.'

'Really? In that case, your callowness must have been truly prodigious.'

'I'm sorry if you don't find my service satisfactory. I'm doing my best.'

'I have no doubt you are – but for whom?'

THIRTY-NINE

'Tell me about this place,' Nish said to Yara the following day. They were riding side by side through tall forest. The canopy was so high and dense that there was little undergrowth, and it was easy riding, as well as delightfully cool. They frequently had to cross rivers, the only hazard they had faced in days, though all proved to be sluggish and the horses were adept at swimming them.

Yara had not thawed. She still watched him every minute, as if she thought he was leading them into a trap, though that was absurd. She was the only one who knew where they were going. He hated being mistrusted. He liked Meriwen and Liliwen, and felt a bond with them from the attack on the way to Kundizand, but whenever he was near them he felt Yara's eyes on him.

'The Worm Wood is one of the greatest forests of Lauralin,' Yara said, checking ahead and over her shoulder. 'Perhaps *the* greatest. From here it stretches unbroken a hundred and twenty leagues to the edge of the Great Mountains. It runs south and north for as great a distance, save for the bite out of it which is the fertile land of Borgistry. Even that is closing up at the southern end, near Clew's Top. Many civilisations lie within the forest, and many ruins. The south-western part of the forest, the uncanny Borgis Woods, surround a high range of white rock, the Peaks of Borg. Not many days' ride from here lies an even stranger place, Booreah Ngurle, the famous Burning Mountain. It is the greatest of many volcanoes that run along either side of the Great Chain of Lakes.'

'I've heard of them,' said Nish.

'The lakes are so long and deep they seem to split the world apart. Warde Yallock is the best part of eighty leagues long, but only five wide. The first city in the world was built there, more than ten thousand years ago, before the Histories began. At the other end of the forest lies Parnggi, almost as long and even deeper, it is said. And certainly stranger – it is a dark, wild, haunted place.'

'And the place we are going to?'

'It is called Morgadis.'

'Is it your family home?'

'Morgadis is the home of my sister, Mira, and she is a woman you will not want to offend.'

'I don't want to offend anyone,' said Nish. 'What is her trouble?'

'She lost her man and all three sons to the war. When the conscriptors came for her youngest she refused to give him up, and he was taken with violence. Since his death she has been bile piled on bitterness.'

'Why are you taking your daughters there?'

'She is my sister,' Yara said simply. 'And Morgadis is the safest place I know. Mira can take care of herself. She is . . . Well, you will see. Just don't mention the war.'

That night they stopped by the ruins of a great monastery. The grass was close-cropped inside the walls by grazing deer. Outside, the forest had obliterated all signs of the farms and vineyards that had once flourished here, apart from a broken stone well that Nish, intent on what lay ahead, almost rode into.

Fortunately the horse was watching its step. Nish yelped, and behind him heard Liliwen's tinkling laughter. He smiled. They had left danger well behind and the surroundings could not be bettered.

'What is this place?' he asked Yara as they dismounted and prepared to make camp in a long roofless hall. A grapevine, so old that its trunk was the size of a tree, scrambled over the walls, covered in tiny bunches of grapes which, unfortunately, would not be ripe for months.

'A monastery that belonged to the Thongi sect, a pacifist pastoral order who worshipped their strange gods here for two thousand years, until not so long ago.'

'Why did they leave?'

'The scrutators burned them out.'

Nish had never heard of such a thing. 'Why?'

'The Thongi questioned the authority of the Council and refused to send their young men to war.'

'That's all?'

'The scrutators like to show their power by making examples. Not a single monk remained. Don't go out of sight, girls,' she called as they wandered in the ruins.

Mounce led the horses down to a rivulet and then on to a river-flat meadow where the grass would be sweetest. Nish gathered wood for the campfire while Yara set up a tent for herself and the girls. After lighting the fire, he glanced up at the sky, which was clear.

'I think I'll sleep in the open tonight.' He walked down to the rivulet with a bucket in each hand. There was no sign of Mounce or the horses. The sun-warmed water looked so refreshing that he stripped off his sweaty clothes and lay in it, since it was only knee-deep. He'd washed his clothes, put them on and was on his way back when a despairing cry rang out.

'Liliwen, Meriwen!'

He dropped the buckets and ran. Yara was down the far end of the roofless hall, looking around frantically.

'Meriwen sang out, then something fell, like a wall toppling. Oh, I *told* them to be careful.'

'Where did the call come from?'

'Down here somewhere.' She swept her arm around a collection of broken walls, all that remained of a building that once had hundreds of rooms. Yara was shaking.

He offered her his hand and she took it gratefully. She could hardly blame Nish, since she had chosen the campsite.

'If we search through there,' said Nish, 'room by room, we must soon find them. And if something's fallen down we'll see it.'

Yara choked back a sob and nodded stiffly. 'I'll take this row, you do the next.'

Nish was halfway up his row when he heard a thin cry. 'Yara – this way!' he yelled. Yara met him down the row. 'It seemed to come from underground.'

They found the place in the next row of ruined rooms – paving stones that covered a vaulted ceiling had collapsed, leaving a neat rectangular hole in the grass. A couple of tall saplings grew in an angle of one wall but the rest of the space was empty. Nish crept to the edge and looked down, for the remaining stones could be just as unstable. The afternoon light did not penetrate very well but he made out a small pile of rubble some distance below. There was no sign of the girls.

'Meriwen, Liliwen!' Yara screeched.

No reply. She looked on the verge of collapse.

'Run back and get the tent ropes,' he said. 'And see if you can find Mounce. He was down along the stream. I'll keep watch.'

She ran. Nish broke off one of the saplings, which was three or four spans long, and reached down to the rubble. The sapling did not look strong enough to support his weight but might do to slide down on. He went down the spindly trunk, burning his hands, and had a good look around.

He expected to find at least one of the girls buried under the rubble, but saw nothing apart from something white over the other side. He was practically standing on it before he made out what it was – a skeleton. He moved smartly away, taking the pole with him. It was an awkward weapon but better than nothing. Nish had a healthy fear of old bones. One of the monks, no doubt. What could have happened to the girls?

The stone was stained with soot from the fire that had destroyed the monastery. Over the other way he saw more bones, the skeletons of at least three people, and two of them were headless. It was too dark to make out tracks. He walked into the gloom, calling the girls' names. Once he passed beyond the lighted area his hackles rose, though he could not tell why. It felt like a place he had no right to be in.

Just enough light penetrated to show that he was in a cellar or basement with lots of long, narrow compartments, each containing something white. Here and there, luminous patches could be seen. It was not a cellar but a mausoleum or catacomb. The white objects were bones.

What a hideous place, and it would be worse when night fell, in about half an hour. 'Liliwen!' he roared, 'Meriwen!' When the echoes died away he heard a faint squeak far off to his right.

Nish turned that way and the floor moved under his foot. A loose flagstone, or was the whole floor unstable? He probed with his foot. The stone collapsed under him and Nish had to leap sideways onto the base of a pillar as a section of floor folded with a crash and rumble that shook dust down on his head. The fire must have damaged the lower levels and the entire ruin could come crashing down.

He should have turned back then, but Nish could not bear to leave the girls in such a dangerous and haunted place. How had they run through here and survived? Nor could he bear to think of Yara's reaction if he came back without them.

He crept backwards to a glowing niche. The luminosity was due to a phosphorescent growth on the bones. Picking up the brightest one, a partly cloven skull, by the eye-holes, he held it high. It gave just enough light to see. Skin-creeping from the look in its empty sockets, he threaded it on a piece of cord around his neck.

Taking the pole in both hands, Nish probed the floor in front of him. It seemed solid. He went forward a couple of steps and probed again. He encountered another unstable section before he got across the chamber, but found a way around it. The floor was most solid next to the pillars. On the far side he came to three passages.

'Girls!' he yelled.

There was a rumble in the distance but no reply. He took the left tunnel – the earlier response had seemed to come from that direction. Halfway along he came to a shallow pit, also full of bones, some savagely hacked and broken. What barbarity had gone on here?

He made his way carefully through a maze of walls and pillars. There could be pits, wells or lower collapsed floors. Twice more the floor caved in under his probing pole, the second time beneath his feet. Nish spun the pole in his hands and managed to span the gap as he fell, though the shock almost tore his grip free. The flag-stones dropped a long way before splashing into water.

Nish hung over the unknown depths, praying that the creak-ing pole would not break, or slide in as he went hand over hand to the edge. It did not, though he had the devil of a time getting up onto solid floor, and after that he was more careful. He threaded his way around objects lying on the floor – thousands of bones and, as far as he could tell, all human. Most bore signs of frenzied sword work.

A long time later, when it must have been dark outside, he found the girls in the middle of a larger catacomb that contained hundreds of burial niches. It was dimly lit by a blue-white phos-phorescent fungus growing on the bones.

Liliwen was sobbing quietly, and Meriwen holding her and trying to be as grown up as she could, though she had bitten through her lip with terror and her eyes were as wide as moons.

'Why didn't you answer?' Nish said gently, giving her his hand. She clung to it as her mother had.

'I tried,' said Meriwen, 'but I was so afraid, Nish. The bones moved as if they were watching us and I was scared that if I made too much noise . . .'

Nish looked over his shoulder. The phosphorescence did shimmer in a way that suggested the bones were moving. He would be glad to get out of here. 'What happened?'

'The ground gave way and we fell down. We weren't hurt but Liliwen saw all those skeletons. Some of them didn't have heads!' she said. 'She ran, and I panicked and ran too. We ended up in here and there were bones everywhere and Liliwen put her foot down on a skull and it rolled under her and she fell and twisted her ankle.' She gasped a breath.

'Calm down,' said Nish. 'Just take it slowly.'

'I could hardly walk,' said Liliwen, snuggling under his arm. 'We tried to find a way back but we were lost. I told Meriwen to go on looking but she wouldn't leave me.'

'Sensible girl,' said Nish. 'I think we'll be right. I'm pretty sure I know how to get back.' He wasn't, but someone had to be the leader.

He picked Liliwen up. A sturdy girl, she was heavier than she looked. She moaned as her ankle was moved, and put both arms around his neck.

'Don't choke me or we'll never get out,' he joked. He put his shoe on something round and bony that rolled underfoot, and nearly dropped her.

'Careful,' said Meriwen. 'if you break your ankle . . .'

'Come close behind,' he said over his shoulder, kicking bones out of the way.

'Don't worry,' Meriwen muttered, taking hold of his belt.

'Is either of you brave enough to hold this skull,' said Nish, 'so we can see?'

Meriwen shuddered, but took it. Nish reached out with his pole and they went forward.

'Hush, I think that's Mother calling,' said Liliwen after a good while.

'She's letting us know the way out.'

They wandered back and forth, Nish probing every ell of the way. If not for Yara calling, he would not have found the exit, for it was dark now. By the time they reached the hole, Mounce was there too. Yara tied the tent ropes together and Mounce pulled the children up.

Nish came up last and he was glad to be out of there, for there were bones everywhere and they had not come from the niches. Either the monks had been massacred in the crypt or their bones had been thrown down afterwards. It made him think.

'No harm done,' he said as Mounce pulled him up. 'Just a sprained ankle and a lot of old bones. All the same, I'd be happier if we camped outside. I'm glad we're not spending the night down *there.*'

Yara searched his face. 'I heard crashes. I was sure you were all dead.'

'The floor collapsed a couple of times,' he said more casually than he felt. 'I had to nip out of the way, quick smart.'

'You could have been killed. And the girls.'

'All of the monks remained here,' he went on quietly. 'They were slaughtered by the scrutators. What a hideous place.'

'You risked your life for my children, Nish,' Yara said. 'I'll never forget it. I'm sorry about before. I was wrong about you.' She gave him a brief, grateful hug. Tears fell on his neck, and that was that.

Nish lay awake for ages that night, watching the wheeling stars and thinking about what he had seen down below. Why had the Council visited such savagery on a harmless, pacifist order? It made a mockery of their claims that they acted only in the best interests of humanity. Nish decided that he had to know more about the scrutators, and what was behind them.

They rode through dense forest for five more days. The weather was good, sunny above the forest but cool and shaded within. It rained once, though only a shower of misty drops reached them.

'How far now?' Nish asked as they were taking breakfast by a stream whose pebbly bottom was perfectly clear. It was broad but shallow; the twins were frolicking in the water.

'We'll be there this afternoon.'

The ground had been climbing for some time, and across the stream they struck a path that wound up into hills that grew ever steeper. When they stopped for lunch the horses were plodding. The trees still extended in every direction, making it impossible to see where they were headed.

At the top they entered a clearing whose edge was marked by an old stone wall, partly collapsed and covered in moss. The trees hung over it. A wooden gate had once closed the path but only rotting timbers hung from the hinges. They rode across a meadow of cropped grass, by a cluster of roofless cottages. The inside walls were scarred by fire. The place made Nish shiver. More work of the scrutators?

On the other side, they looked over a shallow cliff. A river, broad, deep and entrenched into its valley, looped across a green floodplain. Below, the narrowest part of one loop had been cut through to make a dome-shaped island a third of a league across.

It was a pretty place, with orchards and vineyards higher up and lush meadows stretching down to the river. On top of the hill stood a large villa or chateau, built entirely of timber so old that it shone silvery in the sun. It was all verticals. The roofs rose in steeples, at least a dozen of them, covered in shingles. Verandas extended on all sides, in and out and in again. Everywhere he looked was another detail to distract the eye.

'It's stronger than it seems,' said Yara. 'Morgadis has stood for twelve hundred years, and troubled no one in that time.'

'Has anyone troubled it?'

'Many times, but eternal vigilance is our watchword.'

'How pretty and peaceful it appears.'

'No one has worked harder than Mira for peace.'

'And yet she has lost a husband and three sons,' said Nish. 'I would do anything to end this conflict.'

'You will have much to talk about, in that case, though I would advise you to choose your words with particular care.'

FORTY

The river, the principal defence of Morgadis, ran fast and deep. No horse could have swum it, while waterfalls upstream and rapids downstream restricted the use of boats to a couple of leagues either side of the island. A rope bridge, supporting a plank walkway, was the only way in or out. It hung low to the water and Nish did not like the look of it. How was he going to lead his horse across that?

Fortunately he did not have to, for people appeared out of the forest and took the animals away. Mounce went with them. After an exchange of signals with the other side, they went across on foot.

The bridge held no fears for Yara or the children, who had crossed it many times. Nish followed, trying to appear nonchalant. It swayed underfoot and he was uncomfortably aware of the weight of his pack. If he fell in it would take him all the way to the bottom. But then, if he fell in he would drown anyway, for Nish was a poor swimmer.

He reached the other side in safety. To his left was a timber boatshed with two dinghies propped against one wall. Beyond were stacks of sawn timber and a partly erected timber frame, perhaps an extension to the boatshed. He followed the others up the hill, thinking of a cool drink and, with any sort of luck, a long scrub in a hot bath.

Up a steep series of steps, they turned onto a broad veranda. There they were met by a small woman, a head shorter than her sister, trim of figure and with neat, regular features, though set in hard lines. Her eyes were crinkled as though laughter had once not been far away, but no longer. Her lush brown hair was threaded with grey yet she could not have been more than thirty-five. She did not look anything like Yara.

They embraced. 'I thought . . .' the woman bit her lip.

'What?' smiled Yara.

'That I would never see you again, or the twins. Everyone I love goes away and they don't come back.'

'I will always come back,' said Yara. 'Liliwen, Meriwen?'

They embraced their aunt, who then turned, looking questioningly at Nish.

'My sister, Mira,' said Yara. 'Mira, this is Cryl-Nish Hlar, known to his friends as Nish. He has escorted us all this way.'

'I'm pleased to meet you, Mira,' said Nish, holding out his hand.

Mira's hand stopped halfway. 'Hlar?' she said, studying his features. 'Is he related to that warmongering perquisitor, Jal-Nish?'

'His father is Jal-Nish Hlar, now acting scrutator for Einunar,' said Yara.

Mira let her hand fall to her side. 'I'm sorry, Cryl-Nish Hlar, but I don't care what service you have rendered my sister. No Hlar is welcome in my house.'

Nish felt as if he had been slapped across the face. He stepped backwards, gained control of himself and bowed. 'I am not my father, Mira, but if my presence causes you distress I will go at once.'

'Stay,' said Yara, waving her hand at him. 'Mira, know that after the fall of Nilkerrand, Meriwen and Liliwen were lost and wandered alone on the road for a night and a day. Had not Nish befriended them they would have been despoiled and murdered by two of the vilest ruffians in the world. And he has done us further service since. Twice he saved my daughters' lives.'

Mira stared at the girls. She put her hand over her open

405

mouth. Nish thought she was going to scream, though her eyes were as dry as dust.

'They were not harmed,' said Yara, 'though they will remember it to the end of their days.'

Mira threw her arms around the twins and wailed. It went on for ages. Nish looked on uncomfortably. Her eyes were webbed with red.

Yara stood back, head cocked to one side. 'And so,' she said when the embrace finally broke up, 'if Nish is not welcome at your house, neither am I, nor my daughters.'

Nish was astonished. Although Yara had thawed since the monastery, he would never have expected her to defend him against her sister.

Mira pulled away, rubbed her eyes and made a supreme effort which dissolved the lines from her face and for a moment made her seem ten years younger. She must have been a striking woman, he thought, *before*.

'I am sorry, Nish,' she said, giving him her hand. It was deathly cold. 'No doubt my sister has told you of my troubles. The war has torn out my heart and hacked it to pieces, leaving nothing but the curse of my own life. But that is not your affair. You must be weary. Come inside. The hospitality of my house is yours, though I cannot promise you entertainment.'

'All I look forward to,' said Nish, 'is hot food, cool drink, and a bed wherever I may find one. I swear if you propped me against the fence I would go to sleep.'

Mira managed a smile and once again her face was transformed. 'I can promise you all those things. This house has plenty of vacant beds, including my own.' Her face crumpled, she choked back a sob, then froze her face and turned inside.

Yara said something to Nish with her eyes, though he could not read it. He followed her up the steps. The house was large, efficient and well run. Nish was provided with a handsome room lined with boards, walls and ceiling, looking out onto the veranda and down to the river, where mist was already rising with the evening. His dirty clothes were taken away and shortly a servant knocked at the door.

'Your bath is ready,' she said. 'It is the door at the end of the hall.'

Nish sank into the warm scented water with a sigh of bliss. After scrubbing himself until his skin shone, he hung his arms over the side of the tub, closed his eyes and the next he knew the servant girl was knocking on the door. 'If you would come to dinner, Mr Nish.'

Clean clothes were laid out on the end of his bed. Dressing hurriedly, he went down the hall to the stair, where another servant pointed him to the dining hall. This room was long, with panelled walls of dark timber and a steeple roof, also panelled. A fire crackled in a stone fireplace. A long table was set for five people.

Mira came in, wearing a gown of some clinging fabric that revealed a trim figure. Sitting at the head of the table, she indicated the chair to her right. 'Please sit down.'

He hesitated, for Yara and the girls had not yet appeared.

'I do not go in for pointless ceremony,' she said.

Nish sat, looked at Mira, and away. What was he to say? 'I am sorry,' he said, 'to hear about your –'

'You did not know my man or my boys,' she said, not harshly. 'Let us talk of other things.'

Nish was generally comfortable with women of his mother's age, and Mira was nearly that, but there was something about her that tangled his thoughts and he could not think of anything to say. 'What would you like to talk about?'

'Anything but war! What are you, Nish? A warmonger like your father?'

'I am not. How do you know my father?'

'My mother corresponded with every person of note on the continent. I have continued that tradition. And even among the monsters of this world the name Jal-Nish Hlar stands out. But the son is not *necessarily* the father.'

'Do you travel a lot?'

'I do not travel at all. Skeets were first tamed in these mountains by my family, more than eleven hundred years ago. We have been breeding them ever since. It is my sole pleasure, and

I exchange with like-minded people all over the world, as my family have done for thirty-five generations.'

'I never imagined such a thing,' said Nish.

'The Council of Scrutators think they own the world,' said Mira, 'but there are more powers, and older, than they know about.'

'What do you mean by like-minded people?'

'Is that the scrutator's son asking?'

'Of course not.' He flushed.

'I mean those who want peace rather than endless war.'

'But the lyrinx –'

'They did not start the war, and their every peaceful overture has been brutally rejected.'

Nish was staggered. 'Are you saying that the scrutators *want* the war to continue?' Another piece of a puzzle.

'Some do, or did – those at the top. It suited their purpose in the early days, for it gave them control of the world. But control is slipping from their grasp. They cannot lose face by compromising, and the lyrinx no longer wish to. So we must fight until they are extinct, or we are. I do my small best to change that. What is your profession?'

'I was forced to become an artificer at the age of sixteen,' he said carefully, and as her face hardened he rushed out, 'but before that I was a prentice scribe to a merchant of Fassafarn.'

'What name?' she interrupted.

'Egarty Teisseyre. Do you know him?'

'Only by reputation. He is honest enough, for a merchant.'

'I loved being a scribe,' he said wistfully. 'And I was a good one, too.'

'I suppose artificing was your mother's doing, to save you from the army.'

'So it seems, though it was a long time before I realised it. I *hated* being an artificer. I worked hard at it,' he added hastily. 'I did my duty, though I have little talent for that kind of work.'

Yara appeared with the twins, and the talk went on to other matters. It was an uncomfortable dinner, with long silences, and when the girls began yawning uncontrollably Yara rose, saying,

'I will take my leave, sister, for I am quite as tired as they are. Good night.'

Nish rose as well but Mira said, 'Stay awhile, unless you are weary. It is not yet nine.'

'I napped in the bath and feel quite refreshed.'

'Would you care for wine?' The opened flask had been sitting on the table all through dinner but, as Yara had declined, Nish had felt out of politeness that he should do the same.

'I would love some,' he said. 'I seldom get the opportunity to taste good wine.'

'My man loved wine.' She shivered. 'Come, let's sit by the fire.'

Nish was not cold, but he took his wine cup and sat in the other chair.

'Ten years I have lived without my man,' she said. 'No man; no sons.' She dabbed at her eyes with her sleeve.

Again he did not know what to say. They stared at each other.

'What was his name?'

'Chamfry, but I always called him Cham. It was my special name for him. Cham and I did our duty. I bore our first son when I was fifteen, the last three years later. I lost my man when I was twenty-two, my first son seven years after that. Each was fourteen when the war took them, one after the other. They were still children. That is my life, Nish. What is yours?'

Nish began on his tale from the moment he arrived at the manufactory. He told Mira everything, and with complete honesty for the first time in his life. He could not do otherwise, not to someone who had suffered as she had. Nish spoke of his difficulty with women of his own age – that he found himself tongue-tied and speechless. He told her about his crude pursuit of Tiaan, her rejection, and everything that happened afterwards, all the way to Tirthrax.

The level in the flask went down. Mira opened another.

'I'm not a very nice fellow,' he said, a little tipsy, and proceeded to tell her every one of his failings, real and imagined.

Leaning forward, she topped up his cup. 'Go on with your tale, Nish. It quite takes me away from my own troubles.' She pulled her chair closer.

Nish went on with his story, from Tirthrax. She poured, he talked, she listened. It was a kind of confession. The drink had taken away his inhibitions and Nish poured out his entire life to her. He told her about his mother, Ranii, who took every care for his health and welfare but gave him not a second's praise, no matter how hard he worked to please her. 'She was a careful mother, but indifferent. Cold!'

'I was not like that,' she said, looking into the fire. 'My boys were no duty at all. I loved everything about them.'

Nish talked at length about Jal-Nish. 'We were just tools to him, a part of his plan to climb to the top. Dutiful, successful children were required, so he had them, but he never seemed to care about us. Now he is scrutator, I am told, but even that will not satisfy him.

'And yet,' Nish continued, 'he is my father and I love him. When I saw him lying on the edge of the cliff, his face torn to shreds, his arm smashed, I wept. My father begged to be allowed to die, but I could not let him go. Poor man! How he suffers now.'

'I loved my man and my boys too much.' She stared at the flames. 'They are gone but I cannot move beyond. I just don't want to!' she wailed, reaching out until her fingertips touched the fire.

'The war *burns* me, now and forever,' she said. 'I can't get past it either. How *can* there be war? How can we birth our babies, in love and pain, bringing them up as best we can, and then, when they are still children, send them to the slaughterhouse of battle? Where is the meaning in that? I cannot find any.'

'You must despise me,' he said.

'I do not. You have suffered too, Nish, but you have overcome it. I cannot. Their deaths go round and round; I can't break out of the circle. And do you know why? I don't want to, because it would mean leaving behind everything I love.'

She leaned away from him. 'My sister tells me to move on. I am still young and must live. Why? I say. What advice would you give me, Nish?'

'How can I tell you anything? I don't know what you need.'

'What do *you* need?'

410

'I would have swapped everything I've ever had for an embrace with my mother or father.'

'I gave my boys that! It did not save them.'

She bent forward, and in the flickering candlelight the front of her dress hung down and he saw the valley between her breasts. Once he would have feasted on her but now Nish pulled his eyes away. It was not seemly.

She caught the direction of his glance but to Nish's surprise she reached for him. 'Hold me.'

He took her in his arms, but the distracting thoughts refused to go away. When had he last held a woman? Ullii, in the balloon, months ago. He imagined what Mira's dress concealed. She was no girl; Mira was a mature woman, fourteen or fifteen years older than he, yet he desired her. As she drifted her hand across his back, he wondered if she felt the same for him.

Her man had been dead twelve years and she still mourned. But there is truth in wine and she'd had a lot of it. Too much. He desired her but not this way. Pulling back, he reached for his cup. She smoothed her dress at the front.

'You've told me your past, Nish,' she said. 'What of the future? Are you going back to the army, to kill and kill again?' She said it with a bitter twist of the mouth that turned his mood.

'I am ambitious, Mira, as you know. Selfish, too. But I want to stop the war, and I know how it might be done.'

Taking his hand, she drew it to her, examining it in the firelight. Nish had a strong, square hand, not elegant but workmanlike. 'I like you, Nish. Not because you are handsome, or tall, or clever with words. You are none of those things. But you don't lie about yourself. Or to yourself!'

Her words made him think about Ullii. Kindness and gentleness was what she had liked most about him; and yet, when Nish thought about himself neither of those attributes came to mind. He had not thought himself to be particularly honest, either. Privately, Nish considered himself cold, calculating and out for what he could get.

'Honest?' he exclaimed.

'You know all your faults, Nish, and are not afraid to admit them. I know many people who are honest in their business dealings yet lie to themselves all the time.'

He did not answer.

'How can it be done?' she asked.

'What?' He had lost track of the conversation.

'End the war.'

'Vithis wants Tiaan, and especially her marvellous flying construct. If I could find them I would offer them to him in exchange for an alliance against the lyrinx. The war would be over in weeks.'

'So you would end the war by making it worse.'

'Only for a little while.'

'To do so you would sacrifice Tiaan to her enemy?'

'It would not be like that –' he began. He was deluding himself. Vithis would not bargain; he was not that kind of man. And he never forgot an injury. To give Tiaan to him must doom her.

'You're right,' he said. 'You see so much more clearly than I do, Mira.'

'That's because I neither hope nor believe.' She was slurring her words a little. 'So I am worse off than you.'

'Just the construct then,' he said. 'I will just deliver that to him, if I can find it.'

'And you truly believe that will end the war? Do you trust such a man, who has stated that he wants to conquer our world?'

'Then what am I to do?' he cried. 'My every idea you demolish. If I listen to you I will never do anything at all, for fear of doing the wrong thing.'

'Then do not listen to me. Trust your own judgment, Nish. Do what you think is right. And if you fail, at least you will know you tried. I cannot even try any more.'

He looked at her dispassionately. The distracting thoughts had gone away. The flickering firelight blushed her pale cheeks, put a sparkle in eyes that were dead in daylight. Then she leaned toward him and he saw her bosom again.

She caught his eye. Nish flushed. 'Ah, I'm sorry, Mira,' he said. 'I am a man of base desires, and it has been a long time –'

'Why base, Nish?' She swayed in her chair. 'It is a fine thing and you should not apologise for it. It has been a long time for me too. Come here.'

She drew him to her. Nish knew that it was the wrong thing to do, but he'd had nearly as much wine as she had, and lacked the willpower to resist. Mira put his hand to her breast, and while he was occupied there she was working on the fastenings to her gown, all the way down.

The dress fell open. She had the odd scar and stretch mark, but none of that mattered one iota. She pulled him to her breast. Her hand slipped inside his shirt. Nish nibbled at her ear, her throat, her bottom lip. He kissed her eyelids and they fluttered against him. She sighed; she gasped.

'Ah,' she said, easing her knickers out from under her hips and pulling them all the way down.

Nish worked on his belt buckle, which did not want to come undone. She helped him with it, and the trousers, easing them down. They touched, skin to skin, and he wanted to hug her, to touch, to cling, but Mira was impatient now. Sliding her arms around his back, she pulled him down on her.

'Cham,' she said, squeezing him tightly. 'Ah, Cham. Now, now.'

Nish went still in her arms and his desire vanished. She was thinking of her dead partner, not him. His first urge was to tear himself away, but that might hurt her more. Should he pretend he had heard nothing?

He pressed himself against her. She spread her thighs, guiding him, but as soon as he touched her there she cried out 'No! You're dead, Cham!'

Nish reared back, not knowing whether to try to calm her or quietly disappear.

'Dead!' she screamed at the top of her voice. 'You're dead, Cham. Get off! No, no, *no*!'

Down the corridor people began shouting and yelling. Feet thumped along the hall. Nish shook his head, trying to clear the wine away. What would happen when they found him with his trousers around his ankles and Mira naked on the floor, screaming her lungs out? They'd put a rope around his neck and heave him up over the branch of the nearest tree, and nothing he could say would make any difference.

Nish jerked his pants up and hurled himself out the open window just as the servants burst in through the door. Three jumps and he was off the edge of the veranda and pelting for his life down the grassy slope toward the river.

FORTY-ONE

Why did it always have to end with him running for his life? Nish darted along the river edge. It was not far to the rope bridge but he did not see how he was going to get across it. A guard stood at the foot, staring towards the house, and the end of the bridge was well lit. The fellow could summon more guards in an instant. Besides, Nish did not want to compound his crime by attacking anyone.

On the other hand, the island was not a prison. They had boats. He scurried along the shore, crouched low, for cropped grass ran all the way to the river and there was nowhere to hide.

Nish found no boat. Presumably they were in the boatshed. He dared not try to get one out, for lanterns were bobbing all around the house. He slid into the deep shadow between the boatshed and the river, making his way toward the piles of timber on the other side. The river was fast and cold; even a good swimmer might have trouble in the dark. Nish was not a good swimmer and could not possibly survive. Nor could he remain on the island. He would have to find a float.

Someone pounded down the path. No time to waste. Nish lifted the uppermost beam off the pile, staggered to the water with it and slid it in. It went down like a rock.

He cursed. The timber must still be green. He tried several other pieces but they were just as heavy. He felt around. Another stack seemed to be of older material but they were only small pieces.

At least a dozen people were running along the shore with lanterns and what looked like cudgels. Even if they did not kill him, the least he'd get away with would be a sound thrashing.

Well, he'd done what Troist had asked him to do. Nish hefted the largest piece of wood, only the length and width of his torso, clutched it in his arms and slid into the water. It was damned cold.

Kicking away from the bank, he was caught by the current and whirled out into midstream. The timber floated but it was too small for him to climb onto. Nish put his weight on it, it went under and bobbed up again, overturning him. He panicked and sucked water up his nose. Trying to turn over, he went face-down and a squirt rushed down his windpipe.

Nish managed to choke most of it out. He thrashed his legs, desperate to keep on top of the water. Panic was driving him now, but he was tiring rapidly.

'There he is! Bloody fool's in the water.'

'Get the boats.'

Terrified of being caught, he slid under until just his nose and eyes showed. People were running along the shore, holding up lanterns on poles. The current whipped him downstream. Nish discovered that it was easier to keep his head above water when the rest of his body was below it. The piece of wood, held high on his chest, provided plenty of buoyancy. He drew his head down and allowed the water to take him.

The shouts died away, the lights fell behind. They would be lucky to find him now. The water was so cold that it hurt his fingers and toes, and there were rapids downstream. He had to get out, and quickly.

Turning on his back, he kicked toward the other side. This proved ineffective because of his boots, but as he swept around a bend the accelerating current pushed him against the bank. It was a wall of earth with nothing to catch hold of. As the river straightened he kicked hard, just managing to push himself out of the stream into slack water.

Roots stuck out of the bank here. His trailing hand touched one after another but he could not get a grip. Then his shirt caught on a thicker one. Nish let go of his float and grabbed the root.

It was hard to see, the moon being behind clouds. Nish pulled himself up on the root, a good, sturdy one, and felt around for another handhold. There was none. How far was it to the top of the bank? If further than he could reach he was sunk, literally, because his float was gone. In the dark he could not tell, and dared not stand up lest he overbalance.

Nish clung there, shivering. if he got out, what was he to do? It must be a league back to the horses from here and they would be waiting for him. He would have to keep going on foot and trust to his wits.

A pity he had not used them last night, but it was too late for regrets. Nish felt through his pockets. He had nothing but the papers Troist had given him, doubtless sodden and falling to pieces, and the bag of coin. Neither would be any use to him in the forest. He would have traded all the money for a knife or a piece of flint to start a fire with.

The moon came out and Nish discovered that the top of the bank was not far above his head. If he stood up on the root he should be able to reach it. As soon as he did, the root bent under his weight, but he managed to hook his fingers into the springy turf. He dug his toes into the bank and strained, afraid the earth would collapse on him. Dirt crumbled into his eyes but the bank held. He got one leg up and over, the other followed it and he lay gasping on the turf.

When he had his breath back, Nish emptied the water from his boots, wrung his socks out and put them on again, and squelched off into the forest, setting his course by the moon, roughly south. He was not going anywhere in particular, just away from Morgadis.

Daylight found him in the same hilly country, the same dense forest. His belly rumbled but he could find nothing that looked edible. Nish found a hole in the base of a tree, checked that there was no venomous creature inside and curled up on the floor.

Two days later he was still walking, slowly now. It was too early in the season for fruit, nuts or seeds. There could have been all kinds of roots and tubers here but he had no idea how to find them, or which ones were edible and which poisonous. He saw animals and birds all the time but hurled sticks and stones to no avail. His attempts at traps and snares were equally unsuccessful.

Another day went by. Nish could think of nothing but food. He tried some strands of green algae growing in a pond by a creek. It was slimy, tasteless and seemed to have no nutrition in it at all, for he felt just as faint when his belly was full of the stuff.

He was sitting by the creek with his back to a tree, wondering if there were any fish or crustaceans in the water, when he saw a bee emerge from a hole in the trunk of a neighbouring tree. Another followed it, and a third.

He climbed up the knobbed trunk and looked in. It was a hive, thickly clustered with bees. They could be rendered docile by smoke but he'd already failed to strike a single spark from the only iron object he had, his belt buckle. Driven by his flabby stomach, he broke the end off a branch and bashed it with a rock until he had a chisel-shaped point.

Climbing up, he inserted the stick into the opening, found the centre of the nest and prised. The stick stuck in the wax. He prised harder and the bees swarmed toward his face.

He fell out of the tree, picked himself up and raced toward the water. They followed. One stung him on the back of the neck, another on the arm. He splashed into the creek, down to a shallow pool and ducked under. He felt more stings across his neck and shoulders. He must have carried the bees down with him.

Nish tried to brush them off, ran out of air and came up. The swarm, hanging low over the water, went for him. He swam underwater across the pool, coming up on the other side of a log. He clung on there, watching the swarm, which showed no signs of going away.

It was half an hour before he finally emerged from the water.

The bees were gone. He did not feel good at all; he had been stung in at least a dozen places and there were lumps across his back, shoulders and neck.

Sitting on the bank, shivering and trying to warm himself in the sun, Nish noticed that there was something on the end of his stick. It was a large wedge of comb, golden honey oozing from it. He picked off a few dead bees and crammed a chunk into his mouth. As the sweet honey trickled down his throat it felt like a very good day.

It did get better after that. He came upon a solitary nut tree whose bounty from last season, long fallen, had begun to sprout. Nish stuffed his belly to bursting with the mouldy fruit and filled the sleeves of his coat. His stomach ached all night but it kept him going until, after five more days of walking, he reached a fringe of the forest. There he hesitated.

He did not see how Minis was going to find him, one solitary individual in a wilderness. However, the constructs could not readily travel through the dense forest so he'd better keep to the edge.

He crept along the borderlands for another four days, staying to the shadows, heading south. He was wary of being seen, for lone travellers were vulnerable. Nish found enough food to subsist on: a sick rabbit one day, several crayfish in a pond the next.

On the thirteenth day after fleeing Morgadis he was rising from his bed of bracken when a horse whinnied not far away. Taking up a stout stick, he went to investigate. That proved to be a bad decision.

A detachment of soldiers was riding in his direction. They wore a uniform different from Troist's army and were leading a double file of prisoners, looped together. These looked like yokels; farm labourers and the like, all dressed in ragged homespun. It must be a conscriptors' gang, the land equivalent of a naval press gang. Any man between the ages of fourteen and sixty who lacked the necessary papers could be taken by force for the army, and conscripts were the lowest of all soldiers. They began their lives in chains and usually ended them in the belly of a lyrinx. They were paid nothing but their clothing and keep, and once taken, even if in error, were seldom freed.

Nish had experienced enough of the army. He ducked behind a tree but the movement must have caught someone's keen eye. A shout rang out. He ran toward the forest, which unfortunately was thin here. It would be hard to find a decent hiding place. He darted between two trees, turned sharply left behind a screen of pungent pepperbushes and ran on tiptoe across the grass, trying not to make a sound or leave a trail.

At least two mounted soldiers were after him; he could distinguish the hoofbeats. Ahead, the land was flat, though to his right it sloped down to the creek where earlier he had found the crayfish. It was not deep enough to hinder his passage, much less the horses, but the water would hide his tracks if he could get far enough ahead.

They were too close. They would run him down. Nish rolled over a great fallen tree and ducked down behind it, creeping along to the other end where there was space enough underneath to hide.

The horsemen came pounding out of the trees. 'Where's he gone?' cried one, a tall man with long trailing locks and a bushy red beard.

'Not far,' yelled the other, a nuggetty man with a mean look in his dark eyes. 'He couldn't have gotten away. Must be hiding.'

They walked their horses forward, the nuggetty one heading for the fallen tree while the other approached a clump of wiry shrubs. He had a solid stick in his left hand and looked as though he would enjoy using it.

Nish edged back under the trunk. He might just get away from the other side if the man was not too careful in his search. Unfortunately he proved to be meticulous. It was as if the soldier knew Nish was there, for he worked his way along the trunk, leaving nothing to chance. Should he attack the fellow and try to bring him down, or run for it?

If Nish attacked he had to succeed, else the other horseman would have him in seconds. Nish studied the soldier. The fellow looked strong and mean. Backing under the nest of branches, he waited until the man went past, then leapt out at him. The soldier must have seen him from the corner of his eye for he whirled the horse in its tracks. There was no time to run; Nish sent the stick spinning through the air with all his strength.

His aim was high but his luck held. The horse reared, the heavy end of the stick took the nuggetty fellow in the face and he went off backwards. Before he could recover, Nish caught the side of the saddle, threw himself half onto the horse and screamed 'Go!'

The frightened horse bolted through the trees towards the water. As he pulled himself into the saddle, behind him Nish could hear the roars of the unhorsed soldier.

'He went that way!'

The rider came after him. The other fellow would be running for help. When, *if* they caught him, they would beat him senseless for this affront, and to give the other prisoners a lesson they would never forget. No one cared about the fate of a conscript.

Splashing into the water, Nish rode up the centre of the stream. Unlikely it would make any difference with his hunter this close behind, but he needed all the help he could get. The man was not yet in sight but Nish could hear him. Breaking away from the stream, he walked the horse into the deep forest. The trees were closer together here, and it was darker; easier to hide, though the ground was moist and he left clear tracks.

After riding for a good while, he turned into another gully and stopped. He could hear nothing. Had he lost the fellow? It did not seem likely. Perhaps he was waiting for Nish to move.

Walking the horse up the other side, Nish wondered at the unnatural silence. There was not a sound to be heard. He continued up the steep slope, the horse's hooves breaking through leaf litter and slipping on clayey yellow loam. Nish felt vulnerable. The horse was panting as it struggled up the slope.

Nish reined in, cocking his head. Feeling uncomfortable without knowing why, he turned across the slope, and as he did a pair of riders rose up on their stirrups and came at him. Another few steps and he would have walked right between them.

Nish kicked his horse into a run, slipping and sliding across the greasy slope. Passing beside a black-trunked tree, so close that his knee struck it a painful blow, he turned sharply on the other side, angling toward the creek. Going around a tilted standing stone shaped like a tooth, he pounded along the edge of the creek. One rider was close behind. Nish caught occasional glimpses of the other, at the top of the slope.

No use trying to get up that way. He shot by a copse of trees as dark and dense as a wall and looked back. The soldier was gaining. Nish turned sharply along the line of trees, splashed across the creek and up the other side, coming out into open woodland, though the forest continued beyond that. He was halfway across when two more horses appeared on the far side. Nish turned away. The pair who had been following him came out of the trees.

His horse was tiring. No matter what he did, they were going to catch him. No, never give up. If he could get between the pairs, he might make it back into the forest again, and then, who knows?

'Go!' he shouted, kicking the horse into a gallop and putting his head down. 'One last effort!' He patted the heaving neck. The horse responded, running like the wind. Nish had never gone so fast. Both pairs of riders turned to cut him off, but their mounts were tired too. He shot between them with not a dozen paces to spare.

Nish shook his fist in their faces, and now they were slowing, falling back. Another trap? He slowed too, wondering what was going on.

Out of the forest came a construct, its weapons at the ready. Out of the frying-pan . . . Then Nish saw that the machine bore the same colours that Minis's had. Minis had found him.

With a great sigh of relief, Nish walked his horse forward. 'Minis!' he yelled, waving his arm above his head. 'Minis.'

The top of the construct came open and a tall figure stood up on the platform. It was not Minis.

'Hello, *Marshal* Cryl-Nish Hlar,' said Vithis.

FORTY-TWO

The following day, when she had been in Nyriandiol for about a month, Tiaan was permitted to sit upright, though she had to be lifted into position and laid down afterwards. Gilhaelith sat with her, and together they redesigned the wheeled chair so she could move it by herself. It was her most pleasant time since Tirthrax. There were moments when she quite forgot Minis, and once, to her shame, even little Haani was not a lead blanket wrapped around her heart.

It took several days to rebuild the chair, but as soon as the wheels were fitted, its inadequacies became apparent, not least that it was useless anywhere where there were steps, or on the stony ground outside.

'This is no good at all.' Gilhaelith was struggling to get it up the single step from her room.

Tiaan moved uncomfortably in the seat, for the brace was pinching her. 'What about a chair that walks, like a clanker with four legs? I'm sure I can design one. I've seen their workings a hundred times, and whatever I've seen, I can remember perfectly.'

He regarded her, thoughtful. 'No wonder you picked up geomancy so easily.'

'What do you mean?'

'That Art is based on the patterns and forces of the natural world. If you can recall and recognise them, you've already taken the first step.'

'And my work as an artisan was the second . . .'

'Indeed. Geomancy is unlike all other forms of the Secret Art. Perhaps that is why mancers have, as a rule, struggled to master it. It's alien to their way of thinking. Tell me, how would you move such a walker, Tiaan? I don't see –'

'I would build a controller for it, using my hedron to draw power from the field.'

His face lit up. 'I've wondered, sometimes . . .' Pushing her under the shade of the vines, he ran into the house, shortly to return with paper and a piece of charcoal.

Tiaan began to sketch, and after various failures settled on something like a miniature clanker, with two thick legs at the front and another two at the back.

'I don't think we can make that here,' Gilhaelith said. 'What if it were more like this?' He sketched a different arrangement.

She ran it forward and back in her mind. 'The legs will catch. But if we were to make it this way . . .'

They worked well into the night, and though Gurtey's cabal of servants muttered and scowled outside, it was a good day. Gilhaelith must have enjoyed it too, for he lingered afterwards. He seemed less strange, more complete now that he had revealed a little of himself.

The final design did not resemble a clanker at all. The metal legs were spider-slender and placed at four corners of a hardwood frame, for balance. A seat was mounted on the frame so Tiaan's head would be at her head height when standing. The mechanism to drive the legs, a simplified version of a clanker's innards, would go beneath the seat. Gilhaelith's smiths would build it while Tiaan made the controller, and that was such slow work that the walker would likely be finished first.

She worked in her room, which was hard to endure. Over the past six months Tiaan had grown used to being outside in all weather, but with spies about that was not possible.

At first she could work only in short intervals, for her muscles had lost most of their strength. However, she soon began to make progress. Gilhaelith was generally in his organ chamber, working on an unspecified project. Nyrd the gnomish messenger came and went. Tiaan often saw skeets out her window. On the last day of her first month in Nyriandiol, Gilhaelith took dinner with her in her room.

'The Aachim spies have gone, and Vithis has moved his forces north along both sides of Warde Yallock. They must think the thapter crashed in the wild country there.'

'Why would they think that?'

He simply smiled. 'But of course, that won't get rid of them for long. Sooner or later something will tip them off and they will come in force.' His eyes met hers.

'Can your Art still conceal me?' Her opinion of his powers had risen, as his had of hers.

'Not from a direct search, so we must be ready to flee on short notice.'

'But they'll be watching.'

'We'll go in the thapter, if it's ready. If not, I have another way of escape, though it's not so secure now.'

'You would just abandon Nyriandiol, and all you have here?'

'After betraying Scrutator Klarm, and lying to Vithis, there's no choice.'

'Where will you go?'

He looked away. 'I'll decide when the time comes. In the meantime, there's much to do. Shall we get back to work?'

He knows, she thought, but doesn't trust me enough to say. We think the same way on that, too.

He now began to teach her the foundations of geomancy, though in Tiaan's first week of study that Art was not once mentioned. It was like being back in her days as a prentice artisan.

Gilhaelith started with minerals and crystals. Tiaan had expected to find that easy, having spent most of her life working with crystals of various kinds. On the first morning she discovered that she knew nothing at all. Gilhaelith had hundreds of different minerals in boxes, all nested in the pale, papery bark of the sard tree. One entire room was devoted to them, huge specimens as well as little ones. Tiaan had to learn the name of each mineral, and recognise it no matter how poor or damaged the sample. Some came in a bewildering array of forms which seemed to bear no resemblance to each other, defeating even her visual memory.

At the moment she had before her four samples, all supposed to be of ironstone. One was made of a tangle of small dark plates as iridescent as mica, the second was a round crystal with many facets, the third resembled a dark-brown earth, while the last consisted of many small flat crystals grown together like the petals of a rose.

'I don't understand how they can all be the same,' she said.

Her head was throbbing from the effort of remembering them and their geomantic uses. Ironstone had virtues in healing and could also be transformed into lodestone, though Gilhaelith had not told her how. He bade her take particular note of the rosette form, which had a variety of geomantic uses, some belying its appearance.

'There's too much to learn,' she said wearily.

'Just use your memory. Understanding will come in time.'

But there was never enough time. Each morning began with a recognition test, using hundreds of samples, none of which she had seen before. Gilhaelith expected no less than perfection which, even for Tiaan's visual recall, proved impossible. Subsequently she had to list and describe, from memory, every mineral she had previously been shown. She made many mistakes, which did not please her master.

After only a week, he began her on rocks and ores of every conceivable sort, some identified by form, weight and colour, others because of the minerals they were made up of and the way they were arranged. And rocks, a week later, led to the forces that had formed them at the dawn of time, and all the ways that they had been shaped and changed ever since.

Gilhaelith's instruction now became abstract and harder for her to visualise, much less understand. It suited the contortions of his mind, but not her own. As he plunged deep into the patterns of numbers that crystals made, his deficiencies as a teacher became apparent. When she stumbled over a concept or a principle, he simply repeated what he had said before, more loudly. He could not put himself in the mind of a prentice, or see the right way to teach her what had been so easy for him. Incapable of putting technicalities in simple language, he talked in abstruse jargon. Finally, when he was using numbers to explain the forces that caused volcanoes to erupt, and sometimes explode violently, she snapped.

'I have no idea what you're talking about. I haven't understood a thing you've said all morning. *Gilhaelith!*'

He was staring at her bosom, which had grown over the past month. She had put on weight and knew that it suited her. He did not, she now appreciated, look out of lechery, but simply amazement that she could be shaped so differently from him. She had given up reminding him how rude it was.

Gilhaelith looked away, abashed. 'I'm sorry. You are my first prentice and I'm an indifferent teacher. Would you care to come outside?'

'I'd love to, if it's safe.'

'I have guards around the rim. No spy can come up without being seen. I'll take you down into the crater – it may be easier to show than to tell.'

Since Tiaan's controller was not yet ready, she was carried down on the back of a donkey. An uncomfortable journey, it made her back ache within minutes, but she soon forgot about that. Gilhaelith walked beside her, explaining how the lava formed deep in the earth, what force it had taken to blast the crater out, and why its walls had the shape they had. The trip taught her more than she had learned in the previous week.

The sheer cliff below the villa, made of layer upon layer of volcanic rock, looked as if it had been cut with a spade.

'Three hundred years ago, a mighty explosion blasted everything else away,' said Gilhaelith. 'It blocked out the sun for a fortnight and the noise was heard in Tyrkir, hundreds of leagues to the south.'

'And this could happen again?' Tiaan looked around nervously.

'*Will* happen again, and again.'

'Then why risk coming down here?'

'There should be signs for weeks beforehand – earth tremblers, geysers. The lake might boil or drain away.'

So much to learn, so little time.

At the bottom they stopped by a hissing spring surrounded with yellow salts. 'The volcano is only sleeping,' Gilhaelith explained. 'The congealed lava is still liquid underneath, and the solid cap nearly as hot as a fire. The rainwater seeps down, boils and is forced up like water from the spout of a kettle.'

'And these coloured crystals?'

'Hot water dissolves minerals from the rocks. After it spurts out and dries up in the heat, crystals form –'

'Like salt in a dried-up rockpool on the seashore.' Tiaan remembered trips to the sea with her grandmother when she had been little.

'Precisely.'

Further down, the vents were thickly coated with layers of yellow-brown sulphur, the source of much of Gilhaelith's wealth. His workers were hacking it into lumps which they loaded into baskets, some carried on their heads, others on their backs.

They continued to the peculiarly blue waters of the lake. Gilhaelith lifted her off the donkey and to her surprise it felt pleasant in his arms. Setting her down where she could rest against a boulder, he began unpacking a picnic basket. She studied him surreptitiously as he laid food and drink on the cloth, a thick weave patterned with concentric squares in earthy reds, browns and yellows. He still looked awkward but it fitted him better now.

Gilhaelith set down plates, sawed grainy bread into perfect slices and placed two on her plate. He added a handful of a pickled vegetable rather like an olive, white lengths of cheese and slices of cooked gourd, and passed it to her. Looking up, he caught her watching him and grinned self-consciously. Tiaan, for the first time, smiled back. In contradiction of his statement about being indifferent to humanity, he seemed to like her. She discovered that she liked him too, in spite of his failings.

She could almost, *almost* trust him, though she warned herself not to.

It was a pleasant lunch, as long as she did not look too closely at what he was eating. They just talked about whatever came to mind, and Tiaan was sorry when it was over. It was sweltering, without a trace of breeze. There was not a cloud in the sky and the dark rocks radiated heat.

Gilhaelith packed the basket, then said, 'I'll have a swim before we go up.' Stripping off shirt, boots and socks, he waded into the water and began to flap about on his back, sending gouts of water up from hands and feet and blowing like a whale.

As Tiaan watched, her smile faded. It seemed to grow hotter by the second. Sweat ran down her back. Beneath the straps of the brace her skin itched unbearably. A tear stung her eye. She clenched her hands in her lap and waited.

He came out, still blowing and grinning like a loon, water pouring from his skinny chest. 'That's good. Not too warm, not too cool –' He stooped. 'What's the matter, Tiaan?' and slapped his thigh. A few drops landed on her face. 'I'm a damned fool.'

'I enjoyed watching you swim. It's just that – it's so hot . . .' She rubbed her eyes and gave him a wan smile. 'It's all right. I was just feeling sorry for myself.'

'I'd carry you out,' he said, 'but –'

'I don't mind getting my gown wet,' she said eagerly. 'It'd keep me cool on the way up.'

He took off her boots and carried her into the water. It was the perfect temperature – cool enough to be comfortable but not so cool that she could not have stayed in it for hours. The sea near Tiksi, on the few times she had swum in it, had been bone-achingly cold.

Gilhaelith laid her in the water, one hand behind her knees, the other under her back. She floated, weightless and perfectly content. Tiaan splashed water on her face, wiped it off and stared up at the blue sky. It quite took her away from all her troubles.

A droplet on her forehead roused her. 'We'd better go.'

She smacked her cupped hand into the water, splashing him, and laughed. The most extraordinary look crossed his face, like a man trying to climb out through a mask. It tore but re-formed – one hundred and fifty years of self-control could not be broken that easily. He looked so stern that Tiaan quailed. No, she thought, there *is* a human being inside. She swung her arm again and the jet of water caught him right on the bridge of the nose.

Water dripped from his nostrils, hair and chin. He looked so ridiculous that she snorted. He cracked a little, tossing a scoop of water which only dewed her hair. Tiaan attacked him with both hands. Water went everywhere. He splashed her face and this time the mask cracked in two. He whooped. She laughed aloud, going two to his one, until a particularly energetic blow slid her off his arm and she went under. Tiaan did not have time to panic, for he caught her straight away, lifting her out and holding her as if she were a fragile toy.

'Are you all right?'

'Of course,' she said gaily.

'It's late. We'd better go.'

The moment was broken and she was sorry about that, for something had changed between them. They were halfway up the winding track when Tiaan noticed a circling speck, high above. It could have been an eagle but she did not think so. 'Gilhaelith! What do you think that is?'

He stared upwards, shading his eyes with long, knuckly fingers. 'I'd say,' he said slowly, 'that it is a lyrinx.'

'Is it watching us?'

'I think so.'

'Why would a lyrinx be watching Nyriandiol?'

'Sulphur is needed for the war. It would inconvenience humanity if they had to obtain impure stuff from further away.'

'Will they attack, do you think?'

'I doubt it. Despite the war in Almadin, enemy territory is a long way from here. Even if they took this place they could not hold it, for the scrutators have a mighty army in Borgistry. No, they're just spying.'

'Could they recognise me from that height?' she asked

anxiously. Since Kalissin, she lived in fear of being used for flesh-forming again.

'Lyrinx sight is not as good as ours in daytime, but best cover yourself in case it comes lower.' He gave her a scarf to wind around her face.

The donkey grunted and groaned all the way up. The fractured rock and ash kept sliding beneath its weight. Once, the poor beast lost its footing and would have fallen, had not Gilhaelith steadied it.

'The poor thing,' said Tiaan. 'It feels wrong to be on its back, doing nothing while it struggles so hard.'

'It's earning its keep, as we all must do,' said Gilhaelith.

'I'm not earning mine!' she muttered.

'Work hard; master your Art. We've little time left.'

Tiaan had been working hard, but a prentice would have spent years on crystals alone; she'd had a scant week. Even allowing for her experience it was no way to learn the Secret Art, much less master it. But the war, the world, her enemies would not wait.

Alie and Gurteys stood by the front door, and both frowned when they saw the state of Tiaan's gown. She ignored their unfriendly glances. Did they think she was trying to take Gilhaelith away from them?

That night she drove herself harder than usual. She could not bear being dependent. It reminded her of her mother.

The next day Gilhaelith returned Tiaan to her attic hiding place as a local warlord appeared unannounced. He pretended to be checking on an order of brimstone, but as his eyes darted all around and his army of retainers wandered where they were not supposed to, clumsily questioning Gilhaelith's servants, it was clear that he was really looking for the thapter, and Tiaan. Whether for himself, or as a paid informant to Vithis, it did not matter. Tiaan shivered all the while he was there.

Once he had gone the lesser servants, led by Gurteys, stood around talking in low voices, after which they sent a deputation to Gilhaelith. Tiaan was not privy to what was discussed, though afterwards he was unusually silent and distant. She gathered that her presence, and the thapter, threatened everyone.

As she was wheeling down the hall late that night, something struck her painfully on the left ear. It felt like the handle of a broomstick. By the time she recovered and heaved the chair around, the culprit had disappeared in the darkness.

She did not call for a servant to help her to bed; Tiaan felt too afraid. Fortunately, when she was resigned to spending the night in her chair, Gilhaelith came by and lifted her into bed. Her arms were not yet strong enough to do it for herself. She resolved to work on that.

Later, brooding in the darkness, she became aware of an unpleasant smell, like week-old fish. Every time she moved, it grew stronger. Tearing the covers back she dragged herself to the far end. A large and extremely rotten fish had been wedged between the mattress and the end of the bed. Scooping the slimy creature up in one arm, she tossed it out the window. The stench lingered all night.

The unpleasantness, which had begun with the women, soon spread to the male servants, all except Nixx, Foreman Mihail, and Fley. Most of the servants just shunned her, but Gurteys and her friends subjected her to all kinds of torments, including abandoning her in the privy for hours. Tiaan might have spent all day there had Gilhaelith not come looking for her.

Gurteys made an excuse, which Gilhaelith accepted. He took no interest in the servants and had no idea what was going on. Tiaan kept her silence. She had never been one to tell tales. Besides, she understood why they were doing it. They were terrified that Vithis would find her hiding here and put the lot of them to the sword.

Two days later Gilhaelith tightened the last bolt of the walker and tossed his wrench onto the table. 'It's done!'

Tiaan wheeled herself across the tiled basement floor. The walker resembled a four-legged spider and she wasn't sure she wanted to get inside. It would be like being part of a machine. On the other hand, she would not be quite so helpless.

She circled away, going round and round the thapter. Its black metal skin was stacked against the far wall, exposing a mess of mechanical innards. It looked as if it would never move again.

From here, Tiaan could feel the pull of the amplimet, which was back in its cavity. She had not touched it in ages. She occasionally felt twinges of longing for it, though Tiaan was not sure if that was withdrawal. Something had definitely changed since she'd used it in the port-all to create the gate. Not having touched the crystal since she came here, its pull was fading. She would never be free of it but she could, if she so chose, have left it behind. That was just as well since it now belonged to Gilhaelith. She had used her hedron in the controller of the walker.

She longed to be back in the thapter, to soar carefree through the sky. The freedom of the air meant so much more, now that she lacked mobility on the ground. But she had to learn to walk before she could fly – first the repairs must be completed. Then a way must be found to tame, or at least shackle, the treacherous amplimet.

Tiaan had devoted much thought and experimentation to finding a replacement for it, but had found no other crystal that would allow her to draw upon the strong force required for flight. For the time being, she was bound to use the amplimet. Tiaan hated being reliant on it, and it bound her to Gilhaelith too, which did not please her. She liked him now, but since he did not trust her, she was not going to trust him. Heaving the wheels so hard that they spun in place, she headed for the walker.

Shortly, held securely in a webbing of leather and canvas straps, she gripped the controller arm with her right hand and the metal frame with her left. Emptying her mind, Tiaan mentally stroked the hedron into life. The field appeared in her inner eye, here a wavering aurora of pale yellow surrounded by cream, and further off, another wobbling yellow globe. It was rather like a double-yolker egg. Identifying a darker whirlpool, Tiaan caught it as it drifted by, traced a path through ethyric space and tugged gently. Power poured into the crystal and the walker took off with a jerk, its foot pads scraping on the floor.

One limb went one way, its mate the other. The legs splayed and it staggered sideways like a crab, tilting from side to side.

Gilhaelith laughed, which reminded her of her similar experience with the thapter. The wall loomed up. She choked the flow and the walker stalled, canted sideways with its legs unceremoniously spread. Coordinating four legs was harder than she had expected. Tiaan took a deep breath and concentrated, moving one leg at a time, and then the pairs, front and back. They did not want to go the right way, and the back brace, gouging her flesh with every movement, did not help.

Circling around the room, she edged up beside Gilhaelith, moved backwards and forwards without getting any closer, and stopped.

'How is it?' he asked.

'It takes a bit of getting used to.' She moved it sideways and back, which was no better. 'I'm either too close or too far away. But at least I'll be able to work on the thapter.'

He smiled. 'I'm glad. You'll have plenty to do while I'm away.'

The walker jerked, then froze, one leg in the air, as the field vanished from her mind. 'Where are you going?'

'Here, on the top of the mountain, the whole world can see who visits me. Some of my customers don't like other people knowing their business. And nor do I.' He sighed. 'I'll leave you to your work.'

Tiaan watched him go. After all this time she still did not know what he wanted of her, or what his real plans were. Maybe the secret business had to do with her. And what if Vithis came back? The servants would not lie for her.

FORTY-THREE

Only once Gilhaelith had gone did Tiaan appreciate that she was alone in a fortress full of strangers. And they *were* strangers, for while he was there she had been able to ignore them. She wished she had taken the trouble to get to know them at the beginning – she might have made a friend or two. Apart from Nixx, Gurteys, her mute husband Fley, Mihail and Alie, she did not know their names. Tiaan supposed that was part of the problem.

She planned to keep watch on the amplimet while he was away, but could not find it anywhere. Did he not trust it, or her?

On the first morning, Tiaan became so immersed in the disassembly of an intricate part of the thapter that she did not notice the absence of the servants. After lunch, driven by an urgent need to use the privy, she rang the bell beside the door. It was not answered, even after twenty pulls.

There was no trouble getting the walker into the privy chamber, but getting out of the machine by herself proved to be a nightmare. She ended up falling, bruising herself from shoulder to knee. This privy, no more than a squatting hole, was disgusting and using it by herself proved impossible. She ran a piece of cord from a cloak hook on the wall to the door handle and tried to hang on to that. She fell twice, ending up so soiled that it took half the water barrel to clean herself up.

Fortunately no one came by to see her in that state. Weeping with humiliation, she pulled herself into the walker and went to her room. Getting out again, she fell and bruised her other side. Too sore and worn out to heave herself into bed, Tiaan slept on the floor and swore she would overcome her disability. Never again would she endure such helplessness.

She managed to dress herself in the morning, and shortly after, Fley happened to pass by and helped her into the walker. She did not plan to get out until Gilhaelith returned.

As always, her escape was work. Tiaan kept going all day, all night and into the following day, until she could no longer keep her eyes open. At midday she went to her room, locked the door and slept in her harness. She did not use the privy again. When she simply had to urinate she did it outside, which took rather a lot of coordination.

Tiaan, woken one night by a need to relieve herself, crept the walker towards the undulating walkway. She always went that way, knowing she would not meet anyone. As she went through the front door, voices came echoing down the wall.

'. . . heave her, and her wretched thapter, out the window into the lake.'

Tiaan recognised the voice but could not put a face to it.

'There's a price for her, and it,' said another. It sounded like Gurteys.

'I'll not listen to that kind of talk,' snapped a third. 'Gilhaelith has looked after my family for four generations, and I'll –'

'That'll count for naught if the scrutators find it here. We'll die horribly, Iryle. Well, not me!'

'Master has been good to us.'

'And I'd risk my life for him,' said Gurteys. 'Even my family's lives, should it come to that. But I'll not risk so much as a little toe for her.'

'And if we do chance everything,' came an unknown voice, 'where's the reward?'

'Ten thousand gold tells is the price for her,' said Gurteys. 'And the same for her flying machine. Imagine that – two thousand each!'

Tiaan heard a sharp intake of breath, a door banged and the voices were cut off. She headed in the other direction, out behind the skeet houses. Ten thousand gold tells was the worth of a town. No one could resist that kind of temptation. Unable to sleep, she went the long way to the basement to work on the thapter, and made sure she had a long knife within reach at all times.

Despite her efforts, the repairs were going slowly. Tiaan had begun to despair that the thapter would ever be finished. Vithis would return, search Nyriandiol and find it. And her.

The servants did not come after her – perhaps they hadn't yet found the courage to betray their master, or perhaps too many remained loyal. She knew Fley had, for she saw Gurteys abusing him outside her door. Mute Fley said nothing, but the look on his face was savage.

In the morning, Tiaan heard that Gilhaelith was coming up the mountain. She had missed him and was surprised to discover it. She now found it impossible to concentrate on her work and was constantly clacking up the ramps to see if he had arrived. The servants gave one another bitter, knowing glances.

That checked her. Her impulse had been to go flying down the hall, to show how well she could control the walker. Instead she made her face impassive, staying back until he had greeted his servants and handed them a variety of packages.

Gilhaelith turned to her. Tiaan stood where she was, rocking the walker like a boat on the sea. He seemed drawn.

'You look thin, Tiaan.'

'I've been working hard. The walker has done a lot for me. But you appear tired . . . Gilhaelith.' She rarely used his name and it always sounded strange.

'A long journey, and hard bargaining, and bad news at the end of it. The Aachim are preparing to move at last. I believe it means war.'

'On us?' she cried.

'On humanity! But we could well end up casualties.'

'Oh.' She moved the machine back and forth on its spindly legs, conscious that she had not had a bath in a week.

'I must make preparations for the security of Nyriandiol. How goes the thapter?'

'Slowly, though I have spent weary hours at it. It may take another week.'

'I pray we have that long. What assistance I can render is yours to command, though I have many calls on my time. Still,' he smiled tiredly, 'I'm sure we'll find a way. I'd better get started.'

Tiaan wondered if he was putting on a show for the house, for the smile did not reach his eyes and his brow was furrowed.

Late that evening he came to her room, where she sat by the bed in the walker, waiting for him. Tiaan's hands were clenched in her lap. The servants' talk about the reward had so terrified her that she had to take further steps to protect herself. She planned to do something quite foreign to her nature and was not sure how to go about it.

'You look exhausted,' she said. 'Is there more than you have said?'

'There is. The lyrinx are massing in south-west Meldorin, just across the sea from Taltid, where the scrutators have their largest army. Vithis's Aachim are moving down into Almadin. If Aachim and lyrinx unite, they will destroy an army and a civilisation.' He rose.

'G-Gilhaelith?'

He stopped with his hand on the latch. 'Yes, Tiaan?'

'Could you help me?'

'Of course. What can I do for you?'

'Could you help me to get . . . to get ready for bed?' She blushed.

The smile vanished. 'I'll call Gurteys.'

'No!' she cried.

'What's the matter?'

'We don't get on very well,' Tiaan said lamely.

'Sanya then.'

'Sanya?'

'The woman who helps you with your toilet.'

'She and I – don't get on either.'

'Who *would* you would like to attend you?' said Gilhaelith with a trace of irritation.

'I don't want to be attended by *any* of them,' she said, determined to get it out at last. 'They hate me.'

'They will do what they are told.' Gilhaelith strode back and forth, casting her sideways glances. 'What's the matter with . . .?' He seemed to be reassessing her.

'They resent me. They don't like it that you and I are together a lot. They don't want things to change, and they don't think anyone is good enough for you, least of all a *cripple* and a foreigner like me.'

'What do you mean *good enough?*'

Did he really have no idea what they were thinking? She looked into his eyes and saw that he did not. He could read strangers but was blind to his own staff. 'They think,' she said slowly, because just to say it was embarrassing, 'that we will become lovers . . . if we are not already. That I am after you.'

'*After* me?'

'And that when I get you, and become mistress of Nyriandiol, I will dismiss them and bring in my own people.'

'That's absurd. I've never had a lover. Why would I start now?'

You might have put it a bit more kindly, she thought. 'Do you really know so little about human nature? They have never seen you with a woman. Now you are constantly with me.'

'They have nothing to worry about,' he said abruptly.

She had not expected more, nor wanted it. Nonetheless, it was another rejection of her femininity. She was, after all, a cripple. Tiaan took a deep breath. The only way to protect herself was to bind him to her as tightly as possible. She could not risk him taking the servants' side. From here he could probably complete the repairs of the thapter by himself, and if he dared use the amplimet there would be no need for her. The thought made her cold inside. 'And they're afraid.'

'Of what?'

'That Vithis will come, or the scrutator, and destroy everything to get hold of the thapter. And me.'

440

'I can't believe my servants would do anything to harm you.'

She took a deep breath. 'Two nights back I heard Gurteys talking about the reward. Ten thousand gold tells for me and as much again for the thapter. Two thousand each, she said to the others.'

That shocked him. 'I knew about the reward, but even so . . . Perhaps I expect too much. I must think what to do.' He stood there, eyes closed.

Tiaan wanted to scream at him, that the time for thinking was long past. She restrained herself – he was master here. 'If you could just help me to the bath, and then into bed. I'm exhausted.'

Gilhaelith's larynx went up and down. 'But I'm a *man!*'

Her tiredness vanished. She had been awkward with men for so long that the idea of one being uncomfortable with her was a revelation. Minis's rejection, then her injury, had devastated her self-worth. Did Gilhaelith see her as a woman first and a cripple second?

'But while I've been away –'

'I've slept in the walker. I've not had a bath. No one would attend me in the privy.' She looked away.

'My poor Tiaan,' he said.

'I'm tired and I stink, and I'm bruised all over. I just want to bathe and go to bed.'

'But –'

'I would wear a gown in the bath,' she said. 'And you could avert your eyes. Please, Gilhaelith; I can't bear to have them near me.'

'Aren't you . . .? The idea . . .'

Could he possibly be blushing? It gave her the strength to go on. 'Customs are different where I come from,' she said. 'It was so hot near the furnaces of the manufactory that women often worked half-naked.' No matter that *she* never had. 'It does not bother me.' It did, but not so much as it upset him. 'Besides, you are a celibate. Why should I have any fear of you?'

The look he gave her suggested that Gilhaelith was having trouble with his vow. 'I will do as you ask, just this once. Are you ready?'

Still in the walker, she gathered her nightgown and went to the bathing room. Gilhaelith followed, grim of face.

'Would you close the door, please?' she said.

He did so, then waited until she had unbuckled the straps and pushed them aside. Gilhaelith carried her to the travertine platform at the end of the tub.

As she unbuttoned her blouse he whirled to face the wall. She took a guilty pleasure in her power to disturb him. She was using him. But then, he had been born before her great-grandfather. He'd had plenty of time to master his emotions.

Laying the dirty garments beside her, she pulled the gown over her head. 'You'll have to help me.' She indicated her frozen legs.

He came reluctantly, red in the face. She held on while he unfastened the belt and drew her baggy trousers off, looking everywhere but at her. Tiaan, nearly as embarrassed, jerked her gown down. He deposited her into the water and ran for the door.

Bathing in a gown proved to be more difficult than she had imagined, and less enjoyable. She was glad when he knocked on the door again. 'Come in,' she sang out. 'I'm ready.'

He seemed to have gained control of himself. Gilhaelith knelt by the tub, reached down and lifted her onto the platform. There they both realised what they should have been aware of from the beginning. The wet gown was quite transparent.

He stared at her, unable to help himself. He tore his gaze away a dozen times but it kept coming back. Tiaan was self-conscious, yet pleased. She was not just a crippled blob, as she had thought of herself since the accident. She *was* still a woman, and even Gilhaelith the celibate could see it.

'I should have brought an extra gown,' she said.

'I'll run and fetch another.'

'No matter. It's a warm night.'

'The servants –' he said with a strangled gasp.

'Do you care what they think?'

'I don't care what *anyone* thinks. But –' He did not go on.

'But they might think I am your lover?'

'Yes!' he choked.

'Then let them. Would you dry me?'

He did so with such fascinated reluctance that Tiaan was touched. Finally Gilhaelith carried her to her room in her damp gown, studiously avoiding looking down, helped her into a fresh one, then fled.

Tiaan lay awake for hours afterward, amazed by her boldness and thinking about the torment she had put him to. She hardened her heart. He was using her to satisfy his obsession with the great game. Why should she not use him to save her life?

It became a routine after that. He helped her dress and bathe, and took her to the privy. That was even more embarrassing, but better than being waited on by the servants who, even in his presence, could now not conceal their hostility.

Gilhaelith began to teach her the nature of natural fields and the qualities of different kinds of nodes. There was so much to learn, and each day Tiaan realised how little she really knew, and how dangerous her dabblings in geomancy had been. She might have killed herself a dozen times over. Vithis must have known that. And Minis. It made her so angry she could not concentrate. How *could* he have pretended to love her, knowing that what he had asked her to do might destroy her?

Gilhaelith also showed her how to draw power from the field into certain crystals and blast it out again, although he had not yet let her try for herself. It could be used as a weapon, albeit a hazardous one.

Only a few more days and the thapter would be ready for testing. She prayed they had that long. And then?

What if Gilhaelith intended to take the thapter for himself? She must have her own plan and, as soon as the thapter was ready, be prepared to implement it. If Gilhaelith was lying, he might take it and cast her out, and she had to be ready to act first. Dare she steal the thapter while testing it? But what if Gilhaelith was telling the truth? She would be no better than the Aachim she so despised.

Tiaan woke in the night, feeling as though she had just heard the peal of a distant bell. Odd. She'd not heard that sound here before. She wriggled in the brace but could not get comfortable. An hour later, still awake, she decided to continue her work on the thapter. Her arms were strong now and she had perfected a technique for getting in and out of the walker by herself.

She was checking the field when she noticed something strange. It seemed much more regular than usual, and was pulsing gently. She cocked her head, tracing the patterns in her inner eye. The pulsing faded. She continued, but soon heard that peal of bells again. It seemed to be calling to her.

She spidered along the hall of the lowest floor. Up the far end, where she had never been, a vague pool of light spilled from an open door. The walker's rubber feet made no sound on the stone. She reached the door and looked into a vast cavern of a room filled with organ pipes. She knew about the organ, though Gilhaelith never talked of it.

A lantern glowed among the pipes as the far end. She hesitated in the doorway. The bells hinted at something distant, long forgotten and rather sad. She went in a step or two, thinking to ask Gilhaelith about the sounds.

'Gilhaelith?' she called softly.

There was no answer, but at the distant edge of hearing there came another peal. Again a memory struggled fruitlessly to get free. Perhaps he was among the pipes. There were tens of thousands of them – a veritable forest of wood and metal. She edged forward, feeling the thudding of her heart. This was his private place and she should not be here, but the bells called to her and she had to know what they were saying.

The great room was empty, though a two-handled cup of mustard-water steamed on a pedestal next to the organ console, and beside it lay the amplimet. She picked it up. He must have just gone out. She looked around but could not see the bells. Odd. Across the room she made out a great glass sphere, slowly rotating on its stand as if on a cushion of air.

Even from two steps away she could feel the cold. Patches of feathery frost clung to its northern and southern poles, disappearing and re-forming as it turned. Tendrils of vapour drifted lazily away, rising or falling in the air. It looked like some kind of scrying sphere. Edging closer, she reached out with a fingertip, but drew back as pinpoints of light sparkled on a globe of the world, under the glass. Some specks were brighter than others and one, at Tirthrax, positively glowed. Perhaps it was a representation of its node.

Curious, she reached out again. Other bright specks were scattered across Lauralin and the surrounding islands. She was able to pick the node at Booreah Ngurle straight away, though it was far from being one of the brightest. She examined the globe. Kalissin was bright but the node at the manufactory was not visible – not the least pinprick. Cold fear settled over her. Had the manufactory been destroyed, its node drained dry? That might mean Tiksi was gone too – and her mother.

It probably meant nothing of the sort, Tiaan told herself, and there was no way of telling, so it was foolish to construct worries out of light and shadow on the glass. As she turned away, she felt a cold ache in the bones of her left hand, which held the amplimet. She almost dropped it. Tiaan threw her hand up to her chest and the amplimet went out.

Letting out a cry of anguish, she stared at the crystal. There was no glow, no spark, nothing. Had she destroyed it, and all her plans, by bringing it to the globe?

Tiaan closed her fist around the amplimet, squeezing hard. What was she to do? Staring up at the dark ceiling, she noticed a needle-thin blue-white ray reflecting from a point near the skylight. She traced it down to its origin, a point on the globe near the southern pole, which had rotated to the top. A spot on a boomerang-shaped island glowed so brightly that it outshone all other nodes.

She bent towards the globe. The island lay in the centre of a long sea. What was its name? One end was the Kara Ghâshâd, or Burning Sea, the other the Kara Agel, Frozen Sea. The island had a single peak in the centre. It was the Island of Noom. Tiaan knew nothing about the place but as soon as she remembered the name, dread settled over her. She drove the walker backwards by instinct.

Halfway across the room, the slender ray went out, as did all the other specks of light on the globe. She opened her fist, hoping to see the amplimet restored, but it was as dark as before. Still moving, she backed into something she had not seen, for it was covered in a black dustcloth. It gave forth the low, mournful peal she had heard before.

She pulled off the cloth, which could have covered a good-sized shed. Beneath, a carillon of bells was suspended from a small iron tower. Four of the bells were identical, each larger than a witch's cauldron and spaced well apart at the corners of a square. Hanging in the centre was a fifth bell, elongated like a gooseberry and large enough to cover her from head to foot. It was made of glass, though she could not see through it.

Creeping into the middle of the carillon, she lowered the walker to look under the bells. The four metal bells were just like ordinary village bells. The fifth had no clapper and may have been designed to ring in sympathy with the others. The glass was mirror-silvered inside.

Belatedly realising that she had no right to be poking around here, she was turning away when the amplimet shone out and, beneath the glass bell, she saw a lock of black hair which looked just like her own.

She eased in between the bells, spreading the walker's legs until she could pick up the lock. It was her hair, surely. No one in these parts had hair like hers. Coming up again, she happened to glance into the bell and was so struck by the deformed reflections in its mirrored surface that she rose inside to see. Everywhere she looked she saw herself, and every movement twisted and changed her. She went still but the reflections continued to shift, warp and change. Get away quick, she thought, but something pulled her back.

She was looking at a dark-haired man holding a little black-haired baby, which was crying. The amplimet flared and the images dissolved as if she were looking into a soothsayer's crystal ball. A different man turned to her. He wore a half-mask of burnished metal but she knew it was Jal-Nish. The look in his eye made her stomach recoil.

She thrust the amplimet at the reflection. He looked

surprised, then vanished as the light echoed back and forth. It took ages before she made out anything else. The reflections moved like ripples on a pond, slowly clearing to silver. She closed her fist around the amplimet again but the surface stayed bright, as if the light was swirling within the glass.

She made out a tower, twisted like barley sugar, in a frozen landscape of black rocks hung with ice of the same colour. In the distance, the sea was covered with jumbled ice floes and crevasses. The scene dissolved, a new image formed and she was standing at a woman's shoulder as she walked down an endless stair. And someone was behind her but Tiaan was afraid to look back.

Down, down she went, with measured tread, never looking around. The woman came to the bottom, reaching out with old hands for a greatly corroded iron ring on an ancient door that had once been blackened by fire and never cleaned.

Tiaan swallowed. Her hand on the walker's controller was slippery with sweat. What was behind the door?

'No!' someone roared.

A hand went over her hand. The walker dropped and lurched sideways, cracking her head on the rim of the bell. It rang and the vision, or *seeing*, vanished. The walker clattered out from beneath the carillon.

'What do you think you're doing?' Gilhaelith shouted, dragging her away from the bells. The walker's rubber feet skittered on the floor.

It was like being snatched from a dream. 'I –' she said. 'I – I saw a lock of my hair on the floor – and then I looked up. Were you scrying out my life?'

'Of course, as I do everyone who comes within my realm. What did you see?'

'A man with a baby. It might have been my father.' She hoped so. She so longed for him. 'Then Jal-Nish the perquisitor, wearing a metal mask. And lastly, a woman walking down the steps of a bleak tower.'

'The Tower of a Thousand Steps. You are lucky, Tiaan. There are many powers in this world and few as benign as I. They do not like being spied upon. Had I not come back, you would now be wishing you were dead. What were you doing here?'

'I heard the bells. They seemed to be calling to me.'

He started. 'Calling? What then?'

'I was looking at your glass sphere but the amplimet went out and a spot on the globe sent a ray right up to the ceiling.'

'What spot?'

'The Island of Noom,' she whispered.

Uncharacteristically, he shivered. 'Rhymes with *doom*, Tiaan, and for good reason. You are not a true geomancer yet; I fear what you have just told the world about yourself.'

She followed him across the room. 'Where are we going?'

'*You* are going back to bed.'

'And you?'

'I wanted to talk to you, which is why I went to your room, but discovered you gone. However, that must wait. You've left me with much to do tonight. I hope I can cover your tracks.'

'What did you want to talk about?'

'There's no time to discuss it now.'

'Did you discover anything about me, from your scrying?'

'I did, though I don't know what it means. No time for that either.' He saw her into her bed and hurried away.

While she'd been downstairs the weather had changed. Gusts of cold wind had replaced the warm breeze, and the moon was obscured by churning black clouds. Thunder echoed back and forth across the crater, like drumrolls. Hail rattled on the roof, followed by a brief patter of heavy drops.

Tiaan still could not sleep. She pushed herself up in bed, expecting a ferocious thunderstorm like those she had been used to at the manufactory. Lightning lit up the boiling clouds and gave her a show for hours, but there was no more rain. She was sorry about that. It had not rained here since she'd arrived.

The following morning was cool with a heavy overcast hanging low over the mountain, at times descending to the rim and becoming a gentle fog.

'Can I go outside today?' she said to Gilhaelith as they took

448

breakfast together in her room. Tiaan tried not to look at the slugs foaming on his platter. 'I feel so confined.'

'I suppose so. There's little chance of anyone seeing you in this weather, but put on your hat and scarf just in case.'

He helped Tiaan into her walker and they set out along the rim of the crater. Tiaan had to be careful of her footing on the rock-littered ground. Several times, when changing direction too quickly, she went close to tipping the walker over.

She was wrestling with her own dilemma. Dare she take the risk of sticking with Gilhaelith, who might betray her, or should she betray him first and flee in the thapter? If she *had* alerted something to her existence last night, it was now urgent.

'You're very quiet, Tiaan.'

She felt guilty. 'Just thinking.'

'What about?'

'What I did last night.'

'Let's not talk about that now.'

'This weather reminds me of home,' she said with a little sigh. 'It's always raining or foggy at the manufactory. My clothes used to go mouldy in their chest. I never thought I'd miss the place.'

'Home gets into our bones,' said Gilhaelith. 'Nyriandiol has been mine for most of my adult life, but I still feel nostalgic for my homeland.'

'Where was that?' she asked.

'Oh, over on Meldorin Island.' He waved a hand towards the west.

'The name makes it seem like a little place,' she said, trying to envision a map of that part of the world. For once, it would not come. 'It's not though, is it?'

'Meldorin is enormous. A good three hundred leagues from south to north, and a hundred west to east.'

'Whereabouts did you live?'

'Oh, you know!' He waved his long hand again, then fell silent.

A third of the way around the circuit of the crater, Tiaan stopped the walker.

'Something the matter?' Gilhaelith enquired.

'The crutch strap is chafing. I'm not used to such rough ground.'

'Do you want to go back?'

'No. It's lovely out here.'

They picked their way across the stony rim. Billows of mist drifted around them. Tiaan could feel droplets condensing on her eyelashes. The scarf over her face was dripping.

'Gilhaelith?' she said.

'Yes?'

'What did you want to talk to me about?'

He leaned on an elbow-high boulder, staring into the invisible crater. He seemed reluctant to speak.

'Gilhaelith?'

'This is a great gamble, Tiaan. A prodigious gamble, so don't get your hopes up.' Another extended pause. 'I've come across something about broken backs. There is –' His head whipped around. 'What was that? Did you hear it?'

'It sounded like a sheet flapping in the wind.'

'But there's just the gentlest of breezes.'

The mist broke and re-formed. He ran to the outside edge, peering down toward the forest.

'Can you see anything?' she called.

'No. Sometimes you hear funny noises up here,' he said doubtfully. 'I think we should head home, Tiaan.'

She adjusted the chafing strap, rotated the walker and they set off. 'What about my back?'

He was slow to reply. Before they had gone twenty steps she heard that crack again. Gilhaelith went still, his head cocked to one side.

'I think I know what it is.' One hand slid inside his coat.

'What, Gilhaelith?' She turned the walker one way and then the other, but could not see anything.

Before he could answer, a winged shape appeared in the fog right behind him. Another thumped into the ground between him and her, and then two more, one on either side.

Gilhaelith whipped out a stubby rod but the rear lyrinx dropped a rope over his head and jerked it tight around

Gilhaelith's chest. The one to the left struck the rod from his hand.

'What are you doing?' she cried.

They did not answer. Other ropes bound his arms to his chest. He tried to say something, perhaps a geomantic word of power, for a rock exploded into fragments, gashing one of the lyrinx's calves. It ignored the minor wound.

Tiaan hurled the walker forward, recklessly attacking the nearest lyrinx with her fist. It pulled back its arm to deliver a blow that would have torn her head from her shoulders. She skittered sideways, careering towards the second lyrinx.

Gilhaelith shouted something she did not catch. Before he could utter another word, the first lyrinx pulled a hood tight over Gilhaelith's face. She caught a whiff of tar.

Tiaan threw herself at the nearest enemy, who simply put his great clawed hand across her face and pushed. The walker went backwards and toppled. As she crashed down the slope, the last thing Tiaan saw was the four lyrinx lifting off, in perfect formation, carrying Gilhaelith between them.

'Tia –' he yelled.

All further sounds were drowned out by the rush of shattered rock down the slope.

FORTY-FOUR

The scrutator had set up camp in a cave below the steep top of the twin pinnacles at Minnien. Irisis and her team had been working for days, mapping the wisps of field as it strengthened and trying to work out what had happened to it. At the same time, they built a device to read the aura of the node, and hopefully its history. It was a contraption of gold and silver leaf, platinum wire and crystals of various kinds. Jewel-like in its delicacy, it vaguely resembled a dragonfly. It could have had a variety of forms but Irisis had taken her frustrations out by making it as extravagant, and as beautiful, as she could with the materials she had. The work was painstaking, and blindness made it more so, but she would make no concessions to her disability.

They had not seen the lyrinx again, though Irisis felt sure that its visit had something to do with the reappearance of the field, which was clearer and stronger each day.

'It's nearly strong enough to drive a clanker,' she said to Flydd on the fourth morning.

He sat up nakedly in his sleeping pouch. 'Our first piece of luck.' He scratched his scarred, hairless chest. 'How is your aura reader going?'

'Almost finished. The thing that puzzles me, Xervish, is why the Council did not do this a long time ago.'

'Too blinkered,' he said. 'We scrutators think of mancing as the very pinnacle of the Secret Art, and no doubt it is, in terms of sheer power. But it is not a subtle Art, the way we use it, and we do not have the artisan's ability to see the field. We draw on it intuitively; almost blindly. So, when our Art failed to penetrate the node, we did not consider that lesser abilities might succeed.'

'It remains to be seen whether our *minor* talents can.'

'Your humility is admirable,' he said with a twitch of the lips.

'I was taught by a master.'

She began to work another crystal into the dragonfly. Irisis did not need to see for this. As a prentice she had often made jewellery in the dormitory after the lamps had been snuffed out. That craft was her greatest pleasure, though she had little enough time to practise it.

'What are we looking for, precisely?' she asked. 'Or is that another of your scrutator's secrets that can be revealed to none?'

'Several things.' He laid a twisted finger on her bare upper arm. 'Firstly, using my raw power and your subtle device, we will attempt to induce an aura from the node itself. That could reveal its recent history, though auras can be hard to read and even harder to interpret. Tiaan did this with a failed controller crystal, once. But of course, Tiaan . . .' He sighed heavily.

Irisis was heartily sick of Tiaan's marvels. 'Might that not be dangerous?' she said irritably.

'Very. It will take much power and the only place I can get it is from the node, which runs the risk of power feeding back on itself. Such things can get out of control very quickly. Just to induce an aura in something so powerful as a node will be hard. There will be barriers to overcome.'

'And other forces?'

'I was coming to that. The field surrounding a node comes from the weak force that Nunar first described a century ago. But we believe, and it is written in Nunar's *The Mancer's Art*, that stronger forces may also exist. We do not know how to see or draw upon them, though some mancers have accidentally done so. Sadly, none lived to write down what they had discovered.'

'And if you accidentally hit upon one of these forces . . .'

'I will cease to exist even more gorily than that unfortunate mancer up on the aqueduct. And you too, if you're standing too close.' He chuckled.

'Don't get your hopes up,' Irisis snapped. 'I've gone off you, scrutator, since you took my sight away.'

'I warned you, but you were too much of a stickybeak. You had to look back.'

'I was trying to help you!'

'More fool you,' Flydd said cheerfully.

'Oh, go away. I never want to see you again.' Then, realising what she had said, she began to laugh. It was that or burst into tears. He laughed with her.

Irisis worked the last of the crystals into place and checked the device with her fingers. It felt just like a dragonfly now, but with only a single pair of wings.

'I love watching you work.' His voice was rich with good humour. 'You have such beautiful hands. And they move so cleverly.'

She held them up before her blind eyes. 'You just want more of what I did with them the other night.'

'I confess it. After my torment thirty years ago, I never thought I would feel that kind of pleasure again.'

She looked surprised. 'You fasted for thirty years? Surely even an ugly old coot like you must have his pick of lovers. You are scrutator after all, and a lot of women find power rather . . . lubricious.'

'And you're one of them.'

'So it would seem.'

'Until you, I lacked the courage to bare myself.'

'Really? Does the great scrutator confess to a weakness.'

'Ex-scrutator, remember, and you are risking your life by being associated with me.'

'I imagine the price on my head is almost the equal of your own.'

'It isn't, but you will die a most miserable death when they catch you.'

'*When?*' A chill settled over her. She had never heard him talk like that before.

'The scrutators can't afford to be humiliated. They will hunt us down and bring us to justice if it takes the rest of our lives. They never give up.'

'Oh well,' she said casually, 'nothing we can do. Better get on with it. This is ready.'

'I'll call the others.'

She heard him moving away. Irisis began to take deep breaths, calming herself and getting into the right state for sensing. This would be harder than anything she had done before, and she could not afford a mistake. Flydd's life depended on it. She clung to the hope that he could somehow save them, in spite of what he had said. But if he died, they were all doomed.

The party came crunching up the hill, chattering. Flydd gave them their orders. 'Zoyl, I want you to stand here. Oon-Mie, over there. Irisis, stay where you are but get into a comfortable position. This could take a while.'

They moved to their places. 'Shall we begin?' said the scrutator. Despite his demotion, Irisis could not think of Flydd as anything else.

'I'm ready.' Irisis held the reader out.

'I'll take that.' He plucked it from her hands.

'What do you think you're doing?' She felt around in the air for it.

'You know what I'm doing,' he said, '*and* why.' He crunched up to the back wall of the cavern. 'Your turn will come.'

'What am *I* supposed to do?'

'Just keep a close eye on things. *In case.*'

He tossed the dragonfly into the air. It rotated and when it came down again, Zoyl cried out, 'The eyes are glowing.'

'Pipe down, boy,' snapped Flydd. 'You're not at the circus now. Irisis, find the field.'

Taking her pliance between her palms, she visualised. Sight was not required for that. 'I can see it.'

'Tell me what it looks like.'

'The individual wisps are moving faster than before, and

455

there are more of them. They form an almost complete figure-eight now, like two crowns joined at the side.'

'Better, but a long way to go. Keep hold of that image. Oon-Mie?'

'Ready, willing and able, surr,' she said and Irisis could almost see the grin.

There was no humour in Flydd's voice now. 'You will control the flow of power, *very carefully*. If it starts to feed back on itself, it will quickly get out of control and there won't be anything I can do about it. Just trickle it to me. If it starts to flood, clamp down hard.'

'I understand, surr.'

'Aarp, you have the most difficult task of all. I hope you're up to it.'

The lad's chest swelled with pride. 'I won't let you down, Mister Scrutator.'

'See that you don't, or I'll feed you to that lyrinx. Balls first!'

Flydd moved around the cavern and, as he went past Irisis, put his lips to her ear. 'Keep an eye on the boy!'

'I would, if you hadn't destroyed them.'

'You know what I mean,' Flydd growled.

'You haven't told me what to do, surr,' piped Zoyl Aarp. Though a big lad, his voice had not yet broken.

'Haven't I? With this reader I will force power back into the node. That will, I hope, create a faint aura. You are to focus on that, for it is the key to the problem of all failed nodes. Begin!'

Irisis heard the faint tinkle of gold and silver foil. The field brightened, though it was not growing stronger. She was just seeing it more clearly.

'Trickle power to me, Oon-Mie.'

Such a simple skill, and vital for an artisan, yet Irisis could not do it. She envied Oon-Mie; perhaps hated her for it at that instant; then the power began to flow and the feeling was gone.

'I can't see anything,' sang out Zoyl. 'Are you sure –?'

'Shut up, boy!' snapped the scrutator. 'We haven't started yet. I'll tell you –'

Zoyl whimpered. Irisis cleared her throat and Flydd broke off. The boy being highly strung, a little criticism went a long way.

'A trace more, Oon-Mie.'

So it went on, the scrutator calling for more power, working his unspecified magic, Zoyl Aarp looking, 'Still no aura,' then trying harder next time.

'I can't do much more,' said Oon-Mie after half an hour. Her voice was tight, strained. 'It's getting harder to control the flow.'

'Another step, Oon-Mie,' said Flydd. 'We're not getting anything at all.'

'Maybe there's nothing to get,' Irisis mumbled. 'Or maybe it will take more power than the node has in it. What will happen then?'

'Don't tell me my job! I'm not a complete idiot.'

Oon-Mie gave the scrutator another increment of power. 'Anything?' she gasped.

'Not a thing. Zoyl?'

'Nothing, surr.'

'I can't increase it,' said Oon-Mie. 'With the very greatest respect, I'm at my limit, surr.'

'Again!' roared the scrutator. 'Remember we're all under a death sentence.'

Zoyl choked.

'What do you mean?' cried Oon-Mie.

'The scrutator is saying,' Irisis said hastily, 'that Jal-Nish is hunting us. If we do this right, he can't touch us. But if we fail, we will all fall with Scrutator Flydd.' She put one hand on the lad's shoulder.

'Let's make sure we don't fail!' said Flydd. 'Can I rely on you or not, Zoyl?'

'Yes, surr.' There was a quaver in the lad's voice.

'Dare you try one last time, Oon-Mie?' said Flydd. 'I should point out that *I* am the one at most risk.'

'I will try, surr,' she said faintly.

Irisis did not like it. Oon-Mie was her most reliable artisan because she knew her limits and never went beyond them.

'Keep it flowing till I tell you to stop,' said Flydd.

That made Irisis even more uneasy. It was a dangerous escalation of unpredictability.

The power flowed, increased and kept flowing.

'Anything, Aarp?' panted the scrutator.

'No – I mean, there was the very faintest aura but it disappeared right away.'

'Keep it going, Oon-Mie.'

Oon-Mie said nothing but Irisis could feel her tension distorting the field. She did not like what she felt.

'More!' cried the scrutator. 'More, Oon-Mie, damn it!'

The power went up again. Now there was a definite tremor in it. Drops of sweat ran down Irisis's forehead. 'Surr,' she hissed, 'that's enough.'

'Keep it coming!'

Irisis's foreboding grew. The tremor became a shuddering vibration that would have torn a clanker apart.

Zoyl moaned. 'My head hurts. Stop it. Stop it!'

Irisis reached out to him. 'It's all right, Zoyl. The scrutator will look after us.'

Without warning that vibration swelled to gigantic proportions. Oon-Mie tried to clamp down but it was out of control, feeding back on itself and growing catastrophically stronger.

Oon-Mie gave a gurgling, clotted gasp. Zoyl Aarp fell down, wailing. The glow grew so bright that Irisis could feel it on her skin.

The scrutator was just to her left; she could see the distortion in the field. His breath crackled in his sinuses. Irisis caught a whiff of burning hair. 'Flydd?' He did not answer, nor could he. Power coiled around him like a serpent. *Into* him. If she did not do something, they were all going to die.

She thrashed around with her arms and one hand touched the reader, which was burning-hot. Wrenching it from his grasp, she slammed it against the wall of the cave, breaking the metal back of the dragonfly. Delicate silver wires tore. A crystal tinkled to the rocky floor.

The flow stopped at once, the glow faded and all she could hear was Zoyl's stifled moans.

'Oon-Mie?' she called.

'I'm all right,' the artisan rasped, coughing up gobs of phlegm the size of oysters.

'Scrutator?'

His tongue made a series of clicks as if he was having trouble moving it. 'I'll live,' he said thickly.

'Zoyl? *Zoyl!*'

Irisis crawled across to where the lad had been sitting. He lay on his side, knees drawn up.

'Looks like he's had a seizure,' said Oon-Mie.

'Just what we need,' muttered the scrutator, restored to waspish ill-humour.

'Well, *you* caused it,' Irisis flashed.

'We fail, we *die,*' said the scrutator savagely. 'We succeed, we *may* live. Those are the most selfish terms I can put it in. Good enough for you?'

'But you ordered him to risk his life; and Oon-Mie hers.'

'So? Boys his age risk their lives every day in the army.'

'But Zoyl is not in the army.'

'Only because he's got a skill we need. If we fail, everyone will be fighting for their lives, including people like you and Oon-Mie. And me!'

'He's recovering,' said Oon-Mie.

'About time! Sit up, boy, and tell us what you saw.'

'An aura, surr,' Zoyl croaked. 'It was not there long but I saw it clearly.'

'What did you see?'

'The field. And something else. Two planes lay at the centre, one passing through the other at right-angles.'

'Planes?'

'Yes, and they had wiggles all across them.'

'*Is that so?*' breathed the scrutator. 'What about the core of the aura?'

'It was strange, surr. Just for an instant I saw the shadow of a lyrinx, etched in lightning, and behind it the field seemed to flow into a pit. As though it was being sucked into a whirlpool.'

'The *field?*' cried the scrutator.

'Yes,' said Zoyl.

'Someone's coming,' called a guard.

'What is it?' asked Flydd.

'A lyrinx. No, more than one. Two, three. They're heading directly towards us.'

The scrutator cursed. 'To be expected, after the power we've used here. How long till dark?'

'The best part of an hour,' said the guard.

'We can't signal the air-floater till then. Can we defend this place?'

'Not against three, unless you've the power to do it by yourself.'

'At the moment I'd have trouble fighting off a butterfly,' said Flydd. 'We'll head for the top of this peak. They'll have to come at us from below.'

'Unless they've a flier among them,' said Irisis.

'It's the best we can do.'

They headed up, Irisis led by the hand by Oon-Mie.

'That was brave work,' Irisis said to the artisan.

'I thought my brains were going to boil out my ears.'

'But you held your nerve, and that's what made the difference.'

'Had it not been for you –'

'Let's not talk about that. What are the enemy doing?'

Oon-Mie stopped to look. 'Still heading for our cave.'

'Are you sure our work led them to us, scrutator?' Irisis called.

His voice came from just behind her. 'I am.'

'How could they do that?'

'They once had a way of detecting clankers by the aura from the controller. Tiaan fixed that, brilliantly.'

'Bloody Tiaan again,' muttered Irisis.

'But of course you would know that, Irisis,' Flydd said in frosty tones. 'After her crystal madness, you tried to take the credit for it.'

Irisis felt a flush creeping up her cheeks. What fit of stupidity had led her to do that?

Flydd went on. 'I'd say they have a watching device here somewhere, waiting in case we came to investigate.'

It was a considerable climb to the top of the pinnacle and the sun had gone down before they reached it. Irisis was hauled up the last few spans on a rope, dragging roughly across a gritty rock face before being stood on her feet on a mounded surface. A dank wind blew down the back of her neck.

'Don't move,' said Flydd. 'We're standing on top of the pinnacle, a stack of rock whose tip is not much bigger than a bedsheet. Take three steps in any direction and you're over the edge. Zoyl, what the blazes do you think you're doing? Put that rock down.'

Thud.

'Not on my foot, you bloody fool!'

'I was just trying to help, surr.'

'Leave it to those who know how.'

Irisis could *feel* the edge of the drop. Her teeth began to chatter.

One of the soldiers lit a signal lantern. The scrutator held it high, facing across the valley towards the range. He gave a series of flashes, shuttered it completely, then opened it and gave the same sequence again. Irisis could hear the click of the shutter.

'No reply,' he said after a long wait. 'What are the enemy doing?'

'Coming after us,' said Oon-Mie. 'They're nearly within crossbow range.'

'Get your weapons out.'

Swords scraped on scabbards. Someone wound the crank of a crossbow. She felt useless, especially when the enemy were so close that she could hear their claws scraping on the rock. If only she could see. With a crossbow in her hands she'd make them jump.

A crossbow twanged. 'Missed!' the soldier cursed.

'How near do you need to be?' the scrutator said derisively. 'Any closer and you could have picked his nose with it.'

'The light's deceptive, surr.'

'Then hold off until you can see up their nostrils.'

'I don't *ever* want to see up a lyrinx's nostrils,' said Irisis. 'Are any of them fliers, Xervish?'

461

'Doesn't look like it, but once it's fully dark they'll come up the sides without us ever seeing them. And then, my friends, it's dinnertime.' He chuckled grimly.

No one else joined in.

'Look out!' Oon-Mie cried. 'They're throwing rocks!'

Someone pulled Irisis down. There was another thud, a man's cry of pain, then someone went off the side. Irisis heard every pulpy impact until he finally came to rest a long way below.

'Who . . .?' she said fearfully.

'Jarle,' said Flydd. 'A good man. Don't look, Zoyl.'

The sound of rending and feeding began. Bones crunched; gobbets of flesh were swallowed noisily. 'Poor devil,' said Oon-Mie.

'At least he was dead first,' said Flydd heavily. 'Stay down. They'll try again.'

FORTY-FIVE

It was nearly dark now. The lyrinx must charge soon. The soldiers were still shooting but did not seem to be doing any damage. The enemy's claws rasped on the stone, just a few spans below. Oon-Mie was dropping rocks on them. 'Take that, and that!' They weren't big enough to do a lot of damage but Irisis caught one or two cries of pain.

'Can't you do anything, Flydd?' she said. 'What's happened to your famous scrutator magic?'

'I spent it earlier.' He sounded worn out.

'For nothing.'

'Nothing comes for nothing and scrutator magic has painful after-effects, though we don't talk about such things.'

'Why not? To maintain the myth of invulnerability for us peasants?'

'If you like. What's that?'

Irisis could hear it too; the whirr of a rotor. She felt a rush of wind as the air-floater appeared above them.

'Get moving,' yelled Flydd. 'They're charging.'

They scrambled up the ladder, Irisis with a rope around her chest. The machine ticked away rather more quickly than when it had brought them here, such was the strength of the field now.

'That taught us something,' said Flydd, sitting with Irisis down the far end of the cabin in the dark.

'That we should never have been born!' It was just one of her remarks. There was no bitterness behind it. Irisis felt better than she had in ages, though she could not have said why. 'What do you make of what Zoyl saw?'

'I reckon the lyrinx have found a way of draining the node.'

'How?'

'I don't know. We know so little about how they think and work. Some of them are mancers as powerful as any of us scrutators, though they use power differently.'

'They use the field though?'

'Indeed, but not through crystals, controllers or any of the devices we employ.'

'What about those mushroom-shaped spying devices I heard of?'

'Ah, those. We've captured several in the past few years, but we haven't learned how they work.'

'Why not?'

'They're grown, or flesh-formed, for a particular purpose, such as keeping watch. But once we take them they die – if they're actually alive – like a flower plucked from the garden.'

'And you think they've tailored such a device to drain the field out of a node?'

'It's beginning to look that way. It may be that our clankers overloaded this node and drained it, then the lyrinx flesh-formed a device to do the same. It doesn't really matter. What matters is that they can do it.'

'It can't be that easy or they'd be doing it everywhere. How many nodes have gone dead? Four in a year?'

'Five if you count the one at the manufactory, though it hasn't completely failed yet.'

'What I don't understand,' said Irisis, 'is how the air-floater carried us to the node when it was practically dead.'

'Air-floaters are built as light as possible, so it takes little power to turn the rotor. A clanker needs a thousand times as much. And as I said before, we were using a different field.'

'Where are we going now?'

'Further up the coast, to look at another failed node.'

'How far is it?'

'We'll be there before dawn.'

'Good!' She snuggled down against the seat, then sat up again. 'Scrutator?'

'I told you before, I don't like you calling me that in private.'

'I like calling you that in private,' she said, grinning wickedly. 'It makes me feel, well, you know . . .' she leered at him.

'I don't want to know, since there's nothing I can do about it. What did you want, anyway?'

'How come you've still got this air-floater, if you're an outlaw?'

He did not answer.

'Xervish?'

'I still have a few friends where it counts. They do what they can for me.'

'Who?'

'It would not be healthy for you to know.'

Irisis woke in the night, realising that the air-floater was not moving. She was alone, though two people were talking quietly outside the cabin. She began to repair the broken dragonfly reader. Before long, the machine began to move. Irisis finished the job and went back to sleep, to be woken by someone shaking her arm.

'We're here, crafter.' It was Oon-Mie's voice.

'Where's here?'

'I don't think it has a name. The failed node lies inland from a town called Fadd.'

The artisan led her over the side onto rock. It was raining. The air-floater pulled away, its rotor spattering cool drops at them.

'This node is associated with an escarpment that runs inland from the coast,' came Flydd's voice. 'It's quite high here; on a clear day you can see the ocean. At least, you could if you could see.'

Irisis, used to his provocations by now, did not react.

This node proved to be completely dead. There was not a

465

wisp of the field associated with it, nor could they induce any aura, even by a more refined version of the process they had used previously. There was no power to draw upon.

'The node-drainer must still be in place,' said Flydd.

'Are we going to look for it?' asked Oon-Mie.

'It could be anywhere along this escarpment, which runs for a good thirty leagues. We might search for years and not find it.'

'So we haven't learned anything here?' said Irisis.

'Unfortunately not.'

'What were you doing in the night, Xervish? When the air-floater stopped.'

'I had to send a skeet to one of my associates, telling them what we'd discovered. The price of continued support.'

'I hope you didn't tell them where we were, or where we were going.'

'I have to trust someone.'

'Let's hope they're worthy of it.'

The party searched along the nearby part of the escarpment, to fill in the time until dark, when they could signal the air-floater. Irisis was waiting, perched on a rock with her hood over her head to keep off the drifting rain, when something occurred to her.

'Scrutator?' she yelled. 'Anyone know where the scrutator is?'

'He went for a walk in the forest,' said one of the soldiers. 'Probably crapping behind a tree.'

'I was trying to work out the lie of the node, as it happens,' Flydd said with lofty dignity. He had come up on them from behind. 'What is it, Irisis?'

'If there *is* a node-drainer,' she said, 'where is it draining all that power to? And what happens where it comes out – so much power in a small place must have some effect.'

Dead silence. Flydd took her by the arm, shaking her in his excitement. 'That's brilliant!' he cried. 'It has to be going some-where, and that must leave a trace. More than a trace – strange things would happen where all that power was dumped. Such a place can't be hard to find.'

'How would you go about finding it?'

'I'd ask people who live in the area. The local querist or perquisitor, first; it's their job to hear about strange and inexplicable things. If we fly along the edge of the escarpment, we might see something, though I wouldn't want to spend too long doing it. As soon as it's dark I'll signal the air-floater. We'll have a look on the way back, since we're going that direction.'

His words made her uneasy. 'The way back? Where are we going now?'

'Back to the manufactory. To look at its node.'

'The *manufactory*? Are you out of your mind?'

'Shh! Don't alarm the others. There's no choice, Irisis. Only concrete evidence can save me. I have to see a failing node to really understand what's going on. Dead ones are no good at all.'

'After Jal-Nish catches us, *we'll* be the dead ones.'

The problem with the scrutator, as Irisis well knew, was that once he had made his mind up, nothing could shake him. She did not try. Irisis was too afraid. A senile old fool and a blind woman – what a formidable team! Jal-Nish must be quaking in his bed.

They saw no sign of a power seep on the way back, though as the scrutator had said, such a thing need not occur above the ground. It could lie anywhere in the three dimensions.

He roused her in the night. Irisis was lying awake, biting the ends of her fingers. 'We'd better talk about how we're going to do this,' he said.

'You talk! I don't have any ideas and I'm so scared I can't think of anything but which horrible way I'm going to die.'

'There is a way.'

'Good. You can do it. I'm taking my toys and going home.'

He laughed.

'I mean it, scrutator. Everyone has their breaking point and I've reached mine. I can't do this. I'm *blind*, in case you hadn't noticed.'

'We have to. The war depends on it.'

'Would you like to know something?'

'What?'

'I don't give a *slussk* about the war. I've had enough. If we are all to be eaten by the lyrinx, so be it. I don't see that they're any worse than you scrutators and the world you've created, with its breeding factories and Examinations, and its rules for every damned thing. This isn't life, it's misery and I just want it to end. I don't care any more, scrutator!'

He went away and she did not see him for another hour. 'We're not going to the manufactory,' he said. 'At least, not straight away.'

'You've seen some sense, then.'

'No, you've convinced me that I can't rely on you any more and I've got to find another way.'

He went out again. Irisis could not speak, for his words had carved right through her fit of self-pity. She'd let him down. It was the worst thing anyone had ever said to her.

She felt her way through the cabin and out to the open deck, along the rope rails. The rotor was whirring gently. She went up to the stern and his hand – she recognised it by feel – caught her arm.

'If you keep going you'll be over the side,' he said gruffly, 'and what use will that be to me, eh?'

'I'm sorry.' She felt her way to his chest and pressed herself against him. His arms went around her. 'I'm just not as strong as you, Xervish.'

'I'm not as strong as you think.'

'How are we going to do this?'

'Well, I wasn't planning to land at the front gate and ask Jal-Nish to let me in. What ideas do *you* have?'

She pondered for a while. 'What about the old entrance, through the other mine?'

'I believe that's been blocked up.'

She turned her face into the breeze from the rotor. Yellow hair streamed out behind her. 'There are higher entrances, but all would be guarded, and we would still have to go down by the lifts.'

'The guards probably aren't as vigilant as the ones on the main adit.'

'And it would be easier to use some form of deception underground,' she supposed.

'I'll give the order.' He went up toward the pilot.

She did not feel any better. Maybe that was all the planning the scrutator required but Irisis liked everything organised to the tiniest detail, with a variety of contingency plans for when things went wrong. That was how she had survived so long.

The air-floater dropped the two of them on the top of the range, over the hill out of sight of the manufactory and the main adit, just before dawn. It was just the two of them, Irisis and Flydd. They dared take no others into the cramped tunnels.

They hid in an abandoned tunnel all day, and as darkness fell made their way down the hill toward the higher entrance, which was blocked off by a barred gate. The clankers had gone through the mountain that way, in their pursuit of Tiaan last autumn. They eluded the solitary guard and got inside without difficulty, through some magic of Flydd's that he did not explain. These tunnels had been worked out more than a century ago but a decline still led down to the lower mine. They reached the first level without incident. Now their troubles would start; the only way to the lower levels was via the rope lift, which would be guarded.

'You'd think they'd clean up this mess,' Flydd said, after Irisis had stumbled over a tattered length of lift rope, followed by a wooden barrow with a broken wheel. Inside it lay several ragged, greasy miner's aprons.

'Miners don't care about mess.'

'Stop!' he hissed. 'The lift is just around the corner.' He crept forward, then returned to her side. 'The guards are on alert.'

'Well, you're a mancer aren't you?'

'I can't knock them out, else Jal-Nish will soon know we're down there. Our work is going to take hours.'

'Can't you do illusions?'

'It's not a branch of the Art I've ever been much good at.'

'Great!' she said. 'Well, what about a diversion?'

'What did you have in mind?'

'The soldiers would be afraid of fire, down here.'

'So am I.'

'A *small* fire. Lots of smoke.'

'The miners will come rushing up. We won't be able to get down in the lift.'

'I don't think the mine's working at the moment,' she said. 'I can't hear anything.'

'All right. I know just the thing. Come this way.' He set fire to the greasy aprons with his lantern, then piled the rope into the barrow, holding up the strands until they caught.

'I'm worried this will seem suspicious,' said Irisis.

'Oily cloth can catch fire by itself.'

They approached the lift from another direction and waited. Oily smoke began to drift down the tunnel. The leading guard caught a whiff, screamed 'Fire!' and ran for the entrance. Two others followed.

'I think that's all of them,' said Flydd after an interval.

'Seems a bit too easy to me.'

'It probably is. Let's be as quick as we can.'

He wound them down to the ninth level. The crank sounded unusually noisy.

'Do you know the way to the crystal field?'

'I've never been there,' said Flydd. 'I was relying on you.'

'You blinded me, remember?'

'It's your eyes that have gone, not your brain. Just tell me the sequence of turns.'

That was harder than it sounded. Irisis was not used to working that way and when she tried to recall the path it vanished from her mind. She panicked and he had to calm her before they could continue. Precious minutes were lost.

She did not like it down here. Being blind in the tunnels was somehow worse than being lost in the dark. But they eventually found the shaft that the miners had sunk down to the massive crystal. The pumps were working sluggishly, powered by the diminished field. *Thud-thud-THUD; THUD-thud-THUD.*

'Look at *that*!' The scrutator whistled.

'Don't!' she said irritably. 'You've got to *tell* me things.'

'The crystal is gigantic – a perfect prism of quartz as tall as you are.'

'Doesn't necessarily mean it's any good,' she said peevishly. 'Most crystals are useless.'

'This one's different. Even *I* can tell that. Let's get to work. Find the field, quickly.'

With her pliance, Irisis saw it at once. 'It's weak.' It was fluttery and hard to monitor. She was trying to get a good image of it, which proved unexpectedly difficult, when she had the strange sense of being watched from afar. How could that be, through solid rock? She rested her head on the stone, struggling to work out what was going on.

'What's that?' she hissed, facing the other way.

'What?'

'I thought I heard something.'

'I didn't hear anything.'

She paced, trying to extract sense from what her ears were telling her. No, it hadn't been a sound, rather the absence of one. 'The pumps have stopped working.'

'Water's flooding into the bottom of the pit,' said Flydd. 'Check the field.'

She tried. 'There *is* no field now, Xervish.'

'There's got to be something, *this* close to the crystal, if it is actually the node.'

'There's not a trace.'

'It was there a minute ago.'

'Well, it's not there now –' *Thud-thud-THUD.* The pumps were working again. 'I don't understand. How can it be there one minute and gone the next? And . . . it felt as if someone was watching, but from a long way away.'

'Maybe the enemy *is* watching. Maybe they sensed you and turned up their node-drainer.'

'Is there any way to find it?'

'They'd hide it somewhere inconspicuous. It doesn't have to be close to the node, of course, though the closer the better.'

The pumps stopped and a whistling sound arose from low in the pit – threads of water forced through the joins of the metal sleeve. The sound became shrill, then *ping, ping, ping.*

'What's that?' she whispered.

471

'The bolts shearing,' said Flydd. 'The whole thing is failing.'

They tried to induce an aura with the reader but the node was now so dead that they could not draw the required power.

'Now what?' said Irisis.

'We can't do it when there's no field at all. We'll have to wait. If it comes back, even for a minute, we'll try again. Let's scout around and see what we can find in the meantime.'

They went up and down the tunnel, Irisis trying to visualise any kind of power seep, the scrutator searching in his own, mancer's way. Some distance along, the tunnel was blocked by a rockfall. They turned back to the shaft.

'This hasn't been any use either,' said Irisis.

'Oh, I don't know,' replied Jal-Nish, stepping out from behind a pillar. Golden lamplight reflected from the platinum mask. The ragged hole made in the cheekpiece by the crossbow bolt was still there. 'Hard work pays off, if you're patient enough.'

FORTY-SIX

Irisis wanted to die. *Just as well, she thought, since I'm about to do just that.*

Flydd gave a mirthless laugh. 'Good to see you again, *acting scrutator*. You're looking well.'

'I've never felt better,' said Jal-Nish. 'Why have you come back?'

'To make certain of why the nodes are failing.'

Jal-Nish's single eye narrowed. 'And why are they?'

Don't tell him! Irisis prayed. *It's your only bargaining chip.*

'Because the enemy is draining the field from them.'

Jal-Nish's laugh raised hairs on the back of her neck. 'I believe we've already disproved *that* one, Xervish! It's too late; I've had you dismissed. You're not scrutator any more, you're not even a citizen. You're *nothing*! No one will listen to a thing you say. Don't you find that galling? You're an invisible man, Xervish.'

'Considering what the scrutators did to me when I was young, I have no wish to grow old among them.'

'You could have fooled me.'

'*I did*. It wasn't hard. You're a brilliant man, Jal-Nish, no question about it, but you see only what's on the track straight in front of you.'

Jal-Nish yawned. 'The same old flaccid wit and pointless jibes, Xervish. It's so tiresome.'

There was a long silence, in which Irisis felt sure she could hear something ticking. Could it be the crystal? She tried to sense the field but her pliance showed her nothing.

'But you, Irisis, I am prepared to give another chance. It was only during the previous escape that I understood what a talented woman you are. We need people like you.'

What was he talking about? The way she had used the field against that mancer on the aqueduct?

'Take it, Irisis,' Flydd said in a stage whisper. 'It's your only chance.'

'I know what kind of a man you are, Jal-Nish,' she said. 'Do you think I'd give myself into your hands?'

'You're already in them,' said Jal-Nish. 'I'm not alone. How did you think I found you so quickly?'

'No doubt you're about to tell me,' said Flydd. 'You never miss a chance to demonstrate your own cleverness.'

'And you're any different?' Jal-Nish snarled. 'You don't have a choice, Irisis. You're coming with me anyway. But things will be easier if you come willingly.'

'I don't think I'll bother,' she said as casually as she could, taking her cue from Flydd. 'Thanks all the same.'

Jal-Nish must have been expecting that. He snapped his fingers and she heard marching feet. 'A squad of six soldiers, armed with crossbows,' Flydd said in her ear. 'And Ullii behind them.'

Of course. Ullii could see forms of power in her lattice, and people who had it. Jal-Nish would have ordered her to keep watch for them, and as soon as Xervish, or Irisis, appeared in the lattice Ullii knew where to find them. They had walked into a trap. Why hadn't Flydd realised? Why hadn't she?

'This is a mistake,' said Flydd, and now there was a note of desperation in his voice Irisis had never heard before. She hoped he was putting it on. Surely he had not come down here without a plan of escape. He'd better have, because she could think of nothing. 'Jal-Nish –'

'I must say I'm surprised,' said Jal-Nish. 'The great scrutator allowing himself into a situation where there was no way out. It's not like you, Xervish.'

'Only my friends call me Xervish,' said Flydd, seeming to recover his composure.

'And I was never *your* friend, was I, Flydd? You did your best to thwart me from the moment I became perquisitor.'

'That's part of the test, and those who would be scrutator must pass it on their own. You cannot buy the favour of the Council. I knew you'd rise to your level of incompetence without my assistance.'

Jal-Nish showed no sign of being nettled. 'I expected more of you, Flydd. But then, some rise and stay up; others fail as quickly as a salmon after spawning.'

Flydd said jovially. 'Hello, Ullii.'

The little seeker sounded just as cheerful, oblivious that she had betrayed them. 'Hello, Xervish,' she replied. 'Where have you been?'

'Oh, away,' he said. 'Looking at a couple of nodes that failed. Do you know what a node is?'

'Of course. It is a place in the earth where power comes from, like the one down there. It has all sorts of fields –'

'What do you mean, *all sorts* of fields?' said Jal-Nish.

Ullii scuttled backwards and Irisis could hear her barely suppressed panic. Jal-Nish had terrified her even before he'd come back with the mask, and the horror beneath it.

'Th-this node has four fields,' she said. 'There is the weak one you call *the field*. It is dead now – the clawers drained it all away. But there are three more fields, much more powerful. They are like walls going through each other.'

Jal-Nish gave an inarticulate cry of rage. '*The strong forces!* We've been searching for them for a hundred years. Why did you not tell me?'

Flydd chuckled. Ullii was silent. With Jal-Nish she'd learned that no answer was better than the wrong one. 'Because you didn't ask me,' was definitely the wrong answer.

'Can you see these other fields now?' said Jal-Nish.

'Oh yes! They're very bright.'

'What about you, Irisis? What's the matter with your eyes?'

'Silly cow blinded herself up on the aqueduct,' said Flydd.

Jal-Nish laughed nastily. 'The blind leading the blind. Well, Irisis?'

'I've never seen anything but *the field*.' But then she recalled that strange pattern Zoyl Aarp had seen in the aura of the Minnien node.

'Flydd?' said Jal-Nish.

'I'm tempted to say yes, just to annoy you,' said Flydd. 'I've never seen them either. But if Ullii says –'

'I know the seeker is reliable,' Jal-Nish snapped.

'Ullii,' said Flydd, 'can you see a node-drainer near here?'

Silence.

'Well?' cried Jal-Nish. 'Is there such a thing, seeker?'

'Yes,' she whispered.

'Where is it?' He sounded surprised.

'Up the tunnel, past the rockfall.'

'Guards!' Jal-Nish's voice rang out. 'Bind these two.'

Irisis waited for Flydd to attack but still he did nothing. Irisis held out her hands. Ropes were yanked tight around her wrists.

'Bring them!'

She was led up the tunnel on a rope, Flydd's crab-like shuffle sounding beside her. 'We're at the rockfall,' he said, jerking her arm.

Irisis squatted down. The soldiers moved rubble for what seemed like a long time.

'Nearly done,' said Flydd in her ear.

Part of the roof fell, booming, cracking and shaking the floor beneath their feet. 'None fell on his head,' Flydd said regretfully.

The soldiers moved that rubble, too. An interminable wait, before Flydd went on, 'We're in business.'

'Come on!' shouted Jal-Nish.

'Roof looks a little insecure,' came Flydd's amused voice. 'Wouldn't be in such a hurry if I were you.'

'You're going through first, just in case. Soldiers, keep your weapons ready. The enemy may be near.'

Flydd scrabbled across the rubble but no more rock came down. The soldiers followed. 'Out of the way, you old fool!' Jal-Nish pushed past him.

They continued for another twenty minutes, as near as Irisis could judge, when she heard someone gasp.

'What is *that*?' whispered Jal-Nish. 'Bhan and Mord, go and see.'

Flydd's hand gripped Irisis's wrist so hard that it hurt. She froze. 'What?' she whispered. 'What is it, Xervish?'

'Let's wait for Jal-Nish to tell us,' he said softly.

Irisis felt a strange sensation, unlike anything she had experienced before. She seemed to be vibrating inside. The layers of flesh beneath her skin were shivering back and forth. Irisis put her hand on her arm and could feel movement through her skin. Her guts began to churn.

'The very rock is in motion,' said Jal-Nish in awe. 'It's creeping, and swirling, and bubbling, though it's not hot at all. Oh, this is uncanny. I've never heard of such a thing.'

'Nor the Council, either,' Flydd said. 'The scrutators will want to see what's causing it, Jal-Nish, though you're not man enough to take it back.'

'We'll see!' snapped Jal-Nish.

'What are you doing?' Irisis whispered to Flydd.

'Trying to save my old bag of bones, and yours,' he muttered.

'You have a charming turn of phrase.'

'You four, come with me,' said Jal-Nish to the soldiers. 'You two, keep watch on the prisoners, especially the walking corpse. If he tries anything, hit him over the head.'

'Jal-Nish is advancing,' said Flydd. 'The soldiers are just behind.'

'Can you see the node-drainer?'

'No.'

The vibration under her skin ceased, before beginning again in another direction. She could not get used to the feeling. Sparks flashed through her skull. Her eyes began to burn, her nasal passages to itch. Her intestines writhed in her belly, making an audible gurgle. Her stomach contracted sharply, pushing burning acid up into her throat. Was the unreality of the node-drainer slowly peeling her apart, as it had the rock?

'What's going to happen, Xervish?' Her voice sounded blobby.

'I have no idea,' he said, though she was sure that was a lie. 'Jal-Nish has gone up about thirty paces. It's . . . foggy up there, but the fog looks like granite. I can hardly see him.'

'I can see the node-drainer!' came Jal-Nish's cry. His words returned in shredded echoes.

'What's it like?' called Flydd.

Like an excited child, Jal-Nish had to tell someone who would understand, even his enemy. 'It's . . . like a luminous toadstool with a hole in the top, and currents boiling out of it, filled with whirling specks like sparks from a bonfire.'

'I'd keep well clear of it if I were you,' shouted Flydd.

'I'm sure *you* would!' Jal-Nish sneered. 'Soldiers –' His voice was cut off.

'What's happened?' said Irisis.

'I don't know.'

Jal-Nish's cry rang out. 'Just look at *that*!'

'What now?' Flydd called.

'It's – Aah! Help! Pull me out!'

'What's happened?' Irisis repeated.

'Jal-Nish has fallen through the floor; or *into* it.'

'Into solid rock?'

'You asked what it would be like where the node-drainer emptied to. Now we know. It's like nothing on this world.'

'Help, help!' It was a chorus of voices now.

'Better go and rescue them,' said Flydd to the other guards.

A guard screamed, truncated in the middle.

'Hurry!' Flydd snapped.

The soldiers ran off.

'Let's go,' said Flydd. 'Ullii, lead the way.'

They ran, Irisis stumbling along by her lead rope. It was a long hike in the dark and by the time they reached the roof fall she was bruised all over from running into the walls.

'Wait,' she called, her heart hammering wildly. 'I've got to stop for a second.'

'Hear that?' It was a distant wailing cry. 'He's behind us. Come *on*!'

They kept going. Irisis's knees felt like jelly, though at least the weird flesh-shivering had ceased. 'How far to the lift?'

'Too far.'

'Are they catching us, do you think?'

'Can't tell,' he gasped. 'Just keep going.'

Running and running, through the empty dark. Irisis was dragged around a corner and struck her knee on a projecting rock. She cried out.

'What's the matter?'

'Just a broken kneecap!' she said.

'I've climbed mountains with worse. Stop moaning and get on with it.'

'When we get out of here, you hateful man, I'm going to give you the biggest drubbing you've ever had in your life.'

'A *drubbing*?' He smiled. 'I'll look forward to it.'

'Lift's not far ahead now,' he said some time later.

'Where's Ullii?'

'Up ahead. She knows how to take care of herself.'

'But does she know how to take care of us?'

'What do you mean?' They rounded the last corner and Flydd began to laugh.

'What's so funny?'

'We're at the edge of the lift shaft. Don't go forward. The lift's gone. Ullii has wound it up without us.'

'Call her down again.'

'Ullii?' he bawled. The sound echoed and re-echoed in the shaft. 'Bring that lift down again, *right away*!'

Silence, over which she could hear the sound of running feet.

'Ullii?'

She did not reply but the lift rope began to move down. Irisis could hear it swishing through the water, which lay just below the lip of the entrance to their level.

'Hurry up!'

Ullii whimpered. The footsteps came closer. Irisis recognised the wheezing breath of Jal-Nish. She cursed. He'd got out after all.

'Basket's here,' said Flydd, who had freed his hands. He

helped Irisis over the side into the basket, cut her bonds and put her hands on the crank. 'As soon as I give the word, wind like fury.'

'Stop!' panted Jal-Nish. 'Stop or we'll shoot.'

The basket swayed as Flydd sprang in. 'Wind the damn thing! There's only two, Jal-Nish and one soldier.'

Irisis heaved at the crank. The basket jerked up.

'Shoot them!' roared Jal-Nish. 'Shoo – Where's your damned crossbow, soldier?'

'It went under the floor, surr, when I was pulling you out. Sorry, surr . . .'

'Useless fool,' Jal-Nish screamed. 'They're getting away and we can't do anything about it.'

Xervish Flydd laughed fit to burst. 'Goodbye, Jal-Nish. Don't forget to put this in your next despatch to the Council. I'll certainly mention it in mine.'

As they neared the top, Flydd called up to the lift guards, 'Jal-Nish is in trouble at the bottom. Better get down after him.'

The guards whispered to one another. Wasn't Flydd an outlaw now?

'Hurry up!' roared Flydd, helping Irisis over the side. Used to obeying without question, the guards did as they were told.

Once their basket reached the bottom, Flydd cut the lift rope. 'A good evening's work,' he said, whistling jauntily, and headed up the tunnel.

They reached the upper entrance without incident. He flashed the signal lantern and the air-floater came drifting down to the top of the hill.

'What happens now?' said Irisis, snuggling into a canvas seat. Ullii was already hidden in a corner, under the bench.

'We let out all Jal-Nish's skeets, to give us a few extra days, drop Oon-Mie and Zoyl at a safe manufactory, then go to a rendezvous,' said Flydd. 'I don't know what we'll find there. How are your eyes?'

'How do you think they are?' she snapped.

'Have you tried them lately?'

'No. Why would I?'

He untied the bandage and pulled off the pads, which had stuck to her eyelids.

'Ouch!' she said.

'Can you see anything?'

'I can't open my eyes.'

They were gummed shut with yellow secretions. Calling for a bowl of water, he bathed her eyelids until they came ungummed.

'Now try.'

She rubbed her eyes, opened them and stared at where she thought he was. 'I still can't see anything.'

'Of course not. You're looking out into the dark. Turn around.' He turned her. 'There.'

She gazed at him and slowly her eyes began to water. Tears flooded her cheeks.

'I can't be that ugly,' he said gruffly.

'I can see!' she cried. 'I can see!' Throwing her arms around him, she sobbed her heart out.

FORTY-SEVEN

Gilhaelith heard Tiaan's cry as the walker went over the edge, and the crash and rattle of sliding rock, then the four lyrinx took him up so quickly that the noise of their wings drowned out all other sound. He struggled uselessly against his bonds, imagining Tiaan lying bloody and helpless halfway down the crater. With the hood over his head, he could see nothing.

They flew in cloud for a long time – he felt it billowing about them. It was cold. Gilhaelith's clothes hung dankly on him and moisture dripped from the hood down the back of his neck. The great wings went *whoop, whoop*. One lyrinx called to another in their strange tongue. A second snapped back. There seemed to be an argument, at the end of which the lyrinx began to spiral down. They broke out of cloud, the wind lifted his hood and Gilhaelith spied a circular mesa of black rock rising from forest. The lyrinx glided down towards it, resting on the thermals, then landed hard near the edge.

One held Gilhaelith's rope while the other three went into a huddle. Shortly a female put her hands around his wrists and looked into his eyes. 'You called a name as we lifted, "Tia –". Was it Tiaan, the artisan from Tiksi, who fled Tirthrax in a flying construct? Speak truly. I am a truth-reader.'

He hesitated a fraction too long before saying, 'No, it was Tyune, my crippled daughter.'

Orange speckles appeared on her arms. 'He lies,' she called to the others. 'It *was* the artisan we seek. Munnand, go back for her.'

The largest of the four, a male with a brilliant red crest, used the updraught to lift himself in the air and headed north. The truth-reader pulled Gilhaelith's hood down and bound it on. They flew in fog and cloud for many hours more. Gilhaelith could feel the cool, clinging vapour on his skin and the chilly drips down his back.

The lyrinx had surely abducted him in order to use his Art. He felt a stirring of interest. Why did they want him? And if they got what they wanted, what then? Perhaps they would eat him. They'd have to outwit him first! It was the ultimate challenge and Gilhaelith was a master game-player. But this was different. It was personal.

They kept going after dark, but around midnight settled on a crag in the mountains. He was fed, his bonds were checked and he was allowed to lie on the ledge. He barely slept. Gilhaelith realised, to his bemusement, that he was worried about Tiaan, and it was not just for what she could do for him. Nor was it the concern he might feel for an old and faithful servant. It was much more. It was deeper. He actually cared about her!

He explored the strange sensation all the hours of darkness, but when the lyrinx stirred at dawn Gilhaelith was as confused as when he'd begun. They took to the air again, flying all day. He dozed, waking to find that it was dark. Gilhaelith caught an acrid whiff of tar and had a sense of strong forces all around. The air felt close – he was in a cave, or below ground.

Why were they looking for Tiaan? It might have to do with flesh-forming, or with the thapter. If she had not died in the fall, she would now be lying helpless on the slope, waiting to die of thirst. Better that the lyrinx bring her here, whatever they had in store for her.

Gilhaelith was weaponless, since mathemancy could not be used for attack. His geomancy could, though not with his bare hands. He needed particular crystals or artefacts for that.

There were crystals in the rock walls around him, but none suited to geomancy. There was one way, however. Gilhaelith suffered from gallstones, among other ailments. They were hardly crystals but they did have some use in the Secret Art, and nothing could be more attuned to him than a stone from his own body. He sensed out the largest and forced it to wake. It was ill-suited for the purpose, no power in it at all, but he did manage to enhance his awareness with it.

Ghostly images grew behind his closed eyes, swirling currents like a great red fountain, and the shape of a pit. There was a node here, a strong and unstable one, but bound as he was there was no more he could learn about it. It had to be the tar pits of Snizort, a place he knew of, though he had never been here.

He was conveyed down numberless steps, along tunnels that stank of tar, and finally through a series of heavy doors that progressively reduced the smell. His bonds were released, the hood taken off. He blinked at the light of a lantern.

'What do you want of me?' he asked politely. Gilhaelith was always polite when he did not know what he was dealing with.

An elderly lyrinx, a female, said, 'I am Gyrull, Matriarch of Snizort.'

She had a soft voice for a lyrinx, and spoke the language better than most, though her speech was flat, as if she were reciting.

'Matriarch! Are you the supreme ruler of the lyrinx?'

'We do not have a supreme ruler, *tetrarch*. We work collectively to achieve our aims.'

'How do you know what I am?' he cried.

'It was written.'

'Why do you dwell in such a foul place?'

'It occupies a vital part of our life-cycle, or Histories as you call them.'

That made no sense. How could Snizort play any part in the lyrinx Histories, except in the most recent times?

'You understand the earth and the forces that power it, tetrarch,' she went on. 'We seek to know more about this place.'

'What has that to do with me?'

She glanced over his head. Four lyrinx stood behind him, claws extended, alert for any sign of attack.

'Something was lost in the Great Seep. We would very much like to recover it.'

'The Great Seep?'

'The source of the tar at Snizort.'

'What was lost?'

'I cannot say.'

'Big or small?'

'Big enough.'

Gilhaelith rubbed his blocky jaw, wondering what was really going on. 'What are the dimensions of the seep?'

Matriarch Gyrull spoke among the other lyrinx. A small female stepped forward. 'The Great Seep is shaped like this.' She drew an irregular oval on the floor, with a smaller oval budding off one end. 'It is one-and-a-quarter of your leagues long, and seven-eighths of a league wide.'

'And how deep?'

'We do not know. Perhaps a league; perhaps more.'

'What was lost, and where?'

The small lyrinx opened her mouth, then closed it again. The Matriarch pulled her back. 'We cannot tell you that.'

'No matter,' said Gilhaelith. '*Where* it was lost is all that matters; and *when*.'

'It was lost near the centre, as far as I am able to determine.' Gyrull indicated a point with one brittle yellow claw. 'Around here.'

'How big was it? If it was small, the chances of ever finding it are remote.'

'Bigger than a village hut.'

'How long ago?'

Now even the Matriarch looked uneasy. What is it? he thought. They must want it desperately, to have involved an outsider in the search. Gilhaelith was intrigued.

'We cannot be sure,' she said at length. 'Perhaps you can help us. You have the best library in the south-west, we are told.'

Even more puzzling. The lyrinx had come to Santhenar at the time the Way between the Worlds was open, two hundred and seven years ago. The war began in earnest about sixty years later,

485

but the lyrinx had been restricted to Meldorin Island for the first hundred years after their arrival.

'I don't understand,' said Gilhaelith. 'The Histories in my library are mainly of ancient times. How –'

'It might have been lost as recently as seven thousand years ago, or as long ago as ten thousand. We do not have the Histories of that time. I can tell you no more. We brought you here to find out.'

If what she'd said was true, the lyrinx must have visited Santhenar before. He could scarcely believe it. Some creatures of the void had ended up on Santhenar in the distant past, before the time of the Forbidding. The Histories told that such arrivals had been accidental, the intruders slain. Had the lyrinx previously come to Santhenar thousands of years ago, then gone again? It raised many questions. But why would she lie?

'Why should I help you? You are the enemy of all humanity.'

'You traded with us before,' said the Matriarch, watching him with eyes that reflected the light in twin points. 'What is different now? We will pay you well, in whatever currency you demand.' Her eyes held a question.

'I'll consider my price.' It was hard to see how he could get away, weaponless and surrounded by alert guards, but that was not his most pressing concern. He would soon have had to abandon Nyriandiol anyway, but the amplimet was back there, *unguarded*. He had to have it – he had gone too far along that path to retreat now. He must convince them to take him back.

He was also bothered about Tiaan. Gilhaelith prayed that she had survived the fall. Or would it be better if she had died? *No!* He missed her. Astonishing. In all his years at Nyriandiol he had never cared about anyone. He had to know what had happened to her. 'You must take me home first.'

'Why?' Yellow and black patterns moved on her skin – suspicion.

'I haven't read the very ancient Histories in a hundred years, and I can't remember them. I must consult my library. Then I will tell you my price.'

486

They waited for Munnand, the lyrinx who had gone back for Tiaan, but he did not come. The following afternoon they were back in the air, six fliers this time. The Matriarch was one of them, though she took no part in carrying Gilhaelith. Flying into strong headwinds, it took them two days to reach the Burning Mountain. Six days had passed since his abduction. They landed at the point where Tiaan had fallen. There was no sign of her, or her walker, and the rubble showed no tracks. Nyriandiol was unnaturally quiet.

'We will go to your house,' Gyrull said.

They found three bodies on the terrace – Gurteys, Fley and a tall man too clawed to identify. The lyrinx lay on the steps, dead. The chalcedony door had been smashed to pieces and more bodies were sprawled further down the hall. The Matriarch bowed her head over Munnand while Gilhaelith checked the bodies of his retainers. All had died of lyrinx wounds.

'This changes matters,' he said coldly. Going to the front door he shouted, 'Tiaan?' His cry echoed down the hall, but there was no reply.

'Where's Tiaan?' Gilhaelith cried. 'What have you done with her?'

'Munnand lies dead,' said Matriarch Gyrull. The other lyrinx were carrying the body away. 'He was alone. But there are other signs, if you care to look.'

The door had been broken with hammers. There were metal marks on the stone and the lyrinx would not have done that. Inside, muddy bootprints tracked down the hall. They were un- usually long. The Aachim had been here.

'Tiaan!' He raced down the swooping outside platform to the lowest level, at dire risk of going over the edge. The lower door had been smashed. The window was a jagged hole. The room was empty, the thapter gone.

'Vithis has the thapter, and Tiaan!' He clenched his fists, struggling to moderate his emotions so as to give nothing else away. The thapter did not matter but the amplimet was every- thing now.

The Matriarch walked around the room. 'She fought bravely.

See these scars in the wall. She must have used some kind of weapon . . .'

'My crystal rod,' said Gilhaelith. 'She survived the fall, at least.'

'A pity. We could have used her again. To your library, tetrarch.'

He considered refusing and trying to escape but with six lyrinx watching there was no chance. Better to cooperate than be forced. He had to have a safe place to work and, hopefully, scry out where the amplimet had been taken. He was determined to have it back. Moreover, the scrutators would arrive here within days and the evidence of his treachery was everywhere. Why not let Gyrull take him back to Snizort? They could carry the devices he needed, and once there he could use the power of the node to track down the amplimet. And what a strange node it was – that could only add to his knowledge.

He was beginning to see that nodes held part of the secret to the great game, and the more of them he could study, the closer he would be to his goal. Especially such potent nodes as the one at Snizort.

Gilhaelith's library was well organised and it did not take long to collect all the ancient records dealing with the Taltid region of Lauralin. There were not many and all were second-hand, since few original documents had survived for that period. Gyrull sat beside him while he worked, the truth-reader on his other side.

'What, specifically, are you looking for?' Gilhaelith asked.

'Firstly,' said Gyrull, 'all documents from the period ten thousand to seven thousand years before the present day, which deal with Snizort, the tar pits or the people who dwelt in its vicinity. Secondly, reports of wonder-working or the Secret Art from that period. Third – no, that is enough.'

'Here's something,' said Gilhaelith several hours later. He was turning the pages of a chronicle detailing the earliest Histories of the Gospett area. 'It's from nine thousand, three hundred years ago. It mentions the tar seeps, and ghost lights burning at night out in the middle.'

'Ghost lights?' said the Matriarch.

'Like will-o'-the-wisps.'

'Explain, if you please.'

'Ghost lights are gases that catch fire by themselves.'

'Ah, bog vapours.'

The same locality was mentioned several times in the Histories of the next thousand years, but all references related to the tar pits or to products obtained from them. None were of any interest to the Matriarch.

'What does this say?' She pointed to a paragraph on the page opposite the one he had been reading from.

'It talks about yellow crystals – brimstones – found in cavities near some of the smaller seeps.'

'Continue.'

He caught a gleam in her eye and made a mental note to be careful. It would appear Gyrull could read the ancient texts almost as well as he could. What a formidable intellect she must have.

He went through the chronicles, volume by volume. It took all day. Finally, in the year 7327 before the present one, he found something that made the Matriarch sit up.

'The people of the village of Ric Rints, near the tar pits of Snizort, were ordered by the regent to cease their foul sorcery or be put to the sword.'

Gilhaelith explained, 'At this time, mancing was tribal magic and forbidden under the Encial Edict of 7366.'

'What kind of sorcery?' asked the Matriarch.

'A form of shape-changing magic, I'd say. It's not clear what, although almost everyone in the village seems to have had a natural talent, which they focussed using woken brimstones. So close to such a powerful node, they might not have needed anything else. They would require a ready supply of brimstones, though, for such crystals are fragile.'

'Go on.'

'The villagers promised to do no more shape-changing, but later built a floating causeway out to the middle of the lake of tar, where they constructed a village on a cloverleaf platform. Rumours began of sorcerous experiments, right over the Great Seep. One magical

working caused the sky to change colour. Another time, a column of yellow light blasted straight up, brighter than the beam of a lighthouse. Another time, they caused the Great Seep to seethe until hot tar rained down on distant villages. Yet another time the sky opened and closed again, like an eye, and watchers saw stars in the daytime.'

The Matriarch was impassive, save for those gleaming eyes. 'What do you think they were doing?'

'Geomancy,' said Gilhaelith. 'Primitive but no less powerful. This was long before the Forbidding sealed the Way between the Worlds. It sounds as if they discovered how to open the Way. Perhaps they were the very first to do so.' He bent his head to the parchment.

'The regent, furious that they so flagrantly flouted his edict, placed a proscription on the village and began building floating paths out to it. Before he could attack, another great column of yellow light blasted upwards. The sky opened and many of the villagers vanished through it. Under the downblast, the platform broke apart. The village and its remaining inhabitants, more than three hundred children, women and men, were sucked under the tar and never seen again.'

The Matriarch looked to the truth-reader, letting out a great sigh. The truth-reader nodded.

'That is what you are looking for?' said Gilhaelith. 'A village lost seven thousand years ago? Surely their brimstones, and their knowledge, will have been lost with them? It would be easier to –'

'Can you find it?' she said harshly.

'It will not be easy. The tar moves slowly but seven thousand years is a long time.'

'You will try,' she said. 'It must be found.'

He did not ask why. She was not going to tell him. 'I will require a number of scrying and sensing devices,' he said, praying that she would not call his bluff. It was not really a bluff, for all could be used for that purpose, though not all were necessary for it. There would be plenty to do in Snizort, and when all was done, his devices would permit him to break out again, if he could just keep charge of them.

490

Gyrull weighed him for a moment. 'Of course. Indicate what you require and we will carry it.'

He marked a number of items, including his great globe. She frowned at that but did not refuse. The items were packed, the boxed globe secured in rope netting, and they prepared to go.

It was a wrench abandoning everything else, especially the carillon of bells and the great organ, but nothing could be done about it. Those secrets would be in the hands of Scrutator Klarm within days. Gilhaelith wondered what he would make of them.

He considered his options on the long trip back to Snizort. The Matriarch knew more than she was saying. Those villagers must have been better at their Art than anyone imagined. To discover what had been lost that day was going to be a prodigious labour, and it must be a powerful secret. Should he give them what they wanted?

On the other hand, something strange *had* happened out in the Great Seep that day, more than seven thousand years ago, and it had to do with geomancy. It may have been the very foundation of his Art. Gilhaelith's curiosity had been aroused and he had to have it satisfied.

PART FIVE

NODE-DRAINER

FORTY-EIGHT

Tiaan lay in the crashed walker, watching the lyrinx carry Gilhaelith away. Their wings churned the fog, it enveloped them and he was gone. Why had they taken him? And what had he been about to tell her about her back? She dared not hope for a cure, yet hope could not be restrained.

The walker had not fallen far, fortunately, or she would not have survived. It had slid down a few spans until the rubble stopped it. Tiaan was bruised but nothing seemed to be broken.

She felt for the controller hedron, which had fallen out of its socket. Pressing it into place, she attempted to move one mechanical leg without sending the walker further down the slope. Nothing happened. She tried the other legs, one at a time. They did not work either.

'Help!' The fog suffocated her cry.

'Help, help!' It sounded weak and lost. Gilhaelith's servants were inside. They would not hear her, and if they did, who would care? She had to save herself. Tiaan took up the controller again.

Taking it apart, mindful that if she dropped any piece she would never recover it, Tiaan checked everything. The hedron was undamaged but one of the connecting stubs had bent out of place. She straightened it with her teeth. When she reassembled the device the lower leg moved suddenly, rotating the walker on the rubble. She caught her breath but it did not fall. Could she possibly get it upright on this slope? Or move it if she did? The walker was designed for level ground.

Visualising the field, Tiaan selected a whorl that held just a tiny amount of power, trickled it into the controller and spread the legs as far as they would go. That was easy, but to get it upright would not be. The leg beneath her was the key. She extended it a little, starting a miniature rockslide. A little more and the walker rolled sideways. Now the leg had nothing to push against. She would have to work both lower legs at once.

Flexing them at the middle joints so as to reduce their length, she pushed gently. The walker tilted up, one knobbed foot slipped and the machine fell back, starting another slide.

Tiaan tried again and this time got the walker two-thirds upright, though her weight was near to toppling it. If she tried to go further the walker might fall all the way to the bottom of the crater. It would not survive that, and neither would she.

Extending the upslope legs until they were nearly parallel to the slope, she straightened the other pair. The walker edged towards the vertical. The rubble moved beneath one foot. Now the really difficult part. Ever so carefully she pushed with the downslope legs. The walker moved up a little, then stuck. It was like an animal trying to walk on its back legs. How was she to get up the slope? Straight up looked impossibly steep but, if she angled across, Tiaan thought she might just be able to do it.

She pushed off. The walker teetered and Tiaan was sure it was going to go over. She found a little more extension in the up-slope legs. It was just enough. Creeping across the slope like a four-legged crab, she made it to the edge, though she had to go back and forth three times to get up the last bit.

On the rim, bigger challenges awaited her. She did not hold any false hope for Gilhaelith. Few people ever got out of the hands of the lyrinx. She was on her own. Had the thapter been finished she would have fled at once. Since it was not, she must pray for time to complete it.

Tiaan skidded across the terrace and in through the front door. 'Nixx!' she shouted. 'Nixx, quickly.'

The seneschal appeared, quill in one hand, tally sheet in the other. 'What is it? I'm very busy.'

'Gilhaelith has been taken!'

'What?' he cried. 'How?'

'Four lyrinx flew down out of the fog and carried him away. They were so quick he had no chance.'

He dropped the quill. Black ink spattered the tiles. 'When was this?'

'An hour ago.'

'*An hour?*'

She became aware of her wild hair and dirty face. 'My walker went over the edge a long way from here. I called out but no one heard me. They rose straight up into the fog.'

'Show me the place,' he said grimly.

Tiaan led him to the spot and he examined it while she stood by. Reaction had set in and she was trembling.

'Big lyrinx?' Nixx said doubtfully.

'As big as any I've seen.'

'I don't see any tracks. You say you fell?' He sounded doubtful. Surely he did not think she had killed Gilhaelith?

'Down there?' She pointed.

Nixx studied her skid marks just as carefully. He did suspect her. Tiaan was insulted.

He roused out the household to search the rim in a line that extended down each side for about a hundred paces. Every mark and dislodged pebble was noted. It took most of the morning. They recovered Gilhaelith's crystal rod, which did not seem to be damaged. Finally they came back to where Tiaan sat under the vines on the terrace.

'It is as you say,' Nixx said. 'We found unmistakable foot-marks. The lyrinx have taken him.'

'Why?'

'I don't know.'

Nixx sat at the table, staring at his tally sheet. His broad fingers were stained with ink. He seemed not to know what to do. The other servants stood by the door, equally bewildered and fearful. Tiaan could read their faces. Without Gilhaelith, they had nothing.

He had always been here – some families had served him for five generations. Now he was gone and Nyriandiol was unprotected.

The crystal rod lay on the table. It was an elongated prism, translucent and heavy, capped at one end with shiny steel, a basket of which enclosed the striated sides. An ironstone rosette was fixed on the open end. Gilhaelith's teaching had barely touched on such devices, though she knew it could be a weapon in the right hands.

She slipped it into her pocket. 'What are you going to do, Nixx?'

'I can't do anything!' he wailed, still wringing his fleshy hands. 'Four lyrinx might have carried him halfway across the continent.'

Tiaan was back on the terrace, numbly watching the fog wreathe through the vines, when she heard raised voices at the front door.

'The master is lost,' said someone she did not know. 'We will never see him again. Let us take what we can carry and go.'

'He may come back.' Nixx's voice rose above the others. 'We must maintain Nyriandiol for his return –'

'You old fool!' spat Gurteys. 'It's finished. This place will be plundered within days. We've lost everything.'

'We cannot betray our master.'

'We can't hold the place against lyrinx or anyone else. Come on!' she yelled.

'Don't,' he quavered. 'Let me go. Aaah!'

Tiaan knew what was going to happen. Snatching her water bottle, she crabbed sideways toward the path, watching the front door. Shadows moved inside. She sought for a strong part of the field; as powerful as she could bear.

'There she is.' The squat woman, Alie, wielded a kitchen cleaver over her head.

'Don't kill her,' shouted Gurteys. 'She's worth ten thousand gold ones. Knock the metal crab down and break it.'

She ran around the outside of the terrace and stood waiting for Tiaan, holding a wicked two-headed axe. Tiaan stopped. A host of servants were coming up behind, and Fley was running across to join his wife. There was no way past.

But Fley caught Gurteys by the arm, swinging her around. *Run!* he mimed, and as Gurteys swung the flat of the axe at his head, Tiaan slipped through. Fley went down and was trampled as a dozen women stampeded by, brandishing makeshift weapons.

Where were the guards? Perhaps they were already down below, looting. She hoped so, for her sake. Tiaan pulled power into the controller and fled into the fog, moving the four legs by instinct.

She looked back. Any competent archer could have shot her with a crossbow, but fortunately these were mere household servants. Or maybe those who wanted the reward had prevailed. A stick whirled through the air, just missing her. A rain of rocks followed, one whizzing over her shoulder, another striking her back brace so hard that it cracked. Pain jagged up her side.

Realising that she still had Gilhaelith's crystal rod, Tiaan fumbled it out. Just how did one use it? She recalled the lesson about using crystals as weapons, though she'd not had the chance to practise with one. She pointed the crystal at the ground, depressing a strip of metal anchored at one end. A yellow ray burst from the open face of the ironstone rosette. She swung it at the feet of her pursuers. Rocks exploded, flinging gravel everywhere. The servants threw themselves out of the way.

Skilled at operating the walker now, Tiaan fleeted along at running speed until she ran into a wall of fog. She dared another glance over her shoulder. The mob was out of sight, yet she could hear it coming. If she went slowly they might not hear her. The small rubber feet made little noise.

They followed for an hour, after which she heard no more. Perhaps the tireless walker had outdistanced them, or they had given up. That hardly seemed likely: they had much to gain and nothing to lose. She kept going. Later the fog thinned enough for her to see back for half a league. The rim of the crater was empty. She saw no one on the sides, either. Tiaan supposed that they had gone back to wait her out. They knew she couldn't get away.

The bare mountaintop was no place to spend the night. Big cats hunted up here, and other predators. Going carefully down the outer slope, she took refuge in one of the lava tubes that threaded the side of the mountain. From here she could see the rim. No one came after her. Her water bottle was empty and there was no water here. Below, the slope was too steep for the walker so she had no choice. Tiaan climbed back to the rim, clutching the rod. Nyriandiol was a dark shape against the horizon. Not a single light showed, which was strange.

She had to have water and the villa was the only place she could get any. It took hours, feeling her way forward in the dark, afraid she would go over the edge without realising it. Finally she was close enough to see the peaked roof. Still no lights. It had to be a trap.

Then she smelled the blood. Had the burst from her crystal killed someone? The stars gave too little light to see. She continued until one foot of the walker struck something yielding. It was the size and shape of a person.

'Hello?' she whispered.

No reply.

She went around it. Near the paved yard she again smelled blood. Holding the crystal out at a shallow angle, she pressed the metal strip and swept the beam across and back, just for a second. Gurteys lay dead, her neck broken, a bag of gold and silverware clutched to her chest. Fley was nearby, his fingers crooked towards her – in death as in life. By the front door, a lyrinx lay with its head severed from its body. Oddly, it smelled of tar.

Tiaan stood by the bodies, listening in case there were more lyrinx. She heard no sound. Creeping inside, she was going carefully down the hall when someone cried hoarsely, 'Who's there?'

'Nixx?' she whispered. She could see more bodies further along.

'Tiaan?'

She turned into the dark salon. Nixx cowered under a desk. She helped him out. Blood streaked his forehead and left thigh. 'What's happened, Nixx?'

'A lyrinx came looking for you. We managed to kill it but it did a lot of us first. The rest took what they could carry and fled. I can't say I blame them.'

She lit the lamp by the door. 'And you?'

'I am loyal to my master, but what am I to do? I know I'll never see Gilhaelith again. I must run and try to find a new living. It won't be easy, at my age.'

She felt for him – her situation was much the same. All she could do was try to complete the repairs and go . . . where? Borgistry was nearest. She must give the thapter to Scrutator Klarm and throw herself on his mercy – a commodity the scrutators had in short supply at the best of times. Little hope there, but she could not survive on her own.

'Please stay,' she said, 'just until I fix the thapter. It's nearly done.'

'I cannot stay.'

'I beg you – Gilhaelith would expect it. I can't do it alone.'

He agreed, though with an ill grace, and she began.

Why had the lyrinx come back for her? When it did not return, others would follow. And the biggest unanswered question of all – what had Gilhaelith discovered about broken backs? Was that why he had gone to that secret meeting?

If only she knew where they had taken him . . .

Tiaan laboured night and day on the thapter. Four days later it was done, though she still had to test it. And even if it worked, what if the amplimet would not take her where she wanted to go?

She was working up behind the binnacle when a faintly bituminous odour reminded her of something. As Gilhaelith had been taken, and again near the dead lyrinx, she had smelled tar. Going to the front terrace, she checked the body of the beast. Its great feet were deeply stained with tar. She hurtled the walker inside. 'Nixx, Nixx?'

She found him in Gilhaelith's offices, packing coin into a leather bag. 'Nixx,' she cried. 'I've just thought of something.'

'What?' He did not look up.

She told him about the tar. He went out to examine the corpse for himself. 'Looks like it's been walking in tar for years – the stuff is right into the pores of its skin.'

'Where could it have come from?' she asked.

'Only one location I can think of. Snizort.'

'Snizort?'

'A place south of here, famous for its tar pits. It's in the land of Taltid.' He indicated it on a map. 'I'll go through his ledgers and see what I can discover.'

He came down shortly afterwards, finger holding a ledger open. 'Gilhaelith purchased several kinds of bituminous spirits from Snizort. He's made some notes on the place.'

She read them, though they mainly had to do with geography. An arid land, sparsely vegetated, with tar pits and seeps all over the place.

'Oh well,' she said, feigning disinterest. 'He's lost. I'd better keep going. Could you keep watch for me?'

'No. I've done more than my duty, and I can't stay a moment longer.'

'Just for an hour. I'm nearly finished. Please.'

'Oh, very well, for my master's sake. Half an hour only.'

Nixx came running in ten minutes later, his jaw working like a nutcracker. 'Constructs, marm. Lots of them.'

She dropped her wrench, which just missed a fragile glass mechanism. Tiaan reached over to pick it up. 'How many is lots?' she asked, trying to keep her voice steady.

'At least fifty.'

'Where are they?'

'Approaching the foot of the mountain.'

Fear tickled her throat. 'How long will they take to get here?'

'Couple of hours; no more.'

It was not enough; the tests weren't finished. 'You'll have to stall them, Nixx.'

'Can't do it, marm. They'll torture my family if I try. You can't ask that of me.'

'What are you going to do?'

'Run, as fast as I can.'

'Where to?'

'We have a hiding place.' He hesitated. 'An overgrown lava tunnel, way down in the forest.'

'How can I get the thapter out of here?' She should have asked that question a long time ago.

'You can't. We had to remove the window to bring it in.' He was looking increasingly jumpy.

'All right,' she said. 'Go. Save yourself. And thank you, Nixx.'

Offering her a sketchy salute, he ran up the steps. She skittered the walker across to the door and barred it, then raced back to the thapter. There was no time to replace the metal skin sections. She strapped them to the back and got on with the testing. If it did not work the first time, she was finished.

Tiaan was still doing the tests when she heard the echoing whine of constructs coming up the road. Only minutes left. She strapped her walker to the side of the thapter. Pulling herself into its seat, she passed a strap around her, took hold of the trumpet-shaped lever, visualised the field and let the energy flow.

Nothing happened. She tried again with the same result. Had she forgotten something? Yes, the hedron was still in its socket in the walker, and the thapter needed it and the ampliment, to fly. As she climbed out to get it, the Aachim began to smash down the front door.

FORTY-NINE

Nish felt an overwhelming urge to run, but there was nowhere to run to. The horsemen were already melting into the forest. There was just the clearing, Vithis and himself.

'Get down,' said Vithis. 'Send your stolen horse away. You will not be needing it again.'

Nish did so. The horse trotted off.

'Come here.' Vithis leapt to the ground.

Nish came to within an arm's reach of the intimidatingly tall Aachim, who held up his palm. He carried no cane now and the limp was gone. He seemed calmer than before.

'After your previous behaviour, you dared return to my lands?'

'These are not your lands. You're an invader.'

'Force makes them mine,' said Vithis, standing close and looking down on Nish. 'No one has dared oppose me.'

Nish was used to intimidation; his father had done that to him all his life. He had developed a technique to deal with it – he imagined his father failing at what he most wanted. So, what did Vithis most desire, and fear he would never get? A homeland for his people? It gave Nish strength. 'We *will* dare, should it be necessary! But we know Aachim to be human too.'

'I would not have thought it from the way you behaved the other day, Marshal Hlar.'

504

'I am no marshal,' said Nish.

'Indeed! Your speech revealed you to be a most *common* man.'

'I merely reflected your own character back at you,' Nish said coldly. 'If you do not like what you hear, look into your own soul.' He was risking his life, but every word the man said was a wrongness and a goad.

Vithis seemed to grow even taller. 'I could tear you apart with my naked hands.' He held them out and the impossibly long, curving fingers could have spanned Nish's throat.

'It would only carve the bitterness deeper into your heart.'

Vithis whirled and stalked away. Why had he come? Nish had nothing of any use to him. Or was he just looking out for Minis? There were other Aachim in the thapter, and someone behind the javelard in the turret at the back, but it was pointed at the ground. This was between Vithis and him.

'Why do you seek to corrupt my foster-son?' said the Aachim from some distance.

How much did Vithis know? Maybe everything. Nish saw no point in lying, though he was not necessarily going to tell the whole truth either. '*Minis* sought me out,' said Nish. 'We talked. I liked him and we both wanted the same thing.'

'And that was?' Vithis said dangerously.

'To prevent a new war, and end this one that has been going on for generations.'

'We care nothing for your war.'

'Only barbarians could be indifferent to our suffering.'

Nish expected an explosion but it did not come. The Aachim was looking at him thoughtfully. Maybe his defiance had earned a grudging respect.

'Your suffering is insignificant compared to our own. We have lost a world; Minis and I have lost our entire clan – all twenty thousand of First Clan.'

'Why is it called First Clan?'

'Because civilisation was founded on our hearthstone. We built the first city on Aachan. We invented writing, and the wheel, and were the first to discover the Art. We lifted the other clans up from the dirt.'

Nish wondered if the other clans would agree, and how intense their rivalry really was. Perhaps humanity could make use of that.

'What about Clan Elienor? I've heard that they too have a noble history.'

'I have nothing to say of Elienor. They are not of the Eleven Clans. Some of us doubt that they are true Aachim at all.'

'Minis also lost his clan, yet he can still find room in his heart to care about humanity.'

'All Minis wants is to serve his father and do his duty to clan and kind. No Aachim could desire anything else.'

Nish shrugged, trying to seem indifferent. 'Of course you're right. What do I care?'

The Aachim's fingers went down on Nish's shoulders, as hard as iron claws. 'What did my son ask of you?'

'He felt,' said Nish, 'after I had told him my tale, that if anyone could find the flying construct it would be me. Because I know Tiaan well, and because I am courageous and resourceful.'

'I would have said incompetent yet boastful! What did he plan to do with the flier once he had it?'

'Give it to his foster-father, of course.'

The fingers relaxed. 'Minis is a dutiful son. I don't know enough about you, Cryl-Nish Hlar, though I have made many enquiries. Sit down. Be at ease.' He signalled to the construct and a man came forth carrying a cloth and a basket.

Nish sat in the shade of a spreading tree and his racing heart slowly steadied. Perhaps Vithis did not mean to harm him after all. Vithis questioned him on every detail of the past months and the dark eyes never left his face. Nish felt as though the man *was* reading him.

Nish answered truthfully, though not with the same candour as to Mira. Poor, sad Mira. He could not shake that night from his mind. He could not blame her either.

'Hmn,' the Aachim said at the end. 'A fine set of answers! And even if half of them are true, there is something about you, and it agrees with what others have told me. You are resourceful and have a certain rodent-like cunning. I think I will use you after all.'

The word 'use' had an unpleasant ring to it. 'What for?' Nish's voice squeaked as he spoke.

Vithis gave him an amused glance. 'I'm going to take you with me.'

'As what?' said Nish. 'A tame human?'

'I concede to Minis's judgment. You know Tiaan better than we ever could. You will help him search for her and the flying construct. Go up.'

Nish climbed the side of the construct, marvelling at the workmanship, so superior to anything he had seen in the manufactory. The unpainted skin of black metal was polished to such a brilliant shine that he could see his face in it. Such elegant curves could never have been shaped in the manufactory. The joins could hardly be seen.

Vithis handed him inside. Nish recognised a kind of controller lever, though nothing like the ones the clankers used. On the binnacle, glass plates glowed and coloured patterns flowed across them. He wondered if they were projections of the field.

'Go down,' said Vithis.

Nish descended the ladder, finding at the bottom an open space shaped like the inside of an egg. Benched seats might have accommodated as many as ten occupants, crammed together, though at present the space was empty.

The gentle hum that had been in the background all the time swelled to a whine and the construct accelerated smoothly. Nish sat on one of the benches and closed his eyes. He had survived yet again. Someone must be looking out for him. He did not even have the strength to admire.

He woke having no idea where he had been taken, or what time it was. The construct was stationary, silent. Nish climbed the ladder. Vithis was not at the controller and the hatch was open. The construct rested on the ground in the middle of a copse. Beyond, through the trees, Nish made out a glade in whose centre stood a circular wall of cut stone, tapering toward its broken top – the simplest of towers.

He approached it. The tower must have been very old, since

a tree had grown inside it. Its slit entrance had once been blocked with slabs of stone, now scattered on the ground. Nish edged in through the slit. A concentric inner wall followed the outer, inside which was a space a few long strides across, living quarters for the family that had once dwelt here. The trunk of the tree occupied a good fifth of that space, so the structure must have been abandoned for centuries.

Nish climbed the broken inside wall, which formed a series of steps. Peering over the top, he tried to imagine himself here when it was new, looking out in fear for the coming of marauders. Protecting his family.

He could not see much; the forest was too dense. But there might not have been forest here in ancient times. He looked the other way. Vithis and another Aachim stood behind a screen of bushes, as if watching for someone.

Nish became aware that Minis was standing in the clearing, but he had not seen him arrive. Minis crept around the tower. Nish pulled his head low. A dark-haired figure emerged and his heart skipped a beat, thinking it was Tiaan. It was not; the woman's hair was curly and she was smaller, more stocky. She vanished in the dappled shade, appearing on the other side of the clearing next to Minis.

He spoke rapidly to her. Nish did not catch any of it. The woman handed Minis a small packet, Minis dropped something into her hand, then she fleeted across the clearing and vanished.

Vithis came charging out of the bushes. His guard went the other way but neither managed to catch the flying figure. Minis did not move; his young face showed dismay.

'What are you doing here?' Vithis plucked the packet from Minis's unresisting hand.

Minis made no reply. Vithis ripped open the packet, which contained some papers. He read them, tore them to shreds and scattered them on the ground.

'Worthless rubbish! You'll never find it that way.'

'What are you talking about, foster-father?'

'I know what you're up to. Come down!' He looked up, directly at the stone behind which Nish was hidden.

How had he known? Nish climbed down, and when he appeared around the side of the tower, Minis paled.

'What . . .?' he said.

'I know everything, foster-son,' said Vithis, and embraced him, to Minis's surprise. 'You are a dutiful son, Minis. Your loyalty means everything to me; we have only each other. But why did you not tell me what you were planning?'

Minis, clearly, was wondering what his foster-father knew and how much he could safely say. Nish came to his rescue.

'He did not want to raise false hopes. Minis knows it will be difficult to find the flying construct, even with my help.'

Vithis whirled. 'I didn't ask you! Don't speak unless you are spoken to.

'You should have told me, foster-son,' he continued. 'I could have helped you. It fills me with terror to think of you going out, alone. Were this man an enemy, just a single thrust of his knife and Inthis First Clan would be no more.'

'I was not alone, foster-father. I had my personal guard, and Tyara and Vunio too.'

'They are just children!'

'And so must I remain, *foster*-father, unless you let me go. You're suffocating me.'

'I'm doing what I must to ensure the survival of our clan. I am sterile – you know that. It's up to you, Minis. Take one of the partners I have chosen for you. Father children for our clan – and for me!'

Minis's face went blank. 'I don't love them, foster-father.'

'Love has nothing to do with it!' Vithis roared, but he controlled himself and went on, pleadingly. 'Why won't you do your duty, that our clan may live again?'

'I can't, foster-father.'

'Why not?'

'I just can't.'

'Until you do, I shall not give you your freedom.'

Minis stiffened. His eyes darted around – at the trees, the construct, at Nish. He took three deliberate breaths, drew back his shoulders and looked Vithis in the eye.

'You love me too much, foster-father, and it is killing me! If you won't let me be free . . . I shall not live at all.'

Vithis reeled back as if he had been struck. 'No,' he whispered.

'Yes, foster-father, I mean it.'

'But . . . what about Inthis?'

'Our clan is finished. One man cannot bring it back.'

'You must.' Vithis held the young man's gaze and softened his tones. 'Minis, let us not be foes, for all we have is each other. Give me what I want and I will do the same for you. Is what I ask so much?'

Minis gulped as if the air was a stiff drink. 'I . . . I will try, foster-father. It's hard –'

'I know it is, my son.' Vithis smiled. 'But we grow by attempting that which is difficult, not what is easy.'

'I understand that, foster-father. I am working hard to help you with your quest – for Tiaan and the flying machine.'

'I am pleased to hear it.'

'But might is not the answer. There is virtue in subtlety, especially with Tiaan. That is why I asked my friend Nish for help. He knows this world better than any of us. He knows Tiaan, too. He is brave and strong and clever. If anyone can find her, it will be him.'

Vithis tore a strip of bark off the tree, his fingers shredding it into fibres. 'He is an untrustworthy villain and his father has an evil reputation.'

'Nish is an honourable man. Please, foster-father, allow me this. I feel such a failure. I want to do it, for you.'

'You are my son, my heir. You are no failure.'

'I am, *in my own eyes*. I must earn my place like everyone else.'

Vithis stalked across to the construct, laying his hand on the dark metal. It seemed to give him comfort for he turned at once.

'Very well. On one condition.'

'What, foster-father?'

'That when you find her, and the flier, you will do your duty by me and your clan, and father heirs.'

Minis went through another visible struggle, and in the end bowed his head. 'I will do as you say, foster-father.'

Vithis beamed and clapped him on the back. 'You have a month to search out this flying construct for me.'

'Thank you, foster-father.' Minis took his hand. 'I know how hard it is to let your only heir go.'

'You can *never* know what it is like to be alone in the world,' said Vithis.

'I've spent my life that way. I've never had anyone but you.'

'That was hard,' said Vithis, 'but it is harder yet to have had a clan, and to have seen them die before your eyes, every one!'

Minis looked away. Nish did too. Vithis's grief was not something he was able to watch.

'I'll take good care of myself, foster-father,' Minis said after a long interval. 'You'll have nothing to worry about.'

'To be a parent is to worry,' said Vithis. 'I will be in an agony of terror all the time you are separated from me. And as for you, Cryl-Nish Hlar. Should you raise a finger – nay, even raise your voice against my son, I will hunt you down, even if I have to follow you to the bottom of the Well of Echoes!'

'He's finally gone,' said Minis, as the construct whined away. 'I thought he never would. And he has given me my way after all.' He smiled at Nish.

Nish could not smile back. He was no longer a partner with Minis but his servant, perhaps his slave, and if by some chance he did locate Tiaan's construct, Minis would get the credit. He, Nish, would have nothing to bargain with. Vithis would have no need for alliance with either side. The war with the lyrinx would escalate in violence until neither side had anything left, and Vithis would walk in and make Santhenar his own as he had always intended.

How could he turn this situation around? If he could not, better make sure the Aachim did not find Tiaan or the flying construct. That could be the most deadly game of all, in which case he must try to learn all he could about the Aachim, so that when he fled he would have some intelligence to take back. That thought afforded Nish bitter amusement as he followed Minis, whose construct was hidden in the trees some distance away. Nish's life kept cycling back to the beginning. It seemed he was to be a prober, the lowest of the spying rank, after all. He let out an involuntary snort.

Minis turned back. 'Is something the matter, my friend?'

'I was just thinking how hard this job is going to be,' Nish said evasively. 'I've no idea where to begin.'

'We've been looking for Tiaan for some time. There are many people we can talk to.'

'Can you not use your gift, Minis?

'What gift is that?'

'Of foretelling.'

'It is as much a curse as a gift, for it comes only when it wants. I have no control over it. Well, hardly any. There was a time . . .' He looked away.

'What, Minis?'

'It is not right to say.'

He strode ahead and Nish had to trot to keep up with him. Nish felt a creeping unease. 'It's about me, isn't it? You've seen my future. Minis, if you have, you've got to tell me.'

'It doesn't help, Nish. It never can. That is the failing of fore-telling, no matter how much we want otherwise.'

'Please, Minis.'

'It's not you, Nish, but a friend.'

'Who?

'I did not see – only the end.'

'The end?'

'I'm sorry. I wish I'd never mentioned it.'

'You have to tell me now. You saw one of my friends die?'

'Yes,' said Minis sombrely, 'but I cannot tell you who, or how, or when. Do not ask me any more about it.'

Nish did not, but it was never far from his mind that day, and every day thereafter. Who could it be? An old friend or a new, or one not yet made?

As they reached the construct, Minis said quietly, 'Thank you for saying nothing to my father.'

'I beg your pardon?' Nish said, deep in the future.

'About Tiaan. He can never understand what I feel for her. All he can see is that I'm Aachim and she is old human.'

'Many such partnerships are mentioned in our Histories,' said Nish, 'though few were happy ones. And there is the matter of issue. Any children would be blendings, sometimes with unusual talents, but more often mad. And, of course, you live much longer than our kind.'

'None of that matters to me. It would be different with Tiaan; I know it!'

'I hope so,' said Nish, thinking what a fool Minis was. Tiaan would never have him back. Even if she did, Vithis would make Minis's life a misery. The liaison would be a disaster and a true friend would do everything he could to prevent it.

And also, if Minis did find Tiaan, and develop a relationship with her, Vithis would end up with the flying construct. No one could stop that. It could not be allowed to happen. The flying construct would make Vithis too powerful. For the sake of humanity, he, Nish, must prevent it, and so he had to thwart Minis however he could.

He thinks I am his friend, yet secretly I'm working against him. Maybe I'm more like my father than I thought.

FIFTY

'You knew my sight was going to come back all along,' Irisis accused. 'That's why you were so mean to me.'

'I did not, which is why I said nothing. Sight often does come back after that kind of burn. Equally often, it does not.'

'So why *were* you so mean?'

'Perhaps I thought the lesson might be good for you.'

'It wasn't!' she snapped.

'You managed to overcome *that* disability,' Flydd said meaningfully. 'Without you, we would have learned nothing about the nodes.'

They stared over the rail for a while; then the scrutator said, 'On the other hand, maybe I'm just a mean-spirited old sod.'

'Maybe you bloody well are.'

Flydd came over the side. 'Done it – I've set Jal-Nish's skeets free. That'll give us a few more days. Where's Ullii?'

'Usual place,' said Irisis.

Ullii was still hunched up in the corner of the cabin, under one of the canvas benches.

'Come out, Ullii.'

Ullii shook her head.

'What's the matter?'

'Don't beat me,' she whispered.

'Why would I beat you?'

Ullii was not going to answer *that* question. 'Scrutator is angry with me.'

'I've never seen him more cheerful. Come on.'

Ullii emerged reluctantly. 'You look well,' said Irisis. 'I think you might have put on weight lately.'

'Been hungry.'

He put his head around the door of the cabin. 'Hello, Ullii. Have you forgiven *me* yet?' He chuckled at his own wit.

'No,' said Ullii.

Irisis slept what remained of the night and most of the following day, waking to discover that Oon-Mie and Zoyl were gone. She was sorry not to have farewelled them.

Each time she woke the view was much the same – towering peaks clad in snow and ice. From the manufactory the air-floater ran north-west then north, along the rim of the Great Mountains for a hundred leagues. That took two days. They then turned west, to cross at the point where the mountain chain that ran up the east coast of Lauralin, all the way to Crandor, met the vastness of the Great Mountains. The peaks were higher than the air-floater could rise so they had to follow a zigzag course up the valleys and over the lowest passes they could find. It was a wild, rocking ride that left everyone airsick.

'Where are we going?' she asked Flydd on the morning of the fifth day out of the manufactory.

'You'll see when we get there. Pray that Jal-Nish didn't have another skeet hidden somewhere.'

'Why?'

'Because if his version of the tale gets there first, we're done for.'

The air-floater was travelling slowly now, for they were a long way from the nearest node and the field was weak. The machine had descended until it was just skimming the ground. Higher up, the wind blew so strongly from the west that they could not move against it. Down here the wind was erratic, sometimes

515

tossing them on unexpected updraughts, as suddenly ceasing altogether or carrying them as fast as a racing yacht.

Early the following morning, the air-floater turned south and headed towards the ground. The country had changed in the night. There were still mountains all around, but below lay a sunken land, rifted on all sides, with a flat desert bottom upon which lakes glistened. The ones in the middle had dried to salt. Many rivers ran into this desolate lowland but none ran out.

'Kalithras,' said Flydd. 'The Desolation Sink. What a miserable place.'

They were heading towards a dark structure on the southern edge of the sunken land, an escarpment that might have been a thousand spans above the floor of Kalithras, though all around the mountains towered to twice and even thrice that height. Straining her still-sore eyes, Irisis made out an immense fortress or bastion.

'Nennifer,' said Flydd gloomily. 'Our destination.'

A pair of skeets wheeled in the air high above the building, one coming, the other going. Flydd ran up to the pilot, pointing at the descending birds. The air-floater dropped sharply, racing toward Nennifer. A vast square building, four or five storeys high, covered by a mass of steep roofs, it made no concessions to either environment or aesthetics. Plain rectangular windows ran across the front and the front door was set right in the middle. Everything was symmetrical. It looked out of place and was meant to. The scrutators did not have to fit in. They controlled.

Out the front, an area the size of a parade ground was paved with stone all the way to the edge of the escarpment. 'Land there!' Flydd indicated a spot near the brink.

The machine thumped into the ground. Flydd sprang over the side, his eye on the wheeling skeet. Attendants ran out, grasping the tethers and tying them to shiny new brass rings set in the stone.

'Come on, crafter.' Flydd was pacing back and forth, his single eyebrow twitching. 'Ullii, you too. Now we shall see what we see.'

The skeet was gliding towards the rear of the building. Ullii was on the floor of the cabin, searching for her mask. Irisis got down with her.

'What is this place?' she called.

'Nennifer is the hidden bastion of the Council of Scrutators, and I don't expect they'll be pleased to see me. Or you, for that matter. Get a move on.'

'Ullii's lost her mask.' She added, 'I've never heard of Nennifer.'

'It was the most secret place in the world until M'lainte invented the air-floater. I believe it's come as a shock to the Council that Nennifer is no longer hidden.'

'Must have made it difficult for them to rule,' she said, 'being weeks journey from everywhere.'

'They've had plenty of practice. They use hundreds of skeets, as well as . . . never mind. The querists and perquisitors do most of the work, and not all of the scrutators dwell at Nennifer. Only those on the Council.'

'Here it is.' Irisis jumped out, reaching back for her pack.

'You won't need that,' he said. 'We won't be staying. Or if we do, you still won't need it!'

She flinched. 'Sounds ominous.'

'I didn't mean to alarm you.' He linked his arm through hers. 'Don't look nervous. That's a sign of weakness and as such is deadly here. At the Council of Scrutators you must laugh in the face of death.'

'Is that how you got your scars?'

He chuckled mirthlessly. 'I laughed at the wrong moment. Hush! They're coming.'

A big man strode towards them, scarlet robes flowing behind. Broad-shouldered and handsome, with a noble mane of dark hair and a full beard, he looked everything Flydd was not.

'That's Ghorr,' said Flydd. 'Chief of the Council. He is not my friend.'

Ghorr looked thunderous. Another group of robed individuals appeared on the broad steps behind him, ten in all. They were all sizes, shapes and races. Four were women, the rest men. None were young, but neither did any look ancient,

517

though some, including Ghorr, were well over a hundred years old. But what every one of them did have was power. Irisis did not have to touch her pliance to tell that. They exuded power and unchallengeable authority and Irisis, whose contempt for authority ran deep, despised them for it. Authority was the first weapon of the Council and there was not a soul on Lauralin who had not felt it.

'You've got a damned nerve!' said Ghorr, 'coming here after what you've done. Guards!' He signalled over his head.

'Hear me, Ghorr!' Flydd said with magnificent arrogance. 'I may just save the war for you.'

'That's a claim we're accustomed to hearing,' Ghorr retorted. 'From frauds and liars.'

'You've not heard it from me before.'

'You don't have a lot of credibility left, Flydd.'

'If I haven't more than that charlatan, Jal-Nish –'

'I'd advise you not to take that tone,' said Ghorr.

'Are you prepared to listen or not!' Flydd snarled. 'If not, get out of my way and I'll be off again.'

Irisis caught her breath. His arrogance was breathtaking. She prayed he knew what he was doing.

'You won't be going anywhere, Flydd.' Ghorr gripped his arm.

'I would hear what he has to say,' said a small, dark woman named as Halie.

'And I,' said another woman, old and dumpy. Her sandy hair had been teased up into a nest which could not conceal that she was going bald. 'We can't afford to pass up any opportunity, no matter how . . .' she studied Flydd like a small worm on a large hook, '. . . disreputable the messenger.'

'Thank you, T'Lisp.' Flydd bowed in her direction, obsequiously low.

'Don't bother!' T'Lisp snapped. 'I'll be the first to see you flayed should your story fail you.'

'Very well,' said Ghorr. 'I'll give you leave to address the Council, Flydd, though I don't see it doing you any good. Who the hell is this?'

'This is Crafter Irisis Stirm, as you very well know.'

'The woman who slew a mancer though she is not one herself? I will speak to *you* later about that, crafter. And the other?'

'The seeker, Ullii.'

'Ah! Even so, they must stay behind, Flydd. No outsider may enter the Council.'

'Then we'd better meet on the front steps. Irisis and Ullii are vital to the story and there's no time to waste on pointless formalities. The war can be won, or lost, while we're standing here arguing.'

They met on the cold steps, and the displeasure on the faces of the scrutators was manifest. Except for one, little dark Halie who, if not exactly looking pleased to see Xervish Flydd, at least did not appear hostile.

'We have discovered the secret of why the nodes are failing,' said Flydd without preamble.

The group muttered among themselves.

'The Council is listening,' said Ghorr finally, 'but we will not be swayed easily.'

'We have investigated three failed nodes,' Flydd said. 'The first, at Minnien, we found to be regenerating its field.'

'What?' cried Halie. 'This is very good news.'

'Should it prove to be true,' said Ghorr. 'What more have you to say about Minnien?'

'Only that we saw a lyrinx there. It removed an object that had been placed at Minnien some time ago. Afterwards the field quickly grew stronger. It would appear that they have built, or *grown*, a node-draining device.'

'It is as I suspected,' said Halie. 'Show us this object, Flydd.'

The scrutator faltered. 'I . . . don't have it.'

Suddenly every eye was on him and Flydd was no longer a worm on a hook; he was an insect being pinned to a board by a throng of cold-eyed philosophers.

'Why not?' Ghorr said with icy calm.

'They took it away.'

'And you allowed them to?'

'I did not realise the lyrinx had taken anything until later, when the node began to regenerate.'

'A costly failure. Had you brought back such a device, we might have reconsidered your position. As you have no evidence that it even exists, I can only assume you're lying to try to regain your standing. No one has ever found a node-drainer.'

Flydd restrained himself, though not without a struggle. 'They've been looking in the wrong place. It doesn't have to be close to the node.'

'In which case it can be anywhere, and impossible to find.'

'Ah!' said Flydd. 'But we *did* find one.'

That created a sensation. The scrutators began to chatter among themselves. 'He's lying,' said Ghorr.

Halie stood up. 'Where is it, Xervish?'

'In good time, my friend,' said Flydd. 'I must be allowed to give you the full tale.' He called upon Irisis to tell her version of what had happened at Minnien, which she did. One part aroused the interest of all, including the chief scrutator.

'Fields like two planes at right angles,' said Ghorr, glancing at his fellow scrutators. 'Can it be –?'

'We'll come back to that, if you please,' said Flydd.

'So the only evidence of a node-drainer was a few dried-up shreds of leathery plant,' said Halie. 'Not enough, Flydd. Did you do any better at the second node?'

'The one inland from Fadd we found to be completely dead. There was not the least trace of a field.'

'No news there,' said a short man with a black spade beard and a cross-shaped bald patch at the top of an ovoid head. Snake eyes glittered. 'You're not telling us anything we don't know, Ex-Scrutator Flydd.'

'I'm giving a damn sight more than you ever have for your councillor's badge, Fusshte!' said Flydd, so vehemently that the short man drew back. 'It was at Fadd that Crafter Irisis made the breakthrough. Tell them, crafter.'

'I merely wondered,' said Irisis, 'that if a node-drainer *was* at work, what was happening to all the power it drained. Wherever that power was going, there had to be proof of it.'

'Ahhh!' sighed Halie. 'So I was right after all. They do have a node-drainer.' She cast the others a bitter glance. 'Had the Council listened, we might have solved this problem years ago.'

'We hear a dozen crack-brained ideas every week,' said Ghorr. 'And without evidence, that's all they are. Get on with it, crafter.'

No one interrupted as Irisis told her story, after which the Council questioned her. The process was calm and measured, yet Irisis knew she was being weighed by eleven of the sharpest minds on Santhenar. And not just her words. Every flicker of her eyelashes, every drop of sweat on her brow, was evidence in their interrogation.

And all were mancers. All were probing her with the strange version of the Art that was scrutator magic. The waistband of her pants was soaked with perspiration by the time Ghorr signed that they were done. And, to her relief, he seemed satisfied that what she had said was true.

Flydd resumed his tale. 'Finally, we went back to Irisis's manufactory to inspect the node, which lies deep in the hedron mine.'

'That was a foolhardy deed,' said Halie.

'But essential. That node was already weak –'

'So Jal-Nish has told us,' said Ghorr, 'because you failed to protect it from the enemy.'

'I believe that has already been covered in despatches,' said Flydd.

'Not to my satisfaction.'

'As soon as we started to sense the field it went dead. As if someone had been watching and turned it off.'

'Is that all?' cried Fusshte.

'We could find no node-drainer there either,' said Flydd. 'Then Jal-Nish –'

'Jal-Nish was at the node?' someone cried.

'He, er, interrupted us,' said Flydd. 'Jal-Nish asked the seeker a most interesting question. He asked her if she could see the field of the node. Tell the Council what your answer was, Ullii.'

Ullii had been sitting so quietly, hunched up into a little ball, that she was practically invisible. Now she unfolded, gave the assembled scrutators a frightened glance, and said in a wispy little voice, 'I could see all sorts of fields.'

'*Fields?*' cried Ghorr. 'Explain, seeker.'

'The node had four fields,' she said, mimicking his voice. She had not done that in ages. 'There was a weak one that people called *the field*, but it was dead. The clawers had drained it all away.'

'"Clawers" means lyrinx,' said Flydd obsequiously.

'Don't treat us like fools!' said Ghorr. 'Go on with your story, seeker.'

'There were three more fields, like walls going through each other. They were very bright.'

'The *strong* forces,' breathed Ghorr. 'At last! Have you seen such forces before, Ullii?'

'Yes,' she exhaled.

'Where?'

'I can't remember.'

Ullii was looking distressed and Irisis knew why. No one had thought to ask her the question, but she dared not give that answer.

Irisis took the seeker's hand. 'Ullii,' she said kindly, 'what you know about these fields may be vital. Please think where you might have seen them before.'

'I saw them at the cold place where I helped you – where there was an evil node.'

'Up on the icy plateau near the manufactory? When we were trying to get Tiaan back from the lyrinx?'

'Yes,' Ullii whispered, darting anxious glances at the Council.

'Were there also four fields?'

'I think so. The evil node was double. I could not see it clearly.' Her voice was barely audible.

'If these *are* the strong forces, why does she not see them all the time?' said Fusshte.

'Perhaps the weak field obscures them,' said Flydd. 'That would explain why she, and the artisan Zoyl Aarp, only saw them after the node was drained.'

'Perhaps,' said Ghorr dubiously. 'We must investigate this further.'

He questioned the seeker at length, but learned no more. Ullii simply saw; she did not understand.

'I then asked Ullii if she could see what was draining the manufactory node,' said Flydd. 'She told us that the drainer was not far away, up the tunnel beyond a roof fall, no doubt caused by the enemy. We found it. Rather, we discovered where it was, though it was not possible to get to it. It was a most strange place; the fabric of matter did not hold there. Jal-Nish fell right into the floor. The rock could not hold him up.'

'Fascinating,' said Ghorr. 'A marvel, *should it prove to be true*! What happened to the acting scrutator?'

'He survived,' said Flydd regretfully, 'though I'm not sure if all his troops did. He was not a happy man when we left him.' He looked toward the entrance. 'I imagine that will be his despatches now.'

A messenger was hurrying out through the great doors, carrying a sealed skeet packet. Ghorr tore it open and scanned the contents, before passing it to the Council.

'It would appear to confirm the last part of your story,' he said, 'though Jal-Nish takes the credit for it and accuses you . . . Leave us for the moment, Flydd.'

Flydd, Irisis and Ullii strolled on the edge of the precipice, but shortly were called back to the steps.

'We have accepted your account,' said Ghorr, 'and thank you for bringing it to us.' He did not look pleased to be saying it. 'The Council has voted and, despite several . . . er, irregularities in your behaviour, agreed to restore you to your position as scrutator, though not to the Council, of course.'

'Thank you,' said Flydd, bowing to each in turn. 'And Jal-Nish? Does he keep his?'

'The acting scrutator's service has been satisfactory. He maintains that rank.'

Flydd was impassive, though it must have been a blow. While Jal-Nish had any authority at all, he would work to bring Flydd down. 'As the Council pleases.'

'I have not finished. The war is coming to a head in the west. The lyrinx are gathering their strength, across the Sea of Thurkad, for a mighty strike – one we cannot resist. We have two choices: to abandon everything west of Worm Wood, or to make our stand now.'

'We cannot abandon Almadin, Rencid and Taltid,' said Flydd. 'A million people dwell there, plus most of the refugees from Meldorin. Besides –'

'Yes?'

'Even if we did draw the line at Worm Wood, we could not hold it. Nihilnor must fall and Oolo soon after, and within months the whole south-west will be gone. Once that happens, not even the might of Borgistry could stand alone. And if the west is lost, the rest of Lauralin must follow.'

'Indeed,' said Ghorr. 'We *must* make our stand and make it soon. Even so, we are looking at a crushing defeat unless we can convince the Aachim to aid us.'

'Then that must be our primary objective,' said Flydd.

'It is,' Ghorr replied, 'but Vithis of Clan Inthis is a most recalcitrant man.'

'Where is he now?'

'His forces are spread through Almadin, Nihilnor and Borgistry. To the discomfiture of their citizens, it need not be said. His plans for conquest, if that is what they were, appear to be on hold. There is dissension among the Aachim clans which we are hoping to exploit.'

'And the cause of this disagreement?' said Flydd.

'Longstanding clan rivalries, as well as a dispute about their course of action.'

'Please elaborate.'

'Some clans wish to ally with us against the lyrinx, others to take advantage of our present discomfort to seize our best lands for themselves. One or two clans argue that the Aachim cause would be better served by taking the lyrinx side.'

'Does any viewpoint look like prevailing?'

'I cannot say. It is difficult to gain reliable intelligence. But Vithis, as leader of this uneasy coalition, is the key. Presently he has a different agenda, which is why the Aachim have put the invasion on hold. He has sent his entire force after Artisan Tiaan and the flying construct.'

'Ah, yes, the flying construct,' said Halie. 'If we had a dozen of those we would win the war.'

'No doubt Vithis feels the same way.'

'We'd better hope he doesn't find it,' said Flydd. 'If we do attack, where will the battle for the west be fought?'

'There is a place called Snizort, in Taltid,' said Ghorr.

'I know of it,' said Flydd.

'It is the enemy's greatest stronghold on our side of the sea, and where they carry out all sorts of . . . experiments. Snizort also has some kind of mystical significance to them, though we have not discovered what it is. If we could take Snizort it would be a great blow to the enemy. We've been working on a plan to do that.'

'What is it?'

Ghorr drew Flydd away from Irisis's hearing. 'The lyrinx have dug a great system of tunnels into the stone surrounding the tar pits and seeps of Snizort. The area is walled and heavily defended, but the locale has a natural vulnerability –'

'To fire!' said Flydd. 'You plan to set fire to the tar seeps and burn the lyrinx out, straight onto our spears and javelards.'

'Just so.' Ghorr showed his irritation. 'But it will not be easy, even with a mighty army. To get close enough to bombard them with flaming catapult balls will take every man of the sixty thousand we can muster in the west, and the seven thousand clankers that support them. And even that may not be enough. The lyrinx know how susceptible Snizort is, yet they continue to expand it. It does not make sense.'

'Unless it's so vital to them that it's worth any risk. In which case they probably have secret defences,' said Flydd.

'I don't suppose there's any chance of using air-floaters to attack the place?'

'They can't carry enough weight to be useful in an attack. And they're too vulnerable.'

'I thought as much.' Ghorr walked away, then came back. He seemed more tentative now.

'You want something of me?' said Flydd.

Ghorr was staring at the paving stones. 'Your coming is, er, at an opportune moment. The news you bring, even more so. We have a problem. Rather, a fatal flaw in our plan.'

Flydd waited for him to go on.

'The node at Snizort appears to be weakening,' said Ghorr.

'Snizort has one of the greatest of all nodes. That doesn't make any sense.'

'Unless they are drawing more from the field than the node can replenish. If so, what are they doing there? Nothing to our advantage, you can be sure.'

'Or they may have a node-drainer in place,' said Flydd.

'Why would they drain their own node?'

'To siphon power directly, for other purposes. Snizort is known to be a centre for flesh-forming. Perhaps they're flesh-forming an army there.'

'We may suppose any outlandish idea at all, but it won't help us to win the war. We've been planning this assault for months. It was to be the greatest battle of the war, but without a secure field to drive our clankers we dare not move. We've discussed this and . . .'

'You want me to go there?' said Flydd. He did not look surprised.

'As soon as the buoyant air in your floater can be replenished. You will take charge and find out what is happening at the node. Base yourself at Gospett. We have people there. Halie will give you the details. Your main task, which is more vital than all others, will be to make contact with Vithis and bring the Aachim into the war on our side.'

Flydd nodded. 'At any cost?'

After a long silence, with Ghorr consulting his colleagues, he said, 'Yes, at any cost, if there is no other option. You must use your discretion. Don't give up our –'

'I will give away nothing but what it takes to secure the alliance,' said Flydd. 'What else do you require of me?'

'One more task,' said Ghorr. 'If the enemy *have* put a node-drainer in place . . .'

'Yes?'

'Find it, and destroy it.'

Five simple words, so easy to say, but they were his death sentence. No human could get into such a heavily guarded place – Ghorr knew that as well as he did. It was Ghorr's revenge, and it was perfect. Destroying the node-drainer was vital to the war and the chief scrutator had given a direct order. Flydd could not refuse.

He looked into Ghorr's eyes. The man hoped he *would* refuse, so he could dismiss him as a scrutator. A death sentence either way. Flydd was not going to give him the satisfaction.

'If I destroy the node-drainer, *if* there is one, they will simply replace it.'

'If they were easy to make, the lyrinx would have dealt with every node on the planet by now. Since they've only attacked five or six, we must assume that's all the devices they have.'

'Assumptions are perilous things,' said Flydd.

'Destroy it!' said Ghorr.

'That may be . . . *difficult.*'

'I'm sure it will be, but we all have our duty to do and it is frequently difficult. If you are having second thoughts; if you don't have the courage –'

Flydd's eyes met those of Irisis. She read nothing there.

'No,' he said. 'I will take it on, *surr.*'

Ghorr smiled for the first time. Prominent teeth gave him the look of a hyena. 'Good. We'll have dinner inside, brief you fully and then it will be time for you to go. But not you, Irisis. You and Ullii will stay behind.' His smile broadened. 'There is much you two can teach us.'

Ullii gave a terrified squawk and scuttled under Irisis's arm.

FIFTY-ONE

The seeker had been escorted to her own room, away down the other end of Nennifer from Irisis's. It was a cold, shabby little place, suited only for the lowest of servants. That did not bother Ullii, for she took no account of her surroundings. It had a door that kept the sound out, and that was all she cared about. It allowed her to take off the earmuffs she wore everywhere. They were as comfortable as human ingenuity could make them, but still irritated her.

Ullii undressed and washed in a bucket of cold water. She rinsed her spider-silk undergarments, carefully spread a clean set on the bed and lay down on them. She could not bear anything else against her skin. Closing her eyes, she retreated to the security of her mental lattice, a matrix in which she tried to fit all the world within range of her strange talent.

Security would not come. Nennifer was not a pleasant place. It had whole floors of mancers, artisans, artificers and other craft workers, all labouring on devices for spying, control, domination or war. They created such aggressive knots in her lattice that Ullii had to build walls around them, for her own sanity.

And now the scrutator was being sent away. Despite the grudge she held against Flydd for forcing her to search for crystal, months ago, Ullii relied on him. He had been a friend, before he was mean to her. He was still her protector and treated her more kindly than anyone ever had, except her beloved Nish. But Nish was lost and now the scrutator was going away. She relied on Irisis too, but Irisis was being held by wicked Scrutator Ghorr, who was surely going to do something dreadful to her. Who would look after Ullii then?

Who had ever looked after her? In all her previous life, only old Mancer Flammas, who had put her in his dungeon and forgotten all about her. She still thought kindly of him for that. In the cool dark she had found peace from the noise, the sight and smell of humanity, not to mention the world that had so tormented her. In his dungeon no one had troubled her. They gave her food and drink, hosed out her cell at intervals, and left her be.

But that had changed one day when she was sixteen. She had disturbed something unpleasant in her lattice, began to scream and Flammas remembered her. Jal-Nish Hlar took her away and the nightmare of the world resumed. He had treated her kindly at first, though only because he wanted to use her talent. She knew what he was really like. She could *read* the knot he made in her lattice all too clearly.

Ullii's thoughts went back to the years before Flammas's dungeon: that terrible time, beginning just before she was four, when something had woken her hypersensitivity. Life had become such a nightmare that her family, unable to understand what the matter was, or beat it out of her, had cast Ullii out.

She had always avoided thinking about that time. Ullii had blanked it out. Her family had rejected her. And even before *that* she had been abandoned . . .

Ullii drifted into sleep, still thinking about her childhood. She had been happy once, when she was young, but a family crisis had swept it away. She did not know what the crisis had been about, only the consequences. It had been just before her fourth birthday. One day her beloved twin brother, Myllii, had been there. The next day he, and her father, had gone. She never saw either of them again. She missed her father, but words could not describe the loss of Myllii. It was like having a limb torn off.

A week later, an irritating inflammation of the skin had

529

covered her whole body. She screamed with the torment, fell ill, sank into a coma and lay near death for a fortnight. Ullii came out of it unable to talk or walk. Everything had to be learned again. Before she recovered, the sensitivity began to appear. She remembered that with jewel-like clarity. It had begun with loud voices. Everyone seemed to be shouting all the time, and the shouting grew louder and louder until it hurt her. Every time someone spoke, she screamed. Her mother beat her, her brothers and sisters and aunts shouted at her, but she only screamed louder.

Then her sense of touch grew monstrously. Her clothes rasped against her sensitised skin and she took to tearing them off. Her mother and aunts beat her for that too, for they could not understand. The beatings made no difference. They were preferable to the coarse fabric against her skin.

Taste was the next sense to swell out of proportion. The pickled fish and smoked meats the family lived on became unbearable to Ullii. She could eat nothing but fruit and raw vegetables, gruel and an occasional piece of raw fish or flavourless baby lamb.

Her sense of smell attacked her. The odour of people, even those who bathed frequently, became revolting. Her family were not frequent bathers; it was not the custom in the cold land they came from. Though she craved to be held, Ullii could not bear to sit on her mother's lap.

Last and worst was sight. First she could not stand to go outside. The bright sun burned her eyes, the light hurt her sensitive skin. Then she could not be in a lighted room. She began to spend the days in the dark under her bed. Her mother and aunts beat her. Ullii screamed and screamed, and would not stop. The whole world was a torment.

She had wept for Myllii and begged her mother to bring him back, but Myllii had been taken far away and no one knew where he was. Ullii went mad with screaming and her mother and aunts, unable to bear it any longer, eventually put her out the door.

Now she dreamed about her brother, not as a child of four but as the young man Myllii must be, nearly eighteen. She saw him in her dreams and he looked just like her, though his colourless hair was shorter, cut straight across just above his ears. He was a hand's breadth taller than she, with broader shoulders and narrower hips, but his beardless face was like her reflection in the mirror.

Myllii, she sighed, knowing it was just a dream. She could never find him, no matter how she had tried. When first she began to develop her lattice, in Flammas's dungeon, it had been in order to search for Myllii. She would have recognised his knot instantly, but had never seen it. Many times since then she had looked for him, but he was nowhere to be found.

Perhaps he had no talent, though she could not believe that. Her brother and herself had been like two sides of a coin, equal but opposite. Neither had been complete without the other.

She *would* not believe he was dead, for if he was, she must die as well. She could not live knowing that he was gone forever. Most likely he was just too far away, beyond reach of her lattice. She could still hope. She could still search.

The lattice had been her comfort for so long that sometimes she forgot it was there. She had not looked deeply into it for days, not since leaving the manufactory in the air-floater. Now, in her dreams, Ullii did.

The lattice here was profoundly different from the one she was used to. It was almost unfamiliar, being dominated by the geomantic forces that had created the enormous mountains all around, and the sunken land to the north. So much in it was strange that it would take days, even weeks, for her to make sense of it all.

And then there was the might and magic of Nennifer itself, a place dedicated to scrutator magic. Everywhere she looked, Ullii saw the dark knots that signified magical artefacts, devices and implements of war, spying and torment, and the differently shaped knots that represented mancers and other practitioners of the Art. They frightened her. Ullii had suffered at the hands of such people before.

In the maze of knots, lines and other markings, Ullii knew it could take days to find Myllii. She began at once. All through that night she sought him in her dreams, and every minute of the following day. That evening she went to bed early. It was easier to look for him asleep than waking.

Myllii?

Ullii, where have you been? I've been looking for you.

I'm lost without you, Myllii. Ah, Myllii, I nearly died when you were taken away from me.

And so did I. I wept for years.

She did not allow herself to speak, just drew comfort from his existence. Time floated. She felt deliriously happy.

Are you like me, Myllii? Can you go out in the sun, unprotected?

Of course. Can't you?

She felt strangely let down. She wanted them to be alike in everything, even suffering. Especially suffering. She told him how much she had suffered.

Ullii, he said. *If only I had been there. If . . .*

She lost him. Ullii spent the rest of the night searching the lattice but found no trace of Myllii. Perhaps it had just been a dream.

Flydd was delayed and delayed again, though he would not say what the problem was. All Irisis learned was that something was being hastily prepared for him to take to Gospett and it was taking longer than expected to complete.

She was questioned repeatedly about the way she had killed the unnamed mancer on the aqueduct. She had always known that she had done something unusual that day, but not how unusual. With all her other nightmares, she had not spent much time thinking about that one.

'I've gone over it twenty times already,' she said tiredly on the second night. She was walking out the front of Nennifer, along the edge of the pavement with Flydd. 'There's nothing more I can tell them. Why do they keep on about it?'

'Because you did something that has not been done before,' said Flydd, 'and it tips the balance against all mancers. They, *we*, have always seen ourselves as being at the top of the pile. Not invulnerable, certainly, but well protected. If we can be bested at our Art by a mere artisan, a wretched craft worker, it turns our lives upside down. What if the enemy learned to do what you have done? No querist, perquisitor or even scrutator would be safe.'

'Unlikely, since the lyrinx cannot use our Arts.'

'Should they have learned to, they would certainly want us to think they were still incapable. Besides, the lyrinx are adept at finding new ways of doing things.'

'I still don't see why it's such a problem.'

'The Council must also look to a future when they have won the war and their power may be under challenge. They must protect themselves. That means discovering exactly what you did, then making sure that you can't teach anyone else.'

She spun around to face him. 'What?'

'They're not planning to let you leave here alive, Irisis, though they'll wait till I've gone to do the deed. They can't afford to let you live. Keep walking. They may be watching us.'

'What are you going to do about it?'

'I don't know that I can do anything. As soon as everything is ready, I've got to go. I have no choice in the matter.'

After their escape, and getting her sight back, she had allowed herself to enjoy life from day to day, without thinking about the future. She had thought she was safe, under Flydd's protection. Poor fool.

'They're going to *kill* me?'

'They may not,' he said conversationally. 'You can't get away. There's only one path out of here and it's heavily guarded. They have a need for artisans and you're one of the best. And they may want to explore your unexpected talent.'

How could he be so casual? 'They must know that a question mark lies over my abilities. As soon as they discover how I overcame the mancer, they'll have no further use for me.'

'Then you must maintain the secret as long as possible.'

'I've already told them everything.'

'But they haven't been able to reproduce it, so they're sure you're keeping something back. Use it.'

533

'Look what they did to you, when you did that.'

He rubbed a scarred arm. 'Keeping secrets wasn't my failing. It was probing into *their* secrets.'

She couldn't take any more. 'I don't feel that you're being very helpful, Xervish! I feel that you've abandoned me already.'

'I'm under orders. I have to go to Gospett without delay.'

'You've disobeyed Council orders before.'

'If we lose this battle, we lose the west. You mean a lot to me, Irisis, but as I've told you many times, if it ever came to a choice between you and the greater good, I would make that choice. Now I've been put to it. How can I place you above the fate of the world?'

'You don't have to look so pleased about it,' she said.

'Don't be ridiculous. They're watching me every minute of the day, just waiting for me to make one wrong move. Look, Irisis, I'm –'

'Oh, go away!' she snapped. 'Do your precious duty. I always knew you were a true *scrutator*.'

Flydd's normally expressionless face changed. His eyes narrowed to dark crescents beneath that overhanging brow. 'And so I am.' With a mocking bow, he turned swiftly away to the bastion of Nennifer.

Irisis continued along the rim. This was the most extra-ordinary country she had ever been in. Behind Nennifer the mountains marched in ranks as far as she could see, and they were mighty peaks, far greater than the mountains near the manufactory. There was little snow on their steep flanks, though, and the lower slopes of the mountains were brown, arid smears.

Before her, below the escarpment, lay the vast sunken land of Kalithras – the Desolation Sink. It was bounded all around by escarpments like this one, and many rivers ran into it. None ran out, for the land lay below the level of the distant sea. It was as dry a hell-hole as she had seen.

She sat down near the edge, looking over. Her life had to end sometime. And perhaps Flydd was right: there was always the possibility that they would keep her alive. Nennifer must have thousands of workers. After all, she did have other talents.

534

Flydd met Irisis at dinner that night. 'I'm sorry,' he said. 'They're spying on me. I can't do anything for you.'

'Thanks.' She took up her bowl and moved to a table on the far side of the room. She thought she saw hurt in his eyes. Too bad. He'd get over it. And her. He was a scrutator after all, a lying, scheming, cheating manipulator who would do anything, and use anyone, to get what he wanted.

Irisis could normally enjoy eating no matter what her mood, and the food at Nennifer was very good, but she soon pushed the bowl away. She could not taste a thing.

Ullii appeared beside her. Irisis had not heard her coming. She never did. The seeker could move like a ghost when she wanted to, which was most of the time.

'Are you unhappy, Irisis?' Ullii said softly, insinuating her head under the taller woman's arm. She liked to get close to her friends and in this awful place, despite the feelings of jealousy that still plagued her, she felt close to Irisis.

Irisis presumed she was forgiven for pressuring Ullii weeks ago. 'I'm afraid, Ullii. The scrutators won't let me leave here alive.'

Ullii drew in her breath sharply, then rubbed her cheek along Irisis's arm. 'What have you done?'

Irisis explained.

'Mancer was an evil woman,' said the seeker.

'You knew her?'

'I read her knot in my lattice.' The tiny hairs on Ullii's arms stirred.

'You can tell a person's character from the way you see them in your lattice?'

'Of course.'

'What do you think of the scrutator. Is he evil too?'

Ullii gave her an ambiguous look and moved to a chair across the table. 'Scrutator was mean to me.'

Presumably she referred to the time Flydd had forced her to find crystals in the mine. Or perhaps when he'd roared at her to bring down the lift. Ullii did not forget an insult, or an injury. She could not strike back but, where she could get away with it, took pleasure in sullen non-cooperation.

'And Ghorr?' said Irisis.

'He is chief scrutator,' said Ullii, as if that was all there was to say. Perhaps it was.

Irisis was finishing her bowl of tea when Ullii hunched down in the chair with just her eyes showing over the edge of the table. What was it now?

Irisis looked around. The chief scrutator was heading towards her.

'Scurry away, little mouse,' he said contemptuously.

Ullii went sideways off the chair and disappeared among the tables.

Irisis looked Ghorr in the eye. She was almost as afraid of him as she had been of Jal-Nish, but she was damned if she was going to show it. 'Yes?' she said with an imperious tilt of her chin.

'You know what I want.'

'We've been through that.'

'Just tell me how you did it and you can go with Flydd tomorrow.'

'I may be just an artisan, Scrutator Ghorr, but I'm no fool. I know I'm not leaving here alive.'

He evinced no surprise. Ghorr seldom showed any reaction, except deliberately. 'As you wish. But there are more lives on offer than the one you've been leading. With a talent like yours, you could become a *mancer*.' He said it with emphasis, as though it was the pinnacle of everyone's ambition.

'I didn't want to be an artisan,' she said. 'Why would I want to be a mancer?'

'Given the choice between being powerful and powerless, I'm sure you'd make the right decision.'

Irisis knew she should smile and thank him, take what he offered and use it to find a way out for herself. That was the sensible thing. But she just couldn't. She could not ally with a man, and a system, so manifestly corrupt. He wanted to corrupt her too. Besides, they knew her reputation. She had attacked Perquisitor Jal-Nish, disobeyed his lawful orders, killed his mancer in the pursuit of her duty . . . Her list of crimes was endless and it was perfectly clear that she opposed all that the

Council stood for. It was unlikely that they could corrupt her. The offer was a trap.

'Or maybe not,' he said. 'A pity. It would have been easier that way.' Ghorr stood up. 'Come with me, crafter.'

She followed him down the travertine-clad corridor, so long that the other end was just a point. Near the end, he turned into a small, brightly lit room. Each interrogation was held in a different place.

And each ended the same way, with her taunting him and him attacking her with his fists. She was bruised all over, but nowhere visibly. For some reason, Ghorr did not want the Council to know. Irisis would have shown Flydd the marks, had they been on speaking terms.

Afterwards she was taken to another room, several levels down. The door had a simple latch on it, no lock at all.

'Close,' said Ghorr once she was inside.

The door clicked shut and she could not open it. Clever. A crafter with her talents could beat most mechanical locks, but not one based on the Art. However it worked, it was different from anything she had experience with. It did not draw power from the field and she could do nothing about it. Perhaps she should have agreed to do what Ghorr wanted, after all.

Some hours later there was a faint tap at the door. 'Irisis?'

It was the scrutator. He had come for her. 'Yes?' she whispered back. 'How did you find me?'

'With great difficulty. I had to leave a simulacrum of myself back in my room, and employ . . . other scrutator magic to get here unseen. I'm not completely sure that it's worked.'

'Get me out,' she said. 'I can't bear this place.'

'What kind of lock is inside?'

'There is none. Just a simple latch, but it won't lift.'

'I was afraid of that. There's nothing you can remove to open the door?'

'Not without tools. Everything is tightly fixed.'

'And even if you did, I suspect the door still would not open.'

'Ghorr simply said "Close" and went away.'

'Could be any one of a dozen holding or sealing spells,' said Flydd.

'Can't you break it?'

'Depending which spell he used, I might be able to. And then again, I might not. Ghorr is a lot older than I am.'

'He doesn't look it.'

'Rejuvenation is a wonderful thing. He's older, stronger, more powerful . . .'

'If all you can do is make excuses you might as well clear out now.'

'I'm doing my best, crafter,' he said coldly.

She knew that, but it did not help her mood. Irisis had the urge to destroy what she could not save. 'It isn't good enough, *scrutator*.'

He did not answer. All was silent. After a minute or two, she began to fear that he had abandoned her.

'Xervish?' she said softly.

Nothing.

'Xervish, I'm . . . I'm sorry. I can't take this.'

'Just be quiet, will you. I'm trying to work it out.'

'What?' she whispered, relief flooding her. Of course he would not abandon her. They were friends and she had saved his life.

'The holding spell. I think I know what it is.'

'Can you break it?'

'I might be able to. There's a problem, though.'

She waited for him to elaborate. There were some tiny scratchings at the door but nothing else.

'What problem, Xervish?'

'If the spell is broken, it sends an alarm to the person who set the spell. To Ghorr.'

'And you can't break that?'

'Not without alerting him.'

'Then there's nothing you can do.'

'I'd say not.'

'Oh well. You tried.'

'Not much comfort.'

She wanted him gone. If he could do nothing, there was no point him being here, risking himself. She did not want him hanging around just for her sake. 'Off you go then.'

'I –' He seemed disconcerted. 'All right. I'll be on my way.'

'Goodbye.' Just go, dammit.

'I'm sorry, Irisis,' he said softly.

She did not answer.

It was, unquestionably, the most despairing night of her life. Irisis did not take too well to bondage or helplessness. Ghorr appeared early in the morning. The clicking of the latch woke her. She felt as if she'd just got to sleep.

He entered the room. It *was* a room, not a cell. Ghorr was smiling. 'I see you had a visitor during the night.'

'I've no idea what you're talking about,' she said coldly.

'Don't treat me like a fool, Irisis. I haven't got to where I am without knowing everything that goes on, both within my domain and without. I can read when Flydd arrived, what he tried to do and when he left again. It's enough to have him dismissed from the Council and put under a sentence of death.'

'Then why don't you?'

'I've work for him to do first. Work I daren't risk another scrutator on. Come, we must talk some more.'

'I am happy to talk,' she said, 'though I don't think that is what you have in mind at all.'

'What I have in mind, Crafter Irisis, is the employment of certain techniques I have developed, to recover the truth from those who have lost it. Or refuse to give it up.'

FIFTY-TWO

Nish and Minis spent the best part of a week going through all the spies' reports and studying maps of the path Tiaan had taken after assaulting the Aachim camp. Subsequently they went out searching in Minis's construct, with an escort of three others. For another week they slid along the western edge of the vast Worm Wood, investigating sightings, most of which turned out to be hoaxes or natural phenomena. They found nothing, though, because of accidents and breakdowns, Nish learned more than a little about construct artificing. The fields they drew on were weaker than on their home world, and that caused many problems.

They returned to the main camp, currently in northern Almadin, to confess their failure. Having twice been called to account by a furious Vithis, Nish was dreading their next meeting. When a runner summoned him to the command tent, he felt sure he was going to suffer, but Vithis turned out to be in a rare good humour.

'Gilhaelith, the mancer and trader who dwells on Booreah Ngurle, has just been snatched by a band of lyrinx,' said Vithis. He did not say how he knew. 'Do you have any idea why?'

'I've never heard of him,' said Nish.

'It may not have anything to do with the flying construct,' Minis said carefully. 'Maybe the lyrinx want to use him in their own work.'

'Flesh-forming!' Nish said with a shudder. The very idea repelled him.

'It's probably nothing, but you'd better take another look at Booreah Ngurle,' said Vithis. 'Keep me informed. Don't go near Nyriandiol.'

Booreah Ngurle could not be reached directly from the west, the Worm Wood being too dense and rugged for constructs. They followed a winding path east along the rim of Warde Yallock, through a land of volcanic peaks, vertical escarpments and rift valleys tangled with scrub. The surrounding country was so rough that much was accessible only on foot, and would have taken tens of thousands of soldiers to search thoroughly. Beyond the eastern end of the lake, they picked up the Great North Road and followed it south to the point where the track turned off to Booreah Ngurle.

Nish and Minis left the construct in dense forest on the lower skirts of the mountain, with its guard, and continued on foot, taking a curving route up the side. During the afternoon, Minis stopped by a shrub that was bent sideways as if something heavy had gone over it. Further up the slope, another lay flat to the ground, though still living.

'Curious,' said Minis, 'but it could have been a horse or other large animal.'

'An animal would have gone around. Look, there's a broken branch.' Nish pointed up the slope.

The trail led to the mouth of a cave, an old lava tunnel. On a projecting rock Nish found distinct scrape marks.

'Again, it could have been an animal,' said Minis.

'It's got a mighty hard skin, then. No, something was carried this way, weeks ago. Let's see where it came from.'

They backtracked down through the forest and after hours of searching found deep indentations in a pair of fallen, rotting trees. 'There's only one way they could have got there,' said Nish. 'Something big and heavy fell from the sky, and it had the shape of a construct. Gilhaelith was lying. He's got it up there. Or had it – the lyrinx probably have it now.'

'I hope she's all right.' Minis's eyes were ablaze.

541

Nish fought an internal battle. He no longer wanted Vithis to get the flying construct, but it was too late to do anything about that, so he might as well get some credit.

'Let's go up and find out.'

'Foster-father must first be told.'

'If you take the time, you'll lose her,' said Nish.

Minis wavered, but only for a moment. 'Father expressly forbade me to go to Nyriandiol. I cannot defy him.'

'It'll be gone by the time we get back, and so will she.'

It took a day to track Vithis down, for he had taken a contingent to the south-eastern tip of Warde Yallock. Vithis cursed them for not going after her at once.

'But you forbade me . . .' Minis began.

'You've gone past *two thousand* constructs to find me. You might have used a bit of initiative, foster-son!'

Vithis detached sixty constructs from the fleet and they went full speed to the Burning Mountain, travelling day and night, but it still took a day. As they raced up the winding road, Nish knew they were going to be too late. The rotting bodies out the front, and the barred door, only confirmed it.

'Break down the door!' said a grim-faced Vithis.

The chalcedony door proved unexpectedly sturdy; a dozen blows were required to breach it.

'Search every room, every attic, every cellar,' Vithis ordered. 'When I think of that grinning baboon, surring me and seducing you with his talk, foster-son, and all the time he had the construct hidden away here. I'll *destroy* him!'

The upper floors proved to be empty, but during the long search one of the Aachim came running up from the basement. 'There's a barricaded door on the lowest level, Vithis.'

The Aachim's face lit up. 'Smash it in!'

They hurtled down the steps. Nish could not keep up. By the time he reached the door an Aachim was hacking into it with an axe. In between the axe strokes Nish heard a familiar whine.

'It's still here,' Vithis roared. 'Hurry!' Whipping out a violet-coloured rod, he pointed it at the door.

It burst apart. At the other end of a long room sat the construct. Some of the front panels were missing, revealing coiling innards. The metal sheets were strapped to the rear and a strange, four-legged contraption to one side. As they poured through onto a landing, a slender, black-haired woman looked over her shoulder.

'Tiaan!' Minis screamed.

Tiaan had crawled down the side of the construct, taken the hedron out of the walker and dragged herself up again. Climbing in was exhausting work, though she had done it many times now. Her useless legs swung back and forth. She slid into the construct, inserted the hedron in its cup and closed the cap.

As she pulled herself onto her seat, the first blow had struck the basement door. She could see the axe blade shivering the planks, before being wrenched out again. A wedge of timber fell; an eye was put to the hole and the attack had resumed. It would only take another few strokes.

The door was blasted apart. A dozen Aachim were framed in the opening, Vithis at their head. There was no time to complete the test. No time to do up the straps either. Taking the controller arm, she snatched at the field and the mechanism whined into life. The thapter rose to hip height, rocking in the air – but would it fly? She put on the special goggles and visualised the strong forces, which were very strong here.

Vithis shouted, 'Stop!' and raised a rod-shaped device.

Tiaan snatched Gilhaelith's crystal rod off the binnacle, pointed it at the crowd in the door and pressed the metal. The beam blasted rock out of the wall in a curving path before shattering the bottom step. The Aachim sprang back to safety.

She turned the thapter in the air, too hard, for it kept going until it faced the door. The Aachim were creeping forward. She gave them another blast but the beam faded out in a shower of sparks. The stored power in the crystal was gone. Thrusting the controller forward, Tiaan drew power and curved around for the windows overlooking the crater and the lake. Acceleration hurled her against the rear wall of the compartment.

A brilliant violet light bathed her, reflecting back from the binnacle. Tiaan lost the field and the mechanism faltered, but it was too late to stop. She threw one arm across her face as the thapter smashed through the myriad little panes of the window. Timber and glass went everywhere.

As the rain of shards and splinters stopped, Tiaan looked up. The thapter was dropping like a stone. The violet light had lost her, though, and with a wrench she recovered the field. She flicked down the finger lever for flight, pulled up on the controller knob, drew from the strong force, and prayed.

Nothing happened. Had the amplimet rejected her again, or did it feel it had a greater chance of achieving its goal with Vithis? You won't get it this way, she vowed. The thapter will smash, the amplimet sink to the bottom of the lake, and when the volcano erupts, it will be blown to pieces. She hurled all that at the crystal, trying to control or at least influence it.

The machine kept falling towards the brilliant blue lake. The sheer rock walls of the crater flashed past. The violet light played on her again. The field winked out but returned just as swiftly as she fell out of range. It did not help her – the amplimet was not drawing on the strong force. Her impact with the water would be spectacular.

The thapter hit an air pocket, rolled, and she almost fell out. Tiaan clung to the controller, which moved sideways and the thapter crabbed around, skidding like a stone across the air. Something went click in her brain and as the machine came upright she pulled up the knob, all the way. The blood rushed from her head and Tiaan blacked out momentarily, rousing to find herself pressed against the back of the seat. The thapter was going straight up, like a child's skyrocket.

It approached Nyriandiol, which overhung the basalt cliff above the lake. She altered course so as to avoid the shattered window and the Aachim, who were sighting their weapons. Was Minis one of them? The violet light played over her, the whine ceasing for a second as she shot past. Tiaan shook her fist at Vithis, altered course to avoid crashing into the eaves, shot up over the roof and out of their sight.

A wall of cloud was racing in from the south. She plunged into its concealment, climbed through and took her bearings from the sun. She was shaking so violently that the thapter skated back and forth across the sky. Where to go? The largest city of Borgistry was about twenty leagues to the south, but the sky was clear in that direction and Vithis would soon discover where she had gone. He could be there in a day. In his current mood, her presence there could only lead to war.

Or was that just a convenient excuse? Tiaan feared the scrutators, as every sensible person did. She was still a fugitive and must surely be blamed for bringing the Aachim to Santhenar. Her clear duty was to give Scrutator Klarm the thapter and the amplimet, but . . .

She desperately wanted to find Gilhaelith and discover if there was a way to repair her broken back. She would give anything for that. But even if she could find him, a prisoner of the lyrinx could do nothing for her.

Health or duty? Selfish or self-sacrificing? Snizort or Borgistry? How could she decide? The thapter would help end the endless war, and all the human misery it had caused. Against that, her own health was insignificant. It was time to do her duty.

Tiaan turned south to Lybing, the capital of Borgistry. At least, she tried to, but the controls would not let her go that way. The amplimet, clearly, did not want to fall into the hands of the scrutators. Twice it had turned away from them.

Tiaan might have gone down to ground, as she had done before, disabled the flying controls and hovered to Lybing. It was the sensible and responsible thing to do. She hesitated over the choice, but only for a second. The capricious amplimet was all the excuse she needed. Hope triumphed over despair and she turned south-south-east, towards Snizort. She felt guilty about it, but if there was a chance to repair her back . . . Was it so terribly wrong to take it?

As Tiaan vanished from sight, Vithis turned away from the window hole, so angry that he had to sit down. Minis was white and shaking. Despite everything, Nish felt like cheering.

'Watch where she goes,' Vithis screamed. 'Track her! Offer mighty rewards for true information, and dire threats for false. Hunt down the people who once served here. The survivors can't be far away. Take the names of all informants. Han, bring my fleet here and signal to the others. We are going after her with every construct we have.'

He hunted down Gilhaelith's servants, in their cave hideouts, and tortured them. They told him nothing, for no one knew what Tiaan was up to, and Nixx, the only one who might have had an inkling, could not be found.

More than two weeks went by before they discovered their first lead, for Tiaan had flown into thick overcast and her path away from the mountain was unknown. Now they knew that she had gone west and south. The fleet flowed down the Great North Road through Borgistry, to the alarm of its citizens. They had to go that way – there were few paths through Worm Wood and none were suitable for carts, much less constructs.

The convoy swelled as other detachments rejoined Vithis's force. Beyond Clew's Top and The Elbow, his fleet broke into a dozen fronts that spread across a hundred leagues, some going west to Taltid and the lands north of there, some south to Nihilnor and Oolo, and others back east by Saludith and the Moonpath to cover the Borgis Woods and Three Knobs, and even the passage through the mountains to the Misty Meres. A system of flags by day, and flashes by night, enabled communication from unit to unit across that distance. Vithis was determined to find Tiaan no matter which way she fled, though she could be anywhere by now, even over the Sea of Thurkad.

At the end of the third week, an old sighting placed her in the vicinity of Gospett, a town in southern Taltid, not far from Gnulp Forest. The main force headed that way, but near Gospett the trail went cold. Vithis called in the informers and questioned them personally, but could learn nothing more.

'The lyrinx may have her,' he said.

'Send an embassy to the gates of Snizort,' said Tirior. 'Offer a reward for her, and another for the thapter.'

'What reward?' Nish piped up, and immediately regretted it.

Vithis turned a cold eye on him. 'What the blazes are you doing here? Get out!'

As Nish scurried for the door, Vithis said, 'There's only one reward they'd be interested in.'

Nish went cold all over. 'No!' he cried. 'I implore you –'

Vithis strode to the door and hurled him through. 'If the lyrinx *do* have my flying construct, offer them alliance!' he said. 'Against the old humans. And lock up Cryl-Nish Hlar. He is an enemy alien now.'

FIFTY-THREE

Tiaan flew all night and through the following day, taking it slowly and keeping to the clouds. She was afraid that the amplimet would take command, or cut off the force entirely, but it gave her no more trouble. The euphoria of her escape had faded, replaced by an overwhelming worry – how could she possibly find Gilhaelith once she got there? And by irrepressible feelings of guilt – that again she had put self before duty.

It was nearly dusk when she reached Snizort, which lay in the centre of the land called Taltid. From a great height, the tar pits looked like the dark face of the moon. She could see figures moving around on the ground, and some in the air, which meant they were lyrinx. It appeared that Snizort was possessed by the enemy. Nixx had not told her that. What was down there? Walls enclosed a number of tar pits, an area about a league square, though she saw no buildings inside. She dared go no lower before dark.

Taltid proved to be an undulating land whose sandy soils supported only grass, scrub and occasional patches of thorny forest or sand dunes. The flats of a meandering river had once been cultivated but the pattern of fields and hedges was reverting to wasteland. Either the inhabitants had been eaten years ago, or they had fled. Many small, isolated hilltops were capped with round boulders and outcrops of grey stone that might make useful hiding places, if she could get down onto one safely. The area around Snizort was speckled with seeps and boiling springs that stood out from the air in this dry land, surrounded by scrubby forest with blue-grey leaves.

She tried to reconcile what she saw below with what she had read in Nixx's notes. She had to know what she was facing and there were only minutes of daylight left.

In the zone of seeps and pits, the soil, and the sandstone below it, was saturated with seeping tar driven up from some vast underground reservoir. Over aeons the black, reeking muck had spread away from the vents and set hard, though not so hard that it could not be hacked out with spades or, in the winter months, hammer and chisel. The people of Snizort had been digging solidified tar for eight thousand years, until the lyrinx came. In that time they had excavated a series of ragged pits into the sandstone, the deepest of which was more than ninety spans. One pit lay directly below her. Even from this height the bituminous odour tickled Tiaan's nostrils.

In the centre of this desolation, within the walls of Snizort, she made out a vast black cauldron of tar, slightly longer than it was wide – the Great Seep. Its surface was streaked with dust and it had a sullen, ominous liquidity. Wisps of vapour touched the seep. It appeared cold, but Tiaan knew the tar was warm enough to flow.

Smaller seeps, pits and bogs of tar ringed the Great Seep for a league around and she would have to be careful of them, in the dark. Warm tar had spread away from the seeps for several leagues more, turning the land into a sterile wilderness. Tar oozed out of the sides of hills and down the watercourses, taking as much as a week to go a single span. In the winter it did not move at all, but once it went somewhere it was there forever, becoming increasingly brittle and cracked. At least, it remained until ingenious humans found a use for it; gradually, the most accessible supplies had been mined.

Many were not accessible. The larger seeps formed tarry lakes from which the hardened material could be taken from the edges, but no matter how much was removed the level never changed, for warm tar kept seeping from below. Thirsty animals, and the odd reckless child, sometimes ventured onto the crusted surface. Their bodies were never recovered. The clinging tar sucked them under, preserving them perfectly, forever . . .

Tiaan shook herself and came back to the task at hand – to find a hiding place for the night. She had not thought any further ahead. If she had, she would not have dared come at all. What could an unarmed cripple do against a fortress full of lyrinx?

As soon as it was dark, she drifted the thapter towards a cluster of grey boulders, like giant's juggling balls, that topped a hill a good league from the nearest part of the wall of Snizort. Trees stuck up between the rocks: stubble on a shaven head. It was slow and tricky work bringing the thapter down in the gloom, and Tiaan was sweating by the time she eased it in between the boulders.

She moved the thapter under the rocks and trees so it would not be visible from above. Taking out the amplimet, the diamond hedrons and their connectors, she wrapped all carefully and put them in her chest pack. Tiaan laboriously got herself into the walker and inserted the hedron. The field was strange here but it provided the necessary power, which was all that mattered. She covered the thapter with branches, such that only the most determined search would find it. A wedge of moon, falling towards the west, provided a ghostly illumination.

Now what? How *could* she find Gilhaelith in a nest of lyrinx? She had to try. Tiaan had heard horrible rumours about what the lyrinx did to spies. If they caught her, they would tear her apart, and if she went down there they probably *would* catch her. The very idea was madness.

But it was better than being trapped in this body with no hope of recovery. Gilhaelith might be able to free her. What peril would she not face, to have back the use of her legs? She would go down and see what she could discover, and if a lyrinx did attack, well, it would be a merciful release. At least, she tried to tell herself that. It did not lesson the terror.

Tiaan crept, insofar as the walker could creep, through the

scrub. The way down would have been perilous even in daylight, for the hill was capped with a broken layer of sandstone that ended in a cliff a couple of spans high. There was no way she could get the walker down that; however, after circumnavigating the summit several times, she found a crack in the stone that took her to a gully she was able to half-walk, half-slide down.

As the walker's rubber feet sank into the moist earth at the base of the cliff, Tiaan wondered how she would ever get up again. Well, she'd worry about that when she returned – if she did.

A path meandered across the slope and she turned onto it. When it levelled out near the bottom of the hill, she was confronted by a squat-bellied figure standing in a glade. It was just a statue, though an unpleasant one: a bulbous belly, head so narrow that the model must have been bound at birth, and a face that the slanting moonlight showed to be cratered with pox scars. More striking was the fixed, repulsive leer.

Tiaan shivered and passed by. Whoever had made it was long gone. The path ran into another, an animal trail that might also be frequented by hunting lyrinx. The wall of Snizort was an hour's walk from here, through thorny scrub and low forest. She had a feeling that someone was behind her, watching; waiting. Her anxious glances revealed nothing, though a small creature skittered into the bushes as she turned the corner.

After negotiating a network of trails, she emerged in cleared land and saw the wall about a bowshot ahead. It looked some four spans high and was thick enough to support an impenetrable tangle of thornbush at the top. A beaten path ran around the base, presumably where sentries walked. Tiaan felt such a premonition of danger that she almost turned and fled. What stupidity had brought her here?

A shadow flickered in the deeper shade at the base of the wall. This was it. It must see her. She dared not move. It stopped and seemed to be looking in her direction. She thought she caught a glint from its eyes.

Tiaan fingered the crystal rod, knowing it probably would not work, since Gilhaelith had not taught her how to recharge it from the field. Another gleam, then the shadow moved off. She edged back into the scrub. The lyrinx sense of smell was not particularly keen, but it might pick up her scent.

Though Tiaan watched for a long time, she saw no sign of life. Close to midnight, judging by the moon, she turned back. Before she had gone far, the moon fell behind the thornbush wall and it became too dark to see. Tiaan cursed herself for not thinking of that.

Taking a rough bearing from the stars, she headed east, feeling her way forward, and found what seemed to be a track through the scrub. Shortly it came out near the wall again. Continuing along the edge of the cleared zone, she encountered a broad path. To her right, the setting moon streamed through the barred gate of Snizort. Apprehension growing, she headed the other way and collided with a broad figure standing quietly in the darkness. It moved into the light. The moon shone on rows of teeth, glittered in its eyes, revealed its lack of wings.

'I knew you'd bring your crystal back one day, Tiaan,' said Ryll.

She hurled the walker sideways but Ryll thrust out a limb, one metal leg caught and the walker crashed to the ground. Her head struck the frame so hard that she saw stars. She lay still. There was nothing she could do.

'Why are you in this *machine*?' he asked, crouching beside her.

'I broke my back. I can never walk again.'

Ryll's crest glowed pink as he lifted the walker. 'I feel your pain.' His clawed hand closed about her wrist and he thrust his big jaw at her.

'What are you going to do with me?' she said hoarsely.

'I don't know *yet*.'

'Is Gilhaelith here?'

'Ah,' he said. 'The man you travelled across the world to mate with.'

He could still embarrass her. 'No, that was somebody else.'

Ryll looked taken aback. 'The other man did not want to *mate* with you?'

Perception, or a lucky guess? 'He betrayed me,' said Tiaan bitterly.

'I am sorry,' said Ryll, and Tiaan knew he spoke truly. She had not known Ryll to lie, yet he was not, when the situation required it, averse to making misleading statements.

'Gilhaelith?' she repeated.

'The tetrarch is here.'

'What do you mean *tetrarch*?'

'Isn't that what you call him?'

'I call him Gilhaelith. Is he all right?'

'He has been treated well, though he does not appreciate it as he might. You won't try to escape, will you?'

'I've come a long way to find him.'

'As you did for your mate, and he betrayed you. Your loyalty is stronger than your judgment.'

That was certainly true, much as she hated to be reminded of it. They went through the gates, which were guarded by dozens of lyrinx, bearing weapons she could not make out in the gloom. The passage through the wall was an arched tunnel. Inside, the area was dimly lit by flaming bowls the size of cartwheels, set on stone pedestals. Fumes from burning tar drifted across the ground in black wisps and strands. The air reeked.

'This way,' said Ryll.

She followed him along a path, trodden to black tar, that wound through thorny shrubbery. Tar bogs shone ominously in the light of the flickering lamps.

'What are you doing here, Ryll? Are you still *flesh-forming*?'

'It is not my place to tell you such things, Tiaan.'

'You never caught the nylatl, did you?'

'We never did. It disappeared.'

'It killed some good people. I only knew them for a day, but they had become friends.'

'I bitterly regret that I created the beast.' He was much more subdued than before. He seemed, in some strange way, cowed.

'Liett begged you to kill it.'

'I should have listened. I have much to answer for.'

They walked in silence until they came to the edge of a cliff.

At least, that was her first thought, though after they turned onto the sticky steps Tiaan understood that it was one of the pits excavated into the tar-saturated sandstone. In the failing moonlight it looked like a pool of ink.

'I can't walk down steps,' she said.

He picked her up, walker and all, and headed down. Tiaan closed its legs so they would not catch on anything. The steps went halfway around the huge excavation but she could not see them. It was eerily dark. The air reeked of tar; the fumes were making her sick.

'How can you live down here?' she said. 'It would kill me.'

'You'll see.'

Ryll turned left, stooped and bore her into a tunnel through the black sandstone. They went along for ages, his feet making tearing sounds on the sticky floor, and through a series of doors. The tar smell faded. Finally they passed through a metal door where Tiaan felt a flow of fresh air, and began to go up again. The rock here was orange sandstone, so soft that it could be excavated with a mattock. There were lights at intervals, lanterns hung on hooks in the wall.

'Not back there,' he said as if reading her thought. 'The risk of fire is too great.'

They passed small open chambers on either side, looking rather the way she imagined an ants' nest to be. Many contained young lyrinx, playing at games rather like human children. Beyond, Ryll led her into an oval sandstone chamber, carved out by hand.

There were many lyrinx in it, standing around, sitting at benches, or bent over plans or documents. Tiaan recognised none of them. She saw humans too, pale-skinned creatures who appeared to have never seen the sun. Though not manacled or restrained in any way, they had the listless look of slaves. Most were young, none older than middle age. Down the far end of the room stood a tall, dark-skinned woman with frizzy hair and filed teeth – a native of the forests of Crandor. She stood by a large piece of slate, making marks on it while three half-grown lyrinx attempted to reproduce them on smaller slates.

'We teach our brightest children to read and write your common tongues,' said Ryll, noting her interest. He urged her forward.

On the other side of the room, a man was reciting while a group of young lyrinx attempted to speak the words back to him. He waved his arms in the air and they fell silent. His left hand was missing.

'My tutor,' Ryll said. 'He has served and taught us all my life. He is the best teacher I know. We are *almost* friends.' He waved and the man raised his stump.

They continued into another room with a green-crested guard on the door. She allowed them through into a large space crowded with lyrinx. Ryll made a piping whistle and they turned as one. He spoke in his incomprehensible tongue, of which all Tiaan recognised was her name. Everyone stared at her, their skin flashing in lurid, chameleon colours. Tiaan had never learned to read their skin-speech, but it was evident that they were excited. A massive female embraced Ryll, then one by one the others touched him on the shoulder.

Tiaan's skin prickled. She had an overpowering urge to run. Run anywhere, as fast as her legs . . .

Ryll bowed to his fellows and led Tiaan out.

'What are you doing here, Ryll? Snizort is a long way from where we first met.'

'We are great travellers, Tiaan, but as it happens, this is my home. I lived here until I became a man. Snizort is now our most important city on Lauralin.'

'Until two days ago I had not heard of it. Is this where you learned to speak our language?'

'Yes, from infancy. Some prisoners have been here since before I was born.'

'When were you born, Ryll?'

He named the year.

'But that means you're only fourteen,' she cried.

'That is correct.'

'I thought you were an adult.'

The skin of his feet and hands went a pale yellow. 'We are

adults at the age of ten. Most lyrinx my age have been mated long ago. Those who are *whole* and have wings. Unlike me.'

Just before Tiaan had fled Kalissin, it had seemed that Ryll and Liett might be mated, despite their respective disabilities. 'Is Liett here too?'

'She arrived but two days ago.'

'Are you a pair now?'

His brow wrinkled. 'Do you mean, has she accepted me as her mate?'

'Yes.'

'She has not. There have been difficulties.'

'I thought, er, just before I fled Kalissin, that you and Liett were . . . close.'

Colours flickered across his face. 'The Wise Mother withdrew her permission and sent me home in disgrace.'

'That must have hurt you.'

'I am a fool!' Ryll said harshly. 'As well as a wingless wonder. I must take my punishment.' He said no more.

On they went; and down again. It was warmer here. 'Can I see Gilhaelith?' Tiaan asked miserably.

'No, you cannot. We have arrived.'

Ryll thrust open a round door made of wood and ushered her inside. Helping her out of the walker, he sat her on a bench which ran the length of the curved wall. He put her pack beside her, lifted the walker onto his shoulders and turned to go.

'Ah!' He turned back. 'One last thing.'

'Yes?'

'You will give me the crystal.'

There was no choice. Unfastening the chest pack, she put the amplimet into his leathery hand. What would the lyrinx make of it this time? Would they see its strangeness?

'Thank you.' The door was slammed and bolted on the outside.

Tiaan lifted her legs onto the bench and closed her eyes. She had tried it all for nothing and now they were going to use her again. This was the stupidest thing she had ever done. Ryll was right about her lack of judgment. Why, why had she come?

Several hours went by before Ryll carried Tiaan to another place, many winding tunnels away, that she would have had trouble finding on her own. She did her best to memorise the sequence of turns, in the faint hope that, one day, there might be a chance to escape.

It was a dim, moist room, long and wide, with an earthy, peaty odour. Mist wreathed across it, though after some time she made out rows of objects that brought to mind the mechanical devices in the manufactory, except that these looked as if they had been grown of wood and bark, branch and leaf, bone and horn and shell. Each was different in size, colour and form.

She felt something shuddery creeping up her back. 'What are these things?'

Ryll carried her along a row to the second-last object, a throat-high cube of a substance that resembled woody leather, though covered in bulbs and curving indentations. Along the sides were patterns like veins in leaves and gills in mushrooms. A faint spicy odour, like lemony pepper, masked something less pleasant.

'Sit here, please.' Ryll put her on the floor and bent over the cube.

Tiaan tried to see what he was doing. He seemed to be removing a cover; testing the level inside. Something went *glop!* An ominous liquidity.

Across the room, vapour hissed from a dark aperture. A cloud of mist drifted toward the cube.

Ryll stood over her. 'Take your clothes off, please.'

'What?' she cried, her heart thumping.

'Remove your clothes. You won't need them here.'

'Why not?' she screamed. *'What are you going to do to me?'*

'I'm not going to do anything to you.'

Her eyes flicked back and forth. Her skin felt as if hairy caterpillars were swarming on it. 'No!' she gasped. 'You're monsters. I won't help you again.'

'Take your clothes off, Tiaan, or I will have to remove them for you. I'm sure you wouldn't want that. I know how . . . prudish you are.'

She shook her head.

He sighed. 'I have the amplimet, Tiaan. I can force you.'

'I got over withdrawal at Tirthrax. It means nothing to me now.'

'We'll see. Just what did you do there?'

'I opened a gate from Santhenar to Aachan, so the Aachim could bring their constructs through. They've come to wage war, *on you.*'

He frowned. 'We have more skilled questioners than I, Tiaan. They will get the truth from you.'

He did not believe her. That was good.

'Your clothes! Hurry up!'

'I won't!' She folded her arms across her chest.

Ryll bellowed. A small lyrinx came up the row and Tiaan recognised her too. Her thin, translucent skin and the magnificent, colourless wings distinguished her from every other lyrinx. Liett had never liked Tiaan.

'Take her clothes, please,' said Ryll.

Liett, recognising Tiaan, roared with laughter. 'What's the matter with her?'

'She's broken her back.'

The smile vanished. Liett examined Tiaan, then pulled Ryll away and spoke rapidly to him in their own tongue. Tiaan could read his expressions well enough to know that he was troubled. They debated for some minutes, after which Liett began to strip her.

One hand sufficed to hold Tiaan while the other deftly unfastened her coat and shirt down the front. Soon the boots, trousers and underwear had gone the same way.

The lyrinx looked her up and down. 'What pale, helpless creatures you are without your clothes. Shall I put her in?'

'Be quick!' Ryll looked ill-at-ease.

Liett lifted Tiaan in one hand, her useless legs flopping back and forth, carried her to the cube and poked her feet into the top opening. The surface resembled gnarled bark dotted with brown nodules like wooden eyeballs. The peppery smell grew stronger, as did that other, uncomfortable odour.

The cube contained a thick yellow-brown mass. Liett let Tiaan go and she slid into it. It was cool with the texture of jelly, and rose to the level of her armpits. It felt horrible, clinging but slippery. Her skin began to tingle.

'What are you doing?' she cried. 'What is this thing?'

'*You* might call it a patterner,' said Ryll, putting the amplimet around her neck and adjusting it so it hung lower, between her breasts.

'It is going to *pattern* you,' said Liett with a toothy smile.

'No!' screamed Tiaan, and kept screaming until the patterner next to her began to shudder and quake.

Tiaan saw an eye looking at her. Two eyes; another woman, no older than herself. The woman's eyes went wide and she began to scream, a higher, more shrill sound than Tiaan's. The same thing happened on the right.

Shortly the whole room was shuddering and screaming. The patterners must have been sensitive to it, for they began to judder violently.

Ryll ran to Tiaan and shook her by her bare shoulders. 'Stop it!'

She broke off momentarily, but the other women kept on, and soon Tiaan found it easier to scream with them.

'What are we going to do?' Ryll shouted.

Liett yelled back at him but the racket was too loud. She ran out, returning with a bucket whose contents sloshed from side to side. Taking a dipper, she forced some through the bared teeth of the woman at the end of the line. She choked, stopped screaming and her head sagged to one side. Liett did the same to the next and all the others, up the line to Tiaan.

The room was quiet again. Tiaan looked Liett in the eye; Liett looked her back. 'Well?' said Liett.

'I want to see Gilhaelith,' Tiaan said miserably. 'Unless he's being *patterned* as well.'

'He's a *male*!' Liett said scornfully.

'Females are better for patterning,' Ryll explained. 'Only rarely have we found a useful male. If I bring him, will you cooperate?'

'Yes,' said Tiaan. *For the moment.*

Liett resumed her work, whatever that was. Ryll was away a long time. Tiaan resisted the impulse to scream as the jelly slid back and forth across her skin. Small sucker-like objects attached themselves all over, tugging at her skin as the gunk moved in slow swirls.

The door opened. Ryll had Gilhaelith by one arm; he looked frail beside the lyrinx. They came up the row. Tiaan's heart beat wildly. What had he been going to tell her before the lyrinx captured him?

'*Tiaan!*' Gilhaelith staggered and fell against the patterner. 'They caught you after all.'

'I came after you. I'm a fool, aren't I?'

He touched her cheek. Coming from him, it was more powerful than an embrace. 'Why didn't you flee when you had the chance?'

There was no sensible answer to that. 'What are they doing to you, Gilhaelith?' she said softly, expecting to hear some story as horrible as her own.

'Nothing,' he replied. 'They want me too much.'

'What for?'

'They've lost something in the Great Seep and I must find it.'

'*Don't!* I know the price of aiding them.'

'Ah, Tiaan,' he said, 'if only you had not come.'

'You were going to tell me something about my back.'

'I wish I hadn't mentioned it,' he said bitterly. 'I can't do anything for you. You've given yourself into the hands of the enemy for nothing.'

'I must know, Gilhaelith.'

'All right, but it won't do you any good. Far off, across the sea, dwells a great mancer who has devoted his life to the healing Arts. I thought he might be able to do something for you . . .'

'At what price?'

'Seven years service.'

'It would have been worth it.'

'That would depend on what kind of master he was,' said Ryll from the background, 'and what sort of service.'

'It could hardly be worse than what you require of me, for no return,' she flashed.

'It could be very much worse.'

'The matter is irrelevant,' Gilhaelith interrupted. 'Neither you nor I will ever be in a position to meet him.'

He was tall enough to look down into the aperture of the patterner and Tiaan saw that he was staring at her bare chest, only partly concealed by the jelly. It made her angry – even at a time like this, he could not see beyond the physical. The longing in Gilhaelith's eyes was a painful thing to behold. He was practically shaking with desire. Had he really missed her that much?

Then she realised, with utter mortification, that he was not staring at her chest at all. It was the amplimet he wanted, and was determined to have.

Even as Ryll led him away, Gilhaelith kept looking back for it.

FIFTY-FOUR

Ullii woke with a headache and a profound feeling of loss. Somehow the fleeting touch of her brother had made things worse. It *had* been a touch, she felt sure. It was not just a dream. Ullii trusted her instincts. Myllii was out there somewhere and she was going to be reunited with him.

She wandered the echoing halls of Nennifer wearing her earmuffs, and her earplugs and noseplugs, all day. Her sensitivities seemed particularly acute in this place. No one hindered her. They were not troubled by the 'little mouse', as Ghorr so sneeringly referred to her.

Ullii liked the name. Mice knew how to hide and protect their secrets, and the secret of Myllii was one she particularly hugged to herself. Her brother was alive and looking for her. And he had her seeker's talent. She was glad to know that. She wanted him to be just like her. Lacking her supersensitivity, he did not have the talent as strongly as she did. That pleased her selfish heart; a tiny reward for all she had suffered.

She could not find the scrutator or Irisis, though they were both still in Nennifer. She would have known had they been gone. The thought of Xervish Flydd leaving her in this place filled her with terror, and not only because of the Council, who would use her talent then cast her aside. If she remained here, Ullii knew she would never find her brother. She had searched the lattice as far as it reached, but could see no sign of him. He must be far away, and only Flydd and Irisis could take her there.

As she wandered the corridors that evening, a stone's throw down the long hall the Council were trooping into their dining room for dinner. She heard Scrutator Halie mention Irisis's name. The door slammed.

What were they saying about Irisis? Ullii had to know. A thought occurred to her, one that made her quake at her boldness. She was thinking about spying on the Council, a crime certainly punishable by the most hideous torments. She had never done anything like that in her life.

Dare she? She had to know what they were going to do to Irisis. She looked around for a place to hide, and watch. Across the wide hall from their dining room was an open door. Ullii slipped through it. Most of the room was taken up by a long table surrounded by chairs upholstered in crimson leather. Creeping under the table, she took out her earplugs.

Her hearing picked up Ghorr's voice at once, even through the closed door of the dining room. Unfortunately it picked up every other sound as well. The clatter of cutlery was like the clashing of cymbals. The chatter of the scrutators resembled a squad of soldiers marching across a boardwalk. She could hear every chew, every swallow, every grunt and belch.

Ullii endured the cacophony during the interminable dinner, which consisted of eight courses, some so pungent that she could smell them through her noseplugs. When a servant hurried down the hall with hot napkins, the noise was so loud that Ullii almost wept.

There came a single rap, as of a knife on a table, and everyone fell silent.

'We have much to discuss,' echoed Ghorr's voice clearly. He listed a number of items, most having no interest to Ullii, but at the end, 'and what to do about the crafter.'

Irisis. Ullii listened intently, though it was a long time before she heard anything of interest. Ghorr was speaking again.

'The device is finally ready. I will give it to Scrutator Flydd at dawn and he will immediately leave for Snizort.'

The debate went on for another hour before they turned to Irisis. Ullii's ears were throbbing and her headache was worse than ever.

'Ah, now we come to Crafter Irisis,' said Ghorr. 'Scrutator Flydd went to visit her last night.'

A low comment from someone; Ullii could not make out what was said.

Ghorr chuckled. 'If Flydd could have broken the spell on the door he would have taken her. There seems no limit to the man's villainy.'

'It certainly seems that he cannot be trusted,' said another. 'As if we should be in any doubt.'

'I've not trusted him since that incident thirty years ago,' said Ghorr. 'I voted that he be put down then, if you recall.'

'And you were outvoted,' said Halie, 'as *I* recall. The man is a problem, I agree, but that is outweighed by his talent. He has served us well in the years since his . . . punishment. That he survived it shows his indomitable will. We need him until the war is won. After that –'

'After could well be too late,' snapped Ghorr.

'If we lose the war, as is likely without the use of his talents, it will not matter.'

Several people spoke at once and Ullii could not make out what was said, then Ghorr again, with seeming reluctance. 'As you say, he is a problem for another time. Irisis is a problem for now. I have finished my interrogation of her.'

'What did you discover?' came the voice of black-bearded Fusshte.

'I don't think there is any more to learn from her. There is no doubt that she killed the mancer on the aqueduct by manipulating the field. The woman's body was torn apart by explosive anthracism. I've not been able to have our best artisans duplicate it on prisoners, but I was careful not to reveal too much. I'm sure it can be done, though, and that leaves us with a problem.'

'One that's already out in the open,' said Halie.

'Only Irisis knows, and Flydd, Jal-Nish and us. The soldier witnesses can be discounted. Flydd won't spread it around; it threatens him as much as it does us. Jal-Nish likewise. That only leaves Irisis.'

'And the seeker,' said Fusshte in a tone that sent chills up Ullii's back.

'That squeaking little mouse,' sneered Ghorr. 'She can barely dress herself without bursting into tears. Spare me, Fusshte.'

'Besides,' said Halie, 'we plan to use Ullii later on.'

'Irisis must die,' said Ghorr. 'She's too much of a risk. But not tonight. I'll wait till Flydd is safely away. He might become unco-operative, otherwise.'

'A pity,' said Fusshte. 'The woman is a great beauty, and of child-bearing age. And quite a lover, too, I'm told.' He gave a las-civious snort.

'Beauty is everywhere,' said Ghorr coldly, 'if that is *all* that you require. Irisis must die. Agreed?'

The scrutators voted. Most agreed. Several did not, Halie among them.

'Tomorrow,' said Ghorr. 'After he's gone. Keep an extra watch on him tonight. No, lock him in. I wouldn't put it past Flydd to try again.'

Chairs were thrust back all at once, creating such a racket that Ullii had to push in her earplugs. She heard nothing else. She crouched under the table until they were all gone, making sure by the smell of each. Her heart was thumping. Irisis was going to be murdered.

Ullii flooded with memories of all the times the crafter had treated her kindly, most notably when she'd knocked down Jal-Nish after he had struck Ullii. That had been one of the greatest moments of her life: she'd realised she had found a true friend. Since then, Irisis had sometimes treated her unkindly in little ways, but that no longer counted.

Ullii wanted to help her friend, though she would not have dared had it not been for Myllii. She was too selfish – she had to be – and too afraid. She'd always been helpless. What could *she* do, if even the scrutator could not save Irisis?

The seeker spent another hour or two under the table. It was as good a place as any to agonise. Dare she try? She dared not.

She dared. She dared not. As she was sitting there, a mouse emerged from a crack between wall and floor and scurried along the line of chairs, snapping up crumbs and other morsels fallen from the table. There was not much; the room had not been used since breakfast. Ullii smiled and felt in her pocket, where she had a piece of bread. She did not like large meals, preferring to snack through the day.

Breaking a corner off, she flicked it across the floor. The mouse skittered away, then came creeping back and swallowed the morsel before fleeing again. She flicked another piece of bread, not so far. This time the mouse did not run. She rolled out her hand, containing a larger morsel.

The mouse was more wary this time. It sniffed the air as it watched her with little pink eyes. She approved of its caution. Its whiskers twitching, it ran forward, grabbed the piece of bread and ducked behind the leg of a chair.

Very slowly she put out her hand with a length of crust held between two fingers. Ullii had often watched mice in her dungeon cell, and grown friendly with them. This one was young. An older mouse would have been more careful.

She consulted her lattice but of course the mouse did not appear in it. Animals rarely did. Only lyrinx – not that she thought of them as animals, the nylatl, and those flesh-formed monsters in the ice houses.

Claws dug into her fingers, painfully. Ullii had to restrain herself. The mouse had climbed onto her hand and was nibbling at the crust, trying to get it out from between her fingers with its front paws. She held on for a moment, then let it go. The mouse took the morsel in its mouth, swallowed, and sat back on its haunches, staring at her. Its long snout twitched.

What do you want, little mouse? More bread? Then you'll have to trust me. She slowly raised her hand until the mouse was level with her face. Its back legs tensed but it did not spring off. She twitched her nose. It twitched back. It must like her. 'I have some bread in my pocket,' she said softly. 'Would you like it?'

She lowered her hand until it was level with her pocket. The mouse sniffed the fabric, thrusting its snout right against it. Ullii lifted the flap to reveal the opening. The mouse darted inside. She felt it munching at the bread. Ullii sat there while it ate, not wanting to frighten it. She loved the little scurryings and munchings it was making there.

It gave her courage too. If the mouse could be so brave, maybe she could. She crept out from under the table. The mouse tensed, relaxed. There was no one about. She looked through the door into the scrutators' dining hall. The table had not been cleared. She filled her pockets with leftover bread and fruit, then made her way back to her room.

'Well, mouse,' she said, sitting on her bed. 'What can we do?'

It poked its snout out of her pocket. She stroked its brow. The mouse ducked out of sight. Where was Irisis? Ullii searched her lattice and located the crafter, who was away towards the other end of the building, and lower down. The direction was precise but how to get there was unclear.

She went along the hall. The ceiling was nearly six spans above her head and Ullii felt like a little mouse herself, creeping along, ears cocked for anyone coming. She was afraid; there was nowhere to hide. But then, she didn't have to hide. Nobody noticed her.

It took her a long time to get close to the crafter. Ullii felt as though she was walking though a series of endless rectangular tunnels. The lower floors were dark at this time of night. Irisis was that familiar black ball in her lattice, unlike others because it was impenetrable. It covered up a carefully concealed secret.

It was hard to keep Irisis in mind as she walked, for her position in the lattice no longer seemed to match the shape of Nennifer. Ullii went down a set of steps but at the bottom lost the crafter for a moment. She had to crouch down in the dark and search all over again.

Irisis was not there. It was as if her knot had *shifted*. Ullii felt more afraid. Things should not shift in her lattice unless, like airfloaters or flying lyrinx, they were moving away rapidly.

Were they taking Irisis away to be killed? Ghorr had said it would be done after Flydd left in the morning, but maybe that had been a lie. What if Ghorr had known Ullii was out there, spying on them? This might be a trap. Maybe he was hunting her right now. Manipulating her lattice.

She searched it for the chief scrutator. He was up in one of the towers of Nennifer. Relief was followed by panic. Some of the other knots seemed to be moving in her direction.

Ullii resisted the urge to run into the dark. It took all the courage she had, which was not very much. Life had taught her that bravery was stupidity. Were they coming towards her? It was impossible to be sure. Another problem: normal, human, talent-less guards did not show up in her lattice. Ghorr might have a hundred of them hunting her and she would not know it until she heard them coming.

I can't, she thought. It's too hard. Irisis, where are you? Ullii turned left at the bottom of the steps and immediately knew that was the wrong way. She went the other way, then stopped, listening. Was that a boot on the steps far above?

She took off her own boots and socks, tying the boots together by their laces and pressing her socks well inside. She liked the feel of the tiles under her bare feet. It felt more secure. Fleeting down the hall, making no more sound than the mouse in her pocket, Ullii tried to reassure herself. No one here had her talent. They could not track her unless they used dogs, and she had not smelt any in Nennifer.

Ullii scurried upstairs and down, along one corridor after another. She checked the lattice. Those other knots had stopped moving, which was nearly as worrying as having them coming in her direction.

She still could not see Irisis, no matter how hard she looked. Then, it was as if something slipped and she caught a faint glimpse of the black ball. She felt more afraid. Were they hiding Irisis from her? Was Ghorr watching, in some mancerly way, everything she did?

Though Ullii could see most forms of magic, and the people who used it, she did not understand the Secret Art. As far as she was concerned, everything she'd heard about mancers was true. They could do anything.

She began to go down another set of stairs but the terror overcame her and she collapsed halfway. Pulling herself into a ball, Ullii squatted there, rocking. She had an urge to take her clothes off and scream herself into a fit, as she had often done when younger. She could not go on. How she wished Myllii were here. Ullii could not remember his smell, but it must have been much like her own. Myllii, where are you? She did not think she could go on, even for Myllii. Ullii just wanted to run and hide.

The mouse was scratching around in her pocket. She slipped her fingers in and it sniffed at them. Its tongue touched a fingertip. It felt nice; tickly; friendly. For some strange reason the mouse reminded her of Nish, and that brought to mind the attack by the nylatl, where she had saved Nish's life. Though she was little and terrified and weak, she had saved brave, bold Nish, her hero.

The mouse sniffed its way into her hand. She brought it out, cupped in her palms. It had no fear of her. She must have none either. With a swift movement she slipped it back and stood up. She must try to save Irisis.

Ullii searched for that blot in her lattice that seemed to be hiding the crafter. It was hard to locate; it seemed to change shape all the time. She turned her lattice around in her head and saw Irisis's mark at once. The chief scrutator was trying to be too clever, but he did not understand her talent at all.

Her wanderings had carried Ullii down into the lower levels of Nennifer, well below the surface of the ground. These were not dungeons but airy corridors with rooms off them, where people worked during the daytime. Now they were dark.

Irisis's level was lit by lamps at intervals. A guard sat at the far end of the hall. She crept along the wall, in the shadows. He scanned the corridor every so often but did not see her.

She found the room. Ullii could sense Irisis inside. The door was held closed by the Art; she could feel the strength of it without even looking in her lattice. She slid by and kept going. How could she get Irisis out when even the scrutator had failed?

Ullii found an empty room further down, sat in the dark and ate some bread, sharing it with the friend in her pocket.

Surprising how comforting she found him. Ullii knew that it was a him.

She considered the spell on the door. For all that she could see the Art in its myriad forms, Ullii was unable to break the simplest spell and this one, she could tell from the convolutions of its knot in her lattice, was not simple. She rotated the lattice, examining the knot from one side and another. Knots could sometimes be undone, but that was dangerous; she might be attacked by what lay hidden inside.

This knot was beyond her, for its tightly woven structure gave no clue to how it was tied underneath. She left it, looking for the dark ball that was Irisis. She was obscured again. The knot now seemed to surround the space where the crafter was held.

Ullii rotated her lattice again, and from the other side saw an opening, and the crafter within it. It was frustrating to be so close and not be able to get to her. Putting the leftover bread away, she went back to Irisis's door, hoping she might be able to see better from outside. The guard was pacing down the other end of the hall. Ullii could not *see* Irisis at all. In frustration, she did something she had never attempted before. She took hold of the lock's knot in the lattice and tried to move it out of the way.

She felt the strangest sucking sensation, like – a memory from her childhood – trying to pull an octopus off a rock. The door creaked.

Footsteps inside the room. 'Who's there?' came Irisis's voice, flat with hopelessness. 'If that's you again, Ghorr –'

'It's me. Ullii,' she whispered.

'Ullii? What are you doing?'

'They're going to kill you as soon as the scrutator is gone.'

'I thought so.'

'When does he go?'

'Dawn.'

'Four hours left, then.'

Ullii could not think about the death of her friend – finding Myllii occupied her whole mind. 'I need you to help me, Irisis.'

Irisis laughed hollowly. 'I'd be glad to, little seeker. Just name your favour and I will do it. Fly you to the moon? I'm happy to oblige.'

'I want you to find my brother.'

'I didn't know you had one.'

'Myllii is my twin. He was taken away when I was four. He's just like me.'

'Is he now?' said Irisis. 'I wonder if anyone else knows that?'

'Irisis!' Ullii hissed. 'Promise you'll help me find him.'

'Ullii, they're coming for me today. I can't help anyone, even myself.'

'I can open the door,' said Ullii.

The silence from the other side was profound. 'Ullii, if you can get me out of here, I promise I will help find your brother.'

Ullii felt the mouse moving in her pocket. Down the end, the guard pushed back his chair and paced along the hall.

'Guard's coming!' Ullii whispered, scuttling back to the empty room.

He went by, shining his lantern here and there, trying the locked doors. She waited for him to go back the other way. It took a long time.

'Irisis,' she whispered, when the guard had settled back in his chair.

'I'm ready.' Irisis sounded sceptical.

Ullii took hold of the knot. Again that sucking sensation and the lattice blurred in her mind, fragments of the knot waving around her like a handful of worms. The door creaked and groaned. The octopus tightened its grip. She pulled harder but could not budge it.

Ullii sank to the floor. It was not going to work after all. How could she have thought it would?

FIFTY-FIVE

'Ullii?'

She did not answer. Ullii felt too disheartened. The whole world was against her, even her lattice.

Even her lattice? No, that was her own creation: she could change it however she wanted. Not even this spell that wicked Scrutator Ghorr had made could stop her. How dare he invade her personal spaces? She seized hold of the knot and, instead of trying to move it, Ullii held it in place while she shifted the rest of the lattice around it.

The octopus made an agonised squeal as one by one its tentacles tore free. The remaining ones clung more tightly but she controlled the lattice, and with an audible snap the last tentacle let go.

Ullii held her breath. The latch clicked. Irisis slid through the door and was standing beside her. Ullii let go of the knot, which sprang back to where it had been before. The latch clicked again and the door was once more immovably ensorcelled.

'I don't know how you did it,' said Irisis, hugging her gently. 'I'm not sure I want to know. But, thank you.'

Ullii wriggled out of her grip, afraid for the mouse in her pocket.

'Do you know how to get to the air-floater?' Irisis went on.

'No,' Ullii said softly, taking her friend by the hand. 'I have no idea.'

They dared not go up. There were people in the upper halls of Nennifer day and night, and while little Ullii might creep about unseen, Irisis could not. Had Ullii's incomprehensible interference with the door set off Ghorr's alarm? There was no sign of it.

'We'll have to go down, I think,' she said to the seeker. 'Perhaps if we were to look for a privy outlet.'

Ullii gave her a disgusted glare. Even with noseplugs in, she could never escape through such a stinking place.

'Perhaps not,' said Irisis. 'A drainage pipe, then.'

Ullii was not good at finding that kind of thing. After several hours of searching, during which time Irisis's anxiety grew alarmingly, she found the cleaning eye in a conduit that led from the barracks bathhouse above. She lifted it off. The inside was an oval of rough earthenware about the height of a child of ten. Ullii would have to bow her head. Irisis would need to walk doubled over.

Ullii eyed it dubiously. It stank of stagnant water and something else, sweetly rotting. She shook her head. 'Not going in there.'

'We've only an hour till dawn, Ullii. If we don't get to the airfloater before the scrutator goes, we might as well go back and lock ourselves in. There's no other way out of Nennifer.'

'Don't like this way,' Ullii muttered.

Irisis did not either. She imagined it discharged directly over the cliff and when they got to the end there would be no way of getting out. Still, better that than Ghorr's mercies.

'Ghorr will soon be looking for me. We've got to get out of sight, if we *are* to find your brother.'

Irisis had purloined a lantern. She lowered herself into the conduit and Ullii had to follow. Settling the cover back in place, Irisis held up the lantern. The water, a trickle in the bottom of the pipe, flowed back behind her.

'That way.'

The pipe wandered all over the place. Smaller pipes frequently joined it. It did not get any bigger and soon her back was aching. Something trailed across her head as she shuffled along.

The top of the pipe was festooned with grey jelly-like stuff in which matted hairs, bits of toenails and clots and scum of repulsive origin had been caught. More of the gelatinous growth had formed, or congealed, around it. All this has come from people's bodies in the bathhouses, Irisis thought with a shiver of disgust. And what else that we can't see?

The smell grew stronger. Irisis stumbled into a pool of still water where the pipe had subsided. Brown sludge coated her boots. The smell was revolting. Ullii gagged.

After a long interval they began to smell fresh air, carried by a night breeze up the pipe. 'Not far now.'

Ullii grunted.

They reached it suddenly, an oval circle barely lighter than the blackness inside. Dawn was not far off.

'Careful,' said Irisis. 'If you slip . . .'

She needed the warning more than the seeker did. Ullii was surefooted and she never took risks. Irisis edged down to the opening and was glad she had. The floor of the pipe here was covered in a slippery green growth. The pipe ended at the cliff. The lantern light revealed the stream of water arching down, beyond sight and sound, into the Desolation Sink.

She edged up the side of the pipe, where it was dry, and peered out. The cliff towered above her, almost sheer. There was nothing that resembled a ledge or handhold. Without ropes and irons, it was unclimbable.

'I'm sorry, Ullii. We can't get out.'

Ullii crept up beside her. 'Xervish is going.'

'I can't see him.' Irisis craned her head around. Way back to her left a shadow was rising above the escarpment. It was the air-floater. 'Flydd! Flydd!' She waved the lantern as vigorously as she could. 'Flydd.'

The air-floater kept rising. Ullii shrank back into the drain with her hands up over her face, as if to ward something off.

'What is it, Ullii? What's the matter?'

574

'Ghorr!'

Irisis put down the lantern and looked up. Figures moved on the edge. Someone was pointing down at the entrance to the pipe. The lantern must have been perfectly visible against the shadowed rock.

'They're coming,' said Ullii. 'I'll never find Myllii now.'

'By this time tonight, neither of us will have to worry about that,' Irisis muttered. She waved the lantern again, hoping that Flydd might be able to see it, though it was hard to imagine what he could do.

'Ullii, is there any way you can signal the air-floater with your lattice?' On the way, Ullii had attempted to explain what she'd done. It had made no sense to Irisis.

'No one else can see it,' said Ullii, as if she were talking to a fool.

'What if you moved it around Flydd, the way you got me out of my cell?' Irisis knew she was talking nonsense as soon as the words left her mouth.

'Can't,' said Ullii, quivering. She looked like she was going to have one of her fits.

'Where is your little mouse?'

Ullii felt in her pocket and some of the strain faded. 'He's here.'

'Can I see him?'

Ullii brought him out. The little creature gazed steadily at her. Its whiskers twitched.

'He's smiling at you,' Irisis said. 'What a brave little mouse he is.'

Ullii managed a smile of her own as she returned the mouse to her pocket.

People were running above, along the cliff edge, calling out to each other. 'Down there,' Irisis heard someone shout.

'Do you think you can do *anything* to call Flydd?' Irisis said softly.

'Don't know how.'

'Look in your lattice, Ullii. Can you see the air-floater, and Xervish?'

'Yes.'

Why was the seeker so changeable and difficult? 'Do what you did to the door. It may make Flydd realise we're here.'

'Won't,' Ullii said. 'You don't know the lattice.'

'Please try.'

'Can't.'

Ullii's talent was as stubborn as she was. Maybe it, like her courage, appeared only when she had no other option. That was not necessarily when she was threatened; in such cases she normally put her head in the sand. But when someone she cared deeply about was threatened, Ullii could be a tiger. Was her lost brother the key?

'Where is your brother, Ullii?'

'Don't know,' she said sullenly. 'Left me. Hate him.'

'You don't hate him,' said Irisis, waving the lantern with her free hand. The air-floater rose ever higher, well out over the depression of Kalithras. In a few minutes it would be beyond sight or signal. And minutes after that, Ghorr would have soldiers down here on ropes. 'You miss him terribly.'

'Don't!'

'If Myllii has your talent,' Irisis chose her words very carefully, 'the scrutators might be using him too, now that he is grown up. He might be in danger.'

Ullii gasped and shook her head from side to side.

'If we can just get away, in the air-floater we can fly across half of Lauralin. If he's in the east, you'll surely see him in your lattice.'

The seeker was silent. Tears ran down her face.

'Ullii, do something. Try to call the scrutator. He will find your brother, I promise.'

Ullii closed her eyes. A knot appeared on her delicate jawline. Irisis held on to her pliance and tried to follow what she was doing. For an instant faint marks appeared in her mind, surely the lattice, with the colours of the field sweeping through them. One tiny pair of spots among thousands flared bright, the lattice rotated sickeningly and then the glimpse was gone.

There was a roar and blast just outside. Irisis, who also had her eyes closed, thought that Ghorr had dropped some exploding device. A gale of wind slammed her back into the wall of the pipe. Her eyes sprang open as the air-floater materialised beside them, ripples racing across its airbag like waves on the sea. The cabin was right next to her, shuddering violently under the force that had translated it instantly across a thousand spans of space. Flydd stood just a span away, his eyes wide with an expression she had never seen on his face before: sheer, naked terror.

He swore a series of oaths, looked up and saw her there with her mouth open. Reacting instantly, he threw one of the grappling ropes. She grabbed it.

'Ullii,' she screamed. 'Get aboard.'

Ullii was across in an instant, leaping right into the scrutator's arms.

'Spear Irisis!' roared Ghorr from above. 'Don't let her get away.'

'Jump!' yelled Flydd.

Irisis went across in a great leap that took her over the rail, to slam into the canvas wall of the cabin.

Flydd pushed her to one side, threw his arm up and fire roared forth, perilously close to the airbag and its explosive contents. Irisis did not see what happened on the clifftop, for the air-floater gave a mighty lurch, shot away from the cliff and up. As they rose above the edge, soldiers came running across the paved area with spears and crossbows, but by then it was too late. The air-floater was swiftly rising out of range.

Irisis sketched Ghorr an ironic salute, then had to go inside and sit down. Her knees folded up as she reached the bench. Ullii was underneath, in her favourite corner, rolled into an armadillo-like ball.

'I don't know what you just did,' Flydd began, 'but –'

'I didn't do anything, Xervish. Ullii did it. With her lattice.'

'But . . .' Flydd stared at the motionless seeker, 'that's not possible.'

'I know, but she got me out of my cell without breaking Ghorr's spell.'

'*Or* setting off the alarm,' said Flydd, bemused. 'And now this. How was it possible?'

Had Irisis not been so exhausted, she would have laughed at his expression. 'You'll have to ask her yourself, but don't expect to make anything of it. She did it under duress. I forced her, to save her brother.'

'Ah, her brother.'

'You know about Myllii?'

'Of course. As soon as Ullii's talent became apparent, the scrutators went looking for him.'

'And did they find him?'

'I don't know. I was out of favour by then. But if they haven't, they'll spare no effort *after this.*'

'And to get Ullii back too.'

'Indeed. They'll put our little seeker to very good use if they get their hands on her.'

The flight took six days. They curved west then south around the edge of the Great Mountains, since the air-floater could not rise high enough to pass above them. They floated over the plains and braided outwash streams flowing from a hundred glaciers; then, leaving the mountains behind, drifted south-west across the rift valley with its Great Chain of Lakes and its lines of volcanoes. Beyond, they passed south of a smoking Booreah Ngurle. The Great North Road was on their left, running across the downs of Borgistry. The southern section of the Worm Wood curved round in front of them, taking many hours to pass below, before finally they were over the undulating grasslands and scrub of Taltid.

The pilot took them across the fuming pits of Snizort at a great height while the scrutator looked down with his spyglass. Navigator Nivulee stood beside him with her own, preparing a map for later use.

'Precisely where *is* the node here?' asked Irisis.

'I don't know.'

'Should I wake Ullii and ask her to look for it?'

'Let her sleep. When we've seen enough we'll go on to Gospett, which is about twenty leagues south of here, over the

River Zort and the Westway. The perquisitor there will tell us what we need to know.'

The pilot came running. 'Lyrinx taking to the air, surr.'

Flydd focussed his spyglass. 'So they are. Go higher than they can fly. Head for Gospett.'

They were there in a couple of hours. Gospett turned out to be a walled town built of brown stone and orange brick, heavily fortified against attack by lyrinx. Wicked-looking javelards were mounted along the walls, and others set in tall towers clustered inside. The surrounding land was cultivated, though there were signs that more distant holdings had been abandoned.

'How long can Gospett last, with Snizort so near?' said Irisis.

No one bothered to answer.

The air-floater landed in the main street of the town, much to the excitement of a group of children playing a game with a ball made of bound rags. They gathered around in their hundreds until the scrutator came down the ladder and called for someone to take them to the perquisitor's house, whereupon they melted away. Except one, a boy with a twisted leg, not able to dart off like the others.

Flydd grabbed him by the collar. 'What's your name, boy?' he said in the common speech of the south-west.

'Nudl,' said the boy.

'Noodle? Funny name for a boy.'

'That'th what I'm called, thurr.'

'Well, Noodle, I need someone to show me to the perquisitor's house. Can you do that?'

'No, thurr,' said the boy.

'Why the blazes not? Surely you know where it is.' Flydd's continuous eyebrow crumpled up like wet twine.

'Too thcared, thurr.'

'You're afraid of the perquisitor? Why?'

Nudl hesitated. 'Boys put me up to it, thurr.'

'Put you up to what? You're like a limpet, boy.'

'Thank you, thurr. Throwing thtoneth on perquithitor'th roof, thurr. But one mithed and went through the window. Threatened me –'

579

'Yes, yes, I understand! Well, Noodle, I am a scrutator and you know what that means?'

'You eat children, thurr.'

'I don't eat children, Noodle, though I'm bloody well prepared to make an exception, just this once. Take me to the perquisitor's house, *right away*!'

They were there in ten minutes. The house was a relic of better times, a spacious place of orange brick with a high brick fence all around. Wide verandas sheltered all sides but the south. The perquisitor answered the door. She was a small, slight woman, black of hair and with eyes the same colour. Her skin was palest amber, her features delicately proportioned, her manner reserved.

'Well, well, well,' said Flydd. 'This is a pleasant surprise, Fyn-Mah.'

Fyn-Mah smiled, which was rare for her. 'It's good to see you, scrutator. And you, crafter.' She nodded curtly to Irisis, for they disliked each other. 'Let's sit on the porch. It's cooler. I presume, from the Council despatches case in your hand, that you *are* scrutator again?'

Bowing, he passed it to her. 'Indeed I am. What are you doing here? And a perquisitor, no less.'

'You can hardly act surprised, surr, since you recommended my promotion.'

'These days any recommendation of mine is a dubious one. I didn't know you'd been sent west, though I'm very pleased to see you.'

'I've always had a special interest in the enemy flesh-forming art,' said Fyn-Mah. 'There are more flesh-formers at Snizort than anywhere in Lauralin, and their work is well –'

'So I understand. You can brief me about that in private. You may also be interested in what we've got to say.'

'I'm glad you've come,' Fyn-Mah said, 'and I hope it's good news. In my last report –'

'I was briefed before we left Nennifer. Let's see what can be done.'

'Whatever is done,' said Fyn-Mah, 'were well that it be done quickly. The lyrinx are readying for war. The final assault.'

'We'll also talk about that later.'

'There's someone else you'll be pleased to see, surr.' Fyn-Mah called down the hall. 'And you too, Irisis.'

A man came up. Middle-aged and slim, he was dressed in brown homespun leggings and shirt, and grey sandals. Dark hair, cut short, stuck up all over his head. He had a chiselled jaw, prominent cheekbones and a gleam in his grey eyes.

The man put out his hand. 'Scrutator. Irisis.' He sat in an empty chair.

Irisis noticed Flydd inspecting the fellow surreptitiously. She was sure she had never seen him before. Ullii came trailing along the path, where she had been communing with the flowers. She wore her goggles and earmuffs. The man stood up. 'Hello, we haven't met. You must be Ullii.'

Now how had he known that?

Ullii extended her little hand. 'Hello, Mr Muss.'

There was a long silence, then Flydd's laughter came like a thunderclap. 'Oh, well done. Eiryn Muss, the best prober in the business. That's the first time anyone's disguise has fooled me.' He shook the fellow's hand again. 'Ullii, what a marvel you are.'

Irisis inspected the man again. The disguise, or rather trans-formation, was miraculous. There was not a trace of the fat, bald, shambling halfwit from the manufactory, nor the least manner-ism to give him away. But Ullii did not require such things. She could distinguish every human alive by their smell.

Irisis smiled. 'I dare say it would take more than a few bottles of turnip brandy now.'

'Indeed it would, crafter,' said Muss primly, 'since I do not touch spiritous liquors.'

FIFTY-SIX

Gilhaelith was led away, still trying to see the amplimet. Tiaan felt betrayed. He did not care a fig for her, and never had. He had wanted the amplimet all along, and everything else he'd said to her had been to make sure of it. She cursed herself for falling into the trap, once again.

Ryll fed her a bowl of what looked like green porridge but tasted like slimy compost. She could not feed herself, since her arms were trapped inside the patterner. She slept as if she had been drugged, waking with a fuzzy head to find a group of lyrinx gathered around the patterner three down from her. They had bowed heads, deferring to an ancient male whose skin bore a permanent red blush. His flaccid crest angled to the left and he wore a pair of spectacles. The small oval lenses only covered the centre of his eyes and were set in thick frames of leathery hide. Tiaan had not seen a lyrinx wearing glasses before. It looked odd.

The old male was speaking lyrinx, and though Tiaan did not know that language, it was clear that he was unhappy about something. Ryll and the other lyrinx had changed their skin to the colour of sand, as if they were trying to disappear against the walls, and their crests sagged.

The old lyrinx limped towards Tiaan, lifted her out and inspected her minutely. It had happened so often that she was hardly embarrassed at all. Her skin, irritated by the jelly, had gone blotchy. Behind the lenses, the pupils of his yellow eyes narrowed to slits. He swung around to Ryll, questioning him in a raspy staccato. Tiaan recognised her name several times, and once, 'Tiksi'. She supposed Ryll was telling the old lyrinx her history.

The old creature grunted and his wings half unfurled. He snapped them down. 'What have you done with the flying construct?' he asked in her language.

Tiaan had been expecting that question. 'I gave it to Querist Gan'l,' she lied, making up a name at random. There were thousands of querists and he could not know all their names. 'It was near a town south of here.'

Ryll muttered something in the old fellow's ear. He grunted a question. Ryll went out, soon returning with the amplimet on its chain. As the old lyrinx took it, his crest stood up and bright red specks appeared at the tips. He pushed the amplimet away without touching it, his eyes glowing like molten toffee. In Kalissin the lyrinx had not known what the amplimet was. This fellow knew very well, and he was excited about it.

He rapped out a series of instructions in the lyrinx tongue, in which one word, *torgnadr*, was repeated several times. Ryll jumped. Liett ran down the row of patterners. The old lyrinx adjusted his chest plates as if they irritated him and went out, followed by the rest of his group. Ryll bent and began doing something to Tiaan's patterner, below the level of her vision.

'What's going on?' she cried.

'We must begin.'

'Begin what, Ryll?'

'Making a torgnadr.'

'What's that?'

'I . . . may not say. It is to aid us with the war.'

'It's not another monster like your nylatl?' Just the name sent shudders of remembrance up her spine.

Ryll stiffened, closed his heavy-lidded eyes and opened them again. 'Nothing like that. I have . . . I am forbidden to do flesh-forming.'

'Coeland was not pleased with you after the nylatl escaped?'

'The Wise Mother was furious, and so was Liett.'

'So you did not get your heart's desire after all?'

'I am forbidden to mate, not that it matters now. No female would take a wingless travesty like me. My spoiled line must die with me, for the good of all. Ah, but still . . .' He cast a tormented glance down the row, where Tiaan could just see Liett, bent over and displaying her majestic buttocks.

'Are you going to take flesh from me again,' she said, 'to make your torgnadr?'

'Of course not! Torgnadrs are not flesh-formed. Besides, that practice is forbidden.' He bent down to reach something near the floor, then slowly stood up, his eyes ablaze. 'What do you mean *again*?'

Tiaan wished she had not spoken, but from past experience knew that the lyrinx would drag the truth out of her, so she might as well tell him straight away.

'Liett took a small piece of my flesh to make her snizlet.'

'*What?*' At his bellow, Liett leapt up and stared in their direction, but on seeing nothing amiss she bent to her work again. 'She would not dare. That is forbidden.'

'I still have the scar,' said Tiaan. 'On the inside of my arm.'

In one swift movement, Ryll pulled her from the patterner and sat her on top, glistening with the clinging muck. Tiaan looked him in the eye and held out her left arm.

He felt the small circular scar with a fingertip. 'This was not here when I saved you from the frozen river.'

'She put it in her jar to grow the first snizlet. I think she used her own tissue as well.'

Ryll slid Tiaan back into the machine. Without further word he went out, walking proud and tall. Dangerous red slashes seared across his chameleon skin.

What had she done? When Liett came by a few minutes later, Tiaan pretended to be asleep. Shortly the troop of lyrinx reappeared, she was hauled out yet again and the scar inspected.

'Tllrixi Liett!' the old male roared.

Liett came running. There followed a furious exchange, the old lyrinx roaring, Liett shrinking down until her colourless wings rested flat on the floor. Her arms were stretched out and the old lyrinx stabbed a finger at a mark in her armpit. Liett was questioned in her own tongue. She answered in monosyllables, head bowed.

Finally the old lyrinx struck her once on each cheek, a ritual humiliation. She lay on her face even after he had gone. Ryll stood by, speaking softly in the lyrinx tongue. She groaned but did not move. He squatted beside her but she turned her head away. He lifted her in his arms, tenderly. As she sagged there, Liett's eyes fixed on Tiaan, giving her such a baleful glare that Tiaan had to close her eyes.

Liett said not a word to her, though she was always in sight for the rest of the day. Ryll hurried back and forth, carrying containers to one patterner or another. Tiaan could not see what they held. Late in the afternoon, Liett appeared with a pair of barrel-sized glass buckets, which she set on the floor behind Tiaan.

Ryll came in, nodded to Liett, then put his hands on Tiaan's bare shoulders. 'We are going to begin the patterning. Don't be afraid.'

She was terrified. Ryll put the amplimet around her neck and held her head straight. Liett lifted something, resembling an upside-down jellyfish, out of the larger bucket and eased it down over Tiaan's head. Tiaan thrashed her trapped arms. The cool slipperiness cut off her senses one by one, until all she was left with was touch. Strangely, it was not claustrophobic.

Everything felt stronger, more enhanced, from the slippery muck against her belly and back to the clinging, wet-flesh sensation of the tentacled mask over her face. As Tiaan struggled, the amplimet pulsed between her breasts and she began to see the field.

Nothing else happened. She did not draw power, since there was nothing she could do with it in this blind state. Tiaan sensed an immense *flow* of power, far more than it took to drive a clanker, though she could not tell where it was going.

Like looking into the flames of a campfire, the field was endlessly different and fascinating, and stranger than ever here.

She must have watched the play and pattern for hours before it finally flickered out. Tiaan let it go, overcome by melancholy. Everything was so futile, worthless and sad. She wept. She slept.

Tiaan woke just as miserable, and cried for an hour. She did not know why. The mask had been taken off, but something felt different. The smaller glass bucket sat in a recess on top of her patterner, just out of reach, had she been able to reach. Something had begun to grow from its base, rather like a little mushroom. It must be the torgnadr.

A long time ago, back at the manufactory, she had recovered an image of something similar from the aura of a failed controller crystal. It had been a lyrinx spying device. Were they stealing her talent and putting it into this growing torgnadr? If so, why?

The patterning went on once a day, rarely twice, and each time it took a few hours, during which she could feel the amplimet pulsing furiously. After each episode, she woke weeping. They took her out and washed her down periodically, for the jelly irritated her skin. As she finished the sixth patterning, and blinked at the light in her eyes, there came a gasping exhalation from the cube on her right. Rather, it came from the thin-faced woman inside it. As Tiaan stared, the woman's head flopped to the side, smacking against the top of the patterner.

Liett leapt right over the row, hauled the woman out and laid her on the floor on her back. She was a little bony creature, hardly there at all. Liett thrust down her breastbone several times, so hard that ribs cracked. She put her ear to the thin chest, shaking her head as Ryll raced up.

'Another failure, Liett?' he said.

'What am I going to tell Old Hyull?'

'What are you going to tell the Matriarch?'

Liett snapped her magnificent wings at him, hurled the contents of the glass bucket into a slops tank and stalked off, leaving the body lying on the floor.

'Ryll?' Tiaan could only stare at the sad, dead woman and think she would be next. 'Ryll, what happened to her . . .?'

He hunched his shoulders up and down as if his outer skin

plagued him. 'Patterning is hard on humans. In three years we have only created six torgnadrs, and only two at Snizort.'

Tiaan stared at him. 'How many people have you murdered to make them? Hundreds? *Thousands?*'

He shook his head. 'It is dangerous, though usually it is the torgnadrs that fail. Humans rarely die from it. I was against using this one from the start.'

'What are the torgnadrs for, Ryll?' She had often asked that question but never received an answer.

'I can't tell you.'

After that, Ryll and Liett worked with increased urgency. Lyrinx ran in constantly, shouting what could only be exhortations to hurry. The patternings became more frequent and the sessions longer.

Despite Ryll's words, two more people, a man and a woman, died in the patterners in the next three days. Tiaan's melancholy grew worse after each session, and though she knew that it was due mainly to the patterner, she could not stop. Her face was swollen from weeping, her tear ducts so inflamed that it hurt to cry. Ryll added salt to her diet, she had wept so much away.

Tiaan could not eat – the green porridge made her want to vomit. She even gagged on water. Ryll brought women from the other patterners to sit with her. That only made it worse. None could speak her language and none was affected by patterning the way she was. She was different, special, and they seemed to resent her.

The patterning had been going on for well over a week. Tiaan could no longer tell what was day and what was night. She'd lost count after ten sleeps. She felt very weak. Even if she'd had the use of her legs, after so long without activity she could not have stood up. She felt sure she was going to die.

Something was going on – the lyrinx showed skin patterns all the time now, livid, clashing colours and jagged designs, and they ran everywhere. Tiaan discovered, from something Liett had said, that human armies were marching toward Snizort. The lyrinx expected to be slaughtered here, or burned alive, but they seemed less worried about that than about completing their great project before the siege began.

The Matriarch and Old Hyull often came in to inspect her torgnadr. As her melancholy increased, they appeared more frequently, but now their skin colour showed agitation. After their last visit, Ryll had lain prostrate on the floor for an hour, and when he got up his eyes were shrivelled like raisins.

Liett barked at him in the lyrinx tongue. He flashed yellow and black, half-heartedly. She lifted him to his feet and propelled him from the chamber. Shortly she returned to stand by Tiaan's patterner, looking down and clacking her toe claws on the floor.

The silence became uncomfortable. 'What's the matter?' said Tiaan.

Without replying, Liett stalked away.

Tiaan worried about that until Ryll returned with a man she vaguely recognised – the one-handed fellow she had seen as she entered Snizort.

'Tutor speaks your language,' said Ryll, hurrying off.

Tiaan could hardly see the man through her swollen eyes. Thin, a sallow face, dark eyes, dark hair. He said nothing, but after a minute he dabbed at her eyes with a piece of rag. She sniffled. He wiped her nose.

'I'm sorry,' she said. 'I don't know why I'm crying.'

'The patterner occasionally has that effect.'

He spoke the common speech with a familiar accent – the one spoken on the south coast of Einunar. Of course. He had taught Ryll that language. She wept for the joy of hearing the sounds.

'I'm sorry,' she repeated. 'I haven't heard anyone from my own land in half a year.' It filled her with longing for her place in the manufactory. 'What's your name? Or should I call you Tutor?'

'If you like. Tutor is my name; my life. Once I was called Merryl but it doesn't fit any more.'

'What's going on, Tutor?' The name felt wrong. 'Why are the lyrinx so afraid? They're strong.'

'Not so strong that they can hope to defeat the armies moving towards Snizort. They're working on a vital project here, and are afraid they'll never complete it.'

'Can't they take it across the sea where they're safe from attack?'

'I don't know. Since I speak their language, they're specially careful what they say when I'm around.'

'The lyrinx have defeated us so many times already. Why are they afraid now?'

'Because of the Aachim and their constructs.'

Tiaan felt a shiver of fear. Why did the thought of them frighten her more than the lyrinx did? She was sure that Vithis was still after her.

'The lyrinx worry that Aachim and humans will unite to destroy them. Snizort is vulnerable – should they bombard this place with blazing missiles, the tar pits would burn for a hundred years and nothing could extinguish the fires. The lyrinx have a particular terror of fire.'

Tiaan imagined being trapped down here and shuddered. 'So do I.'

'Yet they must complete what they came here to do. That's why your torgnadr is so urgent.'

'What would they have done if I hadn't come?'

'They have a torgnadr here, but it's been in place for years and is rapidly failing. A band of lyrinx was bringing a replacement from across the sea, but something went wrong. The lyrinx carrying the torgnadr fell into the sea from a great height and was killed, and the torgnadr was lost. It was a terrible setback. Then, miraculously, you turned up. With your talent, and the amplimet, it was their chance to make the most powerful torgnadr of all.'

'What are all these torgnadrs for?'

'There's only one – yours.'

'But what about all these other patterners?'

'Their torgnadrs have failed, as nearly all do. They are being repatterned into limnadrs, phynadrs, zygnadrs and other minor devices.'

'Mine is the only one?' she said, wide-eyed.

'Yes. In three years of patterning here they've made thousands of minor devices, but only two torgnadrs, and none in the past year. From what I read of their skin-speech, they have the highest hopes for yours. If it's not ready in time, Snizort must fall.'

'And we will surely be burned to death.'

'Alas.'

To save her life she must hope that the torgnadr grew well and swiftly. But if Snizort survived, the human army might not. In that case it was her duty to destroy or sabotage the growing device.

Tutor fell silent. Tiaan grew uncomfortable, wished he would go, and shortly he did. She started crying again.

In the intervals between patterning she slept or sat staring around her, bored out of her wits. Her appetite came back – eating was the only thing she had any control over. The torgnadr grew as quickly as a mushroom and with every passing hour Tiaan thought more about her duty. After fleeing Kalissin and the horrific result of her unwilling collaboration there, she had vowed she would never aid the lyrinx again. Now here she was, still unwilling, helping them in a way that could be a hundred times worse. Her duty was clear. She must try to destroy the torgnadr.

Yet she could not move while in the patterner, and when they took her out she was carried to another room to sleep. She could not influence the patterner either – it took from her what it required and she did not know what that was.

In the next session, Tiaan watched more closely. She saw the patterner reading her and imprinting the growing torgnadr. She saw the ebb and flow of the field, and the brightening of the amplimet as power was drawn through it. It did not take much power but something else must, for the field was fluctuating erratically. The amplimet began blinking furiously, as it had at Tirthrax. Was it speaking to the node again?

What if she were to draw power into the amplimet and try to damage the torgnadr, or the patterner itself? Tiaan tried to, but her talent could not penetrate the mask. The lyrinx had thought of everything. That day, when the mask and the amplimet were removed, she wept the most helpless tears of all.

By now, the growth so filled its bucket that the bulbous head protruded from the top. At night, when the lights were out, it emitted a faint green glow.

The torgnadr disturbed Tiaan. It seemed to be watching her, trying to copy her talent, though she knew that was ridiculous. There was no brain inside it; no intelligence. Ryll had told her that much. It was simply patterned on her ability to sense the fluctuating field and draw power from it. Nonetheless, the sight of it put her on edge.

Tutor came to see her every day. Though Tiaan knew Ryll had sent him, she looked forward to Tutor's visits. He was cheerful, despite his years of slavery, and talked of places far away and times distant: the Great Tales of the Histories, as well as the minor ones. His presence reminded her of her simple life back in the manufactory. How she yearned for it.

She often saw other humans: prisoners who did menial duties like cleaning, carrying and feeding. Tiaan now recognised a dozen, mostly men, defeated soldiers taken prisoner and afterwards kept because they had some value. They rarely spoke and few knew her language. All seemed beaten down by their servitude.

One was coming now, a slender man of middle age with straight white hair and skin as pallid as a mushroom. He had brought food to her several times, spooning the green muck into her mouth but never meeting her eyes. His left shoulder was missing a chunk of muscle, doubtless an old war wound. The arm hung limp.

'Hello,' she said. 'My name is Tiaan. What's yours?'

'Not allowed – talk,' he muttered in an atrocious accent.

'I'll talk to whoever I want. Hey, come back.'

That was the last she saw of him, or her lunch.

Liett checked the growth and lifted the glass bucket down. Tiaan was about to remark about her missed lunch but thought better of it. The lyrinx looked particularly ferocious today and Tiaan did not want to get the prisoner into trouble.

Not long afterwards the old lyrinx reappeared, along with his bevy of attendants. The torgnadr was set down next to Tiaan. He adjusted his spectacles, pulled something onto the top of his head that rather resembled Tiaan's jellyfish mask, and frowned. At least, she interpreted it as a frown.

Abruptly he wrenched the mask off and spoke to Ryll in an imperative rasp. Ryll answered, again in submissive posture.

'Jjyikk myrr; priffiy tzzukk!' snarled the old fellow.

Ryll sprang up and lifted Tiaan out, holding her with her legs dangling while the old lyrinx examined them, prodding and poking. He snapped at Ryll, who hefted Tiaan and carried her, dripping muck, along many tunnels before going into a long, narrow room shaped like an amputated finger. He laid her on a central table with a bright light above it, face-down. More probing and prodding went on in the middle of her back. She thought they were probing her legs too, though she could feel nothing down there.

Suddenly the room was empty except for Ryll. 'What's the matter?' she whispered, very afraid.

He looked away.

Tiaan caught at his hand. 'Please, Ryll. I saved your life, remember?'

'And I allowed you to escape from Kalissin. The debt is paid.'

'Not the debt of friendship!'

'What?' he exclaimed.

'We worked together for months, Ryll. I was your prisoner, yet there were times when we were friends, were we not? Or were you just pretending, so as to get what you wanted from me?'

He seemed . . . she could not quite say what, perhaps a combination of hurt, embarrassment and revelation. 'You're right. We *were* friends.'

'Then tell me what is going on. Please?'

Again he glanced over his shoulder. 'The torgnadr has a flaw. Old Hyull, Husband of the Matriarch, believes it has developed wrongly because of your broken back.'

Did this mean she was useless to them, except to be eaten? 'What is he going to do?'

'I don't know. The torgnadr is strong; the best yet, but because of the flaw we cannot use it. He is furious. I cannot say any more.'

'But what's going to happen to me?' she cried.

Ryll shook his head and walked away.

FIFTY-SEVEN

'Are we going to look for Myllii today?' The eagerness shone in Ullii's eyes. She had asked the same question every day for a week, usually at the most inopportune times. She searched her lattice for him every night but found nothing. She thought about Nish too, but had no way of looking for him; he did not show in her lattice.

'Not today, Ullii,' the scrutator said in that absent way a parent uses with a nagging child. 'I'm busy with the war right now.'

Ullii was not a child and resented being treated like one. Something died in her eyes. She gave Flydd a bitter glare and turned up the hall. The door of her room was closed without a sound.

'She feels betrayed,' said Irisis. 'And I feel I've betrayed her. I gave her my word.'

'I understand what she's going through, but what can I do? I can't go cruising across Lauralin for a month in the hope she'll find him. I haven't time to scratch myself.'

'I know that, Xervish. Even so . . .'

'You've walked the streets all week, asking after him. I've asked Muss to put Myllii on his list. For the moment, that's all I can do.'

And Ullii could be most uncooperative when thwarted. Irisis hoped they would not have to rely on her for anything important, before Myllii could be found.

Everyone was so frantically busy that Irisis hardly saw the scrutator from one day to the next. The Council had been moving their forces in for weeks. They now had sixty thousand troops within a few days' march of Snizort, escorted by seven thousand clankers. Many of these carried better weapons than before, and were more strongly built, but if the node failed they would be worthless. And without clankers, even that army could not match the twenty-five thousand lyrinx known to be at Snizort.

'And that's not even considering the Aachim.' Flydd was ratcheting back and forth across the veranda, grabbing a tiny break from the endless meetings and messages. She had never seen him so stressed. He could not sit still for an instant. 'If they join up with the enemy we're finished. We probably are anyway.'

'What do you mean?'

'There's something wrong, though . . .'

'What?'

'I think Snizort is a trap and we've put both feet into it.'

'It's not too late to pull back.'

'I've done everything I can to avoid this battle, but Ghorr's orders are specific and I have no discretion. Even if I disobeyed him and retreated, the blow to morale would be disastrous. And the enemy may have an attack plan for that, too.'

'Where are the Aachim now?' Irisis asked.

'Moving down through Borgistry and Almadin, and in from Oolo and Nihilnor, according to our latest intelligence.'

'What do you want me to do?'

'Learn all you can about the node and how its fields are changing. Perquisitor, would you get the Snizort chart?'

Fyn-Mar unrolled it on the boards. 'The node is not actually *at* Snizort, but several leagues to the south, well underground.'

'Underground?' He frowned.

'My predecessor mapped it a few years ago, along with others in the area. Usually nodes are associated with some prominent geographic feature: a hill or volcano, a faultline or canyon. This one is not.'

'What kind of country is it?'

'Rolling hills.'

'Is there limestone?'

'Some.'

'Mines or caves?'

She shrugged. 'I don't know of any.'

'Not much help,' said the scrutator. 'Go to the location of the node, Irisis. Take Ullii and see what you can find. The field is weaker than when we arrived, so they must be taking out more power than ever. See if you can find any sign of a node-drainer.'

'That's lyrinx country. How are we going to get there?'

'The air-floater will drop you there tonight. Signal when you're ready to be picked up but be prepared to come back on your own. Just in case.'

Irisis hoped there would be no such eventuality. The node lay twenty leagues north of Gospett, at least five days' march in this country, even supposing that Ullii would walk at all. She was more sullen and withdrawn than ever.

Irisis and Ullii spent half the night, under a bright full moon, slogging back and forth across the location of the node. Though there was nothing on the surface to indicate its presence, it was one of the strongest Irisis had encountered. Its field extended for nearly twenty leagues in all directions before being over-whelmed by overlapping fields from smaller, more distant nodes. The node itself was compact, little more than a thousand paces across, like the yolk of a fried egg, surrounded by an increasingly tenuous halo of field, the white.

'Any marks on the ground?' Irisis asked Ullii for what seemed the hundredth time. 'Any pits or holes or diggings?'

'No,' said Ullii.

'Any sense of a node-drainer?'

'No! Tired. Want to sleep.'

Ullii always seemed tired lately. It was an added worry.

'Only one line to go,' Irisis said.

Ullii said something rude, but did keep going. They trudged down the line, Ullii sensing the shape of the node, Irisis noting its variations in her book. Finally they got to the end, only a couple of hours before dawn.

'Anything here, Ullii?'

'*No.* Have to sleep.'

'You can lie down right here, if you like. We're finished.'

Irisis signalled into the air. There was no response. She prayed they would not have to walk, for it was a long trek to the Westway, the first place where they could hope to be picked up. She did not fancy that, in lyrinx country.

The work they'd done had confirmed what she already knew. The node was a long way underground and there could be no node-drainer here, else Ullii would have sensed it. They would have to search from the air-floater and hope to come upon signs of strangeness, such as sinking land or a sudden appearance of hot springs, though both were common around Snizort. Ullii had to know where to look.

Irisis sat up until dawn. The air-floater did not come. In the morning Ullii rolled over and was violently ill. She curled up under a tree in the shade, her mask, goggles and earmuffs firmly in place, and could not be convinced to move. Irisis spent a restless, anxious day.

That night she signalled as soon as it grew dark and the air-floater appeared within minutes. 'Where the blazes were you last night?' Flydd said as she climbed over the side.

'Right here!' she snapped. 'Waiting to be picked up.'

'They went back and forth a hundred times but couldn't find you. Got me out of bed to tell me so.'

'Poor you! They must have gone to the wrong spot.'

'Don't see how they could have. They were navigating by the field. Did you find the node?'

'Found it, mapped it. It's small and round, with a broad halo. No sign of any drainer, though.'

'Perhaps they're using all the power for flesh-forming.' He turned to the seeker. 'Ullii?'

'Yes,' she said limply.

'What's the matter?'

'Sick!'

'Can you still see the lattice?'

'Of course!' Ullii said scornfully.

'Well, you couldn't after we lost Nish,' Flydd muttered. 'I want you to look for a node-drainer on the way back. Can you do that?'

'Tired!' Ullii was always snappy with Flydd these days.

'I want you to look. *All right?*'

She'd fought him before, and lost. 'Yes, scrutator.'

They travelled in a direct line from the node towards Gospett. It was a beautiful, moonlit night. The navigator plotted their track on the chart. Ullii could see nothing. They were all depressed.

'What if we flew over Snizort?' Irisis suggested. 'The lyrinx could be dumping surplus power among the tar pits. Ullii might be able to pick that up.'

He considered. 'It's risky on such a clear night. We'd have to stay low for there to be a chance.'

'But –'

'On the other hand, the tar pits would be the perfect place to hide such a flow of force.'

They crossed Snizort from south to north. It was another hot night. The moon reflected off inky-black deposits as shiny as mirrors. Irisis watched Ullii.

'Nothing!'

The air-floater turned and went back the other way. 'Lyrinx,' called Pilot Hila.

Ullii went bolt upright, the moonlight touching her eyes.

'It's all right, Ullii,' said Irisis. 'It's below us. We can go higher than it can.'

'Waves of flesh!' Ullii cried, and fell sideways.

The scrutator caught her and shouted for the pilot to head for home. 'What can that mean?'

Irisis had seen such a reaction before, on the plateau just before they'd attacked the ice houses. 'It means they're flesh-forming down there.'

'We knew that already. Flesh-forming what?'

'It's Tiaan,' Ullii whispered.

Irisis and the scrutator stared at each other. 'Are you sure, Ullii?'

The question was redundant. Ullii had never been known to make a mistake.

'What's Tiaan doing down there?'

The seeker lay back, panting, and did not answer.

'Ullii's been sick all day,' said Irisis. 'She was sick yesterday morning too.'

They exchanged looks. 'I wonder,' said Flydd, 'if she and Nish might have done some flesh-forming of their own?'

'It would explain a lot.'

They travelled the rest of the route in silence. As the air-floater settled down, Fyn-Mah came running out, to speak rapidly in Flydd's ear. He nodded. She went inside.

The scrutator helped Ullii down. 'Do you think you'll be able to look for a node-drainer tomorrow?'

'Found it,' she grunted. 'Tired. Going to bed.'

'What? Where is it?' he and Irisis cried together.

'Tar pits. When lyrinx appeared. Underground. Deep. Very strange.'

Flydd glanced at Irisis. 'What do you mean, Ullii?'

The seeker trotted off without answering. Flydd ran and caught her arm as she was going through the front door. 'Ullii?'

'Goes on and off.' She pulled free and scuttled down the hall.

'Is that good or bad?' Flydd said. 'Either way, it's not a moment too soon.'

'What's the matter now?' said Irisis.

'The Aachim are just over the horizon – the best part of a hundred thousand of them, and as many constructs as we have clankers. And doubtless the rest are on the way.'

'Are they for us or against us?'

'If only I knew. Now be quiet. I've got to think.'

They spent what remained of the night on the veranda with Fyn-Mah. 'So the enemy have Tiaan,' said Flydd. 'How did *that* come about?'

'I haven't discovered,' Fyn-Mah replied. 'Muss is trying to find out.'

'More importantly,' said Irisis, 'what does she have to do with their flesh-forming?'

'They used her talents in Kalissin. Perhaps they're doing it again.'

'What *are* they doing down there?'

Fyn-Mah leaned forward in her chair. 'I don't know, though from what Muss has gleaned from their human slaves, they're close to what they went there for.'

'And that is?' said Irisis.

'A vital breakthrough for the war,' said Flydd. 'Our time has run out. We'll have to attack Snizort, and soon.'

'What are our chances?'

'Of winning this battle? Without aid, rather low.'

Fyn-Mah sat up. 'There is one thing . . .'

'Yes?'

'Vithis is still hunting Tiaan and the flying construct. He's changed all his plans just to find her. So –'

Flydd let out his breath in a sigh that made the candles flicker. 'Of course he is. And we know where she is. I see an opportunity.'

'You wouldn't,' said Irisis.

'What's one life, *any* life, before the whole of humanity?'

Two days later the first and greatest fleet of constructs appeared, some six thousand of them, whining in to camp well south of Snizort, where the Westway crossed the River Zort over a stone bridge of seven arches. Irisis and Flydd watched them from the air-floater.

'Not a comforting sight.' Flydd put down his spyglass. 'Their constructs are . . .'

'Vastly superior to our clankers,' Irisis finished.

'In every respect. And a damn sight more comfortable.'

The soldiers called clankers 'boneshakers', for they were hideously uncomfortable, even on good roads, and prone to breaking down. Constructs, gliding hip-high above the ground, must have been like floating on silk.

'Better go down and see what we can make of the fellow,' said Flydd. 'From what I've heard of Vithis, I can't say I'm optimistic.'

In the next week, five sets of emissaries were turned back by the Aachim. So many spies had been sent out that Irisis wondered if the whole population of Gospett was on the scrutator's payroll. Few returned. Vithis would see no one and no one knew what was going on. One day he was supposed to have allied with the lyrinx, the next planning war on them, with or without human aid. Other rumours held that he was awaiting a signal to strike at humanity all across Santhenar. Only one thing was certain: he was hunting Tiaan. Aachim roved across the land in small groups of constructs, gathering intelligence and seeking information about her.

'Time I went to see Vithis,' said Flydd.

'What if he won't see you?'

'I don't plan to give him the choice. And once there, I dare say he'll be interested in Ullii's discovery.'

'About the node-drainer?' said Irisis.

'Don't mention that! Tiaan is the key. Find her and we'll find the flying construct. Then we can win the war on our own, or offer the flier to Vithis in return for his help. The same result either way.'

'Could be unfortunate for Tiaan,' said Irisis.

'The same applies to all of us.'

The generals argued for making a show of strength and taking a squadron of clankers, but the scrutator vetoed that idea.

'Their constructs are manifestly superior to our machines,' he said. 'It would only prove our unfitness to negotiate as equals. Above all we must not appear weak, nor rustic.'

'Are we to go on horseback then?' said General Tham. 'Or on foot, to be turned away like beggars?'

'We will drop down on them in the air-floater,' said Flydd. 'Equal but different. They may dominate the land but they have not mastered the skies. They want to, desperately.'

'You would fly, unarmed and helpless, into the enemy camp?' said Tham. 'I cannot –'

'They are not our enemy,' said Flydd. 'Yet! And the safest way to approach an Aachim army *is* unarmed.'

'One ill-disciplined soldier, one frightened Aachim youth with a javelard, could destroy the air-floater, and you. And all our hopes.'

'I'm sure no soldier of Vithis is ill-disciplined.'

'Except the one who killed Tiaan's ward, little Haani,' Irisis said to herself. Why would Flydd not listen?

The air-floater was cleaned until it shone and everyone was fitted with freshly tailored uniforms. The embassy went aboard, including Irisis and Ullii, and they rotored gently over the Aachim camp, flying the flag of the Council of Scrutators.

The sight was awesome – thousands of constructs arrayed with military precision around a central heptagon of bare land. That space contained hundreds of tents, as yellow as sulphur and marked with swirling patterns in black. A large tent stood by itself.

The constructs had the same general form, though they were of all sizes up to monsters that might have carried fifty people. Each was armed with weapons, mounted on a platform at the rear, and every weapon was trained on their fragile craft. Irisis held her breath as the air-floater hovered over the tents.

'Take it down next to the command tent there,' Flydd said to Hila. 'And whatever you do, don't hit it.'

She pursed her lips, drifted in and settled the machine in the indicated space so lightly that it would not have cracked an egg. They climbed out, Irisis noting that the javelards still tracked them.

Three Aachim came to meet them, holding themselves erect and walking well apart.

Vithis gave the air-floater a measured sideways glance. 'A remarkable vehicle.' He offered his hand to the scrutator. 'I am Vithis of Clan Inthis, First Clan, at your service. I lead my people, in peace and in war.'

The curly-haired woman to his right scowled. The other man's face was carefully blank.

'Xervish Flydd, Scrutator for Einunar, representing the Council of Scrutators in war. We have not had peace in one hundred and fifty years, and we are prepared to fight as long again, if we must.'

'How does your machine stay in the air?' Vithis asked casually. 'Does it repel the field?'

'It employs a simpler principle. The airbag is filled with a vapour, more buoyant than air, which we obtain from mines deep underground.'

'Ah,' said Vithis, and turned away.

Is he impressed by the simplicity, Irisis wondered, or contemptuous of it?

The subordinates on either side were introduced. These included General Tham and his adjutant, Irisis and Ullii. For the Aachim, Luxor, Tirior and Minis. They retired to a pavilion out of the sun and after refreshments were offered Vithis said, 'Why have you come, Scrutator Flydd?'

'To see if we might be of assistance to each other,' Flydd said.

'You want us to fight your war for you.'

'We don't, though I won't pretend your aid would not be useful. We are both human species and our kinship is close. Should we not stand –?'

'Old humans are legion!' snapped Vithis. 'We are few. Less than one hundred and fifty thousand, many of whom are children. We have much to lose and nothing to gain from an alliance with you.'

'You have everything to lose,' said Flydd. 'Were the lyrinx to defeat us they would attack you at once.'

Vithis shrugged. 'They will get a surprise if they do.'

'We estimate their population at three hundred thousand. If they are not stopped, that number will double in ten years.'

Vithis was shocked but hid it well. 'Do you come here with a proposition? We have much to do this afternoon.'

The scrutator did not react to the breach of civility. 'There are a number of matters we should discuss, but first – I know the whereabouts of Artisan Tiaan Liise-Mar.'

Vithis rose out of his chair like a rock from a catapult. *'Where is she?'*

'I will tell you, should you be willing to help us with our little problem.'

'You know this thieving woman?'

'I do not know Tiaan personally, though my assistant, Crafter Irisis Stirm of the House of Stirm, worked side by side with her for fifteen years.'

Vithis spoke in Minis's ear. He hurried off, soon returning with a bowed figure whose wrists were in manacles.

Ullii, who wore a mask over her goggles, tore off the mask, peered at the prisoner, screamed 'Nish!' and hurled herself at him, knocking him to the ground.

Eventually she was prised free of Nish, who looked bemused. Ullii was led back to her seat, where she kept staring at him. He was not looking at her and her face began to take on an expression Irisis was all too familiar with. Nish had not greeted the seeker with quite the same enthusiasm as she had him. Once again she had built up expectations that could not be fulfilled. She looked let down, angry and confused. Something else to worry about.

'We were sure you were dead.' Irisis took Nish's hand, studying him at arm's length.

He laughed. 'If you knew the half of what I've been through. Oh, Irisis, it's good to see you.'

She took him in her arms, which almost caused an incident. Ullii arched her back, hissing like an angry cat. Flydd stepped up smoothly beside her, his fingers danced on her forehead and the light faded from her eyes. Ullii allowed herself to be sat back in her chair, where she slumped listlessly.

'Quite a family reunion,' said Vithis with curled lip.

'Scrutator,' Nish said, shaking his hand. 'I'd heard you were dis–'

'Never been better, thanks,' Flydd said smoothly. 'We'll talk later.'

Vithis gave him a suspicious glare.

'What the blazes are you doing here, Nish?' the scrutator went on.

'I have been advising Minis on how to find Tiaan.'

'Without success!' Vithis said sourly.

'We would have had her, had Minis been allowed to follow my advice!' Nish snapped.

'Be silent!' said Vithis, 'or you will go back to your cell.' He turned to the scrutator. 'Where is the little thief?'

'If you are referring to Tiaan, I am prepared to tell you . . .'

604

'Your price?' Vithis interrupted.

'Aachim aid in the war.'

'You ask the world, yet offer little, like all your kind.'

'Don't treat me like a fool, Vithis,' Flydd said. 'This flying construct is worth a thousand of yours. If it were not, you would not have broken off your invasion in such a desperate search for it.'

'It is, as you say, valuable to me. And more valuable to you in your situation, so why give it up so easily? I smell deceit. Either that or a man so weak he cannot make use of it. You are desperate, Scrutator Flydd, and desperate men can't afford to bargain.'

'My mechanicians will soon take the flying construct apart and learn how to make more of them, so if you don't wish to deal with me,' Flydd said coolly, 'so be it. Good day.' Nodding formally to Tirior, Luxor and Minis, he rose.

After a moment's hesitation, Vithis said, 'I would be happy to deal with you, scrutator, should we be able to agree on terms. I must have surety before –'

'My word is the only surety I am able to give you. If that is not enough we can deal in nothing.'

'What is your offer?'

'The flying construct in exchange for Aachim support until the lyrinx are defeated. And I would have Tiaan back, plus my servant Nish.'

'You are welcome to the rogue,' said Vithis, 'and I hope he gives you less trouble than he has me. For the rest, you ask too much and offer nothing at all, as the flying construct is Aachim property.'

'Since Tiaan made it from machines abandoned in Tirthrax, one could argue that it is her property.'

'Not by the laws of our world.'

'You are no longer on Aachan.'

'The construct was taken from an Aachim city.'

'Their laws are not yours.'

'Nor yours!'

'Then the only way ownership can be resolved is by Malien, Matah of Tirthrax, who befriended Tiaan in Tirthrax and no doubt helped her to make it.'

Vithis was shocked. 'Tirthrax was empty! No one answered the sentinels.'

'Malien was preparing to go to the Well.'

'Malien has not come forward,' snapped Vithis. 'If she exists! I am within my rights to seize the flying construct.'

Tirior sprang up, but an aide spoke in her ear and she sat down again.

'I would not advise it.' Flydd was a small figure before the tall Aachim, but no less formidable. 'We do not wish to take you on, but you have come to our world uninvited, and not in friendship.'

'Our own world was lost,' said Vithis. 'We had no choice.'

'Granted, but you come armed for war.'

'Who would not? The void is no place for the defenceless.'

'You turn away our emissaries, or treat them with contempt. You rove where you will, deferring to no authority but your own. These are not the actions of a peace-loving people. I would know what your intentions are.'

'Survival!' snapped Vithis.

'By which you mean a piece of Santhenar,' growled Flydd. 'If that is your aim, do me the courtesy of stating it plainly.'

Vithis stood up. 'I will do what –'

Tirior stepped in front of him and when he tried to get by she hissed something that made him leap backwards. 'Scrutator Flydd, be assured that we come in peace and friendship, and that we acknowledge our kinship with old humankind. You have suffered much in your war with the lyrinx, but we have suffered more! Since the Forbidding was broken, two hundred of your years ago, we have seen Aachan torn apart beneath our feet. Nine-tenths of our people are dead. Everything we created in the ten thousand years of our Histories has been lost, save what you see before you. You have Santhenar. We have nothing. And who brought this calamity upon Aachan?'

'The forces of nature, before which the greatest of us are humbled.'

'The Forbidding was broken on Santhenar,' Tirior said force-fully. 'That breaking caused the loss of our world. Santhenar destroyed Aachan. Now Santhenar must provide for its homeless.

You owe us a world, Scrutator Flydd . . .' She met his eye. 'But we will be satisfied with half.'

For a moment, even Flydd was silent. Irisis, sitting next to him, could not believe their arrogance. Did they truly believe humanity would give Santhenar away, or were they so strong that they could take it? She did not think so, else this debate would not be taking place at all. It had to be a bluff.

'The troubles of all the worlds began with the Golden Flute,' said Flydd, 'as you well know. And that was made on Aachan, with Aachim aid. Tensor himself laboured in its forging.'

'The troubles began when the flute was stolen and brought to Santhenar. By *Shuthdar*, one of your own. And Shuthdar created the Forbidding in the first place.'

'Not as I understand the Histories,' said Flydd. 'But we can debate those times until the equator freezes over and we will be no closer to the truth. We were prepared to make you an offer of land, in friendship and acknowledgement of your loss. But we are not to blame for it and we will never submit to demands. We will fight –'

'What offer?' said Vithis, moving out from behind. 'You are late in making one.'

'As are you in putting your true intentions. We were prepared to offer you the land of Carendor, on the eastern side of the Dry Sea.'

'You dare insult us with a desert?' cried Vithis in a rage. 'By –'

'Carendor is an arid land, it is true,' said Flydd, 'yet the fertile valley of the great River Truno runs all the way through it, while the springs and seeps on the slope of the Dry Sea are enough to water a garden a hundred leagues long. Before the war Carendor supported a million people. Its numbers are less now, but even to give that land to you, more than your number must be displaced.'

'Carendor is too hot, dry and barren. We will take nothing less than all that lies south of the fortieth parallel. One half of your lands. That is our price. And the flying construct, of course.'

'Precisely what do you offer in return?' said Flydd.

'Our aid in your coming battle at Snizort. Plus Treacherous Tiaan, and Cryl-Nish Hlar the Rogue.'

'And that is all? I am hard pressed to see any difference between you and the lyrinx, save that they are honest foes.'

The Aachim stiffened as if they had been given a mortal insult. 'You challenge our honesty?' cried Vithis. 'Damn you. The offer is withdrawn. You will regret this insult, scrutator.'

For a moment Flydd did not know what to say, but he was not going to back down. 'You did not deal honestly with Tiaan,' he said mildly. 'Why should you treat us any differently?'

'You will regret impugning our good name, scrutator.'

'I'll make sure you regret it more. You are a *little* force in an unknown land and your supplies are running low. Every man is your enemy; every woman; every child. Even if we took five casualties for every one of yours, you would suffer the greater injury.'

'You reveal yourself,' said Vithis furiously, and now Tirior and Luxor were solidly behind him. 'Your real plan is to eradicate the Aachim and no threat could spur us to greater efforts. We will fight bitterly for our survival, scrutator!'

'I merely point out what is obvious. May I have Artificer Cryl-Nish Hlar?'

'You may not. Begone, Scrutator Flydd, or you will see what our little force can do.'

FIFTY-EIGHT

Irisis was an early riser, normally up long before the scrutator. On going out Fyn-Mah's front door at sunrise a few days later, she was surprised to see Flydd in his chair, staring at a message sheet.

'You look horrible,' she said cheerfully. 'Should have stayed in bed.'

'I haven't been to bed yet.' He did not look up.

'Something else the matter?'

'Ha!' he said savagely.

'What is it?' He was like a barnacle in the mornings.

'Eiryn Muss can't find any way into Snizort. Therefore, I can't carry out my orders – to destroy this strange node-drainer.'

'What about a massed attack?'

'As soon as we begin, they would simply drain the field, stopping the clankers dead. I don't dare.'

'Well, Muss is the best spy there is. He may still find a way.'

'Not in time. Their great project is nearly complete; he knows that much. And the lyrinx are preparing for battle. We must attack now or lose what little advantage we have.'

'But without clankers . . .'

'We're doomed. So I have only one option left.'

'Oh no.'

'I'm afraid so. The node-drainer won't affect constructs since

609

they don't rely on the weak field. I must go back to Vithis on my belly, agree to his demands and beg him for assistance. What price will he put on aid now? I can't bear to think. The scrutators will crucify me after this.'

'And yet you must pay the price,' she said, 'for even a small part of our world is better than none.'

'I must.' He had never looked more haggard or careworn. 'There's only one consolation and I'm sure you saw it too. The Aachim are like warring tribes, forced to unite though they hate each other. We may be able to make use of that, in time.'

'If we get the time.'

Unfortunately the Aachim proved united and inflexible. Flydd had grovelled, a hideous sight; the Aachim had accepted his concessions.

Another four days had gone by before the preparations were complete. Now the battle was about to begin. Irisis was with Flydd at a command post on one of the flat-topped hills overlooking the battleground.

She surveyed the scene through the scrutator's spyglass. Snizort lay on a broad rise with lower, gently undulating land all around, grassland but with patches of scrubby forest, small, mostly boulder-topped hills and isolated clusters of sandstone boulders. The forest near the eastern wall had recently been cleared, the fallen trees forming barriers that clankers would find it difficult to cross. Inside the walls lay the Great Seep, a vast and bottomless mire of liquid tar surrounded by steaming, crystal-crusted vents and a number of pits, some large and deep, from which solidified tar had been mined for thousands of years. Smaller tar bogs and seeps littered the ground inside and outside the walls.

In ancient times, overflowing tar from the seeps had oozed down the low-lying areas, creating a series of black rivers that circled away from Snizort for as much as a league. These had long since dried out, and parts had also been mined, though much remained. Other, smaller seeps and bogs occurred here and there.

The Aachim had planned to attack the western and southern sides of Snizort with their constructs, while the human armies and their clankers struck at the eastern and northern walls, bombarding the land inside with flaming missiles in an attempt to set fire to the tar pits and even the Great Seep. It had not worked out that way. The lyrinx had come over the walls to fight the battle outside, preventing the clankers from getting close enough to fire over the walls.

'This is better than I'd hoped,' said General Tham on the first morning of the battle. 'They're fighting us on our ground in broad daylight and massed formations. We'll slaughter them.'

'Don't be a fool,' growled Flydd. 'They're working to a plan and so far it's going well.'

The struggle began slowly, with catapult barrages from either side, causing little damage, and skirmishes where small groups of soldiers attacked patrols of lyrinx. The lyrinx generally got the best of these encounters. In the afternoon the allies intensified their attacks, using flying wedges of clankers and constructs, though to Irisis the Aachim seemed to be holding back.

'There's a fire in the eastern battlefield,' she called. Irisis was one of many scribes writing orders for the messengers running in and out. 'And spreading fast.'

The scrutator ran his spyglass across the scene. Flames and black smoke were belching up along a line the best part of a league long. Other lines erupted as he watched.

'They've fired the ancient tar runs. Must have used spirits of tar to make it go up so quickly. I knew it could not be so easy.'

'The smoke will disadvantage them too.'

'Not so much as us, since it's blowing our way. And it buys them time. We can't cross the fires, even in clankers. They're like extra walls that will burn for days and then leave the ground impassable. They're breaking up our battle formations.'

'Can we put the fires out and break through?'

He shook his head. 'Even if we could spare the water, it won't put out a tar fire. The only way is to smother it with earth and pack it down hard. If you can find a way to do that in the middle of a battle . . .'

'Surely the constructs could cross the fires?'

'They probably could, but do you imagine Vithis will risk his people if we can't join them?'

The struggle continued. Irisis could only imagine the hell the battlefield must be. The black, stinking smoke, now rising along half a dozen curving lines, provided perfect cover and allowed the lyrinx to fight the way they preferred – from ambush. Being able to hold their breath for five minutes or more, they could take better advantage of it. The human casualties were mounting.

Late in the afternoon, Tham ordered three gigantic catapults to be wheeled up. Teams of brawny men loaded each with a boulder the size of a donkey, then turned capstans as big as cartwheels until the entire structure creaked with tension. The catapult master signalled to the command post. General Tham conferred with Flydd, who nodded. They signalled back.

The first catapult fired. The rock went only a hundred paces to slam into the side of a clanker and knock it onto its roof. The mechanical legs went back and forth in the air. Flydd cursed.

The catapult master ordered the second firer to take up the tension. The capstan was wound another turn but before the catapult could be fired the ropes snapped, scything through the soldiers like a sickle through wheat stalks.

'Order the last catapult to release the tension,' snapped Flydd. 'I thought you'd tested them,' he roared at General Tham.

Too late. The catapult had already fired, its gigantic ball soaring through the air right over the wall of Snizort, to slam into the ground inside. A few seconds later the ground shook, and sometime after that a ragged cheer was heard from the field.

'That's better,' said Flydd, 'but pull them right back for the night.'

As expected, the lyrinx attacked fiercely in the night, though the armies had also made use of fire. The bonfires surrounding their positions made it easy to pick out the enemy. The attack petered out some hours later and the rest of the night was quiet, though few people were able to sleep.

'It's almost as if they're playing for time,' said Flydd the next morning. 'They're not fighting hard at all, just keeping us away from the walls. I wonder what they're up to?'

It could not be called a battle yet. Periodically the ground shook from the impact of the giant missiles. The catapults could no longer get close enough to the walls to aim accurately, yet two lucky shots had broken through. Moreover, the field was constantly fluctuating, one minute allowing the clankers to move at near top speed, the next reducing them to a crawl.

'Is this their doing?' said Flydd, 'or are so many machines taking too much from the field.'

'I've no idea,' Irisis said. It was another worry.

On the third day of the siege the catapults began to use tar-coated missiles, hoping to set fire to the tar mires and pits inside the walls. It was hard to tell if they had succeeded, for there was smoke everywhere, but from the air Flydd's spotters had seen smoke issuing from one of the smaller pits. Flydd was busy in his tent and would not allow anyone in, though Irisis heard cursing from time to time.

Late in the afternoon of the fourth day, Irisis focussed on a convoy of clankers creeping along between the lines of blazing tar. A formation of soldiers, at least a thousand strong, marched behind.

'We're getting through!' she exulted.

The convoy approached an area of bare earth between the lines. The single file of clankers spread out, accelerating toward the waiting lyrinx.

'Now we'll see some action.' General Tham had come up behind them. Flydd was watching from his tent.

The racing clankers had gone out six abreast, firing their javelards in salvo. The lyrinx did not move. The pair of clankers in the middle stopped suddenly, front down as if they had run into a bog. The flanking ones now did the same. The clankers behind swung right and left to avoid them.

'What is it?' cried Tham. 'Spyglass, adjutant!'

He ran out with it. Tham snapped it open.

'Save yourself the trouble, Tham,' said Flydd wearily. 'It's a hidden tar bog covered up with earth. The clankers will never get out. The enemy will fire it, next.'

They watched the clankers' hopeless struggle to extricate themselves. The operators soon gave up, abandoning their machines and climbing back over them in desperate attempts to reach secure ground. Some made it. Many went into sticky tar and became as mired as their machines.

Behind them the rest of the force churned the dry soil to powder as they battled to escape the trap. The lyrinx rained missiles on them with catapults. Less than half the force escaped back into the smoke-wreathed lines.

Tham stalked away, grim-faced. Soon a messenger came running. 'Field's dropped suddenly, surr.' He passed Flydd a sealed packet. 'And there's this from Eiryn Muss.'

'I can see that,' Flydd said gloomily. 'They've divided and demoralised us, made us fear the solid ground beneath our feet. What now? All-out attack, or more of the same?'

'Depends what they want,' said Irisis, handing around mugs of black, sweet tea.

Flydd read the message, then drank the hot tea in a single gulp. 'According to Muss, they are determined to complete their secret project and then annihilate this army so they can move on all the eastern lands.' Flydd thrust the message into a nearby brazier. 'It's no good. They're taking too much from the field. Our clankers can barely go half-pace.'

'Even so, with the support of the Aachim . . .'

He spat on the ground. 'Vithis is only making a token effort, though his constructs have all the power they need. And I suspect . . .'

'What?'

'Once we look like losing he'll make a strategic withdrawal, unscathed, and still demand his share of the bargain. By then we really will be powerless to stop him. I've got to act now.'

'How?'

'It's all or nothing.'

'So you're saying –'

'We're going in to block the node-drainer. Tonight.'

'I thought you said there was no way to get in, secretly?'

'Muss has found one.' His meagre lips were compressed to

614

purple. 'Through the front door, you might say. It requires a particular kind of scrutator magic.'

'I'm delighted to hear of it.'

'You shouldn't be.'

'Why not?'

'I haven't discovered any way of getting back out.'

'What did you mean, *we*? You can't be spared, Xervish.'

'The Council ordered me to. Besides, no one else could get you in there. We're going as soon as it's dark.'

He scribbled a new set of orders and sent them off.

Irisis, Ullii and the scrutator were in the air-floater, hanging silently well above the thorn-covered southern wall of Snizort. It was a dark night with a heavy overcast. The new moon might bring some light when it rose, after midnight. They'd gone up at dusk. The army was supposed to make a diversion but it was nearly midnight and they were still waiting for it.

'I wish they'd get on with it,' said Irisis, looking over the side at the lines of tar fires, and camp fires beyond them.

'You won't once we begin.'

'You keep making these gloomy pronouncements. It quite puts me off my adventuring.'

'I won't dignify that with a response.'

'You used to be fun, Flydd. In a dark, twisted sort of a way.'

'There's no fun left in the world.'

Irisis gave up.

The onslaught began on the eastern side, evidenced by flares and screams. Ullii pressed in her earplugs and covered her eyes, but her face was screwed up in torment.

Irisis stirred. Not yet! Another battle began on the western perimeter. Still Flydd did not give the word. He was waiting for the third. Now it came with a cluster of blazing missiles arcing across the sky from the north.

'That's it,' whispered Irisis. 'And already people are dying to ease our way in.'

'A lot more will die if we fail.' He uttered words of power, scrutator magic she had no comprehension of. The air-floater and everything in it faded until just the faintest edge-shimmer betrayed it. In fog or mist, which they hoped for near to the ground, even that would be invisible.

Flydd gasped. 'Quick now. This is painful magic. I can't hold it long.'

The air-floater drifted high over the southern wall of Snizort, hanging in the dark. Lyrinx swarmed on the wall but did not see them. The battles on the other three sides were picked out by thousands of flares, the blazing tar fires and burning catapult balls, beautiful in the darkness.

'How are we going to find it, surr?' Irisis said.

'Ullii must get us there. You and I will block or destroy the node-drainer, if we can, and we'll try to get out again.'

'With the air-floater?'

He hesitated. 'Possibly.'

Irisis did not like the sound of that. It probably *was* a suicide mission. She said nothing about that to Ullii, who was curled up under the bench, as usual. Irisis felt guilty enough already. Ullii was not speaking to her or Flydd. The meeting with Nish at the Aachim camp had added injury to her previous feelings of betrayal.

The air-floater was now motionless in the still air, invisible in the mist. 'Come out, Ullii,' ordered Flydd. 'Show the pilot where to go.'

Ullii brushed past him, stormy-faced, and stood next to Hila. She said nothing, simply held her arm in the direction they had to go. The air-floater drifted that way. After a few minutes Ullii's arm swung straight down.

The machine dropped through the mist into clear air, settled and rocked gently on its skids. Outside it was as dark as the tar pits. The assault fires were just dull glows beyond the walls. The barrage of blazing balls had stopped.

Ullii moved two steps and disappeared.

'Seeker,' Flydd hissed. 'Stay with us.'

She came back. Ullii knew where *they* were. 'Hate you both,' she said audibly.

'I beg your pardon?' said Flydd.

She did not deign to reply.

Flydd clipped his cord to her belt. Irisis did the same to his. The air-floater lifted, its rotor just ticking over. They felt its wind but could not see it.

'No sound,' warned Flydd. 'They can still hear us.'

'And smell us too,' Irisis muttered. She could feel her heartbeat in her temples. They were going to be caught. They were going to be *eaten*.

'Lead the way, Ullii.' Flydd murmured words that took the spell off the air-floater, restricting it to them alone.

The seeker led them on a meandering route, like a snail trail across a brick path. Most lyrinx appeared in her lattice, so she knew how to avoid them. Most, but not all.

No one saw the lyrinx and of course it could not see them. It came running from the left, hit the cord between Irisis and Flydd, stumbled and fell. The impact sent them all flying. The creature sat up, a shadow that seemed to be feeling its ankle as it looked around in the dark. It had no idea what had happened.

Irisis held her breath. If she moved, it would hear her. She prayed that Ullii would not cry out. She could hear the creature sniffing, trying to work out what was wrong. She hoped it could not pick up their scent in the tar-laden air.

A knife shimmered as though moving by itself. It disappeared; the lyrinx gurgled; she smelt blood. It toppled forward.

'We need to keep a better watch,' said Flydd, wiping his blade on the corpse.

They crept across an open space, holding their staves in front to probe for pits and mires. Ullii's talent could not always pick out physical objects.

'Bog!' She stopped abruptly, extracting her little foot with a sucking sound.

Irisis caught a stronger whiff of tar. There were many tar bogs in this saturated ground. One step too far and it might take five minutes to get out again. If alone, you would never get out.

'What the hell's that?' hissed Flydd, staring back the way they had come.

'Looks like an attack on the southern wall,' said Irisis.

'That's not part of the plan.'

'Maybe it's the Aachim.'

'It had better not be. That'll ruin everything. Hurry, Ullii. I can't hold the cloaking spell much longer.'

Irisis might as well have been blind again; in the next hour she saw nothing at all. Only Ullii knew where they were going, for she was navigating by her lattice. But knowing where they were going was not enough. She had to find a way to get there and that was harder than it seemed. Ullii's mind had a unique and tormented logic.

Fortunately, Flydd had an uncanny grasp of directions and had memorised all the maps they had of Snizort. 'We must go down,' he said as they crouched in the concealment of two spindly thornbushes. 'From the way Ullii's pointing, the location is deep underground.'

'We already knew that.'

'How do we get underground?'

'There are steps down into all the old tar pits,' said Irisis. 'And tunnels leading underground off them.'

'But which pit?' he mused. Flydd stood for a moment, then squatted again. His knees popped in the still night.

A light grew in the sky behind them. A flaming catapult ball swished overhead, to thump into the ground close enough that they felt the impact. Irisis held her breath but the flames went out.

'I thought you gave orders about not firing into Snizort tonight?' she said.

'I did. Bloody rabble. No wonder we're losing the war. Let's try the main pit. Can you find that, Ullii?'

'Yes,' she said almost inaudibly.

It was easy to forget she was with them. They skirted sucking bogs and the edges of pits that quaked like jelly underfoot. They walked trails of sticky tar before descending 741 steps into the biggest of the many pits on the map; they entered a cavern or tunnel that had an eye-stinging, bituminous reek. Irisis could feel the walls with her outstretched hands.

Flydd stopped just inside. 'I'd expect most of the lyrinx to be outside the walls, in the battle,' he whispered into the absolute dark. 'But not all. There will be guards within the tunnels, and other lyrinx moving about. Maybe hundreds. We have to be absolutely quiet.'

You're making all the noise, Irisis thought irritably. She was desperately afraid of this place.

'I'm having trouble holding the concealing glamour,' he went on. 'We'll have to be quick. If I lose it . . .'

They went forward. Most of the tunnels were unlit. Irisis had no idea where they were and she knew Flydd was just as lost.

Ullii saw clearly and moved steadily on. She saw the enemy too. Thrice she alerted them just in time and they huddled in a pungent crevice or dripping hollow while lyrinx hurried by. They wandered a maze of tunnels until Irisis, without touching her pliance, began to *feel* the field swirling all around her. She had never experienced that before. They had been underground well over an hour.

'How far, Ullii?' said Flydd.

She did not answer.

'Surely the place will be guarded,' Irisis said.

'From what? There are twenty-five thousand lyrinx outside. How could any intruder get this far?'

'*We* have! And we guard *our* precious things.'

'Lyrinx are not like us. They do not steal from each other; they do not sabotage or vandalise. Besides . . .'

She detected an ominous note. 'What is it, Flydd? What aren't you telling us?'

'You would not station guards close to a node-drainer. If they were there too long it would begin to . . . *disrupt* them.'

A memory flashed back. 'Like – the way it disrupted the rock of the mine at the manufactory?'

A long pause before he whispered, 'Precisely.'

'So this *is* going to kill us. It'll take our bodies apart.'

'Not if we're quick. Jal-Nish survived it, if you recall.'

She took him by the shoulders. 'How long before it disrupts *us*, Xervish?'

'How the blazes would I know?'

'Ten minutes? An hour? A day?'

'Maybe an hour. Maybe two. Depends how strong it is, and how close we have to get to it.'

She stood in the corridor, unmoving. 'Irisis?' said Flydd.

'So be it.' They continued, but shortly she stopped again, allowing the seeker to move around the corner out of hearing.

'What now?' he said irritably.

'What's it going to do to Ullii's baby?' she said in his ear.

'It will have to take its chances like the rest of us.'

'But it . . . Ullii . . . We've got to tell her. At least give her the choice.'

'We're all soldiers in a war, artisan,' he said harshly. 'You, me, Ullii *and* the child. If we fail, humanity is doomed and where is the child then? We must *all* follow orders. Is that clear?'

'Yes, scrutator.'

They hid from another guard. Flydd's glamour still held, for the lyrinx looked right at them without seeing anything. It peered around uneasily, sniffing the air, its skin patterning in the light of a distant lamp, before hurrying away.

'Glamour's failing!' Flydd was bent over, holding his belly. 'Barely . . . hold it.'

She helped him up and they hurried after Ullii who, no longer roped to them, had disappeared down the tunnel. Irisis was all knotted inside. This was going to go wrong, she knew it.

It began as the merest tickle across her shoulder blades, indicating that they were within the sphere of influence of the node-drainer. The sensation grew stronger. Soon the flesh beneath her skin was shuddering as it was tugged one way and another. Her stomach began to bubble like a brewing vat. Ullii gasped. Her body was racked by sinuous heaves. Flydd groaned and the cloaking spell vanished.

'Watcher!' hissed Ullii, sniffing the air like a dog.

FIFTY-NINE

Before and after his brief meeting with Tiaan, Gilhaelith had spent days surveying the Great Seep, from the ground and the network of tunnels below it, until his maps were as accurate as he could draw them. The lyrinx drove him hard, making it clear that the project was urgent and had priority over every other activity at Snizort. He wondered why.

Gilhaelith was not working as hard as they thought, at least not on their project. He spent every spare moment with his icy scrying globe, pretending to do their work, but really studying the Snizort node, which fascinated him. It turned out to be a very strange one, and the fluctuations in its field were extreme, though that might have been because of the power the lyrinx drew from it for their flesh-forming.

And then again, it might have had something to do with the amplimet, for Gilhaelith suspected it was up to its old tricks again. With the globe he picked up occasional, inexplicable pulses which could hardly be due to anything else.

He went on to sensing out the hot spot that powered the seep. That was not hard for a geomancer of his experience. He had spent more than a century monitoring Booreah Ngurle in a similar way. Finally, most difficult of all, he had to scry out the pattern of slow currents that brought warm tar to the surface of the Great Seep, and carried cooler material down again, in complex whirls and eddies.

The tar moved almost imperceptibly, though over seven thousand years it must have travelled quite a distance. Gilhaelith had brought back much geomantic equipment, but none of his crystals and devices proved sensitive enough for this task. Nor, though he spent ages adjusting it, his globe. He had been here for weeks and Gyrull was angry at the lack of progress.

There was another way – to forecast the path of the currents using mathemancy. He had never used that Art in this kind of endeavour before and was not sure if it would prove any use at all, but what else could he do?

After a night and a day, Gilhaelith set aside his arrays of numbers, checked the map and pointed to a particular location. 'Start digging here, and go in this direction.'

'Are you sure?' asked the truth-reader.

'As sure as I'll ever be.' That was true enough.

Matriarch Gyrull blew on a horn. Lyrinx appeared from everywhere. They went down to the place Gilhaelith had indicated. Gyrull marked the sandstone face with a claw and they began to hack at the soft rock with tools like enormous mattocks, extending a tunnel toward the Great Seep.

The work continued day and night. When Gilhaelith returned in the morning to set up his surveying crystals, they had advanced by sixty paces, incredible progress even under such good conditions. The lyrinx worked as though possessed, and they were – Gyrull never had to remind them how important their work was, or how urgent.

The second day they made nearly as much ground, and the third another forty paces, the work slowing because of the heat, and because the rock here was saturated with tar and difficult to work. At this point Gilhaelith saw the lyrinx's true genius.

Two of the creatures lugged in a metal ring slightly smaller than the diameter of the tunnel. After mounting a mushroom-shaped object called a phynadr in the middle of the ring, they activated it using a long rod. Cold pain sparkled in Gilhaelith's temples, doubling him over. By the time he recovered, the ring was concealed by freezing mist.

The phynadr was powered by the field and drew heat from the area around it. He had no idea how it worked but there was no doubt of its effectiveness. The tarry rock, now frigid, was brittle and easily broken. His crystals told him that the device took prodigious amounts of power from the field, which was weaker than before.

The tunnel went forward in cooling stages followed by excavation. By late that afternoon, the fourth day of tunnelling, they broke through the last of the rock into the pure tar of the Great Seep. Now the work became hazardous in the extreme. Liquid tar was all around them, kept out only by a thin, frozen layer that was, relatively speaking, as fragile as an eggshell. If the pressure found a weakness, or just one of the cooling rings failed, the tunnel would collapse and they would be entombed in hot tar. The floor on which they stood shuddered from time to time.

Gilhaelith was idle now, but never bored. He observed, noted and classified everything around him. The lyrinx were of particular interest, and he saw that they were not completely comfortable in their great bodies or, at least, their outer skin. The lyrinx were constantly scratching, shrugging their shoulders, working their limbs and easing the position of their armour plates. Perhaps there was a disadvantage to all the flesh-forming they had done to their unborn selves, in order to survive in the nightmare environment of the void.

Gilhaelith was working in an embayment down the tunnel, well out of the way of the diggings. He had learned much about the node, another step toward his ultimate goal, but that was as far as he was going to get here. The war drew ever closer and it was time to get out before he was trapped. He felt sure he would be able to escape, despite how carefully the lyrinx watched him. They allowed him unfettered use of his tools, and that should be enough. But before he left he had to get the amplimet. He wished he could free Tiaan too, for he did care about her, but, no matter how much he might regret it, she had to be left behind. He could not carry her as well as his scrying globe, and he could not get out without it.

Adjusting it, and sensitising it with an appropriate crystal, he sought for the amplimet. Gilhaelith found it at once, so quickly that momentarily he wondered if it had found *him*.

His belly throbbed. The colic had been worse than usual since he'd come to Snizort, for which he blamed the bland food they gave him. None of the delicacies he was accustomed to were obtainable here.

The amplimet was around Tiaan's neck in the patterning chamber, and a patterning was going on. He sideslipped that process. Time was everything now and he could not be distracted by irrelevancies. The chamber was empty and there were no guards. Good. He worked out a route to it, and the way out, then scried back to check on the amplimet again.

It was flashing furiously. Was it communicating with the patterner, or the node? It was hard to tell – the patterns seemed deliberately blurred. Surely the node, which seemed more unstable than ever. *And the patterner!* That bothered him. Was it trying to alter the patterning? What for? *And what to?*

Hitherto Gilhaelith had paid no more attention to the patterning chamber than he had to the rooms where the lyrinx carried out flesh-forming and other dubious activities. Now he turned his attention to the growing torgnadr and realised that it was a node-drainer. And if the amplimet controlled such a device, it controlled all the power of the node.

A looming disaster for both lyrinx and humanity, but a fabulous opportunity for himself. It was the chance to learn much more about the amplimet, by seeing exactly what it did.

'No progress today, tetrarch?' snapped Gyrull.

Gilhaelith started and barely managed to control his face, but Gyrull had other things on her mind and kept going. The field was surging erratically and at present the freezing coils were too effective. The lyrinx had broken a number of matlocks, the metal going so brittle in the intense cold that the tools snapped on impact. It was retarding progress and had to be remedied quickly.

He went back to his work, keeping a wary eye out now. His scrying was a delicate business, for he knew not what the amplimet might be capable of, and did not want its attention to turn on him.

However, after several days of such work Gilhaelith grew bolder, for he was beginning to see the pattern. The amplimet seemed to be drawing filaments of force – almost invisible threads of gossamer – out of the field to itself, to the patterner and to many other parts of Snizort. Power did not flow along those threads, yet he could see faint pulses of light. Why this network?

'Come, tetrarch, you are needed at the front,' said Gyrull.

Reluctantly, he began to collect his gear.

'Leave it! There's no time. I'll have it packed for you.'

Packed? Gilhaelith had no choice but to follow. He was not yet ready to break out and could not do it without hours of preparation, but her use of that word alarmed him.

The tunnel extended hour by hour, day by day. Cooling rings were spaced every ten paces along it, each with its mushroom-like phynadr maintaining the cold that kept them alive. The work was slower now; the broken tar had to be removed carefully in case they broke out of the frozen zone. Late on the tenth day of tunnelling, when they were nearly a hundred paces into the seep, Gilhaelith was called to try his scrying crystals again. His worries had proven fruitless; Gyrull still allowed him access to his tools, though only for a few minutes at a time.

In the middle of his reading, the pair of lyrinx at the face ceased their pounding and levered with a bar. A curving slab peeled away to reveal something lifelike embedded in the black material. Putting down his instruments, Gilhaelith went to see what it was.

It turned out to be the body of a wildcat, as long as Gilhaelith was tall, with a huge head and jaws that could have taken his leg off. It was so perfectly preserved that it might have been alive.

The following morning the diggers found another, smaller predator, more like a jackal, and that afternoon a wild bull with long curling horns. 'The beast must have been trapped in the seep,' said Gilhaelith, 'attracting the predators which died the same way.'

'Put two feet in wet tar,' said the lyrinx to his left, 'and you would not have the strength to pull them out.'

Gilhaelith finished his readings and this time did detect something. 'That way.' He pointed left of the tunnel centreline, down at a slight angle.

The lyrinx adjusted their cooling ring and continued. They encountered other dead animals as the tunnel slowly extended: once a pair of seagulls, another time a house cat, and then a pair of snakes the size of pythons, wrapped around each other. After that they continued in clean, glassy tar. By the fourteenth afternoon the tunnel was shuddering all the time.

As Gilhaelith walked back that night, a crack opened in the floor in front of him. A wedge of tar forced its way in, whereupon the lyrinx manning the nearest annulus worked her controls and extended the freezing zone. Another lyrinx broke off the solidified obstacle with a hammer. As Gilhaelith continued he saw other filled cracks. In some places there were more cracks than wall. The shell was barely surviving. The pangs in his belly grew worse.

Gilhaelith tried many times to get back to his own work, but Gyrull always needed him somewhere else, even if just to stand around and watch. At night he was escorted to his room to sleep, without his equipment, and a guard waited outside the door. She was taking no chances. Did she suspect what he was up to? Gilhaelith tried every argument to get his devices back but none availed him, and without them he was helpless. Most nights he lay awake, brooding and suffering pangs of colic. He could do nothing about that either.

He had not seen Tiaan again, and did not expect that he would. Gilhaelith had been touched that she'd cared enough to follow him, whatever her true motivation. She certainly had courage, unfortunately marred by an appalling lack of judgment, but he wished she'd stayed away. He cared about her. Not as much as for the amplimet, of course, but more than he cared for anyone else.

It probably would not matter, in the end. This expedition into the Great Seep was foolhardy in the extreme and the probability was high, his mathemancy told him, that they would all die entombed in hot tar. The lyrinx must have been desperate to attempt the venture. He could only assume that some potent artefact had been lost in the seep in ages past. If they were prepared to risk an army to have it, they must be weaker than anyone expected. Or it must be an object of surpassing power and usefulness to the war.

On they tunnelled, and on. Gilhaelith's existence shrank to a stinking black hole. At night he dreamed he was still in it. They had reached the place his instruments told him to aim for, but found nothing there. The Matriarch was furious.

'Your Art is less than I was led to believe, tetrarch!' she said coldly.

'I told you it would be difficult to find.' Gilhaelith matched her glare, though inwardly he bitterly regretted the failure. If he had to die, he did not want it to be that way. 'The Art is seldom exact.'

'Search again. We're closer now. Hurry!'

'Mathemancy can tell me no more. I'll have to scry with my globe and you must give me more to go on. What am I searching for?'

'I cannot reveal that,' she said.

'Then I cannot help you.' Again he held her gaze.

Gyrull's breast plates mottled green, while her belly went a dull cream and her massive thighs showed tortured patterns – red threads writhing on yellow. Indecision, he thought. She needed to tell him, yet was afraid she would give something away.

'We're looking for the remains of the village,' she said, working her arms vigorously, as if uncomfortable, 'that was built over the tar more than seven thousand years ago.'

'What was in the village? I must have something to scry for.'

'There may be relics,' she said reluctantly. 'Instruments made of brass and precious metals . . .'

'Anything else? Crystals?'

'Perhaps.' Even more reluctantly.

'Crystals are easy to scry for, if I know the kinds.'

She knew but did not want to say. Then it came out. 'Perhaps brimstone.'

'Ah,' he said. 'But that is the one crystal I cannot find.'

Her pupils narrowed to slits. 'Why not, tetrarch? You claim to be a master geomancer.'

'There is brimstone everywhere, here. The tar is full of it, and the hot springs all around.'

'Try!' she said coldly. 'Without your globe.'

So she did fear him using it. 'I will, but should I scry brimstone, remember that it could be anywhere.'

He did his best but, as before, the results were ambiguous. He calculated some random fourth powers, but they were no help at all. 'If I am to help you, I must have my scrying globe.'

Gyrull muttered under her breath but had it brought to him. He sensitised it to brimstone, moved his hands over the frigid surface and closed his eyes. Momentarily he saw those wispy filaments, a shock went though his brain and he envisioned a red-hot crystal above and to the right.

Gilhaelith staggered and fell down. It felt as if his head was on fire. He weakly raised an arm, pointing in a circle. 'That way! No more than ten spans.'

The lyrinx regarded him dubiously but gave the required orders.

Gilhaelith remained on the floor, without the strength to rise. He'd never had an experience like that before. It had been almost mystical, and he did not believe in such things. But he knew he'd found it this time.

Gyrull gave new orders. They were to tunnel out in all directions, like the spokes of a wheel.

'That will magnify the strain on the shell,' said Gilhaelith.

'Always excuses, geomancer.'

'Currents in the seep will break it like a stick and we'll lose everything, including our lives.'

'This is more important than our lives!' she snapped.

A precious artefact indeed. 'Not mine,' he said.

The lyrinx tunnellers set to, showing no fear. Whatever the orders, they carried them out just as enthusiastically. Finding nothing in any of the lower spokes, they allowed these to collapse and began again with a new set, sloping upwards. The pace slowed. It was taking longer than ever to freeze each new section.

'What's the matter?' the Matriarch demanded, late on the seventeenth day of tunnelling, their thirteenth in the Great Seep. At least, Gilhaelith thought it was late. Though he ate and slept at the same time each day, it was hard to keep track of time.

'The field is fading,' said the male in charge of the cooling ring. As they both spoke the common speech, they must have wanted him to know what was going on. 'It's taking an hour to do what once we would have done in minutes. You must beg the channellers to give us more power, else –'

'Keep on,' she said harshly, with a flickering of whites and blues down her front that Gilhaelith was unable to interpret. 'Our enemies have come and their clankers take much from the field.'

'Then we'll never do it.'

'We must, and quickly, else we lose an army for nothing.' She called a messenger and spoke to her for some minutes. The woman hurried away. 'The field must be conserved for us,' Gyrull said to the male. 'Power in Snizort will only be drawn for essentials. We will complete this work no matter what the cost elsewhere. And once that is done, we will drain the node dry and crush the enemy.'

They no longer seemed to require him, so Gilhaelith crept away with his globe, and went back to his watch on the amplimet. Much had changed at the patterner – the torgnadr was gone and Tiaan was patterning another, though this one was not connected to the amplimet at all. Had it done its work here? The filaments were everywhere else, though, and light pulses now flowed furiously along them, so it was still doing something. Well, too bad. It was time to go. He began the laborious working that would, by the morning, get him out of here.

'Come see this, tetrarch!'

A lyrinx dragged him by the wrist down to the excavation face. The tunnellers levered at a cleavage section and the whole face fell down, revealing a wall made of roughly sawn planks fixed to uprights with wooden pegs. The impact sent the tunnel shell into a slow shuddering that moved back and forth like waves along a rope. Cracks appeared along it and molten tar oozed through, before solidifying.

'Matriarch!' the tunneller on the left yelled. 'Look here.'

Exulting, she threw herself at the face and began prying away the timbers. 'This is the place. Call the digging team.'

Before they arrived (a dozen lyrinx equipped with saws, axes, buckets, chests and other equipment, including one who began sketching the scene), Gyrull had taken the timbers apart. They formed one wall of a tar-filled hut. The other walls were partly attached, though the structure had been crushed out of shape. They found nothing inside but household items – a wooden stool, pallets stuffed with straw, blankets and kitchen utensils. Every object was cracked out of the frozen tar, drawn and taken away as if it had some hidden value. Perhaps it did. Who knew what form mancery might have taken, seven thousand years ago?

A tremor passed across the floor. 'The siege has begun,' said Gyrull. 'We must work harder. Let the offshoot tunnels fail. Excavate out around the hut. Quickly, the field is failing.'

Gilhaelith could feel it growing more erratic every minute. 'How many huts would there have been in the village?' he said.

'I don't know.'

He did not get a chance to go back to his mancing. Over the next few days the lyrinx found another seven huts, similar to the first, with the same kinds of possessions in them. The fourth contained a wooden chest which proved to be full of clothes, in perfect condition, as the tar had not penetrated its seals. The clothing aroused considerable interest, for some reason which Gilhaelith could not fathom. The largest of the garments was small.

In the eighth hut they found a body, a boy no more than five. His hair was pale, as was his skin, and his build stocky. He was as perfectly preserved as everything else. The body, still partly encased in tar, was laid on a stretcher and carried away.

The next hut proved empty apart from a wooden bench. The

one after that was full of bodies. The Matriarch carried the first out herself, laying it on the floor of the tunnel. There were twenty-five of them: eight men, seven women and the remainder children. They were a small people. Their skin was stained from the tar, their eyes blue, grey or pale-brown, their hair also light-coloured. They were strong-featured, but rather too stocky to have been called handsome, to Gilhaelith's mind.

The lyrinx gathered around, staring at the bodies. What secret did they conceal? A vibration roused them, teams began to carry the bodies away and the diggers continued with the excavation.

They found no more bodies that night, but did discover some beautiful crystals of yellow brimstone, all broken, as well as a bronze implement consisting of seven concentric circles marked with graduations and symbols. A bronze pin passed through the centre of each circle, allowing them to rotate. Inside the inner circle was another bronze shape, somewhat corroded: a crescent moon, or perhaps the blade of a sickle. Meant to be turned with a fingertip, it was stuck fast.

As far as Gilhaelith could tell, none of these relics was the secret the Matriarch sought, and the excavations continued. It now being the middle of the night, he was escorted to his bed, where his dreams were disturbed by rods of light as thick as tree trunks, and the thrashing of people suffocating in tar.

They came for him a few hours later. He could not see why, for nothing had changed at the face. The floor was piled with mummified bodies, shards of crystal, household objects and other items he had already seen many times.

As he approached the work face, the workers were levering at what appeared to be the wall of a meeting house or chieftain's hut, lying on its side. They pulled off the planks, began to break away the hard tar and suddenly liquid tar began to ooze through a crack.

'Hoy,' the Matriarch roared to the freezing team.

They pushed up the annulus, pointed the mushroom in the right direction and worked their lever. Frost shimmered in the air. Tar continued to ooze through the crack.

'What's the matter?' she shouted.

'There's nothing left in the field.'

'Get some planks over the crack. What's gone wrong?'

'Phynadr's not drawing enough power,' said the operator. 'We must have drained the field.'

'It comes and goes!' said Gyrull. 'Try again.'

This time the annulus worked, though not very well. Behind them, near where the latest bodies and relics lay, a crack opened in the side of the tunnel, allowing in a hot spurt of tar that spattered across the pile. The hole sealed over, only to crack again. The tar kept ebbing in.

This was his last chance. Gilhaelith had just started with the globe, developing the swiftest spell he could manage in the circumstances, when the Matriarch yelled, 'Get the relics out of the tunnel. How are we going, Franll?'

The operator shook his crested head. 'I don't see how we can do any more.'

Cuttlefish waves of colours, pastel blues, greens and pinks, pulsed across her skin. 'We must keep trying. The siege comes to a climax. Move everything to safety, including the tetrarch's devices.'

'And me?' he said hopefully.

'You stay here. Great human armies surround us, tetrarch, and the Aachim with their constructs.' She hacked furiously at the frozen face. 'We will lose Snizort within days. The enemy are trying to set fire to the tar.'

Even Gilhaelith could read the other lyrinx's skin speech – dismay followed by despair.

'I'm afraid for you, Matriarch,' said the operator.

'I merely serve. Should I die, another stands ready to replace me.'

In his mind's eye, Gilhaelith could see himself, an ant at the end of a long, brittle tunnel made from something no stronger than cake icing. It would take no force at all to break it. He was not ready to die. There was so much to do. He felt a sudden pang of fear for Tiaan but there was nothing he could do for her.

A dozen lyrinx were up at the face, furiously excavating. The hut had a circular hole through the roof, or so Gilhaelith interpreted the tangle of shortened framing timbers. Puzzled, he climbed up to take a better look.

'These look as though they've been burned,' he said, 'but see how neatly. As if by a red-hot blade.' The ancient documents had said something about that.

She did not answer. More bodies were removed, all clad in bright, ceremonial vestments. On the far side, another lyrinx was working above his head, trying to free a decorated, coffin-shaped box sealed at either end. He broke the seals, lifted off the lid and grey dust poured out, covering him from crested head to clawed toes. He shook it off, flashed a toothy grin at his fellows and pulled hard. The coffin slid free. There was nothing in it but dust and bones.

The work continued. The Matriarch was busy in a corner of the hut, where the side of a small wooden chest had been dug out. They hacked tar from around it and prised open the lid.

Inside, wrapped in a pale-blue blanket, was a large yellow crystal protected in a golden basket. One of the lyrinx reached for it but she snapped, 'Don't touch! It's very fragile.'

'A brimstone,' said Gilhaelith.

'*The* brimstone.'

'Is that what you came for?'

She opened her mouth and closed it again. Her old face was expressionless but for an instant her shoulder plates sparkled in exhilaration. She seized hold of her breast plates and worked them back and forth, as if to settle them in place.

He tried again, while they were distracted. Gilhaelith closed his eyes, trying to see the web of filaments, but caught only a few unbroken threads, moving as in a wind. The amplimet's work must almost be done.

A spasm of fear struck him. It was finished here, and it was in control of the node. And they were deep in the Great Seep, reliant on power. What was it doing? There had to be more. *He had to see.* Maybe he could draw on it to escape. All his equipment was gone, and all the relics, and there was not so much as a fragment of brimstone left. Only one thing to do. He reached within himself to those ever-troubling gallstones, and forced one to wake.

The tattered webs appeared for a second but they did not show what he was looking for. Only one filament remained unbroken, so fine that he had not seen it before. Light pulsed along it, and it ran into the back of his head.

He tried desperately to see what it was doing, but the gallstone exploded and shrieking agony drove him to his knees. The filament snapped and the tattered webs vanished. It was all too clear now. He had delved too deeply and the amplimet had caught him. How long had it been studying him, and what had it learned?

A loud crack came from behind them. Half a dozen cooling rings back, the floor of the tunnel had sheared in two. Inflooding tar was pushing the sections further apart every second.

'Matriarch!' shouted one of the lyrinx. 'It's failing.'

She closed the chest, tucked it under her arm and sprang down. Her impact with the floor shook the tunnel and one big foot went though the shell. She wrenched it out. Tar oozed up. The other lyrinx ran, carrying as much as they could.

Gilhaelith forced himself to his knees, tripped, and fell sprawling. His insides were in agony, as if the fragments of stone were being forced down tiny ducts. Ahead, tar bubbled through the gap, already a couple of strides wide at the base. The tunnel now cracked at the top and a curtain of tar flooded in.

The Matriarch hurtled past him and burst through the curtain. Gilhaelith followed, but as he tried to jump, the sections were wrenched apart and he plunged to his knees in the warm tar of the Great Seep. He threw out his arms and managed to catch a lump of hard floor. Gilhaelith tried to pull himself out but the tar clung too strongly.

Like a fly on tar paper, he thought. I'm stuck. The lyrinx were already out of sight. Too late he felt the bitterness of regret. The game was lost, and Tiaan. And for what? He hardly dared to think.

SIXTY

Tiaan dreamed that Old Hyull, a glowing mushroom on his head, was stripping her backbone out from its surrounding skin and flesh, smacking his lips as he slurped down the slippery marrow. She woke squirming with horror, but it was only a dream and a ridiculous one. Backbones did not have marrow, did they? Or was it her spinal cord he was devouring?

Later she woke in what she supposed to be a different kind of patterner, hanging upside down in a collection of translucent spheres as green as grass. She felt blurred in the head, as if she'd had too much to drink. It wore off during the day but her back began to throb low down, where she had broken it. The pain grew until it made her cry out, whereupon Liett pulled her mouth open and forced in half a mug of sweet syrup. It sent Tiaan to sleep within minutes. When she woke, the pain was no more than a nagging ache. She felt that days had passed.

Tiaan kept expecting Tutor to appear around the door, but he did not come. She had not seen him for days and missed him.

That afternoon she was taken to another room and put onto a curving platform covered in what felt like hide. It was mottled in shades of grey and was yielding yet firm beneath. Her hands were slid into receptacles like shoulder-length gloves, her legs fed into thigh-high envelopes of similar material. Suckers were attached to the back of her head, her neck and all the way down to her tailbone.

Ryll tightened leather straps across her body and nodded at a lyrinx standing to one side. She reached beneath Tiaan's head. The thigh envelopes began to move in constantly changing directions. Sometimes they went up and down, at other times round and round or from side to side, or made all of those movements at once.

Tiaan cried out as a series of pangs struck her backbone. Liett gave her a half-dose of syrup and her vision faded. People moved across the room from time to time, so slowly that it could not have been real. Time slowed to a standstill.

The exercises went on until Tiaan felt as though her bones were dissolving. She was removed and laid out to sleep on a couch at the far end of the room. As soon as she woke, the exercises began again.

There were many more sessions, over as much as a week, before Old Hyull seemed to be satisfied. Ryll carried Tiaan back to the patterner. The jellyfish mask went over her head and they began to repattern the faulty torgnadr. Again she woke weeping. The top of the device was beaded with her tears.

Tutor was sent for. He dried her face and sat unmoving until she stopped crying. 'Patterning had the same effect on me.'

She raised her head. 'They patterned *you*?'

He smiled. 'They tried everyone, back in the early days when they were learning. They thought torgnadrs were going to win the war in a few weeks, by draining the nodes each time clankers went into battle. They probably would have won, had they been able to pattern enough of them. Fortunately for us, nearly all failed. The lyrinx got no torgnadr out of me, but I cried for a fortnight. I can still remember how it felt.'

'When was that, Tutor?' The title still felt wrong. She did not like using it.

'A long time ago. Five or six years? You lose track of time down here.'

She felt closer to him. Tutor was a nondescript fellow, neither tall nor short, handsome nor ugly. He was thin, but every human here was. And pale; few of the prisoners ever saw the sun. His dark eyes were kindly, his brow lined. His hand was callused – evidently they worked him hard and not only as a teacher.

'This torgnadr of mine, if they succeed with it, will cause the deaths of thousands. Are all these people in the patterners –?'

'No, Tiaan. I told you, torgnadrs are hard to make. The others are just patterning weak devices like limnadrs and phynadrs, and most of those fail too.'

'What are they?'

'Limnadrs are spying devices. They can sense moving clankers, though not well, since the design was changed last year. Phynadrs draw small amounts of power from the field, for one purpose or another. They're a bit like clanker controllers. I think they got a limnadr out of patterning me. Because of my gift for languages, you see – useful for spying.'

'Yes. Do you mind if I call you Merryl? Tutor seems like a slave name.'

'Of course not.' Before he could say any more, Merryl was called away.

He came back several times, when she was overcome by melancholy. They did not talk much but she drew comfort from his presence. The other humans felt alien but he never did.

Tiaan wondered, as she often did, what they were doing with Gilhaelith. He had been kind to her in his own strange way, but in the end, like everyone else, he had made his choice. No doubt he was looking after himself, though she could not see how he could get the amplimet.

Old Hyull now inspected the torgnadr after every patterning session. After the fifth such visit he gave the faintest of toothy smiles as he hefted the bucket, peering through the glass from below.

Ryll spoke to him. Old Hyull shook his head violently. Ryll cast a glance at Tiaan. Old Hyull put down the bucket, rasping a series of orders in which all Tiaan could make out was her name and, once, *torgnadr*. Old Hyull went out with the torgnadr.

'Is it fixed?' Tiaan whispered to Ryll.

637

'No,' he replied, after looking over his shoulder. 'And Old Hyull can't understand why not. But it's better than it was – it will do.'

She wondered what she was responsible for. 'Aren't you going to take me out of the patterner? My skin feels all lumpy and hot.'

'There isn't time. We must pattern another torgnadr from the beginning and hope we can complete it.'

'No,' she whispered. 'I can't take any more, Ryll.'

'You must.' He did not meet her eyes.

The patterning began, exactly as before except that the sessions were much longer. Perhaps it was easier the second time. But if that was so, why did the enemy have so few torgnadrs? Maybe the second time was fatal.

The growing torgnadr was a blob the size of a large melon when the cavern shook, as if something had thumped into the ground overhead. Ryll set down the bucket. His eyes were huge. Threads of red and black inched their way up his arms. The sight made her afraid.

'What is it, Ryll?' she whispered.

'The battle for Snizort has begun and we are not ready.' Ryll closed his eyes. 'I can see Snizort burning. *Fire!*' he gasped, looking around like a desperate animal.

'Ryll?' Too late. He was gone.

Tiaan felt an urge to scream. If Snizort *was* on fire, all she could do was await her death with whatever dignity she could muster. She took deep breaths, which was no help at all. She hoped it would be quick.

Some minutes later, Ryll returned, his skin now showing camouflage colours. He approached, head hanging. 'I'm sorry, Tiaan. I am proven to be a rank coward. Fire is my greatest terror.'

She said nothing. The patterning resumed, but some minutes later the room shook again. Old Hyull bounded through the door and dragged Ryll out, flashing distress markings. Down the row of patterners, someone screamed, but thankfully no one else took it up. The women chattered among themselves in their own language, ignoring Tiaan as usual.

More lyrinx ran in, gathering inside the door and skin-speaking furiously. It looked like a general panic. There were two more thumps. The lyrinx disappeared again.

She was glad when Merryl came up the row a few minutes later.

'What's the matter?' she yelled. 'Are we being attacked?'

'Yes, but we're not in danger yet.'

'Then why the panic?'

'The old torgnadr has finally failed and yours is not proving as effective against the enemy as they had hoped.'

She was pleased to hear it. 'You mean at draining the node?'

'Yes, and channelling power to their great project.'

'How do you know?'

'One picks things up. But –'

He looked around to see if anyone was watching. No one was, though Tiaan was uncomfortably aware of the growing torgnadr beside her, so similar to their spying devices.

'What are they going to do?'

'Their great project is not yet complete, and that they are determined to do. The defenders will fight to make time for it, to the last drop of their purple blood. The battle is going to be vicious.'

'Our people are already dying,' said Tiaan. 'And these torg-nadrs will destroy many more. *My* torgnadrs. I'm sick of being used, Merryl.'

'There's nothing you could have done.'

'If I ever get the chance,' she vowed, 'I'll smash the amplimet to pieces. I would destroy every node on Santhenar if it would only stop this endless war. I mean it, Merryl.' As she spoke, the amplimet flared, then faded, and the skin-creeping feeling re-appeared.

'I know you do, but there are no simple answers.'

'I don't care.' If the field was gone, both clankers and torgnadrs would be useless, and no one would want to use her either. She just wanted to be ordinary; anonymous.

Ryll came hurtling through the door. 'Begone, Tutor!'

The patterning continued, now with breaks of just hours in

between. Her skin chafed constantly, she could not sleep and Tiaan was struck by an old fear that she'd not thought about in her weeks here – what the amplimet was up to. That sudden surge, and the earlier pulsing, suggested that it was watching her. It might not let her destroy it.

'There's not time!' Ryll said to Liett several days later. 'We can't fail now. Not *so* close.' He looked desperate.

The shocks became more frequent. They had been going on for three days, judging by her sleeps. The lyrinx panic grew. Ryll forced the patterning so hard and fast that Tiaan began to have a hallucination. For a few seconds the stone walls thinned to transparency and she saw lyrinx and humans struggling in a long black tunnel. Gilhaelith was among them.

Her viewpoint drifted outside her body. She could see right through the patterner, and her own flesh, to her bones. A hot yellow glow throbbed in the middle, where her back had been broken.

After another hallucination, Ryll realised that she could be driven no further that day. The torgnadr almost filled the bucket, but was still immature. He ended the session but left Tiaan in the patterner. She had been inside for more than a day now.

'Take me out,' she said exhaustedly. 'It feels like beetles are crawling over my skin.' Even with the mask gone, things still seemed strange.

Ryll looked equally worn and, for the first time, showed no skin colour at all. 'We must begin again in three hours.' He held a mug to her mouth.

She gulped it, eager for the oblivion of sleep, but in her dreams the faulty torgnadr was fountaining sparks like a firework. Tiaan was shaken awake. It was deadly wrong, but she could not tell why.

The room shook again, followed by a dull boom. Sand rained down on her hair and, as the shuddering continued, chunks of sandstone began to fall. One smashed a glass bucket further along the row. A line of tar filled a crack in the wall beside her.

A massive blow shook the room, making the walls quiver like

the muck she was suspended in. Lyrinx raced back and forth, yelling and skin-speaking all the colours of the spectrum. A gaggle of humans fled past the open door, including the man with the withered shoulder, urged on by a lyrinx carrying a prod. Ryll raced up the row to Tiaan, but before he reached her Old Hyull roared at him from the doorway. Ryll's eyes met hers. He flashed distress patterns, then pulled the jelly mask over her head.

'Ryll?' she screamed. 'What's going on?' Too late. The mask cut everything off and the patterning resumed, though it did not seem to be working properly. The flow of power kept fluctuating wildly. Was it failing?

Thump! She wanted to scream but couldn't – the patterning had become one continuous hallucination. Battle scenes crashed through her mind: clankers firing blazing missiles over the walls of Snizort; a squad of human soldiers being beaten back by a single, blood-drenched lyrinx; a tar bog ablaze, flames reflecting on it like a black mirror. *Thump!*

Abruptly the mask was ripped from her head and the hallucinations vanished. A strange lyrinx thrust his face at her, grunted and turned away, taking the immature torgnadr. Chunks of roof were falling all around. There was confusion everywhere. The women in the patterners were screaming. Tiaan wanted to scream too.

Thump, thump, thump. She caught sight of Liett down the far end. *'Liett?'*

She was running along the line of patterners, slamming her fist on the release levers. The top of each sprang open. She was about to do Tiaan's when a lyrinx yelled at her from the doorway. Liett lifted Tiaan halfway out but the other lyrinx roared an order. Liett let Tiaan go and ran.

Silence fell, broken by repeated shockwaves that rattled the tops of the patterners and shook down more of the roof. Along her row a woman began to push herself out. She emerged slowly, her big muscular body glistening with muck. After shaking herself, she sprang up on the next patterner and heaved the occupant out. Each then went to another machine. Within minutes, fifteen women and two men, everyone except Tiaan, had been released.

'Hey!' Tiaan yelled. 'What about me?'

The big woman tapped her legs and followed the others. They could not afford to carry anyone.

When Liett dropped her, Tiaan's arms had remained outside the patterner. Instinctively, she felt for the amplimet, and it was there! Ryll always put it around her neck before a patterning session and in the panic both Liett and the other lyrinx had forgotten to take it. As Tiaan touched it, she sensed the field swirling around Snizort like an exploding star. It was strangely deformed and bore a distinct signature that she recognised: the faulty torgnadr. Was the torgnadr deforming the field, or the amplimet deforming both? She did not want to find out.

Tiaan saw points of light in the field – places where the lyrinx, and the human armies, were drawing on it. Another point was in this room, the drain from the patterners, though that was fading.

The field went *whoomph*, like a furnace pumped by a bellows, then dropped to nothing before flaring up again. Something was terribly wrong. Had too much been taken from the node? The draw from all those clankers outside must be monumental. If the node went dead . . .

She tried to push herself out but the muck had too much suction. Tiaan kicked feebly. It made no difference. She was trapped in the patterner. Laying her head on its flat top, she tried to resign herself to her fate. She was wondering what the manner of her death would be when the realisation struck Tiaan like a physical blow. Had she *moved* her legs? It must have been a hallucination. She tried to clench her toes and definitely felt them move.

Tiaan did not allow the hope – soldiers sometimes felt their limbs years after they had been cut off. She kicked herself in the ankle, and felt it, as well as a pain in her toe. It was true! She could move, and feel pain. She was not a cripple any more. She would walk again some day. *Soon,* if she could just get out.

Tiaan slid back down, her mind awhirl. So that's what Old

Hyull had been doing. He'd put her in that other device to pattern, or more likely flesh-form, her severed spine together.

Had she been *flesh-formed*? Tiaan felt sick. Had they used part of some other creature to join the severed ends of her spinal cord? That aching point in her back now seemed to be swelling as if something lay inside, feeding on her. But she had her legs back and, for the moment at least, it seemed worth it.

Tiaan kept trying to push herself out but her arms did not have enough strength to break the suction. She rested her head on the top of the patterner and eventually, in spite of the continuing shocks, exhaustion overwhelmed her.

'Tiaan?'

She roused. It sounded like Merryl's voice. Tiaan opened her eyes. The patterning chamber was full of mist and the air smelled stale, as if the ventilation bellows had stopped working a long time ago.

'Merryl?'

He raced up the line of patterners. 'Tiaan, thank heavens I came back.'

Climbing up, he pulled her out easily, despite his missing hand. Merryl found some rags and she wiped the muck off while he looked for her clothes. Her skin was red and blistered all over.

'What's happening, Merryl?'

'The lyrinx were called out to the battle. It's a desperate struggle out there, and now something has gone wrong down below. There's smoke in the lower tunnels. The remaining lyrinx are abandoning Snizort.'

She wrapped her arms around herself, wary of trusting anyone, even Merryl. 'They just left me behind to die.'

'I'm sure that wasn't meant to happen.'

'Ryll abandoned me!'

'He was sent into battle. I was sure they would have taken you, with the other important prisoners, but in the panic . . .'

'Do you know the way out?'

'Of course . . . if I can get to it.'

She managed to dress herself, but her legs would not support her. He had to carry her and her precious pack. After some minutes, when he began to show the strain, she said, 'Leave me, Merryl. You can't carry me all the way.'

'I'm not going to leave you.'

'You'll die too.'

'I've faced that risk every day since I was captured. I'd sooner die than leave a friend behind.'

'I left mine behind,' she said. 'They were dead.'

They sat on the floor while he got his breath. 'That's a beautiful crystal,' he said.

She touched it. 'It's a special kind of hedron, an amplimet. It can power my walker – do you know where that is?'

'In one of the storerooms near where you were brought in, I'd imagine. But if the field dies it won't be any use.'

'The amplimet is powerful enough to draw on a distant field.' If it could be trusted, and how *could* she trust it? Only because it, too, must want a way out. The heat of the smallest fire would destroy it.

'Then let's see if we can find the walker. I think I know where to look.'

After many dark corridors and crowded storerooms they found it. Merryl helped Tiaan into the seat. She had done up the straps and was just reaching for power when there came a blast and roar that shook the floor and filled her ears with grit. The walker was thrown off its four feet, coming down on Merryl's thigh. He let out a gasp.

'Are you all right?' Tiaan was afraid she'd broken his leg.

He sat up and rolled the walker off. 'Just bruised.' He rubbed his thigh and winced.

Merryl was lifting Tiaan up when a storm of wind roared down the tunnel outside, banging the door of the storeroom. Dust whirled in the air. 'I don't like that, Tiaan. You'd better go.'

'What about you?' She wanted to run, to skip. After weeks when she could do nothing at all, she wanted to race down the tunnels like a child.

'I've one more person to find.'

'Can I help?'

'You probably couldn't get through, in the walker. If you go that way,' he pointed right, 'then left, left, right and left, you'll be on the long passage to the exit into the main pit. I'm afraid for you, Tiaan. I'd go with you but I must look for another friend, and swiftly. Are you sure you can find the way?'

'I've a perfect memory for directions.'

Merryl smiled. His eyes seemed to be summing her up. He gave her his hand. 'After all I've heard about you, I expect you will. Good luck!'

'And you. I hope you find what your heart desires.'

He closed those dark eyes. 'An illusion, I expect, after so long as a slave. But freedom beckons.' He turned away.

Tiaan kept on, following his directions with an increasing sense of foreboding. The air was thicker and hotter here. She wondered how Gilhaelith was faring. He had always looked after himself, and no doubt the lyrinx would take good care of him. But at least he hadn't got the amplimet. Flawed and dangerous though it was, she had it still, and it was going to get her out of here.

She stopped the walker, suddenly uncertain if she was going in the right direction. The strangeness that had pervaded every-thing for days was stronger than ever here. The air was full of floating bubbles of tar, which was impossible, and the whole world seemed to be shaking.

Quite suddenly the strangeness vanished and she stood in a black tunnel where the tar was soft under the feet of the walker. Tiaan flexed her toes, just for the pleasure of feeling them. The tension grew – she could feel it in her knotted stomach muscles; the prickling in the backs of her hands; the dryness in her mouth.

Boom! The walker was hurled against the wall. Had it not been so soft she would have cracked her skull. A gale of sand blasted down the corridor. The rock, solid with tar, emitted tortured groans and with a booming crackle a slab slid across the corridor, partly blocking it.

An even mightier explosion occurred inside her head, so

bright that she almost passed out. Coils of the field wrapped themselves around her skull, dancing in her eyes.

She groaned and shook her head, which was full of cobwebby mirages. Tearing the walker out of the wall, Tiaan continued but before long the air on her face grew warm, the stink of hot tar unbearable. She forced herself around the next corner. Ahead, a red glow danced on the walls. Black, deadly fumes crept along the floor. The tar was on fire.

She fled, retracing the walker's steps as fast as it would go. That was not very fast – it was increasingly difficult to draw from the field. As she reached the place where the wall had fractured, red fire flickered in the fissures. Molten tar dripped in her path. Flame roared forth like the exhalations of a dragon. Forward or back, there was nowhere to go. Then she lost the field, and the walker died.

SIXTY-ONE

Several nights after the scrutator's visit, Nish was lying in his tent, listening to a gentle rain pattering on the canvas, when a signal whistle piped. He did not move. The Aachim were constantly signalling to each other. It did not concern him. The brief hope he'd felt when the scrutator appeared was gone. He was still a prisoner, a pawn in a global struggle. His great plans had failed through no fault of his own.

There seemed to be a lot of activity outside, including the whine of hundreds of constructs. Something was going on. He was just slipping back to sleep when Minis crashed through the opening of the tent. 'Nish! Get up!'

'What's the matter?'

'We march to war against the lyrinx.'

Nish sat up. At last! 'How did this come about?'

'Last night your scrutator agreed to all our demands.'

Nish was shocked. For Flydd to capitulate, after that bitter scene with Vithis, humanity's position must have been hopeless. How Vithis must be crowing.

'Including giving up Tiaan?'

'Yes. Apparently your seeker has located her underground, within the eastern quarter of Snizort.' Minis began to unfasten the manacles.

'And Vithis has agreed to free me?'

647

'A long hesitation. 'Not exactly, though I'm sure if he thought about it . . .'

'What is he going to do in return?' Nish was wondering what he could make out of the situation.

'Attack Snizort.'

'If the lyrinx learn he is after Tiaan,' Nish said carefully, 'and surely they must, it will not go well for her.'

Minis faded to white. 'What do you mean?'

'They will kill her, rather than allow anyone to gain the secret of flight.'

Minis pressed his head into his hands and shook it violently. In times of stress he was given to exaggerated gestures. 'We must save her, Nish.'

'I'm sure Vithis will be careful. Tiaan is no good to him dead.'

Minis's face cracked. Hurling himself across the tent, he wrung Nish's hands. 'Please, Nish. I'm desperate.'

Nish reached for his boots. 'What do you expect me to do?'

'Help me get her out of Snizort.'

The man was such a fool. 'Minis, Snizort is the most carefully guarded fortress in this land. There are twenty-five thousand lyrinx there. It can't be done.'

'I love Tiaan,' Minis said simply. 'I know that now. Foster-father has brought me dozens of partners, all of noble Aachim blood, but none mean anything to me. I look at them and I see Tiaan, only Tiaan. I must find a way, Nish.'

'Vithis has ordered you to take no risks. Would you defy his direct order?'

'To save her life I would do *anything*.' Savage eyes glared out of that young, blanched face. 'I'll hide her away; bargain with foster-father for her.' Minis tried to look implacable but did not succeed.

Nish sighed. Even if they could rescue her, Minis had not considered the most important part of the equation – how Tiaan would react. Whether Minis found her, or Vithis did, he did not want to be there.

By dawn, half of the constructs were gone, and more moved out that morning. The battle was set to begin as soon as they were in position.

The camp was now just a skeleton of its former self. More than four thousand of Vithis's six thousand constructs had gone to Snizort, plus two thousand more from the other fleets. Vithis had accompanied them after many exhortations to his foster-son to take care of himself. The remaining five thousand constructs protected women, children and those too old to go to war. If necessary they would be evacuated to safety in the east.

The Aachim camp was a model of military organisation and no one could move without being checked off a dozen lists. Minis, the only other survivor of Clan Inthis, was not permitted to go near the battlefield. He had promised faithfully that he would not, but planned to break that promise as soon as he was able. The opportunity did not come for days.

On the third night of the siege, Minis and Nish slipped away under cover of a wild thunderstorm, heading for the human headquarters east of Snizort. Nish stood beside the tall Aachim as they floated across the undulating land the following morning. It was summer now and a dry one. The grass was bent and brown; most of the creeks carried no more than a trickle, even after last night's storm. The land was empty. The people who once dwelt here had fled long ago and their mud and thatch huts were crumbling.

Minis consulted a map. 'Your scrutator, and his command post, are here.' He indicated a flyspeck just east of Snizort.

They were moving quickly now and their passage left a furrow in the dry grass. Nish was looking back at it when Minis said, 'I see smoke.'

Smudges of black were rising beyond the hill. 'That's burning tar, not grass. Perhaps they've set fire to Snizort.'

Minis looked around wildly. The construct veered towards a cluster of boulders fallen from a flat-topped hill.

'Look out!' Nish yelled.

Minis jerked the controller and the construct lurched the other way.

'I've heard there's nearly as much tar outside Snizort as in,'

Nish said hastily. 'Maybe the enemy set fire to it to make the battle more difficult.'

They approached the battlefield, which formed a ring around Snizort. Minis took the construct to the top of another of those flat-topped hills. The belching black fumes rose from half a dozen places outside the walls. Vicious struggles were going on all over, though from here it was not possible to tell who had the upper hand. The ground shook from the pounding of mighty catapult balls, many of them tar-coated and blazing.

Nish could imagine what it must be like down there – the dust turning to bloody mud, the shrieks of the dying, and those who could not die quickly enough.

'What is your plan?' Nish asked.

'I was hoping you could advise me. You're so resourceful, Nish.'

'But Minis, I don't know anything about Snizort. This is the first time I've *seen* the place.'

'What are we going to do?' Minis said miserably.

Nish knew what he'd like to do. Run, as far and fast as he could. 'I haven't a clue.'

'I know you can think of a way. I'm relying on you.'

'Well, you shouldn't!' Nish snapped. 'Look how strong the walls are.'

'Please, Nish. You're all I have.'

Nish looked over the side. He did want to do something, if only because the son of the most powerful man on Santhenar was begging him. If he could remain in Minis's favour, one day that could be worth the world to him. 'Let's go and talk to the scrutator, if he's not too busy to see us. Which he surely is.'

Minis headed for the army headquarters, on a higher hill closer to Snizort. They passed through five sets of guards but none hindered the son of Vithis. Unfortunately the scrutator was not at the command tent. He had left in the air-floater earlier that morning.

Nish, walking around the edge of the hill by himself, noticed a pair of officers staring – there was a war on yet he wore no

650

uniform. They began to move toward him. He hurried back to the construct, afraid of being conscripted.

'Come on,' Nish said. 'You'll do no good here.'

They spent the day circling Snizort, well out of catapult range, and at sunset a despairing Minis turned the construct back toward the Aachim camp.

'Let's try the scrutator again,' said Nish.

'You've just missed him,' said Fyn-Mah as the construct pulled up. The air-floater was whirring away to the south.

Minis began to gasp and tear at his hair. Falling to his knees, he reached out to the sky with both arms. His pupils dilated until only the whites of his eyes could be seen. 'I can see the future, Nish, and it's black and red. *Blood-red!*'

'What is it, Minis?' Was he seeing Nish's future, or his friend's death?

'A great bursting!' His staring eyes fixed on Nish.

'What do you mean?'

His eyes rolled up into his head, Minis went stiff and without a sound toppled backwards onto the dry grass, where he lay like a slab of petrified wood.

Fyn-Mah came running back with a bucket of water, which she flung in his face. 'Best cure for hysteria,' she said.

With a gurgling sound, a bubble formed in Minis's mouth. Forcing his jaws open, it squeezed out and drifted away. A rumbling belch followed, Minis's heels drummed on the ground and he opened his eyes. He shuddered, blinked and his eyes rolled down to their normal position. He gave Nish a wan smile. 'It has to do with them.'

'Them?'

The air-floater was now just a speck in the south. 'Your friends – Flydd, the crafter and the seeker. And Snizort.'

'Is that where they've gone?' Nish asked Fyn-Mah.

The perquisitor seemed moved by the young man's distress. 'We believe that the lyrinx have a node-drainer there. Flydd is trying to destroy it.'

It looked as if Minis was going to have another fit. 'What about Tiaan?'

No one said anything.

'I'll go after her, by myself,' said Minis. 'if you don't have the courage to help me.'

'You'd better tell your father, Minis,' said Nish.

'Ha!' said Minis wildly. 'He would be pleased to see Tiaan dead. The only person I trust is Tirior, but . . .'

'What?'

'She's always sneered at my foretellings.'

Nish was fed up with Minis's frailties. 'Are you so afraid that it'll stop you saving the woman you love?'

Tirior was in her tent, reading a despatch. 'It's our first message from Stassor,' she said to Minis, before she was asked. 'At last.'

'Why has it taken so long?' Nish wondered.

'Stassor lies among mountains too rugged for our constructs. Our messengers had to seek it out on foot. The city proved . . . difficult to find.'

'What do the Stassor Aachim say?'

She did not answer. Tirior put the paper aside with a heavy sigh. 'What have you come for, Minis?'

He told her.

She rolled her eyes. 'Your foretellings are no more accurate than tossing a coin.'

'Only when I've allowed my head to rule my heart!' he said angrily. 'When others have tried to force me.'

'Very well! Tell me exactly what you saw.'

'A great, blood-red *bursting*!' he exclaimed. 'Even before I heard that Scrutator Flydd had gone to block the node-drainer –'

'*What?*' Tirior leapt to her feet, scattering papers across the floor of the tent. She gripped Minis by the arm. 'Where did you hear this?'

'At the human-army command tent. Perquisitor Fyn-Mah told us,' said Nish. 'What's the matter?'

Tirior sat down and put her head in her hands. 'When the node-drainer is blocked, it will be like blocking the end of a hose but pumping as hard as ever. Something must give.'

'And when it does?' asked Nish.

'*A great bursting,*' said Tirior. 'It could take half of Snizort with it.'

'Tiaan will be killed,' wept Minis.

'And the secret of her flying construct lost. And that's not the worst that can happen,' said Tirior.

'What *is*?' said Nish, but she did not reply.

'We must save Tiaan.' Tears were streaming down Minis's cheeks. 'We *must*, Tirior. Please.'

'We must try,' she said, 'though I do not see how we can.'

Tirior sent urgent messages to Vithis but received no reply. 'He's right across the battlefield, and sore pressed,' said the messenger. 'I couldn't get through to him.'

'I don't like this at all,' said Tirior.

'Please, Tirior,' begged Minis.

'Be quiet!' She was smoothing down a scroll with her long fingers. The end curled up; she smoothed it down again. 'If I go in, I probably won't come out again. But who among us would have a better chance?'

She inspected Nish dispassionately. 'I must go, whatever the consequences. Nish, you may come with me, if you dare. I'd sooner not risk one of my own. And, after all, you bear some responsibility for this situation.'

'How do you work that out?' said Nish.

'Your scrutator has gone in to commit this insane act. Minis, you will stay behind to advise your father what I have done. I would not have him accuse my clan of wilfully risking his only heir.'

'I must come,' Minis cried. 'You cannot leave me behind.'

Tirior smoothed her scroll again, and for an instant a secret smile played on her full lips. Nish noted it, and wondered. Tirior, it seemed, would not be displeased to see the end of First Clan. But was there more to it? He could almost see her manipulating Minis. What else had she done? Could *she* have made the gate go wrong? Did the clans hate each other that much?

'If you insist, I cannot prevent it. But you must state, in front of two witnesses not of my clan, that you have rejected my advice. And what your intention is.'

Witnesses were called. Tirior formally told Minis that she would not take him into Snizort. Minis just as formally insisted that he was going, and that because of his rank she could not refuse him. The witnesses recorded the statements and took them away, and again there came that satisfied smile.

'We will take my construct,' said Tirior. 'It is . . . more suited to the task.'

'Why is that?' Nish asked, ever curious.

'It's . . . well, you will see.'

The construct, barely half the size of Minis's, made hardly any noise. Even inside, Nish could scarcely hear it. As Tirior touched the controller, a panel in front of them, that Nish had thought was solid metal, became transparent. Outside he could see the lights of battle, a blaze off to their left and others to the right.

Tirior turned a coin-sized dial. The front of the machine, visible through the transparent panel, faded from sight. Even the reflections of the flames disappeared. Nish gaped.

'I use it on . . . covert missions,' she said.

'So you're a spy! Just like I was, once.'

'If you like.' Her distaste for the word was evident.

'Are you planning to drive through the front gate?'

'The concealment is not *that* perfect. It serves on a dark night, as long as the lyrinx don't come too close, but it can still be seen in bright light.'

'What are you going to do?' said Nish.

'Take your cue from Minis, who just listens,' she snapped. 'I have spent much time circling Snizort, watching what the enemy do. I know their secret places.'

They slid through the dark, between patches of stunted trees and clusters of boulders, for more than an hour. They seemed to be heading away from Snizort. Finally Tirior drew up some distance from a boulder-topped hill.

'The lyrinx have a number of secret tunnels out of Snizort and we have surely not found them all. This exit is more than a league from the walls.' She stopped, looking out. 'Keep watch on the hilltop.' Tirior put a spiralling metal cap on her head and stared at the shifting patterns on the green glass.

654

Nish could see nothing but a group of pale boulders, some considerably larger than the construct, between which grew twisted trees. Beside him, Minis was as tense as wire. The scene did not change in the next hour, though the noise of battle, a dull roar in the background, grew louder.

'That'll be our assault on the far side,' she whispered.

'I don't –'

'Shh!' She punched him on the shoulder.

A lyrinx appeared between the boulders as if it had materialised from the air. Another one followed, carrying something between it and a third. They slipped across the open space into the trees.

'Minis?' Tirior said.

Minis had his ear to a funnel-shaped implement. 'They're heading away to the south-west. There were only those three.'

'Can you hear them with that?' Nish asked.

'I can feel their footsteps.'

They waited. Tirior was watching the movement of lines upon the glass.

'What is it?' said Nish.

'They have sentinels – of a sort I'm not sure how to deal with.'

'Sentinels?'

'Patterned devices that sense the aura of the Art and set off an alarm. They never sleep; never fail. Nothing of the Art can get past them.'

Nish asked no more questions.

'Minis?' said Tirior, 'would you go below and bring up the packet on the bench?'

He did so. She handed it to Nish. 'A chance to prove yourself. See that smaller rock, the seventh in from the left-hand side, low down?'

'Er . . . The round one that's narrower underneath?'

'Yes. It's a sentinel. Go up onto the hill and approach it from above, quietly. Unwrap the package before you get there. It contains a net lined with gold foil. Be careful you don't tear it. Slip the net over the sentinel from above and pull it all the way to the ground, leaving no gaps. Then crush this with your fingers and push it under.' She pressed something like a small egg into his hand. 'When I signal, bring back the net and the foil. We may need to use it again.'

'Why me?'

'You bear no trace of the Art.'

'What if there are lyrinx sentries?'

'They'll eat you and I'll have to find another way, which will vex me. Get moving.'

The unpleasant part was, he felt sure she was telling the truth. Nish crept across the dry grass, which crackled alarmingly. His passage was even noisier as he moved up the hill, for the ground was littered with crunchy bark and dry sticks. The piled boulders above would make a perfect place for an ambush.

As he reached the lowest boulder a whiff of something came to him – something strongly, muskily animal. *Lyrinx*. He froze against the rock, head cocked to one side. A breeze stirred the treetops; just a whisper. There was no other sound. The creature, or creatures, could be anywhere. They could probably smell him. And he was unarmed.

But Minis had said they were all gone. He must just be smelling the scent left behind, or from the hole they'd come out of. He waited another minute but heard and smelt nothing more.

Tirior would be getting impatient. Nish had one foot in the air when something thumped onto one of the higher boulders further around the hill. It was definitely a lyrinx – he heard the squeal of its claws against the rock.

Another joined it, followed by three more thumps. Nish did not dare to breathe. Even the most cursory search must find him. There was a mutter in the lyrinx tongue and the unmistakable flap of leather wings unfolding. *Thup-thup, thup-thup*. A lyrinx passed across the sky, and another beside it. They were carrying something between them, suspended in a net. It looked like a long box.

They disappeared into the dark. After a moment's silence the others moved out, one by one. All wore bulky packs. They looked around, then headed down the hill, going west.

Nish counted to five hundred, and even then felt anxious. He had no way to tell if more were coming but the risk had to be taken. He went up among the boulders, unfolded the net carefully and crept toward the sentinel. It looked very rock-like. He studied it closely. It *was* a rock – he was looking at the wrong one.

He found the sentinel. Holding out the net, he tiptoed towards it, whipped the net over and pressed it down. The sentinel did not move, of course. It was not alive, strictly speaking.

Taking the other object from his pocket, he crushed it in his fingers. A nauseating stench wisped out, like the rottenest of rotten eggs, and something slimy clung to his fingers. Nish thrust the mess under the net and held it down. He wiped his fingers repeatedly but could not get rid of the smell.

What now? Tirior was supposed to signal. He climbed onto a rock, looking in the direction of the hidden construct. Nothing. He got down again. The sentinel seemed to be collapsing. Nish was watching it, wondering what to do, when he was seized by the arm. He struggled desperately to get free.

'It's me, Minis,' Minis hissed. 'Why are you waiting here? Come on.'

'I thought you said they were all gone,' Nish grumbled as they went back to the construct.

'I thought they were. Hurry up.'

The construct moved forward until it was between the boulders. Tirior handed Nish what appeared to be a wire helmet. 'Put this on.'

'What is it?'

'Something to stop your little brain melting.'

'I –' He could never tell if she was serious. He put it on.

'Come on,' said Minis.

Nish climbed out after him. 'What are we supposed to be doing?'

'Don't talk! Grab the other side and lift.'

Nish took hold of what looked like solid rock and heaved. It was not rock either and tilted back to reveal a dark cavity.

'Hold it open.'

The little construct, slightly more visible than before, edged forward. Minis thrust his funnel inside the entrance and signalled to Tirior. She stood up, held something elongated to her shoulder and pointed it down the hole. An amber glow spiralled around its length and shot underground. Minis checked again with the funnel. He waved. The construct tilted over the edge and slid down. They followed.

A breeze drifted past, carrying the scent of crushed leaves. The false rock came down over Nish's head, shutting out the light. All was black for an instant, then a light-glass came on at the front of the construct. They clambered inside and the construct moved down the narrow tunnel at walking pace. Shortly they encountered the bodies of two lyrinx by a sentry post.

'If you can kill them so easily,' said Nish, 'why don't you use these weapons in the war?'

'It was not easy,' said a blanched Tirior. 'I will suffer for days, and no one else can use it at all.'

'How did you find this tunnel?' Nish asked.

'Not by flapping my mouth at every opportunity. Minis, go to the firing position.'

Minis jacked up the rear turret, where a pair of devices used compressed springs to fire various kinds of projectiles. He armed both weapons.

'Nish, put your ear to the funnel. Call if you hear anything.'

Nish heard an amplified whine, a *ticker-tick-tick*, but no thumping footsteps. The tunnel wound around as if following weaknesses in the rock, then ran flat and straight for a few minutes before diving steeply and coiling around several times. At this lower level, water was seeping through the roof, making puddles on the floor.

They slid around a corner of yellow rock. Ahead was a second guard post with two lyrinx by it. They had not heard or seen the construct. In the funnel Nish heard *pfft*. The lyrinx in the middle of the tunnel fell, transfixed through the heart. The other hurled himself for the guard post but a spear went through his back, dropping him short. Minis was out of his turret before Nish could blink and killed the struggling creature with a sword blow to the neck.

'Good work,' said Tirior, even paler. 'I don't think it got off a warning. Did you hear anything, Nish?'

'No,' he said, though he'd lifted his ear from the funnel at the first shot.

They continued. The tunnel now ran straight and level. Tirior checked a lodestone. 'We're going in the right direction, at least.'

After half an hour of low-speed movement Nish caught a whiff of bitumen. The tunnel plunged again, levelled out and the walls suddenly became black. The sandstone here was impregnated with tar.

'How do they stand it?' said Nish. The smell was unpleasantly strong.

'I don't know. Few creatures could survive in such a place.'

'I wonder what brought them here?'

'Perhaps a special kind of node,' said Minis.

'How are you going to find the node-drainer?'

'I don't think that will be difficult,' Tirior said dryly.

They passed back into clean sandstone, though not for long. The layers of yellow stone became black-streaked, then banded with tar, and finally completely black. Ebony droplets beaded the walls. From here on they had to go more slowly, for the walls narrowed and sometimes curved in at the sides, as if they were oozing in.

'It's a wonder we haven't run into more of the enemy,' said Nish.

'Everyone who can fight would be outside, and the others have probably evacuated.'

They crept around a corner. 'It can't be far now.' Tirior studied the lines dancing on the grey plate behind her controller. 'I –'

The construct stopped suddenly. Tirior jiggled her controller. Nothing happened. 'What's going on? I can't see any field at all. Minis, can you *feel* anything?'

'No, but we're getting closer. I can almost see the place in my mind's eye, as I saw it in my foretelling.'

'The scrutator must have blocked the node-drainer,' said Nish.

She shook her head. 'That would not affect us. Constructs don't use the weak field. That's why Flydd was so desperate for our support. There's something –'

'What?'

'I don't know, that's the problem. It's . . . a *strangeness*, and I don't like it.' The whine resumed. 'It's back.'

'But for how long?'

Tirior drove the construct through the winding tunnels as fast as was humanly possible. Skidding around a corner, she found a sharp, bulging bend straight ahead. Somehow she got through with no more than a scrape against the sides. They slid around another bend into a cavern that opened out around them. Tirior stopped.

'What is *that*?' said Nish.

The cavern was full of black mist. It took a long time to make out what she was pointing at. It seemed to be a tar fountain in the middle of the floor, a low, bubbling efflorescence about knee high.

'We can go round it,' Nish said.

'There shouldn't be anything like this here,' said Tirior with a worried frown. She consulted the green glass. 'The tar seeps should be a long way away.'

'Maybe they've oozed this way.'

'Not that quickly.' She edged the construct forward. 'See the footprints. They appear to go right through it. This fountain has only just arisen.'

They went around it, but across the far side were struck by floating globules of tar that rolled down the outside of the transparent panel, leaving black trails.

'I didn't know tar floated in air,' Nish said.

'It doesn't!' Tirior muttered, grim-faced.

'What's going on?'

'We've entered the *strangeness* of the node-drainer. The power it's taking from the field has to end up somewhere, and where it does, reality is . . . suspended.'

'We'd better hurry,' said Nish.

'We'll be too late!' Minis cried. 'Quickly, Tirior.'

'I don't dare go any faster.'

'You're going slower all the time!'

'The field we use is weak here.'

'Shouldn't it be getting stronger as we approach the node?' said Nish.

'Constructs don't use node fields. They draw on local stress-fields which are stronger on Aachan but, unfortunately, weaker here. I'm drawing all the power I can but it's barely enough to keep us moving.'

Minis was frantic. 'Something's gone wrong, hasn't it, Tirior?'

'Terribly. The stress-field is fading by the minute.'

'Perhaps the node-drainer is draining *all* the fields,' said Nish.

'I don't see how it could!' she said through clenched teeth. Tirior jerked the controller. The construct lurched forward, stopped, lurched again, and then the whine cut off and it fell, the base smacking against the floor.

'I don't like the sound of that,' said Tirior, picking herself up. 'We didn't crash, we splatted.'

She threw back the hatch and they climbed onto the edge. The air stank of tar. Nish jumped down.

'No!' Tirior yelled.

Too late. His feet went right through the floor. 'Aah.' He sank to his knees in black, oozing tar.

Cursing him, Tirior reached down. Nish took her hand. She tried to pull him out. He did not budge.

'Give me a hand,' she shouted at Minis, who had his hands over his face and was rocking on the rim. 'Minis, *now*!'

Catching Nish under the arms, Minis strained, and slowly Nish's feet emerged from the tar.

'You bloody fool!' Tirior handed him her knife. 'Scrape it off. Remove your boots and trousers before you come inside.'

Nish set to work. Tirior went down the hatch and soon that familiar whine returned. 'The field's back,' she said over the edge. 'At least, part of it. Let's see if we can get ourselves out.'

The whine rose in pitch, until the construct shuddered and pulled free. They continued through the strangeness, which was stranger than ever. The walls oozed and bulged. Layers of soft tar flowed down them, and across, and sometimes up. Clots of tar drifted in the air; hot tar dripped onto the closed hatch.

'How close are we?' Nish yelled.

'There's no need to shout,' she said. 'Another few minutes and we should be there.'

'To Tiaan?' said Nish.

'No, to the node-drainer.'

Minis spun around. 'But, Tirior . . .'

'We've got to stop the scrutator first, Minis.'

'It seems awfully hot in here,' said Nish, mopping his brow. 'It wasn't hot before.'

Something burst through the wall in a spray of sparks. The tunnel vibrated visibly, then the side wall pushed in until it reached the construct. Further ahead, the walls were almost together.

'We can't get through,' said Nish. 'We're going to be –'

A shockwave passed through them. Up ahead the tunnel touched, then peeled apart with a grotesque squelch. The whine disappeared; again the construct splatted to the floor. This time Tirior could not get it up.

'We're stuck,' she said. 'The field is gone.'

They stared at one another. Nish could feel his claustrophobia, never far away when underground, rising like a skyrocket. 'Got to get out,' he gasped.

'We'll have to go the rest of the way on foot, if the floor is solid enough.'

'But without the construct we're –'

'I know!' she snapped, 'but we can't *carry* it.'

'Was that the node-drainer going?' Nish whispered.

She laughed scornfully.

'Then there may still be time.' He put his leg over the side, searching for a patch of floor solid enough to stand on.

Tirior dragged him back. 'Look out!'

A great bulge had developed in the roof, like a wagonload of molasses hanging above him. He threw himself backwards. Tirior slammed the hatch and tightened the clamps. There was an interminable wait before the bulge came down with an oozing splat. It surged across the clear screen; then, with a thump, the rest followed, the level of tar rising until it covered the screen completely.

'We're buried,' said Nish. 'We'll never get out.'

SIXTY-TWO

'Where is the watcher?' whispered Flydd urgently.
'Around corner,' grunted Ullii.

'I told you so,' Irisis muttered. 'What are you going to do now, scrutator?'

'Pipe down. Ullii, come here. You're my eyes and ears into this device.'

He squatted on the floor, knees popping like little fireworks. Ullii crouched beside him, whispering. She seemed quite co-operative now, but Ullii usually was when *she* was in danger.

Flydd rose, rubbing his knees. 'The watcher, or sentinel, is a kind of *growth*. If I attack, it will give an alarm.'

'Can you conceal us from it?' said Irisis.

'No. It picks up the aura of the Art, and we all bear enough of that to set it off.'

'Then we've failed before we begin.'

'There are ways, crafter. I'm just running though a dozen or two. You might as well sit down.'

Looking at the tarry floor with distaste, Irisis leaned against the cleanest wall she could find. Time ticked by, and every moment of delay meant more bloodshed outside. She began to pace up and down. Ullii gestured at her to stop – the watcher might detect it. Irisis returned to her post. Her organs vibrated in her belly and the way the flesh shivered beneath her skin was uncanny. How long would it take before the unreality of the node-drainer pulled her apart?

Flydd's eyes were closed but his lips moved as he ran through all the forms and adaptations of scrutator magic, searching for the right one.

'The spell must disable it instantly, before it can send an alarm.' He sought more precise directions from Ullii. 'I think I have it.' He held out his hands and uttered words in a language Irisis did not know.

'No,' said Ullii, after a long pause.

'Are you sure? . . . Of course you are. Damn it!' he yelped, holding his head.

'What is it?' said Irisis.

'That hurt. I used a spell to freeze it into place. That's a reliable way of attack, as a rule, but the spell hasn't taken.'

'Why not?'

'I don't know. It's as if a similar spell was already at work nearby, but that makes no sense at all. Let me get my strength back and I'll try another.'

Recovering from the spell took so long that Irisis thought it was not going to happen at all. Flydd looked like a man having his leg amputated with a broken bottle. Drops of sweat stood out on his forehead, though in the gloom they had a ruddy look like blood.

'Aargh!' he gasped, spitting gobs on the floor. 'I think I can manage it now.'

He moved his hands and spoke his words of power. They waited, then a *crack-crack-SNAP* came from around the corner.

'It's gone,' said the seeker.

Now there *were* drops of blood on the scrutator's forehead. 'Just as well,' he gasped. 'I could not have done *that* again.'

They went by a mushroom-shaped device that had split down the middle, unable to withstand his evocation that had instantly turned it to stone.

'Anything else, Ullii?' he said hoarsely.

'No,' she whispered back. 'But I see many lyrinx.'

'Coming after us?'

'Not yet.'

'Take us to the node-drainer.'

They turned the corner, passed down a wide tunnel and entered a grotto like the inside of a stubby cross. All was black. The walls were studded with ebony crystals, the roof hung with bituminous stalactites. The floor was strewn with lipped pools, each perfectly circular, that seethed and bubbled like boiling mud ponds.

Flydd stared in wonderment. 'This is it, Irisis.'

In the luminosity of the node-drainer the cavern was eerily beautiful. The walls sparkled like black diamonds, the roof glowed like black pearls, the pools emitted ebony bubbles that drifted around the room, reflecting the light like mirror balls. The node-drainer was, from the vision back at Minnien, just as Irisis expected it to be. It resembled a broad leathery mushroom, white as death, with a circular cap rising to a peak. A hole in the centre, above the stalk, gushed forth energies that flowed and tumbled and shone.

'It's not quite what I expected,' Flydd muttered. 'It's taking power from the node all right, and staggering amounts of it, but channelling most of it away. Where to?'

A hanging funnel made of the same leathery substances collected most of the flow. Irisis could not see where it led to. The leaking field created a foggy unreality at the back of the cavern that blurred everything into the walls.

'I expect they're using it for flesh-forming, and other Arts.'

'No doubt, and if Snizort should survive, we'll have to follow that up.'

Ullii gasped, doubled over and projectile vomited through her legs. Curling into a ball, she rolled forward until she struck the wall, toppled over and lay unmoving. Her eyes were wide open, her arms wrapped protectingly around her belly.

'Myllii?' she whispered. 'Help me, Myllii.'

'Ullii?' whispered Irisis. 'What's wrong?'

'Node-drainer is wrong. *Wrong!*'

'What do you mean, Ullii?'

'Tiaan!'

'What about her?'

Ullii would, or could, say no more.

The seeker did not seem to be harmed so Irisis carried her to the entrance, as far as she could get from the node-drainer. Laying her on the floor, she ran back to the centre.

'How are we supposed to destroy *that*?' She clutched her roiling stomach.

'We discussed it privately at the Council of Scrutators,' said Flydd. 'They had something made up for me in Nennifer.'

From his chest pack he took a device, a sort of metal cap, mirrored on the inside. The rim was set with hedrons made from five perfectly matched blue tourmaline crystals.

'What does it do?' Irisis asked.

'It simply reflects, in a magical sense, the drained power back the way it came. As long as you can tune the crystals to what's left of the field, of course. It requires power to make it work, and a lot of it.'

'What if the power can't *go* back the way it came? And surely it can't, since power will keep flowing the other way.'

'It won't flow back until the power built up within the hedrons is greater than what's coming from the node. Then it will simply burst through, back to the node, burning out the node-drainer.'

'Has such a device ever been tested?' She knew the answer to that.

'How could it be? It was made in Nennifer while we . . . er, waited.'

'About which the least said the better!'

He went to the entrance, crouching beside the seeker and taking her hand. 'Thank you, Ullii. I won't forget what you've done to get us here.'

She snatched it away. 'You are a wicked man. You broke your promise!'

'I do keep my promises, Ullii. You will see. Rest now. You still have to get us out.'

He went back to the centre. 'Irisis, you've got the easiest job of all. I have the hardest – to fit the cap while the drainer is still flowing.'

'What's my job?' Irisis said suspiciously.

'You must tune the node-drainer to the field, draw power into it and make it work.'

It was as if he had raised his sword and cloven her head in two. Irisis fell to her knees in the tar and could not get up.

'Xervish – scrutator – surr.' She stared at him in horror.

'What's the problem, crafter?' As if he did not know.

One minute molten tin was flowing in her veins, the next they were clogged with ice crystals. Her heartbeat sounded like a galloping horse. She licked lips so dry that they crackled. Irisis looked up at the scrutator, standing as implacable as a statue.

'I can't do it, surr. I can't draw power from the field. You know I've lost the talent.'

Flydd, who was staring at the fountaining node-drainer, did not answer.

'Surr, you came here, knowing all the time . . .?'

His head rotated like a sunflower on its stalk. The eyes were like pitch fires in a cauldron. 'You must!'

'You knew my failing, Xervish. Why build a device I cannot use? Why bring me at all?'

'*I didn't build it.* The Council of Scrutators had it made and Ghorr said it was tailored to me alone. He lied. It wasn't until I opened the box this afternoon that I understood how it worked. In the time I could not find another artisan; a *proper* one.'

The insult was like a smack in the mouth. 'Why didn't you warn me?'

'That would have made it worse.'

Then she realised that the solution was right in front of her. 'Surr, Tiaan is in here somewhere. She could use it.'

Hope flared in his eyes, which hurt her too. 'Yes, why didn't I think of that? Ullii? *Ullii?*'

The seeker groaned. Flydd crouched beside her. 'Ullii, can you see Tiaan?'

Ullii was holding her head. 'Myllii, Myllii?'

Flydd and Irisis exchanged glances. He tried again.

'Ullii. We must find Artisan Tiaan. Where is she?'

The seeker's eyes flicked from side to side. 'Long way from here,' she whispered.

'Can you take us there?' said Irisis.

'Too far. Toooo far.' She closed her eyes.

Irisis wept in despair. Flydd dragged her to her feet. 'There's no time for that. Every minute's delay means more dead.'

'Can't *you* use it, surr?' she said desperately. 'You're a powerful mancer.'

'I told you, it's designed for an artisan, not a mancer. Ghorr has betrayed me – he wants me dead and doesn't care if we fail. *Do it!*'

His words froze her to the marrow. That was not Xervish, her friend and one-time lover speaking. It was the scrutator, who broke whomever he had to, to get the job done. She had long dreaded this moment, and surely suffered every pang a mortal human could suffer. If she failed, as she would, she would not have long to regret it. She met his eye.

'I will try, surr.'

'Don't *try*,' he replied, harsh-voiced. 'Succeed. The army, the war, yes, even the survival of humankind is in your hands, Irisis.'

She took the jewelled cap from his hand. Holding it out, she touched her artisan's pliance with her other hand and brought the field into view. Irisis closed her eyes, the better to *see*.

'The field is fading fast. And it's . . . all flabby and warped. I've not seen anything like it. It's hardly got any colour left.'

'Then you'd better work quickly.'

Irisis imaged the field in all directions, then tuned her mind to the blue crystals. That was hard, for she was used to working with one at a time. She traced out paths, through ethyric space, from the field to each of the crystals. It was difficult work, even for her. The knowledge of one path tended to erase the others from her mind.

You must do it! There is no alternative. She struggled on, fixing the first path, holding it while she did the second, the third, the fourth, the fifth. Now the next step. The one she could not do. Opening her eyes, Irisis saw the scrutator staring at her. His mouth moved, as if uttering the word *Hurry*. She heard nothing except the hissing of the node-drainer.

She felt disconnected, as if she was being taken apart muscle by muscle, sinew by sinew, organ by organ. The disruption was beginning. Flydd looked even worse. And it would be worse for him if she succeeded, as he attempted to cap the node-drainer.

Snapping her eyes closed, she felt the blue crystals with her fingertips and imagined power flowing from the field into them. She could see it perfectly. Unfortunately, when she tried to draw on that power, nothing happened. No surprise there. It never had, since that day at her fourth birthday party when she had lost the talent.

SIXTY-THREE

'Why did you lose it?' Flydd said in her ear. His knobbly hands gripped her shoulders, supporting her.

'I wanted it too much,' she whispered, remembering that day so vividly. Desire had burned her.

'*Why*, Irisis?'

'Because I was the best . . . Because it was my destiny –' She broke off, knowing that was wrong.

'Was it? I don't think so. You never wanted to be an artisan at all, *did you*?'

Back in the world of her four-year-old self, Irisis hardly knew what he was saying. 'I do want it!' She stamped one foot in its pretty pink sandal. 'All my life I've wanted it. Mother and father and dear old Uncle Barkus . . .'

A long-suppressed memory exploded into her mind. On the morning of her birthday she had been talking to her mother about being a jeweller when she grew up. Even at four, Irisis had known what she wanted. She had expected her mother to be pleased but Nysygy had slapped her daughter's face.

'Don't be a stupid little girl! Jewelling is cheap, common work for cheap little people. You're going to be crafter one day, like your Uncle Barkus. Only you won't be crafter at a dirty little manufactory. You'll be the most brilliant crafter of all time.'

'But, Mummy,' the four-year-old Irisis had said, bewildered. 'I don't want to be crafter.'

'How dare you,' Nysygy had screamed, shaking Irisis by the shoulders. 'Never mention it again or . . . or I don't know what I'll do to myself.'

Irisis could see her mother's staring eyes, the knife pressed against one slender wrist. 'If I die it will be your fault, you wicked daughter!' she hissed. Her mother was always making threats.

The child could not deal with emotional blackmail. Irisis just knew herself to be an evil little brat who would one day be the death of her mother. Fortunately dear old Barkus had come in. Her mother had tossed the knife on the table and turned to the bottle instead.

Flydd broke into her thoughts. 'What were you *really* feeling, that day of the birthday party when you lost your talent?'

'I was furiously angry, though I knew better than to show it. I hated my family, and most of all my mother.'

'And when you were asked to demonstrate your talent?'

The revelation struck her. 'I wanted to fail. Oh, Xervish, I wanted to fail! It was the only way out of the trap they had built for me.'

'You tried to use your talent but your subconscious mind would not let you. It closed it off and you never found it again.'

'Yes,' Irisis said softly, 'but still I could not escape them. Mother did my trick for me that day, and ever after refused to believe my failure. She was too strong for me. I became a liar and a cheat to cover it up. I had to.'

'What will you do after the war? Will you remain crafter?'

The fiction of 'after the war'. People had been consoling themselves with that phrase for a hundred and fifty years. The reality was different. 'Of course not! There will be no need for clankers then. I will follow my dream. People will want beautiful things again, one day.'

His hand squeezed her shoulders. 'Help us, Irisis. Save the war, then follow your dream.'

She looked within herself. The realisation had not made it

any easier. She still did not know where her lost talent was, or how to recover it.

'Don't think about it,' Flydd said. 'Just do it!'

She tried. Her true calling was a beacon out of the tarry darkness. Irisis reached deep inside herself. She tried harder than she had in her life, searching again and again, but could not uncover her talent. Tears formed in her eyes.

'I can't . . . do it,' she said, the barest exhalation of breath. 'I'm sorry. I don't know where to look.'

He gripped her shoulders again. Those fierce eyes looked into hers and they were blood-red. His lips had gone an ugly blue. A thread of blood appeared in one nostril. The node-drainer was tearing him apart. Flydd turned away. She had let him down.

'Clawers coming!' cried Ullii, who had been motionless in the corner all this time.

'How far?'

'Not far.'

'Give me the cap.' Flydd snatched it from her hands. 'If you can't do it, I'll have to.'

It would kill him. 'Wait, surr!' She had an idea. 'Ullii, remember that time in the clankers, when they lost the field and I had to tune the controllers to that strange double node?'

Ullii's eyes were open and she was staring coldly at Flydd and Irisis. She did not answer.

'Ullii?'

'I remember,' said Ullii.

'How did you –?' Never mind. Can you see where my lost talent is?'

'You're a hard ball in my lattice. Can't see inside.'

'Please try, else the scrutator is going to die.'

'He's a nasty, cruel man,' Ullii snapped.

'But he cares for you, Ullii. He saved you from Jal-Nish.'

'I saved *you* from Scrutator Ghorr. You promised to find Myllii. Hate you too.'

Irisis had no answer to that. She looked desperately at Flydd.

'Ah, but I *have* found Myllii,' he said smoothly.

Ullii rotated to face him, her eyes closed as if she were searching her lattice. 'Myllii,' she whispered. 'Where are you, Myllii?'

'He is far away,' said Flydd. 'Eiryn Muss has found Myllii and will bring him home to you, but it will take many, many days. Now can you *please* help Irisis?'

It was not enough. 'Irisis wants my Nish,' Ullii said sullenly.

'That pimply little runt? I do not,' cried Irisis.

'Saw you at Aachim camp. You were *holding* him.' Her voice rose in outrage.

'Nish is my friend,' said Irisis. 'I don't want him for a lover. Why would I, the little pipsq –' She broke off. Better not insult Nish further. No telling how Ullii would react.

Ullii had her arms crossed about her chest and a stubborn expression on her face.

'Oh, for goodness sake!' cried Flydd. 'You're not a pair of cats in an alley. Irisis, I forbid you, as scrutator, *ever* to be Nish's lover. Will that do, Ullii?'

Ullii gave Irisis a triumphant smile. 'Thank you, Xervish.' Seizing his withered hand, she kissed it. 'You are a kind man. I will do what *you* want.'

Irisis was outraged. How dare any man tell her whom she could take to her bed? 'You'll be sorry, Flydd. Don't think you'll be sharing *my* favours anytime soon.'

He smirked, the effect rather spoiled by the blood at the corner of his mouth. 'Can we get on? I feel I'm being filleted like a fish.'

Ullii put her hands over her eyes. Her arms shook. Her jaw clenched. Irisis felt as if she was picking at a ball made of black string, but it was wound so tightly she could not unravel it. She plucked and plucked, at one place and another, fruitlessly. Then a pair of hands began to work next to hers. Small and slender they were, and they seemed to know what they were doing. In her mind's eye, Irisis followed the movements in and out, back and forth. They eased one thread out of the tangle, leaving it sticking up in the air.

The fingers withdrew. Irisis took hold of the thread and tugged. It unwound, the ball spinning off the other way, growing smaller and smaller until it disappeared, leaving just a pile of shining silver thread. She began to gather it up, for at the end of it must be the key. Or maybe *it* was the key. She began to weave the silver into a bracelet, an exquisite piece of jewellery.

'Clawers, clawers.' The seeker folded up on the floor.

As Irisis slid the bracelet on her wrist she saw the way so clearly that it was like a lifeline stretching out in front of her. She drew power and, to her surprise, her joy, it cascaded into the crystals. They exploded with light and something inside the cap gave forth a low, vibrating hum.

'I've done it! Xervish, I've done it!'

There was no time to enjoy her triumph. Flydd snatched the cap. 'Prepare to defend me!' He ran to the node-drainer.

Irisis whipped out her sword and stood at the entrance, looking up and down and back over her shoulder. There were no lyrinx in sight. She was strangely weak and nauseous. Mancers suffered from aftersickness but this was the first time she had experienced it.

Flydd seemed to be having trouble fitting the cap. Strange energies kept bursting out in all directions. It was like trying to seal a flowing hose. He cursed, forced the cap over the top of the mushroom, and cursed again as it was tossed out of his hands to land on the tarry floor.

Irisis peered out the entrance but could not see any enemy. She crept down the passage to the point where a broad thoroughfare became visible. The disruption was much less here. Some distance away, a lyrinx shadow fleeted across an opening, carrying something that looked like a human body. She edged back. Her sword would not stop a lyrinx, even for a minute.

The lyrinx hurried past, looking neither right nor left. She heard shouting. More enemy shadows ran by, all carrying loads. What was going on? Were they losing the war, or had they already won it? She scuttled back to the cavern. In her absence Flydd must have worked some great scrutator magic, for he cried out, 'It's on! Time to go.'

The energy fountain had disappeared but the room felt stranger than ever. The once solid tar was flowing like water, *up* the walls. The walls expanded and contracted like the chambers of a beating heart.

Irisis fought back the panic, fought the nightmare of being entombed alive, the urge to flee. All this effort must not be wasted for want of courage at the last instant. 'Better be sure it's going to work first.'

'The power's not coming out, so it must go back. They're the only two choices.'

'Then they'll notice the power isn't flowing and come to investigate,' said Irisis. 'They'll take the cap off.'

'There's no way to remove it without breaking it, and if they tamper with anything, it triggers the power stored in the blue hedrons. That would destroy the node-drainer and everything around it.'

'What if they cut off the top of the node-drainer?'

'That will destroy it too. Once the flow is interrupted, anything will.'

'Won't the node-drainer be rather dangerous, then?'

'It shouldn't be if the cap was built right.'

'What if it's not? What if Ghorr deliberately made it wrong?'

'I don't dare think what might happen.'

'In that case, why are we standing here?'

The blue hedrons lit up. The room shook. 'It's working,' said Flydd.

Ullii shrieked, clutched at her temples and fell down.

'What's the matter?' Irisis bent over the seeker. She did not answer. She was unconscious.

'Should have anticipated this,' said Flydd. 'When it turned on, it must have been like an explosion in her lattice. Is she alive?'

'Yes, but she won't be showing us the way out.' Irisis put Ullii over her shoulders. 'Do you remember it, surr?'

She expected him to say no. From the beginning he'd said that it was a suicide mission.

'I know the first part.'

'That's not a lot of help, surr. With all due respect.'

'While we live . . .'

He spoke his words of power, strained, and Ullii became just a shimmer at the edges. The cloaking spell was back. 'Let's see how long I can hold it,' he said ominously.

They struggled along dimly-lit side passages, for the main one was full of lyrinx. For every step of that journey Irisis expected to be torn apart, or burned or buried alive, in some unimaginable disaster connected with the node-drainer.

Flydd's cloaking served them well until they were near the exit, when he let out a groan, fell to one knee and their concealment was gone.

He crouched against the black wall, gasping. His red eyes met hers. 'I feel as if my belly is full of blood.' His mouth and teeth were red.

She felt little better. Her muscles felt like glue. 'There's not far to go, Xervish. Keep on.'

He gave another groan, spat blood on the floor and drew his sword. Irisis could not do the same, for Ullii was a dead weight in her arms. Flydd edged around the door, ducked back, and a minute later looked again.

'It's clear now.'

Before they reached the exit two lyrinx ran in, covered in tar and blood. They stopped, then the first hurled itself at Flydd. The second put hands around its mouth and let out a booming bellow that could have been heard half a league away. Ullii squirmed in Irisis's arms, her eyes flicked open, fixed on the enemy and closed again.

The lyrinx reached Flydd in a couple of bounds. The great arms swung – blows that could kill a man. Somehow Flydd avoided the first and the second, moved in from the side and his sword caught the creature between the plates of the throat.

The second lyrinx proved a harder opponent. A backhanded blow sent Flydd tumbling one way, his sword another. He made no attempt to go for it, but thrust both hands at the creature's feet and screamed a word of power that sprayed blood from his nostrils. The black floor glowed pink for a second, then collapsed. The lyrinx went into it to the hips and, try as it might, could not drag itself out. The tar was already setting.

Flydd wiped blood across his face, staggered to his sword and they lurched towards the exit. 'That was the end of me. I can do no more magic, even to save our lives.'

They emerged at the base of the pit. It was not as black as before, for the rim was lit up by fire and blast. Blazing flares soared across the sky.

'The fools! If one of those falls down here,' gasped Flydd, 'we will die the most horrible death it is possible to imagine.'

'Maybe they've given us up for dead.'

'Maybe we are and just don't know it.'

They staggered up the sticky steps, their feet so clotted with tar that they could barely lift them. Halfway up, a lyrinx came running towards them; Irisis could see the light reflecting off staring eyes and bared teeth. Flydd flattened himself against the pit wall and, as the creature passed, swept his sword at it. It threw up its arms, tried to slash back and went over the edge.

'Easiest victory I've ever had,' he muttered.

'It didn't seem to know we were here.'

'The stink of tar must have kept it from smelling us. You right with her?'

Irisis eased Ullii on her shoulder. 'I'll manage.'

They made the top without further incident and saw fighting everywhere. A force of clankers had broken through the eastern wall of Snizort, near the gate, though they had not gone far. A bitter battle raged there. Other walls had smaller breaches, each with its struggling figures, human, Aachim and lyrinx. The perimeter walls swarmed with enemy, although none looked in their direction. The battle was too desperate.

They headed for a mound, hardly a hill, between the pit and the Great Seep. It was one of several that offered a better view. There was no sign of the air-floater in the cloudy sky and their signals were not answered.

'I didn't expect it would still be around,' said Flydd. 'It's too easy a target.'

'Let's try for the clankers.'

'There's a wall of lyrinx between us and them.'

'We need some kind of diversion,' said Irisis.

'I can't –' Flydd began. 'Well, it looks like you've got one!'

Behind them, above the location of the node-drainer, the ground surface slowly rose until it formed a dome twenty spans across and five high. It changed from tar-black to a dull white, to orange, to red. A single spark burst through in the centre, soaring high, only to wink out. Others followed it, whereupon the ground erupted in a veritable fountain of sparks and colours. It was beautiful; beautiful and deadly.

'This is just the beginning,' said a deathlike Flydd. 'The cap isn't going to burn out the node-drainer at all. It's going to blow it apart and take half of Snizort with it.'

'Shouldn't we run?' Ullii was like lead in her arms.

'There's nowhere to run to. This is it, Irisis. All along I'd hoped we would get away, but that's not going to happen.'

'Oh well.' She embraced him as best she could, still holding the seeker. 'We did our duty. Besides, we've had some good times.'

'Indeed we have. Give her to me.' He took Ullii, who opened her eyes, flipped herself out of his arms and scuttled into the shadows.

'Let her go,' said Irisis. 'We might as well watch the show.'

They stood together, seeing the fountain grow and grow. 'The battle's over. The clankers are pulling back through the wall. They've realised what's going to happen.'

The lyrinx had too, for they were streaming away from the boiling fountain in all directions, passing by as if Irisis and Flydd were not there.

'It won't do them any good,' said Flydd. 'Not even a league will be far enough.'

'Xervish,' Irisis said. 'There's something I don't understand.'

'What's that?'

'About you finding Myllii. You said he was many days away and Muss would bring him. But Muss was at the camp yesterday morning. How did he know?'

Flydd glanced at Ullii, who was pacing around a tar mire some distance away. He lowered his voice. 'I lied.'

679

'What?'

'I had to lie, otherwise she wouldn't have cooperated. I have no idea where Myllii is.'

On the other side of the Mire, Ullii went as still as a shadow. She turned her head to them and fountains of sparks reflected in her colourless eyes. It looked as if she were shooting fire at them. Ullii was not wearing her earplugs and had heard every word.

'Lucky we're all going to die then,' said Irisis.

'Lucky!' Flydd grunted.

The minutes ticked by. Irisis said, 'It doesn't seem to be quite as high as it was.'

The fountain was dying down and now, with an explosion of bubble-clear fire, it burst. The dome began to collapse in on itself like a miniature volcano.

'What's going on?' she cried. 'Is it the end?'

'I don't know. I didn't expect it to go this way.'

'It's our chance.' Opening the shutter of the lantern, she pointed it upwards and began to blink it rapidly.

'They won't come,' he said. 'The lyrinx will have got them.'

'It's worth a try.'

Shortly Irisis heard the faint whirr of the rotor and, in the greatest miracle of all time, the air-floater appeared above them. Ullii sprang up. Irisis threw herself over the side, jerked Flydd in and they were away.

'Drop *all* the ballast,' Flydd shouted to Pilot Hila. 'Up fast and high, away from here. Go! Quick as you can.'

The sandbags went over and the air-floater shot up like a balloon released under water. 'Away!' roared Flydd, pointing south.

Irisis looked down into the collapsed dome chamber, which glowed white, red, and slowly faded. 'It's going out,' she said. 'It must have destroyed itself and plugged up the drainer.'

'It hasn't,' Flydd growled. *'Faster, pilot!'*

'Oh, look!' Irisis was staring beyond the wall, where a glowing speck had appeared a few leagues north. 'Isn't that where the node is –'

'Cover your eyes, everyone,' Flydd roared, casting Ullii onto the floor of the cabin and tossing his coat over her. 'Don't look toward the node.'

'Why not?' Irisis said. 'I –'

His rough hand went over her eyes. 'Do what you're damn well told. *Turn away!*'

Too late. The node erupted in a brilliant purply-white flare that went straight up for a thousand spans. Irisis could see it through her closed eyes; even through the scrutator's fingers. More fire followed it, and more, until it was like a giant needle spanning ground and sky. The needle began to rotate faster and faster, white, blue-white, violet, white again; then it exploded, spinning threads of fire in all directions.

As Flydd threw her through the cabin door, the shockwave hit them with a roar that almost burst her eardrums. The rotor tore away from the air-floater and went spinning into the night. The air-floater turned upside down, dropping them onto the cabin ceiling, then to the floor as the weight righted it. Out of the corner of her eye Irisis saw someone go over the side – one of the soldiers, she thought. Ullii screamed once but the trauma was too much. She collapsed into her silence.

'Are we all right?' Flydd called. He shouted names. All but two answered, the soldier and Navigator Nivulee, who had been at the back when the shockwave hit. She must have been thrown straight out.

'Pull the emergency release, Hila,' said Flydd. 'We've got to go down.'

They drifted away from Snizort toward the rows of clankers on the plain, slowly descending.

'We're going to make it,' said Irisis, reaching out to Flydd. 'Oh, Xervish, we've survived despite everything.'

He pushed past like she was not there, stumbled and clung to the rail. He was panting as if he'd just run a race. She joined him.

They landed hard in the middle of the battlefield, lyrinx to one side, clankers and constructs on the other. The node was an incandescent mass. In the other direction the sun was just tipping the eastern horizon.

Ullii sat up. 'I'm thirsty.'

Irisis hugged her. 'Ullii, thank heavens you're all right.'

The seeker thrust her away so hard that Irisis fell down. 'Liar, liar!' she screamed.

As Irisis rolled over, her hand touched her pliance. 'What's happened to the field?' she said numbly. 'I can't see it.'

'Gone! All fields gone. Node gone.'

'What do you mean, *all gone*?' choked Irisis.

With a great cry, the lyrinx charged. The clankers did not move. Nor did the constructs. They lay flat on the ground, silent and still.

'What have we done?' said Irisis. 'The constructs are not moving *either*.'

'Nor will they, ever again. The node has been destroyed and *all* the fields with it. We've lost the war.' Flydd sank to his knees in the tarry mud. 'We've lost everything.'

THE END
OF VOLUME TWO

VOLUME THREE
SCRUTATOR

continues
THE WELL OF ECHOES QUARTET

GLOSSARY

NAMES (MAIN CHARACTERS IN ITALICS)

Aachim: The human species native to the world of Aachan, once conquered and enslaved by a small force of invading Charon (the Hundred). The Aachim are great artisans and engineers, but melancholy or prone to hubris and arrogance. In ancient times, many were brought to Santhenar by Rulke in the fruitless hunt for the Golden Flute. The Aachim flourished on Santhenar, but were later betrayed by Rulke and ruined in the Clysm. They then withdrew from the world to their hidden mountain cities. The ones remaining on Aachan gained their freedom after the Forbidding was broken, when the surviving Charon went back to the void. Two hundred years later, violent volcanic activity broke out on Aachan, threatening to destroy all life on the planet, and the Aachim sought desperately for a way of escape.

Alie: A servant at Nyriandiol.

Barkus: Deceased master crafter of controllers at the manufactory, uncle of Irisis.

Cloor: Chief Miner at the manufactory mine.

Coeland: Matriarch (Wise Mother) of the lyrinx in Kalissin.

Colm: A resourceful boy who befriends Nish in the refugee camp.

Cryl-Nish Hlar: *A former scribe, a prober in secret and a reluctant artificer, generally known as Nish.*

Dandri: A senior miner and team leader.

Eiryn Muss: Halfwit; an air-moss grower and harmless pervert, he turned out to be the scrutator's prober (spy) in the manufactory, and vanished.

Faellem: A long-lived human species who have passed out of the Histories, though some may still dwell on Santhenar.

Fistila Tyr: An artisan in the manufactory.

Flammas: A kindly, forgetful mancer. Ullii spent years in his dungeon.

Fley: A mute servant at Nyriandiol. Gurtey's husband.

Fransi: Younger sister of Colm.

Fusshte: A treacherous member of the Council of Scrutators.

Fyn-Mah: The querist (chief of municipal intelligence bureau) at Tiksi.

Ghorr: The Chief Scrutator and Flydd's enemy.

Gilhaelith: *An eccentric geomancer and mathemancer who dwells at Nyriandiol and whose obsession is the great game of the earth.*

Gir-Dan: Captain at the manufactory; he has been sent there for 'evaluation'.

Guss: Gilhaelith's foreman.

Gyrull: Matriarch of the lyrinx city at Snizort.

Haani: Tiaan's adopted sister, accidentally killed by the Aachim in Tirthrax.

Halie: A scrutator on the council and supporter of Flydd.

Hila: Flydd's air-floater pilot.

Inthis: Vithis's clan of Aachim, first of the Eleven Clans (First Clan).

Irisis: *Crafter, in charge of the controller artisans at the manufactory; niece of Barkus.*

Jal-Nish Hlar: *The perquisitor for Einunar; Nish's father.*

Joeyn (Joe): An old miner, Tiaan's friend, killed in a roof fall.

Jym: One of Flydd's guards.

Ketila: Elder sister of Colm.

Klarm: Scrutator for Borgistry; a dwarf.

Liett: *A lyrinx with unarmoured skin and no chameleon ability; a talented flesh-former.*

Liliwen: Daughter of Troist and Yara, twin of Meriwen.

Luxor: A conciliatory Aachim clan leader.

Lyrinx: Massive winged humanoids who came out of the void to Santhenar after the Forbidding was broken. Highly intelligent, they are able to utilise the Secret Art, most commonly for keeping their heavy bodies in flight. They have armoured skin and a chameleon-like ability to change their colours and patterns, often used for communication (skin-speech). Some lyrinx are also flesh-formers; they can change small organisms into desired forms using the Art. In the void they used a similar ability to pattern their unborn young so as to survive in that harsh environment. As a consequence, they are not entirely comfortable in their powerful bodies.

Malien: *A venerable but ostracised Aachim living in Tirthrax; a heroine from the time of the Mirror. Also known as the Matah.*

Marnie: Tiaan's mother, a prize breeder of children.

Matron: Woman in charge of the breeding factory at Tiksi.

Meriwen: Daughter of Troist and Yara, twin of Liliwen.

Merryl: A human slave who teaches human languages to the lyrinx. Also known as Tutor.

Mihail: Gilhaelith's manservant.

Minis: *A young Aachim man of high stature and foster-son of Vithis. Also Tiaan's dream lover who was forced to spurn her when the Aachim came through the gate to Tirthrax.*

Mira: Yara's sister who dwells at Morgadis. She is embittered after the loss of her husband and three sons in the war. She communicates by skeet with a coalition of like-minded people.

M'lainte: The mechanician in charge of balloon construction.

Mounce: A disrespectful sergeant in Troist's army.

Munnand: A lyrinx.

Myllii: Ullii's long-lost twin brother.

Nish: *Cryl-Nish's nickname.*

Nivulee: The navigator on Flydd's air-floater.

Nixx: Gilhaelith's seneschal.

Numinator, the: A mysterious figure mentioned by Flydd when in his cups.

Nylatl, the: *A malicious creature created by Ryll and Liett's flesh-forming. It killed Haani's aunts and mother and attacked Tiaan.*

Nyrd: Messenger to Gilhaelith.

Oinan: Father of Colm.

Old Hyull: A venerable lyrinx, husband of Matriarch Gyrull.

Oon-Mie: A cheerful and reliable artisan at the manufactory.

Peate: A resentful senior miner.

Ranii Mhel: An examiner; mother of Nish.

Ranii Shyrr: Troist's envoy.

Rulke: The greatest of all the Charon, he created the first construct.

Ruvix: Flydd's sergeant.

Ryll: *An ostracised wingless lyrinx who captured Tiaan and subsequently used her in flesh-forming. After Tiaan saved his life, he allowed her to escape from Kalissin.*

Seeker: One who can sense use of the Secret Art, or people who have that talent, or even enchanted objects. Ullii is one.

S'lound: A soldier who travelled with Nish in the balloon to Tirthrax. He was killed when it landed.

Tchlrrr: A young soldier in Troist's army.

Tiaan Liise-Mar: *A young artisan; a visual thinker and talented controller-maker. With the amplimet, she picked up Minis's cry for help, fell in love with him and carried the amplimet all the way to Tirthrax, where she used it in opening a gate to Aachan, to save Minis and his people.*

Tinketil: Mother of Colm.

Tirior: An Aachim clan leader.

Troist: An ambitious junior officer in the army destroyed by the lyrinx at Nilkerrand.

Tuniz: A senior artificer from Crandor, now overseer at the manufactory.

Tyara: A young friend of Minis.

Ullii: *A hypersensitive seeker, used by Scrutator Flydd to track Tiaan and the amplimet.*

Vithis: *Minis's foster-father; an Aachim from Aachan and the head of Inthis First Clan. When all First Clan (except Minis) were lost in the gate, he became bitterness steeped in bile.*

Vunio: A young friend of Minis.

Xervish Flydd: *The scrutator (spymaster and master inquisitor) for Einunar. He now leads the hunt for Tiaan and the amplimet and the defence of the manufactory.*

Yara: A brilliant advocate, wife to Troist.

Yorme: One of Flydd's guards.

Zoyl Aarp: A clever but naïve and childish artisan.

Major Artefacts, Forces and Powerful Natural Places

Amplimet: A rare hedron which, even in its natural state, can draw power from the force (the *field*) surrounding and permeating a node. Occasionally can be very powerful.

Anthracism: Human internal combustion due to a mancer or an artisan drawing more power than the body can handle. Invariably fatal (gruesomely).

Booreah Ngurle (the Burning Mountain): A large, double-cratered volcano in northern Worm Wood, with a blue crater lake. It has a strange and powerful double node. Gilhaelith's home, Nyriandiol, is built on the inner rim of the crater.

Clanker (also armoped or thumpeter): An armoured mechanical war cart with six, eight or ten legs and an articulated body, driven by the Secret Art via a controller mechanism which is used by a trained operator. Armed with a rock-throwing catapult and a javelard (heavy spear-thrower) which are fired by a shooter riding on top. Clankers are made under supervision of a mechanician, artisan and weapons artificer. Emergency power is stored in a pair of heavy spinning flywheels, in case the field is interrupted.

Construct: A vehicle powered by the Secret Art, based on some of the secrets of Rulke's legendary vehicle. Unlike Rulke's, those made by the Aachim cannot fly.

Controller: A mind-linked mechanical system of many flexible arms which draws power through a *hedron* and feeds it to the drive mechanisms of a *clanker*. A controller is attuned to a particular hedron, and the operator must be trained to use each controller, which takes time. Operators suffer withdrawal if removed from their machines for long periods, and inconsolable grief when their machines are destroyed, although this may be alleviated if the controller survives and can be installed in another clanker. The term is used in a more general sense, eg. construct controller.

Crystal fever: A hallucinatory madness suffered by artisans and clanker operators, brought on by overuse of a *hedron*. Few recover from it. Mancers can suffer from related ailments.

Field: The diffuse (or weak) force surrounding and permeating (and presumably generated by) a *node*. It is the source of a mancer's *power*. Various stronger forces are also known to exist, although no one knows how to tap them safely. Non-nodal stress-fields also occur, though on Santhenar these are weak and little-used.

Flesh-forming: A branch of the Secret Art that only lyrinx can use. Developed to adapt themselves to the ever-mutable void where they came from, it now involves the slow transformation of a living creature, tailoring it to suit some particular purpose. It is painful for both creature and lyrinx, and can be employed only on small creatures, though the lyrinx seek to change that.

Gate: A portal between one place (or one world) and another, connected by a shifting trans-dimensional 'wormhole'.

Geomancy: The most difficult and powerful of all the Secret Arts. An adept is able to draw upon the forces that move and shape the world. A most dangerous Art to the user.

Hedron: A natural or shaped crystal, formed deep in the earth from fluids that circulate through a natural *node*. Trained artisans can tune a hedron to draw power from the field surrounding a node, via the ethyr. Rutilated quartz, that is, quartz crystal containing dark needles of rutile, is commonly used. The artisan must first 'wake' the crystal using his or her *pliance*. If it is too far from a node, a hedron will be unable to draw power and becomes useless. If a hedron is not used for long periods, it may have to be rewoken by an artisan, though this can be hazardous.

Kalissin: A spire of foamed meteoritic iron arising from the centre of the meteor crater of Lake Kalissi. It has a powerful node and is a centre for lyrinx flesh-forming.

Nennifer: The great bastion of the Council of Scrutators, on the escarpment over Kalithras, the Desolation Sink. Nennifer is home to countless mancers, artisans and artificers, all furiously working to design new kinds of Art-powered devices to aid the war against the lyrinx.

Nigah: A drug used by the army under extreme conditions to combat cold, fatigue and pain, though addiction can make users aggressive, paranoid and delusional.

Nodes: Rare places in the world where the Secret Art works better because of the field surrounding the node. Once identified, a *hedron* (or a mancer) can sometimes draw *power* from the node's field through the ethyr, though the amount diminishes with distance, not always regularly. A *clanker* operator must be alert for the loss and ready to draw on another node, if available. The field can be drained, in which case the node may not be usable for years, or even centuries (cf. Torgnadr). Mancers have long sought the secret of drawing on the far greater power of a node itself (cf. Power, Nunar's *General Theory of Power*) but so far it has eluded them (or maybe those who succeeded did not live to tell about it).

There are also anti-nodes where the Art does not work at all, or is dangerously disrupted. Nodes and anti-nodes are frequently (though not always) associated with natural features or forces such as mountains, faults and hot spots.

Nyriandiol: Gilhaelith's home, fortress and laboratory on top of Booreah Ngurle. The entire building is a geomantic artefact designed to protect him and enhance his work.

Patterner: A semi-organic device developed by the lyrinx to pattern *torgnadrs* and other artefacts used in their Art. The patterner essentially copies a particular human's talent into the growing torgnadr, thereby greatly enhancing the talent and allowing it to be controlled by a lyrinx who is skilled in the Art.

Pliance: A device which enables an artisan to see the *field* and tune a *controller* to it.

Port-all: Tiaan's name for the device she makes in Tirthrax to open the gate.

Power: A mancer, Nunar, codified the laws of mancing, noting how limited it was, mainly because of lack of power. She recognised that mancing was held back because:

- Power came from diffuse and poorly understood sources.
- It all went through the mancer first, causing aftersickness that grew greater the more powerful the source. Eventually power, or aftersickness, would kill the mancer.
- The traditional way around this was to charge up an artefact (such as a mirror, a ring) with power over a long time, and to simply trigger it when needed. This had some advantages, though objects could be hard to control or become corrupted, and once discharged were essentially useless.
- Yet some of the ancients had used devices that held a charge, or perhaps replenished themselves. No one knew how, but it had to be so, else how could they maintain their power for hundreds if not thousands of years (for example, the Mirror of Aachan), or use quite prodigious amounts of power without becoming exhausted (Rulke's legendary construct)?

Nunar assembled a team of mancers utterly devoted to her project (no mean feat) and set out to answer these questions. Mancing was traditionally secretive—practitioners tried (often wasting their lives in dead ends) and usually failed alone. Only the desperate state of the war could have made them work together, sharing their discoveries, until the genius of Nunar put together the *Special Theory of Power*, which described where the diffuse force came from and how a mancer actually tapped it, drawing not through the earthly elements but via the ultradimensional ethyr.

The ultimate goals of theoretical mancers are the *General Theory of Power*, which deals with how *nodes* work and how they might be tapped safely, and, ultimately, the *Unified Power Theory*, which reconciles all fields, weak and strong, in terms of a single force.

Secret Art: The use of magical or sorcerous powers (mancing).

Snizort: A place in Taltid with a potent and concentrated node, near the famous tar pits and seeps.

Strong forces: Powerful planar fields that are speculated to exist at nodes, though no mancer studying them has survived to prove their existence.

Thapter: Tiaan's name for the flying *construct* she and Malien created in Tirthrax.

Torgnadr: Also called node-drainer. A device patterned by the lyrinx to drain a *field* dry, or to channel power from the field for their own purposes. Torgnadrs are extremely difficult to *pattern* and most attempts fail, though some result in weak devices such as phynadrs which can draw small amounts of power for a particular purpose.

Well of Echoes, the: An Aachim concept to do with the reverberation of time, memory and the Histories. Sometimes a place of death and rebirth (to the same cycling fate). Also a sense of being trapped in history, of being helpless to change collective fate (of a family, clan or species). Its origin is sometimes thought to be a sacred well on Aachan, sometimes on Santhenar. The term has become part of Aachim folklore. 'I have looked in the Well of Echoes.' 'I heard it at the Well.' 'I will go to the Well.' Possibly also a source; a great *node*.

The Well is symbolised by the three-dimensional symbol of infinity, the universe and nothingness. A Well of Echoes, trapped in Tirthrax, is held there only by the most powerful magic.